Five *Summers*

Broken Oasis Book One

Eve Campbell

To all those girls who only see their flaws...

Remember that there is someone out there

who will appreciate every part of you.

Chapter 1

Poppy

The sound of my mother's keys jingling at the front door interrupts my usual morning routine of rinsing my breakfast dishes. She's home from her lengthy night shift at the nearby aged care facility. I shove my bowl into the dishwasher and turn to see her eyes on me.

I can already predict what she's about to say before she even says it. It's the same thing over and over, like a broken record.

"You're going to be late?"

Yeah, well, hello to you too, I want to say, but instead of getting into a heated argument with her, I just go with, "Yeah, I know."

As I've grown older, my relationship with my mom is somewhat strained. When I was nine, my mother kicked my father out of the house. Whenever I think of him, a heavy wave of sadness crashes upon me, like a dark storm cloud rolling in, casting a shadow over my heart. Despite not having seen him for years, I miss him, along with the sound of his laugh.

To him, I was his princess, and he was my daddy. He could always make me laugh with his silly stories. He was the best father a girl could ever wish for. He is the reason I have a passion for music.

I have fond memories of the two of us sitting side by side as he patiently taught me the chords on his guitar. He taught me the art of composing music, showing me how to seamlessly merge a melody with lyrics. And then, we would sing the words we had written.

I can still recall the proud look on his face when I totally crushed those high notes.

Too bad my mother couldn't see what we had before she kicked him out. If she did, maybe he would still be here. But thanks to her he's not around now, because he left, and I haven't seen him in years. I guess I wasn't special enough for him to stick around.

With my mom still standing by the door, giving me a watchful glance, I quickly grab my bag and make my way towards her.

"So, have you made a decision yet?" she asks.

Damn, I was hoping I could get through today without her asking me this again. Always the same fucking question.

"Nope, as I've said a hundred times. I have no idea about what I'm going to do when school ends."

Of course, I know what I want to do. I want to pursue music, but I can't bring myself to tell her because I know she'll be livid.

Right before I'm about to walk out the door, I pause.

"Seriously, Mom, stop asking me the same thing every day. Remember, I get to decide what I do. This is my life, not yours."

Frustration and irritation wash over her face, causing her brows to furrow and her lips to tighten. "Poppy, you have no idea what awaits you beyond these walls. It is important to have some qualifications. Don't be as useless as your father."

And there it is. It always circles back to him. She wants me to follow in her footsteps and pursue a career in caring for the elderly, just like she does. That job is okay, I guess. I mean, the elderly are adorable and everything, but it's just not my cup of tea. My true passion lies in music. It's what my dad passed on to me.

I know that music is a touchy subject for her because of my father. He used to be the lead singer of a band.

One day, when she was ranting about him in front of me, she let slip that he had been unfaithful to her multiple times with his groupies. That's why she despises my dad. He shattered her heart into a million pieces. Talking about him causes her to become mad and sometimes unresponsive. That's why I can't talk to her about my desire to pursue music, because she'll only dismiss it as if it holds no importance.

I walk out the open door without even attempting to say goodbye to her.

Walking across the front patio, I rummage through my satchel in search of my car keys. When I can't find them, it finally hits me that I took my shitty Toyota Corolla to the mechanic yesterday afternoon.

Shit. Now I have to catch the bus. The school bus that is full of mean bitches.

The second I step out the front gate, I see the bus approaching. It's only Tuesday and I'm already confronted with a dilemma. I so desperately want the weekend to be here already.

I've got two choices. Either I can sprint my ass down the street - or I can go back inside and ask my annoying mother to give me a ride to school. But that will only result in another lecture about what I'm doing next year. Yeah, it's a no-brainer.

Just so you know, I'm not really a runner or anything. I'm definitely not in shape, far from it. But there's no way I'm dealing with my mom again this morning. Once is bad enough.

I quickly sling my satchel over my shoulder and sprint like a maniac down the street to catch the bus, my feet pounding against the pavement. I'm sure I look ridiculous. I'm not overweight at all. And I guess I'd consider myself average-sized. However, compared to all those Instagram wafer-thin bitches who strive to look like a walking skeleton, people consider me overweight.

So what if I'm not wafer-thin? It just means I don't follow the crowd. But when it comes to feeling vulnerable, I'm just like any other girl my age, worried about my body, my flaws, and all that stuff.

It really hurts my self-esteem when girls, who are more beautiful than me, mock my size.

Every morning, I feel an overwhelming sense of dread as I prepare to go to school. My hate for Eastern High runs deep. Each cruel taunt feels like a bullet piercing my protective shield.

To mask my vulnerability, I adopt a defensive attitude. My words become my weapon, carefully aimed at inflicting the same amount of pain that they have caused me.

I know that this is not the right approach. However, it is the only way I know how to cope.

The bus comes to a halt, and a crowd forms a line, eager to board the bus.

Meanwhile, I still have half a block left to run. I push myself harder, even though I'm already gasping for air. God. I need to get in shape, or perhaps I should cut back on eating those chocolate drops I love so much. Nah, not gonna happen.

As the last person boards the bus, I quickly step on just before the doors close. My heart's going crazy and I'm breathing weird. Bent forward, with my hands on my knees, I suck in great gulps of air.

The bus driver floors the accelerator and pulls away from the curb. The force of gravity propels me forward, causing me to fall to my knees. My hand automatically shoots out to stop me from falling. The echoes of mocking laughter linger in my ears, then followed by their snide remarks.

Fucking bus driver. I bet the asshole did that on purpose.

And then it suddenly dawns on me: my hand is on someone's leg. Scratch that, my hand is on their upper thigh. Whew, that was a close call. An inch higher and I'd be touching his cock. Immediately, I retract my hand and lift my gaze. Oh fuck. Of course, it had to be him.

Xander fucking Williams. The absolute heartthrob and self-declared bad boy of the school, with those stunning dark brown eyes that make all the girls go gaga and, uh, you know, feel a little tingly down there. His cocky grin sends a shiver down my spine, making my throat tighten. The smile that always gets him what he wants. It's no secret that he has hooked up with nearly every girl in our school. It's common knowledge that he's all about casual hook-ups and not into relationships. Oh, and don't forget, he's apparently not into kissing. He basically fucks them and then moves on to the next conquest. Except for Jade and Savannah, who he hooks up with all the time.

But let's be honest. Jade and Savannah are easy and will gladly ride anything that comes their way.

Despite Xander's habit of jumping from one hook-up to another, I have to admit I feel kinda stupid sometimes when I catch myself daydreaming about him.

I like to daydream about all the dirty things I'd want him to do to me if he were mine. It's stupid, I know. Curvy girls like me don't stand a chance with a hot guy like him. Yeah, but a girl can still dream, right?

Feeling flustered and shaking the idea of Xander out of my head, I stand. A rush of heat creeps up my cheeks as I pull on the bottom of my blouse, tugging it down so no one can see.

Jealousy hits me hard when I see who's sitting next to Xander. Jade fucking Wilson. My sworn enemy. Also known as an easy fuck. And enjoys giving blowjobs when requested.

And let's not forget, she's the meanest bitch in the school, at least according to me. Her cruel words cut me to the core.

She's drop-dead gorgeous and adored by everyone. All girls desire to look as beautiful as she does. However, she is fully aware of all of it—the way people gaze at her and follow her trends. The way guys go after her, totally hooked on her oral abilities. Well, that's my opinion. Why else would they hang around with such a bitch?

However, what truly bothers me is the fact that Xander occasionally spends time with her. She must be really good at it, because why else would Xander be hanging out with her for more than a day? That's just not his pattern.

I know. I know. You've probably already figured it out. I have a strong fascination with Xander Williams. However, let me assure you, it doesn't make me some kind of creepy stalker. I mean, who can resist the charm of admiring something so beautiful? And let's be honest, every girl has a weakness for a bad boy.

Xander has been a neighbor of mine for as long as I can remember, living just two doors down. I have to confess, sometimes I hear him strumming his guitar. Sometimes I leave my window open and pretend he's serenading me. I am a bit of a sad sack at times. He is completely unaware of my existence. But not anymore. From now on, he'll know me as the chick who tried to touch his package on the bus.

"Just sit down, you fat cow!" Jade yells, her gaze fixed on me as if I were nothing more than trash. "Everyone here hates you."

"Yeah, I guess I'm not as popular as your mouth," I add, as I move to the only available seat on the bus.

Thank God, I'll have my car back tomorrow afternoon. I'm done with these idiots and their bullshit.

I take a quick look out the window, but my focus shifts back to Xander Williams. He's rocking his usual black attire, looking like he's living his best life. To the outside world, Xander appears to have everything. He's got the looks, and he's on the path to success. It's obvious he should be on stage with his musical talent.

But living two doors down from him, I know it's not all sunshine and rainbows. I hear the loud arguing. I hear his dad, who is drunk all the time, tell Xander he's just a useless piece of shit. It's just the two of them living in that house. When I hear his dad spit those words, I often wonder what happened to Xander's mum. Did she walk out and leave him to deal with his intoxicated father all alone?

Having observed Xander over the years, I believe I have a deeper understanding of him than anyone else. Xander's all about being alone unless he's out looking for some action.

Ace is his only friend. They both love music and have a rebellious side. I've seen how they size people up whenever they approach. Both making it clear that if you fuck with them, there will be trouble.

As I watch him, I notice Jade leaning in closer to talk to him. Ignoring her, Xander shoves his earbuds into his ears and redirects his attention to his music. I can't help but grin. It seems that I'm not the only one who finds her annoying.

The second the bus pulls up out the front of the school, I eagerly race to be the first one to get off. Hiding in classrooms is typically my preferred method for making it through the day. Or find a quiet place to sit on the school grounds where I can read my Kindle and discreetly watch the hottest boy in school.

If you haven't already figured it out. I'm pretty much of a loner myself and I don't have a lot of friends at school. But that's okay with me. I love hanging by myself binging my favorite show - The Real Housewives of Beverly Hills. It's so much better than enduring constant weight taunts all day long.

By the time the school bell rings, I'm completely exhausted. And to make matters worse, I'm pissed that I have to rely on the bus to get home. I've been avoiding the bathroom all day to steer clear of Jade and her friends who hang out there, vaping and giving off bitch face vibes.

But now I gotta pee.

Glancing at my watch, I check the time. Five minutes until the bus leaves. No prob. I'll race to the restroom at the front of the school, the one near the art room that no one ever uses and I'll still make it to the bus.

With my bag slung over my shoulder, I navigate through the bustling hallway, skillfully maneuvering around the throngs of people. Taking another glance at my watch, I still have four minutes remaining. Two minutes to use the restroom, and two minutes to catch the bus. I quickly hustle down the hall.

Using both hands, I forcefully push the door open, then suddenly stop almost causing me to lose my balance on the tile floor. Holy fucking shit. What have I just walked in on?

There's a guy with his back facing me, but I can already tell without seeing his face that it's Xander Williams without a doubt - his signature black clothes and distinctive stance. Wait, did I just walk into the men's restroom? My heart pounds, like a wild stallion galloping in my chest.

"Suck it harder," he says.

His words snap me back to reality. That's when I notice there's a girl on her knees in front of him. But I can't see who it is. I look up and see Xander's brown eyes watching me in the mirror. The seconds continue to pass. I know I should make a run for it. But, for some reason, my feet are stuck to the floor. The passing of seconds continues. And then, I see this sly grin slowly spreading across his beautiful face.

"What are you waiting for, sweet lips? Why don't you come over here and join us?"

His comment, like a sudden clap of thunder, jolts me back to reality.

I know he's fucking with me because that's what he does. He enjoys messing with people for his own entertainment.

"Are you talking to me?" says the girl on her knees, sucking his dick.

That's when I recognize that bitch's mocking voice all too well. It belongs to Savannah Gibson, Jade's best friend, and another one of my bullies. Looks like her boyfriend, who she was just making out with at lunchtime today, isn't much to brag about after all.

"No," he says sharply, his voice oozing with allure, sending a delightful shiver down my spine. "Fucking suck it or I'm out of here," he tells her.

His intense gaze reflected in the mirror feels like a scorching touch, searing through the depths of my soul. As he continues to watch me, he threads his fingers through Savannah's hair. His smirk widens when he thrusts his hips forward, making her gag, all the while giving me a wink.

Oh, my god. Just turn the fuck around and get out of here instead of watching like some pervert. My face flushes with embarrassment as my heart races even faster. The sound of my pounding pulse races through my veins.

I pivot and sprint towards the exit with a surge of adrenaline propelling me forward.

I bolt down the school's front steps, bounding them two at a time, feeling utterly clueless about what I'm supposed to do. My mind feels completely scrambled, replaying Xander's smug smirk and that teasing wink. That asshole. He knew exactly what he was doing.

I sprint towards the bus, my body a mix of embarrassment and excitement from what I just saw. It's hard to put into words, but seeing Xander in that state has an undeniable effect on me. My entire body is still buzzing with excitement, watching him thrust forward while he was looking at me in the mirror.

Once I secure a seat on the overcrowded bus, I cross my legs, silently pleading for a quick journey home. Because damn, I still need to pee.

Jade gets on the bus and stops in the middle of the aisle, holding up everyone behind her. She glances around.

I make sure not to make eye contact with her, so she won't say anything mean. I really can't handle her right now.

"Has anyone seen Xander?" She says.

I cringe at the sound of her voice. It's an irritating, high-pitched noise that seems to go on forever.

"He said he was catching the bus home." She puts her hands on her hips and looks around at the people seated. "Has anyone seen him?"

I'm busting to get back at her. I wanna spill the beans and tell her that he ditched her ass for a little action with her friend, Savannah. I want to let her know she's not as great as she thinks.

"Tobias, have you seen him?" she screeches, moving down the aisle.

Oh, my god, she's clingier than a wet T-shirt in the rain.

"No. He never takes the bus in the afternoon."

"You don't think I'm aware of that," she sharply retorts. "But he did promise me he'd come."

When the bus starts moving, she sits two seats away from me.

I can't help but almost laugh, my mouth twitching with amusement. Oh, you can bet he's coming for sure. Just not in the way she might have imagined. This is the perfect time to get back at her for all the mean shit she's said to me today. I want to give her a harsh reality check, so she knows that Xander Williams doesn't see her as anything but an easy fuck. He's more interested in Savannah's mouth than sitting next to her on the bus. But, for some reason, I really want to keep what I saw today to myself.

CHAPTER 2

Xander

I know that I'm an asshole the second I walk out of the bathroom. However, I couldn't give two flying fucks. If Savannah Gibson wants to be pissed, she can be. She'll eventually move on from it, just like they always do. Those types of chicks don't stay mad for too long. In a few days, or probably tomorrow, all I have to do is whisper something hot and filthy in her ear and she'll eagerly get down on her knees again. They always do.

Ace was correct in his assessment. She's pretty hopeless at swallowing and giving head. But I love the chase. What can I say? I love using my bad boy charm and giving chicks that sly grin. They fall for it every fucking time. Let's be honest, most girls can't resist a bad boy. So, I always use it to my advantage.

I don't want to sound cocky and all, but I have never been rejected by a chick. Sometimes, I turn it into a game just to see how far I can take it. I'm excited to see how far I can push them and what they're willing to do.

My best friend, Ace, often teases me about how my good looks alone can help me score every time, and that it just doesn't seem fair. I had Savannah all hot and bothered, ready and willing to suck my cock. I've fucked her before. Many times, in fact, but she's never given me a blowie.

Ace kept harassing me about letting her suck my dick. After that sad attempt, I just wish I had fucked her instead.

See, Ace and I have this thing where we rate the girls we hook up with. We spill all the juicy details about how easy it is to get with them, what we can make them do, and give them a score out of ten.

Let's just say Ace wasn't wrong about Savannah. That chick can't give a decent blowie, not even if her life depended on it.

And to top it off, she went in for a damn fucking kiss afterward. Fuck me. If that's not giving off clingy vibes, I don't know what the fuck else to call it. I had to bail before I lost my shit because everyone knows I don't kiss any chick. I'm not interested in relationships and never will be. All I'm looking for is a wet, warm spot to sink my dick in. Live it up before Ace and I leave behind this fucked up town.

We're all about the music and nothing can hold us down. Ace and I have been planning it for years. We dream of becoming music legends. Music is our lifeblood, it's what defines us. It's as vital as the air we breathe. And, of course, the idea of scoring with a bunch of groupies is just an added bonus.

As I walk down the hall, I whip out my phone to text Ace.

Xander: FYI Sarah W is no longer in last place.

Ace: Told ya.

Xander: Are you at the car?

Ace: Yeah. You want me to wait.

Xander: Yeah. Be there in five.

Making my way to where I always meet Ace in the school parking lot, I spot him leaning on his car, totally into his phone.

The sound of my footsteps makes him lift his head. He quickly puts his phone in his pocket and smiles, showing the victory in his eyes.

"I fucking told you, bro."

"Yeah! Yeah! You were right," I say, opening the passenger door and carefully putting my guitar in the back seat.

He's got a big smile on his face as he moves around the car and jumps into the driver's seat.

"But you'll never guess what happened while I was in there."

With a turn of the key, the engine springs to life.

"What? You couldn't finish," he says, glancing in my direction. "That happened to me, so I just turned her around and fucked her. You should have tried that."

"Nah, I eventually got there. Poppy Reeves walked in on us."

"No way," his eyebrows raise. "Dude, what the fuck happened?"

I burst into laughter, thinking about how she just stood there. How her breathing got all messed up and her eyes went wide.

At that moment, I knew I could have a bit of fun and fuck with her. I fucking love getting under people's skin. That's why I asked if she wanted to join in. She's most likely better at giving head than Savannah, anyway. No one could be worse than that. But based on what I've seen of Poppy Reeves at school, she doesn't seem easily influenced.

Even though I've never talked to her, I just had this feeling she'd bolt. There's something about Poppy that gives me the impression she's a good, innocent girl. Most likely still a virgin. I suspect she's living a cushy life in that house, all thanks to her mom. Watching her in the mirror made me want to mess with her good-girl vibes. That's why I shoved my dick further down Savannah's throat. I was curious to see how she would react. To see what she would do. But, to my surprise, she stayed there way longer than I expected.

While Poppy Reeves has never really caught my attention, I can't help but admire her sharp wit and clever comebacks. She seems to be in the spotlight for all the wrong reasons. Jade and her mean-girl crew are always after her. They really get a kick out of bullying her.

Jade and her group are thinner than Poppy, but I wouldn't call Poppy fat. She's simply an average-sized girl. If you're a fan of curves, she's got them in all the right spots. But me and Ace barely give her a second look. She's not even on our list of potential hookups. The only time she gets any attention is when Jade rants about her being overweight.

Jade is hot as fuck. It's also a plus that she's super easy. I'm not sure if Jade's jealousy is the reason behind her behavior towards Poppy. Poppy can handle whatever comes at her. She's tough and doesn't let those hurtful words bother her. Despite all the crap she's taken over the years, I can't ever recall seeing Poppy shed a tear. That in itself is impressive. But Jade is weak as fuck and can't make decisions without other people's approval.

Ace turns his gaze towards me, a smile playing on his lips. "What's so funny?" he asks.

"Poppy Reeves just stood there watching me face fuck Savannah's mouth. She didn't leave until I asked if she wanted to join in."

"No way," Ace laughs. "You think she'd be down for shit like that?"

"Nah."

"You never know, she might be up for it."

"Nah, I don't think so. She comes across as a good girl. She's probably still a virgin, anyway."

"Yeah. Fuck no, I refuse to go there."

Ace slams on the brakes at the traffic lights. As people cross the street, I see Ace checking out Nicola, a girl in the year below us.

"Don't go there," I tell him. "If you mess with Noah's little sister, he will completely lose it. Stick to the easy ones."

"Yeah well, it's not as easy for me as it is for you, pretty boy. Plus, I heard she is good at giving head. Nothing gets me more excited than a challenge."

The lights go green and Ace hits the gas.

"Yeah, but... do you really want to risk getting the shit kicked out of you for touching Noah's baby sister?"

"Depends how good the blow job is. I'll give you the scoop when I get one."

"And that there, my friend, is why we should just hang with Jade and her friends. They're always up for anything."

Ace and I have a lot in common. Like me, he's only into casual flings. He can't stand it when girls get clingy. Yeah, what's the big deal if we fuck them?

Doesn't mean we want to date them. We just wanna have a good time before we graduate.

We both come from messed-up homes, and we can't wait to get the hell out of this shithole of a town. Our main thing is our band and our music, even though it's just the two of us for now.

I'm the lead singer with a killer voice, and I love jamming on the guitar. Ace's talent is off the charts. He's a total prodigy on the keyboard and guitar. But what's even more impressive is he's never had a lesson in his life. He's insanely talented and can give our music an awesome vibe.

Ace has never met his dad. He fucked off not long after he was born.

Since I've known Ace, his mom has been going through boyfriends like crazy. His sister, Daisy, was his sole source of guidance. She took care of him, basically raising him while their mom got high and messed around with her boyfriends. But Ace was never the same when his sister bailed on him. At twelve, he was stuck dealing with his drug-addicted mom and the jerks she brought home. Ace hasn't said a word about Daisy since she left, but I could tell he was torn up about it.

I stepped up and tried to fill those shoes, determined to be there and help him get through it. Our connection goes beyond blood ties. We're like true brothers in every way.

Ace's mom is always hammered. Last year, when we got home from school, we walked in on his mom's boyfriend banging her on the kitchen table. That was the final straw for Ace. He's seen some crazy stuff in his life, but that day was on a whole other level. He moved out to the garage in the backyard. He turned it into his crash pad and a spot for us to practice.

Music has this unexplainable effect on us. I know for me that when I sing; it erases all the shitty things in my life. You could say it consumes me, transforming me from Xander Williams, the troubled kid from a fractured home to someone else entirely. It's as if I've left behind the identity of that skinny kid who constantly suffers at the hands of his drunken dad. It's my calling, drawing me in, and leading me to my destined path.

Deep down, I think we yearn to experience a future where our worth is undeniable. My dad constantly hurls insults at me, always calling me worthless. One day I'll fucking show him. One day, he will see that I am something.

But honestly, I gotta get the hell out of this crappy town because I'm scared shitless of turning into a clone of my asshole father. There is no way in hell I will ever let that happen.

Ace turns into the street, the engine purring softly as we move down towards his house. He stops in the middle of the road, staring at the car parked in the driveway, blocking his way to the garage.

"What a fucking asshole," Ace mutters, gripping the steering wheel tightly, his knuckles turning white.

"Who owns that car?" I ask.

"Some new boyfriend. I swear the dipshit intentionally does it to fuck with me." He slams his foot on the accelerator. The car races down the street. "One of these days, I would love to get back at these fucking assholes."

"Where are we going?" I ask.

"I don't fucking know, but anywhere is better than here. When I get back, if that asshole's car is still there, then I'm gonna key it. Let's see how much that jerkoff enjoys parking there, then."

Ace is fuming. And when he gets all mad and starts stewing over things, I always distract him. Try to make him focus on other shit. Just like any brother would do.

"Hey, I worked on some lyrics last night."

"Yeah," he says, looking over at me.

"How about we head to the lake and work on them?"

It seems like what I said made a difference. His shoulders seem more at ease. His grip on the steering wheel loosens. That's what music does to us. It helps us get in a better mindset, shaking off all the crappy things that come our way. But sometimes with Ace when he's so worked up, it's still not enough.

"Yeah. We can do that." He tosses a glance in my direction. "But you should know that I'm texting Jade to see what she's doing. If she gives me the green light, you're on your own, or you can come along if you want."

The fastest way for him to stop overthinking is to hook up. He's always been this way. I knew once we made it to the lake, he'd message Jade anyway, to see what she was doing. In the past, I'd occasionally join him, and we'd fuck her together, but today I'm not feeling up for it. Jade's getting a bit too clingy, and I need to put some space between us.

CHAPTER 3

Xander

I totally called it. Before I even grabbed my guitar, Ace had already texted Jade to hook up. Can't say I'm surprised that Jade agreed to that. I swear, that girl is always craving attention and has more action than a college frat boy.

"So, what's the deal now?" Ace asks, making a U-turn and getting back on the street. "You can tag along if you're up for it. You know she's down for whatever. Remember the last time?"

"Yeah," I say, remembering how we totally railed her.

And the time before that, I snapped a pic on my phone of her on her knees while Ace and I were fucking her. And how every time the bitch pouts when it's time for us to bail.

I glance at my phone to check the time when Ace turns into my street. It's only four in the afternoon.

"You sure you don't want to join us?"

"Nah, I'm good. My old man will still be at work, and then he'll hit the bar, so I'll just relax for a bit and maybe do some writing. But don't sweat it. You can still ditch my ass for some pussy."

"Pussy always comes out on top. You know that," he says pulling up in front of my house.

"Yeah, I'm aware of that. I'm outta here. See you tomorrow!" I lean forward and snatch my guitar from the backseat, then slam the door.

"Catch you later, fucker!" Ace yells, driving away with the windows down.

I stand there for a few seconds, watching him drive down the street until he disappears around the corner. I move down the front path to my house. The paint's all chipped and the yard's full of wild weeds. Unlike all the immaculate houses on this street, all adorned with fresh coats of paint and neatly manicured gardens. Our house used to be just like all the other houses on this block, but that was when Mom was still around.

With a sigh, I trudge up the broken path. I feel a sense of calm as I look at the empty house. The peaceful silence makes me feel at ease because I know my dad won't be here to hurt me with his fists or criticize me for a while.

The front door creaks a little as I push it open. Despite my father's absence, the air is heavy with the overpowering blend of whisky and cigarettes. It's possible that the stench is from all the empty bottles lying around or the overflowing ashtrays. I shut the front door, casting a quick glance towards the lounge. The dent on the couch shows how many nights he's crashed there, too wasted to make it to his room. It's become his domain now, as if he's eagerly awaiting any opportunity to unleash his anger. To remind me once again how small and worthless I am.

Walking down the hall, I glance at the many holes in the drywall my dad has made. Each hole tells a story, a testament to his anger and frustration. The sight of them serves as a constant reminder of the tumultuous moments that have unfolded between us. All the emotions, the hate, and the scars he's left behind.

I enter my bedroom and dump my satchel and guitar on the bed. Then, I eagerly snatch my beloved, worn-out notebook. Its once flawless pages are now a mess of scribbles and thoughts. The ink, slightly smudged from countless entries, tells tales of creativity and inspiration. With my calloused fingers on the guitar strings, I let the music take over and write the next set of heartfelt lyrics.

When I finally sneak a peek at the clock, I'm shocked to see that nearly three hours have gone by without me knowing. The fading sunlight casts eerie shadows, transforming the room.

I put my guitar on the bed, feel a rumble in my stomach, and head towards the front door. Knowing there's nothing to eat in the cupboards, I stick to my usual routine. Every night, I venture two blocks down to the nearby 7-Eleven, where I swipe something to satisfy my hunger.

As soon as I take a step out of the house, loud voices assault my ears, causing me to freeze in place. I'm completely drawn in by the intense scene happening at the house two doors down. Poppy Reeves's voice slices through the air, every word tinged with frustration.

"Oh my god, will you please just stop already?" Poppy shouts, walking down the path towards the gate in front of her house.

I'm on my front patio, unseen, watching everything go down. Why not watch it? I've got nothing better to do. It's looking like this will be my only source of entertainment tonight.

Poppy rushes through the front gate and plops down on the curb, chilling under the cozy glow of the streetlights.

Her mom is hot on her heels, all furious. "If you don't make a decision, you'll waste your life just like your father did," she says, standing at the gate with her hands on her hips. "You have to choose."

"And as I've already said, I'm not doing this right now." Poppy inserts one earbud, deliberately tuning out her mom's never-ending chatter.

"I've had enough of this, Poppy. I need your answer by tomorrow."

"Can you please go away?"

"I mean it. You better give me an answer tomorrow or there will be trouble."

"Yeah, that's not gonna happen," she says with a dismissive tone and a hint of frustration in her voice.

With an eye roll, she inserts the other earbud, blocking out her mother's voice. Then she starts scrolling through her phone.

Poppy's mom walks over and taps her on the shoulder. "Poppy," her mom says, trying to get her attention.

Poppy brushes off the fact that she just spoke and starts singing.

It's "Rebellion" by Arcade Fire. Gotta admit, she's got good taste in music.

"Ugh, why are you so damn stubborn?" Her mother adds, clearly annoyed as she walks away. "You can be so frustrating sometimes. You know that."

From my hidden spot, I spy on her mom as she goes to her car, gets in, slams the door, and quickly backs out of the driveway.

Angry as hell, she steps on the gas and zooms off down the street.

I look over at Poppy, thinking she'll go inside, but she stays put, belting out her tune.

Damn, the girl can sing! I take a few steps forward, closing my eyes to fully absorb the sound of her voice.

As the song ends, there's an eerie silence on the street.

The hunger hits, so I quickly go down the front steps to find some food. I remain vigilant, keeping a close eye on Poppy as I proceed. Once again, her voice resonates, but this time, there's a subtle tinge of sadness that was absent before. Emotion seeps into her voice, causing it to crack as she sings the lyrics to one of my all-time favorite songs: "Creep" by Radiohead.

As she sings, her voice quivers. A delicate tremor, like a whispering breeze, dances upon my ears, sending a shiver down my spine. It is as if every word carried the weight of her emotions, raw and unfiltered. The slight quiver in her voice hints at a tinge of sadness, a longing to find her own place in this world. At that moment, my body moves instinctively, drawn towards her like a magnetic force.

I feel a pang in my chest as I listen to her like she's talking straight to my heart. There's a sadness to her I've never seen before. And, before I know it, I'm standing in front of her, staring at her like a total creep. Luckily, she has her eyes closed.

As she passionately sings the lyrics, her voice captivates all my senses. I stand there, unable to move, unable to tear my eyes away from her. Every note she hits sends shivers down my spine, igniting a surge of emotions. I am completely spellbound, caught in a moment where time stands still

I've never seen her like this before. And I dislike how her husky, seductive voice affects me. This is Poppy Reeves, one of the weirdest chicks at school. However, I cannot dwell on that at the moment. The minuscule cracks in her voice consume my thoughts, which give it a delicate quality, as if her voice could vanish into thin air. Still, it persists and resurfaces, unwavering in its conviction, as if this song was specifically written for her and the burdens she carries. It's a once-in-a-lifetime opportunity to witness this. I've grown accustomed to witnessing her clever remarks and sassy attitude. It's what everyone gets to see. But now, her tough facade is cracking and I see her vulnerable side. Despite our different backgrounds, Poppy Reeves and I share a common desire to conceal our pain behind a mask.

There is something about this girl that deeply stirs my emotions. As she sings, a lump forms in my throat. It's the combination of her voice, her expression, and the overwhelming sense of hopelessness that she portrays. The pain she conveys feels raw and authentic, making it the purest form of art.

The last note of the song sends chills down my spine, causing the hairs on my arms to stand on end. I can't move at all. Because damn... Poppy managed to arouse me without even laying a finger on me. It's as if her seductive and delicate voice wrapped itself around my very being, demanding my undivided attention. This girl is truly talented. Never before have I felt so understood by someone, as if they truly comprehend who I am. Every note that escapes her lips feels like pure magic.

When she opens her eyes, my heart skips a beat, but I play it cool.

With a startled expression, her eyes widen in shock, causing her phone to slip from her grasp and skitter across the road. "Shit!" she says, leaning forward to retrieve it.

I take a step forward, attempting to grab her phone, but she beats me to it. She's totally focused on the screen, wiping away the dirt with her fingers.

"How long have you been standing there?" she asks, her cheeks turning red with embarrassment.

"You were really getting into that song, huh?" I know I'm being a total jerk by messing with her and making her feel embarrassed, but this girl somehow managed to get through to me in a way no one else ever has. I'm always in control, but now I feel the need to regain my power. I give her a sly smirk and casually slide my hands into my pockets. "So, what made you sing in the street? You know everyone can see you, right?"

She exhales deeply through her cheeks before getting to her feet. "What do you want, Xander?"

I can hear the defensiveness in her tone as if her words are covered in a frosty layer. I wish she would drop the facade and be genuine like she was when she sang. Unfortunately, my attempts to assert myself only prompt her to put up her guard again, protecting herself from those around her. "I didn't realize you were a Radiohead fan," I comment.

She sighs, clearly seeing through my act. "And how would you know? It's not like you've ever made an effort to talk to me. Except for today in the bathroom, and that was just to mess with me."

Smart girl. She clearly knew I was fucking with her. Noted. I can't put Poppy in the same box as those other chicks. I need to be smarter if I want to push her boundaries even more.

Ignoring the whole restroom thing, I jut my chin out, pointing towards her phone.

"What else do you have on that?" I ask, my eyes fixed on the phone she holds in her hands.

"You mean music?"

"Yeah! Show me what songs you listen to, Creep?" I respond with another sly smile, playfully making a joke about the song.

Her eyes narrow and I notice her jaw twitch. It's clear that the nickname I used pissed her off. In an attempt to prevent her from telling me to fuck off, I quickly clarify. But as I reflect on my behavior, I can't help but question myself. Insulting people has never bothered me before. I love fucking with them. I have no clue why, but I don't want Poppy Reeves to keep her distance from me. I want her to be as vulnerable as she was just moments ago.

"I only mentioned "Creep" you know because of the song you were singing...that's all," I quickly add.

"Okay," she says, still eyeing me with caution. "What are you doing out here anyway?"

It suddenly dawns on me that she never responded to my previous question. If she's going to play this game, I want her to answer my question first.

"I'll answer your question if you answer mine first.'

I take a step back and begin walking down the street, expecting that she will either call me back or join me like other girls usually do to get my attention. However, as a few seconds pass, I realize that she isn't doing either - no calling out my name or coming after me.

So, I come to a halt and turn around.

I can't help but smile when I see her walking to her gate. Unlike other girls who constantly seek my attention and allow me to have my way, she stands apart. There's something different about her. My usual charms don't seem to have any effect on her. It's a new and unfamiliar experience for me.

"Hey!" I call out, my voice echoing through the serene street.

With her hand resting on the gate, she pauses and glances in my direction.

"Wanna go for a walk?"

"Where?"

"Down to the 7-Eleven?"

She takes a quick glance back at her house, and I'm completely focused on watching her as the seconds tick by. Judging by the amount of time she's taking, I expect her to decline, but to my surprise, she starts making her way towards me.

As I walk down the street, she stays a few strides behind instead of catching up.

We fall into silence as we move down the street; the air filled with an eerie calmness.

Somewhere along the quiet street, I hear the rumble of a car engine come to life. I glance back at Poppy and see her nervously pulling on her shirt, a clear sign she's nervous. I wonder if she's expecting me to say something hurtful, like Jade and the other bitches always do.

As a car zooms past us on the street, the sound of its engine roars in my ears. I lift my head, feeling a rush of wind against my face, and track its movement with my eyes. The vibrant red color of the car races around the corner two blocks away, leaving behind a faint scent of burning rubber.

The sound of Poppy's voice brings me back to the present.

"So, what are you doing down at the 7-Eleven?"

I come to a halt and wait for her to catch up. She deliberately avoids making eye contact and directs her gaze anywhere but at me.

"I'm getting something to eat, Princess."

My words capture her attention as she lifts her head to look up at me. "Why did you call me that?"

"Call you what?" I ask, fully aware of what she's referring to. Once again, I'm fucking with her, and I love it.

"Princess. Why did you call me Princess?" Her tone carries a hint of annoyance.

"Because you are a Princess, right? I've seen your cushy life," I say as I approach the doors of the 7-Eleven.

I decide not to bring up the fact that I saw her and her mom having an argument on the street. It's something I'll keep to myself. Besides, I can't help but wonder what they could possibly be arguing about, given her privileged life and everything.

The glass doors of the shop slide open. I take a step inside, feeling a rush of cool air against my skin. Poppy is right behind, her voice getting drowned out by the background noise.

"Trust me, Xander, I don't live a privileged life. You know absolutely nothing about me."

"You can pretend all you want, Princess, but I've seen your cushy house." I slip through the narrow aisle, carefully watching the cashier.

As the cashier assists a customer, I make my way towards the hot food section. My eyes scan the brightly lit area, hopeful for a mouthwatering find. But nothing. The heating bays stand illuminated but dishearteningly vacant. I let out a sigh and accept the disappointing sight. Determined to satisfy my cravings, I opt for an alternative plan. With speed, I snatch a handful of chocolate bars, their wrappers softly crinkling in my grip. With a mischievous smile, I carefully slip them into my pockets.

As I quickly stuff more goodies into my other pockets, I glance up and catch Poppy's gaze fixed on me.

She marches up the aisle, her eyes locked with mine, burning with intense fury.

As she draws nearer, I become increasingly aware of her stunning beauty. It's not like Jade's, which is instantly noticeable. Poppy is not afraid to stand up for herself, which I think is awesome and refreshing. Yet, there's also a vulnerability about her I simply cannot ignore. All I see is pain in her blue eyes when they meet mine, revealing a depth of emotion that words cannot convey. Her face, with its graceful contours and gentle jawline, exudes a fragility that both intrigues and worries me. It is only now that I realize how her radiant beauty has gone unnoticed before, like a hidden gem waiting to be discovered.

Fuck! You need to stop looking at her that way. Ace would have my balls if he found out all the dirty thoughts racing through my head about what I want to do to Poppy Reeves.

"Get them out of your pants now," she spits, her gaze fixed over my shoulder to the cashier who is still assisting the customer behind me.

Casually, I toss out the following words, carefully watching her reaction to assess whether she might be open to the filthy thoughts crossing my mind.

"Princess, if you wanted me to pull out my cock so you can suck it, you should have mentioned it back at the house."

She clenches her jaw, grinding her teeth together. Her eyes, full of rage, narrow, while her brows furrow. Stepping forward, she closes the gap until our bodies touch. The intensity of her presence sears through me, and my heart starts pounding erratically in my chest. Excitement tingles through every nerve in my body. What the fuck is going on with me?

As her gaze pierces through me, I find myself studying every contour and intricate detail that graces her face. I am captivated by the sight of her mesmerizing eyes, the gentle tremble of her lips, and the graceful curve of her eyebrows.

"You should know, asshole," she hisses at me through clenched teeth. "I choke on small bones."

Filled with anger, she abruptly turns on her heels and strides out of the store. Her actions clearly reveal the depth of her intense frustration.

As I watch her walk away, a mischievous grin forms at the corners of my lips. I can't help but stare at her body, especially her amazing ass. There's something intriguing about Poppy, despite her reputation. She's a total loner at school, with no one to talk to or hang out with. It sucks that people see her as an outcast and always bully her. But she's the only chick in school who's not afraid to speak up.

CHAPTER 4
Poppy

Over the following week, Xander continues with his usual behavior, completely ignoring me at school. I thought it might've changed after he chatted with me on the street. But nope. He didn't even acknowledge me in the slightest.

Sometimes, he'd be with Jade and her friends when they'd make fun of me for being fat. Even though he never joined in, it made me see that Xander would never want to be friends with someone like me. Not with so many pretty girls available to him to do anything he wants. So why would he bother?

Still, I maintain my strength in the face of mockery and insults about my appearance, never revealing to them the deep impact they have on me. Beneath the surface, their cruel words feel like a constant hammer chipping away at the protective armor I have built around myself.

Although I had some reservations, I couldn't help but find pleasure in watching Xander effortlessly manipulate the girls to do whatever he wanted. His mere presence seemed to breathe life into everything, filling my world with vibrant colors and rescuing it from monotony.

I'd spot Xander and Ace, casually smoking and talking to those girls who are known for being easy. His charm is undeniably evident, even from a distance. It didn't take long for me to become familiar with his behavior patterns. Without fail, it played out in the exact same manner every single time. He would lean in, his lips almost brushing against the girl's ear, whispering something secretive. Every once in a while, he'd tuck her hair behind her ear and say a few words before leaving. And I'd see how they would be totally addicted to him.

Then the playful smirk that would appear on his face when the girl called out to him and raced to catch up. For him, it was just a game. A game he played well. I could clearly see that there was some truth to the rumors. Once Xander achieved what he wanted, he would ignore them until he needed it again. No matter how many times I saw him manipulate others, I couldn't resist his captivating charm.

At times, when I glanced in his direction, I would catch him staring at me, which honestly felt a bit peculiar. It made me wonder if he had somehow discovered my secret habit of observing him. In an attempt to divert his attention, I would swiftly shift my gaze or pretend to be engrossed in something else. Yet, no matter how discreet I tried to be, his gaze would unfailingly be fixated on me whenever I looked back.

Sometimes, my obsession went even further. As soon as my mom headed off to work, I would sit by the front window, peering through a tiny hole in the curtain. It became a nightly routine for me, without exception. Every single night, I would watch him strolling toward the nearby 7-Eleven. And like clockwork, within seven short minutes, he would return, indulging in the chocolate bars he no doubt had stolen.

I couldn't understand the reason behind his actions. Was it a compulsion to steal, fueled by the excitement of not getting caught - or perhaps he's simply bored and looking for something to occupy his time?

After spending the entire week observing him, dealing with Jade's cruel taunts, and being constantly nagged by Mom about my future, I feel an overwhelming need to release my anger. I yearn to direct my frustration towards someone or something, anything that can offer some relief from the mounting stress. What infuriated me even more this last week was Xander's complete disregard for my existence, which only made me feel even more insignificant. I'm determined to confront Xander and inquire why he's so fixated on stealing. Moreover, it was an opportunity for me to release all the pent-up emotions I have been holding onto.

Settling into a seat next to the window, I discreetly peer through the partially drawn curtain. When he walks past my house, I quickly go out the front door, standing under the flickering streetlight, waiting for his return.

Finally, after what feels like forever, I see him casually walking towards me on the dimly lit street.

Despite the anger I felt earlier when I came up with this idea to confront him, seeing him now makes me question if I am making the right choice. I bite my nails as a tingling sensation runs down my spine, warning me that this might not be a good idea. This is Xander, the boy whom I have been secretly crushing on for three long years. He's the only person who can make my heart flutter whenever he's around. Yet, he's never spoken to me, except for that one night.

What the fuck am I doing? He has ignored me for years, so why do I suddenly care now?

Before I have a chance to back out, he's already standing before me. His penetrating gaze gives me the sensation that his eyes are searing deep into my soul. I take a brief pause to compose myself, feeling the lump in my throat shift as I swallow.

"What's the reason behind it?" I ask, my voice unintentionally harsher than intended.

"What's behind what?" he asks as he stuffs the crumpled chocolate wrapper into his pocket.

"Do you steal chocolate bars for kicks or some other reason?"

"What?" His brows furrow in concentration. "What's in it for me if I tell you?"

"Are you seriously just playing a messed up game? Are you just bored, or is there more to it?"

A noticeable change in his body language tells me that I have struck a sensitive point. He takes a step forward, positioning himself almost face-to-face. Despite his efforts to intimidate me with his towering presence and fierce expression, I stand my ground and refuse to yield. I remain resolute and unwavering, refusing to give in.

"Why don't you just worry about your own fucking life, Princess? And I'll worry about mine," he scoffs. His voice is laced with a hint of ridicule. The words hang in the air. His eyes narrow, and a flicker of annoyance dances within them. I can feel the weight of his words, like a heavy burden settling on my shoulders, causing my heart to sink.

His eyes continue to roam over every detail of my face, making me wonder what he's up to. Is he trying to distract me from my questions? I shake my head, clearing my mind to refocus.

"Well what is it, or do you just do it to get off?"

He flashes a mischievous smirk. "It would blow your mind what gets me off, Princess."

The impact of his words on me is profound, and all of a sudden, a strong desire arises within me to discover its meaning. However, I quickly suppress that thought and focus on the current topic. "Why do you insist on calling me that?"

"Call you what?"

Watching him, it's evident he's thoroughly enjoying himself, reminiscent of a cat toying with its prey. He swiftly flicks his tongue across his bottom lip.

Oh my god, I can't believe I actually fell for it. I should have known better, considering I know his routine.

He smirks confidently with a lopsided grin. It's clear he's trying to manipulate me, just like he does with those girls from school. However, I refuse to let his charm sway me. I square my shoulders and stand tall, determined to hold my ground.

"You know the name I'm referring to."

"Oh, Princess," he says casually, retrieving another chocolate bar from his pocket. With a slight tilt of his head, he unwraps it, deliberately prolonging my answer.

I release a lengthy sigh of frustration. Having a conversation with Xander when he's in this mood is like having teeth pulled. Fucking painful.

He bites into it, chews for a moment, and then swallows. "I call you that because you chill in your fancy castle, getting all the love and attention from your mother." His shoulders tighten as he gazes down at me, and the intense glare in his eyes pierces right through me. The sheer intensity of his expression sends shivers down my spine. "Plus you have no idea of what it's like to go hungry. And not just a day, but for fucking days at a time. A princess couldn't imagine the hunger that makes your whole body ache. So, don't fucking judge me for the things I do, alright?" He steps in so close that his breath is all up in my face. "You have things that I can only dream of having. You can't judge until you've walked in my shoes. So fuck off to your perfect life and leave me the fuck alone."

Stepping aside, he keeps his gaze fixed on mine while he walks by. Upon hearing his words, I now feel like a hypocrite for judging him without fully understanding his situation. As he strolls home, his footsteps are all that can be heard in the quiet street.

Chapter 5

Xander

Since I saw Poppy singing in the street it did something to me. I don't know what exactly you'd call it, but I've tried to distract myself by fucking every chick I know. But her haunting melody still echoes in my mind. Surprisingly, fucking other girls had no impact on dispelling her presence from my mind. That night, it felt as though she permeated my very soul, infiltrating my life like an unwelcome parasite. This situation is far from what I typically experience. I am not accustomed to such emotions. I like to fuck. So any thoughts of a chick usually revolve around finding something wet and pretty to stick my dick in. So, I have no idea of what the fuck is going on with me?

When she showed up last night, I was so ticked off by her judgment. What the fuck would she know about my life? Sitting in her ivory tower, looking down at me with disdain, treating me like some sort of lowlife. I know that her life isn't as perfect as I made it out to be, with all the sunshine and rainbows. I have noticed that there is a strained relationship between her and her mom. However, when she spoke those words last night, it provided me with the ideal opportunity to express my bottled-up emotions. I hoped that by doing so, I would finally free myself from her grip on my thoughts. I want to purge her from my mind and ensure she stays the fuck out of there.

Unfortunately, my words seemed to have no impact on the situation, regardless of what I said to her. Because this morning, she was the first thought that crossed my mind when I woke up with a raging hard-on. And while I took care of that, I couldn't help but wonder what her smart mouth would feel like wrapped around my cock.

All I can say is it's a good thing I don't see her anymore catching the bus. She's back to driving that green shitbox she calls a car. Thank fuck, because it's bad enough when I see her around the school. I'm aware that she has noticed me watching her, but she has no idea about the filthy, little disturbing thoughts that keep crossing my mind. The desires I have no business entertaining with someone like Poppy. Thoughts of lifting her short skirt and... Oh, damn it, here I go again.

It's lunchtime and I'm frantically banging Savannah in the bathroom in a desperate attempt to once again get Poppy out of my mind.

"Yeah, fuck me like that," Savannah cries out.

Usually, I enjoy it when chicks get loud, but today I'm not in the mood for it. All I want is to remove this bothersome presence of Poppy Reeves from my mind.

"Oh yeah, baby", says Savannah. "That's it. You're gonna make me come."

She tosses her head back and shouts my name. It's clear that she's not even close to coming, just faking it like she always does. It frustrates me how fake she really is, especially with her exaggerated moans. This bitch is getting on my nerves. I'm not into it anymore. The fact that she just called me "baby" and how she's annoying me is enough for me to pull out of her pussy. If I don't get to fucking come, there is no way she pretends to.

"What's the matter, baby?" she asks, as she turns to face me.

"That fucking name for starters." I take a step back to get away from her and dispose of the condom in the trash. As I do so, she turns around, still with her panties around her ankles.

"What do you want, baby?" she whispers, her voice low and filled with desire, completely ignoring what I just said.

For you to fuck off and leave me alone. I tuck my semi-erect dick back into my pants.

"Would you like me to suck your dick?" She trails her fingers up my torso, then lifts herself onto her tiptoes as if she's on the verge of kissing me.

Don't fucking do it. I swear if she does...

She moves in closer, her face so close to mine that our lips almost touch.

Pissed, I quickly turn my head to the side and shove her back.

As I try to move around her, she reaches out and grabs my arm. "Let me help you feel better, baby. Let me give you head."

"No and stop fucking calling me that. I'm not your fucking baby," I assert, forcefully pulling my arm from her grip. I see a hint of disappointment on her face as she adjusts her underwear and straightens her skirt.

"If you're up for it, we could maybe hang out after school."

"No!" I grab my bag and guitar off the bathroom floor. I've had enough. I swing open the door and step out into the hallway. Does she honestly think I'm that desperate to hang out with her? The only reason we've ever been together is for sex, and that one regrettable time she gave me a terrible blowjob. The one

Poppy Reeves happened to walk in on. A smirk forms on my face as I recall her shocked expression. Damn, there I go again, thinking about her. I really need to put a stop to that shit.

Suddenly, I hear the bathroom door creak open, and before I know it, Savannah is right beside me.

"Are you sure you don't want to hang out? My parents won't be home."

Does she genuinely believe that there is something more to this than just a simple transaction? She can't seriously believe she's the only one I'm banging. And why would she think I'd want to hang out with a girl I just hooked up with?

"Savannah, seriously, just fuck off and leave me alone," I say, my voice firm.

"You're a complete asshole," she says angrily, storming away.

"Yeah, so I've been told."

I find Ace in our usual spot, head buried in his phone.

As I approach, Jade and her crew immediately turn their attention towards me. I focus my gaze on Ace, who discreetly conceals a joint in his hand and raises it to his lips for a drag. Setting aside my guitar and bag, I take a seat beside Ace. He glances up and offers me the joint. Inhaling deeply, I raise my head and catch sight of Poppy in her usual spot, leaning against the brick wall. With her eyes closed, she seems immersed in her music, earbuds firmly in place. A sudden curiosity takes hold of me; I can't help but wonder what she's listening to. After all, the songs she played the other night were pretty impressive.

As I pass the joint back to Ace, Jade comes over and sits beside me. I don't bother acknowledging her arrival. My only focus is on Poppy, trying to comprehend why the fuck she's taking up so much of my mental space.

Poppy always keeps to herself and never sits with anyone. I wonder if it's because Jade does some pretty messed up things to her, or maybe she just prefers being alone.

Ace discreetly hands me the joint again.

"Hey, check out Poppy Reeves over there," I mention casually, raising the joint to my lips to see what Ace says about her.

Jade and Ace both turn their heads to look over at her.

"Yeah, what about her?" Ace asks, looking back at me.

Taking a momentary pause, I draw back on the joint and blow out a puff of smoke before speaking. "Have you ever wondered why she always sits alone like that over there?"

"Because she doesn't have any friends, that's why," Jade says. "And on top of that, she's a fat cow. Who would ever want to fuck someone like her?"

I knew Jade picked on Poppy because she felt insecure. However, due to my mood, I can't resist messing with her.

"I'd fuck her," I say, knowing Jade's reaction would be priceless.

Ace, who's caught on to what I'm doing, chimes in and says, "Yep, I'd hit that in a heartbeat."

"Seriously," Jade says, and I can see the shocked, pissed-off look on her face. "You'd fuck her."

"Yep," Ace says, putting out the joint on the seat next to him.

Jade lets out an annoyed sigh and goes over to her group of bitches. Ace laughs and then shifts his attention to me.

"Damn, that was easier than usual to piss her off this time."

As soon as the bell rings for the last lessons of the day. I swiftly snatch my bag and guitar. Casting a quick glance towards Poppy, I see she's already gone. Ace and I go our separate ways to our classes.

The rest of the day drags on slowly. When the bell finally rings, I'm eager to share with Ace, the song I wrote during the last period. Instead of paying attention to the teacher, I found myself immersed in the words I wrote late last night in my room, while my father, as usual, was passed out on the couch.

That's the amazing thing about Ace - his touch on my lyrics always brings out the brilliance in the song. I have full trust in it. It's our reliable method. I take care of the lyrics and jot down some melody notes, while Ace adds those unique elements that take the sound to another level. It's fantastic. Both of us have a strong musical sensibility and we're developing our distinct sound.

As I wait for Ace next to his car, I casually scroll through my phone.

Before long, Ace shows up with Jade accompanying him. In an effort to suppress my irritation, I take a deep breath and try to keep my composure. All I had hoped for this afternoon was to focus on our music. Unfortunately, with Jade around, Ace always has different ideas in store. It's a recurring pattern whenever he brings her along - an untamed and spontaneous adventure.

He grabs his keys from his pocket and unlocks the car. Opening the driver's door, he takes a moment to adjust the seat, pushing it forward creating space for Jade to comfortably sit in the back. In the meantime, I stay put, locked in a tense gaze with him over the roof of the car.

"What?" He smirks. "I thought we could have a little fun. Let's enjoy ourselves first, and then we can practice. It won't hurt." He jumps into the car.

I toss my guitar onto the back seat, narrowly missing Jade, and hop in the car.

Ace starts the engine, and as we leave the school grounds, I light up a joint.

Ace zooms down the street like a maniac. I'm just about to take another hit from my joint when I feel fingers run through my hair.

"Can I have some?" Jade asks.

"No. And move your fucking fingers before I break them."

Passing the joint to Ace, the smoke drifts between us. He takes a swift hit and passes it back.

"Jade, I'm not telling you again. Get your fucking fingers out of my hair," I snap, annoyed.

"Okay," she sighs, slumping into the worn-out seat.

I take another hit; the smoke swirling around me in a hazy cloud.

"Why won't you let me have any?" Jade's whiny voice pierces through my patience.

"Because I don't fucking want to, that's why."

"Well, don't expect me to fuck you later than."

"I'll pass, thanks."

"You didn't tell me that yesterday."

"That was yesterday. Things change." The effects of the joint start to hit and I feel my body relaxing.

"We'll still have fun, won't we, Ace?" Jade says, shifting in the seat, wrapping her arms around him from behind.

"Yeah, we will," he says, glancing at Jade through the rearview mirror before shifting his focus to me. "Are you sure you don't want any?"

"Nah, I'm good, thanks."

Ace brings the vehicle to a halt on the side of the street, directly in front of an empty lot.

"What are you doing?" I ask.

"Let Jade in the front," Ace says.

"What the hell, man," I add, popping open the passenger's side door, fully aware of what's about to happen.

"If you're not gonna join, she might as well start now."

"I'm not sticking around to see that shit, I'm outta here."

"That hasn't stopped you in the past. You always join in. What's up with you, dude?"

I don't even bother giving him a response, I just slam the car door. Lately, I've been asking myself that same question.

I head towards the rear of the car and lean against it. Pulling out my phone, I absentmindedly scroll, attempting to distract myself. It's not that I haven't seen Ace receiving a blowjob before; in fact, I've even fucked her from behind while she was doing it. However, for some reason, today I simply don't feel like participating.

Although I cannot see inside the car, I can hear every detail through the open windows. Typically, my body would respond to the wet sounds coming from Jade's mouth, and I would feel a sudden urge to participate. But my dick must be taking a nap today because those noises aren't doing anything.

"Deeper," Ace demands, and I hear the sounds of Jade gagging.

A few minutes pass.

"Swallow it," Ace says, grunting in pleasure. "That's it. Good girl."

Knowing the routine all too well, I swiftly stashed my phone in my pocket. My friend and I share similar desires - we simply seek to gratify ourselves. Honestly, we don't truly prioritize the need to pleasure chicks, as long as we attain our own satisfaction. We avoid lingering because the girls tend to become overly attached, just like Savannah was today.

Hence, for the time being, Ace will maintain his distance from Jade.

I circle back to the passenger's seat and open the door.

Jade sits up, wipes her mouth with the back of her hand, and grins like she just saved the whole fucking universe.

"Thanks," Ace says, as he tucks his cock back into his pants. "You live somewhere around here, don't you?"

Jade's eyebrows furrow. "Yeah, why?"

"We need to practice. I can drop you home."

Her eyes fixate on him before I notice a flicker of annoyance pass over her expression. "Are you seriously kidding me?" she mutters under her breath. "You complete jerk!" She leans over, retrieves her bag from the back seat, and swiftly exits the vehicle.

Without any hesitation, I hop back into the passenger's seat.

Ace steps on the gas pedal and merges back into traffic.

That's simply our way of doing things. We have absolutely no concern for anyone else. After enduring years of mistreatment and being consistently made to feel insignificant, it becomes ingrained in us to detach ourselves from the emotions of others.

I burst into laughter.

"She's so pissed at you, man."

"Yeah, I'll give her some attention tomorrow, she'll be fine."

As we round the corner, Ace's house comes into view. He lets out a deafening roar upon seeing that car, which is parked right in the center of the driveway, blocking any available space for Ace to park.

"This is complete bullshit," Ace says, as he double parks on the side of the road. "I've reached my limit with this dipshit." He exits the car and heads towards the house.

I quickly step out of the car, hollering at Ace. "Hey, wait up, man. Don't do anything stupid."

Before I can stop him, Ace bursts into the house.

I quickly follow, my focus quickly shifting to Ace's mother, asleep on the couch. The room reeks of booze and weed.

Entering the room, I see a middle-aged man who looks as if he is the leader of an old biker gang. His arms are all decked out with cool tattoos that give off a rebellious vibe. The icy stare in his eyes subtly reveals his twisted pleasure in inflicting pain and suffering upon others.

It's weird to see a car in the driveway with what he's wearing, which suggests he arrived on two wheels.

"Can you find another spot to fucking park?" Ace spits, then his jaw tightens and his fists clench in frustration. "Every damn time I come home, you're parked there." Ace gives him a piercing stare, but he completely ignores him and walks towards the chair where his leather jacket sits.

As he grabs it, he casually adds, "Let her know I'll stop by later."

"I'm not your fucking errand, boy," Ace spits.

Without any warning, the old man immediately strides across the room and forcefully slams Ace against the wall, creating a loud thud.

"Listen to me, you cocky little shit. I won't tolerate your crap like your mother does."

"Screw you!" Ace yells.

I rush over and tug on his tattooed arm. "Let go of him, now."

No matter how hard I try to free Ace, it's impossible because the jerk tightens his grip around Ace's throat. Ace's face turns red as he desperately tries to claw at the hand suffocating him. This situation has the potential to become a real shit show. I need to get Ace and get the fuck out of here.

The wanna-be biker lets out a low growl, sending a shiver down my spine as he releases Ace. Breathing hard, Ace's eyes widen, and he flinches as the guy hurls a punch toward the wall, narrowly missing his head.

Without uttering a single word, he turns around, grabs his jacket, and leaves the house.

Ace and I continue to stare at the door long after he's gone.

"I can't wait to get away from this shithole of a place," says Ace. "I fucking hate my life."

I understand exactly how he feels. It's like being trapped in a pitch-black room, unable to see or hear anything, with a heavy weight crushing your chest, rendering you completely powerless. You have no control over anything in your goddamn fucking life. That's why I also eagerly await my chance to leave this shithole.

CHAPTER 6

Xander

Staying focused during practice is quite a challenge, especially with all the chaos with that biker. However, after Ace's passionate rant about that obnoxious guy, he managed to enter a state of complete concentration. His sound is truly unique, and it complements my lyrics flawlessly. We're making excellent progress.

As Ace drives me home, the silence in the car is deafening, filled with unspoken anger. He's clearly still bothered by what happened earlier, even though he hasn't said a word. Once he drops me off, he'll probably hit up Jade for a distraction. And if Jade's still pissed at him, it will be Savannah or someone else from the group. That's Ace's pattern, hooking up to escape his shitty life.

As we're getting closer to my place, I see Poppy Reeves chilling, sitting on the curb, fully engrossed by her phone. As I take a breath, the haunting melody of her singing that night rushes back to me. Will the sound of her alluring voice ever reach my ears again?

The sight of the empty space in her driveway confirms that her mother must be gone for the night. Maybe they had a fight again, and that's why she's sitting on the side of the road. I don't know why, but all of a sudden, I'm noticing every movement that Poppy makes.

Despite living two doors away from her for years, I've never been tempted to pry into her private life. So, why the fuck do I care now? Maybe it's because I'm still trying to figure out why her voice did something to me the other night when she sang. And maybe the fact that Poppy is throwing me off.

Poppy fucking Reeves, the loner.

That girl doesn't catch the eye of any guy. So why the fuck am I thinking of her in a way I shouldn't?

"Yo, is that Poppy Reeves sitting in the street?" Ace eases off the pedal as he gets closer to my house. "That girl's a fucking freak." He parks the car.

With a jolt of irritation, my eyes lock onto his. For some reason, I kinda wanna tell him to shut the fuck up. Instead, I quickly gather my belongings and get out of the car.

"See ya tomorrow," Ace says out the open window. He zooms off down the street.

As he passes, Poppy's head lifts in curiosity, her eyes watching as he speeds by.

With her eyes now fixed on me, she stands up and quickly slips her phone into her pocket.

All it takes is one look from her and I'm hightailing it out of there. The weight of her gaze stays with me as I make my way up the front path. What the fuck is happening? This chick is stirring up emotions in me that I've never felt before. I'm the one who is always assertive and commanding, always in control. I take what I please, without pause or consideration. They don't even exist until I'm yearning to be balls deep in their wet holes. So why the fuck am I thinking like this? I haven't even gotten a damn hand job from this girl, but she's still all I think about. I need to get my shit together.

My heart starts racing when I hear footsteps coming closer, causing me to stop.

"Xander!" Poppy yells out.

"What?" I'm so pissed off and I can't stand how she makes me feel. I spin around, hoping she'll take one look at me and fuck right off.

She stops immediately and takes a step back, leaving an uncomfortable silence between us. "Um... well..."

I watch Poppy as she fights to find the right words to form a complete thought. Her face flushes with embarrassment. For some reason, I find satisfaction in the knowledge that I've made her uncomfortable.

"I messed up in a big way and now I have way more mac and cheese than I can eat. So, if you would like-"

"Stop," I butt in, knowing she's full of shit. It's all because of what I told her the other night. I step closer, trying to intimidate her, as if it will make her disappear from my mind. "Don't you dare give me your fucking sympathy, Princess?"

"Seriously, stop calling me that, you asshole. Let's get one thing straight. I'm not some fucking princess." Her brows furrow in anger. Her face is like a canvas of frustration. "You'd see that if you pulled your head out of your ass for five seconds. I offered you something to eat, but if you don't want it, then

I'll just throw it away. So go without. See if I care," she says, a bitter edge to her voice. She turns away.

I reach out and grab her arm, feeling the warmth of her skin beneath my fingertips. Her quick glance over her shoulder catches my eye, and for a brief moment, our gazes connect before she shifts her attention down to my hand on her arm.

Just the slightest touch of her sends a small tsunami of goosebumps all over me, leaving my skin tingling with anticipation. A fiery warmth spreads to my cock, igniting my desire. Ah, now it all makes sense. Out of all the girls I could hook up with, my dick is set on Poppy Reeves. Once he gets some relief, all these things I've been dealing with will finally go away.

I purposely keep my hand on her arm, testing the waters, observing her expression as I time how long it takes for her to push me away.

One second, two seconds, three seconds pass.

She takes one look at my face, noticing the mischievous smirk, and hastily pulls her arm away.

"What are you trying to do, Xander?"

Damn, she's clever. Usually, it's a simple touch and they give me what I want. But not with her.

"I never said no to the food. But let me be fucking clear on this. I don't need your pity."

"Listen up, asshole, you won't be getting any pity from me. You can be a real jerk sometimes, you know." She turns and walks away, leaving me alone.

"Yeah, so I've been told," I mutter quietly to myself, as I follow her down the front path. I haven't eaten all day and my hunger is reaching its peak. Plus, I'm up for the challenge of dealing with Poppy if it means I can feast on real food instead of chocolate bars. It's been like forever since I've had a proper meal. Not since Mom passed away. Plus, with the way my dick responded to my hand touching her, maybe I could talk her into doing something to me while I'm there.

Poppy is silent as we walk back to the house.

I walk a few feet behind, stealing glimpses at her ass. Yeah, I can picture grabbing onto it and ramming into her tight pussy from behind.

But first I need to unravel the mystery of Poppy Reeves. I'm clueless when it comes to figuring out how to handle someone like her. She's different from those other girls who always give me what I want. She's not easily manipulated. My usual tricks don't work on her. But believe me, they will eventually.

Time to step up my game. I'm curious how long it will take for her to let her guard down and give me a blowjob with that smart mouth of hers. I suppose only time will tell.

When we get to her house, she moves up the front steps, taking them two at a time. She shoves the black front door open and walks in. With a smile, she holds the door open so I can come in. I step to the side and wait, scanning the area.

As soon as the door clicks shut, Poppy darts right past me, heading further into the house. While Poppy moves over to the kitchen, I take a moment to survey the room.

Placed prominently in the room, the couch is covered with pillows and blankets, creating a cozy vibe. A big-ass TV sits on the back wall, demanding everyone's attention. With the bright lights, all the shiny things in the room sparkle. Yep. Poppy Reeves may not have a castle, but she sure lives like a fucking princess. Nothing like the fucking mess I live in two doors down, with all the walls full of holes and bottles scattered on the floors.

"You can sit on the sofa if you like and I'll bring it over," Poppy yells from the kitchen.

I move over to the couch and drop my bag, feeling the weight lift from my shoulders. I rest my guitar against the side of the couch and take a seat.

Running my hand over the fabric feels like indulging in a lavish treat, with its silky texture under my fingertips.

"Do you want a drink?" Poppy asks, peering into the double-door fridge.

"Yeah, okay."

"What do you want?"

"What have you got?"

"Coke, water, juice."

So many fucking choices. I nailed the fucking name I gave her. She lives like a princess.

"I'll take a coke."

I continue to glance around the room. At least it will be cozy while I hang here a bit. Beats dodging my asshole father's fists at home. Plus, hanging out with her might help me get my head back in the game. It'll serve as a reminder that she's not my type, someone who doesn't matter. Why else would she be the loner of the school? Chillin' with her for like twenty minutes should remind me how boring she is. Then she won't be occupying my thoughts or giving me a boner.

With a can and bowl in hand, Poppy makes her way across the room. Her movements catch my attention by the way her hips effortlessly sway, captivating my senses.

I can feel my body tingling and getting all worked up.

She leans down to pass me the bowl of Mac and Cheese, and I can't help but check out her tits. I have a clear view with the gap in the front of her shirt. Not bad. Not bad at all.

"Thanks," I add, my eyes quickly darting up to her face.

She leaves the can of Coke on the coffee table in front of me and goes back to the kitchen. I can't help but check her out. Fantastic ass, perfectly round and curvy. I'm curious to know if she's ever been hit on before and what she would do if I were to make a move. Would she be open to it or would she shut it down?

She returns, her hands full with a steaming bowl of mac and cheese and a can of coke. When she moves past, I'm hit with a lingering vanilla fragrance.

Fuck she smells really good.

I watch as she sinks into the plush, cozy couch, tucking her legs under her. Leaning forward, she places her coke on the table next to mine and snatches the TV remote.

Even though she's not physically next to me, my body is still alert to her presence.

"Is there anything you want to watch?" she asks, her eyes meeting mine before shifting down to the bowl in my hands. "Why aren't you eating? I thought you were hungry."

I stay quiet and focus on the bowl in my hands, not paying attention to the energy radiating from Poppy. Damn, I thought being here would finally end these messed-up thoughts. But I just wanna get down and dirty with her, corrupt the innocent little princess, and get my fix.

As I grab my fork and stab a piece of pasta, Poppy presses a button on the remote and the TV turns on. When that creamy mac and cheese hits my tongue, I can barely contain my delight. Holy crap, this is good. I take another bite and enjoy the taste.

"Have you ever watched The Real Housewives of Beverly Hills?" she asks, her gaze shifting towards me.

The Real Housewives - I have no fucking idea what show she's talking about.

"Do I look like I'm into that, Princess?" I say with a mouth full of food, ignoring the pissed-off look on her face from the name I've just called her. "But you watch it if you want? I don't care." I shovel more of the mac and cheese into my mouth.

She goes back to watching TV, changes the channel, and throws the remote next to her on the couch. She wastes no time digging her fork into the steaming mac and cheese.

While she eats, I steal glances at her as she remains engrossed in the TV. Holy fuck, the way she sucks the cheese from her fork is turning me on. I'm curious about the sensation of having those plump, pink lips wrapped around my cock. I wonder if she's ever given a blowjob. Probably not. I'm curious to know if she'll kick Savannah out of last place.

While her attention is fixed on the TV, I keep checking her out. The smooth roundness of her face accentuates her natural beauty. As she blinks, her long lashes lightly stroke her smooth ivory skin, beautifully highlighting her big blue eyes.

As she watches something on the screen, a subtle amusement tugs at the corners of her mouth, causing a smile to bloom on her face. Her smile quickly turns into a giggle, ending with a loud snort. The second I hear it, I grin.

Right away, she puts her hand over her mouth and looks towards me. She gets all red-faced and embarrassed.

"Oops, sorry. It just slips out sometimes. This show gets crazy."

With her eyes still on me, I move my hand to the back of the lounge, letting it rest there just behind her neck. I'm curious to see how much I can get away with before she snaps and tells me to fuck off.

Poppy nervously bites her bottom lip, her body subtly trembling as she senses my presence. In an effort to steady herself, she takes a deep breath before refocusing her attention back on the television.

Ahh... yes.

It appears that even this princess is susceptible to my charms. Only she's much better at disguising her true feelings than the others.

I pull my arm back to finish my mac and cheese and focus on the television. Watching these crazy bimbos do some messed up shit to each other is entertaining, and kind of amusing.

It's kinda weird how women can be so mean to each other, like Jade and the girls at school. They're just tearing each other down to boost their own egos.

Before I even realize it, I have become totally invested in the show.

If anyone caught me here with Poppy, eating her mac and cheese and watching The Real Housewives, I'd deny that shit in a heartbeat.

As the show comes to an end, a smile spreads across my face, while Poppy bursts into uncontrollable laughter, amused by the women's sadistic behavior.

The sound of her laughter catches me off guard, like a beautiful melody. It's strange that after all these years of going to school with her, I don't think I've ever heard her laugh.

That's because dipshit you don't have anything to do with her.

With the credits rolling, Poppy leans forward, setting her bowl on the table.

"Should we watch another one or do you have to go?"

I pick up on the hopeful undertone. It's a good sign - she doesn't want me to go. But I can't hang out with her all night. That's not my thing. If I wanna get this show started, it's time for me to make my move.

"Yeah, but first I want to ask you something?" I move my arm back on the couch, right behind her neck.

"Yeah," she says looking confused. She shifts around on the couch to face me. There's a sexy view of her tits through the slight opening in her shirt.

"So, what did you want to ask me?" she says, her voice quivering with uncertainty.

"What went down between you and your mom the other night?"

Pulling her legs in close, she wraps her arms tightly around them, seeking comfort, creating a protective barrier around her.

"My mom is always nagging me to go to college and study aged care, just like her."

"And that's not something you want."

"No. Not at all."

"So, what is it you want to do then, Princess?"

She throws me a "screw you" look but continues to answer my question.

"Well," she says. "Whenever I think about my future, it's all about music. Not in a band or anything like that. But music for children. Musical therapy is a great way to improve the lives of disabled children. I wanna start an organization and make a difference in kids' lives with music."

"Do you even know how to play an instrument?"

"Yes, asshole. Of course, I know how to play. My dad taught me when I was little. He played in a band."

"No way, seriously? How did I not know that?"

Because dickhead, Poppy slipped under your radar. Like she does with every-one else, all except Jade and her bitches.

"Yeah, my dad's band didn't achieve mainstream success, but he still followed his passion."

"So, why not just tell your mom what you wanna do?"

She cocks an eyebrow. "What are you playing twenty questions or something?"

"Yeah, something along those lines. I guess it's a game of Truth or Dare," I say with a sly grin, wanting to test if I could convince her to do what I desired.

"My mom is not a fan of musicians because of my dad." She flicks her tongue over her bottom lip, and my gaze instinctively follows. "Now it's my turn to ask you a question."

"Okay. Truth," I add, yearning to say "Dare" but I need to take small, delicate steps, not wanting to spook her.

"Not to be rude, but why don't you have any food at home? I mean, I've seen your dad leaving for work. So, I don't understand."

She's right. My dad goes to work every morning. It's crazy how he can keep a job and work all day with a hangover.

I look away for a second, trying to figure out what to say and how much to spill. Ace is the only one who knows how messed up my life is. I tend to keep my family issues private, especially with strangers. I don't know why, but I wanted to see how she would react if I told her about it. And since she didn't have any friends at school, I knew she wouldn't spill the beans to anyone. I wanted to see how far I could push her to do what I wanted.

While considering my next words, I run my hands over the luxurious velvet fabric of the couch.

"Yes, you're right. My dad goes to work every day. But to be honest, he doesn't give a fuck anymore. It's been that way ever since my mom passed." The mere mention of my mom causes my throat to tighten, and I instinctively gulp to ease the tension. It's rare for me to mention her to others. As I feel the tension building in my body, I shift the conversation to a different topic.

"Okay, it's your turn now. Truth or dare?" I ask Poppy, a mischievous grin spreading across my face.

"So we are actually playing this game," she says, arching her eyebrow in surprise.

"Yes, now Truth or Dare."

Before answering, Poppy takes a deep breath, clearly not wanting to play. Then she says, "Truth."

"Did you make extra mac and cheese out of pity?"

I notice a flicker of sadness in her eyes as she quickly averts her gaze to something across the room.

"Poppy, I don't need your fucking pity," I say firmly. I can't stand the thought of being seen like that. I make a move to leave, but Poppy's hand on my arm keeps me rooted in place. The anger in me is so overwhelming that I can't even acknowledge the tingling sensation that her gentle touch brings.

"I'm sorry," she mutters softly.

I stand there, the silence hanging heavy between us, waiting for her gaze to meet mine.

When she finally looks up at me, I can see the vulnerability etched on her face and in her eyes, mirroring the raw emotion of the night she sang out in the street. Why does seeing her like that have such an effect on me?

"Xander, I don't feel any pity towards you. I invited you over so you won't go hungry."

"Come on, Princess, that's the definition of pity."

I watch her for a moment longer, savoring the sight of her chest rising and falling with each breath, before settling back down on the couch.

I break the silence with a simple question, "Truth or Dare?" The words linger in the air, waiting for a reply.

As she tucks a strand of hair behind her ear, she utters the word "Truth."

I study her for a moment, weighing the risks of pushing her too far and the potential rewards of getting what I want. I opt to keep it simple for now and stick with a basic question.

"I've noticed you don't hang out with anyone at school. Why is that?"

Her eyes dart away from me, and for a brief moment, I see a flicker of torment on her face. "I used to have friends who were always there for me. But that changed a long time ago." She glances back in my direction and shrugs. "I'm on my own now."

"Is Jade the reason?"

She eyes me for a moment. "You know you asked two questions, right?"

"Quit stalling, Princess. Answer the question."

She gives me a skeptical look, like she's trying to figure out what I'm up to. "Deep down, I know it had something to do with that. My friends never came out and said it. But every time Jade would start, they would distance themselves. I think my friends ditched me because they didn't want to be targeted like I was."

Fuck. I feel bad for her. I can't even wrap my head around having to deal with all that shit. Not to mention her lame-ass friends bailing on her because of it.

She picks up a cushion from the lounge and rests it gently on her lap, blocking my view of her tits. "Truth or Dare," she says.

"Truth," I add.

"What's with all the girl hopping?"

"Because I don't do relationships. Once I'm done with school, Ace and I are outta here." I nearly admitted that I only had an interest in chicks when it came to hooking up, but I didn't want her to assume that was my sole purpose for being here. She doesn't need to know my motives.

"Truth or Dare," I ask.

"Truth."

Her piercing blue eyes hold me captive as she gazes at me. I ask the question that's been nagging me ever since I first entered this house.

"Are you still a virgin?"

I wait, my breath held, preparing myself for her to kick me out of her house, but to my surprise, she doesn't. Instead, she drops her head, her fingers nervously fidgeting on a loose thread on the cushion in her lap.

Her voice, so faint it's almost above a whisper. "Yes."

I don't know why, but it's good to know she hasn't been with anyone else.

'It's my turn,' she says, shifting on the couch. "Truth or dare."

"Truth," I add.

"What's something you're afraid of?"

"Being trapped here and slowly morphing into my father?"

"Then you understand it. You get why I don't wanna be stuck in the same boring job as my mom."

"Yeah, I do," I add, relaxing into the plush lounge, our eyes connecting. "It's your turn."

A mischievous smile dances on her lips as she eagerly challenges. "Dare."

Thank fucking god.

I've been waiting for that word since we started playing this fucking game. I chill for a bit, then position my arm on the back of the couch behind her.

It's clear I'm making Poppy uneasy with my hand near her neck. I try to push it a little further by wrapping my fingers around the ends of her smooth, sun-kissed blonde locks. As I continue to play with the ends of her hair, I marvel at how soft and silky it feels. Glancing up, I notice her eyes fixed on my every move. Her face says it all - she's totally shocked, her mouth hanging open and eyes wide.

"You should be careful with dares, Princess. You might not like what I dare you to do." I run my tongue over my bottom lip. Her eyes flicker down to my mouth. I give her a lopsided smirk, relishing in the satisfaction of knowing that move never fails to work its magic. "I dare you to suck my dick!"

She looks up at me right away. I brace myself for her sharp reply, recalling how she shot me down when I propositioned her at the 7-Eleven the other night.

I watch her swallow, a subtle movement that betrays her unease. Each passing second feels like an eternity, the tension growing as she hesitates to speak. She's in deep thought, just staring at me.

When I can no longer bear the deafening silence, I break it with my voice. "You know the rules, Princess. A dare is a dare."

"I know," she says, her head bobbing in agreement, showing her understanding. With a deep breath, she gathers her strength and stands up from the couch.

I feel the rush of adrenaline coursing through my veins, my heart pounding in anticipation of what's to come. I can't believe Poppy actually agreed to give me a blowie. Fingers crossed, I just hope all the effort I've put in will be worth it in the end.

With a swift movement, she positions herself in front of me and drops to her knees. The sight of her in that position instantly gets me hard. The thought of her mouth wrapped around my cock sends a delicious shiver down my spine. I get comfy on the couch and keep my arm rested on the back cushion.

"Have you done this before?" I ask, eager to find out what's in store for me.

"No," she shakes her head.

Given her lack of experience, I'm pondering whether I should abandon the idea altogether. I don't think I could handle another feeble attempt at a blowie, with half-hearted efforts and a complete lack of technique. I'm still getting over the one Savannah gave me a few days ago.

With Poppy on her knees, her gaze piercing into my soul I succumb to the weight of the moment. I won't know how terrible she is until she actually does it. Furthermore, when she gives me the most unsatisfying blowjob, it will aid in getting her out of my fucking head.

"Well, whenever you're ready Princess," I add, surrendering my control to her.

With a deep breath, she unbuttons my jeans, unzips my pants, and pulls out my throbbing cock. Her fingers on my dick ignite a fire within me, awakening every nerve ending.

Her unwavering stare remains on my firm cock, and I find myself fascinated by her interest. My eyes are fixed on her as she licks her plump lips, and I fight the urge to release a low, throaty groan. The thought of this being her first blowjob is sending my mind into a frenzy. I can't put my finger on why I want to be present for all her firsts, and not just this one.

Pull yourself fucking together. She hasn't even done anything yet, dickhead.

With a tender stroke of her fingertips, she explores the sensitive underside of my cock, unleashing a cascade of pleasurable sensations.

"Fuck," I growl as a groan of delight hisses from my throat.

She meets my gaze, a mischievous twinkle in her eyes, and repeats the action with a playful smile. The slightest touch sets off a chain reaction of bliss, pulsating through every inch of me. The impulse to push her head down and thrust into her mouth flits through my mind, but I quickly dismiss it. I want her to take control and analyze her actions. If her touch gets me this aroused, how intense will it feel in her warm mouth?

She traces her fingers around the tip of my cock, gathering the sticky pre-cum that has formed at the head. With a soft smile, she brings her fingers to her mouth, savoring the taste on her tongue. It's the hottest fucking thing I've seen in my life.

"Fuck!" I hiss.

As she leans forward, I can feel the warmth of her breath on my dick, making me quiver with pleasure as her tongue slides along the shaft. With a swirling motion of her tongue, she explores the flavor on the tip.

When I take a deep breath, I can feel the tension building up inside me, like it's about to burst. And fuck, she hasn't even gone down on me yet.

My breathing, heavy and deep, immediately grabs her attention. She looks up, her eyes sparkling with triumph, and gives me a satisfied smile, knowing she has successfully manipulated me. Her focus shifts back to my cock, and she takes me deep into her mouth.

CHAPTER 7

Poppy

Oh. My. God! If someone had told me this morning that Xander would be chilling in my house, I would've thought they were crazy. But having his dick in my mouth is right off the charts. This is no ordinary person here, people. It's Xander fucking Williams. The guy I've been crushing on forever. No way I was saying no to sucking his cock. But the thing is, what I didn't tell him is that I'm totally clueless about what I am doing. How am I supposed to know how to give head when I haven't even experienced my first kiss yet?

Okay. Stay focused. Just act confident and roll with it. Even if you're winging it, you've still gotta nail this. Just follow his cues and listen to his sounds.

With each inch I take him deeper into my mouth, I can feel his body trembling with pleasure, and I glimpse his hand tightening on the couch beside his leg. Shit. Maybe I'm doing it right after all. This time, I go deeper. Taking him in until he brushes the back of my throat. I pay attention to the sounds he makes, listening for cues about his desires and preferences.

"Fuck me!" He hisses, and I can feel the pressure of his hand tightening around my hair.

If Xander's dick wasn't in my mouth, I'd be high-fiving myself for nailing it.

While I push my mouth back down his shaft and hold him there, I relish the flavor of him and tease the sensitive underside with my tongue.

He moans, his voice echoing through the room, as he tightens his grip on my hair. Wow... He's really getting into this.

As he thrusts his hips forward, my breathing becomes labored, struggling to take in enough air with his cock in my throat. Yet, I suck harder, paying close attention to the erotic noises escaping his lips so I can give him what he craves.

He thrusts into my mouth with a sense of urgency that leaves me breathless.

"Fuck! You're gonna make me come, Princess," he grunts, his voice filled with desire as he thrusts into my mouth.

What the hell do I do? My mind is blank, on what steps to take next. Do I remove his cock from my mouth or leave it there? But when his grip tightens on my hair and he lets out a groan, I allow his release to run down the back of my throat. His face contorts with pleasure as he rides out the wave of his orgasm. Watching him come is the fucking hottest thing I've ever seen.

His breathing slows, and his moans subside before I release him from my mouth with a loud pop.

Xander just sits there, his watchful eyes never leaving me. The intensity in his piercing brown eyes makes me feel vulnerable as if he can peer into the depths of my soul. Did I screw it up? Was I terrible at it? No because if I was bad at it, he wouldn't have come like that or made those sexy sounds.

Unsure of my next move, I lingered between his legs. His chest rises and falls with each breath before he leans forward and, with a gentle touch, he tucks my long blonde hair in behind my ear.

"You sure you've never done that before, Princess?" he says with a smirk.

"No," I whisper, my voice barely audible as I shake my head in disbelief.

With a feather-light touch, he runs his thumb over my bottom lip, sending a pleasurable shiver coursing through my body.

"If you weren't a virgin, I'd bend you over that table and fuck you senseless."

His filthy words make me feel so vulnerable like I'm completely under his power. Despite knowing that I would be just another notch on Xander's belt, I still hoped he'd do what he said.

"You can still do it," I add, dying for him to touch me.

"Nah... Virgins aren't my thing," he says, shifting back on the couch and tucking his cock back into his jeans.

I stand up and plop down on the couch, the heaviness of rejection sinking into my bones. I can't believe I didn't pick up on the obvious signs of his true intentions. I've spent endless hours observing him, studying his behavior. I know that Jade, Savannah, and the other girls he disappears with are just tools for him to satisfy his sexual urges.

Now I'm mad at myself for falling for his charms. I was just a means for him to get off. I'm no different from Jade and those easy girls he hooks up with. I was just a means to satisfy his sexual needs. How the fuck did I fall for that knowing everything that I do from watching him? I know why. Because it was

Xander Williams. But that won't be happening again. I couldn't care less about the attention that jerk gives me next time. He will never fool me again.

As he gets up, I can sense him looming over me, his dark brown eyes never breaking contact with mine. "Well, I'll catch you later, I guess," he says as he heads towards the front door.

That's it. That's all this asshole is going to say to me after I sucked his dick. I refuse to let this jerk treat me like crap when I deserve better. I'm so angry that it feels like every cell in my body is vibrating with rage. Getting up from the couch, I hear the faint creak of the floorboards beneath my feet.

"Seriously, what's your problem, asshole?" I spit out.

He turns to the sound of my voice, a cocky grin on his lips. "What did you expect? You sucked my dick. No biggie. Sorry, but I'm not the marrying kind, Princess."

"You can't help yourself, can you? Just use people for your own pleasure and then treat them like they're worthless."

"Princess, look at this place. You've got it all, but you don't fucking know what it's like to be treated like you're nothing."

"Well, newsflash dickhead, you just did. So get over yourself. I certainly fucking have." I yank the front door open and hold it for him to get the fuck out.

His eyes linger on me briefly before he takes a step forward and walks out through the door.

With a loud thud, I forcefully close the door behind me.

The next day at school, Xander walks right by me, not even acknowledging my presence. I thought at least the sexual favor would earn me more than being ignored. Really I didn't know what to expect. Maybe a nod of his head whenever we crossed paths in the hallway. But in his familiar pattern, he snubbed me yet again, as he has done in the past.

The more I watch him at school, the more I understand that Xander Williams is someone who would never pay attention to someone like me. I knew I would never be special. I'd always be just a face in the crowd. A face that would always fade into the background, never catching anyone's attention. Everyone except Jade and her bitches.

Over the next few days, I keep a watchful eye on Xander's every move. Despite how he treated me the other night, I can't resist the allure of studying him.

Whether it was during lunchtime or while moving through the school grounds, I'm always scanning the area looking for him. You could say I'm a creature of habit, always doing the same thing for so many years. But lately, every time I spot him, I have to quickly look away because he's already staring at me.

Like how he is right now as I sit reading. Despite my attempts to focus on my e-reader, I can feel his gaze piercing into me, leaving me feeling exposed.

While I swipe the screen on my e-reader, I sneak a glance in his direction. Jade is practically grinding on him, in front of the entire school. But it's me he's watching, not her.

Does Jade honestly believe he cares about her in the slightest? Or is she doing it because he's Xander Williams? Just like I did.

Perhaps she does it to gain more admiration from others. She's the type who craves approval from others. I notice it when she taunts me and looks around for reactions.

But that's not me. I don't care what people think and I won't make that mistake with Xander again.

All I can say is that Jade is totally clueless if she thinks she's got some special spot in Xander's heart because of what she does. Xander doesn't care about anyone but himself. Can't she see that he's just using her to get what he wants, just like he did with me? One blowjob with him was enough for me to learn my lesson. And I will not make the same mistake twice. She's either as dumb as she looks or she just doesn't give a damn. Xander may shine like the sun, but his selfishness casts a shadow darker than the night.

As Ace walks over to Xander, I lift my head to watch them, taking in the sight of their easy camaraderie. Before taking a seat beside him, Ace gives him a reassuring pat on the shoulder. With a sudden motion, Ace pulls Jade onto his lap, prompting her to emit a joyful squeal. Despite Jade grinding on Ace's lap, Xander's gaze remains focused on me.

Ace leans over and says something to Xander, then shoots a quick glance in my direction.

Wait, did Xander spill the beans about what I did to him? Is that their deal? That they share stories about their sexual conquests?

My throat gets tight and my heart starts racing as nerves flood through me. That fucking dickbag did. He straight up told him. Because why the hell would

Ace be staring at me when he doesn't even know I exist? I stash my e-reader into my bag and get ready to leave. Who else did he tell?

In an instant, I'm on my feet, ready to flee and hide from the watchful eyes around me.

Each guy I pass deepens my anxiety, fueling my belief that they're aware of what I did to Xander.

I bolt out of school, feeling so relieved when I finally get in my car. I have to get the hell out of here.

CHAPTER 8

Xander

Jade's lap dance did nothing for me. That's usually her way of wanting to hook up. But for some reason, my dick didn't want to play. It was only when I looked across and saw the feisty princess who gave me the best blow job of my life that my dick started to react. I grew rock hard as I watched her, the memory of her warm mouth still fresh in my mind. I'm pretty sure Jade thought she was the reason I was hard.

Yesterday I fucked Ebony Wilson in the girls' bathroom, but while I did it, all I could think about, was the sensation of Poppy's mouth on my cock. My release came swiftly, and Ebony didn't have a chance to put on her usual fake theatrics.

Even though Ace and I share everything. I never told him about the blow job I received from Poppy. For some reason, I couldn't tell him I'd found the first-place champion. If he finds out she's great at giving head, he'll be all over that. And trust me, once he experiences the sensation of Poppy's mouth on his cock, every other blow job pales in comparison. He'll just keep coming back for more, like the way I'm craving it now. And for some odd reason, I don't like the idea of sharing her.

Poppy's mouth was something else. She told me she'd never done it before. But I think that's bullshit. Who gives a blowie so skillfully like that their first time? If what she says is true, just imagine how much better it will get with some practice.

For two days now, I've been constantly thinking about how to convince her to do it again. Yeah, I might have pulled a move on her the other night, but I don't think it would be so easy for her to do it again. When I saw her on her knees after we finished, a strange mix of emotions washed over me. Every touch, every look, every word from her made my heart race with newfound excitement. A flood of unfamiliar emotions washed over me, all because of her. What I was feeling didn't sit well with me. I can't explain it, but the vulnerability in her eyes beckoned me to explore the depths of her emotions. I can see the pain in her eyes. It's as raw as mine. And like me, she holds onto the silence, keeping her thoughts and feelings hidden.

Maybe that makes me a twisted fuck, but I had to get out of there before I did something stupid because of the way I was feeling about her.

It's late when Ace drops me off at my house. Later than usual. We were so invested in refining our sound that we didn't even realize how much time had passed.

As we pull up to my house, Ace turns down the music. In the silence of the dimly lit street, the occasional flicker of the streetlights adds to the already ominous atmosphere.

"You should have just stayed at my house," he says, his tone filled with regret, as his gaze lingers on the house. Ace knows all too well that my father's temper can change in an instant.

I turn my head and follow his gaze.

The house is all dark and quiet, with no signs of life.

"I'm sure it will be fine. The asshole is most likely passed out already."

My eyes move down the street, focusing on the house that is just two doors down. Even though it's getting late, I can still see some lights on in the house from the front windows.

I push open the passenger's side door and get out.

With my pack slung over on my shoulder and my guitar in hand, I bid Ace goodnight as I quietly close the passenger's door.

He slowly drives down the street, the sound of the engine barely audible. Normally, he races down the street. When he drops me off like this, late at a dark house, he just vanishes into the night, without a sound. He doesn't want to draw attention to me, fearing my drunken father might still be awake.

I stay there, watching the red taillights disappear into the distance, merging with the night. I turn and make my way down the front path, feeling the anticipation growing as I approach the front door. I'm waiting, ears on high alert, trying to catch any faint sounds before I go in.

Nothing. It's dead quiet. I lift my hand and turn the doorknob, then step into the quiet house.

The room is pitch black. The microwave clock, usually a source of light in the room, is now completely dark. *Great, the power is fucking off again.*

Closing the door behind me, I navigate the room with uncertain steps. My foot accidentally kicks an empty bottle, making a clinking sound as it slides across the floor. I wait in silence, holding my breath, straining to hear the slightest sound.

Out of nowhere, a voice shatters the silence, catching me off guard.

"Where the fuck have you been?" His voice drips with venomous hatred, like a poisonous serpent ready to strike.

I remain quiet, my heart pounding in anticipation of the impending confrontation. Squinting into the darkness, I strain my eyes, hoping to catch any flicker of movement that might reveal his whereabouts. The last time he caught me like this, the sharp throbbing sting of pain in my face lasted for days. My injuries got everyone at school talking and asking me what happened. There was no way I could tell them the truth. So I lied. I told them I got into a fight with some guy who caught me banging his girlfriend. Only Ace knew the truth. Because he knows my old man's a piece of shit. That's why he worries about me.

My eyes dart around the room, searching for him. And then I hear the unmistakable sound of the whisky bottle slamming onto the table. Fuck he's close. Too close for my comfort. I need to get out of here. I stand still, my mind racing as I contemplate the two choices before me. Either go back the way I came or sprint down the hall to my room. But it doesn't matter which one I choose. He's so close, he'll nab me before I can make a run for it.

"I guess you've been screwing around, just like your mom, no doubt."

His words pierce deep into my heart, bringing forth a flood of memories of my beautiful mother. But now is not the time to linger on that matter. I need to get the fuck away from this psycho.

Moving slowly, I take each step with caution, my breath held tight, afraid of the repercussions if even a whisper escapes me.

One step. All good. Two steps. As I let out a slow breath of relief, I can almost taste the freedom of making it to the hall and then I can flee to my room before the fucker can catch me.

As I take a third step, the floorboards groan under my weight, echoing through the room. But before I can even react, he has me pinned against the wall - his hand tight on my neck.

The impact hits me with such force that my bag and guitar slip from my hands, crashing onto the ground.

With his face inches from mine, his alcohol breath stings my nose.

"You worthless little bastard," he spits out.

"Fuck you, asshole!" I hiss, my voice strained as I struggle against his tight grip.

His grip on my neck tightens, and my pulse becomes a relentless drumbeat in my ears.

"I should've kicked your ass out when your mother died. You worthless fuck."

"I'm not fucking worthless," I say. "Just you wait. One day I'll be something."

"Ha!" He laughs. I feel the wetness of his spit hitting my face. "Dream on big boy, because it ain't gonna happen. Nobody fucking wants you. Not even me, and I thought I was your old man."

"Let me go, you fucking asshole," I manage to gasp out, my nails digging into his hand that refuses to release its grip on my throat.

His fingers relax on my neck, giving me a momentary sense of relief, but he quickly regains his strength and forcefully shoves me back. His face hovers so near to mine that it's almost touching. I can practically feel the waves of anger coming from him as he glares at me.

He despises me with every fiber of his being. I can feel my breath being snatched away as his hands constrict around my throat, my body fighting for oxygen. My vision becomes warped and hazy. I am on the brink of passing out when he retracts his fist and delivers a powerful blow to my face.

Agonizing pain shoots through the side of my face like a fiery spear. I collapse onto the unforgiving floor. My mouth tastes the blood as it flows from my nose, staining my lips. I'm struggling to breathe as I wipe the blood off my nose with the back of my hand.

Despite the darkness, a piercing sound breaks the silence, leaving me even more breathless. It's a jarring sound, like splintering wood. And I know exactly what it is. My heart aches knowing it's my guitar, the one my mother gave me before she passed away.

"How are you gonna make it now big shot without your guitar," he sneers, his words laced with mockery.

What that guitar represents to me is invaluable. It was my ticket out of this place, but, most of all, it was my mom's prized possession. The loss of it reduces me to a whimpering child. Music is not just a hobby or an interest for me - it's my lifeline. Without it, I am nothing but an empty shell.

With each stomp of his foot, my guitar shatters and scatters across the room. By the time he's finished, he's gasping for air and has to stop. Then he wearily collapses onto the couch with a satisfying sigh. "Not so fucking Mr. Big Shot, now are ya?"

Standing up slowly, I lose my balance and make contact with an object near my feet.

Once I hear the sloshing sounds, I know exactly what it is. I snatch it up without thinking. Clutching the bottle tight, I make a mad dash for the front door, seeking solace in the quiet, dimly lit street.

Chapter 9

Xander

I walk down the front path, still crying over the loss of my guitar. I hear a car drive by as I drop down onto the curb. What a fucking asshole! My heart is so sad thinking about my broken guitar.

Under the streetlight, I hold the whisky bottle up and see it's still half full. It's the perfect remedy to escape from all the shit that just happened. To escape the sadness of dwelling on my smashed-up guitar in that fucked up place called home.

I take a deep breath before lifting the bottle to my mouth, bracing myself for the strong taste of the whisky. Despite the burning sensation in my throat, I persist with no signs of slowing down. I keep chugging down until everything becomes a blur and I lose all sense of touch. Fuck, I hate my life. I hate everything about it, except for my music.

As I ponder my next move, I lie back and let the sight of the twinkling stars consume me. What the fuck am I gonna do now? My music is everything. Without it, I won't make it. That asshole did it on purpose, knowing it would break me. What the hell am I going to do with all our new songs now that I don't have a guitar?

Maybe I can just swipe one from the band room at school tomorrow. Yeah, that might work. I let out a laugh, knowing that Poppy would fucking go ape shit if she knew what I was thinking. She totally lost it over some dumb chocolate bars. If she finds out I've stolen a guitar from the music room, she'll lose her fucking mind.

Numb and relaxed, I tip the bottle up, savoring the final few drops as they trickle onto my tongue. As I toss the bottle away, I cringe at the sharp smashing sound it makes as it shatters. I sit up and stare out into the darkness. It's gonna be okay. I'll get Ace to stand guard at the door while I steal a guitar. No one has to know. Especially not Poppy.

The mere thought of her causes me to turn my head.

As my eyesight blurs, I squint in an attempt to focus on her house. There are still lights on in her house. I wonder what she's doing. Probably watching that stupid show with all those mean bitches. She really does like that shit.

The moment I stand up, the world spins, making my drunken shuffle down the street even more challenging.

But I want to know what she's doing. Plus, she might give me another mind-blowing blowjob if I'm lucky. That's if I can convince her to do it again. Fuck, I'm absolutely gonna try.

Balancing myself against the doorframe, I take a deep breath and feel my heart racing as I knock on her front door.

It's a few seconds before Poppy opens the door, revealing her hourglass figure in a tight tank top and short shorts. My eyes roam her body, my desire intensifying as my dick comes to life. How the fuck have I not noticed how fucking hot she is?

"What are you doing here, Xander?" There's a sassy tone in her voice. Annoyed, and I fucking like it. She folds her arms over her chest, pushing her tits up, catching my attention. She takes one look at my face and steps forward. "Oh my god," she whispers, as she takes in the shocking sight of my face.

As she steps forward, her scent fills the air, awakening all my senses.

"Can you do that thing again?" I add, recalling the feel of her mouth during the best blowjob she gave me a week ago. "Will you give me another blowie?"

"Are you drunk?" She's giving me a once-over.

"I don't know. I might be, I might not be." My heart races as I nearly lose my footing on the top step.

In a split second, she reaches out and grabs my arm, steadying me before I have a chance to fall. A flicker of worry passes over her features.

"What happened to your face, Xander? Did you get into a fight?" Her eyes move down to my neck. "And there are dark bruises all over your neck."

"It was just some harmless breath play that got out of hand. The chick went nuts, but fuck, it was hot. Wanna try it with me sometime? So can I come in now?"

"That all depends?"

"On what?"

"If you tell me the truth and stop acting like a jerk."

"You think I'm lying, Princess?"

"Yes, cut the shit, Xander. Be straight with me for once and I might let you in the house."

"Okay," I nod, uncertainty lingering in the air. Other than Ace, Poppy possesses the unique ability to see through my act and call out my bullshit.

"Alright then, you can come in," she says, her hand on the door. The hinges creak as she opens it wider.

As I step into the house, the delicious aroma of freshly baked cookies tickles my nostrils. I haven't eaten all day, and the smell of food is making my mouth water.

"Got any food?" I ask as I settle down on the couch in the exact spot I sat over a week ago. The thought of what went down last time I sat here makes my dick hard. I hope I can talk her into doing it again.

"Sure, I'll grab you something," she says, her voice fading as she walks towards the kitchen.

Her shorts fit snugly around her curves, catching my attention.

"Alright, Xander, spill it," she says, her voice carrying from the kitchen. "Tell me what happened and this time without all the bullshit."

Giving me a quick glance, she reaches for a bowl from the cupboard, then makes her way across to the fridge.

I stay silent, watching her every move, because I've no fucking idea how to tell her the truth. How could she ever understand the shit that engulfs my life when she lives a life full of comfort? Despite her own challenges with her mom, she cannot fathom the daily struggles I endure.

She moves across to the microwave to warm up the food. While it's heating, she turns and leans her hip against the countertop.

"Whenever you're ready."

Normally I would just tell her to fuck off, but I just can't bring myself to do it. Is it because I'm hungry and want to eat? Or is it because I want her to give me another blow job? Or is it something more, something hidden beneath the surface?

I shift my focus to the TV, the flashing images on the screen a welcome distraction from the awkward silence. The bitches from Beverly Hills are back on. The TV is muted, but I can still see the intense drama unfolding on the screen. One crazy bitch is pulling the other bitch's hair.

As I drop my head and pick a loose thread at my jeans, I feel the weight of her gaze on me.

"Me and my dad got into it," I blurt out, the weight of the argument clear in my tone.

Without a word, she walks to the double-door fridge, opens it, and retrieves an object before heading my way.

"Here, put this on your nose," she says, holding out a pack of frozen peas.

I take the cold pack and press it gently against my face, feeling the chill seep into my skin.

At the sound of the microwave beeping, Poppy walks back to the kitchen. With a bowl and fork in hand, she comes back over. As she hands it to me, the delicious aroma of the lasagna fills the air. With a flick of my wrist, I toss the frozen packet of peas onto the coffee table.

Poppy turns away, then returns a few seconds later with a can of Coke and two freshly baked chocolate chip cookies.

As she sets them down on the coffee table, she sits beside me on the couch. My eyes follow her every move as she folds her long legs underneath her. It's hard not to notice that she's created more distance between us on the couch compared to the last time.

With every bite of cheesy lasagna, I feel Poppy's piercing gaze on me. As I fill my mouth with food, I steal a quick glance at her. She focuses on the bruises around my neck.

"Does it hurt?" she asks, her eyes meeting mine with concern.

"Not now, it doesn't."

"Talk to me, Xander. Tell me what really happened?"

"Fuck, we just got into it, okay? You wouldn't understand Princess."

"Try me?"

Her blue eyes hold my gaze as I chew my food. "My old man hates me. Well, one time he didn't, but now he does, now that he knows he isn't my father." I continue to stuff my face with food, my thoughts scattered and unfocused.

As she tries to decipher the words I am uttering, her brow creases with confusion.

"But the worst part is that the asshole smashed my guitar." I try to control my voice as it wavers. "The only way I calm down when he pisses me off is to feel the vibrations of the strings under my fingers. But that's fucked now because I don't have a guitar."

Poppy's gaze lingers on me, and a heavy silence fills the air. Shit, maybe I shouldn't have shared all of that. I knew she wouldn't understand. I don't know why I fucking bothered.

While I load up another forkful of lasagna, ready to eat, she stands and walks down the long hallway.

I let out a long breath, feeling the frustration and confusion build up inside me. With a swift motion, I lean forward, snatch the can from the coffee table, and pop the top.

Right as I'm on the verge of taking a sip, Poppy's footsteps echo down the hall, and my eyes narrow in on the guitar she's holding. I place the can and my bowl on the coffee table and stand up.

"It belonged to my dad," she says, coming towards me. "I saved it just in time before my mom tossed it into the trash." She holds it out for me to grab. "It's yours if you want it."

It's a 2000 Santa Cruz Om guitar. A classic that costs a pretty penny. I glance up and study her, taking in the glistening tears that fill her eyes. Did I hear her correctly? She said it was mine. But the sad look on her face makes me wonder if I should take it. I really want to, but if it's a special gift from her dad like my guitar was from my mom, I know it would really hurt her not to have it here. "Nah, I can't take it," I say.

"Why not?"

"Because it belonged to your dad. It means something to you."

"Take it, Xander," she says. "If my mother finds it here, she'll only destroy it. I want you to have it."

"Wow, your mom must really hate your dad." As I take the guitar, our eyes meet and a wave of emotions washes over me. "Seriously. You're giving it to me."

"Yes."

"Seriously Poppy, why would you give it to me?" This gift is completely unique and unexpected. Despite being a complete jerk to her the other night, this girl is incredibly kind. I can't wrap my head around it. This guitar is amazing. It would thrill any musician to get their hands on a guitar like this. The sound alone will elevate our songs to the next level. I'm surprised by her unexpected gesture. It's pretty amazing that she is giving me something like this.

"I want you to have it. For the past seven years, I've been worried that my mom will find it. And I know you will look after it. But there's one catch."

"Oh, yeah, what's that?"

"I want to hear you play something."

"I can do that," I say with a smile as I sit back down on the couch.

Poppy moves across and sits on the couch.

As I run my hands over the front of the guitar, I find comfort in the smooth texture of the wood grain. Settling it down into my lap, I feel its weight and texture, and straightaway it brings a sense of calm. I position my fingers on the strings as if I'm about to play. I pluck a few notes. The sound of the strings are crisp and clear, each one ringing out beautifully. I lift my head and find her eyes fixed on me.

"Any requests?" I ask, waiting for a response. I can't help but notice the way her delicate features come together to form her pretty face. Her long blonde hair falls in soft waves around her face, framing it beautifully. Her eyes are the color of the ocean on a clear day. A sprinkle of freckles on the bridge of her nose makes her look even more beautiful. Her lips, with their fullness and softness, are irresistible. Despite my strict rule against kissing, I can't help but be curious about the taste of her lips as I gaze upon them.

"No, you decide," she says, sinking back into the couch.

"Okay," I add, my eyes darting from Poppy to the guitar in my lap. I'm excited to share the song Ace and I have been working on for weeks. I'm curious to see how this classic guitar will change the sound of our songs.

As my fingers dance on the strings, the music sweeps me away, and then my voice joins in on the harmony.

As always, the melody pulls me in, drowning out the noise of my troubled life and leaving me with a sense of calm. I close my eyes, and the music engulfs me, cocooning me in its embrace. It's like a warm blanket, wrapping me up and protecting me from the harshness of the outside world.

As the final note fades, I slowly open my eyes and return to the present moment. Poppy sits beside me, her quiet presence soothing. I turn my head to gauge her response.

"Wow! Xander," she says. "I can't find the right words to express how amazing you are. Your music is going to pave the way for endless possibilities."

"You think so," I smile, the corners of my mouth curling up. Never has anyone spoken to me in such a way. The label of being worthless - a no-hoper has been a constant presence in my life. It's a good feeling to hear those words, especially coming from Poppy who is well-versed in music. "Are you sure you don't want to keep it? It's a classic. I understand if you've changed your mind," I ask, admiring the intricate design and details of the guitar.

"No. It'll get destroyed if it stays here. It's yours, Xander."

Carefully placing the guitar next to me, I scoot over to hug Poppy.

"Thank you, Princess. You have no idea how much this means to me. You can trust me with it. I'll never let it out of my sight." I hold her close, feeling the warmth of her embrace, grateful for her kindness. Closing my eyes, I take a deep breath and let the tantalizing scent of her strawberry-scented shampoo fill my senses.

The warmth of her body lingers on my skin when I release her from my embrace and sit back in the plush lounge.

"I was about to have a bowl of ice cream before you knocked. You want some?"

"Yeah, sure," I blurt out.

With a smile, she heads back to the kitchen. I focus on the guitar and run my fingers over the wood, stressing about how to keep it safe from my dad. I'll leave it at Ace's place. That will be the safest option.

Poppy returns with two large bowls of ice cream. The scoops piled high and topped with chocolate topping and whipped cream. After handing me the bowl, she reaches for the TV remote and presses a button to unmute the television. As we eat, we sit watching the Housewives' petty squabbles play out. The entertainment value of this show is off the charts, despite its train wreck nature. I know I shouldn't indulge in shows that thrive on chicks tearing each other down, but damn it, I can't resist. Poppy's infectious giggles fill the air, and I can't help but chuckle along with her as we lounge together.

It's refreshing that Poppy never asks about my father and what went down, leaving the painful memories buried for the night.

As we watch three more episodes, I notice the silence, the absence of Poppy's infectious laughter. I glance over to find her asleep. I look at the clock on the back wall to see it's well past two in the morning. Wow! That time went quick. I've never just hung out with a chick for the sake of enjoying her company.

My movements are deliberate and gentle, ensuring that she remains undisturbed as I get up. I take a moment to gaze at her, listening to the sounds of her steady breathing, before reaching for the cozy throw rug from the back of the lounge. As I tuck the blanket in around her, she stirs slightly but settles back into a peaceful sleep. Moving a strand of her long hair back behind her ear, I notice the peaceful expression on her face. I wonder what she's dreaming about. I reach out and touch her cheek, marveling at the silky feel of her skin beneath my fingertips.

Shaking my head, I pull my hand away, wondering what the fuck possessed me to do such a thing. Wasting no time, I snatch the guitar, my mind already racing to find a secure hiding place in the backyard, far from my father's reach.

Hours later, I wake up early and walk to school trying to avoid seeing my dad. I stand in the usual spot, waiting for Ace to arrive.

Ace's car screeches to a halt in the school parking lot. He looks up through the windscreen and his eyes widen at the sight of the guitar in my hands. Without taking his eyes off it, he jumps out of the car and comes towards me.

"How the fuck did you come across this?" he asks, taking the guitar and running his hands along the surface, feeling the texture of the wood.

"My old man destroyed mine last night."

He looks up. His brows furrow, his eyes narrowing as he finally notices the swollen bruises on my face. "He was awake."

"Yep. Like he was waiting for me."

"You okay, man?"

"Yeah," I confirm with a simple nod of my head.

His eyes linger on me for a moment longer before he shifts his attention back to the guitar. "A 2000 Santa Cruz. How the fuck did you end up with this?" he says, playing a few notes.

"Someone gave it to me."

"Who?" he mumbles, his focus unwavering as he keeps his head down and plucks the strings. "We don't know anyone with this kind of stuff."

Silence follows his question. I'm struggling to find the right words to say to him. I wanted to avoid his interrogation about what I was doing with Poppy. After a brief pause, he raises his head and looks at me, waiting for my answer. Fuck it. I'll just tell him.

"It was from Poppy Reeves."

My answer is so unexpected that his eyes widen in disbelief. "Why did she give you this? What did you fuck her or something?"

"No. Her old man left it behind when her parents split."

"Does she know what it's worth?"

"Yeah, I think so."

"That still doesn't explain how you got it."

I try to evade the question because I don't want to confess about the blowjob or my drunken escapade last night in the hopes of getting another one.

"Apparently, her mom went nuts and kicked out her dad. Her mom trashed everything of her dad's, but Poppy saved this."

His lips curl into a cocky smirk as he continues to watch me. "You still haven't answered my question. Why did she give it to you?"

"Because I told her my dad wrecked mine."

His gaze lingers on me for an uncomfortable amount of time. "Poppy Reeves, huh," he says with a hint of amusement. "Who would have thought? Got any secrets to spill? You two hooking up?"

"She's not really my type, you know."

It didn't sit well with me to lie to my friend. But I couldn't risk divulging too many details about Poppy. I didn't want him to know that I couldn't stop thinking about her - or how I think about her lips wrapped around my cock whenever I jerk off - and how amazing she is at giving head. Because last night, even though I went there hoping for a sexual favor, I ended up just enjoying her company. I don't think he'd understand, because I was having a tough time understanding it myself.

I redirect the conversation to cut off any more of his questions.

"I need a safe place to keep it. Can I leave it at your place?"

"Sure," he says. "But I know you just avoided answering my question."

CHAPTER 10
Poppy

The sound of Xander's voice singing that song last night repeats in my head like an endless echo. There are voices that are good, and then there are those that are simply extraordinary. They are like rare gems, appearing only once in a lifetime, and they truly grace us with their presence. And that's the same with Xander's voice. Anyone with two eyes can see Xander was born for this. His passion and talent shine through in every single one of his movements.

When he opened his mouth, his voice carried a mesmerizing quality that instantly grabbed my attention. Each note he sang seemed to strip away the layers protecting his heart.

Last night, I could feel his unease whenever he spoke about his father. So, I opted to withhold my curiosity and not pursue any additional information. Despite our somewhat friendly relationship, my crush still lingers in the background. Why wouldn't it? He's Xander Williams. The guy other boys wish they could be. The guy every girl wants. Yes, I gave him head once, but I won't allow him to treat me that way again. I'm not a side piece he can toy with whenever he pleases.

Last night, despite his drunken state, I could still see the vulnerability behind the mask he hides behind. I can see he, too, likes to keep things hidden to protect himself. The pain in his eyes was raw and palpable as he told me how his father destroyed the one thing he held closest to his heart.

Without a moment's hesitation, I gifted him my dad's guitar, fully trusting him to protect and care for it. My dad would have staked his claim by now if he wanted it; after all, it's been seven years. Plus, if my mom ever found it, she would just destroy it. It just sits there, hidden away, untouched by anyone, so he may as well make good use of it. The second Xander started strumming it, I knew I had made the right decision.

As always, the moment I arrive at school, I wander the grounds, my eyes scanning, searching for him. But today, he is nowhere to be found, not even in the usual spot where he and Ace always sit together.

With most of the students still outside enjoying the morning before school starts, I move through the busy corridor. That's when I hear it - his raspy voice, the lingering notes of the song he performed last night. Like a magnet, I am drawn towards him, my feet moving as I follow the sound of his voice.

Approaching the music room, his mesmerizing voice fills the air, leaving me in awe. Determined to see more, I lift onto my tippy toes and peer through the small glass window on the door.

With focused attention, Xander sits on a chair, strumming my father's guitar.

His voice washes over me, filling me with a comforting warmth, like a cozy fireplace.

On his left, Ace's fingers danced effortlessly across the keyboard, producing a symphony of rhythmic keystrokes. But my undivided attention is on Xander, my eyes never straying from him.

With each note he plays, he falls deeper into a trance, shutting his eyes as he sings. His voice has a dreamlike quality as if it's weaving a spell around me. His eyes flutter open and he stares to the left. That's when I see the few people watching him from the side. There's a long list of girls he hooks up with, including Jade, Savannah, and many others.

The sight of them gazing at him with adoration in their eyes highlights the contrast in how he treats me compared to those who eagerly submit to him. Even though I gifted him that guitar with no expectations, it hurts to be treated as if I'm invisible. It's during times like this that I long for him to view me through a different lens, as he does with them. By doing that, he would be more open to hanging out with me. I wonder if my body shape and the constant weight-related teasing is what keeps him away, or is it something else? When it's just the two of us, he comfortably engages and has no issue hanging out. But it seems like he never wants to be seen with me in public, always keeping his distance.

Just as I'm about to walk away, he looks up. His eyes widen as he catches sight of me standing there. With every note he sings, his eyes never leave mine.

My throat tightens, and I struggle to swallow over the lump in my throat.

With the last note hanging in the air, Jade's excitement takes hold, propelling her forward in a rush, clapping her hands. Just as I turn to leave, I see Jade extend her arms towards Xander, as if about to embrace him. I don't stick around to witness the exchange of words. I've seen enough to know that he'll never really accept me for who I truly am.

Throughout the rest of the day, I deliberately attempt to distance myself from Xander. Rather than sitting in my usual spot at lunch, I find solace in the quiet corners of the library.

I'd seen enough this morning to put me in a bad mood, and I didn't need a constant reminder every time I saw him with Jade. Plus, it provides me with a quiet space to focus on my homework.

By the time I'm home and my mom's about to head out for work, I'm even more caught up in my self-pity. The lounge becomes my sanctuary as I snuggle under the weighted blanket, relishing in its comforting embrace.

"Are you sure you're, okay?" my mother asks, pausing by the door, her hand on the doorknob.

"Yes Mom, for like the hundredth time. I'm just feeling a little down, that's all."

"Did something happen at school today?'

Yes, everything happened. I was invisible, as always. Instead, I go with, "No, nothing happened. I'll be fine." In order to get her out of the house, I put on a fake smile.

"Okay. If it gets any worse, just give me a ring and I'll come straight back."

"Don't worry, I'll be fine. I'll probably just go to bed."

"Alright then," she says, opening the front door. Just before she steps out, she glances back over her shoulder. "I hope you're not pretending to dodge the conversation I wanted to have today," she says, looking for any trace of deceit. "Because intake has already started."

Oh my god. I can't believe she's doing this right now.

I look away from her, my silence conveying my refusal to answer the question. Sensing my avoidance of answering her, she storms out of the house. The sound of the door slams into the silence.

Before long, a heavy knock sounds, making me wonder if my mother has forgotten her keys again.

With a frustrated huff, I remove the blanket and force myself to get up from the couch. When I get to the door, I yank it open in frustration. To my surprise, it's Xander, with his signature bad-boy grin.

"What do you want, Xander?" I ask, turning around and leaving the front door ajar, inviting him to follow me inside. Despite the events of the day, there's something about him that prevents me from shutting the door in his face.

"I left the guitar at Ace's to keep it safe," he says, closing the door.

Returning to the room, I reclaim my spot on the couch, trying to get comfortable. Xander follows and plops down at the end, making himself comfortable around my feet.

"What! You're not watching Housewives today," he says, glancing at the blank television screen.

"No." I shake my head.

The images of what I saw earlier today still linger in my thoughts. I'm not in the mood for mindless small talk with him. It baffles me why he's even here instead of being with Jade or any of those other bitches.

"What's up?" he asks, his brows furrowing in confusion.

"Nothing," I add, irritated with myself for morphing into one of the girls who desperately seeks his attention. I hate the way he affects me. I yearn for something more than a secret friendship that he keeps hidden from the outside world. But I know who I am, and the thought of him never seeing me in a different light feels like a heavy burden on my heart.

I look up, startled when I feel his intense eyes focused on me. "Tell me what's wrong, Princess?"

"It's nothing!" I shrug, looking down to hide the disappointment in my eyes. I pick at the loose thread on the new couch cushion my mother bought yesterday.

"Poppy," he says facing me, his arm comfortably draping on the back of the lounge.

The sound of my name on his tongue makes my heart skip a beat. He never calls me that. And I treasure the way it sounds, like the voice of an angel singing a holy melody.

I can't tell him how I'm feeling. It's hard to put into words the discomfort I feel when I see all those nasty bitches around him. How it felt today when he poured his soul into singing for them.

The way he looked at me last night while he sang, I felt a connection. As the melody flowed from his lips, his words resonated within me, igniting a tingling sensation that pulsed through my veins. I thought that was a unique moment just for the both of us, but then today, he shared it with all of them. And now, I feel like a foolish idiot, realizing that Xander could never see me in the same way he sees them.

To evade his intense stare and sidestep his question, I get to my feet.

"You hungry?" I say, tossing the blanket onto the lounge.

"Hold on," he says, taking my hand in his.

The moment his fingers make contact with my skin, I feel it everywhere. I freeze, savoring the warmth and comfort of his hand before he lets go.

"Hey!" He shuffles along the couch, trapping me with his legs on either side of mine. With the coffee table acting as a barrier, there is no way for me to make an escape. "What's going on?" He stares up at me with those mesmerizing eyes, the ones that seem to hold a universe of emotions.

Whenever I'm around him, I transform into a version of myself that I can't stand. I'm hooked on his every word and I don't know how to act around him. I know that my feelings for him are hopeless, as his touch sends shivers down my spine, but it means nothing to him.

Within a week, my behavior has experienced a total transformation. Though I longed for him before, it was so much easier when the unattainable boy never even knew I existed. Now he cannot be ignored; his presence at my house has become a regular occurrence, showing up multiple times. I find it difficult to adjust to the new dynamics because I'm constantly plagued by an irresistible yearning for something beyond what's in front of me.

When I don't reply, he tugs on my arm, urging me to come nearer. With a firm yet gentle touch, his hands move to my hips, easing me onto his lap, and positioning me in a straddling position on his lower thighs.

"Do you regret giving me your dad's guitar?" His piercing dark brown eyes lock onto mine, searching for an answer.

"No." I'd rather not open up and share my vulnerabilities with him. I don't want him to know the turmoil he causes within me.

"What then?"

As I gaze at him, I can't help but notice his jawline, sharp and chiseled. But it's his intense gaze that locks me in place, unable to move. I wonder if the dynamics would change if I took on the perspective of someone else. What if I was thinner? Prettier. What if I was special? What if...

In response to my silence, he gently places his hand on my exposed thighs. The moment his touch makes contact, a tingle shoots through me, awakening every nerve in my body. A rush of heat spreads, igniting a fire within me. My mind wanders to the thought of his hands exploring under my skirt. I crave the intimate sensation of his fingers exploring my untouched pussy. How easy would it be for him to make me come? There's no point in considering such a notion because he has no interest in me that way, because of who I am. The outcast. The fat chick. Definitely not one of those super skinny girls that guys are into.

Bitches like Jade and Savannah. I wonder what it would be like to be as bold as them. What if I shamelessly took what I desired from him, mirroring his actions from that night when he dared me to give him a blowjob? Whether or not I do it, the outcome will remain unchanged. Tomorrow, he'll just continue to ignore me, anyway. That way, at least I get what I desire, just like he did from me. Let him experience the same treatment he has been dishing out.

"Is this what you're after?" I query, edging closer, and sinking into his lap. "You want me to act the way they do?" With a subtle movement, I roll my hips forward, feeling the unmistakable hardness of his cock against me.

"You're hard," I say, my eyes widening in disbelief. My voice barely escapes as a whisper.

"You're grinding on my dick in a skirt. What did you expect?"

With a firm grip on my hips, he pulls me towards him, causing our bodies to grind again. This time, when I rub against him, he lets out a sexy groan. His tongue flicks out, leaving a glistening trail of moisture on his bottom lip. The sight of his dilated pupils sends a jolt of desire through my body. And holy fucking hell, I'm just as turned on as he is.

Our eyes remain locked in a heated stare as I grind against him, the tension building with each movement.

His cock presses against me, causing a delicious friction that makes him let out a low, guttural moan. With every movement, the friction ignites a pleasurable response in my body, causing it to pulsate with pleasure. His eyes filled with an undeniable hunger, spur me on.

Another moan of pleasure escapes his lips, leaving me breathless and longing for more.

There's something about the way he reacts to me that fuels a sense of empowerment I can't fully grasp. For so long, I've wished for him to crave me as deeply as I crave him. Given that I can only have him for a short while, I am determined to make the most of every second. I will selfishly claim this pleasure as my own, just as he did with his.

His eyes reveal both desire and vulnerability, creating a compelling mix of emotions. In this moment, he lets his guard down, allowing me to see the person he truly is.

With a firm grip on my hips, he studies every inch of my face with intense curiosity. His lips hover tantalizingly close, tempting me to lean in and savor their velvety touch. The desire to kiss them overwhelms me, even though I know Xander has a strict no-kissing policy. To resist the temptation of tasting his mouth, I shut my eyes and tilt my head back, savoring the intense pleasure coursing through me.

I'm close. So close. I can't believe I'm getting myself off on Xander's lap. But here I am, taking what I want. My body is craving for that release and I'm not stopping until I get it.

CHAPTER 11

Xander

I'm as hard as a fucking steel pipe as she grinds on me. And in a fucking skirt. Face to face. Chest to chest, legs spread, and oh fuck. I've never seen anything hotter in my life.

It's mind-blowingly fantastic. I refuse to blink, terrified of losing out on any part of this experience. I need to see every second of her getting herself off on my cock. Normally I don't care if a chick gets off or not, but watching her do this is so fucking hot. I need to know how she looks when she comes and the sounds she makes when doing so.

As she bites down on her bottom lip, a soft whimper escapes her, breaking the silence.

"You like that, Princess," I ask, a hint of excitement and anticipation hidden within my words. "Open your eyes. Let me watch you because it's fucking hot seeing you enjoy my cock."

My hand rises and I can't resist tracing my fingers along her plump lips, reliving the intoxicating experience her mouth unleashed upon me a week ago.

Her eyes flutter open, and I'm drawn to the strong longing and desire in her gorgeous blue eyes. Holy shit, she's fucking hot, and I'm such a dumbass for never realizing it. This chick doesn't compare to those other dull, self-centered bitches I usually bang. They are nothing compared to her. They're all as fake as their phony orgasms.

She lets out a little moan and picks up the pace, grinding against me even harder. Even though she's getting herself off, she is taking me right along with her. Her body instinctively arches to meet mine. She's practically begging for more, thrusting with all her might. As if she wants even more of me. I never give a shit about whether the girl comes. It's all about me getting off. But fuck me, I'm getting pleasure from just watching her, and I haven't even got my dick in something warm. This girl is blowing my fucking mind, and I can't wait to watch the second she shatters all over my cock.

"Rub that sweet pussy all over me,' I add, my breath quivering with pleasure. "I want to watch you come, Princess. I want to see how beautiful you are when you let go."

"I'm so close," she moans, her voice filled with desperation, as her breath hitches with every word.

As the grinding intensifies, her grip on my shoulders tightens, bordering on pain. I can't explain why, but I have an overwhelming urge to kiss her. The feeling of someone's lips pressed against mine is unfamiliar to me. And I have no clue why I'm desperate to taste her mouth.

But I don't. I hold myself back because I don't do that shit. I prefer to keep it strictly a transaction to fuck them and then leave to avoid any personal interaction. But still, I want to feel her mouth on mine. I want to snake my fingers under her skirt and rub that sensitive spot. Drive my fingers into her hot pussy. But I can't do it. Because it could totally mess up this moment and she might come to her senses. I want her to keep going. To find pleasure on her own terms. I'm desperate to see the moment she comes all over my cock.

Her hips grind up and down, then side to side, finding her rhythm to where it feels best. Harder, then faster. Her pussy driving directly over my dick as she jerks me off through my jeans. The temptation to reach out and touch her is overwhelming, yet I am entranced by the spell she has me entangled in. I want to throw her down on this couch and fuck her in every way I envisioned last night when I was stroking my cock.

"Xander," she cries in a slow, sexy purr. Her body builds as she sinks her nails into my shoulders.

As soon as I hear her say my name, I can't resist the urge to reach out and touch her. With a cautious movement, I slide my hand beneath her skirt, tracing my fingers over her soaked panties.

"Fuck, you're so wet for me," I add, running my thumb over her sensitive nub.

She's totally into it, moaning and biting her lip. Her face is so close to mine, that she is practically breathing on me.

"That's it, baby," I growl, my voice all hoarse. Leaning forward, I press a gentle kiss on the nape of her neck, feeling the heat radiating from her skin. "Fuck me harder. Make us both come."

I rub that little clit faster, knowing she is so close.

"Come for me, Princess. I'm right there with you. Yeah, that's it. Fuck me like that. Can you feel how hard you make me?"

"Xander," she says, leaning in, completely falling apart as she comes.

While I'm mesmerized by her, watching her come, listening to her sexy sounds of arousal, blending with my heavy breaths as hot cum streams over the inside of my jeans. But I don't care. I've had the most intense and unforgettable experience of my life. And my dick wasn't even out of my jeans. I can't remember a time when I've come so hard.

Wait... yes, I do. It was the night Poppy had her hot mouth wrapped around my cock.

Her head drops to my shoulder as she continues to ride out the last of her orgasm.

Instinctively, my arms wrap around her as the pleasures of what just happened pulsate through my body. I bury my face in the warmth of her neck, closing my eyes to savor the delicate fragrance that lingers there. Watching her ride me is the sexiest thing I've ever seen. It feels incredible to witness her intense reaction to me. The way her eyes held her desire. The way she called my name. The way she just let go and took what she wanted. It all fell into place and created an unforgettable moment.

Out of nowhere, she freezes, not making a single movement. As she lifts her head, her eyes widen in surprise when she gazes up at my face. Her body tightens under my fingers.

"Oh my god," she whispers. She's in complete shock and probably feeling a little embarrassed about what she just did.

I watch her face turn a vibrant shade of pink, like a blooming rose. She tries to get up, but I hold on tighter to stop her.

"Don't be embarrassed."

Her eyes wander up and meet mine.

"I should be embarrassed. I'm the one with jizz all down my leg. You made me blow in my pants like a thirteen-year-old boy. That's how fucking hot it was, Princess."

She lets out a giggle that fills the room, her eyes twinkling with delight. Her hand goes over her mouth, trying to muffle the sound.

"No. Go ahead. I'd be laughing too if it wasn't me," I say, smiling at the sound of her laughter.

When her body relaxes, I can see the relief in her expression. I study her pretty face, noticing the delicate curve of her lips and the freckles scattered across her cheeks. Then, out of nowhere, I do something completely out of character. I raise my hand and tuck a strand of her long blonde hair behind her ear.

"I might need to use your bathroom."

She gets up from my lap, her warmth dissipating, leaving an empty space that feels cold.

"It's down the hall. The second door on the right."

I follow her gaze to my lap, where a wet spot on my jeans catches my attention.

Rising from the couch, I inquire, "Is the mess from you or me?"

Her cheeks blush a bright red as a direct response to my comment. Sensing her intention to escape, I interlock my fingers with hers, preventing her from getting away.

"It doesn't matter. It's hot that your cum is mixed with mine." I lean forward, feeling the warmth of her breath and then I kiss her, savoring the gentle touch of her lips. The scent of her perfume lingers in the air, enchanting my senses. As I pull back, the scene before me sharpens into clarity.

Fuck. I totally caved and kissed her, breaking my no-kissing rule. *Seriously, what the hell was I thinking?*

Releasing her hand, I head to the bathroom to tidy myself up. The moment the door clicks shut, I curse myself for my thoughtless action. What in the world is happening? My go-to move is usually to hook up and then disappear. With my palms pressed against the countertop, I raise my head and lock eyes with my reflection in the mirror. Frustrated, I mutter to myself, questioning my actions, "What the fuck are you doing, dipshit? When you go back out there, you're just gonna leave. Like you always do."

Once I've given myself a serious pep talk and cleaned up, I head back out.

Upon my return, I find Poppy still sitting on the couch, her arms crossed over her chest, and her eyes locked on the ground. She remains perfectly still, not even a twitch, as if she has no idea I am standing right next to her. Is she going over in her mind what we just did? Does she regret it?

The mere thought of it makes me feel unsettled as if I don't want her to feel any remorse for what we just did. It was so hot, but I'm glad we did it. Fuck, just thinking about it is making me hard again. *Say something asshole before she looks up and sees you checking her out like some creepy stalker. But remember, you need to get the hell out of here before you do some more crazy shit that you will regret.*

"I meant to ask you the other day," I add, taking a step closer to her, and resisting the urge to sit down, knowing I won't be staying here for long.

"Hmm..." she mutters, shaking her head as if trying to dislodge the thoughts swirling in her mind.

"I said I meant to ask you the other day," I say again.

"Yeah, what's that?" She looks up at me, her face a mask of unreadable emotions.

"You talked about music therapy for kids, but you didn't say what instrument you play."

Her lips curl into a smile. Her eyes twinkle as she gets up from the couch. "Come on, I'll show you."

I feel a magnetic pull as she walks past me, prompting me to disregard my instinct to leave and instead, I follow her down the hall.

I stay silent, my hands buried deep in my pockets, my eyes tracing the curves of her body.

She heads to the third door on the right and holds it open for me to enter. As I enter her bedroom, my eyes land on a keyboard on the left side of the room. Yet, it's the wooden guitar that commands my full attention. Its polished surface catches the light. Its strings shimmer in anticipation, as if silently yearning to be played.

The bedroom walls come alive with vibrant, larger-than-life posters of bands, adding an electric energy to the room. Nirvana, Radiohead, The Cure, The Smashing Pumpkins just to name a few. Each poster fights for your attention. You can feel the rock energy in the air like the music from these legendary bands is still pulsating in the room. Standing in this space, one can't help but feel a surge of excitement, a connection to the music that transcends time.

As I look to the left, I see a bunch of vinyl records, all neatly stacked on three shelves. Without hesitation, I make a beeline towards them, eager to explore the treasures they hold.

The album covers are super eye-catching with their vibrant colors and glossy finish. As I reach out to grab one, I'm filled with anticipation of the melodies they contain. I'm in awe. This collection of classic records is not only worth a small fortune but also a treasure trove for all musicians. To indulge in the nostalgia of these rock classics, with their melodic tunes and infectious guitar riffs.

"Where did you get all these?" I ask, pulling out a Led Zeppelin album. I get a tingly feeling in my fingers as I run my hand over the album's jacket.

"They were my dad's," Poppy says, standing beside me.

"Do you listen to them?" I ask while flipping through a few more albums.

"Yeah, sometimes. Especially when I'm angry with my mom. I pump up the volume to annoy the shit out of her."

"What did your dad do to make your mom so mad?" I grab a handful of vinyls and make my way over to the bed. Putting them on the bed next to me, I grab one and flip it over to see the song list on the back.

When I look up, I see Poppy still standing over where I left her.

"My dad was never home. He spent most of his time on the road chasing his dream. Playing at different venues all over the country. Nothing too fancy, just a couple thousand people, you know." She moves over and sits next to me, watching as I check out another song list on the back of a record. "It was mainly clubs and hotels that had live bands. He was hoping to be discovered. He would have given anything to be the next big thing." She gazes down at the floor, a smile gracing her lips. "I never saw him perform. My mother would never take me. But I remember when he would come home after a gig." Poppy turns her head and looks at me. "There was this one day that instead of taking me to school, we hopped on a train and headed to the city. He took me out to lunch at the Hard Rock Cafe. I'd never seen anything like it. He shared stories with me about the various legends immortalized on the walls. And how much he wanted to be like them."

"So, how come your dad left?"

The room falls silent for a moment, the air heavy with unspoken emotions. She shifts her gaze from me, and I glimpse sorrow flickering in her eyes, casting a shadow over her face.

"My mom is the reason. I think she despised that my father was rarely at home. As he chased his dreams, she shouldered the weight of raising me alone. But that day when he took me to The Hard Rock Cafe, little did I know that would be the last time I'd ever see him. When mom found out I'd skipped school and where my dad had taken me instead, she totally lost it. Even though she sent me to my room, I could still hear the yelling. She told him to leave and never come back. That she was sick to death of always having to do everything herself, while he effortlessly became the fun parent. But the real problem was that he was never a husband to her when he constantly fucked any groupie that looked at him. I was just nine years old and had no clue what a groupie was until I searched it online."

"So after that, you never saw him again."

"No," she shakes her head. I see the tears forming in her eyes. I reach out and intertwine my fingers in hers.

"Did he ever try to make contact?"

"Yes." She swallows, then lets go of my hand.

Bending down, she searches for something under her bed. Then, she pulls out a round lid box as she settles back on her heels. Opening the lid reveals a collection of photographs, birthday cards, and scraps of paper adorned with music lyrics. There are guitar picks and sheeted music, all remnants of her past life. Each tiny treasure holds a story, a precious moment frozen in time. With a sad smile, she rummages through the box.

She grabs a photo and hands it to me. It's a younger version of Poppy, around five or six, sitting in her father's lap. He bears a striking resemblance to her, with his blonde hair and similar features. His arms surround her, embracing her with love and protection as he teaches her how to play the guitar. The radiant smiles on their faces unveil the undeniable bond they share.

But what truly stands out to me in the photo is the guitar. It's the same one I spotted when I walked into the room.

Amidst the assortment of memories, Poppy grabs a birthday card and holds it out for me to take.

"I haven't heard from him since he sent this. I wouldn't have even known he sent anything if I hadn't found it in the trash can. Honestly, I thought he had forgotten my birthday, but my mom kept it from me. I got really mad at her for trying to keep it a secret. The following year, I didn't hear from him at all. I'm not sure if he forgot to send it or if my mom just threw it away."

I open the birthday card and read the message written inside.

To my beautiful Princess,
Hope you have a magnificent day!
I wish I could be there with you today, but I can't because the band has picked up
a few gigs.
I hope you like the package I sent.
I'll see you soon, I promise.
Keep playing that song we worked on and promise to keep doing what you love.
I love you more than anything in this world.
Never forget that. And never forget how special you are.
Love you, Princess, with all my heart and I'll see you soon.
Love always,
Dad

His words bring a smile to my face as I read them, feeling the warmth and love behind them.

I can't help but notice that he refers to her as "Princess" as well. Is that the real reason why she was so mad at me when I first called her that? Her dad used it as a term of endearment, but I use it to call her a spoilt brat.

I hand her the card, observing the way her face transforms into a smile as she opens it, savoring every word written on the page. With utmost care, she returns it to its cherished spot inside the memory box. With a gentle sigh, she closes the lid, then slides the box beneath her bed, the weight of the world hidden away once more.

"What was the gift your dad mentioned?" I ask, my curiosity getting the best of me.

"I do not know. I never got it. My mom refuses to tell me what she did with it."

I stay silent for a moment as she stands and settles herself on the bed beside me.

Standing up, I grab the handful of vinyls and walk back over to return them to the shelf.

"So what song were you and your dad practicing?" I ask while placing the records back onto the shelf.

"It was just something he was working on back then. While he played the guitar, I was on the keyboard."

There is something about this side of Poppy that pulls me in without hesitation. Listening to her sharp tongue and clever comebacks is something I truly enjoy. But recently, now that I've had the chance to witness her vulnerable side, I feel a deeper connection with her. As a means of self-protection, she pushes people away, guarding herself from the pain she once felt when her father left. I can relate. I've never been the same after my mom passed away and my dad turned against me.

"Did you keep practicing?" I plop back onto the bed.

"Yeah, I did, but it was a total waste of time because he never came back."

"Show me," I add, jutting my chin toward the keyboard.

"No." She shakes her head. "Absolutely not."

"Why not? I've already heard you sing. Now I want to see you play."

She locks eyes with me, and I can see the hint of unease as she nervously licks her bottom lip. I've never seen this side of her before. She's always composed, never breaking a sweat, even when dealing with the mean bitches at school when they give her a hard time.

"Come on, Princess. I played for you last night."

She ponders for a few seconds, then gets up and heads towards the keyboard. Her face is pale as if she's on the verge of vomiting. She goes around to the front of the keyboard, takes a big breath, and powers it on.

I flop onto the bed, lying on my side, resting my head on my hand to watch her.

"I haven't played it for some time, so I might be a bit out of practice."

When I don't say anything, she returns her attention back to the keyboard. I know I can be insensitive sometimes, but I'm not the type to offer comforting words.

With her eyes fixed on the keyboard, her fingers move gracefully, creating a beautiful melody that fills the room. As if in a trance, I sit up, utterly captivated by her mere presence. And then, she starts to sing.

Her seductive tone resonates, blending with the slow, enchanting melody. Damn, this girl and that damn fucking voice. Her mother is really a despicable woman, trying to keep her from pursuing her passion when she has this much talent. I'm sure her father recognized it. Just like me as I sit here, watching her infuse every ounce of her being into the song. Her energy is palpable in every breath that she takes. It's like her music has come to life.

I don't move a muscle, just keep my eyes locked on her until she hits that final note.

As the room falls silent, the sound of her voice lingers in my ear like a haunting melody.

The way she sings gives each note so much life, filling the room with a magnetic vibe. Poppy has the power to make any song come alive with that voice.

She hasn't looked my way once since finishing the song, and I haven't said shit because I'm fucking blown away by what I just witnessed. She turns off the keyboard, and with her head down, eyes glued to the floor, she walks back to the bed.

Like some creepy stalker, I can't take my eyes off her. Her performance has left me breathless and craving for more. Poppy fucking Reeves is a mystery I wanna unravel. Why isn't she sharing this talent with the world?

As she sits on the side of the bed, I sit up and simply gaze at her.

"Poppy..." I pause, unsure of what to say. I yearn to tell her that Ace and I frequent the nearby music scene, checking out the competition. But no one can top how she loses herself in her lyrics.

Yet, I refrain from mentioning it, because she probably won't believe me, anyway. How can I give Poppy a compliment without it getting awkward?

Maybe those mean bitches at school make her doubt herself. Plus, I'm not the kind of person who goes gaga over telling someone how amazing they are.

"Don't utter a single word. I told you I'm out of practice." Her eyes lift, and I see the sense of doubt that lingers within.

"It wasn't rusty at all, Princess."

Even if I wanted to sing her praises, I wouldn't know how to articulate the awe-inspiring spectacle I had just witnessed. So instead I go with, "Did you find out if your dad completed that song? Like have you looked online?"

"Yeah, I've looked online, but nothing has turned up. We were so close to it being finished, just needed one more verse and it would've been done."

I'm looking at her and inching closer. This chick has touched my black heart in a way that no one else ever has, and I can't help but wonder if it's because of our shared love for music.

Is that the reason Poppy makes me go against all the rules I've vowed to follow, but now I want to abandon them in a heartbeat? The girl who lives two doors down from me, and I just found out about her. This girl's singing always hits me right in the feels. Without thinking, I reach out and softly caress her face with my hand.

At my touch, she leans in and closes her eyes. It's as if there's a touch of magic in the way she responds to me. Out of all the girls I've fucked over the years, she's the only one who ignites such a powerful response within me. This girl has really gotten under my skin. She's able to bring out emotions I never even knew I had.

Just as I lean in to kiss her, my phone vibrates and snaps me back to reality before our lips meet. I quickly sit up, thankful for the interruption that reminds me I keep breaking my no-kissing rule. I reach into my pocket to grab my phone.

Ace: I'm out the front of your house.

As I'm typing my reply, I notice Poppy leaving the bedroom.

Xander: Be out in a sec.

I stand up and stash my phone in my pocket, feeling super grateful that Ace interrupted me from making the dumbest move of my life. If I kissed her, she might get clingy, and that's not what I want.

As I head back to the main room, I see Poppy grabbing the remote and pointing it at the TV. She ignores me completely as she settles on the couch and watches the TV.

"Catch you later," I say, heading for the door.

"Yeah, whatever," she says, her eyes fixed on the TV, refusing to make eye contact.

Grasping the doorknob, I feel the weight of guilt as her heartbreaking story about her dad lingers in my mind. She bared her soul and confided in me. And I'm just walking away, leaving her alone in an ocean of sadness. I force myself to keep moving, ignoring the urge to glance back because I can't admit I'm sort of into her.

I shut the door and dash across the yard, effortlessly jumping over the little fence. And then it hits me. How the fuck am I going to explain to Ace why I was at Poppy's house?

As I head to the passenger's side door, I feel Ace staring at me through the front windshield. Climbing into the car, the interior light illuminates his face, revealing his intense eyes locked onto mine.

"You've gotta be fucking her."

"No way. Fuck off, asshole. I already told you she's not my type. I was just saying thanks again for the guitar."

"With your dick?"

As soon as I close the car door, the light inside goes off.

"You think I'd get a hard-on from Poppy Reeves?" I laugh out loud and immediately feel a pang of guilt for the way I'm talking about her. But I did it because I didn't want him to catch on to what is happening to me and because I can't even wrap my head around what the hell is going on with me.

"Well, if you didn't fuck then why is there a wet stain?"

Shit, I totally forgot about that. He would've seen the wet spot from the car's headlights beaming down on me when I walked up to him.

"What are you checking out my dick now?"

"Fuck off. Just admit you banged her."

"Just drive, asshole," I say, settling into the passenger's seat.

CHAPTER 12
Poppy

The next day at school, I make it a point to avoid Xander by seeking solace in the library during my free time. I am determined to steer clear of him, as the sight of his face would only serve as a constant reminder of him being a selfish asshole.

My mother has barely left for work when I hear knocking on my front door echoing through the house. Instead of getting up off the couch, I choose to ignore it and focus on the TV. That asshole can go fuck himself. I should've known better than to expect anything else from that jerk. I've studied him enough to figure out he uses people only to get what he wants. I know that once I open that door, his intoxicating presence will draw me in, just as it always does. With just one touch, I know I'll be repeating the same foolish actions from last night. Why does my self-control go out the window every time I'm around him? Although it's thrilling to please Xander, I won't be his go-to person. I won't be one of those girls who just gives him pleasure and then gets tossed aside like a piece of trash. Yeah, I know, I've already said that after the whole blowjob thing, but I won't screw up like that anymore.

Last night, I shared things with him about my father that I've never told anyone else. I opened up my soul to him, only for him to trample all over it with his sudden departure. He dismissed me as if my vulnerability meant nothing.

But that's the issue with someone like Xander, he takes what he wants and then acts like I don't exist. So fuck him and his bad boy ways. I'm no longer the quick fuck when he has nothing better to do. He can go to hell because I'm done with his bullshit.

The sound of knocking on the door intensifies.

"Come on, Princess. I know you're in there."

I grab the TV remote and increase the volume, effectively drowning out his alluring voice. If he can ignore me without a care at school, I can totally do the same.

He pounds harder on the door.

I crank up the volume a few more notches.

The knocking stops, and I can finally relax. Turning down the TV, I grab the big bowl of popcorn I made for myself.

While munching on some popcorn, I'm interrupted by a sudden knock on the window.

Startled, I jump, causing the kernels to scatter all over me and onto the floor. Through the window, I spot his insanely handsome face bursting into fits of laughter.

"Fucking asshole," I mumble, getting up from the couch. I head over to the window.

"I'm sorry," he yells out, bursting into laughter again. "But you should have seen that. It was fucking hilarious."

Once I'm there, I pull down the blind, blocking his view.

"Come on, Poppy. Open the fucking door," he says, banging on the window.

As he keeps knocking, I go around the room and pull down the blinds of the other windows, so he can't see inside.

"I'm sorry, Princess. I didn't mean to freak you out. Please open the door. I have something important to share." He knocks once more.

"Xander, just go home," I call out from behind the blinds of the window he's tapping on. "I'm not in the mood to talk to you."

There's a brief pause before he yells out.

"Why not?"

I don't wanna see you, that's why.

"Is it because of what happened last night?"

"Just go home Xander, I'm not in the mood."

He knocks again, urging me to answer. "Poppy, come on. Open the door. We can talk about it. You know you want to."

"Just go away, Xander," I mutter as I retreat to the lounge. I bend down and pick up all the popcorn on the floor, then tidy up the couch, throwing the spilled popcorn back into the now empty bowl.

Once I've cleaned up, I notice the knocking on the window has stopped.

I move over to the kitchen and throw the popcorn into the trash. Once I turn off the TV, I head to my bedroom. Entertaining myself, I play the keyboard before deciding to call it a night.

School the next day is the absolute worst. From the second I walked through the gate, Jade and Savannah were all over me, tormenting me about my weight. And on top of everything, my blue pen leaked. No need to stress, you say. But it leaked everywhere, and it was a mess. I had to use the bathroom to wash my hands and when I saw myself in the mirror, I almost passed out. My lips were freaking blue. It looked like I had just sucked Papa Smurf off.

While I'm desperately trying to remove the blue ink from my lips, the bell rings stating it's time for class. Feeling a little bummed, I reluctantly give up on trying to make it look better. This will have to do. I scrubbed so much that my lips are now swollen, making them look even bigger. Big blue lips. What the hell am I gonna do now?

When I finally make it to the classroom, I inwardly groan because I'm the last one to show up. All I fucking need is some attention when I'm trying to keep things low-key.

I drop my head and make a beeline for my usual seat, hoping to fly under the radar.

When I pass by Jade, she looks up and catches sight of me. Her eyes widen with delight, and her laughter fills the air, like a signal to let everyone else in on it. "Holy shit, what happened to you, fatty?"

Glancing up, I take in the sea of faces, their mocking laughter filling the air. As I look around the room, my gaze settles on Xander, who sits at the back of the room. Amongst the laughter of others, his face remains devoid of amusement, focused solely on me.

I ignore him and the people staring, and head to my seat. Savannah spins around in her seat to give me a quick look.

"Wow, you're even more uglier than before," she smirks, reveling in her comment, her eyes seeking validation from the room.

"Well, I'm pretty sure you could wipe away ninety percent of your face with a Kleenex," I add, maintaining eye contact with her while casually placing my bag on the floor next to my desk.

My response totally works because she gets up, slams her hands on my desk, and leans in to intimidate me.

"Sit down, Savannah," the teacher yells from the front of the room.

She lets out a breath of frustration, flips her hair, and locks eyes with me as she sits back in her chair.

Just as we're in the middle of our staring battle, my phone pings. I wonder what the hell my mom wants now, since she's the only one who has my number. But I refuse to look away from Savannah, gotta stay strong and show the bully they didn't win.

"Whenever you're ready to turn around, Savannah Gibbons," the teacher says. "I'll wait as long as necessary, and I'm even down for lunch detention if needed."

I keep glaring at Savannah as she turns around.

As the teacher starts talking, I discreetly reach for my phone to check my mother's message. Upon lighting up the screen, I am taken aback by the sight of an unknown number and message. When I open it and read the words. I know exactly who it's from.

Xander: WTF happened 2 u Princess?

Poppy: HTF did u get this number?

The bubbles appear on my screen.

I peek up and see the teacher at the front, recounting some historical event leading up to the war in the 1940s. When he searches for something on his desk, I sneak a peek to see another message from Xander.

Xander: Tell me what happened to your lips and I'll tell you how I got your number.

Poppy: Blow job gone wrong.

Xander: What did the guy have blue balls or something?

I burst into laughter, but hastily attempt to repress it. But it's way too late; both the teacher and all the students sitting in the classroom shift their attention toward me.

"Is something amusing, Miss Reeves?"

"No, sir," I reply, placing my phone face down on my desk.

"Well, you seemed to enjoy something, so do share with us what's so amusing, Miss Reeves."

I look up at him and see everyone staring at me. There's giggling and I can't tell if it's because of my stained lips or if I'm the joke of the day.

I'm sitting there, not saying a word, watching the teacher.

"Out you go," he says, pointing towards the door.

"What?" I ask, not sure if I heard correctly. Savannah's intimidation earlier didn't result in her being sent to the principal's office. However, I am the one who has to go because I refuse to disclose what I was laughing at. This is bullshit.

I'm staying put at my desk, watching him.

When I don't make a move, he signals towards the door. "Get out of my classroom. I won't stand for any disruptive behavior in my class." He walks around his desk and taps on the keyboard of his laptop. "The principal's expecting you."

Man, can this day get any fucking better? I release a frustrated sigh and snatch my bag off the floor as I head towards the door.

As I'm making my way to the principal's office, my phone buzzes.

Xander: I got your number from Zoe Mitchell.

I should've realized that. Zoe Mitchell helps out in the school office every now and then. But Xander doesn't really talk to Zoe. She's not one of the girls he usually hooks up with.

With my thumbs poised ready to ask him how he conned Zoe into giving him my number, another text comes through.

Xander: You won't believe the lengths I went to get your number. So don't ignore me. Answer the fucking door next time.

I don't know how to respond, so I just turn my phone off.

My phone pings again and I'm so tempted to just ignore it, but it's from Xander, the guy who's always on my mind.

Xander: Did my text make you so excited that you died or something? Quit fucking ignoring me.

I smirk as I type out my reply.

Poppy: Sorry, new phone, who's this?

Xander: Well played, Princess. Well played.

CHAPTER 13

Poppy

As usual, my mother has a tendency to lose her temper over the most trivial shit. She got pissed off by a phone call that disturbed her sleep. Unfortunately, it was the principal on the other end, delivering the news that I had detention for the entire week.

Since I arrived home, she has been venting her frustrations about the situation. Thank goodness, the weekend is just a few days away, so I only have to survive two days of detention. Regardless, it's really annoying sitting here and listening to her ramble.

After enduring my mother's incessant rants for another forty minutes, I escape to my room. Determined to avoid her tirades, I focus on watching the clock, eagerly counting down the minutes until she leaves for work.

Suddenly, she taps on my bedroom door and barges in without waiting for an invitation.

"I'm heading to work now," she announces, her eyes lingering on my keyboard. Then, they move slowly to explore the array of posters displayed on my wall.

Finally, her gaze lands on my father's guitar, over in the corner. Her body tenses and her expression becomes stern. Her intense loathing for my father is evident. But still, he is a part of me. Sometimes I wonder if she hates me because of that.

Her gaze shifts back to me, and I can sense a clear sternness in her voice as she addresses me.

"Instead of just sitting around doing nothing. Why not take the initiative to find colleagues for Aged Care like I've been requesting for the past two months?"

I pause for a moment, then respond. "Because I don't want to do that."

She takes a few more steps into the room, folding her arms across her chest. "Since when?"

"Since forever, and you would know that if you bothered to listen to me."

"Are you still going on about that music thing?"

I stand my ground, meeting her gaze.

"Yes, mother. I believe I possess more of my father's qualities than you give me credit for."

I can tell by her body language that my words have an impact. I notice her gulp at the mere mention of my dad.

"You're just as delirious as he was. Music will never bring you money."

"I couldn't care less about the money."

"No, because I'm the one who pays for everything in your life."

"I don't care what you say. I'm choosing music, not aged care."

"You are so much like your father."

"Well, I'd rather be more like him than like you," I remark, standing up from the bed, no longer interested in listening to her. I make my way towards the keyboard as if I'm about to switch it on. I'm aware that my mother will promptly exit my room if she believes I'm going to play. Perhaps I should have gone straight to the keyboard when she first came in. That way, she would've left me alone.

My plan unfolds precisely as expected. With a sudden motion, she abruptly turns, clutching the doorknob firmly. Exiting the room, she forcefully shuts the door behind her, causing a resounding slam that reverberates through the silent space.

Returning to the bed, I plop down and release a sigh. She truly is maddening. If only my dad were here to guide me in pursuing my passions. He would grasp the importance of music. How it has the ability to connect with your soul and evoke a profound sense of calmness. Each note played feels like an extension of oneself, a way to express who you are and share it with the world.

When I hear the front door slam shut, I stay put on the bed, with no intention of moving.

I let out a deep breath and smile when my phone pings I know exactly who it is. Picking up my phone from the bed, I glance at the text message.

Xander: I want to show you something.

Poppy: That's alright. I've already seen it. It's not that impressive.

I pause for a moment, contemplating whether I'm stepping into risky territory by flirting with Xander. But my heart overpowers my rational thoughts, and I ultimately decide to hit the send button.

As I see the bubbles popping up on my phone, I can't help but feel a rush of anticipation, eagerly awaiting his response.

Xander: Really? I'm sure your pussy thinks otherwise.

My cheeks blush as I recall pleasuring myself on his lap. I snap back to reality when I hear my phone ping.

Xander: I'm knocking. Answer the fucking door this time.

With a smile on my face, I slide my phone into my pocket and head straight for the front door.

As always, seeing Xander instantly quickens my heartbeat.

Leaning against the door frame, I can't help but notice the pack hanging over his shoulder.

"What do you want, Xander?" I ask, trying to sound casual. However, the smirk on Xander's face tells me he sees right through my act and isn't buying into this nonsense.

"Ace and I had an amazing session today, and I'm in a great mood. There's something I want to show you."

I turn away from him and head back into the house. "Xander, if this is something sexual, I've already told you I'm not…"

"It's not. I promise it has nothing to do with you wanting to give me a blowjob, but feel free to go ahead and do it again if you want. You won't hear me complaining," he interrupts, raising his eyebrows and giving that arrogant smirk. Then his expression turns serious. "It's something else I want to show you."

"If you don't tell me what it is, I'm not going with you."

"Wow, it seems like surprises aren't your thing, huh?" he remarks.

"I do enjoy surprises, but when it involves you, I'm not sure if it's a genuine surprise or just a sexual favor."

Taking a deep breath, he exhales slowly. "The other day, you opened up to me about your dad. I think it's only fair that I share something about my mom," he says.

Oh, so he was actually listening. It turns out he wasn't just pretending to listen and not caring like I thought.

"Oh, alright then," I reply, making my way towards the couch.

But before I can reach it, Xander steps forward. "No, not here," he says. "I want to show you something. Come on."

Curiosity piqued, I follow him outside.

"So where exactly are you taking me?"

The sun hovers above the horizon, casting a warm, golden glow. I reach for my front door key, hanging from its hook, and with a soft click, I lock the door behind me.

The crisp air fills my lungs as I eagerly bound down the front steps. Xander waits for me in the street, greeting me with that familiar grin.

Together, we stroll along the quiet street, our footsteps echoing softly. I steal a quick glance at him and notice the serious look he has on his face, a side of him I've never seen before. I wonder if he's worried about opening up about his mom.

As we stroll along, we reach the 7-Eleven and continue walking for two more blocks. The faint hum of distant traffic echoes in the background. Eventually, we take a right turn and move down a thin narrow track.

"I used to come here all the time after getting something from the 7-Eleven," he says, giving me a quick glance. "But it's been a while since I've been here. Not since that day when you made the extra mac and cheese."

I stay silent, not knowing what to say because I have no idea where we are going.

We turn right and venture down an unfamiliar path nestled between two houses. A gentle, cool breeze brushes through the air, causing the leaves on the trees to softly rustle. We move through the fading light, making our way through the tall grass until we reach a rock formation. Effortlessly, he climbs up onto a boulder and extends his hand to help me up. I join him, sitting down and letting my legs dangle over the edge.

In the peaceful silence, I'm captivated by the breathtaking scenery. Majestic trees line the lush, emerald-green landscape. Birds gracefully soar through the distant sky. A tranquil serenity surrounds us, only interrupted by the enchanting melody of crickets waiting for the moon.

Out of the corner of my eye, I notice Xander nervously tapping his fingers on his thigh. Every second of silence feels like an eternity. Finally, he speaks, his words stumbling out, unsure and hesitant.

"Do you remember when you mentioned how much you miss your dad?"

"Yeah," I nod.

"Well, I understand how you feel," he says, looking straight ahead, not bothering to make eye contact. I watch as he swallows over the lump in his throat. "Every single day, I miss her. My mother was truly amazing. She's the one who passed her love for music on to me. She taught me how to play, you know. We used to sit together in the kitchen, me on the countertop strumming my guitar while she baked chocolate chip cookies. We would sing, and I cherish those precious moments. But when I was seven, she passed away."

Unsure if he would let me, I reach out and take his hand. Surprisingly, he doesn't pull away; instead, he intertwines his fingers with mine.

"I'm sorry," I whisper. "How did she pass away?"

He finally turns to look at me, and I can't help but notice the sadness in his beautiful eyes.

"She passed from cancer," he says softly.

Then he turns his gaze back to the vast landscape before us. He stays quiet for a bit.

"Before mom died, she asked my dad for forgiveness because she cheated on him. She said he might not be my biological father. After that, my father never looked at me the same. That's when the beatings started."

I hold his hand tighter, hoping to bring him some comfort.

"Sometimes, it was even worse when he didn't beat me because once he did, I knew I would have a few hours of reprieve before it happened again. Instead of anxiously waiting for it, waiting for him to acknowledge my presence in the house..." he falls silent. "People think the worst part is the pain. And it does hurt, christ, it hurts so much sometimes. But the worst part is what he says to me when he's beating me. He calls me a worthless piece of shit. He says I am nothing and will never amount to anything." He glances back at me. "I know that sounds fucked up, because they're just words, but sometimes they hurt even more than his physical punches. Over time, they seep into your soul, penetrating deep within you. And the look in his eyes every time he says those words... he truly despises me." He takes a breath and swallows. "There was a time when he didn't feel that way. Once, he loved me. I was the cherished child, with both my mom and dad by my side. But then, after my mother's comment, everything changed. He hated me as if he wanted to..." Xander falls silent, his gaze fixed on our clasped hands.

My heart genuinely aches for him, recognizing his pain as my own. He had loved his mom and dad just like any child loves their parents, but in return, the man he believed was his father despises him. It's only natural that after all these years, he would want to shield himself and keep hidden what has transpired in his life since his mother's passing.

Taking a deep breath, he admits, "I believe deep down that my dad still loves my mom. He's just angry with her for what she did. My dad has gray eyes, while my mom has blue. However, I have dark brown eyes. Interestingly enough, my dad's best friend also has the exact same brown eyes." His voice tightens as he speaks. "I have no connection with my dad. I am only a constant reminder of what she did, always staring him in the face. As I grew older, I started to resemble my biological father more and more. Then the beatings became worse."

"Xander," I interrupt, catching his attention.

He turns to look at me, and I can't help but notice the anguish in his eyes.

"You didn't do anything wrong. You deserved to be loved. And never, ever think that you're nothing. You're truly something special. I can see it. And so can everyone else." Despite saying these words, I realize that the pain of hearing the opposite for all those years will always be a part of him. It's ingrained in him, inseparable from his being.

As he releases my hand, a sudden thought crosses my mind - did I say something wrong?

"Every time I come here, I sneak a bottle of Jack from my dad." Reaching into his bag, he retrieves a bottle and effortlessly twists off the cap.

'Wanna have a good time?' His playful expression and raised eyebrows successfully mask the vulnerable side he had shown just moments ago.

I burst into laughter. "So, our plan is just to hang out here and get wasted, huh?"

He nods and offers me the bottle. "Yeah, that's pretty much it," he replies. "Once the alcohol kicks in, you stop worrying about that kind of stuff."

Xander watches as I bring the bottle to my lips and take a gulp, unaware that it may not be the wisest choice.

The strong liquor immediately triggers a coughing fit as it goes down my throat. He bursts into laughter.

"Come on, Princess, save some for me!" he playfully teases.

A warm sensation rushes through my veins, and my head feels lighter as I return the bottle to him.

Xander takes a drink from the bottle and then hands it back to me. He turns around to grab a pack of cigarettes from his bag. Placing one between his lips, he lights it.

"Does it bother you when I use the same name your dad used to call you?"

"It did at first, but not anymore," I say as I wipe my mouth with the back of my hand. I hand him the bottle and take the lit cigarette from his mouth. "I thought you called me that because you believed I was spoilt or something."

He nods. "I did at first."

He watches as I bring the cigarette to my lips, draw back on it, and then start coughing, sounding like a cat trying to clear a furball from its throat.

Zander bursts into laughter. "You've never smoked a cigarette before, have you, Princess? But I guess everyone has to start somewhere."

"And do you still think I'm a spoilt princess now?" I hand him the cigarette and quickly grab the bottle from his hand.

"No, not anymore."

Taking another sip from the bottle, I feel a burning sensation in my throat, but this time I manage to suppress the urge to cough. Fueled with newfound courage from the alcohol, I turn to face him. There are a few things I've always wanted to ask but never had the bravery to do so. "Can I ask you something?" I inquire, apprehensive about his response.

"Depends."

"Don't worry about it then."

"Nah, go ahead and ask it."

"But you might not answer. I want you to be completely honest with me."

"Go ahead and just ask, Princess," he says, taking the bottle from my hands. "You might want to take it easy on the alcohol."

I give him the finger before proceeding with my question. "Why Jade and Savannah? Why do you sleep with them?"

"You want to know why I fuck them?"

"Yeah. Why them?"

"Because they're easy," he replies, shrugging his shoulders. "Because they're readily available. I don't need to put in any effort to get my dick wet." He raises the bottle, and I find myself fixated on his lips as they touch the rim. As he brings the bottle back down, he steals a quick glance in my direction before handing it over for me to hold. "Because, honestly, I don't care about chicks. I never have."

Upon hearing his words, I realize that being punched would actually hurt less. I get it. He doesn't give a shit about anyone as long as his needs are looked after. To prevent further emotional distress, I quickly change the subject of our discussion.

"So, where do you see yourself in five years?" I ask, trying to redirect the conversation.

"Well, that's easy," he replies confidently. "I see myself playing my songs to massive stadiums, filled with thousands of people. I want to hear them sing along to the lyrics I've written, especially since they were born out of the most challenging period of my life. I want it all - the fame, the money, the groupies. But above everything else, I want to prove all those assholes wrong who said I was nothing. I want to show them that I'm something."

I interrupt him, reminding him of my previous compliments. "But you are something special, Xander. Your music is a reflection of who you are, and everyone will love you and your music. Oh god did I just slur my words? Did any of that make any sense?"

He laughs. "Yeah, don't worry I understood what you were trying to say. Now it's my turn to ask a question."

"Sure, go ahead. Ask away."

"The blowjob."

"Xander. Don't ask about that because I told you I'm not giving you another one."

"Good to know. Disappointed but that's not what I'm asking."

"What then?" I ask, taking another sip.

I know I should pace myself, but I don't care. I'm young and haven't experienced a drinking binge before. And there's a hot guy sitting next to me, someone I've daydreamed about for years. It's time to embrace life, right?

"You said you've never done it before."

"That's right I haven't."

"Well, I think you're full of shit," he says, flicking the stub of his cigarette forward.

"Oh, really." I burst into laughter.

"Come on, Princess, spill it," he says, grabbing the bottle from my hand. "No more fucking lies."

"I'm not lying, I swear," I say, raising my palm. "Scout's honor." My words blend together, slurring as they leave my lips, and I can hear the distortion in my voice.

"First of all, that's not the signal for scouts' honor. And I'm calling bullshit on your answer."

"I'm serious. Please, look at me. You think anyone wants a fat chick?"

"You're not fat, Poppy. Just 'cause those bitches say it doesn't mean it's true."

"Yeah, I am. Everyone else can see it. Why can't you?" I ask, feeling like the insecure little girl I wish I wasn't. Damn it, Xander is right. Maybe I should cut back on the alcohol because my head is spinning.

I lean back on the boulder and gaze up at the darkened sky. The tiny stars twinkle above me. When was the last time I truly admired the stars? It's been years.

Xander's voice snaps me back to reality. "Come on," he says as he takes hold of my hand and helps me sit up. I see that he's already put on his backpack and the bottle is nowhere in sight.

"Let's get you home."

As Xander helps me down off the boulder, my footing suddenly gives way. I almost lose my balance and stumble forward, but just in the nick of time, a set of strong arms quickly wraps around me, stopping me from tumbling off the ledge.

"Fuck! Are you okay? You nearly fell," he says, his hands gripping my waist tightly, keeping me close.

Feeling his arms around me sends a shiver down my spine. I can't help but steal a glance at him. "Thank you," I say, unable to take my eyes off his beautiful face. I can't help but admire his striking features. "You know, your face is like really pretty, right?" I blurt out, realizing I may be rambling but unable to hold back my words. "Actually, you're hotter than hot." My brows furrow because I'm not sure if that's an actual sentence. But I can't stop my mouth from speaking. "Damn, you're like the hottest person I think I've ever seen."

With his arm still around me, he guides me back in the direction we came from.

"And I was being dishonest earlier. Your... well, your dick is quite impressive. But honestly, I haven't had the chance to compare it to anyone else's. So it might not be that impressive at all."

"Yeah and let's keep it that way, Princess. You don't need to be like those other girls who fuck around. You don't need to be checking out other guy's dicks. Unless it's mine," he says, flashing that arrogant smirk - the one that always manages to stir something within me. "Don't stoop down to the level of those other easy bitches. Because that's not you."

"But you talk to those other bitches at school and completely ignore me," I add, feeling my eyes grow tired. "That's some messed up shit, Xander. The least you could do is acknowledge me with a simple 'hi' when we pass each other in the hallway."

"I suppose I could give that a shot."

With every step, fatigue seeps deeper into my body. My footsteps now falter. Doubt starts to creep in.

"I don't think I can keep walking." I quickly glance around and realize we're on the street, right by the 7-Eleven. "Just leave me here on the side of the road and I'll find my way home soon. I promise."

"I'm not leaving you on the fucking side of the road.

"Why not? I was sitting on the curb when you finally spoke to me, so it's not all bad. But seriously, Xander, just let me lie here for a moment. Then I'll find my way home soon."

Before I can even process what's happening, my legs give out beneath me, and I find myself wrapped in Xander's arms. My head naturally settles into the curve of his neck, finding a comfortable spot.

"You smell amazing. You always do," I whisper, closing my eyes and savoring his intoxicating scent. Nestled securely in his embrace, I feel a sense of solace wash over me.

Chapter 14

Poppy

"What the fuck is that noise?" I mumble, slowly opening one eye. The room is flooded with bright sunlight streaming through the window, and it takes me a moment to realize that I'm sprawled out on the couch, with a blanket draped over me.

A sudden loud noise shatters the silence, causing me to shift my focus to the kitchen. There, my mother is diligently loading dishes into the dishwasher. I wonder what time it is, as it must be late for her to be home from work already.

I quickly scope out the room, looking for my phone, and notice it on the coffee table. Carefully, I reach out to grab it, trying not to alert my mother that I'm awake. Just as I snatch it up, I feel a vibration indicating that there's a text message. I sink deeper into the couch and open my phone to find a message from Xander. I swipe the screen and open the message of a photo he snapped last night.

As I gaze upon it, I see a photo of me asleep lying on the couch. Xander's cheek is squished next to mine, and I take a moment to appreciate his features. He's got such an amazing smile, it's a shame he doesn't show it more often. And his eyes, despite the pain they hold, are still mesmerizing. His tousled hair sticks up, just the way I like it. Finally, I read the caption he has written for the photo.

Xander: Stop begging me, Princess. No, I will not have sex with you.

I let out a chuckle, but immediately wish I hadn't as I try to hide my slip-up. Unfortunately, it's too late, for the noise has already caught my mother's attention. Her anger is palpable as she strides toward me, coming to a halt at the far end of the lounge.

"You're supposed to be at school," my mother says.

"Don't yell," I add, as her shrill voice pierces through my head like a relentless drill, pulsating in all the wrong places.

"What did you get up to last night? I come home and find the place is a mess, and you're asleep on the couch."

I shift my legs over the edge, attempting to get up, but the throbbing sensation in my head forces me to sit back down.

Is it possible I hit my head last night? I tightly shut my eyes and place my hands on either side of my head.

My mother stops complaining and gives a look of concern.

"Poppy, are you okay?" She reaches out and gently grabs my arm.

I pull my arm away from her grip. "It's nothing."

"What's going on?"

"I said, it's nothing." This time, I rise to my feet and remain standing.

"Maybe it would be best if you just stayed home today. I'll book you a doctor's appointment," she says, grabbing her phone from the kitchen counter.

"There's no need, Mom," I add. Not saying more because I don't want to tell her it's probably just a hangover. I don't want her to freak out about that when she's already making a big deal about me crashing on the couch.

But she doesn't pay attention. She just ignores me and starts scrolling through her contacts.

"Mom," I add, louder this time to try to get her attention.

"It's ringing," she informs me.

Frustrated that she never listens to anything I have to say, I snap. "I don't need a doctor, it's just a hangover."

As soon as those words reach her ears, she glares at me and abruptly hangs up the phone.

"You've got a hangover? How did you get your hands on alcohol?"

I just ignore her question and walk away, but she keeps following me ranting and raving.

"Don't even think about staying home from school now."

"I wouldn't dream of it."

"I have no idea what has come over you in these past few weeks."

I make a beeline for my bedroom, attempting to close the door to block out her yelling. But she stops me by placing her hand firmly against it. Usually, I wait for her to vent her pent-up frustration before I go for a shower. But I don't want to hear any of how I'm such a disappointment to her. I turn away, leaving her near the open door still ranting. Lifting my shirt, I head to the bathroom to take a shower.

Standing under the warm water does nothing to drown out her hurtful words. The steam fills the bathroom, offering a temporary escape from the harsh reality outside my bedroom door. I vigorously scrub away the burden of her disappointment, hoping to wash it all away.

As I stand there, head pounding, warm water soothing my body, I couldn't care less if I miss the morning lessons today. I'll get there when I feel like it.

When I finally drag myself out of my room, I make sure to avoid looking at my mom as I walk by her near the couch. Her negative words hang heavy in the air, but I won't let them get to me. I grab my stuff and head to the front door, ready to face whatever comes my way.

CHAPTER 15

Xander

S itting beside Ace in the schoolyard, I can't help but notice Poppy Reeves emerging from her car. It's clear that she's nursing a serious hangover, clutching a water bottle and shielding her eyes with oversized sunglasses. And, as always, she's sporting yet another short skirt that fucking distracts me.

I watch as Poppy settles down across the quad, casually lounging on the grass, leaning against the brick wall. She crosses her legs and makes herself comfy as if she's gonna take a nap.

Without wasting a moment, I grab my phone out of my pocket and quickly send a message.

Xander: Hey Princess, glad you could make it

I look up and notice her reaching into her pocket. After glancing at her phone, she places it face down on the grass next to her. It's really getting on my nerves that she's ignoring me, so I send another text.

Xander: Did you see the drawing I left on your left tit when we were making out last night?

Immediately after pressing send, I glance up, completely zoned out of anything Ace is saying beside me.

I watch as she reaches for her phone, and then quickly drops it in her lap before she peers down the front of her shirt.

Unfortunately, I didn't get an opportunity to see her tits last night. After I helped her settle on the couch, I took a picture of her while she was sleeping. Then I left.

I burst into laughter as I reach for my phone to send her another text, but Ace interrupts me with a question.

"Who the fuck are you texting?" Ace asks. "I know it's not Savannah or Jade since they're right here. So who are you trying to hook up with now?"

"No one," I say, tucking my phone back into my pocket.

"If you're feeling horny, just go for Jade. She'll take care of that."

"Nah, I'm not interested," I reply, dismissing the idea. "She's so fucking annoying, and never shuts up." My phone suddenly pings in my pocket, and I resist the temptation to reach for it, exercising immense self-control.

"Well, there's one way to solve that problem. Stuff your dick in her mouth, then she'll shut up. That always works for me." He stands up and looks down at me. "Well, if you're not gonna do it I might."

"Go for it," I respond.

I'm watching as Ace leans in and whispers a few words in Jade's ear before planting a gentle kiss on her cheek. Then he casually walks away. That fucker just stole my move. Asshole. Well, except for the kiss. I never do that. In a matter of seconds, Jade is already chasing after him, falling for that simple move every single fucking time.

With Ace gone and his attention now solely focused on other things, I finally give in and reach for my phone to read the text from Poppy.

Princess: First of all, asshole, I never beg. And second, do you really think you could fool me that easily?

"Hey Xander," Savannah says, taking a seat beside me.

"Yeah, hey Savannah," I say, keeping my eyes fixed on my phone.

I usually engage with her to get what I want, but not today. I have absolutely no interest in interacting with her.

I totally ignore her and focus on my phone. I don't bother concealing the identity of the person I'm texting, as all she will see is the contact name - Princess. With a grin, I eagerly type out the next text.

Xander: Did you check under the nip?

I push my phone into my pocket and then act all cool, not even bothering to look at Poppy so Savannah doesn't catch on I'm texting her. I casually glance around and then my eyes move to Poppy.

I can't fight the smile tugging on my lips when I see her pulling her shirt out and peering down into it again. I almost burst into laughter but manage to quickly catch myself by biting my bottom lip.

"So," Savannah says, her fingers tracing along my arm. "It seems like Jade and Ace have taken off somewhere together."

"Yeah, so," I say, reaching for my phone as soon as I hear it make a sound.

Princess: You're here, watching me, aren't you, asshole? You saw me do that right?

Xander: Yep but feel free to look again. It's hot watching you check out your tits.

I can't believe I'm hitting on Poppy, of all people.

I look up and see her reading my text, then she just puts the phone down without even responding. The fact that this affects me deeply is something I can't quite comprehend.

Savannah's fingers trace a path up my leg, inching closer to my dick. Back then, I would have jumped at her invitation, looking for some action. But this time, I smack her hand away and turn to face her directly.

"What the fuck do you want, Savannah?"

"Well, you don't have to be so rude," she says standing up, towering over me. "I'm just checking if—"

"No, not interested."

A few people who are near turn their heads, their eyes fixated on the sudden commotion. The air is buzzing with hushed whispers and murmurs, like a soft melody. The crowd becomes a sea of craning necks, each person straining to catch a fleeting glimpse of the unfolding spectacle.

With her hands firmly planted on her hips, Savannah shoots me a piercing glare. Then, she lifts her gaze, scanning the surrounding crowd.

In this situation, there are two potential outcomes. She could opt to gracefully walk away without creating a scene, but given her nature, my intuition tells me that she will resort to her usual tactics. Just like she does with Poppy and her cruel comments, she'll do whatever it takes to come out on top.

"Well, you were interested three days ago."

"Yeah, that was then. This is now, so fuck off and leave me alone."

"Well, your dick never satisfied me anyway, Xander," she says, walking away as if that's the end of the conversation.

"Trust me, my dick could never get satisfied touching that fishy pussy of yours. You have to wonder why I never offered to go down on you." I yell loud enough for all to hear.

Both Savannah and Jade are equally self-centered. I have no desire to go down on a chick. I only said that because I knew deep down that it would hit her where it hurt the most - her fragile ego.

I can hear the crowd laughing, and Savannah's look and teary eyes are meant to make me feel guilty. But all I can think about is karma. It's karma for the years of abuse she throws at Poppy, constantly belittling her in front of everyone. She needs to feel the impact her words have had on Poppy over the years.

Last night, it hit me that Poppy isn't as strong as she pretends to be. I'm not sure if she'll remember confiding in me about how she sees herself. And all of that is because of this self-centered chick and her fake friend Jade.

"Asshole," she snaps, her voice dripping with venom, before storming off in a fury.

The moment I hear my phone sound, my eyes are drawn to it without a second thought.

Princess: So, how bad is the smell, like on a scale of 1 to 10?

My face bursts into a wide smile. Had someone told me a month ago that I would end up befriending Poppy Reeves, and desperately want to fuck her, I would have told them to give me some of the good shit they were smoking. But here we are. My dick's already curious with want, wondering how good it will feel when I finally get to sink into her. But then I remember she's a virgin and that's not my scene.

Screw this shit. I stand up, grab my bag from the ground, and slip my phone into my pocket. Leaving all those fuckheads behind, I head over to where Poppy is leaning against the wall. Her large sunglasses shield her eyes, making it impossible to gauge her reaction to my approach. I casually toss my bag onto the ground and take a seat beside her, paying no attention to the curious onlookers. It has always puzzled me why people feel the need to watch me. Maybe they can sense the vulnerability I carry as a child from a broken home. Regardless, I've become skilled at protecting that part of my life.

There are only two people I've ever confided in and who truly understand the challenges I face in my life: Ace and the girl sitting beside me. Lately, I found the strength to open up to her, revealing things that I have kept hidden from everyone, even from Ace. It was something I thought I had to do, considering she had bravely shared her own experiences with her father. She never judged me or looked at me differently that night when I told her. She had been vulnerable in her words so I thought I might as well do the same.

When she spilled all that about her dad, I didn't know what to do with what she told me. I think because the pain she felt resonated deeply within me, as I had gone through similar feelings for years following the loss of my mother. And then I tried to distract myself from the intense emotions she evoked when I heard her story. That's why I asked her to play that song she wrote with her dad. But I fucked up with it too, because I almost did something completely unexpected - I almost kissed her... again.

When she sang that same night, I felt myself losing control. Her vulnerability in her singing, the rawness of it all, made my walls come down. Thank fuck, Ace's text brought me back to reality, preventing me from making a foolish mistake. I've never had a girlfriend and I'm not interested in having one. That's why I don't kiss, I don't want a girl thinking I'm theirs. That night, I almost messed up big time by giving in to temptation and kissing her again. Instead of having a conversation with her and letting her know we can only be friends, I just ran away. It scared me. She scares me. Whenever I'm with her, she makes me feel things I shouldn't. Emotions I've never felt before. No way I'm gonna let anyone, especially not some chick, come before me, and my dream. And then, the next night she completely ignored me.

Normally, I couldn't give a shit, but that night felt different. She displayed strength and showed that she deserved better than what I had done. That's what I truly admire about Poppy. She's strong and incredibly stubborn. She stands up for herself. So, as a token of appreciation for her honesty with me, I opened up and shared my story about my mom.

"People will see you," Poppy says, staring straight ahead.

"So let them. I don't fucking care."

"I feel terrible," she says.

"Well, I did warn you to take it easy last night, but you didn't listen. What did you have for breakfast this morning?"

"Nothing."

"Well, that's the fucking problem."

"My mom flipped when she found me on the couch."

"Come on," I say, standing up, I hold my hand out towards her. "Let's go."

She grabs my hand and I help her get to her feet.

"Where are we going?" she asks, looking up at me from behind those ridiculous oversized sunglasses.

"You need a greasy burger to help with the hangover."

"Ugh, I really don't think I can handle a greasy burger."

"Trust me, Princess, it'll fix it. Ace gave me twenty bucks this morning, so it'll be my treat for once."

"No, I'll pay. You might need to save the money."

"What the fuck have I said about pitying me," I retort sharply. "I already told you to stop with that shit. I'm paying."

"Yeah, yeah, whatever. I see your lips moving, but all I hear is blah, blah, blah," she says, adjusting her sunglasses and retrieving her bag from off the ground.

I can't help but smirk at her response. While most girls seek my approval, Poppy consistently challenges me and refuses to conform.

Poppy leads the way, walking a bit ahead of me, as we make our way towards the school car park. I can't help but stare at her, checking her out, as she walks to her crappy green car.

Chapter 16

Xander

The car stereo blares "Zombie" by the Cranberries. Despite this old shit box only having a tape deck, it's still going strong. It's surprising to discover that Poppy is into alternative rock - who would have guessed? It makes me curious if her dad was the owner of the tape. I wish I had the chance to meet him; it would have been amazing.

"Take a right up ahead," I say, motioning towards the street up ahead.

As my phone lights up, I quickly glance down to see a text from Ace.

Ace: Where are you? Savannah said you left. What's going on?

Xander: Yeah, won't be back. See you at practice.

I slip my phone into my pocket, and glance back up. "See that red sign there?" I say, pointing ahead to indicate the exact location I'm referring to. "They have the best burgers in town. Have you ever been there?"

I can already predict Poppy's response even before she speaks. This area tends to attract a unique crowd. It's difficult for me to imagine Poppy or her mother ever coming here.

Poppy skillfully maneuvers the battered green car through the crowded parking lot, bringing it to a stop as the engine sputters to a halt. Exiting the car, we are met with the distant hum of traffic and the crisp air tinged with exhaust fumes.

As we step into the dimly lit burger joint, Poppy keeps her sunglasses on. An enticing scent of sizzling patties fills the air. I spot a snug booth hidden in the corner. The speakers reverberate with the energetic beat of rock music, infusing the venue with an electrifying atmosphere.

Poppy raises her glasses and scans the room, taking in her surroundings. The proprietor, Sid, is a seasoned heavy metal rocker. From time to time, he takes a break to entertain the customers, but I've only seen this happen when me and Ace go late at night. However, during the day the vibe totally changes.

The lighting is brighter now and I didn't notice how red the walls were until now.

Poppy settles into her seat, and despite the temptation to sit beside her, I choose the seat opposite her. Already knowing what I want, I give her the menu that's on the table. I watch her closely as she studies the menu. Trying to decide what to order, she wears a frown and anxiously bites her bottom lip.

"So, what do you recommend?" she asks, shifting her gaze to me.

"The triple cheeseburger with a side of fries and a chocolate shake."

"Okay," she says, placing the menu back on the table. "But I might go for a double. I don't think I can fit my mouth around a triple."

My thoughts turn dirty and I can't help but smirk.

"What?" she says.

"Trust me, Princess, I'm pretty sure your mouth can get around anything."

Her cheeks turn red as she looks around the room.

When I glance to my left, I see Tayla, the server approaching. I silently express my frustration because I was hoping she wouldn't be working today, given that she typically works nights. This is gonna be super awkward. We hooked up a few weeks ago. I never called her after she gave me her number. I brought Poppy along today, thinking Tayla wouldn't be working.

"Hey Xander," she says, giving me a smile. "I've been wondering when we would catch up again," she says, shifting her focus to Poppy. "So, who do we have here?" she asks, showing her irritation.

Ignoring her question, I snatch the menu and attempt to order without making eye contact.

But then, Poppy's voice cuts in.

"Hi, I'm Poppy," she says, introducing herself and extending her hand for a handshake.

Tayla hesitates before accepting it. "Tayla," she replies.

To wrap things up and get Tayla to fuck off, I quickly place my order. "I'll take a triple cheeseburger, fries on the side, and a chocolate milkshake," I say, placing the menu back on the table. I take a quick look at Poppy. "And what do you want, Princess?"

As soon as those words leave my mouth, I know I've fucked up.

"Princess," Tayla murmurs, before giving me a stern look. "Xander out of curiosity, does your girlfriend know about what happened between us a few weeks ago? Her focus shifts back to Poppy. "Well, did he tell you about that?"

A surge of tension washes over me, causing the hairs on the back of my neck to stand on end. My only desire is for her to fuck off and stop bothering Poppy.

"Well, first of all, Tayla," I interject. "She's not my girlfriend."

"We're not dating," Poppy chimes in.

Poppy's words hold no significance as Tayla continues to glare at her with a hateful look.

"And let's not forget, it was your idea. You wanted me," I tell her. "It was just a hookup."

A hurt expression appears on Tayla's face as she swallows. Ready to take Poppy's order, she lifts the pen and pad.

"So, what can I get for you?"

"I'll have the same as Xander," Poppy says, putting the menu back onto the table.

After Tayla writes down Poppy's order she turns away without saying a word.

When I glance at Poppy, I notice her looking down at something in her lap. She raises her eyes, searching the room, deliberately avoiding meeting my gaze. I shouldn't let it affect me this much, but damn, it really does. I know she probably thinks I'm a total asshole because of what happened between Tayla and me.

Just as I'm about to start a conversation, I quickly shut my mouth upon seeing Tayla walking towards us with our shakes. Tayla forcefully sets the milkshakes down on the table. She glares at me intensely before walking away. As this is going on, Poppy mindlessly swirls the straw around in her oversized milkshake cup.

"So, another admirer in the Xander Williams hookup club," she remarks, a smile gracing her lips. I watch as she removes her straw from her glass and expertly sucks the cream from the bottom. My dick instantly reacts.

"Yeah, I guess you could say that," I mutter. This is the first time in my life I've experienced such embarrassment from my behavior. I wonder what Poppy thinks of me at this moment.

"So," she says, gazing up at me, still swirling her straw around. "You still haven't told me what you had to do to get my number."

"Yeah," I say, flashing a grin, feeling a sense of relief for a new topic. I'm mesmerized by the way she licks the cream from the straw.

"So what then? What did you do?" She puts the straw back in her shake.

I feel let down because I could sit here all day watching her mouth work its magic.

Leaning in, I place my arms on the table. "Let's just say Zoe Mitchell is a boundary-pushing pro. She wouldn't give me your number unless I went to her cousin's party and acted like her boyfriend."

With a burst of laughter, Poppy snorts and hastily conceals her mouth to suppress her amusement. My face lights up when I hear it.

"Although Zoe wanted me to stay for the entire party, I made it clear that I would only stay for twenty minutes. That's another reason why you shouldn't ignore my texts. I had to put in some work to get that." It's another thing that confuses me. Getting a girl's number has never required this much effort, but with Poppy, I'm completely disregarding my own rules.

"When's the party?' she asks, smirking, then casually sips her milkshake.

"Two weeks from tomorrow," I say, unable to stop staring at the straw in her mouth.

Our server brings our food, and I'm relieved to find out it's not Tayla. Instead, our server is a middle-aged woman with a bob haircut with a touch of gray.

"Here you go, sweetness," she says, sliding the plate in front of Poppy first. "And this one must be for you, handsome." She puts the plate in front of me and grabs the menu off the table. "If you guys need anything else, just give me a holler."

In Poppy's hands, there's a monster-sized burger, it's massive against her palms. "I don't know how you expect me to finish this." Drawing it nearer to her mouth, she sinks her teeth into the mouthwatering patty. "Mmmm... oh my god, this burger is so good."

"I told you it was pretty good," I remark, watching her as she savors every bite.

She lifts her hand and licks the sauce from her fingers, making me instantly aroused. Despite the sauce dribbling down her chin, she remains unfazed. The urge to lean forward and lick it is strong, but I resist and simply smile. I'm glad Poppy doesn't feel the need to hide her eating habits like some other chicks do when they're around guys. With ease, she wipes the sauce off her chin using her finger and then puts it into her mouth. Her finger-sucking skills are a major turn-on.

"Aren't you hungry?" she asks, chewing some fries.

"Nah, I'm hungry," I tell her, taking the salt shaker from the table.

I was so caught up in watching her enjoy her meal that I neglected my own. I can feel her eyes on me as I pour an excessive amount of salt on my fries, as I usually do.

"You know me and my salt addiction," I joke, realizing how dumb it was to say that when we've never eaten out like this before.

It's surprising how much I genuinely enjoy hanging out with Poppy and having conversations about music, my band with Ace, and other interesting subjects. It's on a completely different level compared to the girls I usually fool around with, where I can't wait to get the fuck out of there. But with Poppy, there's none of that. Our chats are always easy and interesting.

"So, tell me how does it work? Do you both write songs together?" She says, before picking up her burger and taking another bite.

"Sort of. I write the lyrics and some music while Ace takes care of the sound, beat, and melody."

"Oh, I totally forgot to ask. So, what's the name of your band?" Poppy asks, casually wiping her fingers on her napkin.

"Ace came up with Broken Oasis. You know, because we both come from broken homes. He thought of it because we're in search of a place where our music can take us. It's like a chill spot, a better life, our own little oasis."

"I really like it. It's a perfect fit for the vision you have for yourself, both now and in the future."

"Yeah, it is," I add. "So what about you? Are you gonna chase your music dreams too?"

"I really want to go for it, but I'm not sure how to approach it. I'm thinking of studying child psychology. You know, so I understand how music benefits children with disabilities. I know I'll never hear the end of it when my mom finds out."

"But it's your life, not hers." I pause for a second, pondering how to approach the subject without upsetting her. "Have you ever considered searching for your dad?"

"Yeah, but I don't know what to do." Her eyes briefly show a hint of pain, making me question whether I should've mentioned it. "I've tried looking him up online. I found a few photos of his band, but there's not much else there to go on. There's no recent information. Only what has always been online. He hasn't been on Facebook for years, but still, it didn't stop me from sending him a message. But that was two years ago, and it is still sitting there unread. It's like he vanished off the face of the earth."

"If I could see my mom again, I'd do it in a heartbeat. Poppy, I hope that one day you find him."

"Thanks. I hope so too,"

She raises her milkshake to her mouth, finishing it off before placing it back on the table.

I glance over at her plate and notice that she has finished her burger, leaving only a handful of fries behind.

"I can't eat another bite," she says, sliding the plate towards me and offering the remaining fries.

I accept her offer of leftover fries and we settle comfortably in the booth, chatting effortlessly.

Our conversations range from discussing our favorite bands to sharing how we handle the loss of our parents. We share funny stories, laugh, and occasionally get teary-eyed. It's crazy how well we connect despite only meeting a few weeks ago. The longer we talk, the more we open up about our hopes, dreams, and struggles. In this booth, we can let our guard down and be ourselves without judgment.

It's only when a new server comes over and asks for our table that I realize how fast time has gone by. It's past four o'clock, and Ace is waiting for me.

We hastily make our way out of the restaurant and jump into Poppy's car, ready to hit the road.

In ten minutes, Poppy reaches Ace's house and parks the car by the curb. I don't go just yet. I can't quite put it into words, but I don't want this day to end.

The soft hum of the engine serves as a gentle reminder it's time to leave. I open the passenger's door and start to get out, but then pause and face Poppy.

"Do you want to come inside and see what we've been working on?" I ask.

"Thanks, but maybe another time," she says. "I think it's time for me to go home and face the music, so to say."

"I wanted to ask you something at the booth, but I didn't get the chance. And I don't want you to get mad at me when I ask."

"Okay... what is it?"

"I want to know why you're still a virgin, or is that bullshit too?" I pause, waiting for her to tell me to fuck off, but she maintains her gaze ahead, staring out through the windshield.

"I told you this the other night, Xander." She looks down at her hands in her lap. "It's because no boy has ever shown an interest in me like that."

I'm clueless about what to say, so I get out of the car and crouch down to look at Poppy. "I'll see you later tonight."

She simply nods.

I close the car door and walk up the driveway towards the garage in the back. While I continue walking, the noise of Poppy's car gradually fades out as it drives away.

Chapter 17

Xander

S tepping into the garage, I am taken aback by the sight of Ace and Jade making out on the old stained couch.

"What the fuck is she doing here?" I blurt out, with no regard for how cruel it might sound.

I set my bag down on the floor and walk over to my guitar, which is resting against the chair in the corner.

When he hears my voice, Ace looks at me. While holding my guitar in my lap, I hear him say something, but it's difficult to understand. I can't stop thinking about Poppy and what she confessed. The reason she's still a virgin is that no guy has shown interest in her. I am filled with sadness for not appreciating the beauty that was right in front of me. The girl who has been my neighbor for my whole life. Now, things are completely different. Now, I can't get her out of my head. If I had seen her back then, like I see her now, I would have selfishly exploited her, just as I do with everyone else. Thank fuck, I've only recently started getting to know her. I would never want to use her in such a way, she deserves so much more than that. Unlike the girl who is currently watching me strum my guitar. The girl who jumps from one guy to another without a second thought.

Poppy is a true friend to me, someone I feel comfortable opening up to and having deep conversations with. Yes, she is attractive, and yes, I'm not denying that I wouldn't fuck her in a heartbeat if given the opportunity. After all, I'm only human. What truly amazes me is her genuine understanding of me. She understands everything - my pain, my struggles, my heartaches, and my aspirations.

I stop playing my guitar and glance up at Ace and Jade who are both staring at me. While seated on his lap, Jade continues to stroke Ace's dick.

"Tell me why the fuck is she here?" I inquire, my frustration clear in my tone.

"Where's your girlfriend?" Ace says, curiosity seeping through his words.

Taking a moment to collect my thoughts, I inhale deeply before responding, "I've already told you she ain't my girlfriend."

It angers me that he brought Jade to our special place. Here is where we come together to make music and strive towards our future goals. Jade doesn't give a shit about music and couldn't care less about the songs we're working on. It's incredibly frustrating. She shouldn't be here, plain and simple.

"I thought Xander didn't do girlfriends," Jade says, lifting her head from Ace's neck.

"I don't," I snap back. "Not that it's any of your fucking business."

"Then who is he talking about?" she asks.

Ignoring the bitch's question, I keep my head down and continue playing the guitar.

If Ace wants to fuck her, that's fine, but he should find somewhere else to do it, not during our practice.

"He's been hanging out with Poppy Reeves?" Ace says, chuckling.

The intensity of my grip on the guitar increases, fueled by the overwhelming urge to grab him by the collar and tell him to fucking shut his mouth. I fight against the urge. Instead, I begin playing a catchy melody that's been stuck in my head.

"You're joking, right?" she says, giving me a disgusted look. "You've been spending time with that fat cow."

"Shut the fuck up, Jade. Just hurry up and suck his cock so you can get the fuck out of here. That's why he brought you here, just so he could get off."

My words have the desired impact.

She glances at Ace. "Is that true?" she asks, her voice all whiny and annoying.

"What the hell, man?" Ace says, throwing me a disapproving look as if to ask why the fuck I would even say that out loud. He shifts his attention back to Jade.

"No, that's not true."

Bullshit. Surely she can see right through this asshole's lies. Is she truly that naïve to think she's something more to us than an easy fuck?

"I wanted you here so you could see us play," he says, tucking her hair behind her ear. "But if you're up to giving me a blowjob now, I won't complain."

"Hold on, so you actually wanted me to watch you guys play?" she asks, her face displaying genuine surprise.

This chick is so fucking dumb. How can she not hear the shit pouring out of his mouth?

I set my guitar aside and quickly grab my phone, feeling an urgent need to leave. My thumbs move quickly as I send a text to Poppy.

Xander: Hey princess, can you come back and pick me up?

I head across the room and grab my bag. When Ace notices what I am doing, he asks, "Where do you think you're going?"

"Out of here. I'm not staying here while you get your dick sucked," I reply, throwing my bag over my shoulder.

"What the fuck is going on with you, Xander," Ace calls out, quickly pushing Jade aside and getting up to join me. "Come on, man. Just stay and the three of us can have a little bit of fun before we practice."

No way. The two of us had a wild time with Jade two months ago when we tag-teamed her. But I'm not going down that road again especially when I can't stand the bitch. I make my way towards the door and push it open.

"Xander," Ace calls out, following me. "Come on, man."

"I'll catch up with you later," I respond, before leaving the garage.

As I feel my phone vibrating, I quickly remove it from my pocket.

Princess: I'll be there in five.

While walking down the long driveway, Ace swiftly catches up and grabs my arm, stopping me.

"What the hell is going on, Xander? Did something happen with your dad again?"

"No." I shake my head and step around him, determined to keep walking. "Practice is a big deal. We need to make sure our sound is flawless before we go. If you're having second thoughts about leaving. I'll just go by myself."

"No way. Why would you even think that? Will you stop walking so we can talk. What makes you think I don't want to leave?"

I turn to face him. "Because you brought that bitch there. That's why."

"What's gotten into you, man? I thought we could relax before jamming, you know, enjoy ourselves. She's always up for anything. Don't forget how amazing it was when we both had her at the same time. I thought we could experience it again."

"Yeah, it was," I reply, recalling the time I snapped that photo of her on my phone. Ace used his phone to record the entire thing. But no matter how incredible that experience was, I want to stay clear of Jade. "She just doesn't do it for me anymore. She's so fucking annoying."

Hearing a car pull up to the curb, I instinctively turned my head. It's Poppy's green beat-up piece of shit.

"Catch you later, man," I say, turning away from him.

"What?" Ace says surprised, as if questioning my decision. "After everything I just said, you're really going to give that up just to hang out with Poppy Reeves?"

I turn, walking backward. "Yep, I guess I am." Pivoting, I make my way towards Poppy's car.

"I can't believe you, man," Ace calls out as I make my way to Poppy's car. "The Xander I know would never pass up an opportunity to get his dick wet."

It's true, and his comment is really frightening because I don't know what's happening to me. But I say nothing to him about that. I just open the door and quickly enter Poppy's car.

As Poppy presses down on the accelerator, I spot Ace standing in the driveway, watching us move down the street. Guilt fills my stomach as I see him in the side mirror. Turning around, he makes his way back towards the house. Maybe he'll reconsider bringing girls to practice in the future.

"So, no practice today?" Poppy asks.

"Nah, not today. How far were you from home?" I ask.

"I changed my mind. Instead of going home, I was going somewhere else. I think my mother can wait a little longer before I face her."

"Where were you going?" I ask.

A radiant, golden hue fills the streets with the afternoon sun.

"To the vacant lot behind Al's. Have you been there?" Poppy responds.

"No. I didn't even know there was a vacant lot there. What do you do there?"

"Nothing really," she replies. "It's quiet. No one ever goes there. Sometimes I go and watch the sunset. It helps clear my mind when I don't want to think about things. I just sit on the hood of my car and unwind."

"Show me," I say, curious to understand what makes that place so fascinating to her. Is it going to be like the place I took her to the other night? Does she go there to think about her dad not being around and wonder about the same "what ifs" as I do when I go to my usual spot feeling down?

"What? You want to go there now?" she responds.

"Yeah, why not? You were going there anyway before. Why not show me?"

With a nod, Poppy activates the indicator and swiftly changes direction.

We spend the next ten minutes passing through vibrant streets on our journey. She drives the car into a narrow lane. It's clear that it's not frequently used, given the overgrown weeds. As we drive on the dusty road, a cloud of dust trails behind us. Poppy finds a hidden spot among the towering trees to park. The peaceful atmosphere instantly soothes my senses. I observe neighboring houses with wooden fences, which adds a sense of safety to their surroundings. Even though I'm far away, I can't help but wonder if my desperate screams would reach someone's ears. Still, in this secret spot, we stay hidden and secluded from the outside world.

"How did you find this place?" I ask, glancing around as Poppy turns off the car.

"About six months ago I found it when I was just driving around, feeling bored."

"How often do you come here?"

"Not that often."

"When was the last time you came here?"

"Oh... about three weeks ago."

"Why? What happened three weeks ago?" I inquire, my voice tinged with curiosity.

"My mom and I'd also had a shit day at school," she responds, her words carrying a touch of sorrow.

I wonder if Jade was the reason her day was shit.

Poppy opens the car door wide, the hinges creaking loudly.

From the passenger seat, I observe her through the windshield as she moves towards the front of the car. Enticed by the warm afternoon sun, she sits on the car's hood.

Driven by an irresistible force, I open the passenger's door and join her. As I sit beside her on the car's hood, I feel the sun's gentle warmth soak into my black t-shirt and jeans. I stay silent and captivated by her presence, observing as she continues to stare at the horizon. The way the sun sets, casting a radiant orange glow on her face, immediately captures my focus. It enhances her beauty, turning her into a breathtaking masterpiece.

As soon as she catches me staring, I swiftly avert my eyes and pull out my pack of cigarettes, lighting one. As I take a slow drag, I admire the tranquil view in front of me.

Poppy grabs my cigarette, and her lips curl around it, releasing a faint trail of smoke.

I can't help but smirk as I eagerly await her cough, just like she did last time. To my surprise, she doesn't. Instead, she keeps her cool and takes another drag, then passes it back to me.

"Are you going to tell me what happened? And spare me the excuses, Xander. I know a musician like you wouldn't just walk away from a jam session for no reason, especially when it means so much to you," she says, gazing out at the scenery.

Damn, it's almost like this girl has the ability to read my mind or has a deeper understanding of me than I previously thought. I take a drag from my cigarette to collect my thoughts and stall for time.

"Ace took Jade there, so we could mess around with her before we started." I can't believe I'm actually telling her this. But what I do notice is that Poppy tenses up as soon as I mention Jade's name. Could it be that Jade's nagging and annoying voice is bothering me more than usual because of her influence on Poppy?

"So, what's the problem with that? I mean, you usually hang out with Jade."

I hold the cigarette out for her to grab. "I didn't want to fool around with her, I just wanted to practice," I explain. "What if we only get one chance to show a talent scout that we're different from all the others trying to get discovered. I just want us to stand out."

"But you do, Xander."

"But you haven't even seen us perform yet."

"No, but I've seen how you become one with your music. You have a special talent that usually takes years to develop. Believe me, Xander, you're destined for greatness."

"You always say that," I respond, raising an eyebrow.

"Say what?" she asks.

"I honestly don't know why..." I shrug.

"Why what?" Her eyes watch me.

"You always believe in me. No one else does. Sometimes I wonder if I'm just kidding myself. If it's all just in my head, a desperate dream to escape my boring reality and prove myself. Like I actually mean something."

"But you are something. When you sing, it's as if you pour your entire essence into those lyrics. It's like a magnetic pull, drawing all of us towards something extraordinary. Believe me, you possess an incredible talent, Xander."

Her words have a profound effect on me, hitting me straight in the heart. I have spent my entire life being called a lowlife, someone without worth. The derogatory comments I've faced didn't just come from the man I thought was my dad, but also from teachers and parents of other kids. Yet, when I look into her eyes, it's not the same. She has a one-of-a-kind perception of me - she sees something in me that is entirely new. She doesn't see the state of my broken home or the challenges I face. What she sees is the real me, the person I aspire to be.

My lips meet hers, prompting a soft gasp to escape her. I gently slide my tongue into her mouth, enjoying the taste. Surrendering to the kiss, I hold her face in my hands. Her mouth, like mine, is warm and needy, igniting a tingling sensation that courses through my entire being. The scent of her perfume permeates the air, adding a delightful sweetness. Our breaths blend together in perfect harmony. Hearing her soft moan snaps me back to reality.

In an instant, I feel a powerful wave of realization crash down on me. The weight of my mistake settles like a heavy burden. Fuck, I kissed her again. My heart sinks as I realize I've broken my number one rule once again.

I swiftly move back, noticing that her breath is as labored as mine. Her intense blue eyes meet mine, locking in a heated gaze. It's impossible for me to control my body's reaction to her, no matter how hard I try. My desire for her surpasses any longing I've ever experienced. My heart races within me, overwhelmed by the intense arousal I feel for this person. Music is my passion. That's what I strive to do. However, the attraction I feel for her is different. She possesses a unique quality that sets her apart.

I don't know why, but I suddenly feel an overwhelming need to express how stunning she is. The way she holds her head high, even in the face of torment and criticism, fills me with such admiration. I have this intense desire to pour out all my emotions to her, but I'm having difficulty finding the right words. This is a completely new experience for me because I've never been this open or felt this way about someone before. I feel unsure and hesitant about the vulnerability that comes with allowing someone to get closer to me than anyone else ever has before.

However, there's something about Poppy that compels me to establish a much deeper connection with her. It's like she has become intertwined with my thoughts, merging with the core of my being.

I'm still so close to her that I can almost taste the warmth of her breath lingering on my lips. Her chest's gentle rise and fall is captivating to behold. Still, there is a sense of stillness as she gazes at me, studying me as if trying to read my expression.

Silently, she raises her hand and threads her fingers in my hair. She firmly clutches the back of my head, pulling me closer to her.

Our lips collide in a hungry kiss. It's wild, desperate and holy mother of God, so fucking incredibly hot. I love it. I choose to ignore all the rules I should abide by. My brain screams no, but my cock refuses to listen. He's tired of seeing the inside of my fist. He yearns to sink into her. To succumb to the irresistible sensation of her tight pussy.

Then I realize that she's a virgin. I don't do virgins. A better man would distance himself. Poppy Reeves deserves someone better than me, a complete jerk who fucks anything he can. Although I am aware that one day she will resent me for taking her virginity, all I want to do is claim her as mine.

I trail my tongue along her jawline, down her neck, and across her collarbone. "You have no idea how much I want to fuck you right now." I confess, grabbing her breast.

She responds eagerly, emitting a seductive sound when I give it a gentle squeeze.

Wow, if just pinching her nipple gets that reaction, I can only imagine the pleasure I would experience exploring every inch of her body. The very idea of it makes my cock harder, almost to the point of discomfort. If she were some other chick, I would have shoved my dick in her hand, her mouth, or any other hole I could stick it in to get what I desired.

However, Poppy is not like any other chick. There's no one else like her, she's in a class of her own.

"I've fucking fantasized about touching you so many times. All I can think about is slipping my hands under your short skirt to see how wet I can make you," I confess, my voice barely above a whisper as if carried away by a gentle breeze.

"Then do it."

With a cocky grin, I plant another kiss on her collarbone, then get up.

Her eyes remain fixed on me as I grab her legs, coaxing her towards me and helping her lie down on the hood of the car. My hands glide along the smooth contours of her inner thighs, feeling the warmth radiating through my fingertips with every move. The mix of anticipation and fear causes her to tremble in response, unlike anything I've seen before. I know I'm her first and I want to make sure she enjoys it.

Slowly, my fingertips glide beneath the fabric of her skirt, igniting a surge of anticipation. The moment my fingers brush against her wet spot, she lets out a hiss.

A confident smirk tugs at the corners of my mouth. "You're so fucking wet already," I remark.

She bites down on her bottom lip and challenges me. "So, how do you intend to handle that?"

Her feistiness is such a turn-on.

I lift her skirt and can't help but groan at the sight of her black lace panties, completely transparent and leaving nothing to the imagination.

Who would have thought that Poppy Reeves, the virgin, would wear something like this? My fingertips trace the intricate patterns of the delicate lace as I gaze at her smooth, shaved pussy. Slipping my fingers under the waistband, I slowly slide them down over her thighs, past her knees, and eventually reach her ankles.

And just like the pervert I am, I quickly stash them in my pocket, intending to keep them as a memento to get myself off later.

A deep groan escapes me as she willingly opens her legs for me. The sight of her glistening pussy is irresistible, begging me to indulge in some playful exploration.

"Tell me, Princess, let me know if you want me to stop," I say, praying like fuck she doesn't say no.

When she remains silent, I gently let the pad of my finger glide across her damp, slick flesh, teasing her and feeling the warmth and wetness beneath my touch. As I watch her, she bites down on her bottom lip, releasing a moan.

My dick aches with need, with want. My desire intensifies, aching and craving for more. It consumes me, an insatiable hunger that I have never experienced before. Deep within me lies a place untouched, a territory I have never dared to explore. The desire to please her surpasses anything I have ever felt. The air carries a faint aroma, tantalizing my senses with unexplored possibilities. I yearn to fully immerse myself in this uncharted territory, embracing the unknown with open arms.

I gently insert a finger inside her, overwhelmed by how fucking incredibly tight she feels. A moan escapes her lips, sending a shiver down my spine. And I swear hearing her sultry sound will drive me to the brink of insanity. Her velvety walls grip me intensely. If she doesn't ask me to stop soon, I won't be able to control myself. Her moans intensify as my thumb grazes her clit.

With each rhythmic movement of my fingers, her seductive sounds have me entranced, as if under a spell. The graceful sway of her body as I pleasure her holds me captive, mesmerized by the enchanting world of Poppy.

My heart races, my breath quickens, and I am utterly captivated, lost in this otherworldly moment.

"Fuck, you feel amazing," I whisper, my gaze locked on her, unable to look away for even a moment.

"Xander," she breathes, her voice instantly sends shivers down my spine.

Hearing her say my name makes me feel powerful. I can sense her nearing the peak, her walls tightening around my fingers. "That's it, Princess, just let go," I encourage her.

And she does, her face contorting in a mesmerizing display of beauty, like a delicate dance of emotions. The subtle lines around her eyes deepen, revealing the intensity of her orgasm. The soft sounds of her moans escaping through her parted lips add a melodic quality to the moment. It's awe-inspiring to witness her come down from that high. I'm rock hard as I slide my fingers back in, observing her as she rides out the waves of her orgasm.

I pull out and bring my fingers to her mouth.

"Open," I demand. "I want you to taste yourself."

When she does, I slip my fingers in her mouth.

"Damn," I add, as desire courses through me when she eagerly sucks her arousal from my fingers. She sucks with intensity, savoring every drop. Removing my fingers, I lean in and passionately kiss her.

Nervous anticipation fills my belly as her fingertips locate the zipper on my jeans and tugs it down. She then boldly slips her hand inside and grasps my hard cock. Despite my desire to keep going, I wrestle with every ounce of my being to reach out and make her stop.

"Wait," I say, my breath heavy, as I grasp her hand. Gasping for air, I press my forehead against hers, feeling the warmth of our skin melding together. "You know, if you pull out my cock, I won't be able to resist. I will fuck you right here on top of this car."

"That's what I want Xander," she replies, her eyes aflame with desire.

I pause for a moment, knowing that I shouldn't do it, but the way she makes my mind go crazy there is no way I can stop myself from wanting to be balls-deep in that tight pussy.

"Are you sure?"

She nods, her eyes sparkling with understanding and her head gently bobbing up and down.

"No, you gotta say it, Princess. I need to hear you say it," I insist, still breathing hard with my forehead against hers.

"You're the one I want to be my first, Xander. So, fuck me… please."

Her being a virgin makes me worry, which is the reasoning behind why I always avoided inexperienced partners. But for some reason, I long to be her first.

"I'll be right back," I assure her, moving around the car. I retrieve my bag from the back seat where I had tossed it earlier. Grabbing out the bottle of whisky, I return to Poppy. If I was going to take her V-card, I wanted to do it properly, not just for my own selfish desires.

Returning to the front of the car, I notice her sitting upright with her skirt neatly pulled down over her legs, her eyes fixed on my every move. I extend my hand, offering her the bottle of whisky.

"If we're gonna do this, you need to relax. Now drink."

Glancing briefly at the bottle, she reaches out and takes it. She takes a big swig of whisky, downing it quickly. Then passes it back to me.

I take a gulp and then hand it back fast. "Drink some more."

My intention is to help ease her pain from her first sexual experience, but not to the point where she would forget it because she's too intoxicated. I have a rule of not hooking up with chicks who are drunk.

As I watch her, she raises the bottle to her lips and delicately wraps them around its rim. After she takes a satisfying gulp from the bottle, I take it from her and securely screw on the lid.

"So, when are we going to do this?" she asks.

My heart pounds, slow and heavy, in my chest. My desire grows stronger. I catch a whiff of her delicate, feminine scent, overpowering my senses.

"You sure about this?" I ask again, just to double-check if she's changed her mind. "Once we do this there's no going back." I can't believe I'm saying this, but I didn't want her to regret giving me her virginity.

"Seriously, Xander, just do it already and quit asking," she says impatiently.

With a smug grin on my face, our eyes meet, a silent intensity passing between us for what feels like forever. My heart races, while her breaths become shallow. And then, without a second thought, I crossed that forbidden line. I press my lips against hers, exploring her mouth with my tongue, relishing the taste.

I don't care about the consequences, about how wrong it is for me to be with her. Ignoring everything, I kiss her and carefully lower her onto the hood of the car. But it isn't just a simple kiss; it is an all-consuming collision of desire. I part her lips with mine, delving deeper, pressing my body against hers. She moans as I begin grinding my hips, my cock rubbing against her soft pussy.

She gasps and squirms beneath me as I move my hips, seeking to find that sweet spot. I am fucking relentless in my pursuit. She said she wanted me. And let's be fucking honest, this is who I truly am - the guy who lives for music and loves to fuck. I kiss her with hunger, moving my hips, grinding against her. And she's totally into it, grinding against me, kissing me back.

My cock strains against her. My balls throb. I'm so fucking horny, everything in me zeroes in on her pussy. All I can think about is getting inside her. Fuck yes, that's what I want.

I drift my fingertips over her clit, eliciting a pleasurable groan from her. She moves her hips, rocking, eagerly seeking more of my touch. I watch her intently as I continue to explore her. With each stroke, I increase the pressure, knowing that it will heighten her arousal. I move my fingers in small, circular motions over her clit, causing her to tremble.

"Oh God," she blurts out.

"I'm not going to make you come," I tell her. "I want you turned on before we do it. Apparently, it hurts less if you're all worked up."

"I know it's gonna hurt at first," she says, gasping, clearly loving what I'm doing to her.

My gaze wanders down her body before finally meeting her eyes. In this very moment, she is fucking breathtaking, seeing her openness and vulnerability. It's almost as if I am orchestrating her like a musical instrument, coaxing out the most delightful erotic sounds from her. I am tempted to tell her how beautiful she is, but I don't know how to say all that mushy shit.

I just wanna slam into her and make her scream my name while she tells me how much she's been thinking about me, just like I've been thinking about her, and she wants to do every dirty thing I've ever dreamt about doing to her.

As she lays before me, her breath quickening, her gaze burning with desire, I notice her hard nipples, a clear reflection of her arousal. She so fucking close and I love it.

CHAPTER 18

Poppy

I'm in a state of euphoria as if I am floating on a cloud. The moment our eyes lock, my heart races and my excitement reaches overwhelming levels. A soft whimper escapes my lips as he gently lifts me up, intensifying the feeling. His deliberate and torturous circles on my swollen little nub send waves of pleasure crashing through me. However, to my frustration, the asshole suddenly stops. What the fuck. I release a frustrated breath.

With a mischievous grin, he runs his tongue along his lower lip and winks at me. "Hang tight Princess, we'll get there eventually," he says with that damn cocky grin. "I don't want all my efforts to be in vain."

"You're such an asshole, you know that."

He bursts into laughter. "You can only come when I have my cock buried deep inside you. Take this off, I want to see your tits," he demands, his voice deep and raspy, the kind that could convince any woman to comply with his desires.

His magnetic eyes remain focused on me as I slowly unbutton my shirt. But apparently, I'm not doing it fast enough for him, because he helps and the last two buttons pop off.

With a swift motion, he reaches behind and unclasps my bra, displaying his skill and speed. Holy shit, he's a pro at that. I lie there, my skirt bunched up around my waist, and see the subtle change in his expression. His jaw tenses and a flicker of emotion dances across his beautiful face, but I can't quite decipher it. The tendons in his throat tighten as he swallows, adding to the intensity of the moment. I hold his gaze, feeling my heart pounding painfully against my chest. His eyes roam over every part of my body, and despite the urge to cover myself up, I stay there, arms by my side. I hope he doesn't see what Jade and her friends always gossip about.

His eyes narrow into mysterious slits, exuding an enigmatic aura as they fixate on mine. A sudden longing awakens within me, a yearning to witness every facet of his being. If I am naked, I also yearn to see him in the same vulnerable state. I crave the sight of his magnificent form, to explore every aspect of what he has to offer.

"Take that off," I tell him, motioning towards his shirt.

"You're a pushy little thing, aren't you? I like it," he says, with a sly grin spreading across his face. He reaches up and effortlessly pulls his black t-shirt over his head, casually discarding it on the ground.

My gaze lingers on his chest, which is just as breathtaking as the rest of him - slim, with a few well-defined muscles.

"Get rid of those," I insist, motioning to his jeans.

That cocky grin reappears. He quickly unbuttons his jeans and takes them off in a flash, like he's on fire.

As he stands in front of me, I avert my gaze downwards. His presence is commanding, and his size is undeniable. Through his heavy eyelids, he looks down at me, his gaze filled with desire. His hands delicately trace up my waist, before grasping my breasts, gently squeezing my nipples and sending waves of pleasure through my body.

My lips part, releasing a moan that I can't control.

"I knew you would like that," he growls, as if he is fully aware of the effect he has on me.

The blaring sound of his ringtone breaks the silence while he stands there, watching me.

"Do you need to get that?" I ask.

"Fuck no." He leans forward, pressing his lips against mine. The sensation of his velvety lips and the forceful thrust of his tongue intertwining with mine overwhelms me. His hands firmly grip my hips, leaving a mark on my skin.

After breaking the kiss, his warm breath tickles my ear, leaving me breathless. "Lift your legs so I can slide in and make you come on my cock."

Just the thought of what he wants to do to me makes me weak in the knees. Who would have guessed that Filthy-Mouth Xander could be even hotter than regular Xander? I love everything about it. Xander Williams is a pure sex machine, and I can't get enough. I moan without even meaning to.

He is unbelievably hot. I've never felt like such a naughty girl before. But at this moment... just fuck me. That's what I want to be. His naughty girl. With my legs spread wide, I feel sinful, mischievous, filthy, and it feels absolutely incredible.

Lying on my back, I gaze up at him towering over me while he stands in between my legs, my knees resting on either side of his hips.

When our eyes meet, I feel all these crazy feelings rushing through me, my body buzzing with excitement. He takes his time, lowering himself and sensually licking my left nipple, giving me the chills.

His touch becomes exploratory, his hands tracing the curve of my hip, the contours of my waist and down towards my pussy. His eyes shift from my body to my face, as if he were deciphering my reactions.

Then proceeds to kiss my body again. His intimate touch holds me prisoner, my hands splayed on the hood of the car. Oh, god I wish I had something to hold onto.

He twirls his tongue slowly around my nipple, sending a rush of tingles coursing through me. When he starts sucking on it, I can't help but feel a jolt of electricity shoot through my body, causing me to tense up. Holy crap. I squirm beneath him, breathless as he continues to play with my nipple - alternating between licking and sucking until the other nipple yearns for his attention. And as if he can read my thoughts, or perhaps my body, he shifts his hand over to it and gives it a squeeze.

Holy fuck. Xander Williams is sucking on my tits. That thought alone is almost unbearable. How can he remain so calm? That's because he's done this countless times before like it's his signature routine with every other girl he's been with.

As he leans over me, I can feel his arousal pressing against my thigh, sending a surge of excitement coursing through my body. His slow, deep breaths and the heat radiating from his body intensifies the sensations. I can't help but squirm, almost on the verge of hyperventilating. Why wouldn't he just fuck me already? I am incredibly wet, my pussy pulsating with desire, and the slippery warmth between my legs only intensifies. Shifting his position, he extends his arm to retrieve something, and it is then that the condom packet in his hand catches my attention. Holy fuck this is happening?

He tears open the packet and smooths the condom down over his dick with his hands. It must be a satisfying feeling, because his mouth falls open.

I am so freaking turned on. I've never realized that witnessing a guy so aroused could arouse me to such an extent.

Again he seems to understand my needs and glides his hand down between my legs. His tender touch cups my most intimate area, and he skillfully massages me there. It feels so different from when I touch myself. It's so much better, more exhilarating because he is in control. The worst part is not knowing what he'll do next or how softly he'll touch me, and it's driving me wild with longing.

A whimper escapes my lips as my body trembles uncontrollably. Leaning down, he plants a kiss between my breasts. My breaths come out in shaky, desperate gasps, while an intense longing for him surges within me. I need to feel him inside me. I want him to fill me up. With a subtle movement, he nudges my legs wider and moves in closer.

Raising my head, I glance down to where his dick is positioned at my entrance. Holy shit. He's huge. I already knew that when I gave him a blowie. But how the fuck is that going to fit in there? Shit, this is really happening. I am about to lose my virginity to Xander Williams.

His hand moves down to hold his dick, angling it between my legs. My anticipation grows as I feel the tip pressing against me, causing me to suck in a deep breath.

"Take a breath, Princess. Relax," he whispers, his spare hand caressing my body with gentle strokes. "I won't move until you're ready."

I try to relax. Try to calm myself and get ready for what's to come, but my excitement gets the better of me. I'm nervous too and scared as hell. I try to steady myself, ready for him, but he doesn't push inside. Instead, he leans forward, kissing me once more with intense passion. It's as if he can't get enough of me. Despite that, he resists the urge to push himself inside me.

"I need you to relax, Princess," he says. "You're overthinking it." Fisting his cock, he runs it through my wetness.

My lips tremble as he leisurely traces circles around my sensitive nub with his shaft.

"Oh, god," I moan softly, his teasing is driving me crazy. "Just fuck me already, Xander."

He laughs and pushes into me.

I cry out, gasping and screaming simultaneously, creating a... gasp-scream. Yeah, it's a gasp-scream that's all I can call it. Suddenly, he comes to an abrupt halt.

We both freeze, remaining completely motionless. My breath escapes me as if I'm in a state of shock. Is he inside? Yeah, he's definitely inside. A strange sensation makes me squirm slightly.

"Are you okay?" he whispers, planting a gentle kiss on my lips.

"Hmm," I say, because my brain has just stopped working.

"Does it hurt?" He hesitates, studying my face all intense-like.

"Not really, to be honest. It feels really... I don't know... weird."

"How so?"

"I don't know," I say.

"Will I keep going?"

"What?" I hear my voice, all high-pitched and trembling.

"Should I push in further?"

"Seriously, aren't you already in?"

His expression softens as that self-assured smirk reappears. It's not exactly a smile, more like a conceited grin. I realize that I've inadvertently stroked his ego.

Leaning closer, he plants a tender kiss on my lips. His tongue delicately explores my mouth, intertwining with mine. The unhurried pace of his kisses calms my body, inducing a state of relaxation. Then he fucks me, slowly, gently, pulling nearly all the way out and then easing back in. He breaks our kiss, but his face remains close to mine. I can feel his warm breath on my face. Every time he pushes inside, it feels like he goes a little deeper. Each time, I let out a breath, a mix of pain, pressure, warmth, and desire.

"You doing okay?" he murmurs, his face filled with concern as he continues to move in a slow and steady rhythm.

I nod.

"Use your words."

"I'm fine," I respond.

"You ready for more?"

More. More of his dick. Where on earth does he plan to put that?

With a gentle push, he slides all the way inside me. Wow, it's intense. He's in deep, his balls are squishing up against me. Everything feels weird and new.

"Fuck, you feel amazing," he whispers, his body pressed tightly against mine. "Just hold on a sec before I lose it and finish inside you like a horny teenager."

I burst into a giggle and hastily cover my mouth.

He lifts his head from my neck and gives me a grin. "Yeah, laugh all you want. Don't hold back," he says. "Because it's the fucking truth."

After a few seconds, he resumes a slow rhythm, thrusting against me, filling me.

It feels a bit strange, but it's also kind of pleasurable.

"Fuck, you're so tight. I love how it feels. Want more?"

I'm nodding, totally speechless from the amazing sensations he's giving me.

He slides his arm beneath me, wrapping it around my waist, lifting me so that my shoulders remain on the car hood. My back arches, with his cock still inside me.

"What are you…" I protest, but my words fade away as he effortlessly finds that sweet spot. "Oh God, please keep going," I plead, my voice dripping with desire.

His other hand glides lower, tracing a path along my belly, before skillfully stimulating my clit with his thumb.

"When you come, I want you on my cock. Just get used to this feeling," he whispers, his voice sending a shudder through me.

Oh hell yeah, I can certainly get accustomed to this incredible feeling, this mind-blowing sensation.

I sense him deep within me, as pleasure surges beneath his touch, rapidly intensifying. It doesn't take long for me to reach that point of relaxation, where I can fully enjoy every sensation, especially with his intense gaze fixed upon me, observing my every move with his desire-filled eyes.

As the pleasure intensifies, I feel my body responding, my pussy clenching around him, tightening around him, reaching its peak, sending waves of ecstasy rushing through me. Gasping for air, my body moves with urgency as my inner muscles maintain a tight hold on him.

"Fuck," Xander groans, his intense gaze locked on me. "That's it, let go. Let this cock be the first to satisfy you."

I moan in ecstasy as waves of pleasure ripple through my body. However, my vision is obscured. Everything appears as a hazy blur of light. The only clear image is his body hovering above mine. Our eyes lock. His thrusts intensify, delivering immense pleasure. All I can see is him, ravishing me, fucking me. His lustful eyes watch me as he stimulates my clit. My pussy quivers and clenches around his cock, sending tiny spasms of delight. If this is what sex is like, it's no wonder Xander indulges in it with anyone who catches his eye. I want to keep doing this with him over and over again until my body can no longer endure it.

And then my whole body gets all warm and tingly, and I feel this amazing rush of pleasure. It's as if a fiery sensation is coursing through every nerve ending. He increases the speed of rubbing my swollen nub, and I can feel myself pulsating around his cock.

I keep my eyes locked on Xander, who is watching me with intense fascination, as I cry out in ecstasy.

"Oh my fucking god, Xander!"

He continues to stimulate my clit until the waves of pleasure gradually subside.

"Fuck," he groans, his face contorting beautifully as he leans into me and releases his seed. I can feel the tremor in him, his breath coming out in short bursts against my neck as he slowly rides out the rest of his orgasm.

He stays like that, his face nestled in the curve of my neck, as he inhales deeply. It feels like my legs are disconnected from the rest of my body, completely devoid of any sensation. After that intense orgasm, my entire body feels relaxed and limp, as if it has turned to jelly. It takes me a while to register that Xander has spoken.

"Are you okay, Princess?" he asks, keeping his face in the crook of my neck.

When I don't answer, he lifts his body up to look at me.

"Poppy," he says in a worried tone, his fingers softly stroking my cheek.

As our eyes meet, a warm smile spreads across my face. "You know, you're pretty good at that," I tell him, not sure why I'm saying it out loud. It feels like something that should stay in my head.

His face lights up with a confident, cocky grin. "I might have a few moves," he says teasingly, leaning in to kiss me. "You sure you're alright?"

"Yes, I'm fine," I assure him.

He softly kisses my lips and then pulls out. He turns away to discard the condom, hiding it in the nearby bush concealed among the towering trees.

Feeling suddenly awkward, I have no clue what to do now. I have no idea what to do after sex. Will things now get awkward between us? And what will Xander do? What if he just takes off? I remember him mentioning that he simply finds a wet spot to satisfy his needs and then he bails. Even though it's my first time, I can't expect him to be any different from his usual self - a guy who doesn't seem to give a damn about anyone.

I take advantage of Xander's back turned to me. Sitting up, I adjust my skirt and retrieve my bra from the hood of the car.

Glancing up, I notice Xander has already put on his jeans and is reaching for his shirt.

Once I'm dressed, I climb down from the hood of the car, feeling uncertain about my next move. I avoid making eye contact with Xander, not knowing how to behave or which emotions I should be feeling.

"Can I have my underwear, please?" I ask, the frustration evident in my voice as I extend my palm up towards him.

When he doesn't answer, I look up and notice how intensely he's staring at me.

"No, I'm keeping them," he says, zipping up his jeans.

"Why?"

"Because they belong to me."

Pervert. I suddenly wonder if he has some twisted habit of keeping souvenirs from the girls he's fucked.

Without uttering a word, I watch him walk toward the rear of the car to retrieve his bag from the back seat. I assume he's about to leave like he said he typically does, but to my surprise, he comes back to the front of the vehicle where I am standing. He snatches the whisky bottle from off the hood and stuffs it into his satchel, then pulls out a pack of cigarettes.

The air crackles with tension as he lights up a cigarette. I'm at a loss for both words and actions because, deep down, I know that despite the incredible orgasm I just experienced with Xander; I am merely another name on his extensive list of conquests.

"What's the problem, Princess?" he asks, a cigarette hanging from the corner of his mouth. His gaze remains fixed on the landscape ahead.

"Nothing," I reply, my voice catching in my throat as I swallow hard.

He takes another drag of his cigarette and blows out a plume of smoke before speaking again. "So what's with the attitude, then?"

I turn away. "I don't know, Xander. Maybe I'm annoyed at myself for being just another conquest on your long list."

"And this is why I never stick the fuck around," he says, blowing smoke rings into the air. "Fuck this," he says, flicking the cigarette to the ground and slinging his bag over his shoulder.

"Yeah, that's it. Walk away. I always knew you were an asshole!" I shout after him, my voice carrying over the car as he walks away from me.

Tears glisten in my eyes, but I don't bother wiping them away, not even when Xander glances back over his shoulder. It pains my heart to see him walking away, though I don't know what I expected. Everyone knows that Xander doesn't do relationships. Yet, there are rumors that he doesn't kiss, and yet he does that.

I move to the car and climb in, slamming the door in the process. Starting the engine, I quickly turn the car around and drive past Xander as he makes his way down the dirt track.

Through my blurred vision, I watch him slowly fade into the distance, becoming a mere speck in the rearview mirror.

CHAPTER 19

Poppy

I can't help but feel frustrated with myself. Ever since I had sex with Xander two days ago, I've been feeling on edge. Whenever my mother tries to talk to me, I've end up shouting at her. But now, she's finally giving me some space.

When I arrived home that night after Xander walked away, I cried myself to sleep. I didn't know what I'd expect would happen. No, I knew exactly what would happen. He walked away once he got what he wanted. After watching him all these years, I'm familiar with his patterns. However, despite feeling pissed at him, pissed at myself, and pissed at the world, I can't get it out of my head that I had sex with Xander. The hottest guy in school, and my ultimate crush.

My thoughts are constantly playing tricks on me as I try to distance myself from him. However, memories of how amazing he made me feel and the way he touched my body keep replaying in my mind.

It's frustrating that he hasn't even bothered to text, but in all fairness, I haven't reached out to him either. I suppose I finally understand where I stand. He got what he wanted and now he's off to find another wet hole to stick his dick into, as he always does.

Glancing up from my E-reader at school today, I noticed him sitting with Ace in his usual spot, engrossed in conversation. Jade was also sitting there next to him. The mere thought of him doing to her what he did to me fills me with anger and jealousy. But the best part was when Jade tried to give him a lap dance, and he shoved her off. She ended up falling flat on her butt. I nearly laughed my ass off because she totally deserved it.

And then there was this one moment when he was sitting there all alone, just watching me. The second our eyes met, I swiftly gathered my stuff and hightailed it out of there, making sure he didn't see my tears. Yeah, my dumbass tears over some guy who doesn't give a shit about me and probably never will.

Every day that's gone by, I can feel myself weakening, wanting to give in and talk to him. I can't help but wonder if he's eating. I've even started watching through the window again, just to see if he's heading to the 7-Eleven for a quick bite. All I want is for us to be friends again like we were before. If only I had been more cautious with my silly crush. Maybe then, all of this could've been prevented.

By the fifth day, my mind becomes overwhelmed with a torrent of racing thoughts, suffocating me entirely. Jade and her bitches persist in their cruelty, showing no signs of relenting. I am too exhausted to summon the strength to fight back, so I simply turn and walk away, while she revels in the laughter. Has Xander Williams truly broken me?

Then, for a few more days, after school, I end up driving around aimlessly, trying to delay going home and having to face my mom. I simply cannot endure another day of her incessantly questioning me about what's bothering me, or her relentless belief that pursuing a career in music would be the gravest mistake I could ever make.

It's been over a week since I had sex with Xander, and I'm feeling incredibly down. I can't seem to focus or enjoy watching my favorite TV show. Everyday tasks feel overwhelming, and I'm struggling to function normally. How did I end up in this state of mind?

Today has been the worst day so far. Jade not only confronted me, but she also ratted me out for skipping English class and hanging out in the girls' bathroom, which led to a week of detention. I just didn't want to be around Xander during that class. I naively thought it would be fine to relax in the girls' bathroom and scroll through my phone. However, I never considered the consequences of someone spotting me there, especially Jade, who I'm certain figured out I was in there and snitched to the teacher.

Finally, I let out a long, exhausted breath as the school bell signals the end of the day. All I want is to escape from this place. I casually sling my bag over my shoulder and make my way to my locker. Once everything is sorted, I quickly stuff the homework that's due tomorrow into my bag, and then head out of school.

In the car park, there's a bustle of activity. I navigate around a group of guys engrossed in a conversation about meeting up somewhere.

As I search through my bag for my keys, I glance back up and catch sight of Xander casually leaning against the side of my car. My steps falter, and a surge of emotions washes over me. He is completely absorbed in his phone, oblivious to my presence. With a mix of anticipation and uncertainty, I stand there for a moment. My heart races as I gather the courage to approach him. But if he honestly thinks he can simply hook up with me again, he is mistaken.

As I draw closer, he lifts his head, the sound of my footsteps grabbing his attention. When our eyes meet, a jolt of electricity races through me, stimulating every fiber of my being. He rises and effortlessly slips his phone into his pocket.

"Hey," he says, his eyes scanning my body with intensity.

"What do you want, Xander?" I continue walking past him, heading towards the driver's door.

"I want to talk," he says, following closely behind.

"There's nothing to talk about," I declare, opening the door and casually tossing my bag onto the back seat.

"Come on, Princess, we need to have this conversation," he insists, reaching out to touch my arm.

I swallow hard, determined to push the overwhelming feeling aside. I take a deep breath and remind myself to focus on the task. Though the sensation lingers, weighing heavily on my chest, I refuse to let it distract me.

With a firm tug, I yank my arm away from him, resolute in my decision to get into the car. "You made your feelings quite clear the other day," I add.

"Fuck," he mutters, clearly annoyed. Stepping forward, he effectively traps me in place, rendering me unable to move. "Quit being stubborn, alright?"

"Well, stop being a complete asshole," I retort, my gaze locked on his as I get right up close in his face.

His lips curl up into a cocky grin, revealing a row of perfectly white teeth. The gleam in his eyes adds to the arrogance emanating from his face. I can almost hear the smugness in his smirk as he looks at me.

"I just want to talk," he says.

"Well, I don't."

With a gentle touch, he raises his hand, delicately tucking a strand of hair behind my ear.

I'm mad at myself for liking how it feels when his fingers brush against my skin.

His confident, cocky grin gets even cockier, somehow becoming even more self-assured as he witnesses the effect he has on me.

"You should know, Princess, I never do this. But I'm sorry for bailing on you."

"Why should it matter? Isn't that what you usually do when you hook up?"

"Yeah, but this should've gone down differently."

"What? Because I gave you my V Card," I hear my voice waver as I struggle to keep it under control. "Don't sweat it, Xander. You're off the hook."

I see something flicker on his face like I've accidentally hit a nerve. "I wanna make things right with you."

"Why does it matter?" I ask, the frustration evident in my voice.

"Because it just fucking does," he replies, his voice laced with frustration. He shuts his eyes, leans in closer, and rests his forehead against mine. The subtle aroma of his cologne hangs in the air. "You drive me so fucking crazy at times, you know that," he murmurs, his voice a blend of frustration and longing.

"What the fuck?" a voice interjects, echoing from somewhere nearby.

Xander and I quickly straighten, both of us turning towards the voice. Standing there is Jade, her arms folded across her chest, glaring at us.

"Is this why you keep avoiding me? You'd rather spend time with this fat cow than with me," she accuses.

Xander steps back, creating some space. "Nah, Jade. I'm staying away from you because I can't get a boner whenever you're around."

Xander's comment has a real impact on Jade. Her expression changes instantly. "And you expect me to believe that she can? Just look at her!"

Xander storms over to her, his footsteps echoing angrily on the ground. He leans in so close that their noses nearly touch, his face contorts with rage. "If you talk about her like that again, or say the mean shit you usually do, I'll have Ace send that video to everyone in school. You know the one I'm talking about. Do you fucking hear me?"

Jade's eyes widen, and her mouth hangs open in utter disbelief.

"So back up and stay the fuck away from me. And that goes for Poppy as well."

Jade takes a few steps back, quickly shifting her gaze towards me. Without uttering a word, she lowers her head and makes her way to her over pricey car her dad bought her.

I'm at a loss as to what to make of these feelings swirling through my body after just witnessing Xander stand up for me against the biggest bitch in the school, but damn that was hot watching it go down.

He doesn't take his eyes off Jade until she leaves the school. Then he turns his attention back to me. "I'll see you at seven," he says with a touch of cocky arrogance.

I nod, still shocked by his confrontation with Jade. Words fail me as I watch him stride toward the other side of the parking lot, where Ace's car is still parked.

It's around six when I make my way home. Just one hour of dealing with my mom before she leaves for work.

When I walk through the door, I find Mom sitting at the table, all ready for work and chowing down on takeout. I prepare myself for the onslaught on where I've been but to my surprise, she gives a warm smile, then nudges the burger box towards my usual spot at the table. "I got you some."

I toss my bag to the side before making my way over to the table. Sitting down, I eagerly unwrap the burger and take a satisfying bite. All at once I get this weird feeling. I lift my eyes to see her watching me.

"What?" I ask.

"Where have you been?"

With my mouth full, I mutter. "Nowhere. Just driving around." I take another bite.

I watch as she cleans her fingers with a napkin and raises an eyebrow. "So do you want to fill me in on what's been going on with you lately?"

"There's nothing going on," I say, getting up to grab a can of Coke from the fridge.

She tidies up the table and swiftly tosses the empty boxes into the recycling bin. I can tell that she wants to ask something more, but she's hesitant because she's afraid I'll snap at her, as I have been doing for the past few days.

I let out a deep breath, knowing that this is going down whether I like it or not. "Just speak your mind so we can get this over with," I say, opening my can and returning to the table to finish my burger.

"You'll be wasting your life if you follow in your father's footsteps." She comes back to the table and sits across from me.

"Really? We're back onto this," I add, pausing mid-bite. "It's a bit dramatic, don't you think? I wouldn't say it's wasting my life."

Her mouth tightens, showing her anger, and I can sense she's restraining herself from screaming at me. She takes a deep breath, trying to compose herself. After a brief pause, she finally speaks up.

"Poppy, I need you to listen to me without becoming defensive or interrupting me."

"Well, that applies to you too. You can't always have things your way."

"See, you've just done it again. I don't know how to talk to you anymore."

"That's because you only see things from your side. You're never interested in listening to what I have to say."

I feel my phone vibrate in my pocket. Without hesitation, I reach for it.

My mother immediately interrupts me. "Don't even think about grabbing that phone. We haven't discussed what I need to talk to you about."

"I've heard it all before, Mom," I respond, rolling my eyes, ignoring the stern look on her face.

Xander: The Rock. Be there at 7.

Poppy: Why?

As I'm about to place my phone face down on the table, I suddenly notice tiny bubbles appearing on the screen.

Xander: Just come the fuck here, Princess.

Poppy: Okay.

I slip my phone back into my pocket and confront my mother's intense glare.

"Who was that?"

"None of your business. Are we finished yet?"

"No, Poppy, we haven't even started."

Releasing a weary breath, I exhale through my cheeks.

"I'm curious about where this idea came from. Why the sudden interest in music?" she asks.

"Oh my god, are you serious? You know, I've always loved music. But I guess you don't really care, since you never listen to me."

"Why do you always depict me as the bad guy or someone who is so insufferable to live with."

"Well, sometimes you are," I reply, causing her to cross her arms over her chest.

"Poppy, you're young and clueless, and you have no clue about the realities of living in this world. The responsibilities of being a grown-up. How essential money is to function in today's society. Nothing comes for free. You need a regular nine-to-five job."

"But I plan to have a nine-to-five job in music therapy. Once I establish my own business, I'll have the freedom to work whenever I choose."

"You just don't get it, do you?" she says, frustration evident in the sharpness of her voice with the creases forming on her forehead.

"Get what?" I inquire, trying to read her eyes for any sign of understanding.

"Your dream is just a fantasy," she asserts.

It's so annoying when she brushes my dreams off like that. As if they are nothing.

"And I've already told you, your opinion doesn't matter to me," I declare, standing up from the table, picking up the empty burger box, and tossing it into the bin. "Why can't you just accept what I want?"

"Because I will always be the one bailing you out when the bills come in, Poppy," she responds. "And I'm not willing to do that for the rest of your life. You're almost an adult, so start acting like one."

"Oh, don't you worry about that? I will be an adult, and I will have the freedom to choose what I want for my life." I grab my bag from the floor and head towards my room.

"This is not the end of it, Poppy," my mother yells as I walk away.

"Oh, yes, it is," I mutter quietly as I stride into my room, forcefully slamming the door behind me. Frustration lingers in the air as I toss my bag onto the bed and head over to my keyboard. I feel like getting lost in music and also pissing off my mom, so I turn on the keyboard.

Regaining my composure, I channel all my anger into my music, repeatedly going through the song my dad and I were writing.

Glancing at the clock, I realize it's already seven-thirty. Picking up my phone from the bed, next to my bag where I left it earlier, I notice two missed messages from Xander.

Xander: Are you almost here?

Xander: What the fuck are you doing?

I text him straight away.

Poppy: Sorry, be there in a minute. Got held up.

In a hurry, I sprint out of my bedroom, making a beeline for the front door.

Chapter 20

Xander

Since I fucked Poppy last week, I had hoped that having her would finally suppress the constant desire that I feel for her whenever she's around. Unfortunately, that wasn't the outcome. She remains deeply ingrained in my thoughts, unchanged. I'm so pissed at myself for ditching her the way I did that day. She deserves someone much better than me. But that's my pattern. Whenever things become too difficult I just walk away.

I honestly thought that distancing myself would help me avoid the uncomfortable feelings that have been arising. However, the absence of not being near, not talking to her is making it incredibly difficult to stay away.

Every evening, as I pass by her house on my way to the 7-Eleven, an intense urge would spring up inside me, compelling me to knock on her door and apologize for leaving. It's not in my nature to apologize easily, so this uncharted territory left me feeling unsure of how to navigate it. Consequently, I would simply continue walking, not wanting to become the kind of person who seeks attention from girls or easily succumbs to their influence. However, these unexpected emotions have completely consumed me, and it's unusual for me to give much thought to such matters.

Like earlier today, my focus was protecting Poppy from the heartless insults that Jade was throwing at her. I don't get into petty shit like that. But I did because it was Poppy. That's why I threatened to release that video Ace has on his phone. Of course, it's just an empty threat. Despite being the asshole I am, I would never embarrass a chick like that. I only said it because of what she said to Poppy.

Sitting on this massive rock, I gaze towards the distant ridge, eagerly anticipating a glimpse of Poppy coming down the path. Since seven o'clock tonight, I've repeatedly glanced in that direction, more times than I'd like to admit.

Taking a deep breath, I turn my head, scouring the surroundings once again for any signs of activity.

Seeing her approach, I quickly shift my attention back to the guitar she had gifted me, pretending that I hadn't noticed her. I do this more for my own reasons, as I prefer to avoid her becoming one of those clingy girls. However, I must admit, Poppy Reeves doesn't strike me as the clingy type either. She's nothing like Jade or those other girls.

Whenever I hooked up with Jade, she always believed there was something more between us. But with Poppy, she just doesn't give off that kind of vibe. Since my mistake of walking away from her the other day, she hasn't attempted to call me at all. So there's that. Totally different. She doesn't smother me like other chicks do once we've hooked up.

Strumming my guitar, I continue working on the melody that has been constantly looping through my head. However, when I notice her standing there, I pause and glance up.

"That sounds good," she says, climbing up the rock to sit beside me.

"Yeah, it's just something I've been working on." I turn my attention back to the guitar and continue playing. "What took you so long?" I ask, casually.

"Mom and I got into it again."

I pause playing the guitar and lift my head to look at her. "You guys fight a lot, huh?"

"Yeah. Hey, I thought you were leaving this at Ace's," she says, gesturing towards the guitar, attempting to change the subject.

"I usually do, but I needed it today. Plus I wanted to keep working on this melody that's stuck in my head. Do you think you could look after the guitar for me until tomorrow, like maybe leave it in your car or something?"

She nods in agreement, but I can sense that something is bothering her. I refocus my attention on the guitar and begin strumming a few chords.

"What's on your mind, Princess?"

"I don't know just the usual stuff." Sitting beside me, her legs dangle over the edge, swinging back and forth.

As I strum the guitar, the strings vibrate against my fingertips, filling the air with harmonious melodies. As I raise my head, my heart skips a beat, completely captivated by her beauty. Her eyes, like mirrors, reflect the sun's golden rays as it sets below the horizon, casting a warm glow upon us. A gentle breeze carries the alluring scent of her perfume, intoxicating my senses. As I study her face, my fingers abruptly halt on the taut strings. I lift my hand and trace my fingertips along the side of her face, feeling the smoothness beneath my touch while a heavy weight settles in my chest as regret floods over me, realizing my foolish blindness all these years. I never truly saw who she really is.

"That sounds really great, Xander," she says, her voice pulling me back into the moment.

In that instant, I am reminded once again that I have returned to that forbidden place. I remove my hand from her face and gaze out over the landscape.

"Thanks. Ace thinks it's the best thing I've written so far, and the lyrics are top-notch too."

"Can I hear it?"

"We don't play this sort of music usually, but we're trying to mix things up a bit. We need to have a variety of songs for when we audition for agents."

"Will you play it for me?"

"Yeah, if you spill the beans about what's bothering you."

"My mom has been hassling me again about what I'm gonna do next year. That's all. So can I hear it?"

"It's not finished yet."

"That doesn't matter, I'm curious to hear what you've come up with."

"Why?"

"I'm so glad I'm here to see your talent, Xander."

I glance down at my guitar, uncertain of what to say in response to those rare words that I seldom hear.

However, when it comes to her, she never fails to remind me of how talented and how unique I am.

"You can never take a compliment, can you?"

"No." I lift my head and meet her gaze. "Not when you've been told most of your life that you're worthless. You tend to believe it sometimes," I confess.

"But don't ever believe that shit, Xander. One day, you'll see yourself the way I see you. How everyone sees you."

Remaining silent, I watch her closely. "I truly hope that someday I can see myself through your eyes. But for now, it's easier to accept what people have been calling me all these years."

"It saddens me that you can't see your own worth." Tears well up in her eyes.

"You know how I feel about pity, Princess. I fucking hate it." I lean in closer, cupping the back of her neck, and resting my forehead against hers. A single tear trails down her cheek. I press my lips gently against hers, savoring the sweet taste. "Now, do you want to see what I have been working on?"

"Yes," she nods.

Refocusing on the guitar, my fingers find the strings, and I strum the opening chords. The sound fills the space, resonating with a melodic rhythm.

"Feel the heartbeat in every strike,
In the thunderous roar, we find what we like.
Lightning flashes, an electric spear,
Can you feel the thunder, drawing near?

Cracks in the silence, the storm's embrace,
In the echoes, our hearts find a place.
Guitars screaming, breaking through the night,
A symphony of emotions, taking flight.

Thunder rolling, breaking the chains,
A symphony of rebellion in our veins.
Feel the power, the energy, the fear,
Can you feel the thunder, drawing near?

Pounding hearts, echoes in the night,
A fierce storm, emotions taking flight.
The storm subsides, but the echoes persist,
In the aftermath, our bond exists."

I stop playing and look at Poppy who still watches me. "That's all I've got so far."

"Wow, that is really good, Xander. How long have you been working on it?"

"The tune has been stuck in my head for a while, but I only started writing the lyrics yesterday."

"It's really good. I can't wait to hear the rest of it when you finish it."

Compliments have always been hard for me to believe, so I shift my attention to the vibrant colors splashed across the sky.

"So why are we meeting here tonight?" Poppy asks.

"Today's my mom's birthday," I whisper, my throat tightening as the overwhelming sense of loss and longing for her resurfaces.

"Today! Your mom's birthday is today."

"Yep," I reply, trying to keep my emotions in check.

She extends her hand towards me, and I feel solace in her touch as our fingers entwine. "How old would she have been today?"

"Thirty-nine." I pause, briefly collecting my thoughts. "On her birthday, we would always sit side by side, strumming our guitars and singing."

"Oh, I get now why you have your guitar."

I nod.

"What's your mom's favorite song?"

"Well, her favorite band was Radiohead," I reply. "So, any of those, but I know one that we can sing."

Her lips curl into a smile. "Creep!"

I nod and shift my gaze downwards, ready to play the first few notes on the guitar. With fingers poised, I eagerly anticipate the melody, determined to bring it to life.

As the music begins, Poppy's seductive voice sings with mine, creating a mesmerizing connection. Our eyes lock, and together, our voices blend harmoniously, weaving a tapestry of emotions through the air. The energy intensifies with each strum of the guitar, igniting a profound passion within me.

As the song continues, our voices intertwine like vines, effortlessly harmonizing. Poppy's sultry voice adds depth and allure, beautifully contrasting with the raw intensity of my own. Our eyes hold, a magnetic force pulling us closer. In that instant, the world around us fades into insignificance, leaving only the music and this single moment of time.

When the final notes hang in the air, a quiet stillness descends upon us. The bond of singing to my mother lingers, a palpable energy that leaves us breathless. "Thank you," I add, my voice choking with emotion. Tears come to my eyes as I envision how deeply my mother would have treasured this moment. I look away, hoping to conceal my vulnerability from Poppy. "Tell me more about what happened with your mom tonight?" I inquire, eager to shift my focus onto something else.

"Well, I told her about my plans a little while back and she was pissed. Has been every day since. And when she started on me again, I made it clear that it's my life and I will do what I want."

"Good. You need to do whatever makes you happy, Poppy. No matter how much your mom pressures you, don't give in."

"I won't."

When a cool breeze sweeps in, I notice Poppy shivering. She raises her hands and gently glides them over her arms, trying to soothe the prickling goosebumps on her skin.

"Come on, let's go," I say, getting on my feet. With my guitar in one hand, I reach out my other hand to offer her support.

"Are you sure?" she asks, taking my hand to get up. "It's your mom's birthday. I don't want you to leave because of me."

"It's fine. I came straight here after school."

As I walk home with my guitar in hand, Poppy by my side, we reach the 7-Eleven. In a hurry, I hand my guitar to Poppy and head into the store. I carefully stash a couple of chocolate bars in my pockets and rush out. Poppy's disapproving look says it all - she knows about my little adventure.

Not uttering a single word, she hands me the guitar and moves down the street with me following closely behind. Arriving at the front of her house she turns to face me.

"Are you coming in?"

"Sure," I reply, following her down the front path and into the house.

Inside I rush to the couch, while Poppy shuts the front door. I carefully place my guitar against the couch. The minute Poppy walks by, my instincts take over. I wrap my arm around her and bring her in for that long-awaited kiss. Since I saw her tonight, I've been wanting this moment so badly, trying to resist my urges.

The kiss is hot and needy, igniting a fiery passion within me. Instantly, I'm rock hard. The intensity of our connection electrifies the air, sending delightful shivers down my spine. It's a kiss that leaves me breathless, yearning for more. Filled with desire and hunger, I gently caress the side of her face with one hand while the other rests on her hip, walking her backward towards the couch.

Keeping our lips locked, I carefully guide her to the couch and settle on top of her. "You can't even imagine all the things I wanna do to you," I say in between kisses. "I want to touch you everywhere. With my fingers, my tongue, my cock." I grind against her, so she can feel how much she turns me on.

As soon as my lips touch hers, she instantly comes alive. Her arms wrap around me tightly, and her tongue passionately meets mine. I grip her hip firmly, feeling the intensity of the moment. She digs her nails into my scalp, both of us wanting more. The intense desire surges through me as she rubs herself against the undeniable bulge in my jeans.

"Fuck!" A low growl escapes my chest as she continues to grind against me, igniting a wild desire within. Thankfully, we're lying down because my mind is in chaos. I run my nose along her neck, captivated by her intoxicating scent. I crave to explore and possess every inch of her.

Since I saw her in that fucking short skirt, I've been rock hard, yearning to be deep inside her. And she wants it too. I know it. It's clear by the way she's kissing me.

Suppressing a groan, I slide my hands up her silky thighs, causing her to tremble even more. My lips brush against her ear, while her sharp teeth graze the skin of my throat. My hand slips under her shirt, dragging it up to expose more of her stunning body. I firmly hold her waist and my thumb brushes against the delicate skin under her bra, making her melt.

"Lift," I add, more a demand than a request, tugging at the end of her shirt. She lifts herself a little, making space for me to pull it up over her head and toss it somewhere in the room. But honestly, I'm too distracted by the gorgeous black lace bra to pay attention to where it lands. I then focus on the side zipper of her short skirt, carefully undoing it as she lifts herself a bit to make it easier to take off. I can't take my eyes off her, lying there in that sexy black lace bra and panties.

With one quick movement, I reveal her by pulling down the cups of her bra, then seal my mouth over her taut nipple.

The desperate, arousing sound that escapes her lips only adds to the allure. I let out a husky grunt as I flick my tongue against her nipple. I suck harder, so hard that it pulls a soft sexy moan from her that consumes my every thought.

"Take it off!" I grunt, eagerly tugging at the delicate lace of her bra. She reaches behind and unhooks her bra, causing her tits to press against my face.

A deep growl of desire escapes my lips. "I love your tits," I whisper.

The idea of my jizz all over them gets me fired up. Lowering myself, I trail soft kisses along her skin, savoring every inch. Her body squirms as I teasingly graze her lower stomach with my teeth.

"I can smell how much you want me," I say, running my tongue along the edge of her underwear. Her whimper fills the air as I bury my face between her legs, pressing my nose against her pussy and inhaling deeply. Hooking my fingers on the sides of her panties, I slide them down her thighs, eliminating any obstacle that is between us. Now, I have a full view of her. She lies there, gazing up at me.

My gaze slowly moves down over her naked body. "Fuck, look at you," I say, desire written all over my face as I focus on her pussy.

She attempts to cover herself, but I take hold of her hands before she can.

"You don't have to hide from me. You're fucking perfect. You hear me," I declare, running a finger along her slit. "Now spread your legs," I tell her, and she complies.

"Wider," I demand, watching as she hooks her arms under her knees, fully exposing herself.

"Good girl," I whisper, my lips trailing along the inside of her thigh.

That is her only warning before I put my lips on her pussy. She tastes incredibly delicious, like sweet honey. Although this is my first time eating out a chick, I've watched enough porn in my life to know how to get her off using my tongue.

I can't help but moan as I skillfully suck and tease her, ending each wet motion with a gentle flick to her sensitive clit.

"Oh god," she moans, and I enjoy every sound she makes as she moves her body while I devour her.

My fingers firmly press into her thighs holding her in place as I suck her clit in my mouth.

She moans and holds onto my hair, begging me to keep going.

"Fuck yeah," I add, smirking against her wet pussy. It's fucking hot witnessing the effect I have on her, to watch her surrender to the sensations I create. "Keep making those hot sexy sounds for me," I encourage her. And when she does, my tongue explores even more, enjoying her fully, so she never wants it to end.

I slide my finger into the mix, moving in sync with the intense flicks of my tongue. She moves her hips eagerly against my face. Damn, this girl is smoking hot when she lets herself go. I can feel the pulsating sensitivity of her swollen center and sense her nearing the point where I yearn to take her. I passionately kiss her, just as I do with her mouth - intense, hot, and filthy.

Panting, Poppy tightly grabs my hair in her fist. "I'm close," she says, all breathy.

"I know," I say with an arrogant smirk, my mouth glistening as I glance at her. "Keep your eyes on me until you come," I tell her, the wet sounds filling the air as I find a rhythm that makes her squirm. I curl my fingers inside her, making her gasp.

"Oh, my god," she whispers, grinding against my jaw. The sensation of her tight inner walls gripping my fingers makes me crave her even more. Unintelligible sounds escape her lips as her thighs tremble. My fingers and tongue seem to have found the perfect spot. Shamelessly, she rides my face, and I fucking love it. And then, she explodes, her orgasm crashing over me, filling my mouth. I don't stop licking until she comes down from her high. Each soft, gentle lick gives her a pleasurable shudder.

"Damn, that was hot," I say with a mischievous grin.

Leaning forward, I kiss her lips, allowing her to see how amazing she tastes.

As I pull away, she gazes up at me. I softly run my thumb along her bottom lip, knowing how badly I've been craving one of those amazing blowjobs she gives.

"Open up, so I can feed you my cock."

CHAPTER 21
Poppy

Xander's dirty mouth leaves me totally smitten. He leans forward and kisses me hard. No time for second thoughts. I mirror his fervent tongue movements with equal intensity and desire as I reach out and touch the bulge in his jeans. He pulls back and watches me closely as I undo his button and lower the zipper.

As I slide my hand inside, I notice the muscles in his throat tighten, filling me with a mix of anticipation and excitement. I lower my gaze, marveling at his impressive, pulsating cock that fills my hand. It's long, thick, veiny, and undeniably intimidating... yet still incredibly beautiful. I stroke him from the base to the tip. Deep throating is not an option given its impressive size, but I am determined to give it my all.

"Kiss it," he commands, gripping the base of his cock.

I'm overcome with longing as I give a gentle kiss to the wide tip. Looking up, I smirk, knowing he wants so much more than what I just offered.

"Quit playing games and give me more," he demands, his velvety voice enveloping me like an electric current. "Kiss it the way you did that first time you sucked my cock."

It's amazing how Xander becomes so vulnerable to my touch. I absolutely love it. I lick my lips and savor the sweet milky drop forming on the tip.

He lets out a satisfied hum and gives himself a slow stroke. "Good girl, keep going," he murmurs, causing me to almost purr in response.

Continuing my exploration, I gently swirl my tongue around the end of his sensitive tip. He lets out a deep, guttural groan, urging me to repeat the motion. His throat muscles contract as he swallows, craving for more. Craving for me.

I carefully suck, causing him to pulsate against the roof of my mouth. With one hand he runs his fingers through my hair while the other hand holds his cock. I widen my mouth, allowing him to slowly enter, stretching my lips.

His jaw tenses as he goes deeper, reaching the depths of my throat and causing me to gag.

"Damn," he groans, pulling out completely, causing a strand of saliva to form between us. "Do you know how fucking sexy you look right now with my cock in your mouth?" He thrusts back into my mouth, and I savor the way his body tenses.

He closes his eyes, enjoying the feeling, and then opens them as if he doesn't want to miss a second of what I'm doing.

The second I make eye contact with him, a primal growl escapes his lips as he tightly grips my hair in his fist. It's the only warning I receive before he forcefully thrusts in and out of my mouth, with untamed intensity. I ease my throat, accommodating his increased pace.

"Holy fuck, it feels so good. I wanna feed you my cock every fucking day. Do you like the taste of my cock, Princess?"

Fuck me. Xander's dirty mouth has a way of arousing my senses. Saliva drips down my chin and tears escape from my eyes as I nod.

His chest heaves with a ragged inhale. "Then prove to me how much you enjoy it."

Lifting myself higher on my knees, I take him in as deep as possible, savoring every inch.

I have never felt such a strong desire for someone like I do in this moment, and it's all because of him. I increase the intensity of my suction, moving faster.

He lets out a moan, clearly enjoying what I'm doing. "Damn," he breathes, thrusting his hips forward. "You're going to make me come." Another moan fuels my desire, urging me to pick up the pace.

"Fucking hell, Poppy," he says, his muscles straining, and I can tell he's so close. I savor the way my name rolls off his tongue The tongue that expertly teased and pleased me until I couldn't hold back any longer.

Xander withdraws from my mouth. One hand squeezes my nipple while the other frantically works over his length, causing those prominent tendons and veins to flex.

"I'm dying to see your sexy tits covered in my cum."

I lean back, arching my spine, raising them higher. My mind and heart are just bursting with excitement.

Pleasure floods his face as a muffled moan escapes his lips, and his milky liquid splashes onto my chest.

I feel a rush of heat as he spreads his release with his fingers. "Open your mouth," he demands, his voice filled with authority.

When I comply, he pushes his fingers into my mouth. I eagerly suck them, cleaning off his taste.

A smug grin forms on his face. "That's my dirty little princess," he says, pulling me onto his lap and kissing me. "You're a real wild one, aren't you," he remarks, giving me a thorough look, absorbing every little detail of my face. "You're fucking perfect."

Having faced numerous comments about my weight throughout the years, I am well aware that I am not perfect. However, the way he says it and the way he's looking at me at this moment makes me feel like I just might be.

He embraces me tightly, planting a tender kiss on my shoulder before gently guiding me to the side. As he slips his hand into his pocket, I assume he's retrieving a condom. However, to my astonishment, he pulls out two chocolate bars instead.

"Want one?" he asks, holding it out in front of me.

"Yeah, even though I know you never paid for it," I laugh, playfully grabbing the chocolate bar from him.

Chapter 22

Poppy

Another day goes by and my mother continues to give me the silent treatment. On the third day, just before she leaves for work, she finally breaks her silence and turns towards me.

"So, are you still being defiant? You know pursuing music will never bring you happiness. It won't lead you anywhere."

I look at my mother, her words piercing through me. The silent treatment was one thing, but now she's attacking my dreams. Taking a deep breath, I calmly reply.

"Mom, I get it, but music is my thing. It makes me happy, and I think others can benefit from it too."

She scoffs, and with a shake of her head says, "You're just wasting your time. Choosing a career in music is a risky move. You should think about your future and pursue something more stable."

"I told you already that I don't want a job like yours." I return my attention to my e-reader. I snuggle into the comfy couch. "I'm done discussing this with you," I add, my eyes still focused on the screen in front of me. Feeling frustrated, I let out a sigh. It's tiring having the same back and forth with her over and over again.

Why won't she let me do what I want?

I sense her presence, lingering close by, watching me intently, eager to speak. Yet, I choose to keep my focus on the novel I hold in my hands. It's my refuge and escape from the ongoing argument.

"You're impossible," she mutters, grabbing her keys from the countertop. With a pissed look on her face, she heads towards the door, forcefully slamming it shut as she leaves.

I glance up from my e-reader and look through the front window to see her walking towards her car. The cloudy, gray sky hangs above, mirroring the inner turmoil swirling within me. There's a tangible sense of anticipation in the air, as if even nature itself is pausing, waiting with bated breath.

Taking a deep breath, I feel the weight of my dreams, pressing down on my chest. I can't help but wonder if my father experienced the same emotions whenever she criticized his love for music.

The car engine roars to life, and within seconds, it speeds off down the street.

I shut off my e-reader, get up from the couch, and head to my bedroom. Just as I reach the middle of the hallway, I come to a sudden stop upon hearing a knock at the front door. A smile spreads across my face because I already know who it is. I race towards the door, casually tossing my e-reader onto the couch as I pass by.

The door swings open with a forceful pull, and I am instantly breathless at the sight of him. Xander always has that effect on me. His tousled hair falls over his forehead, adding to his irresistible charm. A mischievous grin lights up his handsome face, sending a thrill through me.

In one swift motion, he lunges forward, his eyes ablaze with desire. The air crackles with electrifying energy as our lips collide, sparks flying in every direction. Our hearts pound, syncing in perfect rhythm. I find myself completely immersed in the kiss, consumed by its intensity and the way he kisses me.

As he pulls back, he leans his forehead against mine, his breath coming out in heavy spurts.

"I've been itching to get you out of that skirt and have a wild time every time I saw you today."

After Jade caught Xander and me next to my car, I was sure she would expose us, considering what she had seen. But, to my surprise, she hasn't said a word to anyone. Not only that, her hurtful cruel words about my weight have also stopped.

Nevertheless, Xander prefers to keep our activities and our relationship, or whatever this is under the radar. I'm not even sure if he's mentioned anything to Ace. I don't know if he's embarrassed about people finding out what we're doing, but I don't care. I get to spend time with Xander. His gaze never suggests he is embarrassed by me. Every time we are together, I can see a burning desire in his eyes, the way he yearns for me. No one has ever looked at me like that. And I gotta say, I fucking love it.

I also have a feeling that he's not hooking up with any other girls like he used to. I've noticed that he hasn't disappeared with Jade or any of those other easy bitches. Whenever I see him at school, he's sitting with Ace, completely ignoring all the other girls he used to hang out with.

But what I do know is that our time is limited. He'll be leaving soon to chase his dreams. Meanwhile, I will cherish every moment I get to spend with Xander until the day he eventually leaves or starts questioning why the hell he's spending time with me.

The sound of rain on the roof echoes throughout the entire house.

"Oh my god, it's raining!" I say, grabbing his hand and pulling him through the house.

"Yeah, so what? It's just rain."

I lead him onto the back patio, where the gentle rain falls, creating a symphony of pitter-patter sounds all around.

Releasing his hand, I run down the back steps, taking them two at a time, to stand in the rain.

Xander remains on the patio, his brows furrowing in confusion, questioning my motives amidst the downpour.

Closing my eyes, I tilt my head back, letting the cool raindrops fall on my face. The rhythmic patter of rain creates a soothing melody, calming my racing thoughts and turmoil caused by my mother.

In this crazy moment, I find peace and clarity.

Xander's voice breaks the silence. "What the fuck are you doing?"

"Enjoying the rain," I say, opening my eyes, only to find his intense, piercing dark brown eyes locked onto me. The sheer power in his gaze electrifies my veins, awakening my senses and filling me with a profound sense of excitement.

The combination of liquid courage and lust has me feeling unusually daring. Xander seriously got to me earlier when he grabbed me in the house and kissed me with such intensity. Now, it's my turn to make him feel the same way.

I twist and wiggle, searching for the zipper on my damp skirt. Xander keeps an impassive expression, but I can sense his mind working, curious about what I'm planning. The truth will reveal itself in due time. While he watches me, I slowly lower my skirt and let it fall onto the wet ground. Then, move on to unbuttoning my shirt.

As he takes a deep breath, his nostrils widen. A surge of excitement courses through me as his gaze travels over my entire body, lingering on my bra and then my panties. There is an undeniable intensity in his eyes, as though I am the most beautiful thing he has ever seen. Nevertheless, he remains stationary beneath the back patio, carefully observing my every action.

I have a strong desire to see Xander Williams completely lose control. I yearn to witness the deep longing reflected in his eyes, to evoke in him the same intense passion that his touch always ignites within me.

Driven by this motivation, I slowly trace a fingernail down my stomach. Any doubts I may have had about my weight vanish completely at this moment. His gaze on me, his eyes hooded, almost dare me to continue. As I playfully trace my fingertips along the waistband of my panties, a surge of exhilaration washes over me, setting my stomach abuzz with intense fluttering butterflies.

Without warning, he swiftly moves his hand down and begins to stroke himself through his jeans.

With an intense gaze, he watches me as I rub myself through my panties, my mind consumed with thoughts of him touching me. As I notice a shift in his breathing, it becomes clear to me that his self-control is slowly weakening. In response, I choose to push the boundaries even further.

With a smile on my face, I casually slip my hand into the waistband of my panties. Excitement and desire course through every cell of my being. As I slide a finger into my wetness, a sharp breath escapes my parted lips.

His jaw tightens as his eyes examine my body, lingering at the space between my legs. My heart races as I inhale quickly, closing my eyes tightly.

When I reopen them, he's directly in front of me, kneeling and looking at me with a desire that seems to plead, as if he wants to devour me entirely.

"Move your fucking hand now!" His voice breaks through the silence. His words resonate firmly in my ears, leaving no room for negotiation. I immediately surrender to his command.

A sudden, sharp tug on my ankle startles me, causing a squeak to escape my lips. His handsome face, wet from the rain, is just inches away from me.

"Stay still," he demands, his voice velvety and raspy, while the fiery intensity in his eyes sends an electrifying shiver down my spine. Every nerve in my body tenses, yearning for his touch, but it never comes.

He lifts his head staring up at me, blinking through the rain. The longing in his eyes is unmistakable - he wants me, and it's impossible to ignore. He lowers his face again, fixing his gaze upon my pussy. The feeling of anticipation builds within me, filling me with exhilaration, as I eagerly await his touch.

A shiver runs through me as his fingertips delicately glide over the inside of my wet thigh. A tightness settles across his face, a sign of his self-control. My senses heighten, and my heart pounds like a drum as he leans in, replacing his fingers with his skillful tongue.

The sensation of his tongue on my inner thigh is utterly captivating, almost heavenly, arousing me with every deliberate stroke. I willingly submit to him, longing to be his instrument, eager to be played. The intense sensation of his touch, coupled with the way he gazes up at me, results in a seriously hot experience. My heart dances with excitement as he keeps eye contact, leisurely tracing his tongue along the delicate flesh of my inner thighs.

With every glide over a new spot, he plants a sweet little kiss on it. A shiver runs down my spine, causing goosebumps to appear on my skin. And whenever he discovers a spot that elicits a reaction from me, he revisits it once more.

Again and again.

He is becoming increasingly familiar with my body, utilizing all the things that bring me pleasure to push me to the brink of madness. I tightly shut my eyes and clench my hands, exerting every ounce of effort to resist the urge to react.

"Xander," I add, my voice barely a whisper when his tongue traces the edge of my panties.

Knowing exactly what he's doing, he gives me that cocky grin, purposefully fueling my anticipation and creating an irresistible desire for more.

As frustration builds up within me, he changes his direction and proceeds to plant a series of tender kisses along my hip. However, he skillfully avoids the area that is pulsating with desire. Unable to control myself, a small whimper of irritation escapes my lips.

"Please," I gasp, biting down on my lip so hard that it sends a sharp pain coursing through me. Finally, I feel his touch where I ache the most. My thighs quiver as he delicately explores the contours of my most intimate area with his tongue. I am overcome by a powerful combination of arousal and wetness that takes over my senses.

Suddenly, Xander's movements halt abruptly. He draws his face closer, inhaling my scent deeply. A low, guttural groan escapes his lips, causing my nipples to harden and my heart to race.

There is something incredibly satisfying about the way he responds to me like I am exactly what he wants.

"Xander," I squirm as he pulls my soaked underwear to one side and slowly trails his tongue along the length of my folds. His eyes remain fixed on me as he skillfully teases me, causing an incoherent sound to escape my lips. Overwhelmed with pleasure, I grip the top of his head as he changes direction, tormenting me with slow, torturous circles of his tongue.

He stops once more, his methods of torment stirring both love and hate within me. I release a tense breath through clenched teeth, observing as his smirk curls at the corner of his mouth. The jerk knows exactly what he's doing. He finds pleasure in teasing me. Unexpectedly, he surprises me by exhaling a warm breath onto my pussy, causing a whirlwind of sensations to surge through my body. The contrast of the cold rain and his heated breath sets a fire ablaze within me. With his skilled touch, he begins to pleasure me, expertly licking my clit, causing me to writhe and whimper involuntarily.

I am consumed by waves of pleasure, each moment growing more intense than the last. I cannot suppress my helpless moans, as the overwhelming pleasure he brings me takes control. Eventually, I reach the pinnacle, an orgasm so powerful that it takes me several minutes to collect myself. Once I do, I discover him staring up at me with a predatory gaze, his expression exuding undeniable arrogance. He gently adjusts my panties back into position and tenderly places a soft kiss on the lace.

"Now, stick your finger back in," he says in a raspy voice.

Taking a deep breath, I slide my hand beneath the waistband of my underwear, following his instructions to collect my wetness. I'm remarkably slick. As soon as I comply, he snatches my hand. A rush of warmth floods my cheeks as he runs his nose along my finger before closing his mouth around it. Standing up abruptly, he captures my mouth with his own, leaving me speechless. The moment his tongue explores my mouth, I yield completely to him. Heaven help me, this man is like quicksand, and I'm falling, descending, sinking deeper and deeper.

Chapter 23

Xander

I can't take my eyes off this beautiful girl standing before me. Drenched from the downpour, seeing her like this radiates a heat that drives me wild. Her long, blonde hair clings to her body, forming a mesmerizing curtain that falls over her tits. The wetness adds an irresistible allure, igniting a deep desire within me. The way she moved and pleasured herself in the rain is an image that will forever be burned in my mind. This girl has a power over me that leaves me completely undone every single time. I haven't fucked another chick in four weeks, which is totally out of character for me. But who would want to fuck someone else when I can be with this girl who gets me all riled up every time, I lay eyes on her?

I glide my tongue slowly across my parted lips, savoring the delightful lingering flavor of her coming on my mouth. Her alluring and sweet nectar always leaves me wanting more.

As I exhale, my fingers glide along her damp jaw, tracing a path down to her neck. Gradually, I move my hand towards her breasts, delicately caressing the curves with the tips of my fingers. Her tits never fail to leave me in awe. They're fucking amazing.

As much as I want to sink my teeth into those babies, my dick has other plans. I desperately want to be balls deep inside her, to ease this throbbing ache in my cock. I move my fingers away from her tits and cradle her face. When her tongue darts out to taste her wet lips, I let out a groan.

I wrap my arm around her waist and lead her towards the back patio. Taking a seat, I gently pull her onto my lap.

"Ride me," I command.

She tries to guide me into her pussy, slowly, but I'm extremely aroused, and patience has never been my strong point. Plus, the intense desire to fully connect with her becomes unbearable. Lifting my hips, I penetrate her with force, eliciting synchronized moans from both of us. Her eyes slowly shut, and she rests her hands on my chest for stability.

"Take me for a ride, Princess," I say, desperately wanting her to be in control and give me pleasure until I come inside her.

My whole body tingles when she slides along my shaft. Leaning forward, I suck her wet neck, not caring if I leave a mark.

I pull back, utterly captivated by the mesmerizing sight of her riding me. Her hair, still damp, cascades down in gentle waves, with droplets of water gracefully falling from its ends. Her cheeks are flushed, and her eyes reflect a profound craving and desire that is solely directed towards me. It baffles me how this beautiful girl could ever doubt her own perfection. In my chest, I feel a tightness, as if an invisible force is constricting my lungs, making each breath a struggle. How will I ever say goodbye to her in just two months?

The moment our eyes lock, the thought quickly fades away. Her hip movements make me groan out loud. I grab her ass with one hand and squeeze her nipple with the other. My heart pounds as she amps up her moves, making me hold on to her tighter.

"I'm close," she says, almost breathless.

Now that she's nice and relaxed, I bring my middle finger to my lips, and then open my mouth.

She watches me as I pull it from my mouth and reach around and slide it up and down her ass crack.

She suddenly stops. "What are you doing?" she asks, her brows furrowing as she looks at me.

"Just trust me," I assure her. "Keep going."

She eyes me for a few more moments before moving again. As I approach her entrance, I gently navigate around the narrow opening, allowing her to get accustomed to the feeling.

Taking a shaky breath, she rides me, finding a rhythm that brings her pleasure, her eyes close.

With caution, I insert the tip of my finger inside. She opens her eyes and stares at me. Slowly, I withdraw my finger, only to push it back in, this time going a little deeper.

She matches my pace, and I continue the process, gradually increasing the depth with each movement. When she lets out a little moan, I can't help but grin.

"I knew you'd like that," I say, cocky and confident. "Now fuck me harder and don't stop until we come."

With her hands placed on my chest, she moves in a rhythmic motion on top of me, chasing her pleasure from the sensation. Simultaneously, I carefully insert my finger deeper into her tight hole. Her breathing becomes erratic, and her body arches, completely consumed by the intense moment.

"Oh my god, it feels fucking amazing," she says, increasing her pace and riding me with intense pleasure. As I watch her, the sensations she evokes in my body are overwhelming, and I can tell she's on the brink of falling apart.

"Are you almost there? Because I'm about to..." She doesn't even have a chance to finish her sentence. Her mouth drops open and her face lights up with a beautiful expression as she comes. A soft moan escapes her lips as she tightens around me, gripping me firmly while her juices flow down onto my balls. Now that she's satisfied, I increase the speed of my thrusts.

Normally, I would be consumed by my own desires, but with her, it's different. Poppy Reeves has this amazing ability to make me forget about myself and focus entirely on her pleasure.

Once her orgasm fades, she sits up straight and starts riding me.

"That's it, babe, go all out. Fuck me like there's no tomorrow."

The intense combination of desire and heat causes my head to tilt back in pleasure. It's an incredible sensation. As she rides me, a pulsating sensation rushes through my body, causing my abs to tighten and my cock to throb. Poppy grabs my hair and pulls me closer, our lips meeting in a passionate kiss that consumes my every thought. She slips her tongue into my mouth, and I eagerly reciprocate. A primal and insatiable desire takes over as our kiss leaves me breathless. Her nails dig into my skin as our tongues dance together, completely possessing me at the moment.

It feels as if time is against us, and we're racing against the clock. Tremors and spasms ripple through my body as she continues to ride me harder and faster. My muscles tense, and my body craves more, more of her, hungry for her touch. The rain adds a slickness to our skin as I desperately try to hold on. The pressure within me builds as we move in perfect synchrony, like a flawless harmony. A whirlwind of emotions crashes in my chest when I hear her softly whisper my name.

As she experiences another orgasm, her lips part and her brows furrow, capturing my undivided attention. I can't look away from her face as I burst inside her. Our eyes lock, and in that moment, time seems to stand still. A surge of conflicting emotions washes over me, tempting me to ask her to come with me when I leave this shitty place, but I can't bring myself to say it. Instead, I choose to suppress them, unwilling to acknowledge their existence.

How on earth am I supposed to tell Ace that I want Poppy to join us? I want her to be around so we can continue what we have, not only the hot sex, but I want to hear her laughter and most of all, I want to support her in pursuing her music dreams. But I can't say anything because it's not who I am. That person I yearn to be for her will never exist. Because I crave it all - the fame, the groupies, the validation of being someone in this fucked up world. I'm not one for committed relationships, so why the fuck do I feel the urge to invite her to come with me.

Pull yourself together, you idiot. There will be other women to fuck. However, deep down, I know there will never be another woman quite like Poppy Reeves.

Chapter 24

Xander

Right now, I'm with Ace and I see Poppy chilling in her usual spot, totally engrossed in her e-reader. To see Poppy dancing in the rain and touching herself was mind-blowing. When she was riding me, I felt an overwhelming surge of emotion towards her. An impulsive thought almost led me to make a big mistake by suggesting she come along with us. It caught me off guard, and I'm relieved I didn't invite her to join us. I need to keep that shit in check. Thankfully, I came to my senses and didn't follow through on that crap. When I got home, I had a serious chat with myself, to make sure it didn't happen again.

"Hey," Ace interrupts, bringing me back to the present moment.

"Hmmm," I respond, turning to him. I notice the mischievous grin on his face and instantly anticipate what he's about to ask. It's the same question he's been pestering me with for weeks now.

"Why don't you just admit that you're fucking her? What other reason do you have for constantly staring at Poppy Reeves?"

"All right, fine. I'm fucking her. Are you satisfied now?" I snap back, feeling both frustrated and relieved that I don't have to lie anymore.

"You gotta tell me, man! Where does she rank? And do you think she'd be down for a threesome like Jade?" he suggests mischief in his voice.

Hearing Ace talk about sharing Poppy stirs something inside me. It's annoying and it seriously pisses me off because I don't want anyone else touching her except me. I don't want him to see her that way, like the other girls who are so quick to give it away. I suppress my emotions, hiding the turmoil inside so that Ace remains oblivious to how I feel about Poppy. I don't want him to think there's more to it than there is, because honestly, I can't figure out what the fuck is going on with me, either. The confusion is overwhelming.

"Nah, I don't think she's into that," I add, trying to keep my voice even to act like this conversation doesn't bother me. It pushes me to the point where I want to tell him to just shut the fuck up about Poppy. But I don't because I don't want to bring attention to any of it. I fold my arms over my chest, attempting to release the tension rising in my body. But it does nothing.

"Well, have you even asked if she's interested?"

The lump in my throat makes it difficult for me to swallow, a physical manifestation of the tension I feel.

"Yeah, I might have mentioned it," I reply, avoiding eye contact desperately hoping he doesn't catch onto my lie.

It pains me to deceive Ace, my best friend since forever, who has always been by my side through thick and thin. We've endured lives filled with constant misery, thanks to our equally shitty lives. We've shared everything, all the pain, the anger, how we feel about ourselves. However, I can't have the same discussions about Poppy with him as we did in the past, rating girls and sharing our thoughts. There's no way I can do that to her.

"Well, she must be good if you're going back for more," he says. "I know you haven't been messing around with Jade or Savannah because they told me."

"So you're keeping tabs on how many chicks I fuck these days?"

"No, fuck off. You're not usually like this, man. What's going on?"

"Nothing is going on."

I sense him watching me, waiting for my reaction, trying to figure it out. I don't know what to say to him. How can I tell him, yeah, she's fucking incredible? That she never fails to blow my mind every time we're together. However, I must remain silent about all of that, understanding that if I were to reveal anything, he would eagerly want to join in on the action and pursue her. Instead, I casually lift my shoulders in a shrug, downplaying the situation.

"She's alright, I guess," I add.

Ace smirks, and at that moment, I wonder if he can see right through my lies.

"She's right there, two doors down, so I don't have to go far to hook up. Plus, I get a free meal out of it while I'm there." I can't stand talking about Poppy like this, but it was the only way to get Ace to back off.

"So, if I'm feeling horny, do you think she'd be up for it?" Ace asks.

"Nah, I've already told you she's not into that." My voice comes out firm, laced with a bit of anger because I don't want him anywhere near her.

"Relax, dude, she's all yours," he says, raising an eyebrow and smirking.

I know he's fucking with me and he can totally see right through my bullshit.

"If you're horny, go see Jade," I add. Turning slightly, I notice Jade standing off to one side. "Jade!" I call out.

"What are you doing man?" Ace asks.

Jade immediately turns around to the sound of my voice. "Yeah," she responds, her face lighting up as she runs over.

"You want to hook up?" I ask, keeping my eye on Ace, who gives me a puzzled expression, clearly wondering what the fuck I'm up to.

"Of course I do. I'm always down for it, with you, Xander," she says, sitting next to me, sliding her fingers up my thigh.

Her touch makes my skin crawl. It repulses me, but I am forced to suppress my urge to push her away with Ace's eyes fixed on me. All I desire is the touch of my sassy princess.

"Ace is looking to hook up," I mention.

"Oh," she responds, the disappointment clear in her voice. "Okay," she says, glancing over at Ace and then looking back at me. "So are you going to join us?"

"Nah, not today. Maybe another time," I add.

Ace glares at me while he speaks to Jade. "Go. I'll meet you in our usual spot."

With a nod, Jade stands up, sparing a quick glance in my direction before she heads off.

"It wasn't Jade that I was interested in fucking. I wanted to know what's been holding your interest lately. But it seems like you're not into the idea of sharing. That's okay bro, but next time, just tell me the fucking truth instead of avoiding my questions." Ace gets up and walks off in the direction that Jade went just moments ago.

I feel like the biggest asshole for lying to Ace, especially since how easily he saw through my lies.

Later that night, at Poppy's place, we enjoy another meal she put together and watch a bit of The Real Housewives, which, secretly; I'm fucking hooked. I find amusement in the outrageous antics those wealthy bitches engage in for our entertainment.

I arrived at Poppy's house earlier straight after her mom left, once again driven by an intense desire to see her, plus a desperate need to sink my dick in her and indulge in the wild experiences we come to share whenever.

However, tonight I've chosen to be a little patient.

Apart from a hot as fuck kiss I gave her when I walked through the front door, I've not made any further moves. And what the fuck is up with that shit? Every time we're alone, I get this intense urge to kiss her as soon as I see her. It's crazy how something so simple can be so damn hot. And the way she kisses me back almost every time leaves me breathless and my dick craves so much more.

Poppy's on the couch next to me, seeming distant and zoned out, with a furrowed brow and frown that suggests she's troubled. It's clear her mom is getting on her nerves again like she always does. Sometimes I just want to confront that overbearing woman and tell her what I think, but I don't want her to know about me and her daughter's secret activities.

Standing, I reach for her hand. "Come on, let's go listen to some music," I say, pulling her off the couch.

Ever since I saw Poppy's vinyl collection a few months ago, we've been listening to classic rock almost every night. We step into her room and, just like she always does, she closes the door. I'm not really sure why she does that when it's just us, but maybe it's a habit to keep her mom from hearing the music and getting mad.

I sit on the bed, eyeing her as she heads to the shelf, picking out the next vinyl from our long list that we're dying to listen to.

The sound of The Smashing Pumpkins fills the room as she moves over to the bed and plops down beside me, lying on her back.

"What's the matter, Princess?" I ask her. "Is it your mom again?"

"Yeah. I'm so sick of hearing how I'm going to waste my life. It should be my choice, not hers."

I lie back next to her, propping myself up on my elbow, just watching her. As I talk, I casually start unbuttoning her shirt.

"Just remember, if you want something, you gotta fight for it." One more button opens up, giving a sneak peek of her soft, tempting skin. "Nothing is worth it if it's too easy." I lean forward and press a kiss to the top of her breast, then open another button.

"I get that," she says, turning to me, her hair flowing around her. She's so beautiful, like a masterpiece come to life. "I'm willing to put in the work. I want to, but it is the constant way she keeps discouraging me, saying I'm wasting my life with music that brings me down. Sometimes I wonder if it's all worth the battle."

"It is. And you know it is. You're talented, Poppy," I assure her, opening up her shirt. My eyes go straight to her sexy bra and flawless tits. "Your mom's opinion doesn't matter, just do what you want."

I lean down and playfully lick her hard nipple through her lacy bra.

A moan escapes her lips as I suck on her pert nipple.

As her fingers explore, she finds my hard cock, skillfully stroking it through my jeans. "You're hard," she says. "You're always hard."

With a smug smirk, I motion towards my cock with a suggestive move. "Don't hesitate, Princess, go ahead and take what you like."

She swiftly flips me onto my back, straddling me and holding me down on the bed. Her newfound confidence in her own sexuality is incredibly arousing. She gazes down at me, then leans forward, tangling her fingers in my hair as she claims my mouth. A rush of desire courses through my veins as her tongue glides over mine, and her hand continues to stimulate me through the fabric of my jeans, driving me into a state of frenzy.

I slip my hand in under that fucking short skirt. She gasps when I slide two fingers inside her with one smooth motion. I withdraw them and flash a cocky grin as she looks down at me, clearly wanting more. I playfully tease her by running my fingers along the length of her wetness, spreading her arousal. And then I abruptly stop. Running my tongue over my lips, I watch as she glares at me, clearly thinking I'm the biggest asshole.

"Oh, you want to play that game, huh?" she says, moving away from my body and positioning herself between my legs.

I casually prop myself up and enjoy the view as she unbuttons and unzips my jeans.

"Lift up," she asserts, her tone leaving no room for negotiation. I find myself drawn to this side of Poppy, the naughty seductive side that is unafraid to explore new boundaries.

Complying with her demand, I raise my hips, allowing her to effortlessly remove my jeans and boxers, discarding them somewhere in the room. My eyes remain fixed on her as she hungrily gazes at my cock, and an intense desire surges hoping that she will indulge in it. She pauses momentarily, teasing me with tantalizing anticipation.

Unable to withstand the suspense any longer, I reach down and grab my throbbing cock, bringing it close to her lips. "Open," I tell her, gently nudging my cock against the softness of her mouth.

She looks at me with a mischievous grin, and I can tell she's teasing me just like I was teasing her. Purposefully, she runs her tongue along the bottom of her lip, leaving it moist and shiny. I let out a longing groan, yearning for her to take my cock into her mouth.

"Oh, you want me to suck it?" she asks, smirking.

"What the fuck do you think?"

She laughs softly when she sees me getting frustrated, knowing how much I want her to fulfill my filthy thoughts.

"I bet you by the end of this, you'll be the one begging for me to suck your cock," she teases, biting down on her bottom lip. It's incredibly arousing, watching her torment me like this, knowing that I enjoy tormenting her just as much.

"You have high expectations there, princess," I reply, stoking the fire and encouraging her to continue.

"Is that a challenge I hear?" she says, leaning closer. She playfully teases me with a long, sensual lick along my shaft.

I let out a hiss.

"Or, how about this," she says, her lips forming a tight seal around the tip and she sucks, exerting such intensity that I can't help but cry out.

"Holy fuck," I groan, overwhelmed by the incredible sensation she's granting me.

With a loud pop, she releases me. "Or perhaps I could simply walk away and binge-watch some Real Housewives," she suggests casually, shrugging. She rests her palms on my bare thighs and rises to her feet. At that moment I know she's won. The cunning little vixen. It's astounding to think that just two months ago, she was a virgin, and now she possesses the perfect knowledge on how to play me, the seasoned player.

I sit up, grab her wrist, and pull her down onto the bed. Our gazes meet, and in that moment, an unspoken connection forms between us.

Her eyes search mine as she reaches out, brushing her hand against the side of my face. She's got this wild hunger in her eyes as she pulls me closer by grabbing the back of my neck. Our lips crash together in a fiery kiss that steals my breath away. My heart thumps like crazy as we briefly let go, letting Poppy take off my shirt. The air crackles with intensity as her gaze scans every part of my body, leaving a trail of heightened awareness in its wake.

Lowering myself to my knees, I press my lips against her body, showering her with gentle kisses.

No more games, no more teasing. I want to feel her. I want to experience her fully, to feel every connection between us. A soft needy sound escapes her lips as I cup her breast in my hand and flick my tongue against the sensitive clit before taking it into my mouth.

She always enjoys that, and I'm obsessed with the sounds she always makes. My ears crave to hear the intoxicating symphony of her sexy sounds.

With my hands firmly gripping her hips, I move her over to the edge of the bed. I hook my fingers on the side of her panties and slowly peel them down her legs.

"Do you want me to take off the skirt?" she asks.

"Fuck no, leave it on," I add, bunching it up around her waist. I don't think she understands the power that those short skirts have on me. Maybe she fucking does, and that's why she wears them, to ignite a longing, a desire for her in my body.

My heated gaze sweeps over her, appreciating every aspect of her perfection. Emotion clogs my throat as I continue to stare. *What the fuck is wrong with you asshole? Pull yourself together. Dude, you're acting like a simp. No girl should have this much control over you.*

Suddenly, our eyes meet. The raw desire in her expression and the longing in her eyes - it's different from anyone else I know who I've hooked up with.

It's as if she sees the true me, the vulnerable and the broken. The ruthless side that takes what he wants, never caring about how others feel. But not with her. Never with her. I lean in closer, planting kisses along her inner thigh. As I reach that sensitive spot, the tip of my tongue flicks out, teasing her clit before diving inside.

She lets out a moan and her legs tremble. My heart races as I pleasure her skillfully, using my tongue to its full extent and then circling her sensitive spot. I can see her studying me as I tend to her needs. With each lick, suck, and playful movement, I respond to the sounds she enjoys the most. She's so close, she's on the verge of coming.

"Oh god, Xander," she yells, as I skillfully pleasure her clit, applying just the right amount of pressure to give her what she desires. Her body trembles against mine, her fingers tightly gripping my hair as she experiences a powerful orgasm. I fight to catch my breath while she grinds her pussy against my face. It's so fucking hot watching her take what she wants.

As she comes down from her climax, I rise to my feet and position myself on top of her, pressing my hard cock against her.

"I'm gonna make you scream, Princess, but first, I want your mouth on my cock," I confidently state, smirking.

Lying on the bed, I give myself a stroke. Poppy gets up and positions herself between my legs. Out of all the blowjob experiences I've had, and believe me, there have been so many, no one can compare to her incredible skills. I find myself captivated as she expertly smears the precum from my cock onto her fingers and then seductively licks them clean.

A deep groan escapes my lips. Fuck, it's hot when she does that. It's undeniably arousing. I never tire of witnessing that tantalizing sight when she does the unexpected. No matter how many times I see her do that, my reaction remains unchanged - a surge of excitement and anticipation. She ignites a fiery desire within me, pushing my longing for her to dangerous heights.

She is the one currently in charge, holding the control over me. It's quite surprising how she manipulates me into doing whatever she desires. When did I lose my dominance in these sexual encounters? I've always been the one in control.

As she lowers her head, I instinctively grip the base of my cock, spreading the pre-cum along her lips. It's arousing to witness her relishing my taste as she licks it off.

"Open," I say in a deep gravelly voice from deep in my chest.

When she opens her mouth, I slowly guide my cock into it. Her lips stretch wide, and I'm not sure if it hurts her or not, but damn, it feels good when her tongue slides along the underside of my shaft. I thrust my hips forward, reaching the back of her throat. She increases her suction, and I hear her gag as she takes me in deep.

Pleasure contorts my face, and I let out a moan. She's so fucking hot when she sucks me off and looks up at me. I wanna etch this image into my brain, so I won't forget it when I'm gone. I need to remember how incredible she looks with my cock in her mouth.

She eagerly sucks me harder and faster, as if she can't get enough.

The muscles in my thighs tighten, and I release a growl. I quickly pull out of her mouth, realizing that I'll finish any second if we keep going like this.

"Get the fuck over here now."

When she doesn't move fast enough, I forcefully tug her towards me, causing her to stumble and fall onto me. Our lips connect, and my tongue explores the depths of her mouth as I shift our positions, with me ending up on top of her. The way I press against her entrance spreads her wetness and makes it feel amazing. The urgency in her movements becomes palpable, her desire evident as she reaches for me, ready to slip my cock into her. But I swiftly grasp her wrist, halting her advances. With a firm grip, I lift her wrist and secure it above her head.

Pausing for a moment, I take in her face, memorizing every detail. Her eyes hold a depth that captivates me, her cheekbones exude elegance, and her lips have an irresistible allure. But a sudden pang strikes my chest as I realize that in just five weeks' time, I won't be able to do this anymore. Because I will be gone, and it's likely that I'll never see her again. I close my eyes, trying to push away these overwhelming thoughts and emotions that are surging through me. I have to stop this shit now. This is not who I am.

"Xander," she says.

I open my eyes and take a deep breath, gazing at her. Her eyes, filled with desire, look back at me. It's impossible for me not to feel this way. However, I refuse to let these overwhelming emotions consume me while I fuck her.

I swiftly flip her over onto her stomach on the bed. That way, she won't be able to make eye contact with me, and I hope it'll help sort out these confusing emotions.

I take hold of her hips and lift her ass in the air, exposing her bare pussy, ready and waiting. I grab a condom, tear the packet open with my teeth, and slide it on.

As I slip inside her, she lets out a soft moan, savoring every inch until I am buried deep inside her. She feels so good. It always feels freaking incredible inside her tight little pussy. My chest tightens, knowing that no other experience will compare to being inside her. Our bodies fit perfectly like she was made for me. On a strangled groan, I withdraw ever so slowly before thrusting back in.

Poppy's moans echo through the room as she tightly grips the sheets, matching the rhythm of my thrust. Time seems to stand still as if it is just the two of us. With every thrust, I can feel her pussy squeezing me tighter, deepening the connection. Leaning in, I gently plant a kiss on her spine as I continue to claim her from behind. As our desire intensifies, our bodies collide with a fervent passion, perfectly synchronized in our motions. I wrap my arm around her waist, pulling her closer to my chest, longing for even deeper penetration in this position.

She turns her head and kisses me, her tongue slipping inside my mouth. With every movement, my core tightens with anticipation, begging for release.

Our skin glistens with sweat as Poppy's fingers grip the sheet even tighter. We move together in perfect harmony, our movements synchronized like a flawless song.

As she reaches her peak, her inner walls tighten and she whispers my name in a breathless plea. The way she comes like that is seriously breathtaking.

A wave of pleasure washes over me, causing my lips to part and my brows to furrow. I release my warm load inside her, gently biting down on her shoulder blade, blending a touch of pain with pleasure. As I move in and out of her, I can feel the pulsating sensations of her inner walls, amplifying the lingering pleasure of our orgasms.

Gasping for air, I gently kiss her spine, not wanting to let her go. But then, a crashing reality hits me like a tidal wave. I need to get the fuck out of here right now. This shouldn't be how I feel. What the hell am I doing? I pull out of her, causing her to collapse on the bed, gasping for air. I move over and toss the condom into the trash. Scanning the room, I locate my shirt and put it on. It's imperative that I get out of here right now before I completely lose it.

Poppy sits up on the bed and watches me closely. "What are you doing?" she asks.

Come up with some excuse to tell her. In a split second, I fabricate a lie as I quickly put on my shirt. "I have to go. I just remembered I've got something important to do."

"Xander," Poppy yells out.

I pause over at the door, my hand resting on the doorknob, prepared to open it. However, upon hearing her call my name, I turn my head to look back. As I do, my gaze unintentionally drifts down to admire her stunning tits, all while trying to disregard the bewildered expression on her face.

"I'll see you later," I say, opening the door and racing down the hall.

I grab my shoes from their usual spot by the front door and leave. How did things escalate to this point? It was supposed to be just a casual hook-up, a bit of fun, but it's spiraled out of control. How the fuck do I put an end to this?

I step onto the street, hoping to find some relief. Slipping one shoe on, and then the other, I'm filled with desperation as I walk down the street. I'm determined to break free and clear my head from all this emotional baggage. The only place I know where I'll find solace awaits me, where I can be alone with my thoughts, and usually, where I reflect on my mother. But tonight, I need to divert my thoughts elsewhere. I've gotta figure out a way to get all this crap out of my head.

Chapter 25
Poppy

I can't fathom why Xander left like that. It's total bullshit what he said about forgetting to do something. I can always sense when he lies, and that excuse was a complete fabrication. I gaze at the door, hoping he might reconsider. However, as soon as I hear the front door slam shut, I realize he won't be returning.

I'm aware that he occasionally acts this way, but tonight it caught me off guard. It hasn't happened since the time we had sex on my car I have no clue what triggered it.

Lately, though, I've noticed a change in our sexual encounters compared to how they were at the beginning. I understand that it's purely physical for him, but sometimes I get the sense that there might be something more going on. He has never said anything to suggest otherwise, but I can see it in the way he is with me. The way he gazes at me during sex makes me feel like I'm the most beautiful person in his eyes. It's a confidence boost for me to explore my sexuality. However, I can't allow myself to entertain the idea that it could be more than just sex because it would shatter me if I let myself believe that. Plus, in just five weeks, he'll be leaving anyway. So, why should I entertain these thoughts and only end up hurting myself more when the day comes for him to leave?

I get out of bed and carefully tug the fitted sheet back on the edge of the mattress. It's the first time I've ever done this. It's not that Xander doesn't always bring me immense pleasure whenever we have sex, because he definitely does. But this time, the intensity was on a whole different level. It felt like electricity coursing through my entire being, and when he bit into my shoulder, it only heightened the already exquisite sensation that surged through me.

Once I've tidied up the bed, I make my way across the room to pick up the bra, panties, and shirt that Xander carelessly threw when he undressed me. Tossing them into the dirty clothes hamper, I steal a quick glance at the clock. It's only nine-thirty, and I can't help but wonder what Xander is up to right now. I know he won't go home just yet. He's told me a few more stories of his dad over the last few weeks, so I know he rarely goes inside the house before eleven-thirty.

With my hair tied up in a messy knot, I head straight to the shower.

I'm awake before the sun rises the next morning, unable to sleep due to constant thoughts about what I may have done wrong for Xander to leave. Maybe I didn't do anything wrong, or maybe he had something else going on. Who knows, he's been acting a bit odd lately. However, last night felt different, not like our usual encounters. Maybe he's growing tired of our casual flings and wants to return to hooking up with random people. I really hope not. It would be difficult for my heart to handle seeing him with Jade or Savannah again. I like being the only girl he's been with lately. That might be why he's been acting so weird. Maybe he wants more than just me.

After getting dressed and making sure I choose one of the skirts I know Xander loves, I make my way to the kitchen to have breakfast. As I eat, I repeatedly glance at my phone, fighting the powerful urge to send a text to Xander. Each time I'm about to give in, I quickly place my phone face down on the table and then resume eating my cereal.

The cycle repeats so frequently that I'm tempted to fling my phone across the room.

As I finish washing my bowl and place it in the dishwasher, my primary goal is to leave before my mother returns home. However, my efforts prove futile when I hear her entering the house. I'm super annoyed, cursing myself for not leaving sooner. I really don't want to endure another lecture about my plans for next year. If only I hadn't been so distracted by my phone, I could have made my escape sooner. While my attention is on the dishwasher, I hear her keys dropping into the bowl near the front door.

Closing the dishwasher, I fix the dish towel that I left on the counter, putting it back where it belongs.

As she enters the room, I sneak a glance at her before turning to grab my bag from the couch. Feeling her eyes on me, I sling the bag over my shoulder and get ready to leave.

"Poppy," she interjects, "please, just stop."

I come to a halt, but I don't turn around to face her. "I don't want to argue, Mom."

"Neither do I," she replies.

Finally, I turn towards her and notice her leaning against the back of the couch.

"All I ask is that you consider your actions," she says.

And there it is. It's the same old topic she always ends up talking about.

"Why can't you just be happy for me? Let me pursue what I want instead of trying to force me into something I don't want to do."

She gazes at me, a brief moment of silence passing between us.

"I see a lot of your dad in you, and it frightens me."

It's the first time she has mentioned my dad without belittling him or calling him worthless. I stay silent, curious about where this conversation is heading.

"I genuinely want you to be happy. It's just I don't want you to go into music."

And just like that, she's back to telling me that I'm wasting my life by pursuing my passion for music. She fails to understand that it's not the same as what my dad did. I have no desire to join a band. All I truly want is to use music to help children, especially those who are trapped in their bodies and unable to communicate. I want to provide them with a connection to something, anything, that allows them to express themselves. Without saying a word, I turn and head towards the door, completely disregarding her voice as she calls out to me.

When I arrive at school, I'm still seething with anger. I park my beat-up green shitbox of a car in its usual spot and turn off the engine. Retrieving my bag from the back seat where I had angrily tossed it earlier, I make sure to lock the car, just in case someone like Jade or the other mean girls decide to play a prank on me. I wouldn't put it past them to pull a prank like hiding a smelly fish or doing something else awful just for laughs.

As I make my way to my usual spot, where I like to read and lean against the brick wall, I spot Xander sitting beside Ace in their usual spot. When he notices me, he quickly looks away. It's different from our usual morning interaction of exchanging long glances. There's definitely something going on with him.

I place my bag down gently on the soft grass, taking a seat. With a sense of anticipation, I begin to search through my bag, my goal being to find my e-reader.

After a brief moment, I finally locate it. Leaning comfortably against the sturdy brick wall, I pause before turning it on. As I lift my head, I catch his gaze once again on me. And just like before, he quickly glances away. What the hell? Confusion floods my mind. What is happening with him? It feels reminiscent of when he manipulated me into giving him that first blow job. Why can't he bring himself to look at me now, especially after all the hot, wild sex we've shared? I believed he was enjoying it as much as I was. Was I mistaken?

I try to push the thoughts out of my head and focus on my e-reader, but I find myself going back over each line I read because I can't concentrate. Feeling frustrated, I tuck my e-reader back into my bag and look up.

This time I see that Xander has turned around in his seat, his back facing me, like he doesn't want to look at me, but I can tell he's engaged in a conversation with Ace based on how Ace is interacting with him.

Jade and her friends make their way over to where Xander is seated. I notice Jade inching closer to him, but not before she shoots a glance in my direction. It's obvious she knows I'm watching. She deliberately runs a finger down Xander's black t-shirt, catching his attention. Leaning in close to his ear, she whispers something to him. The sight of her touching him and having his undivided attention fills me with a painful wave of jealousy. I know what comes next, as I've observed him closely over the years. They both get up and leave together. My heart aches as I anxiously wait for them to rise from their seats. Why did I think he would never reconnect with her? My heart pounds with anticipation as I sit there, observing their interaction.

But to my surprise, Xander abruptly retreats and forcefully pushes her away.

"Stay the fuck away from me," he shouts in a loud and intimidating tone, causing everyone nearby to stop and stare.

Ace places his hand on Xander's shoulder, attempting to calm him. Meanwhile, Jade stands up from the ground, straightens her dress, and turns, clearly embarrassed. I must admit, while everyone watches her walk away from Xander, I can't help but rejoice inwardly. That nasty bitch is getting what she deserves. Finally, she's humiliated in front of everyone.

Jade shoots a look my way, and I respond with a smug smirk. Right before she averts her gaze, she flips me off. People turn their heads towards me, but I couldn't care less because Xander didn't want her after all.

As soon as the bell rings, I swiftly pick up my bag from the ground and make my way to my first class.

Xander completely ignores me during the first two lessons, and then he disappears. Ace is gone too. Maybe they bailed on school and went somewhere else. Nevertheless, I constantly check my phone like some pathetic girl, eagerly waiting for a text from him. All I want is for this day to be over so that I can confront him about what's going on when he comes by later at seven like he always does.

It's already nine o'clock at night and there's still no sign of Xander, I've reached my limit. I can't take it anymore. I grab my phone and send him a text.

Poppy: What the fuck is happening?

I try to concentrate on the TV, trying to get into my favorite show. There's so much I need to catch Xander up on about this episode.

But my eyes keep shifting back to my phone. I see the message bubbles appear and then disappear, but I wait in vain for a text that never comes. What the hell? I'm tempted to march over to his place and demand to know why he's ghosting me. But the fear of running into his drunken father terrifies me. I've seen the constant bruises on Xander from his father's unprovoked attacks. It breaks my heart to see how he's treated. No one should ever endure that kind of abuse. It's no wonder he struggles with self-esteem and why it hurts him so much when his father calls him worthless. I know deep down that Xander's drive to be famous stems from his father's lifelong criticism. However, I hope that someday, when he achieves his dreams, he realizes he was always something special.

I lift my head and attempt to concentrate on the show, but again it's no use. Other thoughts occupy my mind.

At the stroke of ten, a sinking feeling settles within me, acknowledging that Xander won't be showing up at the house, nor will he be answering my text. With a heavy heart, I head to bed, feeling let down.

CHAPTER 26

Xander

It's been one day of trying to ignore her, but she's the only thing on my mind. For the past few months, we've been fucking like rabbits, all over her house - the kitchen bench top, the couch, her bathroom shower, even in the backyard during another downpour. That memory is permanently etched in my mind, and whenever I think about it, it still arouses me.

During lunch today, all I wanted was a break from school and the drama that comes with girls like Jade, who constantly want to hook up. It's been over three months since I last fucked any of them, yet they keep coming back.

Ace could sense that something was bothering me, but I couldn't confide in him. I can't admit that every time I'm with Poppy, the sex intensifies, and the pleasure keeps escalating. I just love how I can explore every inch of her body and bring her to a point where she screams my name, genuinely, unlike those other girls who fake all their orgasms. It just keeps getting hotter and hotter. Like everything else, she surpasses everyone I've been with before.

Last night, when she screamed my name as I bit down on her shoulder, I couldn't hold back, and I blew my release inside her. I yearn to keep fucking her over and over again. However, the predicament lies in the fact that my black heart is starting to feel something deeper for her. It's more than just physical satisfaction now. And that's something I can't allow. I can't risk jeopardizing everything Ace and I have worked so hard for.

Ace and I made a pact years ago, promising that nothing would come before our dreams.

Lately, I can tell that Ace has noticed a change in me. He hasn't said anything directly, but I can see him observing me, wondering why I've been quiet at times, much like I was today. Maybe that's why he suggested skipping the second half of school and heading straight to practice. It's the only place where I can clear my mind and escape the thoughts racing through my head.

As we played music and added the final touches to the song I finished writing the other day, I tried my best not to think about her. But it's difficult when, deep down, I know that the songs I've been writing are about her. I never even realized it until today, not even when I sang her part of the song all those months ago when we first started fooling around.

I set my guitar aside and make my way over to the couch, taking a seat next to Ace. He's just lit a joint, which I promptly take from his mouth. As I inhale, a light-headed feeling washes over me. After another drag, I pass it back to him, blowing the smoke out of my mouth.

"I've been scouring the internet for affordable apartments, and it looks like there are a few we can rent," Ace says.

"I don't have much money, just seventy dollars," I admit, realizing now that maybe I should have found a job instead of wasting time with Poppy. If I had, I wouldn't be feeling the way I do.

He hands me the joint, and I bring it up to my mouth.

"I've got around two grand," Ace says.

When I hear the amount he has saved, I cough and choke on the smoke in my lungs. "Two grand," I say, coughing again, handing him back the joint. "How the fuck did you manage to save that much?"

"You remember that old asshole bikie wannabe dickhead? Whenever he left, he always left a few dollars on the table for my mother, as if she was some kind of whore. Once I realized what he was doing, I'd wait until that fuckhead was gone, then sneak inside and take a few bills from the pile."

"And your mom never found out?"

"No," he says, shaking his head. "She was always too fucking high to notice. So, when we find a place, we should have enough for rent for a few weeks and by then we'll find some paying gigs. We just need to find a drummer and a bass guitarist when we get there."

"And what if we can't find them?" I ask.

"Then we'll need to find some way to make money until we find the perfect people to join our band, but only if they're the right fit. I don't want just anyone to join us. We still have five weeks until we leave, so I might be able to save another two or three hundred dollars by then." Ace glances at the clock. "Damn, it's already three in the morning. You might as well stay here tonight."

The following day, Ace and I decided to sleep in and skip school altogether. I didn't really mind, as I had no desire to see Poppy anyway. However, I couldn't help but keep glancing at the unanswered text message.

To take my mind off things, I get lost in the music again, writing more songs while Ace adds his awesome sounds to the mix.

As the clock strikes eleven at night, a wave of fatigue washes over me, mingling with a gratifying sense of achievement. We had successfully worked on and completed another song, which was now ready to be shown to any label who shows interest. And yes, once again, it's a song about "her". I'm certain that Ace has caught on to this pattern, but he hasn't said a word. I don't think he knows how to approach the subject, and honestly, I would probably lash out at him if he ever brought it up. It's a subject that we both consciously avoid.

As Ace drives down the darkened street towards my house, I can't help but wonder if Poppy waited for me again, like she did two nights ago. I haven't received another text from her. Yeah, I did check, and I'm annoyed at myself for doing that.

Ace pulls up to the curb and looks at me as I gaze two doors down towards Poppy's house. All the lights are off.

Ace's voice catches my attention, and I turn to look at him. "You can tell me about her if you want."

"There's nothing to talk about. I've already told you she's not my type," I reply.

I open the door, ready to get out, but pause when he speaks again.

"But if there's something on your mind, you know you can always talk to me. I'm here for you, man."

"See ya later, Ace."

As I step out of the car, I shut the door and stand on the sidewalk, keeping an eye on him until he disappears around the corner. Only then do I turn and make my way towards the house.

As usual, the lights in my house are out. The hinges of the screen door screech into the silence. I cautiously open the door and step inside. Almost immediately after shutting the door, I feel it - a sudden impact from behind. The force of the blow drills into my side, causing me to stumble. Instinctively, I raise my hands to shield my body. But it's too late, my father has me trapped against the wall. His arm forcefully presses against my back, while my chest and face are forcefully pushed against the hard surface. I'm grateful that I left my guitar at Ace's place.

"Where have you been?" he barks angrily. "Off fucking some little slut."

With each word, he increases the pressure of his arm against my back, causing my head to repeatedly bang against the wall in front of me.

"Let me fucking go, asshole."

"You're just a useless piece of crap. I wish I found out I wasn't your father before your mother died, because I would have thrown her skanky ass and her bastard kid out long ago." His face inches closer, and the stench of alcohol on his breath overwhelms me, instantly making me sick. He makes me feel like barfing the pizza that Ace ordered using the cash he took from his mom's new boyfriend, while they were banging in the shower tonight.

I can't move, not with the way he has me pinned against the wall. History serves as a reminder that resisting only escalates to more violence. In just over five weeks, I'll finally be able to escape this shithole and never lay eyes on this asshole again. For now, I must simply keep quiet and bide my time. That's how I'll endure these last five weeks.

His face remains close to mine. And the seconds seem to stretch on as the pain in my body continues. Suddenly, I feel his arm loosen its grip on my shoulder. Just as I'm about to step away, he forcefully grabs my hair and slams my head against the wall. The impact causes the drywall to crack, joining the countless other holes scattered throughout the room, remnants of my father's fits of anger and violence. With a cruel laugh, the fucking bastard walks away, seemingly satisfied with his cruel act.

I remain there standing, still propped against the wall, desperately trying to suppress the pain as the throbbing ache intensifies in my head. Surprisingly, my legs manage to hold me upright, refusing to give way. I catch a glimpse of his silhouette as he moves down the hallway, watching him as he exits the room.

Trying to regain my balance, I notice a slight dizziness creeping in. Carefully, I take a few steps forward, desperately searching for something to hold onto. To my surprise, my hand lands on one of the whisky bottles that he always keeps on the coffee table in the room. Without a second thought, I swiftly grab the bottle and quickly leave, my head still spinning. I make my way out of the front door and onto the street, desperate to escape before he comes back and realizes one of his bottles is missing.

Unscrewing the lid, I indulge in the alcohol to numb the throbbing pain in my head.

I waste no time drowning my sorrows to numb the pain of what just went down. I despise him and everything he represents. The kind man he used to be, is now a distant memory. It's as if that version of him faded away, replaced by this despicable asshole. Why did my mother have to reveal her secret? That's when everything changed. That's when his animosity towards me began and has been festering ever since.

With the bottle now half empty, my headache has subsided and my body feels more at ease. One day, I hope he faces the consequences he deserves. I can only hope that I am the one who brings him down a notch by proving my worth to the world. He will see me the way Poppy sees me, acknowledging that I am truly something.

With thoughts of Poppy consuming my mind, I roll onto my side and glance towards her house. Bringing the bottle to my lips, I take a large gulp. A sharp ache courses through my body as I fixate on her home. It's a debilitating and relentless pain, gnawing at my gut for the way I've treated her since that night I walked out of her room.

Is this what love feels like? An ache deep within your soul? If it is, I want no part of it.

I close my eyes and envision what it will be like in a few weeks when I walk away from her. The feeling is soul-crushing. It's like I've been torn open, left with an immense void that's bleeding out my very essence. My eyes snap open. How the fuck did I let this happen? I've made a terrible mistake. She never should have infiltrated my heart so deeply.

Guzzling down another gulp, I get up off the curb. I'm on my way to Poppy's house, feeling an overwhelming need to see her right now, as if my life depends on it. I know she must be angry with me for ghosting her, but I hope she can channel that sharp tongue of hers in a different way. Instead of yelling at me, she could use it to get me off. All I want is to kiss her, to feel her touch. I want to encourage her to follow her dreams and stand up against her mother, who constantly belittles her. Maybe I'll even have the guts to tell her mother to back off before Poppy does.

Noticing that all the lights are off, I decide not to bother with the front door since I know Poppy is already asleep in her room. I proceed to walk around to the back of the yard. Finishing the last drop, I casually toss the bottle aside and search for something to use as a step.

As soon as I notice a wooden crate by the back door, I make my way around the side of the house, struggling a bit and stumbling a couple of times. My goal is to reach Poppy's bedroom window.

After finally managing to position the crate in the right spot, I attempt to stand on it, needing two tries to find my balance. With great care, I slip my fingers under her slightly ajar window and lift it up, allowing me room to climb inside.

As I slide the window open, I become a shadow in the night, maneuvering my way inside. With a burst of strength in my arms, I pull myself up, only to clumsily stumble and fall into the room.

Lying on the carpet, I gaze up at the ceiling above. "Don't worry, it's only me," I slur.

"Xander," she says, and suddenly, the lamp beside the bed flicks on.

I hastily shield my eyes, giving them time to adapt before I unveil them and gaze towards her. As she sits in the bed, her tousled hair cascades over her shoulders, and I feel my heart skip a beat, captivated by her beauty at this very moment.

"Xander, what are you doing?"

Carefully, I listen to every word she utters, paying close attention to the tone of her voice. Nope, she's not even a little pissed at me. I turn over onto my stomach and slowly get to my feet.

"Have you been drinking?" she asks.

I simply nod in response.

As I make my way toward the bed, I urgently kick off my shoes, longing to lie beside her and express all the thoughts that have been swirling in my mind. I want to convey how much I desire her, and how much I need her. I want to pour out my heart and then some. However, I'm fucking clueless about how to navigate this unfamiliar situation I've stumbled upon.

I position myself beside her on the bed and instinctively, my arms wrap around her. Nestling into the curve of her neck, I breathe in her intoxicating scent, finding solace in its familiarity as it eases the tension in my body.

"You have no idea how much I want to fuck you right now, Princess. I can't get you out of my fucking head. You've really messed me up. No matter what, I don't know how to rid myself of you."

"Xander, you're not making any sense."

"It's quite simple, can't you see? You've completely ruined me. I have no fucking clue what I'm doing."

"You're slurring your words. I can't understand what you're trying to say."

She looks incredibly adorable as she gazes at me, her eyebrows furrowing, her hair tousled from sleep. I lean in and softly kiss her neck. When I gently bite her skin, she releases a moan.

Smirking, I whisper. "I love it when you do that."

Being near her ignites an immediate sense of desire, causing my dick to get hard. I gently roll us in the bed, positioning myself on top of her. I grind against her.

"Look how hard you make me. You drive me fucking crazy sometimes, Princess" I murmur, as my hands move to explore her body.

Slowly, I trace downwards until I find that intoxicating wetness that always drives me wild. Slipping my hand in under her underwear, I tease her clit. And like always, she eagerly opens for me. The sounds she makes and the way she pushes down on my fingers make me feel like my dick is about to burst. I gently withdraw my fingers and proceed to remove her panties, followed by taking off my jeans. I position myself between her legs.

As I hold her arms above her head, I guide my hard cock into her wet, tight pussy.

A moan escapes her lips, and my head spins with desire.

"Do you know how fucking sexy you are when you make that sound?" I pull back and push in, slowly.

Every time I thrust inside her, she moans, intensifying the sensation. Sex with her is mind-blowing. I could do this for the rest of my life. Listening to the sounds she makes as I fuck her.

She spreads her legs wider. I wouldn't dare to close my eyes and miss a single moment of this.

"Open your eyes, Princess," I request when she shuts her eyes enjoying the sensation. "Tell me how much you like my cock."

When her eyes flutter open, I'm lost in her beautiful blue gaze. It's filled with longing, and desire, as if I am the only one she craves. This girl, she's a damn goddess and I know I'm screwed.

I quicken my pace. She lets out a soft gasp. Her body naturally curves towards mine.

"Oh, God," she moans.

"Let go, baby. You are always beautiful when you let go."

"Xander," she moans my name in a sultry, seductive purr. Her body trembles with anticipation each time I thrust inside her.

"That's it, baby," I groan hoarsely. "You feel fucking amazing."

"Yes," she hisses, her body quivering. "I'm so close."

"I know, I can feel it. I'm right there with you."

"Oh, yeah, just like that," she murmurs, biting her bottom lip. "Xander," she cries out, her face twisting in pleasure as she shatters on my cock.

As I come inside her, I gently press the side of my face against the curve of her neck. It's a moment I wish could last forever, lost in the intimacy we share. Her body is like a warm embrace and her scent wraps around me. Breathing heavily, I remain there, savoring every precious second I have with her, aware that our time together is drawing to a close.

Still catching my breath, I lift my head and study her stunning face. Her rosy cheeks and glistening sweat droplets add to the whirlwind of unexpected emotions swirling inside me. I lift my hand and brush a stray strand of hair away from her face. "You're so beautiful. You know that."

And I can hear the slur in my voice, but I want her to know that I'm not saying it because I'm drunk. It's the truth. Damn, did I already mention that earlier? Maybe I didn't.

"Well anyway, I think you're beautiful," I say.

She bursts into laughter, and hearing it puts a smile on my face. "I think you've had way too much to drink," she says.

"Yeah, maybe." I gently press a kiss to her nose and roll off of her, immediately pulling her close to my side. The comforting touch of her warm, naked body brings me solace as I snuggle my face into the curve of her neck.

That's when it hits me, like a ton of bricks. Damn, I'm head over heels for this girl. She's mine, and I want to keep it that way. The thought of not being with her just doesn't sit right with me. How can I simply walk away from the incredible connection we share, something I've never experienced with anyone else? But first, how the hell am I going to break the news to Ace? How do I tell him that I've messed up and that I want Poppy to join us when we go?

I don't care, I'll find a way.

Lying there, I snuggle up to Poppy, just soaking it in. Gradually, her breathing deepens, becoming synchronized with the gentle rhythm of a peaceful sleep. Holding her close, I press my lips softly against her delicate skin, savoring its softness. "I love you," I whisper, my voice barely audible, as if afraid of the weight of those words.

CHAPTER 27
Poppy

The sudden noise of my bedroom door swinging open startles me, and then I hear it - her voice, piercing and shrieking. Panic overwhelms me as I realize I've overslept. And to add to the chaos, Xander is lying naked beside me.

"What in the world is happening?" my mom screams, making me jump out of bed, fully aware of my latest screw-up. My cheeks burn with shame as I stand naked before my mother. But she's not paying attention to me. Instead, her attention is on Xander, who absentmindedly scratches his groin while frantically searching through the disarray of clothes on the floor. And to add to my shock, he's sporting a raging erection.

"Get out of here now!" she yells, her voice filled with panic. "Get out or I'll call the cops."

Xander's sudden display of nudity in front of my mother completely catches me off guard, causing me to momentarily forget that I'm also unclothed. It's only when she glances back at me that I snap back to reality. Hastily, I grab the oversized crumpled t-shirt resting at the edge of the bed and swiftly pull it over my head.

Xander hastily pulls on his jeans, but he's not fast enough, leaving his ass on display. All I can do is stare at it. *Come on, Poppy. Get your shit together. Now is not the time to check out his ass. Your mother is right there, after all.*

I suddenly snap out of my daze and nervously shift my gaze towards my furious mother, who is giving me a deathly glare. Yeah, she totally caught me shamelessly checking out his butt.

"I told you to get the hell out of my house," my mom shouts. She's super pissed, I think she's about to explode.

Xander, in a rush, quickly throws on his shirt and then steals a glance at me from across the bed.

"Catch you later, Princess," he mutters, and heads towards the window.

He opens the window and slips through, leaving me alone with my mother's seething anger.

As I stand there in the uncomfortable silence, I'm unsure where to direct my gaze. Briefly, my eyes glance at the floor before shifting to the untidy bed. I can't help but notice that the fitted sheet has once again come loose from the corner, most likely due to the wild night I had with Xander. The mere thought of what he did to my body and the mind-blowing orgasm he gave me sends a wave of tingling sensations rushing through me. Being with him feels like my body is a finely tuned instrument, and he is the skilled maestro coaxing out every sound and sensation it can produce.

I turn my head and watch as my mother walks over to the window that Xander just slipped through. With a firm grip, she shuts it and locks it.

"So, this is how you choose to spend your time when I'm not here," she remarks, her words dripping with disdain.

Her eyes meet mine, but I quickly divert my gaze, unable to hold her stare. "I never raised you to be a promiscuous little slut, but unfortunately, that seems to be the case now. And to top it off, it had to be with a loser like him."

Her words cut through me like sharp daggers. While the unfounded accusation of me being promiscuous didn't bother me, it was when she labeled Xander as a loser that truly hurt. It bugs me she doesn't have her own point of view and just sees things the way Xander says people see him. It's not his fault his life turned upside down when his mom passed away.

"His name is Xander, and he is anything but a loser," I add, feeling annoyed.

"I know exactly who he is, damn it. The entire neighborhood knows about that boy," she exclaims, ranting and pacing around the room. Suddenly, she pauses, taking a moment to gather her thoughts. "Wait, is he the one who influenced you to change your plans for next year?" Without waiting for my response, she continues her rant, pacing back and forth. "That's why I couldn't reach you. It's all his fault."

"No, Mother, he didn't influence me. He simply made me realize the importance of standing up for what I want," I explain. Her constant blaming of Xander is truly starting to irritate me. I walk over to the bed and neatly arrange the sheets, deliberately avoiding any further discussion on the topic. Yep, she busted me sleeping with Xander, and I take responsibility for getting caught, but I wish she'd move on already.

"I'm amazed at how naïve you are. Do you truly believe that he actually cares about you? Brace yourself for a harsh reality check because the truth is, he's only using you, and you've fallen for it. Can't you see that he's just like your father? That boy will never genuinely care for you, no matter what he says. It's all just empty lines that they feed you, my dear, foolish girl."

"Seriously, it's time to move on. It's been over eight years since you and Dad were together. Your constant dwelling on him is getting exhausting." My comment takes her by surprise. "Honestly, I can't handle hearing about how he messed up and hurt you anymore. It's totally wearing me out."

"Do you honestly think things will change with that boy? Wake up. He's simply toying with you. Can't you see that?"

"You don't know who he is, so keep your opinions to yourself. Are we done here?" With the bed now tidied up, I stand, hoping she'll grasp my subtle hint and leave my room, thus putting an end to this conversation. However, she remains unmoved, giving me a chilling stare.

"No, we can't just drop this conversation. Come out to the family room immediately. I can't be in here, aware of what you did with that boy in your bed."

"Sorry, but I'm done talking about this. Feel free to close the door when you leave, because I'm finished." I turn and flop on the bed.

"You have two choices here, Poppy. Either you come talk to me now or I'll call the police and let them know that the scumbag from two doors down broke into our house. It's your choice."

Seriously, is she for fucking real? I give her the death stare. I'm so pissed off that it's come to that. "You can't be serious?"

"Yes, Poppy, I'm serious. If you don't get out into that room now, I'll make that call." With those words, she walks out of my room.

Standing there, I can't help but feel a wave of worry as I watch the doorway long after she's gone. The time has come for me to step out of the safety of my room and confront her anger head-on. It's a simple decision, really. I have to go out there because if I don't, she'll start causing trouble for Xander. And that's something I absolutely cannot allow to happen.

Xander has so many aspirations, and so many dreams he wants to pursue. Life hasn't been kind to him so far, and if my mother were to interfere, it would be an absolute disaster. Xander would be stuck with a criminal record before he even gets a shot at chasing his dream of fame, his music career. Just imagine how a record label would view that, especially with a breaking-and-entering charge hanging over his head. It's no wonder my dad walked away. I'm willing to bet he couldn't handle the constant turmoil my mother put him through.

I let out a groan as I get up off the bed and make my way down the hallway.

As I step into the family room, the sound of clattering dishes in the kitchen fills my ears, serving as a reminder of the mess I left behind last night.

My plan was to get up early and clean it all before my mom came home. But with Xander showing up and keeping me awake all night, everything got messed up.

I'm just standing there, watching her as she fills a glass at the sink.

She drinks the water, puts the glass upside down on the sink, and then turns to look at me. She points to the table. "Take a seat," she instructs.

I make my way over and sit in my usual spot at the table.

"How long has this been going on?" she asks, taking a seat across from me.

The tension in the room is palpable, like an electric current crackling through the air.

"How long has what been going on?" I play dumb on purpose, acting like I know nothing. If she's gonna act like a bitch, I will too.

"Stop it with the games, Poppy."

Glancing at my hands, I can't help but notice the faint marks left behind by my nails digging into my palms ever since she caught Xander and me in the room.

"About a week or so," I say, not letting on that it had really been just over three months.

"Can you tell me how it started?" She gets up and slowly walks around the table, her footsteps echoing on the tiles.

"I don't know," I shrug, not in the mood to engage in this conversation with her. It was none of her business what I did while I was here alone. If she hadn't found us this morning, she wouldn't have a clue about what was happening. There was no way I could tell her that Xander had been coming here for months. She'd be furious if she ever found out. I've never had the kind of relationship with my mother where I could openly share things. That dynamic was always reserved for my dad.

"What do you mean you don't know?" she asks, coming back to the table and bending down to look into my face, as if attempting to intimidate me into answering. "You must know, I'm not that naïve, Poppy."

"I don't know what you want me to say."

"Well, you're not to see that boy anymore. You hear me."

"You can't stop me." I get up from my seat, ready to leave the room.

"Oh yes I can, you're only seventeen."

"I'm eighteen in two weeks. And then, I'm free to do whatever I want."

"While you're under this roof, you will do as I say. Are we clear?"

"Well, maybe I don't want to live here anymore," I add. The thought of losing Xander in a matter of weeks was already distressing, but the notion of not being able to see him before he left was inconceivable. Furthermore, even after he left, I still wanted to keep in contact with him to hear about his new life and how things were progressing for him.

"Do you understand what I am saying, or do I need to make that call?"

I fight the urge to scream at her. "Yes, I understand. I will stay away from him."

I maintain a poker face to prevent revealing my lie. The mere thought of being apart from Xander is unfathomable. The impending end of school fills me with dread, knowing that his departure will shatter my heart. However, for now, I cherish having him in my life, despite the possibility that he might forget me once he achieves his fame. Until then, for the next five weeks, until he departs, we can secretly continue this friendship/relationship without getting caught. We just have to exercise extreme caution to avoid getting caught, like we did this morning.

"Poppy, can you guarantee you won't break your promise? I can always swing by during work hours to make sure you're keeping your word."

Drawing on my personal experiences over the years, I knew that she wouldn't simply drop by to check on me. Her work schedule lacks flexibility, making it difficult for her to leave whenever she wants. In my younger years, I often longed for her presence at my school events, but she couldn't leave work. So, why should this occasion be any different?

"Yes, Mom. I will stay away."

My comment brings a smile to her face, yet beneath the surface, I feel a twinge of shame for deceiving her. As she nods, I can't help but feel the weight of guilt as her blue eyes remain fixed on mine. But I knew the guilt would fade because Xander would be leaving soon, leaving my lie hidden.

"Can I go now?" I ask.

"I hate to say it, but you've disappointed me, Poppy," she sighs sadly.

I don't respond because I'm sure she'll totally see through me, see my lies.

"Hurry up and get to school," she says.

"I just need to quickly shower before I go," I explain, leaving her alone in the room.

Thank God, going to school suddenly seems like the best option to avoid her never-ending interrogation. She can't help herself. She always jumps on the bandwagon about something. But at least this way, I can still hang out with Xander, even if we don't really have conversations at school.

CHAPTER 28

Xander

What the fuck did I just do? The atmosphere in that room was so fucking tense, filled with the bitter scent of anger and disappointment. I made the mistake of leaving Poppy there alone to deal with her unpredictable mother, whose voice cut through the air like shattered glass.

I should have quietly slipped away last night while Poppy was sleeping, but my mind was clouded. All I wanted was a little more time with her, and in my intoxicated state, I must have dozed off. Instead of staying and facing the consequences, I did what I always do - I run when things get tough. Now, the weight of regret hangs over me like a suffocating cloak, knowing that I abandoned Poppy to handle everything alone. I should've just stuck around and dealt with the anger.

I've been pacing back and forth for the past half hour, contemplating whether I should go back and confess to her mother that it was my fault. I'm the one who initiated everything with Poppy. But how the fuck can I confess that I was the one who influenced her daughter to engage in those actions? And now, it has transformed into something else, something that stirs deep emotions.

Feeling frustrated, I kick one of the many whisky bottles strewn across the floor. When I got home this morning, my dad had already left for work, so I didn't have to worry about him being here. It never ceases to amaze me how he miraculously manages to pull himself together to head off to work.

Making my way towards the front door, I pull it open, knowing I need to go over there and have a conversation with her mother. It's crucial for her to know that things aren't what she thinks. I can already anticipate the things going through her mind, as people always assume the worst about me. Maybe it's because of my appearance or the fact that I usually don't care about anything or anyone. I must admit, I used to be that person, but now, I genuinely care about Poppy. How the fuck am I supposed to tell her any of this? I've never encountered a situation like this before, and honestly, I have no idea how to handle it.

Feeling the nerves coiling in my stomach, I gather my courage and make my way down to Poppy's house. The look her mom gave me this morning lingers in my mind. It made me feel worthless, like a hopeless case, as if I shouldn't even exist in this world. That look brought back so many memories of the insults my dad has thrown at me over the years, weakening my defenses even further.

Is this how life will always be, or is it just the people in this shitty town who perceive me this way? But this time, I'm determined to prove to Poppy's mother that I am something more, someone who won't simply walk away. She needs to know that I care about her daughter and that this is not just a casual hookup like she probably believes.

Last night, while I watched Poppy sleeping, I made up my mind to invite her to come along when we leave. I'm tired of hiding everything and, honestly, I couldn't care less about Ace's opinion because Poppy is my everything.

With a lump in my throat, I summon the courage to approach the house. My objective is to ease any worries Poppy's mother may have and reassure her that Poppy holds immense importance in my life. I must convey that I would never take advantage of her or harm her in any way. I know exactly how parents see me when I'm near their daughters.

I lift my head to glance at Poppy's house and catch sight of her mom glaring at me through the front window. Nervously, I gulp and mentally brace myself for whatever awaits me. Her intense stare adds an unexpected challenge to this task. With my hands securely tucked into my pockets, I cautiously take a step forward.

As I make my way down the front path, she vanishes from view.

Within seconds, she bursts out of the front door, swiftly shutting it behind her. Descending the three steps, she blocks my way to the house. She's staring me down with pure hate.

"What the hell do you want?" she hisses, suspicion narrowing in her eyes.

I fidget under her intense gaze as I absentmindedly run my hand over the rough stubble on my chin. "I apologize for leaving. It was a mistake. I want you to know that Poppy means a lot to me."

"Yeah, right! I know exactly the kind of person you are," she scoffs, bursting into laughter. "You must think I'm some sort of fool."

I find her mocking laughter incredibly irritating. It's disheartening that despite mustering up all my courage to express how much her daughter means to me, she continues to be so judgmental. It's frustrating.

"It's not a lie. Laugh all you want; I don't give a damn about what you think. I know the truth, and that truth is that Poppy means more to me than you can understand."

"Yeah, until the next girl comes around, and then you'll just toss her aside like you guys always do."

It really bothers me how she's talking about Poppy like that, but I choose to remain silent because I want to convey that she's mistaken. "You're right, that's how it was for me in the past. But things have changed. I'm not the same person anymore, and I have her to thank for that." I can't express my love for her daughter because I've never said those words to anyone other than when I whispered them to her last night when she was asleep. Even that was fucking scary to say out loud.

"Seriously, do you honestly believe that by saying that you can change the way I see you?"

"Probably not. Honestly, whatever I say won't change your opinion of me. I'm here because I didn't want her to face this by herself. I take the blame too, and I want you to know that."

She crosses her arms over her chest, a defensive gesture that clearly indicates her lack of interest in this conversation. "I couldn't give a damn about what you want. I'm telling you, keep your distance from my daughter."

"I'm sorry, I can't do that," I say, shaking my head.

If only she knew I've tried that already and it didn't work out.

I'm trying to stay calm to make the situation better for Poppy, but everything I say just seems to annoy this woman more.

Her face transforms into a piercing expression, her lips gradually thinning. "People like you just want to ruin everything for others because you're bored. You've got nothing going for you, yet you're trying to bring down someone who has a bright future ahead. I will not allow it."

Her words hit me like a punch, practically knocking me down, reminding me once again how worthless I am. "I think I've got a better grasp on Poppy's ambitions than you."

"You have no clue about my daughter. You don't know what's best for her."

"I know music is her passion and maybe you're a bit hesitant because she got it from her dad."

"You don't know anything about me or my daughter," she hisses, her voice laced with venom.

"You're wrong about that. I know more about her than you do."

She scans me, observing every inch of my being. "You haven't changed," she comments, her words dripping with disdain. "Your arrogance suggests you believe you're someone exceptional. Allow me to clarify that you hold no significance in this world. And you never will."

Each word she speaks effortlessly pierces through the barriers of my protective armor.

"Poppy is currently in the dark about who you truly are, but there will come a time when she realizes. She'll see how small you are in the grand scheme of things, just like the rest of us." She takes a step forward, fueled with anger, causing me to take a step back. "Your father sees it, too. We've all heard him calling you a worthless scumbag. And soon enough, I'll make sure Poppy sees it too. She'll see how you manipulate and exploit everyone and everything for your selfish gain. She'll see how you played her. And when that day comes, she'll see you in a whole new light. She'll realize what a lowlife you really are."

Her words pierce through me like a searing flame, leaving behind an agonizing ache in my chest. The mere thought of Poppy, with her kind nature and gentle eyes, perceiving me as insignificant is a notion too painful to handle. Despite her constant reassurance that I held value in her world, I couldn't fathom the possibility, nor did I wish to comprehend she would see what everyone else sees.

"Fuck you!" I spit. "You know fucking nothing about me?"

As I turn to leave, a surge of anger rushes through me, my face turning red in response to her hurtful words that continue to pour out without mercy.

"I'll make a point of telling her every day about how worthless you are until she gets it. Hopefully, she'll grasp the truth before you take everything from her. You'll ruin her whole life, and she'll never forgive you for it," she snaps, following me down the front path. "Let her go and move on with your life. Don't let her life be destroyed because of you."

My blood boils as I swiftly turn back to face her, causing her to halt in her tracks. "Fuck you. You think you know what's best for her? You don't even listen when she tells you what she wants to do," I snap. I've reached my limit. "I don't need to put up with your annoying shit any longer."

I suddenly wonder what Poppy is doing while all this is going on. Was she in the house listening? I glance at the front of the house to see if I can catch a glimpse of her.

"She's inside and does not wish to see you. Soon, you will hold no significance to her. Do yourself a favor and leave her alone before it's too late."

"Screw you," I hiss and turn away.

It's only now that I've realized my love for her, even though I've never expressed it. But is that truly enough in the harsh reality of life? I used to believe it was enough for my parents, but just look at how that shit turned out. Years of love disappeared in an instant, replaced by hate. Ace's parents faced a similar fate. I couldn't bear it if Poppy ended up hating me like that. I don't want her to see me like everyone else. I can't give her a good life yet, not until I make it. Once that happens, she'll see that I'm not the loser everyone thinks I am. She'll eventually see that I'm good enough for her.

Using the back of my hand, I gently wipe away a stray tear that rolls down my face. If I choose to stay in this shitty town, I know that resisting her will be nearly impossible. The magnetic pull between us is simply too strong. Over the past few months, she has had a profound impact on me, to the extent that I yearn for her presence. I ache to hear her infectious laughter, her clever remarks. I crave the beautiful sounds of her moans when I pleasure her body. I long to engage in conversation, to share the same breath, to become a part of her world. She means everything to me. She is everything I could ever want, and more. But once she sees me through the lens her mother predicts and perceives the same judgment of others, I fear I won't be able to bear it when she decides to walk out of my life.

I must leave immediately. I must create some distance between Poppy and myself. Whether or not Ace comes with me, I don't care, I need to leave. I cannot stay here any longer. The magnetic pull Poppy has on me is overpowering. I have to give her the freedom to live her own life, to discover her own path. Once I have accomplished my goals, I'll come back for her. That's when I'll be worthy of her.

When I arrive home, I forcefully push open the front door and then slam it shut, allowing the tears to stream down my face. The pain in my chest is excruciating as if someone has mercilessly scooped out my heart with a spoon.

I quickly pull out my phone from my pocket and text Ace.

Xander: Got to get out of this fucking town right now. You in, or am I going without you?

In just a few seconds, my phone screen lights up. Ace is calling me.

"What the fuck is going on?" Ace says.

"I'm done with this, man. It's a simple question. You in or out."

"Did your dad give you trouble again?"

"Just answer the damn question, Ace. In or out?"

"But I thought we were going to wait-"

"Plans change." I cut him off.

"Just tell me what the fuck happened, man."

"Don't sweat it. I'll pick up my guitar and head out on my own."

"I'm coming with you asshole. It's our dream."

"What are you doing now?" I ask, pacing the room. I kick an empty whisky bottle across the floor.

"Nothing. Just at school."

"I'll meet you at your place within the hour," I inform him.

"I'll swing by and pick you up. You at home?"

"Yeah, I'll start walking."

"Okay. See ya soon." He hangs up the call.

Heading to my room, I gather all my belongings, hastily stuffing clothes, guitar picks, and notebooks filled with years' worth of lyrics. Stepping out onto the street, I start walking towards Ace's house, knowing he'll come from that direction. I never once glance back at Poppy's house as I continue along the street. It's killing me that I'm walking away from her without saying goodbye or even letting her know I'm going.

Lost in my thoughts, I barely register Ace's car pulling up beside me. The scent of exhaust fumes hangs in the air as I navigate my way to the passenger's side. I open the door and settle into the well-worn leather seat, keeping my bag on my lap.

"Care to fill me in on what went down?" he asks, eyeing me.

"No."

"Is it something to do with Poppy?" he asks, watching me while I keep staring out the front windscreen.

"No, and I've already fucking told you a hundred times she's not my girlfriend. She isn't my type."

I can't even look at him, because he'll see right through me.

"Why don't you cut the crap and just tell me the fucking truth already?" He steps on the gas, speeding down the street.

"There's nothing to tell, that's why."

My phone vibrates in my pocket, but I don't bother to check it because I already know who it's from.

In silence, we sit in the car, Ace is clearly pissed at me for lying. I have no intention to tell him any of it.

At last, we reach Ace's garage. He parks the car and then gets out. I pause for a moment, watching him through the windshield as he strides forward and disappears into the garage. I take a deep breath, open the car door, and casually throw my bag in the back seat.

As I enter the garage, I immediately spot Ace packing up his keyboard. Though he briefly glances up, I find it hard to meet his gaze. The last thing I want is to tell him what's happened, fearing that I'll completely fall apart in front of him. All I can think about is getting away from this place, no matter what it takes. Moving towards the area where I keep Poppy's father's guitar, I pause for a moment, overwhelmed by guilt for what I'm about to put her through. I can feel Ace's eyes still fixed on me as I move forward.

My phone pings again, reminding me of the unread message.

"You gonna get that or keep dodging it like this fucking conversation?" Ace remarks, neatly rolling up the keyboard cord.

Slipping my hand into my pocket, I glance at my phone, feeling Ace's unwavering stare. Even though I haven't mentioned anything about Poppy to him, I'm certain he knows the message is from her, because of my resistance to check it earlier. But I won't let him see the extent of my heartbreak over this girl, as he would never truly understand what we had. Poppy's message crashes over me like a tidal wave of anguish, causing my knees to nearly buckle.

Princess: Hey. I'm still alive and kicking. See you at school.

I slide my phone into my pocket. "You ready?" I ask, grabbing my guitar.

"Do I look fucking ready?" he snaps. "I still gotta pack clothes, sort out the mic, and get some other shit together."

I put my guitar on the worn-out couch and walk over to the mic. As I pack it up, I feel Ace's intense gaze. "Can you stop fucking staring at me?"

"Not until you tell me what went down."

"Nothing happened. I just want out of this bullshit town. That's all."

"That's a load of crap. I know you, Xander. I can tell when something's off. Now, give it to me straight."

"I'll meet you in the car," I say, grabbing the mic and my guitar, and swiftly making my way out the door.

As I wait for Ace, I grab my phone and open the message from Poppy. My fingers effortlessly glide over the keys as I start typing a reply.

Xander: Sorry, but I have to go. Ace and I are hitting the road. Catch you later.

But my fingers freeze up and I hit the back button, deleting all my words. I stop for a second, my head all jumbled up with different thoughts. Should I even send a message? I can't send that to her like she's just some random chick. But then again, I'm leaving without even saying anything to her. That's a total dog move on my part.

Taking a deep breath, I try once again, my fingers moving slowly this time.

Xander: Hey Poppy, Ace and I are leaving town today. Bye.

As I reach the end of my message, a wave of hesitation washes over me. My finger hovers with uncertainty above the send button, unsure of what to do. Doubt begins to creep in once again, making me question whether I should send this to her. How the fuck can I do it? Sending this message will undoubtedly cause her pain, but leaving without telling her would also inflict a different kind of hurt.

Taking a deep breath, I'm unsure of what to do. Normally, I wouldn't think twice about causing someone harm, but with her, it just doesn't sit well. I pause, my finger hovering over the back button, contemplating whether or not to send the message. I decide against it and delete it, tucking my phone back into my pocket. Now all I can do is hope that Poppy will eventually be okay with me leaving. If we ever cross paths again, I'll have the opportunity to explain everything to her then.

Ace appears, a large bag hanging from his shoulder and his reliable keyboard grasped in his hands. He heads towards the back of the car, cautiously placing everything into the trunk. After a short pause, he goes back inside the building, only to emerge again carrying his electric guitar and another armful of possessions. Eventually, he shuts the trunk and settles himself in the driver's seat, plopping down with a sigh.

"You sure about this?" he asks.

"Yeah, I'm sure," I reply.

Despite the overwhelming heartbreak, I find solace in the fact that this tough decision will allow Poppy to chase her own happiness, proving her mother wrong. I will always hold her dear to my heart, and I am determined to enrich her life. If that means I have to step away, then I will do so selflessly.

CHAPTER 29
Poppy

It's been two days already, and I have received no response from Xander. I haven't seen him at school, and the same goes for Ace. Ever since that morning when my mother caught us, Xander hasn't bothered to come to the house.

Initially, I assumed he was intentionally keeping a low profile. However, as rumors started circulating around school, with Jade discovering Xander and Ace's departure, it deeply affected me. The rumors seemed all too real, especially since I hadn't even caught a glimpse of Xander walking down to the 7-Eleven. I must admit, I even sat by the window, hoping to see him pass by. It's pathetic, I know. But when the truth finally hit me that he was truly gone, it genuinely hurt. It hit me on a personal level that Xander didn't have the courtesy of letting me know he was leaving.

I honestly thought he cared about me. It was clear in the tenderness of his touch and the warmth in his gaze. But now, his silence hits hard, making it clear to me that I mean nothing to him.

It's surreal to consider how different life was before Xander came along.

Now, I'm struggling to manage without him. The past few months of having him with me constantly have truly changed me. I always knew our time together would be short-lived, and I understood that I'd have to adjust when it ended. However, I never expected it to be this difficult.

As I make my way through the school corridor, I can't help but feel a deep void of pain. I really don't want to think about anything right now. It's like the hurt is suffocating me. All I want is to find a quiet place and cry my heart out. I've shed so many tears already. I keep wondering, why would he do this to me? Why did he keep hanging out with me, only to end up tossing me aside?

Nevertheless, the agony amplifies as Jade reveals to the entire group she has had contact with Xander, and he is thriving. She mentions that they have found a place to live and are eagerly waiting for an opportunity to be discovered.

Standing alone at my locker, I feel the pain of her words, as if they were stabbing my heart. The sound of her voice carries across the hallway, spreading the news to everyone nearby. So I just stand there and endure the torment in silence.

It's a never-ending pain, knowing he lied to me. How he callously cast me aside, treating me as if I held no value. On top of the pain of losing him, I also have to deal with my mom who keeps verbally bashing Xander and questioning my judgment.

At first, I had his back and would defend him, but now it's easier to just walk away in case I say something I'll regret. I'm constantly angry, mostly with myself, but especially with him.

Now that the fear of Xander's threat to expose Ace's video has diminished, Jade has resumed her relentless teasing about my weight. As I walk closer, I see Jade, Savannah, and their little group up ahead. Usually, I would steer clear of this area to avoid any run-ins with them, but today, it doesn't really matter. They can say whatever they want because their words can't hurt me any more than I'm already hurting.

"Hey, fatty," Jade sneers. "You've been so quiet. Is your mouth still stuffed with food?"

The group bursts into laughter, their mocking taunts resonating through the air.

I try to go around them, but they step forward and block the path.

"What's the matter? No witty comeback? Are you going into shock because you haven't eaten in, like, the last ten seconds?"

That's enough. I can't handle her relentless, fat-shaming remarks anymore. I've truly had my fill of her today. Consumed by anger, I grab hold of the ridiculous shirt she's wearing today and forcefully slam her against the lockers.

The shock in her eyes is evident as she struggles to comprehend what the fuck I'm doing, and honestly, I'm just as surprised by my actions. It's as if I've become a ticking time bomb, ready to explode at any given moment.

"Shut your fucking mouth," I hiss. "Or I'll do it for you."

Behind me, I hear a firm voice.

"Poppy Reeves, get to the principal's office now."

I release a long breath. Just what I need, more ammunition for my mother to manipulate me into doing what she wants after I graduate. My grip on Jade's shirt tightens, my eyes lock on her with intense, burning hatred. "If you ever talk to me like that again, bitch, I won't just grab your shirt the next time."

"Let go, Miss Reeves!" Mr. Simpson shouts, coming up behind me. I can feel him towering over me. I let go of her shirt but stay put for now.

"He s-said to get away from me." I can hear the fear in Jade's voice, and I like it. Maybe now she'll think twice before stirring up more trouble.

Stepping back, I navigate through the crowd as they part to let me walk down the corridor toward the principal's office. People start chatting behind me, and I can feel them staring. But I couldn't care less about it.

As my week-long suspension is coming to an end, my mother wastes no time putting me to work, just as she promised. She took some extra time off, so today I spent most of the day assisting her with spring cleaning. Essentially, we were decluttering the accumulation of things she had gathered over the years. Sometimes, it feels like she purposely does this to annoy me. However, amidst all the unnecessary items, I stumble upon a few belongings that were once my father's, which I did not know she had kept. Of course, she remains completely unaware that I discovered them. As far as she knows, we discarded them in the trash.

The dynamics of our conversation have undergone a shift. Rather than criticizing my father, she now focuses on belittling Xander, making him the primary topic of discussion. She constantly reminds me that I held no significance to him. She tells me that after he got what he wanted, he distanced himself from me completely, taking advantage of me. Occasionally, her words hold some truth, as there are moments when I believe they are accurate and that he had manipulated me like he manipulates everyone. However, deep down, I can't help but feel that it was more than just manipulation. Our connection surpassed that. It was something greater, something that she or anyone else could never truly comprehend.

CHAPTER 30

Xander

It has been three weeks since Ace and I left, and during this time, my meals have been scarce. The persistent hunger that plagued me for years has finally vanished. I now have more urgent matters to attend to instead of constantly fixating on my next meal. Nevertheless, I have been consuming excessive amounts of alcohol as a coping mechanism. It helps alleviate the pain, but I still cannot stop thinking about all the texts Poppy has sent. All of which I leave unanswered.

Ace totally lost it yesterday, accusing me of turning into my father. When he said that, it hit me hard and made me realize I need to change. There's no way I'm ever going to be anything like that heartless prick.

So, I finally got off my lazy ass and found a job as a kitchen hand. I have to admit, I truly detest it. The primary focus of this job mainly centers on washing dishes, but I suppose it's only a temporary gig until we can come across our lucky break.

Sadly, Ace and I are living in the biggest dump that surpasses anything I've encountered before. And trust me, I've seen some shady shit. The place is deteriorating, with walls riddled with holes and the sound of clanging pipes whenever the water is turned on. Adding to that, this apartment is infested with shady characters, like drug dealers, prostitutes, and folks from all walks of life. I suppose if my father or even Poppy's mother were to witness my current living situation, they would probably deem it a perfect match for me.

Ace bolted out of our apartment yesterday when he heard someone playing the drums. Turns out, the music was coming from the apartment upstairs. By sheer luck, Nate, a skilled drummer, and Theo, a talented bass player, were actually seeking to form a band. Can you believe the odds of that? Suddenly, we stumbled upon the perfect additions to our band, the ones Ace and I were eagerly waiting for. Unfortunately, I haven't had a chance to meet them that day because I was totally wasted.

But today Ace is taking me upstairs to meet these two guys. I know I should be more excited about it because everything is finally falling into place. However, there's a dark storm cloud hanging over my head as I step into each new day.

I haven't touched my guitar since we got here, it's just too painful. Whenever I see that guitar, I feel so guilty because it reminds me of what I did. But Ace said I had to bring it along with me when I meet these two guys today. I just hope the effort today pays off in the end, and why the fuck did he not bring along his own guitar?

I'm standing next to Ace, gripping my guitar tightly, as he knocks on the door of the apartment above ours.

He looks my way. "You could show a little more excitement. These two inside might be the perfect fit we've been looking for."

I opt to remain silent, still angry with Ace for texting Jade and filling her in on the recent events. I have no doubt that Jade, being the gossip she is, would eagerly share the details with everyone. If word of this reaches Poppy, I don't even want to imagine what she must be thinking. Before Ace can say anything else, the door swings open.

In front of me stands a guy with short blond hair, proudly displaying his tattooed chest while wearing a pair of sweatpants. There's another guy next to him, with shoulder-length brown hair, same style as mine, also shirtless and only wearing boxers. They both seem to be around the same age as Ace and me. The guy in boxers has his arm around a cute little blonde, who is wearing a snug red dress that clings to her figure. And I notice straight away she's way too skinny, her figure resembling a stick with no curves whatsoever.

"Hey," says the first guy in surprise when he spots Ace and me standing by the door.

I see the blonde girl lean in and give the boxer guy a kiss, leaving a smudge of red lipstick on his cheek. Then she goes to the other guy holding the door and also kisses him.

"Don't forget to call me," she says, running her fingers down his tattooed chest.

The blonde gives Ace a once-over, and then her blue eyes meet mine. She smirks in a playful way, letting me know she's interested. But I choose to look down, focusing on the floor in front. I used to be all about that, looking for a place to put my cock, but now I can't even bring myself to do that. I'm totally screwed. Completely broken. And it's killing me.

"Xander, this is Nate," Ace says, introducing the first guy in sweatpants.

"Hey," I add, shaking his hand.

"And this is Theo," Nate says, pointing at the guy next to him.

"Hey," I add, reaching out to shake his hand.

"Theo plays bass and Nate's on drums," says Ace.

"Hey, cool guitar, dude," Theo says. "You guys want to come in?"

Nate steps back, holding the door open wider for us to come in.

"Sure," Ace says, entering the room.

As I venture further into the small apartment, I can't help but notice how similar it is to our own less-than-ideal living space. Countertops cluttered with pizza boxes and beer bottles, clothes and miscellaneous items strewn across the floor. Positioned near the back window is a set of drums, providing these guys with a view of the nearby park. In contrast, the window in our shabby apartment falls short, unable to offer a glimpse beyond a boring brick wall.

With his guitar in hand, Theo walks out of the room and takes a seat beside me. I'm taken aback by his spontaneous gesture of offering me his guitar, which leaves me pondering his intentions. However, he quickly breaks into a mischievous grin. "I'll show you mine if you show me yours," he playfully remarks.

His playful joke makes me laugh. Right from the start, I instantly take a liking to Theo, but I'm not quite certain about the other guy, Nate. Personally, I think Nate's a bit too serious for me.

I pass my guitar to Theo, and in exchange, I grab hold of his. Resting it on my lap, I strum a few chords. It's pleasant, but it doesn't quite compare to the guitar that Poppy gifted me. Casting a glance at Theo, I witness his fingers gracefully pluck the strings, and a smile appears on his face when our eyes connect. He, like me, truly appreciates the craftsmanship of a well-made guitar.

As we jam on our guitars, our fingers effortlessly slide across the frets, creating a sweet rhythm.

Meanwhile, seated on the adjacent couch, Nate and Ace are engrossed in a deep conversation about the band, the music, and various other topics. Every now and then, they pause their discussion to watch Theo and me playing our guitars.

Theo and I spend a few hours jamming together, and I take the chance to teach him a few chords from my songs. He catches on quickly, and soon we're jamming together. Nate wastes no time and joins in, getting up from the couch and heading over to his drum set. His exceptional drumming skills make it clear why Ace wanted to get to know him before anyone else could snatch him up.

Ace heads down, grabs his guitar, and then we jam for the rest of the afternoon. The way these two boys interact and support each other is truly remarkable, making them the perfect duo for our band, Broken Oasis. We instantly connect, and it's clear that Nate and Theo are enthusiastic about joining our band and learning more of our music.

As I play the guitar and sing, it feels good, and the familiar melody takes me to a peaceful place. Deep down, I know it'll take time to heal and let go of Poppy. However, with our band members now in place, I can effortlessly immerse myself in the power of music.

The room overflows with music as we keep playing our instruments, and without realizing it, the sun disappears, and darkness envelops the world beyond.

We bring the evening to a close with a late-night jam session, indulging in pizza and savoring beers. Our band takes center stage in our conversation, but the threat of our neighbors calling the cops forces us to tone it down.

Despite Ace and I seeing our dreams come true and everything falling into place, there's still a lingering gloom that I can't seem to shake off.

CHAPTER 31
Poppy

With only a week left of school, I'm counting down the days until I can finally escape this awful place and its awful bitches.

It's odd how Jade consistently narrates Xander and Ace's activities as if she's bursting to tell everyone the gossip. It always hurts to hear that she's been in touch with them. Nevertheless, I make it a point to linger near my locker every morning, just to eavesdrop on their latest updates. However, it's always the same tired story on repeat. They're still figuring things out, hoping that their band will get discovered any day now.

However, the biggest thing I've been avoiding is the fact that my period is two weeks late. Deep down, I know I should go and get a pregnancy test, but there's a part of me that just wants to ignore the whole situation. If it turns out to be positive and I am indeed pregnant, I have absolutely no idea what I'm going to do.

My mother keeps reminding me every day how close I came to ruining my life if she hadn't stepped in. I'm not entirely sure what she means by that since she didn't actually prevent anything. Xander was the one who walked away. I have no idea what I will do if I am pregnant with Xander's child. I don't know what my next steps should be. He hasn't even responded to any of my texts. All I can say for certain is that my mother will be furious and make my life even more of a nightmare than it already is. I just pray to God that I'm not pregnant.

Maybe I'm not pregnant after all. It could just result from the stress I've been dealing with lately. Xander always used a condom, but that one night we were together, he was drunk, and now I can't be certain. I've been trying to replay that night in my mind, desperately trying to remember if he used one. But I can't say for sure. The rush of seeing him again caught me off guard when he climbed through my window. He was so wasted, the most intoxicated I've ever seen him, even worse than that time when his father hurt him. So maybe he wore a condom and I have nothing to worry about... or maybe he didn't. Oh, damn, I don't even want to think about that.

However, I can no longer avoid dealing with this matter. It is time for me to confront it directly. Today, I will gather the courage to face this issue head-on. Once school is over, I will head to the pharmacy to buy what I need. Later, when my mother is at work, I will take the test. By doing it this way, if the result turns out positive, I can spare myself from breaking down in front of her.

With the school day finally over, I have reached my breaking point with Jade's relentless name-calling. Sneaking into the pharmacy without drawing any attention to myself, I feel an overwhelming sense of panic as I hastily grab three pregnancy tests. Three, because I need to be absolutely certain. I quickly pay with my card, grab the three boxes, and get ready to bolt out of the pharmacy.

My goal is to reach home before my mother can once again lecture me for being a few minutes late from school. It feels like she's constantly watching my every move, suspicious that I might be up to no good. But as I spin around, ready to dash out, I see Mrs. Reynolds standing right behind me, smiling.

Oh no. Out of everyone in this town, it had to be her standing there. Mrs. Reynolds happens to be a friend of my mother's and also the town gossip.

"Oh, hi Poppy," she greets me, tilting her head to catch a peek at what I'm holding.

I quickly shift my hands behind my back, attempting to hide the pregnancy tests from view, desperately hoping they go unnoticed. However, to my disappointment, it's clear from the surprised look on her face that she's already seen them.

Our eyes meet in an instant. "Does your mother know about this?"

Without knowing what to say to her, I instinctively blurt out the first thing that pops into my head. "Oh, these aren't mine. I'm just grabbing them for a friend," I hastily reply.

Her eyes filled with skepticism, narrow with doubt. "Then why isn't your friend here getting them with you?" she questions, her tone revealing her disbelief.

Oh, crap. I instantly regret my impulsive response.

"Next!" The girl at the counter yells and I let out a sigh of relief, glad I don't have to answer a bunch of questions.

When Mrs. Reynolds passes, I quickly run down the aisle and rush to my car. As I reach my car, I quickly open the door and practically dive inside, seeking refuge from the outside world. In a hurry, I stash all three pregnancy kits in the glove compartment, start the engine, and head home. Throughout the drive home, I silently pray that my mom's nosy friend will keep today's incident to herself. Maybe she bought my lies, or maybe she'll just forget about it. God, I really hope so. The last thing I want is for my mother to find out that I might be pregnant. But keeping it quiet won't matter if I'm pregnant because she'll find out, eventually. Still, until I know for sure, I've got to keep it quiet. I park my car in the driveway, in my usual spot, and shut off the engine.

As I lean forward to retrieve my bag from the footwell on the passenger side floor, I completely overlook my mother standing on the patio, patiently awaiting my arrival. The stern expression on her face indicates that something is amiss. Could it be possible that Mrs. Reynolds has already spilled the beans? *Just stay calm, she might not know yet.*

I get out of the car, sling my bag on my shoulder, and close the door. Walking towards the house, I see her intense stare and know trouble's coming.

In an effort to deflect her intense glare, I reach into my pocket and casually pull out my phone. I begin absentmindedly scrolling through it, pretending to be deeply engrossed in something important.

After a quick moment, I slide my phone back into my pocket and rush up the stairs, taking them two at a time.

"Poppy," she says, arms crossed. "Is there something you want to share?"

"No," I declare, pushing past her.

"Poppy," she says again, firmer this time. She snatches my arm, halting me in my tracks. I feel her strong, insistent grip on my arm, knowing that my mother won't let go until she finds out what she needs to know. "Show me your bag," she demands.

"Why?" And I can already foresee what is about to happen. I've never been a fan of that nosy bitch, Mrs. Reynolds. She always interferes with everyone's business. But it's unbelievable that in under ten minutes, she has already snitched on me.

My mother forcefully pulls my bag off my shoulder and starts searching through my satchel, clearly determined to find the pregnancy tests. After failing to locate them, she looks up.

"Where are they?"

"Where are what?"

She sighs, clearly frustrated. "Poppy, Andrea phoned me. Why didn't you just tell me?"

I'm contemplating the idea of lying about the pregnancy tests and pretending they were for a friend. But what if it turns out to be true and I am pregnant? Perhaps it would be better to be honest now rather than later.

"How Mom? How could I tell you when all you do is criticize Xander? You clearly hate him. How can I explain to you that I'm hurting because he's gone and that there's a possibility I might be pregnant?"

"And that's where the problem lies, my dear. That's exactly why you should have stayed away from him. Look at the mess you're in now, all because of that lowlife."

I knew that attempting to engage her in conversation would only result in another onslaught of hurtful words aimed at Xander. I have no interest in enduring her relentless ranting about him, especially since I have more pressing matters to attend to. It truly puzzles me why I even entertained the idea of discussing my problems with her.

With a surge of anger, I forcefully snatch my satchel from her hand and head back to the car. After I open the passenger's door, I retrieve the three pregnancy tests from the glove compartment. Their weight serves as a poignant reminder of the significance of this moment. As I near the house, I sense my mother's eyes tracking my every move. When I reach her on the front patio, I quickly walk around her and enter the house, leaving her standing outside.

The sound of her rapid footsteps echoes behind me, but luckily, I am faster. I quickly make my way to my room and swiftly enter the bathroom, ensuring to turn the lock just in time before my mother approaches. With my heart pounding in my chest, I grab the pregnancy test and tear open the box.

Ignoring the persistent knocking on the bathroom door from my mother, I stare at myself in the mirror. I feel a strong urge to confront this situation head-on. I have no clue how my life will change if the results are positive. But one thing I know is that if I am pregnant, I'll be trapped under my mom's control, with no other choices or places to go.

Letting out a sigh, I release the breath I've been holding and make my way over to the toilet to take the test.

"Poppy, open this door right now!" my mother demands, pounding her palm forcefully against it.

Tearing open the plastic sleeve, I retrieve the test and pee on the stick, attempting to block out my mother's voice and her pounding on the door.

Desperately, I pray to God, hoping that my lateness is just a delay and not a pregnancy. Please, please, please don't let me be pregnant.

The knocking abruptly ceases, leaving a chilling stillness on the other side of the door. I can't help but wonder if my mother has finally left my room.

In an attempt to distract myself, I reach for my phone, set the timer, and settle onto the tiles, leaning against the vanity. The wait is excruciating, each passing second stretching on like an eternity. If I am pregnant, what will I do? Xander has been avoiding my calls and texts ever since he left. I have no clue how else to get in touch with him to let him know.

As soon as the timer goes off, I am immediately brought back to reality, and a shiver runs down my spine. Despite the lump forming in my throat, I muster up the strength to stand, prepared to confront the test results with a newfound sense of bravery. I understand that these next few seconds possess the potential to alter the course of my life.

My heart pounds and the nerves consume me, as I approach the spot where I left the test beside the bathtub. The sight of the word "pregnant" sends my heart sinking, and in an instant, tears flood my eyes. Panic washes over me like a crashing wave. With a heavy heart, I sit on the edge of the bathtub, totally focused on the test. The results leave me in utter disbelief. Oh My God... I'm pregnant.

How on earth did this happen? Now what am I supposed to do? How can I tell my mom without getting an earful about my screw-up?

Feeling overwhelmed by the fear of how my mother will react, I quickly brush away my tears using the back of my hand. I can't help but wonder if she's still out there waiting for me to share the information with her.

Slowly, I make my way across to the door.

With my ear pressed against it, I eagerly listen for any sounds coming from the other side. After confirming that it's safe, I cautiously unlock the door, preparing myself for any unexpected noises or movements. Much to my astonishment, I discover my mother sitting on the edge of my bed.

As the door creaks open, she lifts her head and her gaze falls upon my tear-streaked face, a clear indication of my sorrow. Anticipating a barrage of angry and hurtful words, I steel myself for the storm. However, much to my surprise, she stands before me, arms wide open, ready to embrace me.

"Oh, come here, my child."

I approach her slowly, tears streaming down my face. In that rare moment, I find solace in the warmth of my mother's comforting embrace as tears flow uncontrollably.

Chapter 32

Xander

Every Sunday night, Nate and Theo throw a party, just like they've been doing since the day we met them. Although I wouldn't necessarily call it a full-blown party. It's mostly just the two of them, Ace, me, and a few adventurous girls who are up for anything.

I'm currently lounging on the couch, taking sips from a bottle of Jack and indulging in a joint while Ace happily entertains himself with two girls on the nearby couch.

Nate and Theo are huddled together in a dimly lit corner of the room, with a girl squeezed between them. They always prefer to share a girl rather than going solo, and it's surprising to see how much the girls seem to enjoy it based on the noises they make.

There's a blonde next to me on the couch, rubbing my cock through my jeans, trying to get me aroused, but it's not working. Once again, my cock is a no-show for the party.

Taking a sip of whisky and inhaling from my joint, I close my eyes and focus on her touch as she strokes my cock. Maybe if I could just fuck someone else, then maybe I could move on from this fucked up mess in my head. Although her touch doesn't turn me on, the feeling of her hand on my cock is pleasant and soothing. Not at all like Poppy, who was on a whole other level. Just being in her presence got me so damn horny, and when she touched me, I went fucking wild. I feel my dick thicken, coming to life just at the thought of the things we did. Maybe I'll give this chick beside me a shot. It might help me get back on track and finally move on from Poppy. Leaning my head back against the couch, I surrender to the soothing sensations of her touch.

"You like that," she whispers, sensing my arousal.

"Shh, don't speak," I respond, not wanting her to ruin the moment for my dick down there to realize it's not who he thinks it is.

"Want me to suck your dick?"

"No," I firmly tell her. "Now shut the fuck up."

No chance I can let some girl give me head when I can't even handle a simple hookup without freaking out. But one day, I'll be my old self again. I just need a bit of time. But nothing and no one will ever compare to the mind-blowing blowjobs Poppy used to give me. Just thinking about her lips on my cock gets me rock hard. But this girl next to me stroking my cock seems to think it's because of her. She shifts and I feel her getting closer, her tits touching my arm. I crack one eye open, wondering what the fuck she is doing, only to realize she's going in for a kiss.

What the fuck does she think she's playing at? I quickly turn my head to avoid her lips, but they unexpectedly land on the side of my face. Anger overwhelms me, and I forcefully push her away.

"What the fuck are you doing?" I yell, causing her to fall to the floor, landing on her ass.

As I rise from the couch, anger courses through me as I cast my gaze upon her. It's unbelievable that this girl would even dare to kiss me. I simply have no desire for any more hookups that involve kissing.

On the couch opposite, Ace leans forward, his eyes sweeping the room before coming back to me. The two girls seated on either side of him pause briefly, intrigued by my actions.

Breaking the silence, Ace speaks up. "What's the problem?"

The girl who had just moments ago been stroking my cock suddenly stands up and glares at me, clearly annoyed.

"Wow, I can't believe I was going to fuck you, you jerk," she snaps.

She stomps across the room and sits down next to her friend on the couch beside Ace.

Honestly, I couldn't care less. Let him have her. I'm not bothered. She was never the right fit for me, anyway. Sure, she may have been blonde, but something just didn't feel right about her. Even my dick could tell, because I had to close my eyes and picture someone else just to get turned on.

"Chill out, man," Ace says, coming over to me with his boner poking out, and the three girls on the couch all look at me.

"Fuck it, I'm done," I announce, making a beeline for the exit. I quickly grab my jacket but decide against putting it on, unwilling to let go of the whiskey bottle and the joint. All I crave right now is to escape this place. I thought I was getting better, but that text from Poppy earlier today has sent me spiraling back into despair. All I want tonight is to get high and momentarily escape from the problems of this world.

For weeks now, Ace has been determined to get me laid. He's introduced me to several chicks, and there have been many opportunities to hook up at the parties organized by Nate and Theo. However, I just haven't been able to bring myself to take part. Even tonight, when that girl started messing around with my cock, I knew she was a sure thing, but I wasn't into it. I wish I could go back to the days when I could fuck anyone before Poppy entered my life. I just wanna get laid and be done with it, but it's proving to be a challenge. Poppy's presence still lingers in my thoughts. I can recall the feeling of her body under my touch, her unique scent, the sounds she made, and how I couldn't tear my gaze away from her beautiful face when she came on my cock.

Even the noises coming from the chick Nate and Theo had over in the corner were messing with my head. There's no way I could hang around and be reminded of what I left behind. It's just too painful.

Making my way downstairs to the ground floor, I navigate through a crowd of people who are passed out or completely wasted. Since I arrived, I've been intentionally ignoring a girl who has been giving me flirty looks, clearly showing her interest in hooking up. She's a gothic chick, the type of person I usually find intriguing and could have a wild time with. However, even that no longer holds any appeal for me.

Tonight, as a gentle coolness fills the air, I pause to slip on my jacket. I flip up the collar, determined to shield myself from the cold. With a purposeful stride, I make my way toward my secluded sanctuary - the refuge I seek when I need to be alone with my thoughts.

I settle on the hill, ready to immerse myself in the soothing embrace of alcohol, hoping it will ease the weight of my sorrow.

Each time I come to this place, I am drawn to the breathtaking city down below. The shimmering lights gracefully dance upon the water's surface, creating a captivating reflection.

Even in the late hour and darkness, the streets are alive with the bustling presence of people, jogging, and walking their dogs. I can't help but stare at the electrifying flashes of lightning in the distance, telling me a storm is coming. The air carries a faint scent of rain, heightening the anticipation of the impending downpour.

As I retrieve my phone from my pocket, my attention is captivated by the image of Poppy that I had been admiring earlier. It's the snapshot taken when I brought her home, a memory that was once cherished and proudly displayed as my screensaver, now absent due to our separation. My gaze wanders over the contours of her face, appreciating the gentle slope of her chin, the elegant prominence of her cheekbones. Her hair playfully covering her eyes while she's asleep.

It's almost cruel how my mind continuously tortures me, reminding me of every contour of her body and every tiny flaw she despised, which I thought was nothing less than perfection. In an attempt to find solace, I switch over to the text message she sent me earlier today.

Princess: Xander, ring me or answer your phone, please. We need to talk ASAP. It can't wait.

I unscrew the lid and take another guzzle, the warm, brown liquid soothes my throat, fulfilling the craving I've had since I walked away from her. Each gulp slowly eases the pain. While enjoying the effects of another hit from my joint, I casually scroll through the many text messages she's sent me over the weeks, messages that I've neglected to respond to. Guilt seeps in like a relentless poison, intertwining its presence within the very essence of my being. She's the first girl who's made me feel something, but I just tossed her aside like she was meaningless. Perhaps she hates me now. Maybe these last few weeks have shown her how worthless I really am.

With another sip of whisky, I summon the courage to dial her number. It rings twice before she picks up.

"Oh my God, Xander," her voice resonates, causing a rush of memories to swirl in my mind like a hurricane. The way she effortlessly pronounces my name with those lips sends a chilling sensation down my spine. Her voice serves as a constant reminder of the pain in my chest, the agonizing guilt that courses through my body for abandoning her.

Then I can't help but recall the hurtful words uttered by her mother, words that have haunted me ever since. They serve as a constant reminder that I am not good enough for Poppy. I fear that one day she will realize what everyone else sees - that I am a worthless, insignificant person in this world. It's as if I will never measure up to the person I should be for her. Swallowing becomes a struggle as a lump forms in my throat, hindering my ability to speak. I no longer feel like a man, but rather a feeble, voiceless coward who is unable to stand up for himself. It seems that I am incapable of providing anything for her, not even my own voice.

"Xander, are you still there?" she asks, her voice trembling with an unmistakable sense of desperation.

I cut off the call, but the echo of her melodic voice lingers in my mind like a haunting symphony. I let out a deep sigh and cover my face with my hands, feeling the weight of regret seeping through my fingertips.

The piercing sound of my phone ringing, loud and distinct, cuts through the peaceful silence. I let it ring, while my eyes stay on her photo displayed on the screen. I hesitate to answer, because what could I possibly say to her? How can I find the right words to explain my reasons for walking away? Perhaps one day, my newfound fame will validate me, proving that I am now deserving of her. Maybe, just maybe, she will find it in her heart to forgive me for all the terrible things I have done to her.

Instead of answering, I let the call go to voicemail. But, to my surprise, the phone won't quit ringing. In frustration, I press the reject button. The ringing persists, now reaching its fourth cycle, pushing me to my breaking point. I suddenly rise, leaving my bottle of Jack on the hill, and hastily head towards the water. I can't take this torment anymore. There is only one way to bring an end to it all.

"Please Princess, don't hate me for what I've done," I murmur, my voice tinged with sorrow, tears pooling in my eyes. With a heavy heart, I fling my phone towards the murky depths of the water, its screen flickering to life once again with yet another incoming call. A distant splash reverberates through the air, intensifying the pain in my chest.

I dream of being by her side someday, and I'm getting more desperate with each passing second. Yet, I am afraid of her witnessing the version her mother predicted she would eventually encounter. I never want to see that look on her face when she realizes everyone is correct. Especially since she's always seen me in a different light, appreciating my individuality and assuring me I'm truly something special.

"I'm so sorry, Princess. I need to put myself first so we can have a future. Then I'll be good enough for you."

As the gentle drizzle lightly kisses the earth, I redirect my focus back towards the hill, ready to sit in the rain and relish every drop of whisky left in my bottle.

CHAPTER 33

Ace

It's been six months since we got here to chase our dreams, and Xander still isn't himself. I know for a fact he hasn't hooked up with anyone during this time. Despite the many attempts from eager girls, he prefers getting wasted on his bottle of Jack or smoking a joint. This behavior is unlike the Xander I know. He's definitely not okay. He's become more of a loner, keeping to himself most of the time. We hardly talk anymore and our experiences aren't the same. I miss the connection I had with my brother, the one who used to confide in me.

I'm not sure what went down between him and Poppy Reeves that made him so determined to leave earlier than we planned. I've asked him multiple times, but he just tells me to leave him alone. So I haven't brought it up for months now. However, there's still a noticeable tension in the air, almost like he's hiding something and doesn't want to talk about it.

It turned out to be fortunate that we left when we did because everything fell into place. If we hadn't, I'm confident that Nate Reynolds, the drummer, would have been recruited by another band. Now, he and his friend Theo are part of Broken Oasis, and I must say, they fit in perfectly. Although Xander now spends more time with Theo than with me, they enjoy hanging out, having a drink, sharing a joint, and jamming on their guitars together. I do miss the good old days when Xander and I used to do that. However, at least he's slowly getting back to some sense of normalcy and no longer sitting there, feeling miserable like he did during the first month after we arrived.

The past few months have been a whirlwind for us. I kicked things off by leaving demo tapes at local bars and ended up getting us two gigs per week. Suddenly, everything took off at full speed.

At first, we performed for small crowds of around ten or fifteen people. However, as word spread, more and more people started showing up. Eventually, the demand grew so much that the bar had to sell tickets, and every night became a sold-out show. It's insane to see how much attention we were getting. Before we knew it, record labels started showing interest.

Just last week, we officially signed our very first album contract with Victory Records. And you won't believe what's happening next week - we're heading to the studio to record our debut album! I am absolutely bursting with excitement! Xander and I have been dreaming about this moment since we were just twelve-year-old boys, and now, finally, it's becoming a reality. It's crazy to think that two boys from broken homes, who everyone in town thought were worthless, got discovered by a record label that's worked with some of the biggest bands. All I can say is that we are on our way up, and there is absolutely nothing that can stand in our way now.

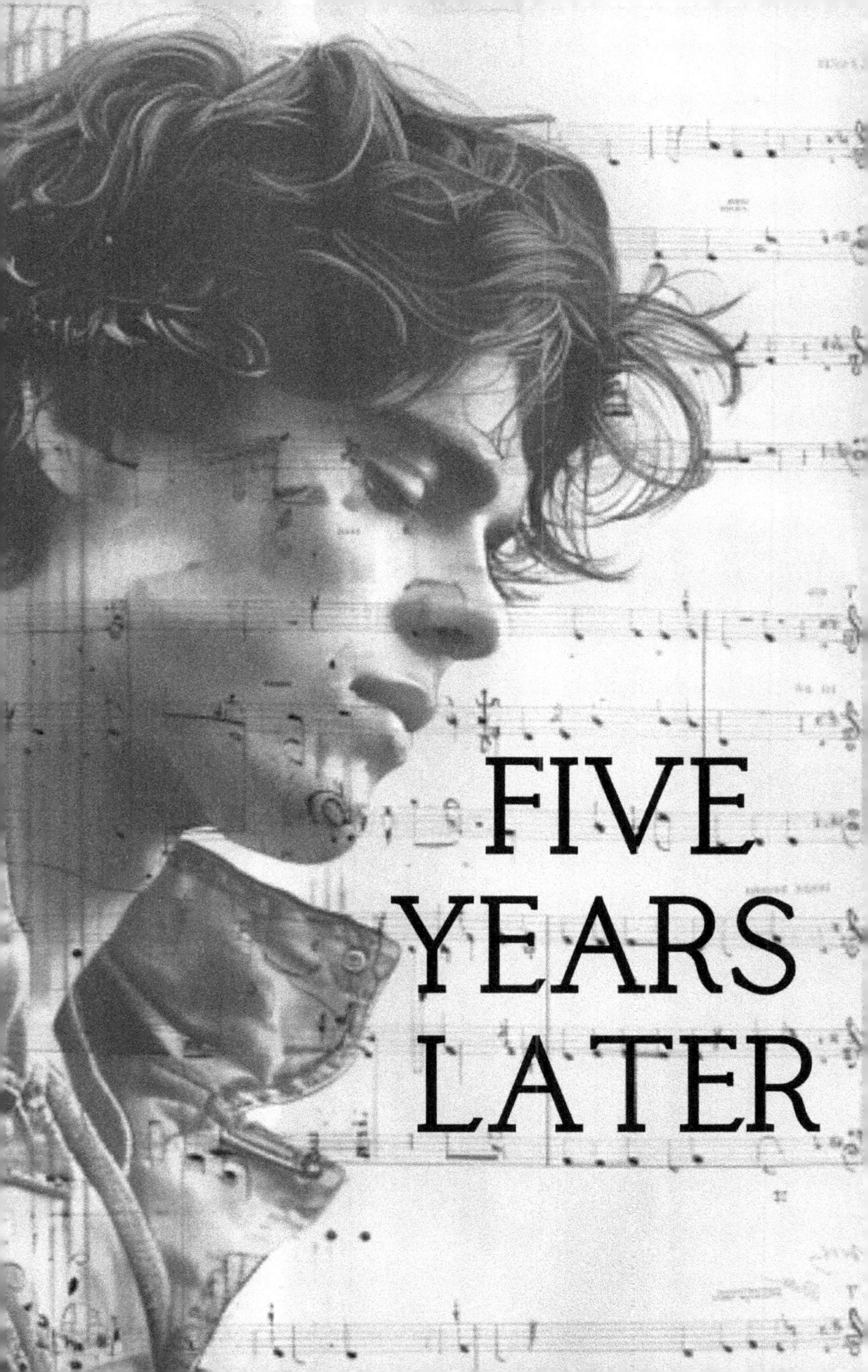

FIVE
YEARS
LATER

CHAPTER 34

Xander

As the stage lights fade to darkness, the deafening roars of the crowd intensify, becoming even more thunderous. I take a deep breath, preparing myself to sing the last song of the night. My heart is pounding, and I'm covered in sweat from giving it my all in front of eighty thousand people. As the crowd cheers, my body feels their energy, feeling the vibrations ripple through my skin. Their excitement peaks as they chant the name of our band.

"Broken Oasis! Broken Oasis!"

Suddenly, the lights come back to life, bathing the stage in a warm orange glow, and the audience erupts in thunderous applause.

"Creep! Creep! Creep!" they chant, their clapping echoing throughout the stadium.

I stand with Ace, Nate, and Theo, the other members of the band, as we look out over the endless sea of phones poised ready to capture this last song. But it's fucked up. The last song they want to hear isn't even our song. It's only a cover.

Last year in one of my drunken states, I sang Creep to the audience just so I could feel close to her. But all that did was create some fucking viral video. Sales went up. Management loved the money and told us we had to sing that as our sign-off song for every performance. It pisses me off because it breaks my heart for so many reasons. Not only because it was my mother's favorite song, but it's a constant reminder of the girl I left behind.

However, I've never been one to follow the fucking rules, neither has the band and I don't see that changing any time soon. We've already generated millions for the label, so we couldn't care less about their orders.

However, what caught me off guard after I sang that song was the moment the lights abruptly went out, and the entire crowd began chanting "Creep," repeatedly. It was then I realized I couldn't let our fans down. Whenever I sing that song, it just hits me with a wave of sadness and guilt for what I did to her. Thank God, I'm usually wasted, so it's easier.

Willis, our stage manager, brings out my guitar. It's the one that I cherish, the one that Poppy gave me. He carefully places it down on the stool in front of the mic while I quickly finish the last of my water, or rather, Vodka disguised as water. I've always had a deep love for playing the guitar, but ever since the label signed us up, I rarely get the chance to play it because I'm always on vocals.

Tossing the empty bottle aside, I make my way over to the stool and put my precious guitar on my lap, preparing to play. As my fingers strum the strings, the crowd erupts into a thunderous roar. Every chord I play, the crowd gets louder, and then it happens every fucking time, nothing but silence as I deliver the first line into the microphone.

As I sing this song, memories trickle in. That first day when I saw Poppy sitting on the side of the road. Of how we sang it together that night on the rock to my mother. I didn't know it back then. I was a dumbass, but that night when I first heard her sing this song, it changed my fucking life. The memories of the way she poured her heart out, and I saw how vulnerable she was. That tough girl with a sharp tongue had her vulnerabilities, just like me. Just thinking about it causes a pang in my chest.

When I hear my voice falter, I push those sad painful memories aside and do what I need to do, and that's singing this song to our fans.

As Nate skillfully handles the drums, Ace joins me, his guitar slung across his shoulder, filling the air with its melodic sounds. As I look around, I see Theo not far behind me, playing bass.

Though not related by blood, these guys have become my brothers, and I know they will always have my back. We understand each other. They get me, but only Theo comprehends the underlying reasons for my behavior when I first met him.

Over these past few years, I've had it with the record label trying to control things, doing anything to make headlines to get more sales. I don't give a damn about meeting their expectations anymore. Despite having wealth and fame, I still experience a sense of emptiness. People only hang out with us because we're a famous rock band with a sick record of twenty number-one hits all over the world. Groupies merely allow us to fuck them so they can boast about hooking up with someone famous. However, there is an undeniable void in my life, and deep down, I know exactly what it is, even though I struggle to admit it aloud.

When the ache in my chest becomes unbearable, I find solace by drinking my sorrows away.

Ace has often referred to me as my father, and because of that, our arguments often escalate into physical confrontations. However, the reality of being a number one-selling rockstar is not at all what I had imagined.

I realize now that the record company couldn't care less about us as long as we generate profits for them. Our songs, no let me rephrase that. My songs, the ones I pour my heart into, aren't mine anymore. The label completely fucked us over when we signed our first contract. I despise how my life has unfolded, and there seems to be nothing I can do about it.

They have complete ownership over us, dictating our every moment basically, from the moment I wake up to the second I fall asleep. The only way I can regain some sense of control is by doing things my way, even if it attracts attention for the wrong reasons. Screw them.

Ace is always going on about how we're gonna lose our contract. Who cares if they threaten to rip it up? We are the hottest band at this label, even the fucking planet, and they'd be stupid to miss out on the millions we make for them every year. So let them fucking try.

As the last note of the song sounds, the audience erupts in applause that echoes throughout the entire stadium. It has been an incredible night. I cherish the sensation of being on stage, doing what I was born to do. Only one more show tomorrow night, and then we'll take a two-week break before our eight-week Australian tour.

My eyes lift and I see a drop-dead gorgeous blonde in the front row. I give her a flirty smirk. She fearlessly lifts her shirt, exposing a huge rack. Not bad. Not bad at all.

Tonight, she will be my source of enjoyment. Groupies like her are always eager to please. And tonight will be no exception. She will worship me. This is the typical behavior of these groupies. She will surrender on her knees, her mouth yearning to satisfy.

I point towards her, motioning for our security Neil, who is well acquainted with my preferences and knows exactly what I'm looking for. He understands the type of person I want to spend my evening with - a blonde with considerable assets.

It's well-known that our band relishes in the company of women and enjoys partying. After all, we are revered as rock gods by the world. People no longer perceive us as mere individuals, so it's only natural that we indulge ourselves and have fun with groupies. They willingly offer themselves to us, so why shouldn't we partake in the fun? So, I'm gonna get high and have a good time. Seriously, what else am I supposed to do?

The four of us move to the front of the stage, acknowledging the applauding crowd with a final wave goodnight. Then, we turn and exit the stage.

Out in the hall, Nate and Theo lead the way, eagerly hoping to choose a groupie to share.

Meanwhile, Ace, my trusted companion since our school days, patiently walks at my side. His face says it all, telling me I've had way too much to drink.

"Great show tonight, man," he says, giving me a reassuring pat on the back. I can sense that he wants to say more, but he's hesitant, afraid of once again triggering a negative reaction from me.

"You good?" He asks me that question every time, fully aware that singing that song brings a deep pain to my heart.

Back in our younger years, I told him that it's my mother's favorite song. But he doesn't know the real reason for my pain. He doesn't know that it's because of Poppy, the only girl I've ever loved. I messed up big time with that amazing girl and treated her like she didn't matter.

"Yeah," I lie, absentmindedly rubbing the hollow feeling in my chest. "I'm ready to party," I say, avoiding eye contact with Ace so he doesn't see right through my bullshit.

"We totally crushed it tonight," he says, like he knows he should change the subject.

"I'm not so sure about that," I shrug. "The guitar solos seemed a bit off." I give him a smug smile.

"Fuck you, man." He jokingly traps me in a headlock with his thick tattooed arm.

I burst out laughing because I knew he would react that way.

"Have you changed your mind about the event?" Ace asks.

For the past few months, the subject has been a sensitive issue between Ace and me. The label owner Lionel and the mayor of the messed up town I grew up in are cousins. In a show of gratitude, the town wanted to commemorate the accomplishments of the two golden boys who had found success. Where were they when I was growing up in a fucked up home and looked down upon my entire damn life? It's because they want to highlight how fucking amazing that shitty town is. That's another thing that pisses me off, is that people only notice us now because of who we have become.

"I not fucking doing it, Ace. I can't stand that place."

"Yeah, I know, I'm the same, but you know it's gonna cause problems if you're not there."

"I don't fucking care."

"Xander, what you choose impacts the rest of us. We've already had management on our backs about the crap you do."

"So. I'm not going back there, Ace. They couldn't give a shit about us when we fucking lived there, so why now?"

"Xander, do us all a favor and don't resist it. We'll only have to show up for a couple of hours at most. Don't start any trouble. Come on, do it for the rest of your band and avoid the drama."

I turn my head and observe his expression. I know he's worried about us losing the contract, and when I go against the label, I stress him out. Ace is the glue, keeping us together, and I know I've made things tough for him in the past five years. But I'm annoyed with him because he never listens. He only cares about the label, and that's been causing some problems in the band.

I really want us to be like we were before, when we could share everything. If I go along with what he wants, maybe things will start to shift between us.

"Fine," I add, giving in. "But if my fucked-up excuse for a father shows up, I'm gone."

"Deal," Ace says with a grin, clearly relieved that I'm not causing any problems.

I only agree, so hopefully I can fix things between Ace and me, and also I know it's unlikely to run into Poppy Reeves after five years.

She's moved on and is probably happy with someone else. She was just as eager as me to leave that shitty place and follow her dreams. I haven't had the courage to see how she's doing, afraid she might hate me now - see me like everyone else, as worthless and insignificant. But all these years I've always wondered if she had the guts to go after her dream or if her mom kept calling the shots.

Ace opens the door to the backstage party room and I'm right behind him.

As we step inside, we're greeted by a bunch of stunning groupies. Nate and Theo already have their tattooed arms wrapped around a voluptuous brunette who wears a satisfied smile on her face, clearly ready to indulge in their pleasure. Nate leans in, whispering something into the groupie's ear, and she nods in agreement. They guide her towards the door at the back of the room. These guys are ready to get down to business, just like me. We just wanna savor the high energy from our performance for as long as we can.

Ace, being his usual grumpy self, is acting out of character tonight, obviously on the prowl looking to get laid. He throws his arms out and shouts.

"Okay, ladies," he shouts, halting in the center of the room. "Who's up for a party?"

The groupies squeal and rush into his welcoming embrace. They're all vying for his attention, pushing and shoving. Little do they know, Ace thrives on adoration, so those who are willing to worship him will be the chosen ones. He once confided in me the more groupies at once, the better. He gets a thrill watching girl-on-girl action, and his devoted followers will go to great lengths to please their idol.

Personally, I'm not interested in that scene.

Instead, I immediately head towards the alluring blonde who is standing at the side of the room, quietly observing all the groupies vying for Ace's attention. Even though I know she won't measure up to what I had before, I can't resist approaching this blonde. But, history has shown me they always end up being the same. Their voice feels off, their touch feels wrong, and their scent is unfamiliar. It's like I keep punishing myself, going through the same cycle over and over. It's like that insane line I've heard countless times, but I can't seem to break free from this pattern.

On my way over, I quickly grab a full bottle of Jack from the table. Tonight, all I want is to escape into a haze of smoke and alcohol, numbing myself to the touch of this blonde groupie. However, deep down, I yearn to slip back into my usual routine of imagining the soft touch of Poppy against my skin.

Without saying a word, I take her hand and lead her to the door Nate and Theo went through. I don't give a damn that management is coming soon and there's only one band member left to entertain the guests. All I desire is to return to the hotel room, get wasted, and let this girl satisfy me, so I can temporarily forget who I am for the night.

CHAPTER 35

Poppy

As soon as little Alex starts coughing in his sleep, I lift my head to look at him. It has been four days since he first fell ill. Thankfully, the medicine has made him slightly better today. As he drifts off to sleep, I focus on the pile of bills in front of me.

Rent is due soon, and the other overdue bills are starting to accumulate. These past four days of missed work and docked pay have made it even more challenging for me to stay on top of these expenses. However, my son's well-being is my top priority, above everything else in the world. My love for him surpasses all other things in this world.

As I calculate the numbers in my head, I realize that I won't be able to cover all the overdue bills. Unfortunately, I can't skip work tonight, especially because this event is a huge deal for the restaurant I work at and I really need the money. But if I don't show up, I'll definitely get fired.

Ideally, I had hoped to call in sick because I can't be there when Broken Oasis receives a town recognition for their success. It's going to be really difficult for me to handle seeing Xander again at the special event tonight. I honestly have no desire to see that prick, especially considering the fact that he has completely ignored me for the past five years. Despite my many attempts to reach out and inform him about his son, he has deliberately changed his phone number or something to avoid any contact with me.

I reach for my wallet and glance at the notes inside. There's no way I can afford to dye my hair darker, hoping Xander won't recognize me. Maybe he'll have a swarm of adoring groupies around him, just like the ones I've seen in those glossy celebrity magazines. He probably won't even spare a glance in my direction. No doubt he'll simply brush me aside and ignore me, just like he did when we were younger. Nevertheless, despite still harboring anger towards him and myself for letting things unfold the way they did, I cannot be upset about what he left behind. I cherish my son and am grateful for the precious gift Xander gave me to remember him by.

As I glance around the room, I can't help but wonder if there's anything I can sell. Last year, when I was struggling to keep up with the bills, I had no choice but to part with my beloved keyboard. It was an incredibly heartbreaking experience for me. I remember crying my eyes out for an entire week over that loss. I guess I could've sold my guitar, the one I used to jam with my dad, but instead, I'm selling his vinyl collection to keep us afloat. If things don't turn around soon, I'll have nothing to remember my dad by.

When Alex was just nine months old, I left my mother's house because I couldn't handle the situation any longer. It was crucial for me to make that move when I did. It was hard because my mom wouldn't stop telling Alex how terrible his dad was.

I wanted to shield him from that negativity, but I promise to share all the amazing things about Xander when he's old enough. Right now, Alex only knows that his dad is away, involved in something really important. I don't want Alex to have a negative opinion of Xander, as I truly hope they will meet someday. Hopefully, in the future, Xander will have the opportunity to know his wonderful son and see how truly beautiful he is.

As Alex continues to grow, I can't help but notice more and more of Xander's features shining through. Whether it's his dark eyes, his hair, or that mischievous grin, they all remind me of him.

Alex's passion for music truly comes to life when he talks about his favorite songs. His eyes light up with excitement, and he absolutely adores it when we play my dad's vinyls and joyfully dance around the room together. Alex is my everything - my heart, the reason I breathe.

These days, I don't really have much to do with my mom, unless it's absolutely necessary. It all started when I was struggling to pay my bills, and I reached out to her for some financial help to get back on my feet. Sadly, she turned me down, stating that I had made my decision and I must face the consequences. This left me with no other choice but to part ways with my cherished keyboard.

So, now my mom wants nothing to do with Alex. Because of that, he doesn't get to see his grandma anymore.

When we first moved here, she didn't want to come over because she didn't like how our place looked. I would take Alex to his grandma's so they could spend time together. However, I stopped doing that because of the constant taunts she made about Xander. It made me realize that if she truly wanted to spend time with Alex, she would make the effort regardless of where we lived. So, I decided not to take him there anymore. Surprisingly, she didn't even bother to call and ask why I did that.

From the start, my intention was to escape my mother's control. Though this apartment may not be anything extraordinary, it has become my sanctuary. Initially, I had planned to reside here for only twelve months, so I could save up to secure a better place for us. But when my first job fell through, all my dreams of a better life and a career in musical therapy went out the window. My current job doesn't offer a high salary, but the tips can vary and sometimes help cover the bills. I have contemplated taking on a second job, but that would mean sacrificing time with Alex, and I refuse to become one of those mothers who are constantly working and hardly ever see their child.

When I go to work, Alex hangs out with my neighbor, Mrs. Baxter, or Mrs. B. as I call her, who's older than my mom. She's the sweetest old lady you'll ever meet. She's basically Alex's grandma now. Mrs. Baxter is truly wonderful. Alex totally loves her, and honestly, I get along better with her than my own mother. I told her everything about Xander and what happened between us. The best thing is that she just sat and listened, never saying anything bad about Xander. It feels like I can confide in her about all the things I've never been able to share with my mother.

I shuffle the bills scattered on the table, overwhelmed by the sheer number. I quickly grab my phone and pay the one bill I can't put off for another week.

Glancing at the clock, I realize that it's time to get ready for tonight. My body is buzzing with nerves, just thinking about seeing him again. Once again, I make a mental note to shield my heart from potential pain.

Throughout the years, I've never been involved in a romantic relationship. I've only had one man in my life, and that's Xander. Honestly, I never really cared about finding someone to date because Alex was always my top priority. However, at work, there's Tom, the sleazy bartender who constantly flirts and makes inappropriate comments. His behavior is enough to deter me from wanting anyone to look at me the way I used to desire.

With a sigh and knowing that I cannot put it off any longer, I finally get up and quickly hide the bills in the kitchen drawer.

Once I've changed into my work clothes and tied my long hair into its usual ponytail, I walk over to the couch to check on Alex. The moment I touch his forehead to check his fever, his eyes open, revealing his deep brown gaze. When he notices me sitting beside him, a smile spreads across his face, reminding me of Xander.

"Hey buddy, how are you feeling?" I ask, feeling relieved to see that he might be a little better than he was a few hours ago.

"I'm thirsty," he replies.

I reach over and grab the glass of water I left on the table beside him.

He sits up and I help him take a big sip of water.

I hear a soft tap on the front door, indicating that Mrs. Baxter has arrived to take care of Alex while I go to work. I put the glass back on the table and head toward the door, ready to welcome her.

"Hi," I say, smiling, holding the door open for her to come in.

"How is he doing?" she asks.

"Better. Not as bad as before," I reply, closing the door.

"Oh, that's great news, Poppy. I've been so worried about him. And how are you feeling about tonight?" she asks.

"I'm a little nervous," I admit.

"Don't worry, you'll be fine, sweetie," she reassures me, reaching out to rest her hand on my arm. "Just go with it and see what happens. That's all you can do."

"I know," I nod, giving her a false smile. "But honestly, I'm freaking out about seeing Xander again. I'm not sure if I can handle another rejection from him."

"It will work out exactly how it's supposed to,' she reassures me.

The sound of little feet walking on the wooden floor has us turning around.

"GG," Alex says, as he comes over and wraps his arms around Mrs. B.'s legs.

I can't help but smile at the endearing name Alex has given her. The name they came up with when he asked if she was his grandma a while ago. I remember feeling at a loss for words that day, but Mrs. B. reassured Alex that even though she wasn't his biological grandmother, that would make their bond just as special.

"Are you feeling better today?" she asks, stooping down to lift him and carry him into the next room.

I follow them, listening to their conversation about a book that Alex wants her to read to him later tonight. Mrs. B settles Alex into one of the chairs at the table.

"Now, his dinner is in the fridge. It just needs to be heated," I mention, grabbing my keys from the counter and my handbag from its usual spot on one of the old worn-out chairs. "I'm hoping I won't be home too late."

"It's okay, sweetie. Don't worry about it. Whenever you come home, it'll be fine."

I walk over to Alex with a smile, and he watches me as I go around the table. "Now you be a good boy for GG," I add, leaning down to kiss him on the head. "Love you."

"Love you too, Mommy," Alex replies.

I give Mrs. B a quick smile and head towards the door.

I don't waste any time hopping in my old, crappy car and driving to work. The whole time, I can't stop stressing about how the next few hours will go down.

Ten minutes later, I'm parked in my usual spot behind the restaurant. Tonight is huge! Everyone in town is talking about the local boys who've become rock icons.

The streets are packed with extra cars, but luckily the bar staff doesn't have to come in as early as the wait staff. I highly doubt that the band has even shown up yet. Judging by the headlines I've read over the years, Xander is probably already off somewhere, engaging in his typical activities. Sleeping with anyone who catches his eye. It's frustrating to witness how the girls constantly chase after him.

I step out of my car, fully aware that I shouldn't bother locking it. Like, who would wanna steal this old shit box? But if someone actually takes it, I'll have to come up with more money. Honestly, it's tough enough without having to pay for a car on top of everything else.

As I sneak into the restaurant through the back door and hustle through the kitchen, my nerves go crazy. All the chatter in the kitchen is freaking me out.

I know my boss, Nicole, will be somewhere around here, and I do my best to avoid her. She's always up my ass about something. I know she'll probably make some snide remark about me taking a few days off because of Alex being sick. It's just what she does. Thanking my lucky stars that I've not seen her, I quickly stash my bag in my locker and head towards the bar.

Just as I'm about to enter the bar, I pause for a moment. Nerves churn in my stomach as I gently push the door open, peering through the crack in an attempt to catch a glimpse of him. Instead, I see Ace, engaged in conversation with an older man, both leaning against the bar. Ace is all grown up now, nothing like the kid I remember. His arms are a canvas of intricate, vibrant tattoos. Margo, the bartender, hands them their drinks while a steady stream of people pour in through the double doors.

Soft music fills the room, creating a soothing ambiance.

Slowly, I push the door open a little further, and that's when I see him. Xander's right there, sitting on a bar stool, totally absorbed in the chat with a group of girls. Maybe they're his entertainment for the night. Theo, from the band, sits right beside him. I know this because I made the mistake of reading those fancy magazines I bought at the supermarket whenever I saw Xander making headlines on the cover. I shouldn't torture myself like that, but I just need to know what's happening in his life, even if he doesn't want me. Though his back is facing me, I would recognize him anywhere. My heart skips a beat when they say goodbye to the girls and turn back to the bar, swiftly downing one of the many shots lined up in front of him. He looks so different now, more like a man than the boy I remember. With all that ink on his arms, fuck me, he's hotter than hell.

I swallow the lump in my throat, knowing I have to go out there. But for some reason, I can't bring myself to move. Who am I kidding? He probably won't even recognize me. I was just a plaything, someone he messed around with until it was time for him to leave. My hair is much longer now, and after having Alex, my hips have filled out more, my boobs are bigger, and I'm not the same girl he would remember. I'm just a blip in the life he once had. And why would he want to remember me now that he's a successful rock star with the world at his feet and an ego to match.

I push open the door, holding my head high as I make my way out to help Margo with the swelling crowd at the bar.

I move to the opposite end of the bar, positioning myself so I'm not anywhere near Xander.

CHAPTER 36

Xander

Fuck, I completely forgot how boring this town is, and to make matters worse, Jade is here. I forgot how annoying this chick is with her never-ending chit-chat. It's all coming back to me now, why I used to shut her up by shoving my cock in her mouth. It was the only way to stop her from babbling about all kinds of shit.

I grab my shot glass from the bar and down it, relishing the burn in my throat. I just need to get numb so I can get through this shitty night. I never wanted to come here in the first place, but Ace convinced me. Perhaps I'll talk to that cute bartender at the end of the bar and see if she's down to have some fun later. My eyes wander over her figure. Her long blonde hair, tied in a ponytail, cascades down her back, just above her hot ass, which is exactly my type. Damn, I might even grab hold of that ponytail and have some wild fun until I'm too wasted to realize she's not who I really desire.

The record label owner, and the biggest pain in my ass, Lionel, is here annoying the shit out of me, as he has done since we first signed with the label. I've been eyeing him all night, sitting with his idiot cousin, the mayor of this fucked up town. He expects me to go around shaking hands and bowing to everyone, but honestly, he can suck on my dick for all I care. Our band is his biggest money maker, so I can do whatever the hell I want. I'm not going to suck up to anyone, especially not to these fake ass people in this shitty town who never gave a damn about me or my life. It's already hard enough dealing with people who only want to be around us now that we've become rock gods. Where were they when my life was a living hell? So, no, I'm not going to suck up and shake hands with those stuffy corporate guys in their expensive suits. Screw that.

Reg, the band manager, and Ace are sitting four seats away from me, but I can still hear them yabbering on to some hotshot in a suit, accompanied by his wife or girlfriend in six-inch "come fuck me" heels. Ace introduced me to them ten minutes ago, but I wasn't interested in hearing from these boring people. I wonder how he'd feel if I fucked his gold-digging girlfriend. Judging by the way she looked at me earlier, I know all I have to do is say something in her ear and she'd be purring for my affection. But she doesn't interest me. She's not my type - too snooty and thinks her shit doesn't stink. But I can still pretend to be interested just to fuck with that egotistical bastard and all the others who think I'm something special now just because I'm important.

Well, fuck them and their egos. I'm Xander fucking Williams. I don't bow or scrape to anyone. I made myself who I am because of hard work, not because of them.

When we arrived in this town earlier today, my immediate reaction was to confront Poppy's mother and prove her wrong. Tell her that I am someone of significance, someone who is admired. So, to all those bitter old women out there who looked down on me all those years ago, you can all suck my cock.

Then, my father came to mind. But the idea of seeing him again and the immense anger I have towards him, I knew the second I saw that fuckers face, I wouldn't stop. I'm pretty sure I would have killed him the second I saw him. But I stayed away from those two opinionated assholes. They are the ones who are truly unworthy of my time. Just like all the assholes here tonight sucking off our fame.

There were only two people who saw me in a different light compared to everyone else. First, there was Ace, my faithful and trusted best friend. And then there was the girl whose heart I unintentionally shattered, causing my own heart to break in the process.

Not this annoying skank Jade, sitting next to me, thinking we were high school sweethearts. She's just here, wanting attention and to feel important. Even Theo isn't flirting with her, and he flirts with every girl he sees.

That's how fucking annoying she is.

Downing another shot, I quickly follow it with another, hoping to drown out the incessant bitching coming from the person sitting next to me. Left with only two shots, I grab them and get out of my seat. Jade reaches out her hand to stop me.

"Where are you going, Xander?" she asks, looking up at me and keeping her hand on my arm.

I glance at her hand and then give her a dirty look. "Back the fuck off, and get your fucking hand off me now," I yell, not caring about those who turn their heads to see what's going on.

As soon as she removes her hand, I turn and make my way to the empty seat next to Ace, who's engrossed in a conversation with Reg about some stuff for the upcoming tour. I want to hear what's going on, due to Ace not sharing things with the band. We're heading to Australia for a seven-week tour, followed by a week in New Zealand and I want to know what the fuck is going on. What interviews they are forcing on us. Our schedule is always jam-packed, and it never seems to let up. I hate giving interviews. All I crave is being on that stage, soaking up all the energy that comes with being in the spotlight.

Despite our first album being our best, and how the label now owns my songs, I wasn't letting that happen again. I've told the label that I can't write anymore. It's a lie of course I still write every day.

The label now pays someone else to write our songs, and I fucking hate it. I hate that I have no say over what I sing. We have a different sound now to the one we originally had. Sadly, it feels like Broken Oasis has lost its essence. Even though the media has never mentioned it, I can sense it. The rest of the guys can feel it too.

"Hey, man," I say, settling down next to Ace without even glancing at him. Instead, my attention is fixed on the blonde bartender as she skillfully serves the numerous guests at the far end of the bar. Her soft, feminine curves captivate my gaze, causing my dick to become interested.

"How many is that?" Ace asks.

Lately, all he does is complain about my drinking.

"You might need to slow down, Xander," says the asshole, Reg. I'd rather drive nails into my ears than follow his instructions. "Don't mess up tonight, Xander, seriously. Not here. Lionel is already furious with all your outbursts and the negative attention it brings to the band. He's been on my ass about all the trouble you've caused in the past few months."

Ace chimes in with Reg, adding his thoughts. "It's not just about you, you know. Your actions affect all of us."

"You ought to talk asshole, when half the time, you're the problem," I tell Reg, knowing that he is behind most of the shit that goes down.

"Xander," Ace says, and instead of listening to the asshole give me a lecture, I fix my attention back to the blonde bartender at the end of the bar.

I watch her for a moment moving around, chatting, filling up glasses, and then I hear her laugh. Suddenly, my heart starts racing in my chest. Fucking hell, it can't be. She couldn't possibly still be here in this shitty town, no way. She should be out there chasing her dreams.

I swallow over the thickness in my throat as I watch her intensely, completely disregarding everything else around me. I'm freaking out just by looking at her, to the point where my leg won't stop bouncing. I wonder if she's noticed me sitting here. No way she hasn't. The Poppy Reeves I know would've totally called me out with her sharp tongue. She would've called me the biggest scumbag by now.

Wanting to confirm that the alcohol hasn't affected my vision and it's really her, I get off my stool, hoping to get a closer look. But before I can take a step in her direction, I freeze when I catch the sound of a familiar voice - one that I wish to never hear again in my life.

"Don't you wanna say hi to your old man?"

With a sense of urgency, I swiftly turn towards him, and spit my words that reflect the intensity of my anger.

"What the fuck are you doing here?"

I can't help but notice the heavy silence that hangs in the room. But I don't care. It's no surprise that my asshole father has chosen this exact moment to cause a scene. And, of course, once again, all eyes turn towards me because they think I have something fucking important to say.

He smirks and takes a stumbling step forward. "Just came to see my boy," he slurs.

I feel Ace's hand grip my arm, trying to get my attention. But I don't bother to look in his direction.

"As you've constantly reminded me, I'm not your son." I spit the words at him. My lips tighten, and my fists involuntarily clench at my sides, memories of the beatings this jerk subjected me to flood my mind, all because he discovered I wasn't his biological child.

His bloodshot eyes lock onto me. "You always were a little cunt of a kid. And now, hotshot, I see nothing has changed."

With a glance, I observe the stains on his shirt and the greasy, disheveled state of his hair. He appears significantly older than I remember, maybe the alcohol has finally taken its toll.

"Your old man is having some money problems. You owe me a favor after all I did for you."

And there it is. This asshole didn't want anything to do with me when I needed him the most, especially on the day my mother passed away. Instead, he constantly abused me, day in and day out, and now he expects me to help him out.

Fuck no.

My anger rises to the surface that this asshole now wants to call me his son. I don't care about the executives from the label, the mayor, or any other high-profile person who thinks they know me because of my success.

Ace places his hand on my shoulder. "Come on, Xander, it's not worth it."

Despite Ace's effort to prevent a public showdown, I am too angry to listen. The intensity of his cruelty fuels a growing rage within me, urging me to unleash my true feelings - to tell him what he told me, that he is insignificant, a worthless asshole, and he will be now and forever.

I forcefully shake Ace's hand off my shoulder and move forward, my face burning with anger. Strong feelings consume me as I recall the words, I've rehearsed for years to tell him if I ever saw him again. Ignoring the spectators in the room, and the phones pointed in my direction does nothing to stop me from lashing out.

"Fuck you!"

Reg moves in front of me, his hands outstretched, desperately trying to silence me and avoid any commotion, but his attempts are in vain as I am determined to speak my mind. I know well that once this situation unfolds, it will be plastered across the media. My every action seems to find its way into magazines, although most of the content is nothing but lies. It's just another means for them to profit off of me, much like this record label.

My father looks around the room at the many people watching. "This is the fucking hotshot at his best." He looks back at me with that smirk, that same one he always gave when he was satisfied with the beatings he gave me.

How dare the asshole come here asking for a handout, when I'm the one who has put in all the hard work? It's seriously mind-boggling that he would even dare to refer to me as his son after all the cruelty he inflicted.

Reg and Ace attempt to drag me away, but it's already too late. I open my mouth, prepared to express clearly that he has never been a father. And how he will forever remain the asshole who made my life a living hell.

"Xander!"

I hear her voice and instantly freeze as she gently places her palm against my chest.

Ace and Reg release their grip on me, and both look down at Poppy, who is standing in front of me.

"Not here in front of everyone," says Poppy.

Her voice has a profound effect on me, especially when she speaks my name. However, it's the sensation of her hand on my chest that sends shivers through my entire body, just like it did years ago when she used to touch me. Her touch has a grounding effect on me.

As she draws near, I take a deep breath in. I shift my gaze downwards and meet her captivating blue eyes, feeling a lump in my throat. Surprisingly, there is no hint of hatred in her eyes, contrary to what I had expected when I first saw her. What strikes me the most, though, is how she has become even more beautiful than I remember. There are a few additional freckles sprinkled across her nose. However, she doesn't allow me to admire her face for long, as she redirects her attention back to my father.

"Back off, now," she warns my piece of shit father. She then directs her gaze towards the security guard, who has been silently observing the entire situation unfold. "Warren, remove this person from the bar immediately, or I will involve the police."

Approaching the scene, Warren, the security guard, whose bald head and substantial muscular build cannot be ignored.

"Listen here, bitch," my father angrily retorts. "This is between my son and me. It's got nothing to do with you."

I take a step forward, fully prepared to deliver a punch to my father's face for calling Poppy by that name. But Poppy removes her hand from my chest and boldly steps forward, confronting him with her gaze. It's the same Poppy I remember from our school days but now she's bolder, more self-assured - always ready with a sharp retort.

"We know what kind of asshole father you were to Xander. Now get the fuck out of here, or I'll have your ass thrown in jail."

It's truly unbelievable to see Poppy in the first place, but it's even more surprising to watch her defend me, especially after what I've done to her.

Warren, the useless security guard, takes hold of my father's arms and spins him around.

"You self-righteous prick," my father yells at me, his voice echoing through the room. Warren forcefully shoves him towards the exit, and the shocked crowd parts, making way for him to be escorted out.

As everyone watches my dad get kicked out, I can't take my eyes off Poppy. I can't believe what she just did. Not after everything that went down between us.

Poppy's gaze meets mine briefly as she turns around. In that moment, a surge of emotions overwhelms me, as memories flood my heart. However, she immediately looks away and walks back to the bar.

The murmurs of the crowd sound in my ears, their penetrating stares fixed upon me.

"You alright, man?" Ace inquires, standing by my side as Theo and Nate approach.

Nodding, my mind goes blank, and I can't find the right words to say. I simply wish to follow her, but I am unsure of how to express myself. It's all too much to handle, and I'm in desperate need of a drink.

"Damn, who's the blonde spitfire over there?" Theo asks, his gaze fixed on the bar.

I open my mouth to tell him to drop it, but I don't get a chance because Ace answers for me.

"That's Poppy Reeves," Ace says, glancing over at the bar where Poppy is now serving drinks. "She used to go to our school."

Hearing her name, Theo glances my way. "You mean that Poppy," he comments.

I nod to confirm, and Ace gives me a puzzled look because I didn't tell him anything about Poppy when he asked. But I've already told Theo everything.

"Fuck!" Theo mutters, knowing all about our history.

CHAPTER 37

Poppy

Oh my God! I can't believe what I just did. What's wrong with me? One moment, I was serving customers at the bar, and the next, I'm standing in front of Xander, desperately trying to calm him down. Maybe I should have just stayed out of it, but I couldn't ignore the protective instinct that surged through my body when I thought his father had returned to belittle him.

I'm not sure as to why I did it - perhaps it's because Xander has been through so much with his dad, or maybe it's because he looks so much like my son, and I would do anything to protect him from assholes like that in this messed up world.

I knew that as soon as Xander's dad approached him, his reaction would be explosive. I'm certain that what just occurred is already circulating on multiple social media platforms. Xander shouldn't face unjust criticism for circumstances beyond his control. He can't help it if he has an asshole for a father. Despite Xander breaking my heart, he is still the father of my child, even if he doesn't care about our sweet little boy.

Once I'm back behind the bar, my boss, Nicole, comes over and stands next to me. I brace myself for her harsh words, expecting her to tell me I should've stayed behind the bar, but what she says catches me off guard.

"I had no idea you knew Xander Williams. How exactly do you know him?'"

"I don't want to talk about it," I tell her.

I can't go back to my previous spot at the end of the bar because Sienna is now serving there. I reluctantly walk to the other end of the bar, only to see Xander and the rest of the band huddled together a few feet away, having a serious talk. No matter how hard I try to calm my racing heart, it's useless. Being in close proximity to him triggers a rush of memories that I'd rather not revisit. I refuse to go through that pain again.

"I want you to introduce me to him," Nicole says, as she follows me. I groan inwardly as I notice the stuffy-suited asshole who asked for my number earlier is now sitting in my section. When I turn my head, I see all the members of Broken Oasis looking at me. I curse silently, wondering what he's saying about me. Is he spreading rumors that I'm easy? That he used me and left me like I meant nothing? I resist the urge to give Xander Williams the finger and tell him to fuck off. Instead, I just focus on my job.

The uptight, suited asshole beckons me over, and I reluctantly make my way towards him.

Out of the corner of my eye, I notice Theo, the bass guitarist, making his way towards the bar. I feel a sense of relief knowing that Nicole is the one who goes over to serve him, as I had no intention of answering any of her questions about Xander. It's quite surprising to see how she is around them.

"What can I get you?" I ask abruptly, recalling the unpleasant memory of asking the same question to this jerk who responded with something inappropriate and sexual.

"Just your phone number, sweetheart."

Rolling my eyes, I refuse to tolerate this drunken idiot. I wait, impatiently tapping my nails on the bar. All I want is for this night to end, so I don't have to put up with these assholes or face the man who broke my heart and took a piece of it with him when he left.

"What would you like?" I ask again, my tone harsher than before.

He smirks mischievously and replies, "How about you sit on my face, beautiful?"

This guy is so full of himself, thinking he can say whatever he wants to women. I refuse to tolerate this disrespectful behavior.

"Why is your nose bigger than your dick?" I retort, moving across to serve the next patron, fed up with these assholes who think they can say whatever they damn well please. All I want is to work and not be subjected to this kind of crap.

Theo cracks up and snatches the drink Nicole sets down on the bar. I don't know if he's laughing at me or something she said.

I move to the next customer, and I immediately recognize him as the older man who was with Xander when I tried to help calm him down earlier. I think he has something to do with the band.

"What can I get you?" I inquire.

"I'll have a Jack and coke," he says, perched on the bar stool.

I grab a glass, fill it, and bring it back to the customer.

"It's Poppy, right?" he says, reaching his hand out to me.

I place the glass down in front of him and reach out to shake his hand.

"I'm Reg," he says. "The manager of Broken Oasis."

I let go of his hand, questioning why the hell he feels the need to disclose that to me. My gaze swiftly shifts to Ace, who slides into the neighboring seat at the bar.

"Hey Poppy, long time no see," Ace says.

"Hi Ace," I say, my confusion growing at this unexpected interaction. I can't help but wonder what on earth is happening. Ace has never spoken to me before, let alone acknowledged my existence at school. What in the world has Xander said about me? And why are they both here, staring at me?

"Do you want anything from the bar?" I ask Ace, eager to escape the intense scrutiny of their watchful gazes.

"Yeah, a beer, thanks Poppy," Ace replies.

I turn away and notice Nicole standing nearby, observing me with a hint of curiosity, seemingly hoping that I will introduce her to Ace.

Ace has transformed since high school. He's way taller now and super ripped, like he's always at the gym. Meanwhile, Xander is still tall and lanky, with a slightly edgier vibe than before.

As I bring Ace his beer, my eyes instinctively scan the area where Xander was just moments ago, only to discover that he, along with the other two band members, are no longer there.

'Thanks, Poppy,' says Ace.

I start to step away, but I stop in my tracks when Ace speaks. "Do you have a few minutes to talk?" he asks.

"No, I'm sorry, I'm really busy," I reply.

"It's alright, Poppy," Nicole chimes in as she listens in on our conversation. "I'm here for you. Chat, and once you're finished, maybe you can introduce me to this handsome man," she adds, making her way over to attend to the customers patiently waiting to place their orders.

I always had a feeling that she was a flirt. It was clear in the way she openly laughed whenever attractive men walked into the bar. Normally, she would constantly push me to work faster, but now she suddenly wants me to take a break, even though the bar is insanely busy with customers waiting to order their drinks. First, she asked me to introduce her to Xander, and now it's Ace. It's like she effortlessly moves from one man to another without any hesitation. What the hell is going on with this woman?

"You want something to drink?" Ace asks me.

"Nah, I'm good," I reply, not intending to stay long and therefore not needing a drink. Leaning forward on my elbows at the bar, I position myself closer to Ace to hear him speak over the noisy crowd.

CHAPTER 38

Ace

Over the past five years, I've witnessed Xander's downward spiral. He never opened up to me about what really happened between him and Poppy, but based on what I just witnessed a few minutes ago, it seems like there's more to the story than he's let on.

Reg and I have been doing our best to keep him on the right track and prevent him from ruining everything. Just last week, Lionel from Victory Records called me and Reg in to let us know that if Xander doesn't start showing improvement soon, they might have no choice but to cancel our contract.

Despite the fact that we generate millions for them each year, the constant negative media coverage, the never-ending expenses of hiring lawyers to resolve issues and non-disclosure agreements (NDIs), are starting to have a significant impact. Just last week, Xander, under the influence, took one of his sports cars out for a drive and ended up crashing it. Thankfully, no one was injured. Thanks to our legal team and a settlement with the affected family, this incident hasn't made headlines yet. However, like everything else, it's only a matter of time before the world becomes aware of it.

Not only has Reg attempted to address Xander's behavior over the years, our attempts have proven futile. Xander acts according to his own will, disregarding any consequences. It feels as if he's a ticking time bomb, threatening to dismantle all the achievements we've worked tirelessly to attain.

Lionel said they couldn't care less if we stopped producing albums. There's always the next best thing to take over the music industry. They can continue to make millions without worrying about paying the NDI's and lawyer fees for all the messed up things Xander keeps getting himself into. That's why they don't give a damn if we're no longer part of their label. They own the rights to all our songs. What we didn't realize back then was that we were signing away all our rights. Xander was furious when I told him about it because he poured his heart out to create them. I believe that might have been the starting point for all this chaos.

When Reg and I saw Xander's confrontation with his father earlier, I knew it would be a challenge to calm him down considering his strong feelings towards his father. Unfortunately, Reg didn't react when I told him to grab Xander, maybe he didn't hear me. My only goal was to remove Xander from that situation, knowing that he was about to lose control, and the media would exploit it for days. However, to our surprise, things unfolded in a different way, rendering our intervention unnecessary.

I've never seen him change that way before. He's always been hotheaded, but when this little blonde came over and said his name and placed her hand on his chest, he instantly stopped. It was as if Poppy Reeves had cast a magical calming spell that made everything come to a halt. As Xander's best friend, I have never witnessed anything like it before. That's when I told Reg we needed to bring Poppy on board. Maybe with Poppy around Xander will stop engaging in his reckless behavior.

Reg initially didn't approve of it, but when I warned him that I would reveal his affair with Lionel's wife, he finally agreed to have a conversation with Poppy. I am completely lost about what actions to take. All I am aware of is that my brother is spiraling, and I need to take responsibility and intervene.

We are about to start a seven-week tour in Australia, and then we'll spend another week in New Zealand. I've heard that the Australian Police are quite strict and shouldn't be underestimated. The law is enforced rigorously there, regardless of someone's status or influence. So, I've come up with a solution to this dilemma. Now, I just hope that Poppy Reeves is willing to be a part of it. No matter how much it costs me. I am prepared to pay her whatever it costs to save our contract and prevent my best friend from going off the rails.

"I have a proposition for you," I say, leaning in close to ensure she can hear me.

CHAPTER 39

Poppy

"N ot interested," I tell him, wondering if this has something to do with what Xander was telling them earlier. Knowing how Ace was at school, if he's looking for a hook-up, I'll fucking punch him in his face, I don't care how big he's gotten and I don't care who's watching.

"No, just hear me out," Ace says.

I let out a sigh. "You've got two minutes, that's it. Then I'm going."

"So, you and Xander have a long history," Reg says.

"Yeah, so," I say, getting all defensive and crossing my arms. I've turned off that part of me, never wanting to go through that again, so I don't feel the pain.

"Before you say anything, just hear me out," Ace says. "I'm not sure if you've kept track of us over the years."

"No, I haven't," I lie, not revealing that I've actually seen the headlines about the trouble Xander has been getting into lately.

"Well, Xander has been spiraling out of control recently," Ace remarks.

"And what does this have to do with me?"

"I'd say more than you think, considering what I just saw," Ace says.

Confused by his cryptic statement, I choose to remain silent, observing him as he reaches for his beer and takes a sip. His intense gaze meets mine as he peers over the rim of his glass, leaving me to ponder whether I should just walk away.

"We're on the verge of losing everything," Ace says, putting his glass back on the bar. "With the way Xander is at the moment, it's likely that we'll never get signed by another label again if we lose that."

"Well, that's not my problem. Take it up with Xander."

"We have, but he won't listen to us. But he did it for you," Ace says. "You prevented a disaster from unfolding. There's no way he would have listened to either of us. He would have completely lost his shit and caused another issue for the label."

"Well, I didn't do anything."

"Yeah, but you did, Poppy. Xander was on the verge of exploding at his father. I think you might know what went on with his dad."

"Yeah, I know."

"Back then earlier, he wouldn't listen to me or Reg when we tried to calm him down. I can't reach him anymore. And Reg and I were discussing..." He shifts his focus to Reg, leaving the conversation unfinished.

Reg and Ace hold each other's gaze for a moment, something passing between them like each one is waiting for the other one to tell me what this bright idea is. Finally, Ace speaks.

"That you help out until Xander gets his shit together."

"No way," I add, raising my palms in a defensive gesture and taking a few cautious steps back. I had no intention of being a part of this preposterous plan. How could I possibly be around Xander, considering the immense pain I still harbor? I have deliberately shut my heart off because of him, from the possibility of ever opening it up again. Subjecting myself to the constant proximity of him would only inflict more agony than I ever wished to endure. Going back to that level of hurt was simply out of the question. And there is no way I want to see him with all those other women, who he's constantly photographed with.

"You can name your price, Poppy. No matter the cost, it's all yours," Ace declares.

The thought of Ace just casually throwing money at me and expecting me to give in annoys me. I wasn't some gold digger lacking morals. "No, please stop. This isn't going to happen. Trust me. Xander and I aren't friends anymore."

"Just say you'll think about it."

"No. I can't I'm sorry."

"I'm not aware of the details regarding your situation with Xander, but I believe you understand that this has always been our shared dream, Poppy. Xander's actions are jeopardizing his own dreams, as well as those of the other band members."

I didn't want to hear any of it. At least Xander had achieved his dreams. He wasn't the one living day by day, struggling to make ends meet. I had texted him numerous times, informing him that I was pregnant after that one time he called and never said a single word to me. He even ignored the texts that I sent telling him he had a son, and his name was Alexander, but he didn't even acknowledge it. So no, I didn't give a fuck if Xander was having a hard time dealing with all the fame and money.

"Stop asking Ace. There is no way I can do what you're asking me to do."

Ace shoots Reg a look as if silently instructing him to say something. "You're not interested in helping, huh?" He turns his attention back to me.

"You're observant. What gave it away?" I add with a hint of sarcasm in my voice.

"Most bands don't have the kind of talent that these four boys possess. It would be a shame to see it all go to waste because of one band member who can't seem to get their shit together. Xander continuously drags his name through the tabloids, going from one scandal to another. He has never shown any remorse for his actions. He's always high and couldn't care less about who he hurts or what he does."

"It's true Poppy," says Ace. "Tonight, I saw a different side of Xander. He was eager to listen to what you had to say. Maybe you don't see it, but right there I saw the significant impact you had on him."

"Again, I'm not interested."

"I'm sure you know back before we left how much Xander needs his music," Ace adds. "I'm pretty sure you know that without it, he won't survive. It's a part of who he is."

Hearing those words, I remember the deep pain Xander felt when he appeared on my doorstep the night his father destroyed his mother's guitar. I witnessed his shattered state, as he felt completely lost without his music. That night, I saw the broken boy who believed he had lost everything and how his music instantly soothed him once he held my father's guitar in his hands. I hate myself for caring about how he will feel if he loses his music. Especially after everything he has done to me, and to Alex.

"Name the amount, Poppy. I don't care how much it is. It's yours if you want it." Ace adds.

While the idea of not having to struggle day by day to make ends meet and worry myself sick about paying the bills is tempting, I can't bring myself to let my guard down. I just can't act like nothing happened. I can't pretend that he had rejected the both of us. But I can't help but wonder what they wanted me to do. Taking a deep breath, I ask.

"So, hypothetically speaking, if I were to do what you're asking - and I'm not saying I will - what exactly would be required of me?"

Ace throws a quick glance at Reg before he speaks. "We have an eight-week tour. Seven weeks in Australia, followed by another week in New Zealand. I'd really like it if you would join us."

"I'm sorry, but I can't do that." I raise my hand to interrupt him. "I have a child."

Ace's eyes widen in shock as my words sink in, and instantly I feel a surge of anger. Xander hasn't even mentioned our son to his best friend.

"You name your price, Poppy. Anything you want. I'll sign off on it right now, no problem," Ace says.

As I lock eyes with him for a moment, I sense the desperation in Ace's gaze, a clear indication of his urgency to bring Xander under control. It dawns on me that I could ask for any amount. The money could truly resolve all the problems that have been constantly weighing on my mind. However, the thought of being separated from my son for eight weeks is simply out of the question.

"She's considering it," Ace says with a grin.

"No, sorry I can't," I respond, taking a step back.

"Poppy, please wait," Ace says, his voice filled with urgency, making me pause. He glances over at Reg. "Give me one of your business cards."

I see Reg reach into his jacket pocket, retrieve a card, and hand it to Ace, who is already holding a pen.

"Here's my cell number," Ace says, jotting it down on the back of the card. "Don't decide now. Sleep on it and tell me your decision tomorrow."

I look at the card in his fingers, pausing briefly before accepting it. I slide it into my back pocket, dead set on tossing it in the trash later when everyone's gone, so no one, especially Nicole, gets to snag Ace's number.

"Please, consider it, Poppy," Ace asks, as I turn away to resume my duties at the bar.

CHAPTER 40

Xander

After briefly stepping outside to get some fresh air and gather my thoughts with Theo, I make my way back into the bar. Unfortunately, the detour only made things worse as fans crowded us for photos. I can't believe that Poppy's here. I want to know why the fuck she's working behind a bar instead of pursuing her dream. I suspect her mother has played a role in influencing her life choices. Why else would she be stuck here, getting hit on every fucking night by some drunk asshole?

I halt my steps right before I reach the double glass front doors and look towards the bar. The crowd inside makes it impossible to catch a glimpse of her.

"You okay, man?" Theo asks, coming to my side, casting a quick glance through the glass pane at the lively scene beyond the doors.

"Yeah," I nod. "I always thought she would move on to bigger things, you know. Not stick around in this shitty town, working in a bar to be constantly hit on."

"Don't stress, she can handle herself. When some creepy dude hit on her at the bar, she put him in his place." Theo rests his hand on my shoulder. "Go talk to her man."

"And what the fuck am I supposed to say? Hey, hello, remember me? I'm the asshole who left all those years ago without saying goodbye."

"Yeah, pretty much. It's a start."

"Yeah, I'm pretty sure she never wants to see or talk to me again."

"You won't know standing out here like some pussy on the other side of the door. Besides, standing up to your old man took some guts. I don't think she would have done that if she didn't care."

As I listen to Theo utter those words, I can feel a surge of emotions welling inside me. All this time, I've held onto the hope that she didn't hate me for leaving her without an explanation or a proper goodbye.

"Come on," Theo says, making his way towards the door. "If you don't go chat to the little spitfire, then I definitely will," he adds, with a smirk on his face.

I swear the teasing asshole does it on purpose knowing how I feel about Poppy. There is no way he's going anywhere near her.

After a year of knowing Theo, I had to tell him about Poppy when he asked me if I was gay because I wasn't hooking up with any girls. I was honest and shared all the details about Poppy. I confessed to him about falling in love with her, which terrified me since I had never experienced such emotions. How she is really into music and how talented she is. The guitar that I play every day and still cherish was once her dad's. Also, how she accepted me for who I truly am, broken and all. Lastly, I poured my heart out and told him how guilty I felt for leaving, explaining why I did what I did. Telling him all the hurtful words her mother said. But I shared none of the intimate moments or any of the amazing sex we had because that was just something between Poppy and me, nobody else.

I walk into the room, determined to go talk to Poppy. People always stare when we enter a room. I always imagined fame to be cool, but I never considered that everyone would be obsessively tracking our every move.

As we walk through the crowd, I find Ace and Reg talking with Poppy at the bar. When Ace hands her a card, I watch her take it and then turn away. That fucker better not be hitting on her.

As she goes to the next customer at the bar, I can't take my eyes off her. Her presence is just so captivating, especially when she flashes that beautiful smile. It reminds me of how she used to smile at me, just like that.

Man, I'm feeling super anxious right now. It's crazy how I can own the stage in front of thousands of people, but right now I'm losing my shit just thinking about talking to her. What if she straight up tells me to go fuck myself? I stay there, watching her for a few more seconds as she moves on to the next customer.

Ace and Reg get up and head over to the wankers in the suits who paid extra to be here tonight.

Wiping my sweaty palms on my jeans, I make my way over, aware of all the eyes on me.

I keep walking, not looking at anyone, just watching Poppy as she pours drinks at the bar. My throat is so dry and my heart is pounding so loud in my chest, that I can hear my blood pumping.

I've always wondered if I should reach out to her and see if she still has any feelings for me. However, I never did because I was afraid that she'd finally figure it out. That I was a lowlife like everyone said.

Upon reaching the bar, I swiftly take the seat that Ace was sitting in.

From there, I watch attentively as she interacts with the other patrons. I can't help but notice that she has aged a little, but the essence of the beautiful Poppy I remember from what feels like a lifetime ago is still there. Nervously, I tap my fingers on the bar, catching her attention. She gives me a quick look before passing a beer to the irritating dude in a suit who wanted a photo with me earlier. He keeps staring at Poppy as she turns away, and I can't stand the way he checks her out, examining every part of her. If the fucker doesn't look away soon, he'll feel my fist in his face.

As she makes her way towards me, my throat suddenly feels dry.

Standing before me, she swallows, her gulp appearing painful. Her eyes lock on mine for a moment before she looks away.

"What can I get you?" she asks. Though she never utters my name, her voice carries an impersonal, robotic tone, as if she's repeated these words countless times tonight, treating me like just another customer, much like the fuckhead in the suit two seats down.

"Hey, Princess," I say nervously, worried about how she might react to being called that.

"What can I do for you, Xander?" she asks, giving me a scrutinizing look that hints her patience is wearing thin as if she's desperate to distance herself from me.

"I'll have a bourbon, without ice," I say, feeling uncertain about what to say in front of all these people, especially with the moron in the suit still staring at me.

She turns around and prepares the drink.

With a forceful motion, she places it on the bar, causing it to spill over the edge of the glass. "Is there anything else?" She asks, her tone noticeably colder than before. It's a stark contrast to how she used to respond to Jade and others. It feels like a stab in the heart when she acts cold towards me. Nevertheless, I don't want her to walk away.

"Yeah, give me another one," I say, grabbing the glass and quickly downing the drink.

Poppy stares at me, like she's wondering what I'm up to. She waits for a second, then grabs another glass and fills it up. I really hope she stays and talks with me. I need to know why she's working here instead of pursuing her dream.

She returns, setting the bourbon down before taking hold of the empty glass and turning away.

Unable to contain my curiosity any longer, I ask. "Why do you work here?"

She stops and turns back, giving me a skeptical look. "Seriously, Xander? You think you can ask me that? It's none of your business what I do now." She turns to walk away.

"Wait, I'll have another," I add, desperate for her to stay. I've already had my fair share of drinks tonight to get through this event. Ace will lose his shit when he catches me slamming down every drink she puts in front of me, but I don't give a fuck. I need to talk to her.

She rolls her eyes, a characteristic reminiscent of our younger days, before turning away to get me another drink. I can't help but smile at the comforting familiarity of that simple gesture.

"She won't give you her number," remarks the asshole two seats away. "But hey, you might have a chance, since you're famous and everything. I bet she's a wild one in the sheets," he says, loud enough for people nearby to hear.

I'm so mad I could explode. Without thinking twice, I get up to confront this asshole who dares to disrespect Poppy like that. I snatch his shirt collar and bring him closer, our faces inches apart.

"You better listen, asshole," I yell, seething with anger. "Don't you dare disrespect her or I'll fuck you up."

The asshole's eyes go wide, and I feel his alcoholic breath on my face, triggering memories of the beatings my old man gave me.

Out of nowhere, Reg and Ace come over and drag me away from the jerk. The room goes dead silent again, but I don't give a damn. If he talks about Poppy like that again, I'll punch this jerk in the face.

"Come on," Ace urges. "You need to calm the fuck down, Xander."

"You better fucking apologize for talking about her like that," I yell, eyeing the asshole while I'm being dragged away from him.

The guy gives me a look like I'm out of my fucking mind. He thinks my statement is completely ridiculous. Ace and Reg let me go, but they're keeping an eye on me to make sure I don't go back and finish this guy off.

Without even needing to glance over, I can already feel Poppy nearby.

"You better fucking say it, dude, or else I'll come back over there," I tell him.

The asshole's gaze moves from me to Poppy.

"Sorry," he says, his apology carrying a half-hearted vibe.

"What for, dickhead?" I add.

He glances at me, but I give him a death stare and he immediately looks away and focuses on Poppy. "I'm sorry for disrespecting you tonight."

Poppy stays quiet and just glares at him like he's not even worth the effort to respond. She moves over and puts my drink next to the one that's already there.

I shove past Ace, making my way back to my seat. He follows me, ready to intervene if I go to punch that asshole again. But I totally ignore him and focus on Poppy.

"This is the shit I'm talking about," Ace says to Poppy. And I can't help but wonder what the fuck is going on.

"Can we talk?" I ask, sliding back onto the bar stool.

"Nah, sorry, I can't. I'm working," she says, her dismissive tone catching my attention.

"Why are you working here?" I ask again, curious to know why she's working here and hoping to learn more about her life.

"It's not your concern anymore. Plus, I don't think there's anything left to discuss. You made it crystal clear ages ago that you wanted nothing to do with me or care about what I had to say, so I don't have time to catch you up on my life."

"Princess," I say, a sharp ache piercing my chest. I never wanted her to see me as a worthless asshole, but now she does. How do I even tell her I left so she could have a better life, but it didn't work out like I thought?

"Let's make something clear, Xander," she says, placing her palms on the countertop of the bar. As soon as she leans forward, the scent of her perfume immediately transports me. "I'm not your fucking princess. I'm just some chick you fucked back in the day, same as all the others."

"No fucking way. I didn't think of you like that at all." Her words cut like tiny blades. Is that truly what she thinks? Does she really think that's all she meant to me?

"Your actions say it all. Just leave me alone, Xander."

She walks away, making me want to scream and tell her she's completely wrong. I wanna spill everything to her. How leaving her was the biggest mistake of my life. That the pain of my broken heart has forever changed me. But deep down, I know that no matter what I say, she won't believe me. Instead, I snatch the two bourbons from the bar and make my way back to where Theo and Nate are deeply engaged in conversation, captivating a small crowd at their table.

I walk past them and head to the empty table on the side of the room. I just want to be alone, and get fucking wasted.

As soon as I take a seat, I hastily gulp down one of the drinks, realizing that time has slipped away. There's no going back. It turns out her mother was right all along. She sees me exactly as she had predicted. Just like everyone else. The worst scum of the earth.

I quickly down the other drink, feeling its warmth spread through my body, and catch the waitress walking past.

"I'll give you a hundred bucks if you can score me a full bottle of Jack," I say to her.

She nods and heads to the bar.

Earlier, Ace lectured me about mingling with those who have paid a high price to be here tonight, but fuck that.

"It didn't go well," Theo says, passing me a glass of bourbon and plopping down in the chair next to me.

"What do you think?" I grab the glass and quickly consume its contents, hoping the alcohol will dull the ache, fully aware it's over. Poppy Reeves will never be in my life again.

CHAPTER 41
Poppy

As I drive back home, tears stream down my face at the thought of seeing Xander again. It's been five long years since he's been near me, and I had forgotten how his presence could make my body come alive. The way he used to look at me made my heart race like I was his entire world. There's still that look in his eyes that makes me feel like the most precious thing on earth, but deep down, I know it's just an act. He totally rocked that act in high school, using it to manipulate girls and get what he wanted.

Tonight, I didn't fall for it, even though part of me wanted to hear all about his new life. I was curious about how he's feeling now that he's made it big, and if it's everything he ever hoped it would be. But I didn't wanna risk being tossed aside once again, so I played it safe. This time, I have Alex to think about, and if his father is not interested in getting to know him, then I can't go down that road. Besides, he was probably looking for a hook-up for the night, and tomorrow he'll leave without giving me another thought.

I swipe the back of my hand across my face, trying to wipe away the tears as I fight to keep my attention on the dimly lit street in front of me through the windshield. All I need is to make it to the opposite side of town so I can finally get home.

My mother always cautioned me about the dangers that lurked in this rough part of town. She strongly believed that Alex and I shouldn't live here, but circumstances left me with no choice but to escape her tyrannical influence. As I continue driving, fresh tears cascade down my face as I catch sight of the vibrant neon sign of the burger joint ahead. It's the very same spot where Xander once treated me to delicious burgers and made me feel cherished.

"Stop it this instant," I say to myself. "Quit crying over someone who never cared about you. You're stronger than that."

Parking my car among the other dilapidated vehicles in the car park, I lock it up and head towards the entrance doors. Climbing the steps up to the twelfth floor, I retrieve my keys from my bag and unlock the door. The serene silence inside reassures me that Alex must already be asleep, given the late hour.

The room is bathed in a warm glow from the kitchen light, which illuminates the area. As I glance over, I notice Mrs. B. peacefully asleep on the couch, her head resting against the back. Her glasses are slightly askew, and her mouth is open. It truly astonishes me how this remarkable woman goes above and beyond, exceeding anything I could ever ask of my mother, despite not being related to me. It's already one-thirty in the morning, and I can't help but ponder how, if it were my own mother, she would have incessantly called me, asking when I'll be coming home.

I carefully place my bag on the table, followed by my keys, hoping to avoid making any noise. Unfortunately, my attempts are futile as Mrs. B. wakes up and glances over at me.

"I'm sorry. I didn't mean to wake you," I quickly apologize.

"No, you didn't. I just closed my eyes for a few minutes," she explains, getting up from the couch and coming over. Her movements are slow, and her aging body shows signs of stiffness.

"How was he tonight?" I ask, hoping Alex is doing better.

"He seemed more energetic tonight. We read a story and put together a puzzle. Then he asked me to take a seat so he could play something on his guitar."

I smile with relief as I hear him returning to his usual self.

"But he barely touched his dinner. How was your night?"

I walk towards the sink, my hand reaching out for a glass of water, uncertain of how to convey to her the immense wave of emotions that washed over me upon seeing Xander again. It was like my heart had been shattered all over again.

"That bad, huh," she says when I don't answer. She gets how much Xander's actions hurt me with how he won't even be there for his own kid.

"Are you okay?" Mrs. Baxter asks.

With a glass in hand, I turn towards her. Nodding, I raise the glass to my lips and take a large gulp of water, desperately attempting to suppress the tears that are forming in my eyes. Yet, it proves to be in vain; Mrs. B has already detected my distress.

"Come here, love," she says, her arms wide open.

As I set the glass down on the sink, I find solace in her comforting embrace, tears flowing freely down my face. This vulnerable side of me, I've only shown her once before, when I couldn't keep it inside any longer, and I revealed the painful truth of what happened five years ago - when Xander left me, and I found out I was pregnant. "The most messed up thing is, Ace from the band actually offered me a job," I say, wiping my nose and trying to hold back tears.

"What kind of job?" she asks.

"I don't know exactly. Something about just being around."

"They want you to be around Xander after everything that has happened."

"Yep," I say, grabbing the card from my back pocket and giving it to her.

When she gives it back, I go over to the trash and toss it in. "I don't think I can deal with that. It hurts to see him. He tried to talk to me tonight, but I just couldn't do it. Ace wants me to come along on their Australia and New Zealand tour."

She looks at me, totally confused.

"I know, right? It's absurd," I add.

"I'm totally confused. Why do they want you to go on tour?"

As I sit at the table, a deep sigh escapes me, as I feel the weight of the night settling upon my shoulders. "Well, tonight there was an incident. Xander's father unexpectedly showed up and caused trouble. Xander was furious when he saw his dad. Ace and another guy attempted to calm him down, but he refused to listen. It was only when I approached him and intervened that he finally stopped. I know it might have been foolish of me to get involved. I should have just stayed out of it. However, seeing his father there and knowing what he's been through, I couldn't just stand idly by and do nothing."

Mrs. B takes a seat beside me. "So, let me get this straight, Xander only stopped when you told him to?"

"Yes."

"And the others told him to stop, but he wouldn't listen?"

"Yep, that's right," I say, feeling kind of confused about where this conversation is going. "What's your point?"

"It's nothing," she says, a mischievous smirk playing on her lips, hinting at an undisclosed secret. "You should think about it."

"Think about what, exactly?" I inquire, rising from my seat and making my way towards the kitchen. Unsure of how to proceed, I pick up a dish towel from the kitchen counter and neatly place it on the hook.

"Consider going."

I turn around, staring at her as if she has grown another head. A laugh escapes me, finding the idea completely ridiculous. "Eight weeks? How in the world could I ever be away from Alex for that long? It's just not possible."

"So how much are they offering you?" She raises an eyebrow, intrigued.

"I can have whatever I want," I say, leaning against the kitchen counter with my arms crossed. "Ace said to name my price."

"Can't you see, Poppy? Remember, a few years back when you said you wanted to find a special place for Alex to have amazing childhood memories? You wanted him to have a big backyard to play, ride a bike, and have a tree swing. This is your chance to make that dream come true."

"No. I can't be near a man who didn't want me or our child."

"Just put that aside and focus on the result. Eight weeks isn't that long if you really think about it. If you pass on this chance now for a better future, will you regret it later? Alex is fine to stay with me."

She was correct. I must consider the larger perspective. There's a chance I could get enough money to buy a house in a more desirable neighborhood. Then Alex can hang out with other kids his age and learn how to ride a bike. The current situation here is extremely dangerous, so it is too risky to let him venture out into the hallway.

Can I truly accomplish this? Can I spend eight weeks with Xander? Is it possible for me to stay strong and resist his charm?

As I turn my head to think, a large cockroach scuttling across the floor in front of me abruptly captures my attention. Just the sight of it sends shivers down my spine. This place is truly unbearable.

Within days of moving in, I realized that coming here was the biggest mistake of my life. However, I had no other option but to stay, as I couldn't go back to my mother's place. I couldn't subject Alex to the constant negativity and relentless criticism of Xander. I longed to provide him with a much better life than the one we had while living at my mother's house.

This place was meant to be a temporary fix until I could find a better alternative, but unfortunately, that never happened. I now have an incredible chance to rectify the situation. I have this amazing chance to spend eight weeks on something I don't want to do, but it could change our lives and give us a place to call home.

I quickly squash the cockroach, getting rid of the disgusting creature. If I never have to come across another one again, I would be happy. Just seeing a cockroach crawling on the edge of my bed two days after moving in made me feel disgusted and repulsed. I need to get out of this place.

As I glance back at Mrs. B, I notice her watching me. And she's right. I can handle this for eight weeks. All I have to do is stay focused, keep my guard up, and make sure I keep my distance from Xander.

I walk over to the trash can, grab the card, and then my phone. It's already past two. It's late, but I send a text anyway.

Poppy: Hey Ace, it's Poppy. Alright, I'm game, but I've got a couple of conditions. First, you need to offer me a dollar amount I can't refuse. Also, I need $10,000 upfront to cover rent and support for my son while I'm gone.

After sending the message, I gently set my phone down on the table, knowing well that I won't hear back until tomorrow.

Mrs. B gets up from her seat and says, "You're making the right decision, Poppy. You're thinking about your future."

My phone makes a noise, and Mrs. B glances at it. I snatch my phone and check the message, reading it aloud.

Ace: Cool, let's meet up at the Astor Hotel tomorrow at 10.

The next morning, after leaving Alex with Mrs. B, I make my way towards the hotel. Uncertainty fills me, and I do not know what to expect. I couldn't sleep at all last night, constantly questioning if going back to Xander's realm is the right choice. But deep down, I have a firm belief that whatever awaits me after eight weeks will be worth it. I keep reminding myself that I'm only doing it for the money, and that's the only reason.

Pulling up in front of the hotel, I switch off the engine and feel a surge of nerves wash over me. Leaning forward, I take a deep breath in an attempt to calm myself, but before I can fully compose myself, a sudden knock on my window startles me. Glancing over, I see a hotel employee dressed in their uniform. Eagerly, I roll down the window, wondering if Ace or Reg had sent them to guide me.

"Sorry, but you can't park that vehicle here."

"Why?"

"Because..." The employee pauses, and I quickly glance around. The surroundings are filled with luxurious, shiny cars that exude prestige, making my green clunker look more like an abandoned vehicle. I roll up the window, totally ignoring him. Without hesitation, I push open the door, causing him to take a step back as I get out of my car.

No matter how tempting it may be to snatch one of the many flashy cars out here, I make sure to lock up my trusty old shitbox. Despite its lackluster appearance, it holds immense sentimental value for me. Sadly, I cannot afford insurance, so the thought of replacing it would be an unbearable financial burden.

"Miss, I told you to move your car," he says, chasing after me as I walk towards the hotel entrance.

"I don't give a damn about what you want. It's there now, so just deal with it," I say, throwing the words over my shoulder.

"Miss, you're not listening to me."

"And you're not listening to me. My car is going to be there for at least twenty minutes. I'll move it once this meeting is done. That is, if the old junk starts," I throw out, chuckling, trying to get under his skin. So what if my car isn't up to par? This is just how my life is, and he'll have to deal with it.

With confidence, I stride through the automatic double doors that effortlessly slide open.

When my name is called, I immediately turn to the left and see Reg and Ace sitting at a table. The table is placed against a glass window, which provides a beautiful view of a lively garden. On the round glass table, there are two coffee cups and a noticeably large yellow envelope. As I walk closer, both men get to their feet.

"So happy you could join us," Ace says. "Do you want coffee?"

I give a nod, and a server comes over. Ace makes sure she takes my order. It's hard to fathom that the person sitting beside me is the same Ace I used to know in school. He appears softer, more compassionate, and thoughtful. "I was hoping you'd reconsider," Ace says, grinning.

"Honestly, I'm still uncertain. But if I choose to go through with it, it'll be for my son."

"Alright," Reg says, opening a folder. "I received the papers this morning. It's pretty straightforward, as you can see." He slides the papers in front of me. "On the first page, you'll find a list of demands. If you agree, you can sign on the second page. I assure you, the amount we're offering is quite generous."

As I wait for my coffee, I read the page. Right at the top, I see my name and my position - Band assistant. Below that, there's a list outlining my duties.

When I see something I don't understand, I pause and look up at Ace. "What exactly does it mean to be available when the band needs me?" I inquire.

Ace locks eyes with me and explains, "If Xander spirals, we'll need you to help calm him down. Of course, there may be times when we can handle it on our own. But, given Xander's recent behavior, we might need you in the beginning."

I take a moment to think and then pose the question. "But what if in the end, I don't make any difference to Xander and last night was just a one-time thing?"

"Poppy, trust me, if you hadn't stepped in when Xander got all fired up last night, things would've gone terrible with the label. We would've lost everything. I've known Xander for most of my life and what I saw last night just confirms that you're the only one who's been able to get through to him in ages. He listens to you."

"The next clause states you must not engage in any sexual activity with any of the band members," Reg explains. "Break this rule and the contract is non-negotiable. You'll be asked to leave with no payment."

"You don't have to worry about that?" I reassure Reg, looking directly at him.

"Alright," he says, diverting his attention to the paper and flipping to the following page. "Here's the amount we're willing to pay you for completing the task. If you're happy with everything in this agreement, just sign on the line below."

As I reach for the pen on the table, I steal a glance at Ace, who nods in approval.

Two hundred thousand dollars. That's the exact sum stated at the top of the contract. This amount has the power to transform our lives completely. A strange blend of excitement and worry wash over me as I sign my name. Thoughts of Xander still linger in my mind, but I remind myself to stay strong and keep my guard up against his charms, just as I did last night.

Yes, I can do this.

Once I sign, Reg quickly gathers the papers and tucks them into his briefcase. As I reach for my coffee and take a sip, I continue to contemplate whether I have made the right decision. Yet, the idea of offering Alex a better life in a better home and neighborhood reassures me I am indeed on the right path.

"Here's the cash you wanted," Reg says, sliding the yellow envelope over to me.

"Thank you so much," I say, happily accepting the envelope and tucking it away in my handbag. "This will totally help with the rent and cover some expenses for my son while I'm gone."

"Right. Welcome to the tour," Reg says, his hand outstretched towards me, but his tone leaves me uncertain if he truly wants me here.

With that, Reg stands up and makes his way toward the elevators, leaving Ace and me alone. It dawns on me that I've never really had a proper conversation with Ace before, and I can't help but ponder what Xander might have shared about me with him throughout the years.

"Is your son gonna crash at your mom's while you're gone?"

"No, he'll stay with someone else,' I say, grabbing my coffee. "Hey, I forgot to ask, what date do we fly out?"

"October twenty-fourth. It's two weeks away. I'll text you the details about what time a car will pick you up for the airport."

I nod as I put my cup back on the table.

"I have no idea what went down between you and Xander, he never told me. But I want you to know that if you need anything, don't go to Reg. Come to me, Theo, or Nate. If you talk to Reg, it might go back to the label, so I'd prefer to handle it ourselves if we can."

"Does Xander know what's going on?"

"No. Xander has no clue. Maybe that's a good thing," he says as he gets up.

I down the last of my coffee and get up.

"I'll be in touch, Poppy. I appreciate your help with this. Sorry to rush you, but we need to leave soon to catch our flight."

I walk beside Ace as he leads me towards the glass doors. They slide open, and right before I take a step outside, Ace speaks up.

"Thanks again, Poppy, for doing this."

I say nothing to Ace because I wasn't doing it for them. I was doing it for myself and my son. It was our chance to have a better life. Nodding, I walk out of the hotel and make my way to my car.

The hotel parking attendant from earlier gives me a dirty look and keeps his eyes on me as I walk to my car.

CHAPTER 42

Xander

There's a sudden knock on my hotel door, and I don't feel like dealing with it. Whoever is on the other side, I wish they would just fuck off and leave me alone. I'm suffering from a killer hangover.

The knocking intensifies, turning into forceful thumping. "Xander, get the fuck up now and answer this door!" Ace shouts from the other side, his thumping growing louder by the second, aggravating the throbbing ache pulsating through my head. "We're all downstairs waiting for you, asshole."

Shifting my legs to the side of the bed, I run my hands through my hair as his relentless thumping persists. "For fuck sake, Xander!"

"Yeah, alright, I'm coming, asshole." I muster the energy to push myself up from the bed and stride towards the door. With a forceful pull, I swing it open, desperate to halt the pounding that feels like a drill piercing my brain.

Ace glances down. "Put some clothes on, man. I don't want to see your fucking junk. Now hurry up." He walks into the room ahead of me.

Closing the door behind me, I turn around only to find a pair of jeans thrown at me, landing on my chest.

"Put these on now and hurry the fuck up. Reg is already pissed."

"So what? The asshole can wait."

I try to put on my jeans but almost fall over because I'm still feeling the effects of last night's alcohol. Damn, I bet I'd still be over the limit if I had to take a breath test.

"We were supposed to leave forty minutes ago. Why the hell didn't you answer your phone?" Ace asks, gathering my belongings from the floor as he moves around the room.

He throws me a crumpled shirt, signaling for me to put it on. I have a clean shirt in my bag that I never bothered to unpack, but I'm feeling too drained to retrieve it. The one I wore yesterday will do because I can't wait to get out of this fucked up town that always brings me down.

"There's something we need to discuss," Ace says, walking over to the couch and hastily gathering all the items of mine that are scattered on the floor, stuffing them into a bag.

"Yeah, I get it, asshole. I need to quit drinking." My mimicking tone echoes the words I've heard from him countless times over the past five years. "Or else I'll end up like my father. I've heard this shit before. It's time for a new subject."

"No," Ace replies. "Well, yes, you really should quit drinking. I already talked to Theo about keeping you supplied with bourbon all night."

"Yeah, I never thought you'd become such a boring old fart at twenty-four, always bothering me with nothing else to do," I snap back.

"And I never thought I'd be the one to call out my friend for ruining our dream."

"Fuck you."

"Put on some shoes, asshole," Ace says, when all my things are loaded up in my bag.

In an attempt to defy him, I act like a spoiled child as I walk over and grab my shoes.

With determination not to comply with his request, I slip my phone into my pocket while holding the shoes in my hand. Making my way towards the door, I prepare to leave.

The atmosphere in the elevator is tense and quiet, and I can sense that Ace is itching to criticize all of my flaws. It's such a stark contrast to how he used to be in our school days when we would hang out together. He embraced me, faults and all, understanding that this was the real me. But now, it's clear that the mere thought of my actions annoys him endlessly.

As the elevator doors open, my head is pounding like crazy, and I'm immediately met with deafening shrieks that threaten to make my head explode. Five girls sprint towards Ace and me.

"Hey, Xander, can you sign these?" One girl passes me a marker and lifts her top for me to sign her skin.

Back in the day when Ace and I used to talk about our groupies and fame, I always imagined these moments to be fulfilling. I believed it would make me happy to have the world at my feet and the power to have any girl I wanted. I had this vision of attaining a god-like status, adored by millions. But to be honest, it hasn't lived up to my expectations. These girls only desire the version of Xander they see on stage, the persona portrayed to the public. None of them truly understands the real me, the one burdened with deep scars. The one who sometimes struggles to breathe. The one who yearns for something more meaningful than the life I find myself in. This empty feeling that's been haunting me for years.

After snapping a few more pics and signing some more tits, Ace and I head towards the side door where Reg and the rest of the band are waiting. The rest of the group is already in the car. Reg stands alone, his gaze fixed on his phone.

As soon as we approach, Reg turns around. Even with those sunglasses and his wannabe security guard vibe, I can tell he's pissed. I've seen that look on his face so many times in the past three years, ever since I found out the record label was screwing us over and now I refuse to comply.

"Where the fuck have you been?" he asks, his voice filled with irritation.

"Avoiding you, asshole." I move past him and get in the car beside Theo.

Once Ace and Reg get in, the car takes off to the airport. I stare out the window, purposely avoiding eye contact with Reg. I know that if I turn my head, he'll be glaring at me. One of these days, I swear I'm gonna lose my shit at him.

"Well, have you told him?" Reg asks, no doubt just wanting to hear himself speak. He always enjoys doing that.

"No," Ace responds. "I don't think now's the right time."

I glance at Ace, who is looking at Reg with a silent plea for him to be quiet.

"What do you have to tell me?" I ask. My voice carries a sharp edge as I lock eyes with my childhood friend. There are moments when I feel like I don't even recognize this guy anymore. He has changed, and not for the better. I sometimes wonder if he enjoys being controlled by the label that owns us, since he always does everything they tell him to do. The Ace I used to know never gave a damn about authority or the rules. This version of Ace is incredibly embarrassing compared to the hot-headed, rule-breaking kid who used to be my friend. It's like he's completely sold his soul to the label.

"What's going on?" Nate asks.

"Nothing that affects you?" Reg says.

"Hey, listen up, fucker," says Nate. "If something affects Xander, it affects all of us. You can't just throw out a comment like that and keep us in the dark."

Lately, Theo, Nate, and I have been having conversations about where the record label is taking us, and we're not happy with it. Unfortunately, we feel powerless to do anything about it. On top of that, everyone here thinks Reg is a complete asshole, all except for Ace.

"We have a few matters to discuss concerning the upcoming tour," Reg states. "On Thursday, the label wants to address a few things—"

"The rules, you mean. Just say it straight. It's all about the rules," interrupts Nate.

"Come on," says Ace. "We can sort everything out at the meeting."

I eye Ace for a brief moment before redirecting my attention back towards the window. There's no point in arguing or trying to make my point heard because, regardless of what I, Nate, or Theo say, no one listens. We're merely humble puppets to be manipulated by the damn label. Sometimes, I wish I could boldly tell them to go screw themselves and that they can stick their contract where the sun doesn't shine. However, I could never do that to the rest of the band, including Ace.

Soon enough, we reach the airport and board the company plane. At least this way, I can create some distance between myself, Reg, and Ace for the next couple of hours, until we finally touch down.

CHAPTER 43

Poppy

Over the next week, I handle all the arrangements. I pay the rent in advance and stock up the food shelves, since Mrs. B will be staying for the entire duration while I'm away. Every day, I try to spend as much time as possible with Alex because the mere thought of being separated from him is unbearable.

Yesterday, I had a conversation with my boss, Nicole, about taking some unpaid time off. However, it didn't go as I had expected. I think she is still upset with me because I failed to introduce her to Ace or Xander. Unfortunately, this situation has led to my decision to finish my current job by the end of this week. It's disheartening to know that when I return, I will have the added stress of finding a job.

Earlier today, I got a text from Ace, asking for my address so he could arrange a car to pick me up and take me to the airport. In response, I asked if Xander knew I was coming on the tour. Ace told me that Xander still does not know. I hope they tell him soon because I don't know how he'll react when he sees me getting on the plane. I know for a fact that he'll be pissed.

With just four days remaining until I depart, there's still a lot of tasks left to complete. I haven't even begun packing because I still need to buy a new suitcase. The stitching on the zipper of my old one came undone.

While I patiently wait for Alex to put on his socks and shoes, I suddenly hear a knock at the door. I quickly move over, eager to find out who it could be. But as soon as I see Mrs. B, with tears in her eyes and a troubled look, I know something's wrong.

"What's happened?" I ask, taking a step back to let her come inside.

"It's my daughter. I just got a phone call from Simon."

I'm familiar with Simon, Mrs. B's son-in-law. She can't stop talking about how great he is with her daughter and grandkids.

"It's Sienna. She's been in a car accident. Simon rang a few minutes ago. He's booked me a flight out this afternoon."

"Oh, I'm so sorry," I say, stepping forward to give her a hug. "Is she going to be okay?" I ask, taking a step back.

"I'm not sure," Mrs. B says, lifting her glasses and wiping her eyes. "She hit her head and Simon said they're gonna operate, so I won't have more information until I'm there. I'm so sorry, Poppy. I have no idea how long I'll be gone for."

"Don't worry about me," I reassure her. "Go, be there for your daughter."

Just then, Alex comes running into the room. "GG," he says as he approaches.

"Hello sweetheart," Mrs. B says, with a faint smile, trying to put on a happy face.

"So, what time is your flight?" I ask.

"The flight is at two. I'll have to pack and leave shortly."

"I'll give you a lift to the airport," I offer, feeling indebted to Mrs. B for everything she has done for us throughout the years.

She reaches out and grasps my hand. "If it's not too much trouble, I would like that. Again, I'm sorry."

"Don't apologize for taking care of your family. I completely understand. Let me know if there is anything I can do to help?"

I open the door, allowing her to move out of the apartment. "Just knock on the door when you're ready to leave."

"Thank you, dear," she responds, then heads to her apartment across the hall.

After she shuts her door, I close ours and head back to the table where Alex is engrossed in the puzzle we had started earlier. I suddenly feel trapped, with no escape in sight. The ten grand that Reg gave me has already been spent, and now I have to figure out a way to repay it. But what if they demand the full amount all at once? It's completely impossible for me to come up with that kind of money. And to make matters worse, I've already lost my job. They brought in a new girl last week, and I was the one training her. What the hell am I supposed to do now?

I grab my phone off the table, determined to text Ace to let him know I might not make it if I can't figure out a solution to my problem. But then Alex comes over and jumps on my lap, so I stop.

"Why was GG crying?" he asks.

"Her daughter was in a car accident today and she's worried about her."

"Is she gonna die?" He gives me a stare with those familiar brown eyes.

"I hope not. But don't ask GG that, okay. It might upset her."

He nods and goes back to his puzzle.

When Mrs. B knocks, Alex swiftly gets up from my lap and hurries to open the door. I quickly lock my apartment as I step out, taking Mrs. B's suitcase. She holds Alex's hand and guides us to the elevator, the two of them chatting along the way.

I hate seeing Mrs. B so upset. On the way to the airport, I saw she was trying to act happy whenever she spoke to Alex.

After saying our goodbye, Alex and I sit, gazing out the glass windows watching the planes take off. Alex just sits there all afternoon, wanting to watch the planes. It's crazy how something so small can hold his attention for so long. Meanwhile, I've been sitting here, attempting to text Ace to tell him I can't make it, but I keep chickening out and deleting it every time.

The only option I have is to find another babysitter for Alex, and unfortunately, the only person I know is the last person I ever wanted to leave him with. My mother. But I have no choice. Not after I've already spent the ten thousand. I have to go to my mother and see if she would be willing to watch her grandson. It might only be for a few days anyway. Mrs. B said that as soon as she has more information she will let me know. It's possible that Alex will only be at my mom's for a week, tops, and then Mrs. B might be back.

As I drive to my mom's house, I'm feeling anxious as I go over the verses in my head, rehearsing the words I will say to her. It's been over two years since I last saw her. Since I stopped taking Alex over to see her. I'm not sure how she'll react when she sees me. And especially when she hears the job is music related.

As I pull up to the curb, a lump forms in my throat as I spot her out the front of the house, tending to the garden. When she turns around and spots my car, I see the shock on her face. Resisting the powerful urge to flee, I turn off the car engine. I take a deep breath and force myself to open the car door. As soon as I get out, I go around the car to open the back passenger door for Alex to get out.

While we head towards the front gate, my mother keeps a close eye on us. The moment we reach the gate, she swiftly removes her gardening gloves and approaches us. Although no one has spoken, I can already feel the tension in the air.

"Hey, Mom," I say, trying to make things less awkward.

"Hey Poppy, what brings you here?" she asks, glancing down at Alex. "He looks more like his father every day." I pick up on the tone in her voice. Under her intense stare, Alex finds refuge behind my legs. I'm tempted to just quit and not bother asking her, but I've already spent the ten thousand dollars.

"Can we talk?" I ask, noticing she's blocking the gate, not allowing us to walk through. Taking a brief pause, she continues to gaze at Alex, before eventually granting us access by opening the gate.

Alex and I move through the gate and wait off to one side.

"Hello Alex," my mother says with a warm smile as she closes the gate behind us.

"Hi," Alex's tiny voice sounds from behind my leg.

Mom moves around us and leads us to the front steps. When she gets to the front door, she takes off her gardening gloves and puts them on the small table on the patio, before she heads into the house.

I close the door behind us and move further into the house. I see that the interior of the house is still the same as before.

"You never said why you were here?" she asks, making her way to the kitchen.

"You won't believe it, but I've got an opportunity to make a huge differ-ence in our lives."

She walks around to the other side of the kitchen counter as if to put a barrier between us. I try to keep it positive because as soon as I tell her what it is, she'll be annoyed.

"So, what's this opportunity?" she asks.

"This is a real chance for me to get us into a house."

"Okay. So what do you need from me?"

She gets straight to the point.

As I look at her and listen to her tone, I notice she has become even more hardened since the last time I saw her.

When I first brought Alex home after he was born, she offered no help whatsoever because he shared the same name as his father. Every day, she kept pestering me to change it, but I wanted their names to be linked. Eventually, she realized that I would not change Alex's name, so she gave me some help, but it was minimal. I never want to follow in my mom's footsteps with how she would avoid talking about my dad. I didn't want that for Alex.

Even though Xander doesn't care about us, I've always been honest with Alex about his dad.

Well, at least as much as I can be. I haven't broken the news that his dad wants nothing to do with him. But he knows who his dad is, and I've told him he's doing something really important. When he's older, he can ask Xander all the questions he needs. Hopefully, Xander will be interested in meeting him someday.

"I was wondering if you could do me a favor and look after Alex for a few days. The lady who was supposed to watch him had to leave for a family emergency. Hopefully, she'll be back in a few days."

"Why? Where are you going?"

I swallow hard as I'm about to drop this bombshell. "I've been offered a chance to go to Australia and New Zealand for eight weeks."

"Eight weeks?"

"Yes," I respond. "However, Mrs. B, who lives across the hall, is more than willing to take care of Alex for the majority of the time. Unfortunately, her daughter had an accident and she had to leave unexpectedly today." I realize I'm waffling but I can't seem to stop. "It's just for a few days until she returns, and then she'll be able to stay at the apartment to look after Alex." I let out a sigh and finally shut my mouth.

"So essentially, you need me now because the person you initially asked is unable to do it at the moment."

I can't help but notice the sarcasm in her voice.

"Well, that's one way to look at it but-."

"So, why are you heading to the other side of the world?" She cuts me off.

Here we go. I lick my lips, feeling unsure of what to say to her because I know that as soon as she hears this news, it will make her mad. "So, here's the deal. I've been offered a position to join a band on tour," I finally say.

In an instant, she withdraws into herself. Her face becomes rigid, her body tenses up, and she folds her arms tightly.

"Mom, it's a great opportunity. I can't pass it up."

"How much are they paying you?" I can't help but notice her snarky tone.

"Once the tour is over, they will pay me two hundred thousand."

She stays silent for a moment, and I can tell that she is somewhat taken aback by the substantial sum of money. She knows how money can make a difference - she inherited her grandmother's life savings not long after Alex was born and she quit her job.

"Mom, getting this money means we can finally leave the apartment and move into a house," I say, trying to emphasize the importance of how things could change for us. "And as you can see-" I don't even get to finish the sentence because once again she interrupts me.

"So, which band wants you to go on tour and what will you even be doing since you don't have any skills?"

I hold back my response to her snarky comment, opting to bite my tongue. Thank goodness Alex's stay will be short and then he can return to the apartment with Mrs. B. For the time being, I prefer to remain silent, as I'm not prepared to engage in a heated argument with her.

"It's him, isn't it? That lowlife," she says when I don't answer her previous question. "It all makes sense now. He was here two weeks ago. Because who else would offer you something like that."

"It's Xander's band, yes, but he has no clue that the label is paying me to go."

"So, what will you be doing while you're there?" she asks. "It's obvious you're back with him. Why else would they offer you a position?"

There was no way I could tell her about what happened with Xander's dad and that I was the only one who could get through to him, because I knew she would only mock it. Anything to do with Xander and she doesn't listen.

"No Mom. I promise you, it's not at all what you think. I'm not back with Xander."

"I still can't figure out why they'd want you."

That's the thing about my mother. She's never been my biggest supporter. "So, do you think you could look after Alex for a few days until Mrs. B comes home?"

By now, Alex has moved out from behind my legs and is looking around the room. My mother stares at Alex for a long time before she looks back at me.

"Well, I guess so," she says. "It'll be nice finally getting to know my grandchild since you always keep me away."

I'm about to open my mouth and tell her I never stopped her from seeing him, but I decide against it. Engaging in an argument with her in front of Alex is something I want to avoid.

"So, when do you leave?"

"In three days. And trust me, Mom, I have no desire to be with someone who hasn't even made an effort to get to know Alex."

She gazes at me for a moment and then nods as if believing the truth in my words. "Okay," she says, glancing at Alex, who stands next to me staring up at her.

"Hey Alex, do you like milkshakes?" she asks, smiling as she moves back around the kitchen cupboard and comes to stand in front of us.

It's surprising to see her like this because I haven't seen her smile like that since my dad was around.

Alex looks up at me as if asking for my approval. I nod, giving him the go-ahead.

He moves over and my mother holds her hand out for Alex to take.

I stand there watching as they walk back around the other side of the kitchen counter.

I move onto one of the stools, watching the interaction between my mother and her grandson.

I send Ace a text with the new address for the car to pick me up. My mother's address. I've been spending time with my mom so she and Alex can bond. He's way more comfortable with her now than when we first came back here. She's been good with him. The only time she brings up Xander is when she's talking about how Alex looks.

When we came back the next day, my mom told me she got in touch with a handyman to build a sandpit for Alex in the backyard. She didn't have to do that, but I'm so thankful. At least Alex will have something to do while I'm gone.

He's really excited to come to my mom's today because the sandpit is finally done.

As I wait for the town car to arrive, Alex is happily playing in the sandpit. It's so great to see him playing outside and what I'm doing for the next eight weeks is all for him, so he can do this every day.

Yesterday I heard from Mrs. B. She was so upset. She rang to tell me that her daughter suffered a stroke during her surgery and she needs to be with her family. And that it could be a few more weeks before she returned. Surprisingly my mother was happy to have Alex for that length of time.

"I'm pretty sure I didn't forget anything for Alex," I say, coming out the back door to stand with my mom as she watches Alex play in the sandpit. "I think I'll stand over there so I can see when the car arrives." I move to the side of the yard for a better view of the street.

My mother walks over and waits with me.

"I'm going to call you every night." When I hear a car pulling up, I quickly turn my head. "That's my ride," I say, moving in to hug my mom. "Thanks, Mom, for doing this for me," I say.

I release the hug and notice the driver is already out of the car.

"I'll be there in a second," I shout out, before going over to say goodbye to Alex. It's heartbreaking that I won't be with him, but I have to do this for our future.

"Alright, buddy, I'm gonna go now," I say, tears welling up.

He stands and rushes over, his arms and legs covered in sand, but I don't mind because as a mother, those little things no longer bother me. Not anymore. There was this one time when Alex was a baby that I went to the supermarket and unknowingly had baby vomit in my hair.

"Bye Alex," I say, holding him in a tight embrace. However, I can feel his excitement to get back to the sandpit. "I love you." The moment I release him, he dashes off, as if the sandpit holds the utmost significance in his world.

"I love you too!" he shouts, grabbing the red bucket and spade, and returning to his digging.

I make my way back to where my mom is and continue circling the house. Just as I'm about to enter the front yard, I pause for a moment to steal one last glance at Alex. He's got his head down, totally engrossed in the sand. I turn away, grab my bag from the front patio, and head towards the front gate, where the driver patiently waits for me.

"Miss Poppy Reeves," the driver says.

"Yes," I add.

"Hi, I'm Nigel, and I'll be chauffeuring you to the airport."

He takes my bag, heads to the car, and pops open the back door so I can get in.

As I settle into my seat, he shuts the door. I steal a quick look toward the spot where my mother was standing earlier, only to find she's already left.

Once Nigel puts my suitcase in the trunk, he hops in and starts the engine. I give my old childhood home one last look as the car leaves, already missing my son.

Four hours later, following a business class flight and another town car ride from the airport, I've checked into the most luxurious hotel I've ever laid eyes on. Without wasting any time, I indulge in a delicious meal and take full advantage of the mini bar, while treating myself to a binge-watching session of the latest season of my all-time favorite show, The Real Housewives of Beverly Hills. It's a rare opportunity for me to catch up, as it has been years since I've had the chance to sit and enjoy a binge-watch marathon like this.

Ace kindly left an envelope for me at the front desk, informing me that a car would pick me up early in the morning. So, I avoid drinking any alcohol, as I certainly don't want to oversleep and miss my wake-up call.

Chapter 44

Xander

For the past two weeks, the walls of my house have felt suffocating. I know it's too big for just one person, but that's what you do when you have money and come from nothing. You splurge because you never want to go back to that.

Years ago, we stumbled upon a large block of land and decided to divide it, constructing three houses on that block. We never fenced off our houses, so the environment felt like a family estate for me and the rest of the band members. My house is positioned in the middle. It's slightly smaller than Ace's, which has a recording studio. Theo and Nate live on the other side of me.

Each of us needs our own space, and we've agreed not to bring any chicks or groupies back to our sanctuary. This place is our haven, where we can be our true selves, flaws and all. Over time, our bond has strengthened to where we feel like a family, the four of us. Out of all of us, Nate was the lucky one who had a supportive family that pushed him to chase his dreams, and from what I've heard, his parents practically raised Theo. He used to live three doors down the street from Nate. I thought my childhood was tough growing up with an asshole of a father, but the night Theo opened up and shared his childhood experiences, it was nothing compared to what he went through.

I have more respect for Nate's family after hearing that. I enjoy it when they come to visit. Even though they've been here only a few times in the last three years, his mom reminds me a lot of my mom in the way she takes care of her son. His dad is really funny, and I enjoy sitting and having a few beers with him. I haven't met his younger sister yet, but from what I've heard, she's following in her brother's footsteps. Word has it she's killer on the drums and determined to make a name for herself in the music scene.

Sitting on my couch in nothing but my sweatpants, I gaze at the white grand piano that takes up most of the room. I impulsively bought it when I moved into this place. It was a foolish decision to invest in an instrument that serves as nothing more than a dust collector. I suck at playing the damn thing.

Still today I have no fucking idea why I bought it in the first place. I've tinkered with it a few times and honestly thought I could teach myself to play, but man, the piano is a whole different ball game compared to a guitar. I think watching Poppy easily switch between the keyboard and guitar made me think I could do it too, but it never worked out. She's super talented in that area compared to me.

Ever since I saw her the other night, I've been spiraling downward again. It's a tough pill to swallow knowing she doesn't want anything to do with me. And honestly, who can blame her after what I put her through. But what I love is she's still that fiery girl I remember, the one with the sharp tongue who refuses to tolerate anyone's shit.

I find myself absentmindedly soothing the pain in my chest, near the tattoo etched on my skin. I got it years ago and only Theo knows its significance. The music staff, embellished with music notes, wraps around a flower - a red poppy. In addition to the intricate design, there are also tiny inscriptions, but you need to get up close to read them.

I hide it away from the prying eyes of the media, ensuring its secrecy. I always make sure it remains out of sight. This tattoo serves as a reminder of what we used to have. How she carved her name into the depths of my heart, and it has never faded.

As the afternoon goes on, I try to distract myself.

Tomorrow's tour looms, so I pack. I play my guitar, jotting down additional lyrics in my old notebook.

Despite my efforts, the loneliness persists, so I retreat to my oversized pool, immersing myself in its refreshing waters, praying it will bring me some peace.

By late afternoon, I'm back on the couch once again staring at the grand piano.

The sound of my front door opening and closing catches my attention and I already anticipate who it is. Theo usually comes over at this time of the afternoon.

Theo gives me his usual smile as he comes into the room, holding two beers. "I gotta tell you something because I don't want you blindsided when you find out," he says, passing me a beer.

I twist the lid off my beer and toss the cap on the coffee table. "What is it?" I ask, lifting the bottle to my mouth.

Theo plops down on the other couch next to me. "It is serious. I've only just found out. Well Nate found out when he was talking to Ace, but I just thought-"

"What the fuck Theo, just tell me," I cut in.

"You're not going to like it. Or you might. I'm not sure."

"Seriously, just tell me already."

He eyes me for a moment. "We've got someone joining us on the tour."

"If it's Lionel, I'll fucking lose it," I say, taking another drink of my beer.

Theo drinks his beer, then puts it on the coffee table before pulling out a joint and lighting it up. "Nah, it's someone you know, someone you've mentioned a lot." He leans forward to hand me the joint and I take a hit.

"Who?" I ask, blowing out smoke. I take another hit and pass it back.

"Spitfire," says Theo.

My heart races and my stomach tightens. No, Theo's just fucking with me like he always does. I stay silent and wait to see what he's gonna say because none of it makes any sense. Why would she join us on tour?

I hear someone coming in through the front door, but I don't take my eyes off Theo, trying to figure him out. He's lacking that cocky grin that he usually wears when he wants to mess with me.

Nate enters the room and sits on the couch beside Theo. "So did you tell him?" Nate asks, reaching over and taking the joint from Theo.

"Yep," answers Theo. "That's why the fucker looks so stunned. He hasn't said a word since I told him."

"You're fucking serious?" I ask, struggling to grasp the reality that this isn't some kind of prank or elaborate setup. Knowing how serious Nate always is, I realize Theo's telling me the truth. Throughout all our usual shenanigans and teasing banter, never once has Theo included Nate.

"Told ya he wouldn't like it," Nate says, passing the joint back to Theo.

Hearing Nate's words only confirms my suspicion. That he knows about what happened between Poppy and me, including my feelings towards her. I can't focus on that now, I'll address that with Theo later.

I lean forward and put my empty beer bottle on the table in front. "Is it the label or Ace?" I ask, shifting my gaze between them.

'Both," Nate replies.

"Why the fuck would they ask Poppy to come along when they don't even know her?" I get up off the couch, determined to get to the bottom of this. I can't see her every day for eight weeks. I saw her for one night and it fucking wrecked me.

"Where are you going?" Nate yells, turning in his seat.

"To get some damn answers," I spit out.

Footsteps sound behind me on the marble tiles and just as I'm about to open the door, a hand seizes my shoulder, forcing me to stop.

"Xander, hold the fuck up," Nate says.

"What?" I ask, turning abruptly, desperate to go over to Ace's house to find out what the hell is happening.

Theo stands further down the hall, watching.

"Don't go over there like this," Nate warns. "I'll call Ace and tell him to come over so we can get to the bottom of it." He wraps his arm around my shoulder, guiding me back to the couch. On the way there, he pulls out his phone and calls Ace. "Hey man, we're hanging out at Xander's. Can you pop over for a quick band meeting?"

I can hear the muffle of Ace's voice, but I can't hear what he is saying.

"Yeah, see you soon," Nate says, ending the call and slipping the phone into his pocket.

"He's on his way. Sit down and we'll clear everything up."

I nod and plop onto the couch, still fuming about the surprise that was set up behind my back. If it wasn't for Theo and Nate dropping by to give me the lowdown, I would've been totally clueless.

Nate goes to my fridge, grabs a six-pack, and brings it over. Once he hands out the beers, he plops down next to Theo on the couch across from me.

"Just wait to see what he has to say," Nate says, eyeing me. He can clearly see that I'm pissed.

"We didn't want you to board that plane tomorrow and be caught off guard when you see Poppy there."

"You know about Poppy?" I ask, giving Nate a look.

"Yeah, he knows. I already filled him in," Theo chimes in.

"Chill out, I kept bugging him until he spilled about the girl at the bar. That's why he told me," Nate says.

The front door swings open and Ace comes in with a big ass smile, plopping down on the couch next to me. I resist the temptation to punch the asshole for hiding this shit from me.

"Hey, what's up, fuckers?" Ace says, leaning in and grabbing a beer off the table.

"He's in the loop," says Theo.

The look on Ace's face says it all when he meets my eyes. I glare at the jerk, feeling totally betrayed. Even though I never told him what happened between

Poppy and me, he must have suspected something since he asked if we were hooking up.

"Which one of you spilled the secret?" Ace asks, turning to look at Nate.

"We both did," Nate answers.

"Why?"

"Because he fucking needs to know this shit, Ace," says Nate.

I can't handle this conversation anymore, so I turn to look at him on the couch. "Seriously, when were you gonna give me a heads up, or did you just not fucking care?"

He doesn't say anything, but his face tells me everything - he never intended to tell me any of this.

"Fuck you, man. I thought we were like family. Family doesn't do shit like this to each other and you know it."

"Seriously, Xander, what else am I supposed to do when you're constantly fucking up?"

"Fucking up, you mean by your standards and the labels."

"We're going to lose our contract. There's already talk about replacing you."

I can tell by the expression on his face that he's let something slip. This is news to me, once again left in the dark. What else is he hiding from me? Let those bastards even try to replace me. This is my fucking band. The band I created.

"Wait a second," Nate cuts in. "What do you mean there's talk of replacing Xander?"

Nate and Theo shoot Ace a death glare. Obviously, they had no clue what was happening.

Ace pauses for a second, scanning the group.

"Answer the fucking question, Ace," Nate demands, his tone sharp and straight to the point.

"Lionel's found two singers who he thinks can take over Xander's role if he keeps causing trouble."

I get up from the couch, so mad that my brother didn't fill me in on any of this.

"So, you're okay with that?" Theo asks, sounding just as annoyed as me.

"No, I'm not fucking okay with it."

Nate gets up from the couch and towers over Ace, giving him an intense stare. "Hey, asshole," he says, his voice all loud and demanding. "Next time this shit comes up, you better tell Lionel or Reg, or whoever the fuck you're talking to, if Xander goes, I'm gone too. No way am I letting another frontman join

Broken Oasis. We joined this band because we loved hanging out and playing music. It was all about the lyrics Xander wrote and the music we made together. Now it's all about kissing the label's ass. We've totally lost ourselves because of them. Ace, it's about time you stood up to the label and fought for what we want, instead of taking their fucking side."

"It's not that easy," says Ace. "We could lose everything."

"Yeah, so what?" Nate's voice drips with anger. "Stop being a fucking pussy. Who cares if we lose our contract? We'll just start our own damn label. What was the point of building that recording studio if we're never gonna use it?"

Ace doesn't even have time to answer Nate's question before I butt in, because I'm dying to know. "Why is Poppy Reeves joining the tour?"

Nate and Theo quit staring at Ace and look over at me.

"I can tell you, but it will piss you off," Ace says.

"I'm already pissed, so spill the beans or I'll beat it out of you." I move back over and take my seat on the couch.

Letting out a long sigh, Ace glances down at the beer bottle in his hands before answering. Nate sits in the lounge waiting to see what Ace has to say.

"We've been trying to get you to fall in line for years," Ace admits, avoiding eye contact and staring at the bottle in his hands. "But that night, when your old man showed up at the event, you didn't pay attention to Reg or me. You only stopped when Poppy told you." Finally, he looks up. "We just figured if she was there, you might actually listen to someone."

"You brought her along to keep me in line?"

"Yeah," he says, looking down at the bottle.

I shake my head in disbelief, trying to process why. I admit I fucked up with the car accident, but everything else is not on me. "Tell her you don't need her to come," I add, getting up off the couch.

"It's too late. The contract's signed and she's already in the hotel room."

"Fuck!" I say as I start pacing. It's gonna hurt to see Poppy every day, knowing how much she hates me. I turn around and head for the door.

'Where are you going?" Theo shouts after me.

"Away from this fucking asshole," I add, storming out and leaving them behind.

I head out to the backyard, take off my sweatpants, and dive into the pool, butt naked. I swim laps to calm down and find some peace. My mind won't calm down. I keep obsessing about how I'll handle the next eight weeks with Poppy. That night at the bar keeps replaying in my mind and it still bugs me.

Chapter 45

Xander

I'm anxious about seeing her again. As the company car arrives at the airport, and we exit, a sudden thought crosses my mind - what if she's changed her mind? Honestly, I wouldn't even care if she did. Then I wouldn't have to keep feeling guilty about what I did to her back then.

After a sleepless night, I come up with a plan to move on.

I'm gonna brush her off and pretend she doesn't matter. I'll just treat her like any other chick. That's the only way I can stop my heart from shattering.

The car door opens, and we all step out. I'm on edge, scanning the tarmac for any signs of her.

"She's still coming," Theo says. "I heard Reg saying to Ace she'll be here soon."

"I don't fucking care," I say, shrugging like I couldn't care less, but the asshole Theo just smirks at me.

Movement out of the corner of my eye has me turning my head. A sleek black town car pulls up next to ours, and Poppy steps out. Seeing her in that short skirt gets me all hot and bothered.

Is she intentionally messing with me, knowing I had a thing for her when she wore those fucking short skirts? I always had the urge to slide my hands under them, curious to see if she was wet for me. Fuck, she's just arrived and I'm already feeling all these crazy emotions. Seriously, how can I handle the next eight weeks with a constant boner?

Out of nowhere, a light breeze comes along and lifts her skirt, showing off her black thong. Without delay, she hastily pushes it down.

I let out a frustrated sigh, knowing this girl is gonna be the death of me. I can see it now. The words on my tombstone: "Xander Williams. Died from a raging boner".

"Damn," Theo says next to me.

I shoot him a fiery glare. He looks at me for a second, then smirks. I swear the asshole thrives on riling me up. If I give the prick a good punch, he'll quickly get the message.

He laughs out loud and starts making his way to the plane.

Ace rushes off towards her, and I curse myself for not being the one to help with her damn suitcase. I should be the one helping her, not him. If he thinks he's having some fun with her, he's in for a fucking surprise. I'd rather cut his dick off than let that happen.

I keep a watchful eye on Poppy as Ace approaches. When she hears his voice, she turns and gives him that smile. The same smile she used to give me. The same smile I yearn to see directed at me again, but deep down, I know it's never going to happen. She fucking hates me for what I did to her. Little does she know, I hate myself even more for my actions.

As they approach, she glances up and the second our eyes meet, my heart races. My palms become sweaty. Why does she make me so fucking nervous?

Because she's Poppy Reeves, you idiot - a little voice in my head reminds me. *The only girl you've ever been in love with. The only girl who doesn't hang onto your every word. The only girl who dares to challenge you. The one who truly knows you, faults and all. And the one person in this world who will always have your heart.*

Ace says something to her, and she bursts into laughter. My fists, tightly clenched at my sides, reflect the intense urge I feel to punch him. It should be me making her laugh, not him.

"Come on man," Nate says, as if reading my thoughts. "Let's get on the plane."

Pissed off, I turn away from the asshole hitting on my girl and join Nate as we board the plane.

Upon entering, I notice Reg already sitting in his usual spot, leisurely sipping his drink with his laptop open on the table before him. Nate walks over to Theo who's busy flirting with the hostess. The way she giggles and flirts, it's obvious she's totally into Theo. Very few women can resist his smooth talk.

I bet by the middle of the flight, Nate and Theo will be banging her, just like all the other hostesses the label hired. I mean, who the fuck hires these groupies?

I'm anxious. I can feel the tension building in my body. I just need a damn drink to numb these fucking emotions.

"Hey, before you start sucking their dicks, grab me a bourbon?" I cut in when the hostess laughs at Theo's joke.

The hostess shoots me a disapproving glare, then heads to the next room to fetch me a drink.

I hear Ace's voice as he boards the plane, with Poppy by his side.

"So, how did he handle the news about you being away for the next eight weeks?" Ace asks.

WTF? Don't tell me she's taken, or even worse, married or engaged. I quickly glance at her hands, praying there's no ring. I feel at ease when I notice she's not wearing any rings. Can't spare a dime, you jerk. If she was mine, she'd be rocking rings on all her fingers.

"He didn't even seem upset when I left. I was expecting him to cry, but he didn't," Poppy says, coming to a stop next to Ace.

Cry. What a fucking pussy? I mean, I cried for months after I left her, but that was different. But this dickhead sounds like a loser. I would have thought my Princess would be with someone who challenges her, not some weak fuck who cries when his girl is gone for less than two months.

Ace passes her bag off to one of the staff members.

"Hey there, spitfire," Theo says, coming forward now, reaching out to take her hand. "I'm Theo, the bass guitarist." He lifts her hand to his lips, planting a kiss on the back of it, before flashing me a shit-eating grin.

Can't the idiot see I'm two seconds away from punching him in the fucking face?

"Spitfire?" Poppy questions, her brows furrowing as she drops his hand.

Nate steps forward and shakes her hand. "Hi," he says, introducing himself. "I'm Nate, the drummer."

Poppy gives him a big, dazzling smile. Normally I'd be annoyed, but Nate is too shy and serious to make a move. It's always Theo who is the biggest flirt.

"And you know Xander of course," Ace says.

"Sure," she says, giving me a quick look before flashing a smile at the group. Her eyes dart from face to face.

It bugs me that when her gaze returns to me, her smile fades.

"Looking for a cock, Princess," I say, clearly annoyed.

A look of annoyance manifests on her face. "No, but it looks like I found a dick."

I hear Theo's hearty chuckle, but he swiftly puts his hand over his mouth to stifle it. The fucking asshole.

"Which way should I go?" Poppy asks, turning to Ace.

Ace points to the left. "Through that door over there. Your room is the second door on the right."

"Thanks," Poppy says, heading for the door.

Nate, Theo, and Ace's eyes are glued to her as they shamelessly check her out.

Don't they know I'll rip their fucking eyeballs out if they keep pulling that shit?

"Damn," Theo mutters.

Once he's had his fill, he locks eyes with me. "If you're not going to make a move, mind if we share her?" That smart-ass grin returns like he's fucking with me all over again.

"You better fucking listen. No one touches her," I tell them. "If anyone lays a fucking finger on her-"

Theo's laughter cuts me off mid-sentence. "Just kidding, man," he chuckles. "Man, your totally fucked up."

"Leave him alone," Nate says, slapping me on the shoulder.

"Chill, man, I'll be busy keeping the hostess entertained," Theo says. "Where is she, by the way?" He heads over to the door she went through earlier. "You coming to have fun?" he says to Nate.

Nate moves forward as Theo opens the door.

"Tell her I'm still waiting for my fucking drink!" I yell out to them before Nate closes the door.

"Xander, can we talk?" Ace says.

I shoot him a glare, still pissed he didn't keep me in the loop about Poppy.

"Please, brother," he says. "It's about Poppy."

"I don't want to hear it," I add, moving over to sit in a chair.

"Cut Poppy some slack. She's a mom now."

Those words hit me hard, cutting deep with the news. A kid. She's got a fucking kid. She left me behind and moved on. She's made a family with that weak-ass pussy of a man. I can't help but rub my chest where the pain's been stuck for the last five years. I'm a fucking idiot. I gave up on the only good thing in my life.

"Seriously, she has a kid?" I confirm just to make sure I got it right.

"A son," Ace informs me.

I get up out of the seat and head for the door that Nate and Theo had exited just moments ago.

"Where are you going, Xander," Ace calls out after me.

"Nate and Theo won't be getting any action until I get my fucking drink."

CHAPTER 46
Poppy

For the past two hours, I've been sitting in my assigned room, simply wasting time. I can't bring myself to go out there and face him. But it's my job. It's what I'm being paid to do. It's the very reason why I'm here in the first place. Once this job is over, then I'll never have to see him again. I'll have my house and the freedom I've longed for since moving out of my mother's house all those years ago.

I hop off the bed, grab my phone, and slide it into my pocket. As I walk down the corridor, I hear music coming from the other side of the door. The guitar stops playing for a bit and then starts again.

I open the door and suddenly freeze.

There, sitting on the edge of the lounge, is Xander. A notebook is open beside him, a pencil tucked behind his ear, as he plucks the strings of my father's guitar. The sight brings forth a flood of emotions. Not just because of my father, but also because Xander has kept his guitar all this time. Despite his fame and wealth, he still treasures that one symbol of our past.

I swallow hard, trying to push down the painful lump in my throat as I stand there, watching him. He strums a few chords, then pulls the pencil from behind his ear and scribbles in the notepad. With him momentarily distracted, I take the opportunity to study him, something I haven't had a chance to do since I've seen him. I check out his strong jawline and how his hair falls into his eyes. He's no longer the boy I remember, but a man, edgier and undeniably more attractive. I can't help but check out the muscles in his arms as he reaches for the bottle of Jack on the table in front. He tilts his head back and takes a long swig before putting the bottle on the table with a loud thud. Then, he focuses on the guitar. This time around, he's singing. I shiver as I hear his sultry voice, memories flooding back to all the times he serenaded me.

Every time my mind wanders,
it always brings me back to you,
But as I can see,
you long forgot about me.

The moment I enter the room, he looks up.

As I come closer, I can feel Xander watching me as I search for coffee. I make a point to not make eye contact with him, instead choosing to focus on anything else in the room.

Where the hell is that hostess who was here earlier when I got on the plane?

"What are you looking for, Princess?" Xander asks.

Closing my eyes, I remember how that word sounded on his lips all those years ago. Initially, I despised that name because of its implications, but as time went by, I grew to adore the seductive and playful tone with which he used to say it. I shove those memories aside, throw up my walls, and turn to face him.

"Coffee. I need coffee."

Without saying a word, he grabs the phone on the cupboard next to him. He pushes a button and puts the phone to his ear.

"Hey, Theo. You guys finished yet, it's been two hours."

After a momentary pause, a grin spreads across his face.

I used to love that smile, with how it lit up his face.

"Alright," he says, looking up at me. "Yeah, coffee. Cream and one sugar." He raises an eyebrow in my direction, and I give a nod, surprised that he still remembers my coffee preference. He hangs up the phone and focuses on his guitar. "You might wanna grab a seat. They said she wouldn't be too long, but you never know with Theo." He casually plucks a string on the guitar.

"I'm surprised you've still got it," I state, sitting on the couch opposite him.

He glances up and when his brows furrow, I point to the guitar.

"Yeah, I couldn't bear to part with it," he says, shifting his focus back to the guitar.

No, but you could leave me pregnant and heartbroken.

The silence between us grows more awkward by the second.

I shift in my chair, wondering if he's annoyed that I'm on the plane, given our history.

I wonder if it's because I remind him of the girls he used and discarded as if we were nothing. I'm not that naive girl anymore. His looks, charm, voice, or words won't fool me. So what if he's Xander fucking Williams, the rock god of today? I'll never fall for his manipulative charms again.

Bored, I strum my fingers on my lap, contemplating whether I should say something or just get up and walk away. As I am contemplating my next move, he breaks the silence.

"Mind if I ask you something?" he asks, not bothering to lift his gaze from his guitar.

"Yeah, I guess," I say, not sure where this conversation is headed.

"Are you and your son's dad still a thing?" He lifts his gaze and locks eyes with me.

What the actual fuck? Is he serious right now? Why is he asking me this? Does he still think I'm some easy girl who'll just sleep with him because I'm here for the next eight weeks?

"No," I snap, my voice warning not to mess with me.

Without uttering a word, he nods and reaches for the bottle of Jack on the table before him. He takes a long swig, and I watch his throat as it moves while he swallows. His gaze remains fixed on me as he places the bottle back on the table and resumes strumming his guitar.

While we're sitting there, the door behind me swings open and the hostess shows up, looking like a mess. She looks like she's just rolled out of bed as she hands me a cup of coffee. As I take it, her shirt catches my attention - one side of it is buttoned unevenly.

"Thank you," I say, feeling the warmth of the steaming cup of coffee in my hands.

"Can I get you anything else? Perhaps some chocolate cake?"

"No thank you," I say, before blowing gently on my hot coffee to cool it down.

"And how about you, Mr. Williams, is there anything I can get for you?" the attendant inquires, standing by the edge of the couch.

As I wait for Xander to answer, I keep my eyes fixed on my cup. When Xander doesn't respond, I lift my eyes to see him watching me with a smirk on his face, clearly amused. He always found it amusing when I blew on my coffee, thinking it would magically cool down.

"What?" I ask.

"Nothing," he says grinning.

"Sir," the flight attendant says again, her voice slightly raised this time as if Xander is stopping her from her duties.

"No, now fuck off," Xander replies. "Make the most of banging the band members, because this is your last shift on this fucking plane."

Yep. There he is. The rude asshole who doesn't give two shits about what he says or how he says it.

The hostess's face goes red, and she quickly goes back through the door she came from.

"That was a little too harsh, don't you think?" I comment, taking another sip of my coffee.

He puts down his guitar and grabs the bottle, then settles back on the couch. His intense gaze scans my body, and I have to stop myself from fidgeting or pulling down my shirt to hide my stomach. It's no secret Xander's been photographed with beautiful women. Last year, I saw the headlines of him with some model on a magazine cover. When I saw it, I went home and bawled my eyes out because, even though he dumped me, I still clung to the hope that he'd come back someday. But when I saw that picture, I realized it was a lost cause. He's a total celeb, living his dream life, while I'm just plain old me - someone he used to know. A nobody. Just a girl who lived two doors down.

"Why?" he remarks. "She's supposed to be here doing her job, not just a plaything for two band members."

"But isn't that what you guys do? Or is it a problem because she's not your plaything?" I interject.

With a faint smirk on his face, he watches me. "Just because you see it doesn't make it true. Don't believe everything you read in the papers, Princess," he adds, taking a gulp from the bottle.

There's that name again, the one that sends goosebumps across my skin.

"Yeah, just like all those other girls you've been caught on camera with."

He flashes me that sexy grin, and I realize my mistake. I've fucked up.

"Sounds like you're jealous, Princess. Don't stress, I'll make sure there's enough room for you to be my plaything."

"Sorry, did I look interested? My bad."

That smirk is back on his face, but this time it's even bigger. I try my best to shake off the intense rush of desire that sweeps through me.

I lean forward and put my empty coffee cup on the table. "Well, it's been an interesting chat, I guess." I stand up and make my way to my room, fully aware he's checking out my ass.

CHAPTER 47

Xander

Fuck her and her smart mouth and those witty remarks. Since the moment she walked onto this plane, my dick's been throbbing. I thought drowning myself in alcohol would numb these fucking feelings, but it hasn't worked. I've already jacked off twice to get my dick to calm down, but now, as I watch her walk away, I'm getting aroused again. While many women desire me, it's amazing how just a few sassy words from her smart mouth can make my desire for her skyrocket. After all these years, how the fuck does she still hold so much power over me?

Ace walks through the door, smiles at Poppy, then comes over and flops down in the chair.

"Is the hostess still in there with those two idiots?" He asks.

"Yep," I down more of my drink, not taking my eyes off the door even after Poppy's gone.

"Every fucking time those assholes do that. Well, that's another hostess gone. What's that, eight now in the past year because they can't resist being in a Nate and Theo sandwich?" He chuckles to himself as if sharing an inside joke.

I wish he'd fuck off and leave me alone. Go talk to his buddy, Reg, if he wants to chat.

"So, did you come up with anything?" Ace asks, nodding towards the guitar sitting beside me on the seat.

I eye him for a moment, wondering if I should say anything because he could go back and tell the label.

"I might have," I shrug. "And no, I won't be handing it over to the fucking label."

"I'll be back in a minute," he says getting up off the couch. He moves back out through the door.

Within seconds, he reappears with a guitar in his hand. I watch him intently as he settles down on the couch directly across from me. We haven't jammed together like this, just him and me with our guitars in ages, not since high school.

He plucks at his guitar, then stops and looks up at me.

"What have you got?" He asks.

I eye him for a second longer, lifting the bottle to my mouth and drinking it, contemplating whether or not to show him. Leaning forward, I put the bottle down, then grab my guitar to show him what I've been working on.

When I play, he's super focused on the music, adding his own special touch to take it to the next level. It feels great to be back together, just like the old days when we were inseparable, making music and dreaming of making it big.

The hours quickly slip away as Ace and I spend our time playing, singing, and getting lost in our music. After five hours, I feel on top of the world. It feels like a piece of me is finally back, after being gone for so long. Theo and Nate join us. Theo is on bass, while Nate beats his drumsticks on the coffee table, making his own sick beat. Jamming out with my bros to the music is exactly what I need. In those moments, the pressures of the media, the label's expectations, and the never-ending demands all vanish from my mind.

I look up and see Poppy sitting in the back of the room, watching us do our thing.

Ace sets his guitar aside and gets up from his seat. "We need to celebrate with a drink," he declares. "And no," he looks my way. "Before you ask, I'm not telling the label we have a song." He gives me a nod, showing he's being honest. "Great job, brother. I really miss the old days." Then Ace turns around, scanning the room. "Where the fuck is that damn hostess."

Theo and Nate share a look. "Well, she's a little bit tied up, you could say?" Theo laughs as he looks around the group.

"I told him not to, but you know how he is. He never listens," Nate says, giving Theo a disapproving look.

"No. He never fucking does," I add.

"Don't stress. I know exactly where the booze is," Theo says, jumping up and heading for the door at the back of the room.

Within seconds, he comes back, holding several bottles in his arms. He passes them out, giving one to me first, then to Ace, and finally to Nate.

Theo then playfully focuses on Poppy, flashing a mischievous grin.

"Come on over, pretty girl," he calls out, gesturing for her to join us. "Come on over and celebrate. We still have another eight hours on this darn plane."

Poppy gets up and joins us.

Theo unscrews the lid and passes the bottle to Poppy when she approaches. Ace scoots over to make room for her on the couch.

She takes a drink from the bottle as she sits and I half-expect her to wince at the burn in her throat like she did that night at the rock when I had to carry her home, but she doesn't. I guess her life's changed too, just like mine.

I'm just sitting there, getting more and more wasted, as Poppy and my brothers keep talking. Her face is so beautiful, I can't help but study it, along with her captivating eyes and flowing long hair. She's even more stunning now than when I left. Guilt, my old companion, settles beneath my skin, taunting me, reminding me she's someone I can never have again.

When she laughs at what Theo says, I can't help but feel a surge of warmth. Her laughter is like music to my ears. Something I could listen to for the rest of my days. I want to record it and use it as my ringtone, but the thought only serves as a painful reminder of what I've done and all that I've lost.

I turn my head and catch Ace checking me out. Don't tell me the bastard knows the thoughts running through my head. He's always had a knack for infiltrating my thoughts, delving into the depths of my mind.

Theo's question catches my attention, causing my ears to perk up.

"So, what's your son's name?" he asks.

Poppy shoots me a quick look before turning her attention back to Theo. "His name is Alex."

"Cool name," Nate chimes in.

"Cool kid," Poppy adds with a smile, and I can see the love in her eyes as she talks about her son. It brings back memories of my mom's love for me. This kid is so lucky to have her in their life.

"So you all went to school together?" Nate asks.

"Yeah, we did," Poppy answers, glancing at Ace and then over at me.

Under her scrutinizing gaze, I feel a lump in my throat.

Theo shifts his attention to me. "So, who was that girl at the bar claiming to be your childhood sweetheart?"

I shoot him a death glare. The fucker already knows who she is because he asked if I wanted to join him and Nate fuck her in the men's restroom. I'm tempted to punch that smug look right off his face, but Ace's words snap me back to reality.

"That was Jade," Ace bursts into laughter. "No way. Did she actually say that, for real?" Ace laughs so hard that it makes him slump over in a fit of laughter. Finally, when he regains control of his laughter, he adds. "Xander and her were never a thing growing up. She was super easy. She was everyone's hookup."

"From what I remember," says Poppy, slurring her words. "She was a total bitch. She was hell-bent on making my life miserable for years."

"Yeah, but I remember how you always shut her down with your quick comebacks," I add.

Her piercing blue eyes lock onto mine, and a surge of awareness sends my heart racing in my chest.

"Yeah," Ace chuckles. "I remember that. Some days, putting her in her place was the highlight of my day."

"Well, the bitch deserved it," Poppy shrugs.

We keep talking for another hour, getting even more wasted.

With only six more hours left, Theo and Nate go back to the girl they've tied up in their bed. Ace, however, grabs his guitar and goes to his room to get some much-needed sleep. Now it's just me and Poppy. Every time we lock eyes, it's like a rollercoaster of emotions and my heart aches when I think about my actions.

"I get that me being here is awkward," she says.

"It's not awkward."

She chuckles softly. "I can tell this is making you uncomfortable... Anyway," she trails off, cutting herself off mid-sentence, and then gets up. "I really should get some rest."

She turns and heads towards the door, and before I realize it, I'm following. As she reaches the door, I wrap my arms around her waist, causing her to let out a startled gasp, when I pull her back against my chest. The overwhelming feeling of being able to touch her again sends my mind into a whirlwind. I nuzzle my nose against her neck and get lost in the way she smells - a mix of innocence and temptation. I yearn to explore every inch of her, to possess, to consume her, succumbing to the desire to corrupt every inch of her completely.

"What are you doing?" she asks.

"You wanted to know if it felt awkward. The only awkward thing, Princess, is this," I say, pressing my lips to her neck as I grind my hard cock against her ass. "Feel that? The only awkward thing right now is how deep I want to be buried in you."

Her skin breaks out in goosebumps as she arches her back. And I'm loving how I'm affecting her.

"Yeah, that's what I thought," I whisper, feeling the warmth of her skin as my lips brush against the sensitive spot beneath her ear. "I'm dying to fuck you."

I graze my teeth on her shoulder, then slide my hand in under her skirt and run my finger up her thighs. "Remember how much fun we had when you got off on my cock?" I run my finger along her wetness, exploring her slit.

She hisses when I touch her, and I love that I'm getting to her.

"Oh yeah, I remember all the stuff you used to love," she says, teasingly rubbing her ass against me.

"Fuck!" I hiss, closing my eyes as a flood of memories come racing back. The way she takes charge and teases me with her body has always fascinated me. It's so fucking hot.

"I remember a lot of things about you, Xander," she says, her eyes lingering on me as she glances back over her shoulder. "But now, none of that matters. Get it through your fucking head. I will never be one of your groupies." She forcefully shoves my hand, walks forward, opens the door, and then slams it in my face.

The world is full of women I can pursue, but none will ever come close to evoking even a fraction of the emotions Poppy Reeves stirs within me. Her presence is like a magnetic force that pulls me in. What's worse is she's the one person on this planet that I can't have, and it drives me fucking crazy.

Chapter 48

Poppy

I make every effort to avoid Xander. The memory of his body pressed against mine plays tricks on my mind. The lingering sensation of his breath on my skin is hard to shake off. But I'm proud I remained strong, resisting the temptation to surrender and relive the moments we once shared. And still, after all this time I want him. Want him with everything within me. But I can't go back to the way things used to be between us. I refuse to relive those memories where he manipulated me into thinking I'm the center of his universe, the most beautiful girl he's ever laid eyes on because it's all an act. I'm not falling for that shit again.

Upon landing in Australia, I purposely keep my distance from him and the band, silently asserting my need for personal space. But every time he looks at me, I can feel it, like a physical touch.

As we make our way through the airport, it becomes increasingly apparent the enormity of what I've gotten myself into and the chaotic frenzy that lies ahead. A sea of fans, comprising both girls and boys, eagerly await the band from behind the barricades.

Their screams are so loud that I almost cover my ears. Some of them hold signs that say, "Marry me, Xander," while others offer to do sexual activities with the band - "I'll let you stick it anywhere" or "I'm down for anything."

I can't help but wonder if any of these requests actually happen. I watch from afar as the band members happily mingle with fans, taking selfies and signing stuff, even various body parts.

Seeing all this, makes me wonder why Xander would flirt with me on the plane when it's obvious he could have any girl he desires. The adoration and screams from the fans imply that these men could easily satisfy all their sexual fantasies whenever they please.

Watching Xander mingle with his fans, I realize he's living his dream, the life he's always wanted - a life where fans admire and adore him, all while doing what he loves - music. While I'm thrilled about his achievements, it's a little heartbreaking knowing that I was not there to share his dream and celebrate his victories.

Lost in my thoughts, observing how these four guys effortlessly attract all the love, I'm startled when Reg suddenly appears right beside me.

"This is how it starts," he says, looking down at his phone.

Curious, I inquire, "How what starts?"

"You'll find out soon enough. Just remember, your job here is to keep him in line. If you fail, the contract will be considered non-valid," he says, walking away towards the guys. I can't help but wonder if there was some kind of threat in his comment.

Asshole. I watch him as he makes his way towards the security guards, who are positioned near the band.

"Don't worry about that asshole." A voice sounds behind me.

I glance behind to see a woman in her early thirties making her way towards me. She has short, dyed blonde hair and three facial piercings—eyebrow, nose, and lip.

"Poppy isn't it?" she says, extending her hand to me. "I'm Kit."

"Hi," I shake her hand, curious about how she knows my name.

Kit cracks up laughing when she notices the confused look on my face. "No, I'm not a stalker. I got an email that you were coming on the tour."

"Oh, okay," I reply, still unsure about who she is or what she does since I didn't see her on the plane at all.

"I imagine it's quite overwhelming to witness all of this, but it's practically their daily life while they're on tour," she explains, gesturing towards the fans vying for the attention of the four guys. "Things have gotten even crazier in recent years. Some fans are incredibly obsessive. Let's hope the Aussies aren't as wild."

"So you've been with the guys for a while, huh?" I inquire.

"Yep, ever since they got signed and started touring," she says, turning back to look at the band. "I make sure the guys know what's happening with their daily schedule, and I fix or change it if there are any issues. I take care of all the media stuff and publicity during their tour. Stuff like that, you know."

"Right. Bet your job keeps you busy. I didn't see you on the plane."

"Those of us who work behind the scenes, we don't really mingle with the band. Company rules. We were all up in the lounge towards the front of the plane," she explains. She takes out her phone, swiftly types something, and then puts it back into her pocket.

"The band is about to head out to meet the press, so we should follow them. Down there where the vehicles are waiting," she says, pointing.

I turn my gaze in that direction and notice several camera crews from various news outlets, eagerly awaiting the band's arrival. I look back to see Reg nodding, and immediately the six security guards spring into action, leading the band forward.

Kit grabs my arm and urges me to follow as the security guards behind us move ahead.

"Just a quick tip, Poppy," she says. "If you want to avoid being on television and social media, I suggest hanging back with Neil over there," she points to a large, bald security guard who is still wearing wrap-around sunglasses inside the airport. "Well, it was nice to meet you, Poppy. We'll probably head down to the bar tonight at the hotel. Come down and meet everyone if you like." She gives me a quick smile and hurries ahead to catch up with Reg.

Neil and I exchange glances, and I offer him a smile. However, he remains completely unresponsive. His commanding stature and strong build emit an intimidating aura, clearly deterring anyone from crossing his path. He maintains his unwavering gaze on me until I avert my eyes. Meanwhile, the band, Reg, and Kit all move forward towards the press, who are eagerly waiting.

I stay back, away from the cameras and reporters who are moving forward with their microphones to question Xander and the other band members. Following Kit's advice, I move to Neil, ensuring I stay out of the shot but close enough to hear the reporter's questions.

"Xander, since this is your first time in Australia, can you let your fans know what you'll be up to while you're here?"

"I'll be singing."

The reporter chuckles before asking another question. "Well, I guess you must be quite busy with all those sold-out concerts. C'mon, give your fans a little sneak peek at what you've got planned while you're here!"

Xander responds with his trademark grin. "Why spoil the surprise by revealing everything now?"

He's a pro at giving the media what they want.

"You'll have to wait and find out," he says, smirking and giving a cheeky wink.

This version of Xander I'm seeing right now is not the one I know. It's a show for the media, and if I didn't know the real Xander, I would mistake this imposter for the genuine one. He flashes his sexy smile and hops into the waiting black limo, with the door already open.

The rest of the band answers a few more questions, and then they pile into the limo with Xander. Reg gets in and shuts the door. Kit comes over to where Neil and I are standing.

The limo pulls out from the curb.

"Alright, our car is this way," Kit says, gesturing further down. However, before we can take a step in that direction, the black limo abruptly screeches to a halt. Its front end juts out into the traffic, causing a complete halt in the flow of cars.

With the press standing there, their cameras still rolling, everyone wonders what the hell is going on. Suddenly, horns blare, urging the black limo to get out of the way. Equally puzzled, I observe the scene. Just then, Kit's phone rings and she quickly answers it. While on the phone, she looks over at me.

"That was Reg," she says, hanging up the phone and slipping it back into her pocket. "You're to get your ass in that car now. His words, not mine. Come on," she grabs my hand and pulls me towards the car.

Luckily, the press is too busy to notice us slipping through the crowd. Chattered whispers start the second Reg gets out of the car, looking around, no doubt searching for me. Judging by the bulging vein on his forehead, he's pissed. A camera almost hits me in the face as it turns towards us. As soon as he spots Kit pulling me forward, he moves to the side, allowing space for me to get in. I claim the seat next to Ace. Reg climbs back in and closes the door, sitting next to me. Sitting opposite me, Nate and Theo watch me, and Xander looks annoyed. I feel foolish, my cheeks burning with embarrassment. No one gave me the heads-up that I was supposed to travel with the band. The vehicle moves forward.

"I'm sorry, I didn't know—" I don't get to finish my sentence because Reg cuts me off.

"Don't tell me you're going to cause more problems for me than you're worth."

"Don't you fucking speak to her like that," Xander says, moving forward in his seat. His eyes burn with a fiery rage.

The tension in the vehicle is palpable like there's a ticking bomb ready to explode.

"She needs to understand I haven't got time to babysit her ass."

"Watch your fucking mouth or I'll kick your ass for disrespecting her," Xander says, getting more pissed by the second.

I take a quick look at the rest of the group, and they appear completely unfazed as if this is a common occurrence for them.

Reg laughs out loud. "Yeah, come on, big guy, you want to do this in front of her. You didn't even want her to come in the first place."

"Yeah, but now that she's here, she stays with us, so I know she's safe, asshole." Xander's words are fierce and filled with fury, serving as a clear warning not to fuck with him.

Reg glances my way. "Are you gonna deal with him or what? It's your job to call out his inappropriate behavior."

This asshole is taking it out on me because Xander called him out for talking to me like that.

I meet Reg's glare. "Yeah, too bad I don't get paid to call out your rudeness. Because we'd be here all fucking night."

Theo laughs out loud and tries to stifle it behind his hand, but it's too late; we've all heard it.

"One word from me and your contract will be gone," Reg spits out in response to my comment.

"Reg," Nate says. "Cut her some slack. She just fucking got here. She doesn't know how things work around here."

As I observe from an outsider's standpoint, it appears that Nate and Theo have developed a closer relationship with Xander. It makes me wonder what might have happened over the years for Ace to become more distant. If my memory serves me right, Ace and Xander were inseparable, like brothers, relying on each other for support in every aspect of their lives.

Reg remains silent for now, studying the three men. Their expressions show a readiness for a fierce confrontation.

There's an undeniable sense of unease beyond what just happened with me not joining them in the car. It's as if there's an additional layer of tension lingering in the air.

Without uttering a single word, Reg swiftly retrieves his phone from his jacket pocket and unlocks it.

I look up and see Theo smirking at me.

"Spitfire," he whispers.

I'm completely confused about why he calls me that.

I discreetly sneak a peek at Xander and notice him gazing out the tinted window. Intrigued, I watch him for a moment, finding his side profile just as captivating as his front view. His long lashes catch my attention as I watch him blink. I can't help but notice the defined edges of his jawline as my eyes wander over his face. Suddenly, it seems like he senses my eyes on him as he turns his head. In a hurry, I redirect my attention, only to catch Theo and Nate watching me. My cheeks flush with embarrassment at the thought of them watching me check out Xander.

The hotel is the fanciest I've ever seen. The room is practically the same size as my apartment. After enduring that terrible place for three years, being surrounded by luxury makes me feel like a queen. The queen-size bed is so inviting, it's practically begging me to crash as soon as I checked in this afternoon. But instead, I resist the urge because I know it would mess up my sleep to adjust to this new time zone.

It's crazy to think that it's already tomorrow here like I've time-traveled into the future.

After I shower, I throw on some tights and a comfy top, then flop onto the bed. Right when I'm about to call Alex, there's a knock on my door. Opening it, I'm totally surprised to find Kit standing there.

"I know it's early, but I need a drink. You wanna come?"

To be honest, all I feel like doing is sitting down, flipping through the channels, and perhaps indulging in the mini bar. Earlier, I noticed some crisps and peanuts that I was quite eager to munch on. However, this is my opportunity to connect with someone outside of the band on this tour. It wouldn't hurt to go downstairs for a few hours and have a drink.

"Sure, sounds good," I say, walking over to the bed to get my phone that I threw when I heard a knock at the door.

Kit turns away and waits for me by the elevator.

As I walk up, I see her pushing the elevator button over and over. As soon as I get there, the doors slide open, and we step inside.

"I bet Reg had a total meltdown when you got in the limo," she says, keeping her eyes on the bright red floor numbers going down.

"You can say that," I add.

"I know what it's like when Reg gets angry. He can be quite an asshole."

"Yeah, I'm starting to see that."

"Neil's meeting us at the bar. He might seem scary, but don't be fooled. Once you get to know him, he's like a little puppy dog."

"More like an angry bear scoping out a picnic basket," I say, laughing.

Kit smiles. "You'll see what I mean. He really is just a gentle giant."

As the elevator bell dings and the doors open, we step out onto the second floor. Kit leads me through a set of double glass doors. It's like being transported into a classic Hollywood film, with its old-school piano bar charm.

At the heart of the room, an exquisite grand piano commands attention. I'm brimming with excitement, eagerly awaiting when the enchanting melodies fill the space, creating an ambiance that is simply magical. The melodic notes produced by the piano never fail to enthrall me; they have always held a special place in my heart. However, a tinge of sorrow lingers within me, as I no longer have the pleasure of feeling the keys beneath my fingertips since I sold my keyboard.

As we approach the bar, Neil sits alone with a half-finished beer, engaged in conversation with the bartender.

Kit slides onto the stool next to him, and I climb onto the one beside her.

"Yeah, I bet," says the bartender. "Tell me, what's the weirdest request you've ever been asked?"

"Well, there was this woman in her forties who told me she'd give me a blowjob if I would sneak her into Xander's room."

"No shit." The bartender laughs.

"No lie, my friend."

"Ladies, what can I get you?" The bartender asks.

"Surprise us," Kit replies.

Neil lets out a laugh while grabbing his beer, and I can't help but smile at the sight of this burly man laughing so freely.

"Don't sweat it, dude. She's always pulling that one," Neil says, lifting the glass to his mouth.

The bartender studies Kit for a moment, before shifting his attention to me. After a moment, he turns away.

"I bet the shit hit the fan inside that limo," Neil comments, leaning forward to look at me.

"Yeah, you could say that."

"Don't let the asshole get to you. It's just his vibrant personality," he says.

It's so weird to see him sitting here, all smiley, after that intense encounter we had earlier today where he couldn't even crack a smile when we locked eyes.

The bartender comes back with two glasses - one with ice and what looks like whiskey, and he puts it in front of Kit.

"Whiskey," says Kit.

"Well done, man," says Neil. "That's what she always orders."

In the bartender's other hand, there's a cocktail glass with a strawberry and a cute little umbrella.

"I made you a strawberry mango daiquiri," he says, placing it down in front of me.

I can't help but smile. The drink looks so good.

"I've never tried this," I say, meeting the bartender's friendly, blue gaze.

I can feel all their eyes on me as I grab the cocktail, carefully putting the straw in my mouth, and taking a sip. My eyes light up with joy as I gulp down the refreshing sweetness.

"Thank you. It's delicious." I place my drink on the bar.

"Whenever you're ready for a refill, just give me a shout," he says, grabbing the cloth from his shoulder. He then turns and walks down the bar to dry a few glasses.

The three of us spend the next few hours chatting. Kit is absolutely right—Neil is like a big teddy bear. Once I'm done with my daiquiri, I'll switch to soda so I'm not even a little tipsy when I call my mom later to talk to Alex.

Meanwhile, Kit and Neil persist in ordering round after round of whisky and beer.

As the night goes on, Neil's voice trembles as he opens up about the heart-wrenching situation of not being able to see his son since he was five. That was seven years ago. He shares the pain of being excluded from his son's life, all because of his ex-wife's choices. As he talks about his pain, I can see the vulnerability in his eyes, evoking a deep sympathy within me for this gentle giant.

Kit too shares some heartbreaking news about her recent break up with her girlfriend of six years.

I can't help but feel a fondness for the two of them. They are so genuine and down-to-earth. However, when they ask me questions about my role in the band, I struggle to open up and often evade the topic about my history with Xander. Whenever the conversation turns to Alex, I carefully steer clear of bringing up the fact that Xander is his father.

It just feels right to keep that information to myself, as I don't want to bring unnecessary trouble into Xander's world. The fewer people who know, the better, especially considering that I'll be leaving and Xander will continue working with these people.

As the doors of the piano bar swing open and the crowd pours in, we make our way to a booth, eager to soak up the music. Sitting there, surrounded by the cozy vibes, I feel soothed by the melodic piano music. The piano's captivating sound has always held a special place in my heart, completely captivating me.

My phone interrupts the peaceful serenity - it's Reg calling.

I quickly swipe the screen and answer, curious about what he wants after the crazy limo incident earlier.

"Hello."

"Tell me he's with you?" he spits into the phone.

Glancing up at Neil, I'm unsure who Reg is referring to.

Neil and Kit's eyes are watching me.

"Wait, are you talking about Neil?" I ask to clarify.

"No, I'm not fucking talking about Neil. I'm talking about Xander."

I feel like hanging up on this asshole because of his aggressive tone, but I stay on the line because I have no idea what's happening with Xander.

"No, I haven't seen Xander," I tell him.

"Well, that's just fantastic," he says. "We hired you to deal with situations like this." He vents his frustration before cutting off the call.

"God, what was that about?" Kit asks.

I place my phone face down on the table. "Apparently, Xander is missing," I add, then finish the last of my soda.

Neil reaches into his pocket and grabs his phone.

"I should go look for him. Honestly, I have no clue where to look. Does he usually disappear like this?" I ask, not wanting to know if he's off getting busy with a groupie.

"Sometimes," Kit replies.

I turn my attention to Neil, who's messing around with Google Maps, and I'm curious about what he's doing. Just as I'm about to ask him if he knows where Xander is, my phone pings.

Ace: Hey Poppy, do you know where Xander is?

I quickly type out my reply, not sure why he assumes I know where he is.

Poppy: No. I'll let you know if I see him.

I put my phone back in my pocket and watched Neil chug down his beer.

"Come on," he says, getting up and making his way through the crowd of people chatting and listening to the music.

I sneak a look at Kit.

"Go follow him," she says.

I quickly go after Neil as he heads to the elevators.

"Do you have any idea where he went?" I inquire, trying to keep up with him.

"Perhaps," he responds.

The elevator doors smoothly open, and we enter.

As we leave the motel, we weave through the busy sidewalks, skillfully maneuvering through the vibrant lights, traffic, and bustling crowds. The shops blast lively music, filling the air with its rhythmic melodies. I pick up the pace to keep in step with Neil, staying right behind him as we maneuver through the crowd.

After strolling for four blocks, we arrive at a set of traffic lights, briefly stopping until the green light allows us to safely cross.

"Do you seriously think he'd be down here?" I ask, trying to catch my breath. "Xander's most likely just hanging with some groupie. That's it. Once he's done, he'll make an appearance."

Neil locks eyes with me, and as we find ourselves in a public setting once again, he seamlessly transitions back into his customary stoic and emotionless demeanor. I can't help but ponder if this is the persona he presents to the world, his public facade.

When the traffic stops, the lights turn green and it's time to cross the street. We then divert onto a slender pathway, which leads up to a beautiful park.

People walk arm in arm, and Neil and I step around them onto the lush green grass. Filled with curiosity, I can't help but wonder where he might be going. People lounge on comfortable blankets, their silhouettes illuminated by the soft glow of the park lights, adding a touch of mystery.

I steal a glance at Neil, noticing how his eyes dart around, taking in the sights as he walks.

We walk past all the pretty flowers and find a more private spot. A couple cozily sits on a bench, wrapped up in each other's arms. There's this other couple with their kids playing happily close by. I pause for a moment as the children run past me, their laughter filling the air as they chase after one another. It makes me miss Alex even more. I make a mental note to call him once I return to the hotel.

Hastily catching up to Neil, I nearly collide with his back when he suddenly halts. His finger points to the left, drawing attention to someone lying on the grass, their hands relaxed behind their head. I have doubts about it being Xander, especially because the person on the grass has blonde hair and wears a cap, which is visible in the faint light from the nearby park lamp.

I have the urge to tell Neil that it's not Xander, but the more I observe him, the more I start to consider the possibility that it might be.

As I was showering in my hotel room earlier, I pondered the notion of reconciling with Xander. Considering that we will be working together for the next eight weeks, now might be the perfect time to put that idea into action. I know it won't be easy, given our complicated history, but it's something I feel compelled to do. It's time to let go of all the old grudges and move on. It's time to move forward. Being in his presence might just mend my broken heart. The hard part is trying to look at him without feeling the painful ache of missing him. Pushing aside my hurt is the only way to move forward and get on with living my life.

I slowly walk closer, not knowing if it's really Xander.

Chapter 49

Xander

As I lie on the grass, I casually cross my legs at the ankles and simply relax, taking in the breathtaking view of the stars above.

I've heard in this part of the world, the stars are bigger and more breathtaking, and the view certainly lives up to all the hype. This is my one and only chance to escape and enjoy some alone time before the crazy schedule of upcoming shows and the tour bus ride across Australia.

I just need a moment to sit, think, and calm my racing thoughts.

I know that the minute I step back into the hotel, Reg will completely lose his shit. It's always the same whenever I do something like this. He'll demand to know where I've been. And as always, I'll respond like I always do, by telling him to fuck off.

Raising my hand, I scratch underneath the blonde wig. I know it must look completely ridiculous, this unconventional choice of a blonde wig. However, I always bring it along during tours as it grants me the precious opportunity to escape and enjoy some alone time. It's the only time when I can think freely, without the relentless pressure of meeting everyone's expectations.

Whenever we go touring, I never fail to stumble upon places like this, where I can truly indulge in deep reflection. It brings back memories of the moments when I would sit on the rock, pondering life's mysteries, and reminiscing about my dear mother.

Suddenly, a voice breaks through my thoughts.

"Hey."

My heart races as I recognize the voice. I turn my head to see Poppy standing just a few feet away.

"It is you?" she says, a smile spreading across her beautiful face as if she has caught onto my secret.

I remain silent, simply watching her as she comes over and sits beside me.

"Nice cap and wig, by the way. You had me fooled," she says. "But Neil knew it was you."

Observing her as she leans back on her elbow, I check out her tits, noticing that they are slightly bigger than before.

"It's nice out here," she says, scanning the area.

A strand of hair falls across her face, and as she raises her hand to brush it aside, I catch a glimpse of a tattoo on the inside of her wrist. It reads the name "Alex."

"Alright, spill it. Why are you out here?" she asks.

I turn my head and gaze up at the stars. Even though I'm not looking at her, I can feel the weight of her stare. I place my hands on my chest, closing my eyes, relishing the comforting sensation of her presence nearby.

"Okay," she says. "All we need now is a bottle of whisky to complete the night."

Glancing at her, I glimpse a remorseful expression on her face, as if she instantly regrets her words. Swiftly, she diverts her focus back to the sky above.

"Reg is looking for you," she casually mentions.

"Yeah, so," I add, "I don't care."

"Well, he certainly seems like a dick," she says.

"You nailed it, Princess. He is a dick." I'm waiting for her to tell me she's not my princess like she did the last time I called her that. But she doesn't.

"You still haven't answered my question," she asks, turning her head to look at me. "Why are you here?"

I pause for a moment, then turn my head to meet her gaze. "When I'm on tour, I just need some alone time to gather my thoughts."

"Sorry, I can go if you'd prefer," she says.

As she sits up, a desperate longing to keep her close compels me to reach out and gently grasp her wrist. It may seem strange, given that we aren't on speaking terms, yet having her here is comforting. I can't bear the thought of her leaving.

"Stay," I tell her.

"Or I can just wait over with Neil if you'd like."

If anyone needed to locate me urgently, I knew Neil would be the one to track me down. He understands my need for a peaceful spot where I can be by myself. That's why I like Neil; he never rats me out, unlike that asshole Trevor who runs to Reg whenever he sees me in my disguise, thinking I'm up to no good.

I choose not to respond to Poppy's question; instead, I simply grasp her wrist.

Whenever I touch her, it's as if memories from the past blend with the present. I long to return to those days when I was younger. I wish I could go back and tell my foolish, aspiring rockstar self that leaving her behind would be the biggest mistake of my life. If I had the opportunity to redo it all, I would have stayed with her or asked her to come with me. Because all this time, all I've ever wanted was to call her and share my success.

The satisfaction of achieving my dreams and growing into the person I am today has never been as fulfilling as it could have been if she had been there with me, celebrating those moments of success together. With every milestone I reached, every chart-topping song, and every sold-out performance, all I wanted was to reach out and find out if she was proud of me, to know if she truly believed that I deserved her love and admiration.

She lays back on the ground, her eyes fixed on the sky overhead. Moments pass before she finally speaks.

"Is it always this hectic, like it was today?" she asks.

"Yeah, pretty much," I respond.

I can sense her uncertainty as if struggling to find the right words to say. It's unlike her to be so cautious. I miss the confident, smart-mouthed girl with all her sass.

Just like today, I couldn't help but feel super proud of her when she completely shut Reg down for being an asshole. It's reassuring to see that her weak-ass boyfriend hasn't extinguished the fiery spirit inside her yet.

"How did you find me," I ask to fill in the silence, even though I know the answer to that question. I just want to move on from this tension and talk like we used to.

"Neil." She props up onto one elbow and looks around the area. "It's pretty here. I'd love to see it in the day."

"Yeah, I'm sure it is, but I'll never get to see that. Sadly, I'll never get to see it unless I'm looking out the limo's window."

She glances in my direction. "Do you ever have any time for yourself?"

"Not really. And even if I did, it's not like I could simply stroll around like everyone else," I respond, keeping my eyes on her.

She nods and then lies back down.

All I want to do is turn over and bury my face in the curve of her neck, savoring her scent just like I used to enjoy doing when we were younger.

"So that's the reason for the wig and the cap."

"Yeah. I know it looks pretty ridiculous, but it's my go-to move, along with these sunglasses." I hold them up to show her. "People still stare, amused by how stupid I look, yet they can't quite pinpoint who's hiding underneath. So, it works, no matter how ridiculous it may seem."

"Do you ever get tired of all the fame?" she asks. "I remember that's what you wanted."

"Yeah, it's not exactly what I had in mind. Don't get me wrong, I'm grateful that I still get to make music and all, but it's not what I thought it would be."

"How so?" she asks.

"It's just that I feel like I have no control over any of it. All we are to the label is a product. In the beginning, it was fine because we were pursuing our passion, chasing our dream, but now it's lost its allure. Sometimes it seems like the label owns every part of me, and that's something I can't handle. It's like we're no longer seen as individuals, but merely a money-making machine."

She keeps quiet for the moment as if considering my comment. She crosses her arms and rests them on her stomach, turning her gaze back to me.

"Regardless of all of that, you still wouldn't change it, though, right?"

"No, probably not. But if I had known what I know now, maybe things would have turned out differently. I would have made different choices."

"But you still did it, Xander. You followed through with everything you said you would. I'm sure your mom would be incredibly proud of you," she remarks.

And at this moment, I find myself unable to speak. Emotion tightens my throat. Since the last time I was with Poppy, I haven't discussed my mother with anyone. Not being able to talk about her has been difficult for me. But that's the special thing about Poppy - she understands the loss of losing someone so significant in my life. She turns her head towards me, and I feel the weight of her stare.

"I'm sure your mom would be so proud of the success you've achieved. I bet she never imagined that when she gave you your first guitar, you'd become the envy of the world. Now, I'll say this once, and I won't say it again because I'm still mad at you for ditching me, but I've been keeping up with your success online. I'm super proud of what you've done. You did it. You pursued your dream."

To hear her say that brings an ache to my heart, but I'm glad she has been keeping up with my progress and achievements. There have been countless moments when I achieved milestones and instinctively reached for my phone to call her, only to remember that I didn't have her number because I threw my phone in the lake. Another regret of my life, and I've been annoyed at myself for years for another foolish mistake.

"So, will you tell me now why you never pursued your dream? Why were you working at the bar instead?"

Right away, I see her shutting down when I mention it.

"I don't think it's any of your business what happens in my life. Especially after you just walked away without ever wanting to know about it before," she says, sitting up and hugging her legs close to her chest as if protecting herself.

She's right. I really shouldn't have asked, especially considering how long it's been since we last spoke. But as she takes out her phone, I am captivated by her gorgeous face, illuminated by the screen. I quickly glance down and notice that she's texting Ace.

Poppy: I found him. He's okay.

It's frustrating that Ace knows her number, but not me. I should be the one who has her number. A small voice in my head reminds me that I messed up by throwing it away. I'll ask him for her number later; it's the least he can do after all the crap he's been pulling lately.

Poppy's gaze remains fixated on her screen, clearly anticipating Ace's response.

In a matter of seconds, it finally arrives.

Ace: Where is he?

I watch, curious to see if she will disclose my current location. I hope she doesn't, as I can do without the chaos of the media, exposing my ridiculous disguise all because Reg wants to forcefully return me to the hotel, just like he did in the past when he contacted Neil.

Poppy's fingers glide effortlessly across the screen, and I observe as she composes the following message.

Poppy: It's under control. He's fine. I'll text you when he's back at the hotel.

I smile, seeing that she hasn't changed a bit. She remains loyal, steadfast and doesn't let others sway her.

She locks her phone and places it face down on the ground next to her. After taking a moment to observe the peaceful surroundings of the park, the tranquility is abruptly shattered by the loud ring of her phone. She wastes no time and flips the phone over, and there it is. That asshole Reg calling her. Taking in a deep breath, she answers the call.

"Hello," Poppy says.

"Where the fuck is he?" Reg's voice roars through the phone, reaching my ears. I make a mental note to give him a piece of my mind when I get back.

Poppy moves the phone away from her ear, abruptly ending the call. Once more, she switches it off and is about to place it face down on the ground next to her. However, just as she's about to do so, the phone suddenly lights up again, accompanied by her distinctive ringtone.

"Reg, just listen," she says, her voice filled with frustration.

"Don't you dare tell me to fucking listen. You had one job."

Poppy disconnects the call once more, but this time she grips the phone, anticipating another incoming call.

Without delay, the phone rings again, and she answers it. "If you persist in yelling at me, I'll simply keep ending the conversation. However, if you're open to having a respectful discussion, I'm willing to talk to you."

I'm on the verge of bursting into laughter, as I can't help but be in awe of her sassy attitude. Even someone as infuriating as Reg, a man who has intimidated countless others with his rage, is completely powerless against the feisty sass of my princess. Having her around will be entertaining, just to witness how she toys with Reg.

His booming voice is noticeably absent from the phone, implying that he might have to control himself this time. Instead, it is Poppy's voice that I hear.

"Yes, he's fine. And no, I won't tell you where he is. You're paying me to handle this, so please allow me the freedom to do just that."

"Tell me right now where the hell he is," Reg's voice booms through the phone.

"I don't remember any part of the contract saying I have to keep you updated on everything."

"For fuck sake, we're paying you for-"

Poppy ends the call and turns off her phone.

Spontaneous laughter bursts out of me, a liberating sensation that has been absent from my life for so many years.

"Don't laugh," she says, playfully slapping my arm. "I could totally get my ass handed to me when I go back to the hotel, or worse, get sent packing."

"Don't worry. No one is going to make you leave."

"How can you be so sure about that, especially when dealing with Reg? That man's temper is off the charts. When I first met him, he was good at hiding his hot temper."

"Yeah, he acts all professional when he's in the spotlight. But in private, he becomes a total asshole, spewing a bunch of crap."

A ringing phone grabs our attention, causing us to turn our heads to see Neil answer his phone.

"What's up?" Neil greets, his deep voice resonating.

"That's probably Reg," Poppy says. "He's probably asking Neil the same question."

"No, Sir. I haven't seen Xander," Neil replies. "But if I do, I'll keep you updated."

Poppy giggles, her shoulders shaking with laughter. "Why am I suddenly having so much fun annoying Reg?"

I know I should head back to the hotel because Reg can be a real pain and he won't quit searching. But screw it, all I want is more time with Poppy. I love when she lets her guard down and talks with no animosity. I've been dying to kiss her ever since I saw her at the bar that night.

Damn, I'm already back to that with her. She's the only one I've locked lips with. Many have tried, but I've never felt such a strong desire to be close to someone like I do with her. The urge to lean in and kiss her is undeniable, even though she has made it clear that she wants nothing to do with me now. But you know what? I don't care. So fuck it. I won't let that stop me from trying. Holding back has never been my style, and this is a chance to find out if she truly hates me.

I sit up, fixing my wig so I don't blow my cover and ruin this moment of kissing her. The last thing I want is some groupie barging in and wrecking the moment. As I move closer to her, I see this confused look on her face, like she's trying to figure out what I'm doing.

I seize the chance and make my move.

As I hold the side of her face, our lips meet, igniting a powerful surge of desire within me. For a brief moment, she hesitates, her body tensing before completely surrendering. The warmth of her lips against mine triggers a rush of familiarity, and I cherish the soft moan as I tenderly explore her mouth with my tongue. As the kiss deepens, she matches my passion, and at that moment, I find my answer. She still desires me just as strongly as I desire her. Despite her outward demeanor suggesting otherwise, her actions unveil the truth.

As my hand moves over her body, I can feel the warmth radiating from her skin through the thin fabric of her shirt. The thought of undressing her consumes my mind, as I yearn to relive the fervor of our past encounters. But as quickly as that thought enters my head, her hands come in between us and she forcefully pushes me away.

"God, what am I doing? This can't be happening again," she says, her face displaying complete disbelief at her own behavior. Her expression swiftly shifts from shock to anger. With a stern look, she fixes me with a serious glare.

"You can pretend all you want, Princess," I say, smirking. "I can see through your act. Quit playing games and be real."

"An act? You honestly think this is all an act?" Her voice escalates, and I can tell she's struggling to find the right words.

It's a little disappointing because I was hoping for her usual sassy come-back. However, she shakes her head, trying to regain control of her emotions. I'm still in disbelief that she kissed me back. I can't help but smirk, knowing that if she felt nothing for me, she would have reacted angrily and left. Yet, here she is, still sitting beside me. It gives me all the answers I need and makes me realize that there's still a chance for a fresh start with her. This time, there is no way I'm going to fuck it up.

"Stop staring at me like that," she snaps back, her irritation prompting a reaction.

"Enough of this crap already," I respond.

"You're the one talking crap," she replies, crossing her arms, clearly annoyed.

I lean forward, closing the gap between us until our faces are almost touching.

She takes a sharp inhale in response to my close proximity.

"Yeah, that's what I thought, Princess. You can pretend all you want, but there's no denying it." I lean in and press a kiss to the side of her face. "Let me know when you're ready to admit the truth. Goodnight, Princess. Get some rest; we have a busy day tomorrow." I get up and leave her there alone on the grass as I make my way over to Neil.

"Asshole!" Poppy says, letting me know I've hit a nerve.

I can't help but grin, relishing in the impact of the truth now that it's out there.

I stop in front of Neil. "I'll be good getting back to the hotel. Stay with Poppy and please let me know when she is back safe in her room."

"Yes, Sir," Neil says, acknowledging my request with a nod.

I continue walking past him and navigate my way through the park. Retrieving my phone from my pocket, I swiftly check the time. It's getting late, much later than I had initially planned to be out.

Chapter 50

Poppy

In the aftermath of that lingering kiss, I find it difficult to maintain eye contact with Xander the following day. Yet, I can feel his presence close by.

Reluctantly, I join the band at sound check the next day, even though I can't understand why I have to go. But Reg made a big deal about it. So here I am. Sitting in the stands of the venue, I am completely captivated by Xander's powerful voice as he sings. The band's undeniable collective talent and captivating stage presence are evident, but my focus remains unwaveringly on Xander throughout it all.

As he belts out their greatest hit, the very song he sang to me on that unforgettable night on the rock, my tears threaten to spill. A whirlwind of emotions and memories wash over me, transporting me back to the carefree moments we once shared. The way he opened up to me, sharing personal things, I believe only Ace was aware of.

How did we go from that profound connection to our current predicament? My longing for him intensifies even more after our recent kiss, and I struggle to suppress this overpowering attraction. These feelings for him have been with me since I was fourteen, and I cannot simply switch them off because of what has happened between us. I just need to get better at not letting him see how I really feel.

Kit takes a seat beside me, her eyes captivated by the band as they deliver another powerful song.

"This is why they're the best," she comments, turning her head and smiling. As soon as her eyes meet mine, her smile falters. "Are you alright?" she asks, lightly rubbing my arm.

"Yeah," I sniffle, swiping a finger under my eye to stop a stray tear from falling. "Just memories."

"I've heard some rumors about you and Xander having a past. Well, that's what people are saying. It's nothing scandalous, if that's what you were expecting. It's just this rumor going around that you and Xander were involved, and apparently, he hasn't been the same since you two broke up."

I can't help but burst into laughter at how ridiculous these speculations are.

Kit smiles at me and asks, "So, I take it there's absolutely no truth to those rumors?"

"No, not at all." I quickly reply.

The song comes to an end and we redirect our attention back to the stage.

Xander walks over to the half stage where Nate's drums are placed, picking up the half-empty bottle of water. After chugging it down, he grabs a stool and returns to the microphone, but not before he gives a look in my direction.

Kit settles back in her seat, getting comfortable as if she plans to stay for a while. "I absolutely adore the way he sings this song."

As the music begins, my throat tightens upon hearing the opening notes, especially when Xander's eyes shift toward me, and he starts singing the first line of Creep.

He keeps eye contact with me the whole time during the first verse.

The rush of emotions overwhelms me as I recall all the times we sang that song together. I remember that day on the street when he first spoke to me, and the time we performed it on the rock for his mother's birthday. There were countless other moments in my room when he would grab my guitar and play it. It's all too much, these intense memories flooding back. I have to leave before I completely break down and he realizes the power he still has over me.

In one swift motion, I snatch my bag and get to my feet, fully prepared to make a quick exit.

Just then, Kit's voice pierces through the music, shouting from behind, "Where are you going?"

With tears welling up, I press on, navigating through the rows of seats, my pace quickening as I make my way towards the exit, a sense of urgency propelling me forward.

Xander's eyes track my every step, intensifying my awareness of his gaze. Despite knowing that the band's sign-off song was coming, hearing it live, and locking eyes with him as he sings it, brings back the memories I cannot brush aside.

Out of nowhere, the song comes to an abrupt halt, causing me to quickly turn my head in Xander's direction. He gets up from the stool and makes his way towards the side of the stage.

Oh my god. That's the last thing I wanted to happen.

In a hurry, I rush into the large foyer, ready to bury my head in shame. I can't understand why I ever thought I could handle any of this. I should be back home with my son, not here, where every memory painfully tugs at my heart. Maybe I should just go find Ace and confess that I can't bear this any longer because it's too agonizing. I'm freaking out because I don't know where I'm going, and I can't believe I messed up sound check.

As I turn the corner, I abruptly halt upon seeing Reg. He's on his phone, but we lock eyes when he sees me there. His gaze narrows, studying me as he comes forward. I quickly turn, discreetly wiping away the tears streaming down my face. I can't afford to let him witness my vulnerability; undoubtedly, things will take a turn for the worse once he discovers that I've ruined sound check. It's just one more issue to add to the lengthy list of problems he has with me. It's only been three days, yet I already feel like I'm crumbling from within.

"We need to discuss what happened last night," he tells me as he ends the call.

Shit. I had successfully avoided him last night and this morning at the hotel, and now he wants to bring it up when I'm feeling my worst.

"I never should have come. I just want to go home," I blurt out before he can even begin to criticize me.

The expression on his face says it all. His jaw tightens, his lips narrow. "You must be joking. After all the arrangements that have been made, you choose to bail now. Just three days into it," he responds, clearly frustrated. "You've already been paid the ten thousand dollars, Poppy. If you leave now, you'll have to pay it all back, and you'll also have to find your own way home. The label won't be providing any money for your return trip. Ace said you were tough, but clearly, he didn't know you at all. So why don't you just go back to your insignificant life that means nothing to anyone? After what you did last night, I'm better off without you," he says.

The term "insignificant" evokes a strong reaction in me. Just because I'm not a wealthy rockstar doesn't mean I'm a nobody. It fuels a fire within me, similar to when Jade used to constantly target me with hurtful comments about my weight.

Screw him. He has no right to speak to me like that. Sure, I may have broken down and shown vulnerability in the face of overwhelming emotions, but I need to toughen up and confront this jerk who won't stop yelling at me.

"Fuck you. If you want me to do this job, then you need to stop being so demanding and let me do it. You can't scream at me down the phone just because I won't give in to your demands like everyone else."

Footsteps sound on the hard cement floor, prompting Reg to turn around to see who's approaching. I cast a glance over Reg's shoulder to see Xander. His gaze meets mine, then shifts to Reg, as if he yearns to find out what's going on.

Reg glances at his watch. "You haven't finished sound check yet," he says, eyeing Xander.

"I'm done," Xander says, his eyes locked on me as he approaches. Reg opens his mouth to protest, but Xander beats him to it. "Don't say a fucking word, I swear to god, Reg."

Reg takes a step back, watching as Xander grabs my hand and pulls me forward.

As we make our way down the long corridor, he finally spots a restroom and quickly ushers me inside, locking the door behind us.

Leaning against the door, he watches me for a moment before he speaks. "What's wrong, Princess?"

"Don't worry about it," I mutter, keeping my head down, feeling embarrassed for letting myself fall apart.

"It's the song, right?" he says.

I lift my head in response to his words, but I find it difficult to articulate my feelings. Hearing him sing that song hurts me deeply. It feels like our special song, or at least it was to me.

"Singing that song hurts me too," he admits.

I get it. The pain of losing his mother is just as intense as my longing for my father.

"You didn't have to come after me," I say, trying to divert the conversation. "You could have continued with sound check. Now I'll be blamed for messing that up."

"You're not to blame," he says, pushing off the door, coming towards me. "I canceled sound check because I wanted to, and believe me, no one will say a fucking word about it." He walks over and positions himself directly in front of me. His eyes scan my face, as if examining every tiny feature.

He raises his hand and gently caresses the side of my face.

"I can't do this, Xander."

"If you want me to stop, just say the word," he says.

I swallow, not wanting to say those words but knowing that I have to. I can't just be his convenient hookup for the next month or two. Allowing that to happen would shatter my heart beyond repair.

He leans in, running his nose over the shell of my ear. I close my eyes at the sensation of feeling him again—the smell of him, the touch of him. His other hand rests gently on my hip. "I want you, Princess," he whispers close to my ear. "I want you in every way possible. Not just you coming on my cock, but everything. And when you're ready to forgive me for what I've done, we need to talk." He plants a soft kiss on my cheek and turns away, unlocking the door and stepping outside.

I recognize that move. It's the one I've witnessed countless times for years when I watched him. He did it with Jade, Savannah, and all the other girls he hooked up with.

I make my way over to the sink, place my palms on the counter, and fix my gaze on my reflection in the mirror. Through my tear-stained eyes, I notice my mascara has smudged. Flicking on the tap, I cup my hands and let the water cascade over my face. Get your shit together, Poppy. You're tougher than this.

Three days later, the crowd's roar pulsates in my ears as I watch Xander move around the stage. The dazzling lights cast a radiant glow on his figure, and despite the scorching heat surrounding me, a chill runs down my spine.

It's been over two hours, yet he continues to pour his heart and soul into his performance. It is both mesmerizing and intimidating to witness how effortlessly he commands the attention of over eighty thousand people. He's in his element as if he was born to thrive in this very moment.

"I love you, Xander," someone shouts from the crowd.

"I want to have your babies."

"I'll let you stick it anywhere," another woman at the front of the crowd yells.

I can't help but roll my eyes when he gives her a panty-melting smile.

He grabs the mic in a crude gesture and the crowd cheers get even louder. And he just stands there - like some important world figure. Absorbing the energy, biding his time until the tension, the anticipation becomes so intense that you can hear the rapid beating of hearts belonging to every girl in the crowd.

Another moment slips away. Electricity surges through me like a live wire. Quietly, I scold myself for the way my body reacts to him.

With a sudden turn of his head, he catches sight of me standing there. Our eyes lock, and he playfully runs his tongue over his bottom lip in a suggestive manner, igniting a surge of desire within me. Memories flood back of that skilled tongue and all the pleasurable things it can do. His eyes narrow, and he gives me a self-satisfied smile, while Nate sets a slow beat on the drums, followed by Theo on bass and Ace on the guitar. Yet, his gaze remains fixed on me, his seductive, sexy lopsided grin never wavering. Cocky asshole.

I used to adore the way he was - unapologetic and unaffected by others' opinions. His rawness and that dirty way of speaking captivated me. Oh, that mouth. The very thought of it would invade my thoughts as I lay alone in bed at night. And even though he projected toughness, he slowly let me in to see the tender parts that had caused his scars.

What the hell was I thinking when I said yes to Theo's request to watch the show? I should have stayed in the green room like I have every other night.

I've been avoiding Xander at all costs ever since he dragged me into the restroom. It took every ounce of strength to resist the temptation of indulging in him and using him the way he used me. But I couldn't, as it would only reopen old wounds and painful memories.

My phone suddenly vibrates in my pocket, prompting me to quickly pull it out. To my surprise, the caller ID displays my mother's name. This is unusual since she never calls me. It's always me calling her to check on Alex.

A rush of anxiety courses through me, wondering if something is wrong. As I glance up, I notice that Xander's gaze is still fixed on me. The only noticeable change is the concern etched on his face, replacing his previous smug expression.

I quickly distance myself, sprinting away from the stage so I can answer my phone and listen to my mother amidst the deafening music.

"Hold on!" I shout, plugging my other ear with my finger and racing towards the green room to ensure I can hear her. "Is everything okay?"

"Yes, but try not to panic when I tell you this," she says, her words instantly sending waves of panic through my body. My heart beats loudly, like it's about to hammer its way out of my chest.

"Just tell me, Mom," I demand.

"We're at the hospital. But don't worry, Alex is okay. He had an accident when he fell off his bike on the sidewalk. The doctors said he needs surgery and they need your insurance information."

"A bike? But he doesn't even have one, let alone know how to ride it. How did he even get on a bike?"

I'm rambling, unable to fully grasp how this situation even happened. Tears fill my eyes as I agonize over my son's injuries. In all the chaos of getting everything ready, I forgot to give my mother the insurance details. How could I have overlooked such an important thing? However, the greater worry lingers:

why was my son riding a bike? What other secrets has my mother been keeping from me?

"Hang on, Mom. I'll get them," I say, realizing that all our bags from the hotel are now loaded on the tour bus.

With my phone pressed to my ear, I quickly approach Robbo, one of the many friendly Australian security guards the band has hired while here in Australia.

"Hey Robbo, it's an emergency. I need to get to the bus right away."

Noticing my distress, he pivots and guides me towards a locked door, leading us through a narrow, fenced-off section to reach the bus waiting at the back of the building.

"Alex has been asking for you," my mother mentions, adding yet another layer of pain.

Great mom. Push the knife a little deeper into my heart. "Can I talk to him?"

"No, they're preparing him for surgery."

In a rush, I board the bus and find our luggage already placed at the front of the bus.

There I see a well-equipped kitchenette with a spacious dining area. Next to that, is a cozy sitting area with two inviting couches, accompanied by a television and an Xbox console.

"What? He's going into surgery now?"

"Soon. That's why I'm calling you."

I reach into my bag, searching for my wallet to locate my insurance card. "Alright, I found it," I say as I pull it out.

"Just a moment, I'll pass you over to the nurse."

"Hello," a high-pitched voice greets me on the other end of the phone. Once I've provided the necessary information, I ask the questions my mother refuses to answer. "Is Alex okay?"

"Yes, Alex is all set for surgery. He has what we call a displaced fracture. Which means that Alex's bone in his arm needs to be realigned."

Right then, Xander rushes onto the bus and stops, his eyes fixed on me as I keep listening to the nurse on the phone, silent tears rolling down my cheeks.

"Is he in pain?" I ask.

"No, not at the moment. We have made him comfortable, so he isn't feeling any pain. He should be going into surgery within the next twenty minutes."

"Okay, thank you," I reply, as a wave of relief washes over me.

"I'll hand you back to your mom now," the nurse says.

Waiting on the line for my mum's voice, I'm met with nothing but silence.

"Mom…" I say, waiting for a response. But when I pull the phone away from my ear to look at the screen, I see the call has been disconnected. I can't understand why my mother would do such a thing to me.

With Xander observing me, I dial her number. It goes straight to voicemail. It's clear now that she has intentionally turned off her phone.

Feeling frustrated and angry, I collapse onto the lounge, burying my head in my hands and sobbing. I can't help but wonder why she's using this situation to retaliate against me. Just because I went against her wishes of coming here doesn't justify her actions. As I'm lost in my thoughts, I feel the couch shift beside me, letting me know Xander has taken a seat.

To create a sense of distance and regain control of my emotions, I stand up. How can I possibly discuss our son without completely falling apart in front of him? Just as I'm trying to gather my thoughts, Xander's hand gently wraps around my wrist, offering support.

"Talk to me, Princess," he says, standing up and lifting my chin to meet his gaze. His calloused fingertips gently wipe away my tears. "Please talk to me."

"It's… my son," I confess, my voice trembling. "He's injured. His arm is broken, and he needs surgery to realign it. As for my mother… well she was never in favor of me coming here, and now…" I pause, sniffling. "Now she refuses to share any information with me about what's going on. It was the nurse who let me know Alex is about to go into surgery when I gave her my insurance details."

"When is he having surgery?" Xander asks.

"She said in twenty minutes. My mother called only because I forgot to leave my insurance details and…" Tears well up, and I cover my face with my hands.

I never thought I would pour my heart out to Xander again, especially not about my little boy. The little boy he continues to never acknowledge.

"Just give me a moment, Princess," he says, planting a kiss on the top of my head.

As I gaze up at him, he pulls out his phone from his pocket and walks off the bus. What the fuck? I just poured my heart out to him, and now he's walking away.

Outside the bus, I hear someone yelling - it's Reg. "You need to get your ass into that fucking green room right now to greet those VIP Ticket holders."

"Fuck off. I'm busy," Xander snaps back.

"Xander, I swear to god, if you don't go back in there, there will be consequences."

I glance out the window and see Xander walking alongside the bus, phone pressed to his ear, completely ignoring Reg as he continues his rant.

Annoyed that Xander is ignoring him, Reg storms onto the bus, stopping right in front of me. "You were supposed to be here to address this behavior. Get out and do your job."

Sniffling, I quickly wipe my eyes, ready to tell him to fuck off as I have urgent matters to attend to. However, before I can utter a word, Xander comes back onto the bus, phone still pressed to his ear. He firmly grabs Reg by the collar and forcefully pulls him back. "If you ever fucking speak to her like that again, it will be the last thing you do," Xander declares, his voice seething with anger. He then yanks Reg down the front steps of the bus.

"Get your hands off me!" Reg demands, struggling against Xander's grip. "I fucking mean it, Xander."

Peering through the side window, I watch Xander forcefully shove Reg against the bus. He keeps him pinned there momentarily, engrossed in the phone conversation while giving Reg an intense glare. Eventually, Xander releases his grip and proceeds along the side of the bus, still holding the phone to his ear.

With a few quick adjustments to his suit, Reg returns to the building.

A wave of urgency washes over me, prompting me to grab my phone and search for information on a displaced fracture. I feel immediate regret when I discover the severity of my son's injury.

While consumed by distressing thoughts, the sound of footsteps makes me lift my head.

"Here," Xander says, handing me his phone. "A nurse will call you every half hour to give you updates on your son."

"How...," I say, staring up at him in disbelief.

"Just grab it, Princess," he urges, pushing the phone towards me once more.

I reach out and take his phone.

"She'll call right away when your son goes into surgery. That's her private number. If you have any questions, just call her."

"How did you do that? How did you just-"

"Princess, when you've got money and fame, you can pretty much get whatever you want. Well, almost anything."

I can't even put into words how thankful I am to him for doing this.

"I gotta get back in there before Reg explodes and takes it out on the guys. You gonna be okay?"

I give a nod, overwhelmed by him doing this, helping me to find information about our son.

"I'll be out as soon as I can. If you need me, text Ace."

I nod, appreciating what he's done. Although, I can't understand why he's bothering to help when he acts like our son doesn't exist. That's something we need to discuss, but that will have to wait.

"Everything will be alright," he says, moving his thumb across my cheek. "I've arranged for the best surgeon to operate." He leans in and kisses me on my forehead. And then he turns away and rushes off the bus.

I clutch his phone to my chest, collapsing on the couch, not sure what else to do.

I've had two conversations with the nurse in the past two hours, her kind words providing comfort during this difficult time.

The first time, I called her in a panic, unable to bear the uncertainty of not knowing what was happening. The second time was when she called me to say Alex was going into surgery.

The whole time, I anxiously waited, my heart pounding with each passing second, my eyes glued to my phone, desperately hoping for my mother's call with an update on Alex. Sadly, she never does.

While I'm on the phone with Nurse Sally, Xander comes back on the bus. While I listen to what she has to say, my gaze stays on Xander, and I can't help but notice the way his eyes explore every inch of my face.

When she finally tells me that Alex is fine, I let out a sigh of relief.

"Alex is sleeping now," she tells me.

"How long will he stay in the hospital?"

"We'll keep him here overnight and evaluate him in the morning. If everything looks good, he should be able to go home. Do you want me to call you when he wakes up?"

"Would you mind?"

"Not at all. Oh, and before you go, can you please let Mr. Williams know my son is super excited about his guitar lesson?"

It's in these precious moments when Xander shows such kindness that tears well up in my eyes, my throat tightens with emotion. It's hard to believe that this man is the same person who has caused me so much pain.

"Okay, I will let him know. Thank you again, Nurse Sally."

"Don't worry, Poppy. Alex is in good hands. I promise."

Taking a deep breath, I finish the call and glance up at Xander.

"Everything's fine. The surgery was successful. She'll give me a call when he wakes up." I get up from the couch and hold his phone out towards him. "Thank you."

"No, you hold onto it." He pushes my hand back towards me.

"Are you sure? What if one of your groupies rings for a booty call or something?"

I watch as irritation washes over his face, causing his features to contort, and at that moment, I deeply regret what I said.

"Princess, don't believe everything you read," he retorts, his voice filled with frustration and a hint of anger. He strides over to the refrigerator and grabs a bottle of water.

My attention shifts to the three other band members making their way onto the bus, with four excited groupies. I notice their wide-eyed expressions on their faces as they spot Xander, leaning against the kitchen cupboard, gulping down his water.

Suddenly, Reg storms onto the bus.

"No. There are to be no groupies on this bus. Seriously, how many times do I have to say it? Everyone get out now!" He points towards the door, gesturing for them to leave.

A busty blonde groupie looks my way, clearly annoyed. "Why does she get to stay on then?" she says, her tone resembling that of a tantrum-throwing toddler.

Xander tosses the empty bottle into the sink and comes forward. "She's not some fucking groupie. Get off this bus right now before I kick your skanky ass."

"Relax, man," Theo interjects. "They're leaving, right, baby?" He kisses her and walks her down the steps.

The other three groupies quickly exit the bus the second Xander strides across.

Ace and Nate grab their bags and make their way towards the closed door halfway down the bus.

It's only a few seconds and then Theo returns.

"You totally killed my vibe, Regie boy," he says, snatching his bag. Then he throws a smirk Xander's way. "I might have to find my fun somewhere else." Then he glances my way. "What about it, Spitfire? Can you handle ten inches?"

I know he's just messing with me. I've already figured out who Theo is. He enjoys messing with people, just like Xander did for his own entertainment.

"Well, Theo, if it's really that big, you'll have no problem shoving it up your own ass," I reply.

He pauses, smirks, and gives Xander a quick look. "I like her. She's a keeper. For fuck's sake, don't screw it up this time." Moving ahead, he goes through the same door Ace and Nate went through earlier.

Theo's words won't leave my head. Does everyone here know what Xander did to me back in the day? Did he blab that I was just a high school fling? Do they actually think I'm crushing on Xander, like Jade does? Yes, I still have feelings for him, but it's more than that. He shared things with me he told no one else, except for Ace.

"Come on," Xander says, grabbing our bags. "I'll show you where your bunk is."

CHAPTER 51

Xander

It's the middle of the night and I suddenly hear my ringtone. I've been lying awake, unable to sleep, knowing that Poppy is just across from me in the bunk. It must be the nurse calling Poppy to give her an update about her son.

Curiosity gets the better of me and I pull back the curtain just enough to catch her getting out of her bunk. She looks so hot in her sleep shorts and tight tank top, my dick can't help but react. Despite my intense stare, she's too busy on the phone to notice. She stops in her tracks when she almost steps on Theo, who, as usual, has somehow ended up in Nate's bottom bunk.

Those two idiots think we don't know what's going on. Every morning, Theo rushes back to his bunk to hide what's going on, but they're wrong if they think we don't know. All I know is that Nate is the only one who can calm Theo when things get too intense. I know Theo has nightmares that haunt him from his painful past. Apart from them sharing girls and Theo ending up in Nate's bunk, there are no clear signs that they are in a relationship. Even if they were, I wouldn't care. Their sexual status would never change the way I feel about them.

As soon as Poppy leaves, I swiftly get out of bed, being careful not to step on Theo, who has his ass hanging out over the bunk. In a rush, I grab a shirt and put it on, desperate to cover up the tattoo on my chest before Poppy sees it. I step over Theo and make my way to the front of the bus.

I quietly approach the slightly open door, staying hidden in the shadows, observing Poppy as she sits back on the couch. Holding her phone up, she glances at her son's image on the screen. Because she's facing me, I can't see him, but I can hear his tiny voice.

"I'm fine, mommy. It hurt before, but it doesn't hurt anymore."

"I'm sorry I wasn't there, sweetie."

"It's okay. I got a huge pile of ice cream from Nurse Sally.

"Eat as much as you want to feel better."

She's beaming with joy, showing how much she loves that little boy. I can't help but admire her, smiling in awe, wishing I could join this amazing family. If only it were Alex, Poppy, and me. Regret consumes me. Was it a waste for me to leave her when I could have had this with her? She never pursued her dream, and I didn't stop her like her mom thought I would. Now that I have everything I could ever ask for, the one thing I desire most in this world feels out of reach. The longing to provide her with everything still lingers, but now I fear it may be too late.

"Have you seen a kangaroo yet?" Alex asks.

"No, not yet. But I promise to snap some shots when I do."

"And don't forget to get one of a koala. I like koala's too."

"I promise I will if I get the chance. I'm not sure if I'll be able to get some time off to see them."

In the background, I hear music—a catchy tune, like the opening credits of a kids' television show.

"Is that Bluey I can hear in the background?"'

"Yeah. Nurse Sally put it on. I might go to watch it, Mommy."

"Okay. Make sure you're careful with your arm when Grandma takes you home."

"Bye, Mom."

"Bye, sweetie. I love you."

"I love you too, Mommy."

Poppy brushes away a tear that's rolling down her cheek. All I want to do is rush in there and hold her and tell her everything will be alright.

"He's doing well," Nurse Sally says, coming onto the call. "You don't have to worry. We'll take good care of him."

"I'm so grateful for all you've done," Poppy says, her voice filled with thanks.

"You're welcome," Nurse Sally replies before ending the call.

Poppy lets out a long sigh, her gaze falls on the floor in front.

Entering the room, I stretch my body as if I have just gotten out of my bunk bed. I notice her quickly wiping her eyes before she looks at me.

"Xander," she says. "I know what you did for me, and I want to-"

"It's alright, Princess." I interrupt, walking to the refrigerator. "Do you want some water?"

"Please," she responds.

Grabbing two bottles, I make my way over and hand her one, settling down on the smaller couch opposite her.

"I've been so worried since my mom called," she admits, her voice shaking. All at once, she bursts into tears, like she's been holding it in. I don't even think twice. I throw away the unopened water bottle and rush over to her, hugging her tightly while she lets it all out. As I bring her onto my lap, I can't help but run my fingers through her silky soft hair. She leans into me, resting the side of her face against my chest. All I want is to make everything right for her.

"It's okay, Princess," I reassure her, running my hand down over her back. Seeing her so upset causes me unbearable pain. "He'll be okay. I'll text Nurse Sally soon, to see if she'll let you know when he leaves the hospital so you can talk to him."

"Thank you," she says, pulling back to look at me. I lift my hand and gently wipe the tears from her cheeks.

"Xander, I don't know what to say... You..." As she pauses, her eyes fixate on my face, carefully studying every intricate detail.

Nervously, I swallow, feeling the weight of the moment.

My stomach flutters when her fingers trail up the side of my neck. I'm craving her so badly, it's causing a surge of lust to pulsate in my groin. I know she feels every inch thickening, as my growing arousal would be poking her in her ass by now. The ache in my balls intensifies, craving the friction that only she can provide. My damn brain tells me to fuck her right here right now, but I know that acting on it would only push her away.

I don't want that, especially now that she's finally starting to trust and see the real me. I need that trust. So instead, I fight against every instinct that screams at me to strip her naked and possess every inch of her body to satisfy my own selfish desires.

Shifting positions, I gently lay us down on the couch, turning her so her back is pressed against my chest, spooning her in a way that I know will bring her comfort in this moment. I want to soothe her emotions, which have been on a rollercoaster ride over the past few hours. I resist the temptation to give in to my own needs, seeking my own release. But next time, I can't promise I'll be as patient.

As we lie here, she remains silent, letting me bury my face in the soft curve of her neck. I inhale her scent, relishing the familiarity that I've missed so much. I've missed the way we used to effortlessly connect with each other. And now, my head is all messed up with feelings and memories.

The bus moves along the road, its constant hum providing a soothing backdrop as we lay together. The rhythm of her pulse lulls me to sleep as my eyelids grow heavy.

Chapter 52

Poppy

I curse myself for almost giving in to temptation last night. If he hadn't moved me onto the couch when he did, I'm certain I would have fucked him. The way he looked at me with those dark lustful eyes, and when I felt his dick grow hard under my ass, had me craving a release that only he could give me.

Thankfully, it didn't happen because that would mean I've fallen back into the same old pattern.

Once this tour is over, he'll be gone again. But I still need to discuss our son, especially after everything he did for me with Alex. But a part of me is hesitant. I'm afraid of the rejection that may come when he tells me that nothing has changed with our son.

When the bus made a pit stop for gas early this morning, I realized I needed to leave before the others caught sight of us lying together. If they saw us, they might assume we had sex. And I don't want them to think that. Especially Reg. I'm here to focus on my job. Yesterday, all I did was cry, but I will not let that happen again.

Leaning against the sink, sipping my coffee, I hear faint whispers coming from the direction of the bunks. I think it's Theo and Nate, but I can't be certain, because I can't make out what they're saying.

From the same direction, Ace yells, "If you're not sleeping, get the fuck out!"

A smile creeps across my face as I recall the tough, no-nonsense Ace I knew back in school. He always spoke his mind without caring about anyone's opinion.

A few seconds pass, and then Theo emerges wearing sweatpants. He stretches his arms overhead, a smile spreading across his face as he notices me standing there.

My gaze is drawn to his tattooed chest.

"Like what you see, Spitfire?" he teases, a mischievous smirk forming on his lips as he effortlessly takes my coffee mug from my hands. After taking a sip, he hands it back.

"I just made a pot. You want one," I offer.

"Yeah," he responds, walking over to the table.

I turn and grab a cup, filling it with the freshly brewed coffee. Grabbing my own mug from the counter, I join Theo at the table.

The sound of footsteps grows louder, prompting me to turn my head to see Ace. Dressed only in his boxers, his inked arms stretched overhead. My eyes widen, and a moment of awkwardness washes over me as I glance away. Ace is there, sporting a noticeable boner.

I grip my coffee cup, trying to regain my composure, and unintentionally lock eyes with Theo, who sports a sly smirk.

"You better get used to it. That thing greets everyone every damn morning," he casually remarks.

Ace strides over to the coffee pot, pouring himself a cup. He then joins us at the table, settling in as if it's just another ordinary morning.

"How's the little man?" Ace asks, twisting his head to the side, causing his neck to crack.

"He's referring to Alex, not the two-inch dick you saw in his pants," Theo comments, but Ace chooses to ignore it. As do I.

"He seemed okay when I talked to him through the night."

"I understand it's difficult being away from him, but you're already making a positive impact here, you know."

"I'm not so sure about that." I ponder on his words, because all I've done is get upset and scream at Reg.

"His writing again," he nods towards Xander, who's still asleep on the couch. "He hasn't done that in years. The label has been pressuring him for ages, but he couldn't come up with anything."

Theo gets up and rummages through one of the top cupboards above the sink. After he finds what he's looking for he moves over to Xander asleep on the couch. When he's in front of him, he crouches down. I wonder what he is up to because I can't see what it is from this angle.

"He'll fucking throttle you when he sees it,' Nate says as he comes through the door, and approaches the table, joining Ace and me. He grabs Theo's coffee and takes a drink.

Theo steps back, holding a black marker in his hand. After he examines his work, he walks away. I nearly spit my coffee out onto the table when I notice what he has done. On Xander's left cheek, there's an outline of a sizable dick, with droplets dripping into his mouth.

"If Reg sees that, he'll totally lose it," Ace says.

"But how will he know it's me?"

"He'll know," Nate says.

Right on cue, the side door swings open and Reg emerges, engrossed in his phone. Seizing the opportunity, I have a quick look in the room through the open door. Inside, I spot a cozy double bed and a compact wardrobe. It seems way more comfortable than the tight bunk beds in the enclosed area at the back, where the money-makers sleep.

The bus starts to slow down and eventually stops.

I turn my head and gaze out of the window, taking in the large roadhouse where we have stopped.

"Kit reserved the entire cafe. So make sure you're in there in the next ten minutes," Reg says, not bothering to acknowledge any of the guys as he exits the bus.

"Yeah, good morning to you too, asshole," Nate says, as he finishes Theo's coffee.

"Yo, Xander, wake the fuck up," Theo yells, throwing an empty water bottle in his direction.

Reg comes back onto the bus. He slips his phone into his pocket and looks around the group.

When he looks at Xander, his brows furrow, and he gets this pissed-off look before he turns to Theo.

"What the fuck have you done?" He yells. His voice is so loud that he wakes up Xander. "He's the fucking lead singer, center stage, performing in the spotlight in front of thousands of fans!"

"Why do you just assume I'm the one to blame?"

"Because, who else could it be?"

"Chill out, it's not like it's a permanent marker," Theo says.

Xander, still half-asleep, sits up and rubs his eyes before looking up.

Ace accidentally spits out his coffee, causing some of it to land on Reg.

"What the fuck, man?" Reg says, eyeing his pricey shoes, before re-entering his room and closing the door.

Theo and Nate erupt into laughter, catching Xander's attention. He shoots Theo a stern glare, his eyes narrowing as he senses something amiss. Determined to find out, he rises from the couch and strides towards the restroom. Once he arrives, he forcefully opens the door.

We're all waiting, giving each other looks, waiting for Xander to come back.

"You better run you fucking asshole," Xander yells.

"Well, it's been nice knowing you," Theo says, grabbing his shirt from the back of the couch. "See ya at breakfast." He bolts off the bus.

"Where is he? Where's that little prick gone?" Xander says, coming back out.

Reg opens his door, and I notice he's wearing different shoes.

"Remove that shit off your face before you go in there," Reg says. "I've already cleaned up enough of your mistakes in the media."

Xander moves forward, and I can tell from the way he's staring at Reg that a fight is about to break out.

"Time to go," I butt in, tugging Xander's hand and leading him toward the restroom to ease the tension.

He willingly comes, even though he is still angry. I can feel the tension in his arm as I lead him into the restroom and close the door behind us. His presence makes the already tight space feel even more confined. Being this close to him sparks a strange sensation in my body.

"Do you guys always pull pranks on each other like this?" I open a drawer to locate a washcloth.

"No," he says firmly. "Theo's the only idiot who pulls this kind of crap."

I turn on the tap, feeling the cool rush of water against my hand as I wet the washcloth.

"Sit," I say, motioning for him to take a seat on the toilet lid. It's not a request, but a demand.

As I gently move the washcloth across his cheek, his captivating dark brown eyes meet mine. I swallow hard, attempting to hold back the intense sensation building in my chest. My attention is solely on his striking face and the task of erasing the drawing of a large penis from his cheek. I try my best to disregard the way his fingers delicately brush against the back of my leg. Though I should speak up and ask him to stop, my voice fails me.

The silence stretches between us, growing heavier with each passing moment. I hold my breath as his fingers slowly travel up my leg, inching beneath my skirt. He watches me, waiting for a reaction. When I stay quiet, he dares to go higher, causing goosebumps to rise on my skin as he approaches that sensitive area. My breathing becomes irregular as I attempt to remove the black marker from his face, but he's distracting me with his actions.

He gazes at me, as if he is attempting to decipher my desires. He has always possessed a talent for understanding what my body wants. I close my eyes, eagerly anticipating his touch, yet at the same time wishing I didn't yearn for it so intensely.

As if he can delve into my deepest thoughts, a wave of longing rushes through me when his thumb brushes against the edge of my underwear.

"Xander," I whisper.

Opening my eyes, I'm captivated by the intensity of his lustful stare. In that instant, I can feel his longing, his deep desire, yearning for me. It has been such a long time since I've shared an intimate moment with a man, ever since he walked away from my life. The sensation of being touched in this manner, by him, has become a distant memory, one I've almost forgotten.

Feeling his thumb circling my clit brings a delightful sensation, carrying me to a new level of pleasure. I can't help but moan as I bite down on my bottom lip, surrendering to the irresistible pleasure he gives me. Despite knowing I should stop, an unexplainable desire consumes me. I long for him. I ache for the release.

I let out a small whimper as he gently pulls aside my panties and slides a finger inside me, followed by another. His fingers move in a rhythmic motion, sending waves of pleasure coursing through my body. As he lifts my shirt, he tenderly places a soft kiss on my stomach, causing a shiver of anticipation to run down my spine. The warmth of his breath against my skin drives me wild. The sensation of his fingers surpasses any pleasure a sex toy could ever provide. My thoughts become scattered, consumed by the overwhelming sensations building within me. Just as I feel myself reaching the edge, a desperate moan escapes me when Xander removes his hand.

As I glance down, I can't help but notice that cocky grin on his face, which only adds to my annoyance. He laughs and pulls me onto his lap, bringing us closer so that I'm straddling him.

"If you want it, Princess," he whispers. As he leans forward, he presses a soft kiss to the side of my neck. Closing my eyes, I surrendered to the pleasure of his sensual touch. "Then take it. Let go on my cock, just like you used to."

As his hands find the back of my neck, I can sense his desire for control, his need to keep me exactly where he wants me. With force, his lips collide with mine. The intensity of his kiss matches his dominant nature. A deep groan escapes his chest as he hungrily explores my mouth with his tongue, his grip on my hips tightening as he moves me against him. "I know what you want,

Princess, because I fucking want it too. Now ride me. Bring out that wild side of yours again."

His words cause me to arch my back slightly, overwhelmed with excitement. A surge of heat rushes through me, causing my nipples to harden. Slipping my hands into the waistband of his sweatpants, I free his hard cock. He moans as I tease him with gentle strokes, feeling the heat build between us, before sliding my panties to the side. His intense gaze locks onto me as I lower myself onto his shaft, feeling every inch of him stretching me.

"Fuck," he says, skimming his nose along the column of my throat. "You feel so fucking good. So much better than I fucking remember."

As I move my hips, a sensation of tightness spreads through my body from his touch. I am fully captivated by the sexy sounds that escape his lips as I keep moving. The pleasure intensifies, causing my body to coil even more tightly with each passing moment.

With a deep, sensual growl, Xander firmly winds my ponytail around his fist, using it to steady me, ensuring our gazes remain locked.

I pick up the pace, targeting that specific spot that ignites a blazing fire within my body. Each downward thrust sends waves of pleasure coursing through me, until finally, my orgasm consumes me and I'm crying out his name in sheer ecstasy.

With a forceful grunt, he grips my ass, hoisting me up and pinning me against the wall, asserting his dominance. I spread my legs wider, eagerly aiming to fulfill his cravings. Bliss alters his expression, and a deep, throaty sound escapes him. He's teetering on the brink.

"I'm on birth control," I hastily add, not wanting to lose the intimate connection we share.

His lips collide with mine in a powerful, all-encompassing kiss. I swallow down his primal moan as he thrusts into me one last time. I bite down on his lip as he finishes inside me. Breathless, with his hands still gripping my ass, he rests his head on the curve of my neck. Slowly, he moves in and out of me, savoring the aftershocks of his orgasm. The feeling of his warm breath on my neck offers comfort and security, a constant reminder of his presence.

After a few seconds, he lifts his head and gives me a mischievous grin. It's then that I spot the outline of the drawing on the side of his face, reminding me of the reason we came in here. The mere thought of everyone hearing what we've just done makes me cringe.

"Oh, God," I whisper, taking in a sudden, sharp breath. "What have I done?"

As his brows furrow, the tendons in his neck strain as he swallows. "Don't fucking freak out now, Princess."

"Put me down," I say.

All the reasons why I shouldn't be doing this come rushing back. All the restraint I had to get him out of my system. What the fuck have I done? And what if Reg is out there and heard everything we just did? But above all, how could I have been so foolish to fall for his charms all over again?

CHAPTER 53

Xander

For the next three days, Poppy consistently ignores me. Most of the time, she remains in her hotel room, only coming out occasionally when Reg insists she joins us for the day. I know she regrets fucking me. But I have no regrets whatsoever. I relive it every night with my fist around my cock.

Girls can scream at me on stage and tell me all the dirty things they want me to do to them, but it's that morning on the bus in the bathroom with Poppy and how she got herself off on my cock that gets me hard. Not some superficial groupie who only wants to be with me for the sake of bragging to their friends that they fucked a rockstar. They couldn't care less about me. They don't give a shit about the person behind the mask. They have no idea of what scars I've endured in the process to get where I am today. No, they only see Xander Williams, the frontman of Broken Oasis. Beyond that, they don't give two fucks about me.

Poppy is the only person who has ever taken the time to truly understand me. It's fucking weird that even after all this time, she still gets me. And she accepts everything ugly in my soul, all those dark demons that haunt me. She was the only one who believed in my talent, even when others couldn't give a fuck if I lived or died in the curb. She was the only one who cared if I had something to eat, who could read my mood, and understand that the demons within me never truly disappear.

And still today, having all the money and fame, that sense of worthlessness lingers. In my mind, I will always see myself as the useless piece of shit my father told me I am.

Now, the person who holds the utmost significance in my life is intentionally avoiding me, and it is incredibly painful. But one thing Poppy can't deny is the strong connection between us.

I haven't seen her since Thursday, which was three days ago when I saw her at an event that Reg said she had to attend. But already, I miss her and crave her presence. Thank fuck that tonight, after the show, we will all be back on the bus together. There's no way to avoid me there. I really need to talk to her and make things right. I need to explain why I walked away and clear up our past. I need to make amends and rectify this situation.

The thunderous roar of the crowd echoes in my ears as I prepare for the last song of the night.

This is what I live for – being on this stage, living my dream, and savoring the exhilarating sensation of truly being alive. It's about being someone, feeling the surge of adrenaline coursing through my veins. This is the essence of our band's existence, the four of us bound together. Through sheer determination and hard work, we overcame countless obstacles.

However, something feels off tonight. Throughout the entire evening, my gaze has repeatedly drifted toward the side of the stage, hoping to catch a glimpse of Poppy standing there. Each time, a pang of disappointment engulfs me as she remains absent.

As Nate lays down the soft beat of his drums, I wait for Ace and Theo to join in. It's the well-known cover that the crowd always looks forward to. Stepping up to the microphone, I pour my soul out. With each lyric, memories trickle back to that night on the curb. It feels like a lifetime ago

The crowd erupts in cheers, and I suddenly fall silent as thousands of voices harmonize the next verse of a song. It holds a deep significance for me, a cherished place in my heart that represents my history. I regret the night I got drunk on that fucking stage and sang it as a farewell to her. Little did I know, it would take on a life of its own. If only I could turn back time, I would keep it to myself, preserving the memory of her solely for me. That special moment when I came across that extraordinary girl sitting on the curb, who transformed my life like no one else ever could. I know I need to fix this fucked up situation between us, but I don't know how. Doing this sort of shit has never come easy for me, but the one thing I'm sure about is that I know she still desires me, just as I yearn for her. But she struggles to accept it.

As the echoes of the last cheers fade away into the darkness, we take our final bow and make our way to the side of the stage.

"Great show?" Ace says, slapping my sweaty shoulder.

"Yeah," I reply with a smile, using my t-shirt to wipe the sweat from my face.

"Green room now," Reg says, pointing at me. "Be there for the next two hours, or you'll receive a call from the record label. And Xander, make sure you engage with your fans."

He's been on my back ever since that night I kicked him off the bus for yelling at Poppy. In fact, the tension between us has been constant for years. However, what he said to her that night was completely unacceptable. It pisses me off that he hasn't even apologized to her yet, so I don't give a shit about being polite to him anymore. He needs to understand that there are more important things in life than just him bossing everyone around and seeking a bigger bonus from the money we earn. Seriously, our schedule has been incredibly hectic. I've been meaning to talk to Kit about who's pushing us so relentlessly without giving us any time to relax.

During our trip from Adelaide to Melbourne, we were busy with more than twenty radio interviews in different towns.

Not only that, but we also had to stay back and hand out merchandise to competition winners. We even had to take photos for our social media and advertising.

Who in the world has time to do that? Other than our fucking label pushing us with every marketing opportunity to get more sales. None of us actually enjoy this stuff, but I guess it's all just part of the job.

Theo busts into the green room and as usual girls scream and all that other shit. At first, it was great to have people fawning over us, looking up to us, admiring us like we were something special. But after a few years, it became clear that it was only because of who they think we are. Theo and Nate are always keen to share a groupie. Ace occasionally does when he needs to get laid. I'll admit, I've had my fair share of blowjobs, more than the average guy gets in a lifetime, but I never fuck them like I used to dream about when I was younger. I've lost count of how many pairs of tits I've had to sign my name on. But over the years, the novelty of it all has worn thin. We see groupies the same way they see us - just something to derive pleasure from.

"Keep it down, for fuck's sake," Ace yells. I can't help but smirk as the perpetually grumpy Ace shows his true colors.

Immediately, my eyes scan the room, searching for Poppy. It comes as no surprise that she's not here tonight. When we first started the tour, she used to come to the green room almost every night, except for the night her mother called to inform her about Alex.

Those first few nights in the green room, two groupies approached me. Curiously, I observed Poppy's reaction, and I must confess, I felt a sense of satisfaction when I noticed her jealousy. As the two groupies shamelessly voiced all the dirty things they wanted to do to me, Poppy abruptly got up and left the green room.

Ace heads straight for the table where the drinks and food are located. I follow closely behind, pausing when a blonde woman in a short dress suddenly rushes over and jumps on me. She wraps her legs around my waist and kisses me. I pull back, intending to tell her to get the fuck off and express my outrage that she kissed me, but before I can say a word, she forcefully kisses me again.

Reacting quickly, I push her away, disregarding the fact that she falls to the floor with a loud thud.

That's when I notice Nicole, the PR girl, taking a photo with her phone. Frustration wells up inside me as I approach her. I've had enough of this shit. All these staged pictures of me with random chicks, it's not real. I wouldn't be surprised if the damn label orchestrated this whole thing, using scandals to boost sales.

"What the fuck, Nicole?" I grab her phone, swiftly deleting the photo.

The room falls silent, and I can sense all eyes fixed on me. I'm not concerned about anyone capturing this outburst because, as a condition of being in the green room, everyone has to surrender their phones before entering.

"I'm sorry, Xander," she says, glancing at Reg and then back at me.

I remain silent, returning her phone without uttering a word. That fucking asshole, Reg, will go to any lengths for publicity.

"I'm outta here," I yell to Reg, frustration evident in my voice. "I've had enough of this shit. And you can go to fucking hell."

As I make my way towards the door, a forceful hand yanks me back, stopping me in my tracks.

"Walk out of this room now, and it will be the last thing you do," he shouts angrily.

Determined, I break free from his grip and continue through the doorway. I hear footsteps trailing behind me. Just as I'm about to unleash my anger on Reg, a hand gently lands on my shoulder. A familiar hand. Ace.

"That guy seriously annoys me on purpose," I comment "He's willing to do whatever it takes to get shit in the media. I can't deal with him anymore. Last week, I almost lost it when he started on Poppy."

"Yeah, I can see it now. He was totally out of line in there."

"We gotta do something, Ace. It's spiraling out of control."

"I totally agree. We need to have a band meeting, and Reg shouldn't be there. I'll head back in and sort it out," Ace says as we get to the door.

Pushing open the exit door, I feel the refreshing coolness of the night air against my sweaty skin, providing much-needed relief. I swiftly make my way down the steps, taking them two at a time, and step onto the bus. Instantly, my eyes scan the area, desperately searching for Poppy. My heart drops when I don't see her, knowing she's still avoiding me. It's so frustrating not having her by my side.

The sound of heavy footsteps reaches my ears, but I don't bother to turn and see who's boarding the bus.

"Get your ass back in there and greet your fans," Reg's voice commands.

"Fuck off," I add, reaching for a bottle of whisky from my secret stash. I asked Kit to make sure it was fully stocked for our next trip on the tour.

"You have a contract. Don't think I won't make a call," he yells.

I snatch the bottle up and unscrew the lid. "Fuck off, Reg. Yeah, so what? I didn't sign a contract that says you organize groupies to do whatever the fuck they want."

"I won't say it again, Xander. Get back in there."

"And I'll tell you again, Reg, go fuck yourself. Because I ain't doing shit."

"Where the fuck is she?" he yells, making his way towards the back of the bus.

Acting on instinct, I stride across and firmly grasp his arm, yanking him back. A look of shock spreads across his face.

"You go anywhere near her, and my fist will fuck up your face," I shout, my words forcefully spewing out.

Reg's eyes widen at the intensity of my threat. "She was hired to keep you under control, not to be your fuck buddy. And by the way, she has already violated her contract."

I forcefully push him into a panel on the side of the wall, my hand twisting his shirt. "You leave her out of this, you hear me? This is strictly between you and me, asshole. It always has been. And we both know that none of this would've happened if you didn't pull the shit you do." My face is inches from his.

"You dare lay a finger on me, and it will be the end of you."

"No, it will be the fucking end for you if you try that shit again, like you just did in there."

'Xander, stop,' Poppy says from somewhere in the bus.

As soon as I hear Poppy's voice, my senses snap back into focus. I turn my head to find her standing there, clearly having witnessed everything unfold. However, that is not my immediate concern. What worries me is her pale complexion and disheveled hair, which is sticking to the side of her sweaty face.

Without hesitation, I release my grip on Reg, pushing him back into the wall.

'Asshole,' he grumbles.

Normally, I wouldn't let that slide, but my immediate concern is for Poppy.

"Are you sick?" I ask.

"No, I'm fine," she replies.

"Don't lie to me, Princess," I add sternly. "I can clearly see you're not."

I grab her arm and gently lead her to the big couch. Reg stands nearby, silent, knowing that if he dares to speak up, he'll quickly feel the force of my fist.

"It's okay, Xander, there's no need to make a big deal out of it," she says, her tone indicating that she simply wants me to let it go.

"You heard the girl. She's fine," Reg adds.

I don't bother looking at him, but I can feel his scrutinizing gaze on my skin. If I were to look at him now, I would completely lose it, but right now, all I care about is Poppy.

Ace, Theo, and Nate make their way onto the bus.

"What the hell are you doing here?" Reg spits out, moving towards the three of them.

"After that stunt you just pulled, we decided to call it a night," Ace responds.

Ace's unexpected response and tone towards Reg catches me off guard. As I glance up, I notice that Theo and Nate are equally taken aback. It has always been Ace who has supported Reg and the label for the past few years. Therefore, seeing him react in this manner is new to all of us.

"Don't you fucking start. You know what's a stake," Reg snaps back with a glare.

"Yeah, well, maybe there's a few things you've been doing that the label needs to know about," I add, gently lowering Poppy onto the couch. Her skin feels feverish and clammy as if she's running a high temperature. "How long have you been feeling like this?" I ask Poppy, my tone firmer.

"I'm fine, Xander. Just stop fussing."

"How fucking long, Princess," I insist.

"Since yesterday."

"Fantastic!" Reg interrupts. "Since you fucked her, you'll probably get what she has. That's just perfect, having to cancel the tour."

I choose to ignore the jerk for now because my main concern is Poppy. I'll deal with him later for making that comment in front of everyone.

"You should have said you were sick," I remark.

"I'm fine," she replies, slightly annoyed.

"You're not fine," Ace interrupts. "You look like shit."

"Wow, don't you know how to make a girl feel special," she says.

"That's not what I meant, Poppy. It's just..."

"It's cool, Ace," she responds with a slight smile. "I'm just messing with you."

I move across and grab a bottle from the fridge. Returning, I hand the bottle to Poppy. She takes it but doesn't drink it; instead, she holds the cold bottle against her forehead and then moves it down to her neck.

"I'll be back in a second," I say, leaving her on the couch.

Moving down the front steps, I step outside in search of Kit. After a while, I finally spot her by the side of another bus, casually taking a drag from a cigarette as she chats with a group of people.

As I get closer, the conversation fades away. Kit offers me a cigarette, but I decline politely. With our busy schedules with upcoming radio interviews and a sold-out concert in a smaller city on the way to Melbourne, I let Kit know what I need from the pharmacy and ask her to organize a doctor in case Poppy's condition worsens in the next few days.

Making my way back onto the bus, I notice that Theo, Nate, and Ace have taken seats on the opposite couch from Poppy. Reg sits alone at the table, engrossed in his laptop. He glances up as I approach, and I purposely ignore making eye contact, because shit will hit the fan if he says anything. Instead, I settle down on the floor, leaning against the couch where Poppy has peacefully drifted off to sleep.

Clearly annoyed, Reg closes his laptop and heads to his room. Thank fuck for that, because I really don't want to hear him complain about meaningless shit.

Now that the band is on the bus, our bus driver, Rob, joins us. "Kit said we're good to roll. Just making sure everyone is here," he says.

"Yeah," Ace replies, "Everyone is here."

Nodding, he gets into the driver's seat.

Within minutes, the engine roars to life, and the bus departs from the venue.

A large sigh escapes Ace's lips, drawing everyone's attention. "I'm sorry, guys," he says, scanning the group. "I made a mistake by listening to the damn label. It's clear now that we're the ones who know where our band should be heading."

"Wow! What a complete fucking turnaround," Nate states. "So, what made you change your mind?"

"I've been reflecting on everything we discussed that day at Xander's. I stepped back and observed the situation. Watching that train wreck with Xander tonight, I see I was wrong. We can't keep going on like this."

"Holy shit," Theo says, sliding his hand into his pocket. "Wait up. I gotta capture this moment. Ace admitting he messed up? That's rare."

Nate and I burst into laughter.

"Man, fuck you," Ace says, pushing Theo's phone away. "I now realize that half of the shit Reg told me isn't Xander's fault. I'm sorry, man. I should have talked to you first."

"So, what's the plan now?" Nate asks.

"Don't know yet. But I think we should schedule a meeting with Lionel once we're back and insist on having more control over our work," Ace suggests.

"You really think that'll change anything? Lionel is raking in the cash from our hard work, and he couldn't care less about giving us a break or dealing with Reg," I interject, grabbing my whisky bottle from the table.

"Well if he doesn't, we go out on our own," Ace declares.

Nate leans forward in his seat to look at Ace. "Seriously?"

"Yeah, like you guys said, what's the point of having a recording studio if it ain't being used. Maybe it's time we give it a shot."

"Hey Ace, I gotta confess something I didn't want the label to know - I never actually stopped writing," I admit. "I just said that so they wouldn't make me give them all my songs."

"Wait, so you've been writing all this time?"

"Yep. We have enough songs for at least four albums."

"No shit," Ace says, smiling.

I lean forward, extending my hand across the coffee table towards Ace. "It's great to have you back, brother," I say. He glances down at my hand and then shakes it.

We sit there, just talking, like the old days when we lived in our dilapidated apartments. Back before our fame. It's great to witness Ace's return, effortlessly blending in as he always did. It is comforting to see him reclaiming his role as the brother I've always believed him to be.

CHAPTER 54

Xander

I keep a close eye on Poppy as she sleeps on the couch throughout the night. I'm exhausted, but after a quick shower, we arrive in some random town in the middle of nowhere for one of many radio interviews. I don't understand why these interviews have to be in person instead of over the phone like we usually do in the States, but we just follow Reg's instructions. Speaking of which, where the fuck is he? It's not a big deal if he stops nagging me, but he's usually here to keep me in line.

The rest of the band sits at the table eating breakfast and drinking coffee. Theo's spouting his usual bullshit. Nate's just doing his usual thing, sitting and watching. Ace looks like crap, so he must've pulled another all-nighter - his childhood monsters are back to haunt him again. No matter how much he drinks, they always find a way to break through.

As I make my way towards the others, my legs inexplicably lead me to Poppy instead. She looks so still sleeping on the couch. Her fever has vanished and her complexion is no longer pale and clammy. I find myself captivated by her beautiful face, gently brushing aside a strand of her hair that hides her features. Lost in my focus on Poppy, I fail to notice the conversation at the table has come to a stop. With tenderness, I caress her cheek with the back of my fingers, savoring the comforting sensation of finally being able to touch her again.

"When are you going to tell her how you feel?" Nate asks.

I retract my hand and notice three pairs of eyes fixed on me. I slide my hands into my pockets and take a seat on the opposite couch, not uttering a single word.

"You'll end up losing her again if you don't tell her," Ace remarks, his words hitting me. How the fuck does he know? I give Theo a glare, the idiot who can't keep his trap shut.

He throws his hands up like he's surrendering. "I swear, I didn't say anything," he insists.

I can't discuss this with them. I can't go there emotionally. There is an undeniable chemistry between Poppy and me. But it feels like I'm losing her again because she can't stand to be near me. Even though the sex was amazing, I know she regrets it.

"Talk to her, dipshit," Theo says. "Grow some balls and tell her you love her."

I turn my attention back to the group, and they're all staring at me with intense curiosity. "It's complicated."

"It won't be if you tell her how you feel," Nate says.

"And when was the last time you were a fucking Romeo, asshole?" I add.

As Nate and Theo lock eyes, a silent exchange passes between them, leaving me with a nagging feeling that I may have misspoken.

Reg enters the room, talking on the phone.

"Lower your voice," Theo grumbles. "Some of us are trying to sleep."

Reg glances at Theo, who points to Poppy peacefully snoozing on the couch. "Yeah, right," he says to the person on the other end of the phone. "I'll deal with it." He ends the call and slides his phone into his pocket. "Fuck!" he yells, his hands pulling on his hair.

"Reg's world looks like so much fun," says Theo, with a smug grin.

Ignoring Theo's comment, Reg turns in my direction. "There's been a development," he says, his eyes piercing into mine for a few prolonged seconds.

Ace, impatient as ever, jumps in. "Well, are you going to tell us, or do we have to be fucking mind readers?"

Reg opens his mouth, but then quickly closes it. I'm taken aback by his uncharacteristic silence. It's rare to see him at a loss for words, so whatever he has to say must be significant. Finally, he breaks the silence, his gaze fixed on me. "You know that groupie you pushed to the floor yesterday," he remarks, his gaze fixed on me, studying my reaction.

"You mean the groupie you set up?" I snap back, making it clear that I had absolutely no part in it. He did it, so he's the one to blame. I want him to realize it all falls back on him.

He acknowledges my words with a nod.

"Yeah, what about it?" I ask, wondering what the fuck it's got to do with me.

Taking a moment to gather his thoughts, he inhales deeply; the uncertainty written on his face.

"Just spit it fucking out," I tell him. "If she's saying I hurt her, then just pay her off."

"She's threatening to go to the media," Reg yells, pacing back and forth. I can sense that something serious is happening.

From the corner of my eye, I notice Poppy sitting up, undoubtedly awakened by Reg's loud outburst.

"So let her go to the press, Xander didn't do anything," Nate states.

"She is threatening to sell her story about how Xander kissed her."

"I didn't fucking kiss her. You-" I stand up from my seat, furious that I am being blamed yet again for something I never did.

"She's planning to sell her story about Xander mistaking her for a groupie, asking for sex, and then kissing her."

"I didn't do any of that fucking shit. Why the fuck would I kiss her, damn it."

"She was only fifteen," Reg says, running his hands through his hair.

Ace hastily stands up, inadvertently jostling the table and causing coffee to spill from the mugs. I make my way towards Reg, intending to confront him, but Ace beats me to it.

Ace approaches Reg, his voice filled with fury. "Let me make sure I understand this correctly. You deliberately arranged for an underage groupie to approach Xander just to generate some media attention, and you didn't even bother to check her age?" I recognize the familiar anger in his tone, the same rage he used to direct towards his mother's boyfriends who would push his buttons. I know I have to intervene before things escalate like Ace throwing Reg off a moving bus. I can already envision the headlines: "Ace Roberts, Lead Guitarist of Broken Oasis, Kills Idiotic Manager."

I step forward to intervene, but Nate beats me to it. "Come on, man. He's not worth any of this. Remember what we discussed last night. That's all that really matters."

Ace takes a few calming breaths and nods.

"So, with this problem hanging over our heads, how do you propose to fix it, asshole?" I ask, fully aware that there's no way we can possibly do the ten press interviews that Kit mentioned last night.

"She's threatening to go to the press, so I might as well try to win her over with some merch or free concert tickets in Melbourne," he says, grabbing his phone and heading back to his room.

Poppy rises from the couch and discreetly heads towards the rear of the bus. I suppress the temptation to follow her, but we must come up with a plan in case Reg cannot get this situation under control and everything goes haywire.

Chapter 55

Poppy

I've been completely out of it all night, barely aware of what's happened. Apart from Xander waking me up to give me water and a couple of pills that he somehow managed to find, I've woken up to a chaotic situation. The tension in the air is palpable.

Something has occurred, and it must be really bad because Reg and Ace are at each other. They're not the united front they usually are. It's about some incident involving Xander. I'm surprised Reg hasn't asked me to stop being a lazy bitch and do my job, but he hasn't.

I've never liked Reg, especially after the way he spoke to me on the day Alex broke his arm. If Xander hadn't dealt with him the way he did, I would have told him to go fuck himself.

I smile at the memory of Xander grabbing him by the shirt and throwing his ass off the bus. It was so fucking hot when Xander did that. I can see that fame hasn't changed him because I still see glimpses of his old self.

I'm really angry at myself for what happened that morning on the bus. Whenever I'm around him, it's like I easily slip back into our old routine. I crave to be with him and for him to love me. Deep down, it's him I truly desire, but I know it's an impossible dream. Although he may give off signals he wants me, I know it's only temporary because I'm with the band on tour and our paths will soon diverge. He's a true rock star in every way. Women are mesmerized by him, and I could never compete with that. Just look at how it affected my mother; she became distant and resentful, and I never want to end up like her.

As I pull the curtain aside on my bunk, I realize that yet another day has already slipped away. Those pills must have really knocked me out. My eyes immediately focus on Theo, who is standing there shirtless. The ink decorating his chest catches my attention. Magnificent wings span across his chest, accompanied by the words "freedom," "hope," and "loyalty." When I lift my gaze, there's a large grin on his face.

"Just let me know when you're ready, Spitfire," he playfully taunts with a laugh. "How are you feeling?"

"Better. But I'm desperate for a shower."

"We should reach the hotel in about an hour."

Raised voices come from the front of the bus, specifically from Xander and Ace. However, it doesn't seem like they are arguing. It's more like they are standing up to someone.

Curious, I say, "What's happening?"

"Oh, just the usual shit show. Nothing to worry about."

"That doesn't give me any information," I chuckle, my stomach grumbling. I swiftly cover my belly with my hand, feeling slightly embarrassed.

"Nate's making some tacos."

Shifting my legs to the edge of the bed, I get down. As I lift my head, I can't help but notice Theo's gaze fixed on my chest.

"Hey, buddy, eyes up here."

That smug sexy grin of his appears. "I'm just returning the favor and checking if you have any ink," he says.

"Asshole," I reply, turning around and searching for my sweater. I glance around the end of my bunk bed and then check the floor in case it fell.

"Here," Theo says, handing me a sweater with the words "Broken Oasis" written on the front.

I swiftly pull the hoodie over my head and slide my arms through, all the while feeling Theo's scrutinizing gaze. It fits perfectly, just the way I prefer it - snug and comfortable. Its length cleverly conceals my ass, which is a bonus. Folding up the sleeves, I make my way toward the front of the bus, immediately enticed by the mouthwatering aroma of food. Once again, my stomach growls, reminding me I haven't eaten in two days.

As soon as I step through the door and into the main area, the conversation abruptly halts and all eyes quickly shift in my direction. Reg, being the first to break the silence, finally finds his voice.

"No one mentions a word about this to anyone."

In other words, I'm pretty sure he doesn't want anyone to mention this to me.

Reg retrieves his phone, punches in a series of digits, and raises it to his ear before retreating into his room.

Xander keeps his silence, fixating his gaze on me, causing my heart to race uncontrollably beneath his piercing, intense eyes.

"It's ready," Nate declares, as he brings all the food to the table. He turns towards me and inquires, "Would you like some, Poppy? There's plenty here."

"Yeah, it smells amazing. Thank you."

I make my way over to the couch where I left the paracetamol earlier before I fell asleep. Just as I reach the other side of the bus, Xander suddenly approaches. He stands in front of me, blocking my path, and raises his arms, effectively trapping me against the wall. I try to glance over his shoulder to see if anyone else is watching, but his close proximity and hunched posture make it challenging to get a clear view.

He gives me a seductive smile as he leans in, his lips lightly brushing against my ear. "I wanna strip you down and fuck you senseless in nothing but my sweater," he whispers, his voice deep and filled with longing. He tugs at the bottom of the sweater, slipping his fingers beneath it, to touch my bare skin.

I stifle the moan that threatens to escape my lips. Wait. What? His sweater. That asshole Theo gave me Xander's sweater. The intense heat between my thighs from his touch tries to distract me, but I ignore it and keep going.

"Your sweater. I thought it was one that everyone shared."

Theo yells from somewhere over at the table. "If she's into sharing then-"

"She's not," Xander snaps.

"I'm just saying if she is."

Xander rolls his eyes and pushes off the wall with a groan. "For fuck's sake, Theo. How many times do I have to tell you?"

"Yeah, I hear ya. But you're not doing shit about it, asshole."

"About what?" I ask, moving towards the table. "Is there something I should know? I feel like you're referring to me, but I'm totally lost."

Theo opens his mouth to speak, but Xander interrupts him. "No!"

What are they keeping from me? I wonder.

"Come on, let's just eat," Ace suggests, trying to change the conversation.

Xander and Theo share tense glances, their eyes locked in what feels like a never-ending staring contest. Suddenly, Theo smirks and breaks his gaze, opting to take a seat beside Nate at the table. Meanwhile, Xander navigates his way over to me and settles down right beside me.

We enjoy our meal in silence, relishing the delicious tacos that Nate has expertly prepared. His culinary skills are so impressive that I can't help but envision him as a professional chef, even though he's already an amazing drummer. As I savor each bite, Xander's unwavering gaze remains fixed on me, just like that time he took me out for a burger when I was hungover at school.

The guys discuss the need for a band meeting, ensuring that Reg isn't present. I can't help but feel curious and wonder what the heck is going on. I haven't been involved with the band for nearly four days now - three days of avoiding Xander and a day of being sick on the bus. But it seems like a lot has transpired during my absence.

Chapter 56

Xander

Two hours before sound check, I'm pacing in my hotel room. The problem is, Poppy's staying in the room next door. I feel the urgent need to talk to her and address all the issues that led me to leave her. I've been meaning to do this for a few days, but she's been avoiding me and she's been sick, so I never had the chance. This morning, when I saw her wearing my fucking sweater, something possessive welled up inside me. I almost lost control and it's been driving me crazy ever since.

Twice now, I have stood at my door, ready to step outside, only to hesitate and turn back out of the fear that perhaps Poppy doesn't want anything to do with me. I'm familiar with every inch of her body, every sound she makes. Yet Poppy Reeves terrifies me like nothing else in this world. I'm scared to get too close, in case she says those awful words, telling me she hates me and will never trust my pathetic ass again. But despite all of this, I cannot deny the undeniable attraction I feel towards her.

Whenever she is around, I'm unable to look away from her. Every feminine aspect of her body and every intricate detail of her beautiful face captivates me. The very first time I laid eyes on her in the street, I remember thinking she was flawless. Her voice, her vulnerability, and her face all had a hold on me. I can't believe that I went for years without noticing her. Those feelings that I felt for her back then have not changed. However, there is a difference now compared to the arrogant prick I used to be. It's not just her physical beauty that arouses me anymore. It's everything about her. The person she is on the inside is just as captivating and stunning as the outside. I wish I could tell her that I have loved her all these years, but it's difficult because I've never allowed myself to be so vulnerable with anyone. The fear of being ridiculed if she were to laugh in my face is what holds me back.

Fuck it. Just go for it, asshole. If you don't open up, you'll never know how she feels. You lost her before because you couldn't step up.

I stride towards the door, forcefully pulling it open, my heart racing. As I make my way down the hallway to her room, my nerves send waves of anticipation through my body. Upon reaching her door, I pause for a few agonizing seconds. *Come on, get your shit together. Tell her how you feel.*

I lift my hand and give the door a knock. Damn, that was louder than I expected.

The wait feels like forever until she finally opens the door. My eyes trace over her figure, admiring every graceful curve. A pleasant warmth stirs deep within my stomach. My dick thickens when I notice she's still wearing her sleep shorts and tank top, revealing a hint of skin near her hip. Although she's smoking hot, I can't help but feel a bit bummed that she's not wearing my sweater anymore.

"Can we talk?" I ask, pushing past her, so she can't refuse and slam the door in my face.

With a sarcastic tone, she replies, "Sure, why not come in and make yourself at home." She closes the door behind me.

I only realize she isn't following me when I sit on the couch and glance up. As my eyes scan the room, they land on her, standing off to the side, slipping her arms into a cardigan.

Disappointment floods through me when I realize she's trying to cover herself up. She doesn't want me to see her like that.

Clutching the cardigan tightly against her body, she settles into the chair across from me.

Leaning forward, I run my hands through my hair, feeling the weight of the situation. Damn, this is going to be more challenging than I thought.

"Xander," she says, eyeing me.

"Yeah."

"What's going on?"

I sigh, releasing the breath I've been holding. *Just do it, man. Just tell her how you feel.*

When I finally find my courage, I open my mouth to speak but before I can Poppy interrupts and all the thoughts scatter from my mind.

"I know there's something going on with the band. Please tell me what it is."

I eye her for a moment. "There was this incident in the green room involving something Reg did, and there's a possibility that it might be leaked to the press. He's working on fixing it, but there's a chance it could get out, and it's bad. Like really bad."

Getting up from the couch, I nervously run my hands through my hair while pacing back and forth. I'm clueless about how to open up and express my love and tell her I want to be with her. Sensing her gaze on me, I continue to move around.

"I have something important to tell you," I say, worried that she might laugh in my face. "Please, let me finish before you say anything."

"Okay," she says, sounding unsure, like she doesn't know where this conversation is going.

Taking a moment to gather my thoughts, I return to the couch. Nervously, my leg bobs up and down.

"Xander, you're scaring me," she says, her voice tinged with concern.

"Yeah, I'm kind of scaring myself, too." A nervous laugh escapes me, and upon hearing it, I realize how ridiculous I sound.

How the fuck do I do this? How can I summon the strength to share my true feelings with her? I mentioned it once, but I waited until she was asleep because to voice it out loud was difficult. But my love for her persists, and if I continue to withhold this truth, I fear losing her again. But how the fuck can I open up and tell her that?

My mouth opens, words hovering on the tip of my tongue, yet I hesitate and close it without uttering anything. Inhaling deeply, I exhale slowly, pausing for a few seconds. *Just do it dipshit. Man up and tell her how you feel.*

"Remember when I said we needed to talk?"

"Yeah."

"Can you forgive me? Can you forgive me for bailing on you?"

She lowers her head, absently picking at a loose thread on her cardigan. The pain on her face is clear, and it cuts me to the core, knowing I caused her this pain.

I stay silent, giving her the time to respond.

Finally, she lifts her head and asks, "Why did you do it? I could have understood if you had left early, but you simply vanished without saying anything."

"I know. I'm sorry. It's a burden I've carried for years, Princess."

"Why did you leave like that?"

"Because when things get hard, that's what I fucking do. You know that? And after what your mother said-"

She lifts her head. "Wait!" she interrupts me, studying me for a moment, and I see the confused look on her face. "When did you see my mother?"

"That morning, she caught us. I returned to the house so that you wouldn't get all the blame."

"Wait?" she says, her brows furrowing. "On the morning we were caught in my room, you came back to the house?"

"Yes."

She blinks like she's trying to put the pieces together in her head.

"As I was walking down the front path, your mom came out of the front door and blocked me." From the way she's looking at me, it's clear she has no idea what I'm talking about. The thought crosses my mind that Poppy's mother might have been lying and that Poppy wasn't watching from inside, as she had said.

"What exactly did my mother say to you?"

"She told me I was nothing but a fuck up. Someone who will only continue to screw your life up, because that's the person I am. Someone who always brings you down."

"Why didn't you tell me?" she says, tears forming in her eyes.

All I want to do is go over and protect her from this pain. But I have to keep pushing forward. I can't hold back now.

"She said you were inside and sent her out to tell me that. And that she would remind you every day how much of a lowlife I was."

"I've never thought of you like that, Xander. You know that. No matter what anyone says." A stray tear slides down her cheek.

I go to the bed and sit beside her, holding her hand to comfort her because if I touch her any other way, I'll be distracted and won't continue to open up.

"I wasn't aware of that, Poppy. I didn't want you to think of me like everyone else did, as a lowlife. Not you. I thought it would be better if I left, so you'd never see it."

I thread my fingers through hers and stare at our joined hands.

"But that doesn't explain why you ignored my texts when I told you I was pregnant and again on the day Alex was born?"

I lift my head in response, as though she's speaking a different language. I blink, feeling dumbfounded, with the words lingering in my mind.

"I texted you, Xander, to let you know I was pregnant. And again the day Alex was born. But you ghosted me. Why?" She stares at me.

"Because I didn't fucking know," I mutter, scanning the room in disbelief. My stomach churns with sickness. The sensation of the room spinning overwhelms me. All this time, and I didn't fucking know.

"But how, when I sent you those messages? I texted you the night you called me and didn't speak."

"Because after that call, I threw my fucking phone into the lake straight after I called you. I did it to let you go." I release her hand and get up from the bed, pacing back and forth across the room.

Little did I know she had been pregnant with my son. All these years passing without knowing I had a kid because I was a fucking idiot, unable to bear the pain of losing her and resorting to drastic measures of throwing my phone in the lake.

What the fuck have I done? She's done it all by herself while I've been living my dream. Suddenly, I turn towards her.

"So, that's why you never pursued your dreams and ended up working in a bar?" I ask.

She stares at me, and I see her swallow.

"Answer the fucking question, Poppy."

"Yes."

Her response hits me hard. Her mother was right. I was the lowlife who would alter her life and sabotage her dreams. She never had the opportunity to pursue any of the things she wanted. It's too much, knowing that it's all my fault. My heart is racing, and I can't catch my breath. I need to get the hell out of here before I break down in front of her.

"I have to go," I state, rushing over to the door and letting myself out. I need to get the fuck away from here and think.

I rush down the hall with no idea of where I'm going. After what Poppy just said, I need to get out of here. I'm not angry that she told me. I'm angry at myself because it's just another asshole move I pulled on her all those years ago. She was pregnant. We should have been going through it together, instead, I left her alone to deal with it all by herself. The overwhelming sense of guilt and shame washes over me, making me feel like a complete asshole.

I stride quickly down the street. Fuck, I should have grabbed my wig and cap. Just something to avoid catching people's attention so I don't have phones pointing in my direction. I can't deal with that shit at the moment of some fan wanting a photo.

"Hey, man," says someone.

And that's the problem with fame. No matter how awful or messed up you feel, everyone expects you to put on an act for their benefit. Well, fuck it. I'm not in the mood. I need to get away from here and think.

"Fucking asshole!" I hear the same voice shout behind me because I didn't stop and make his day so he can brag to his friends.

If I were just an average guy, I'd turn around and tell him to fuck right off. But I can't because I don't want to make a scene right now.

I hear my phone ping, and I don't bother checking it. Whatever it is can wait. I pick up the pace and sprint down the street, racing toward the taxi pulling up to the curb.

I'm standing there, waiting for the door to open, when this girl gets out and does a double take the moment she spots me. She flashes me an excited smile, but I brush her off and jump into the taxi, slamming the door.

"Where to?" The taxi driver asks. He's middle-aged, and judging by the way he's looking at me, I can tell he has no idea who I am. Thank God I don't have to deal with all the fanboying shit while feeling this way.

"Anywhere," I add, not caring about the destination. I just need time to think.

"You need to give me somewhere, man, otherwise we'll just drive around."

"Just take me somewhere quiet where I can be alone and think. Where people won't annoy me."

"Okay, you got it." He turns left at the next intersection, and we continue to drive.

There's music playing on the radio, and normally, I enjoy listening to random tunes, trying to guess the song by its opening ten seconds. But today, with everything on my mind, I can't even focus on that.

For all this time, I've had a son out there. My son. My own flesh and blood. Just last week, when I heard Poppy talking to her son, I yearned to be a part of that world. Now I am. He's my son, and I belong to their special bond.

Guilt, my old friend, brings up all these old feelings, making me feel like the biggest piece of shit for what I did, not only to Poppy but to Alex as well. It highlights how I've messed up bigger than I thought. Poppy has been handling all of this on her own. I should have stayed back at the hotel and asked her more questions about everything, but I couldn't think, and I did what I always do. I ran. I regret not answering her calls years ago, believing that with me out of the picture, I was improving her life, when in reality, I only fucked it up. Made it more difficult. I should have been there all along for her, for our son, acting as a father figure. Fuck, I'm no better than my asshole father. What the fuck is wrong with me? All I do is hurt people, especially the people I love.

My father and Poppy's mother are right. I am a piece of shit. I've hurt the only girl I've ever loved so much more than I thought. I messed up her dream, and now she's probably been busting her ass to make ends meet, and that's why she's stuck at that damn bar. God, that alone is enough reason for her to hate me.

The taxi comes to a halt, and I come back to reality. We've stopped in a park with a water view. Thank God he's not been one of those taxi drivers who talk for hours and hours.

"Is this okay?" he asks.

I look out the window and see a few people in the park.

"It's great. Thanks, man." I quickly grab my phone, pay, and open the car door. Right as I'm about to get out, the driver speaks.

"If you want a cab back, go one block down that way." He points down the street on the left.

"Thanks again, man," I say, getting out and closing the door.

As the taxi pulls out and returns to the street, the driver gives me a quick wave.

As I sit on the grassy slope by the water's edge, I wonder how the fuck I can make it up to Poppy and Alex for the years of abandonment and how to mend our fractured relationship.

Chapter 57

Poppy

I've shed an ocean of tears since Xander walked out that door. Why is it that all I do is cry on this trip to Australia? I haven't cried this much since Xander left me and I found out I was pregnant. But that's what Xander does—he just leaves when he can't handle shit.

I'm so pissed at what my mother did. Not once did she tell me about Xander coming back. She knew how much he meant to me. She saw how much I cried when she consoled me when I found out I was pregnant. She never let on that she was the reason behind Xander leaving in the first place. It all makes sense now when she continually said that she helped me get my life back on track. I often wondered what she meant by that. But I never put the pieces together until now. Not even when she wouldn't stop shitting on Xander.

The fact that he never knew about Alex makes me happy yet a little sad. I'm relieved to find out that Xander never rejected him, but it's also saddening that Xander has missed out on so much of his life already.

Grabbing my phone, I feel a wave of anger wash over me. I swipe the screen, navigate to my contacts, and locate my mother's number. The fact that I never knew what she had done weighs heavily on my heart.

However, as I press the call button, I quickly reconsider. With the time difference, it's the middle of the night, and I don't want to disturb Alex's sleep.

Frustrated, I toss my phone onto the bed and get up, making my way to the bathroom. Seeking solace, I reach for the washcloth, run it under warm water, and gently dab it over my puffy eyes.

I've shed so many tears for this man for years, yearning for his love and affection. Discovering that he returned that morning, along with the things my mother said to him, makes me want to break down and cry for all the time we've lost. Xander coming back to talk to my mom tells me I meant more to him than I realized. There's no way he would put himself through that if he didn't care.

I rush out of the bathroom when I hear my phone ringing, thinking it might be Xander. I know I haven't given him my number yet, but as history has shown me, he has ways of getting what he wants.

I'm disappointed when I see it's Ace calling. Worry washes over me as I wonder what is going on. The only time I ever hear from Ace is when something is wrong.

"Hello," I answer.

"Hey Poppy, is Xander with you?"

"No, why?"

"Is he with her?" I hear Reg ask in the background. By his tone, I can hear he's ticked off about something.

"No!" Ace says. "He's not with her."

"Well, tell her to get the fuck down here and find him. That's what she's paid to do."

"Calm the fuck down!" Ace spits. "Any idea where he might be?"

"No… but…" I pause for a moment, unsure if I should tell Ace what happened. But I know they'll be heading to sound check soon "I need to tell you something, but I don't want Reg to hear it. Can you come up here, and make sure Reg doesn't come with you. I don't want him here when I tell you what happened."

"Okay, I'll be there soon."

After I hang up the phone, I start pacing the room, anxiously waiting for Ace to show up.

A few moments later, I hear a knock on the door and quickly go to open it, revealing the rest of the band. Ace enters first, followed by Theo and Nate.

"Sorry, Poppy, they insisted on coming," Ace apologizes.

"Do you know where Xander is?" Theo asks, with a hint of concern in his voice.

They all take a seat on the couch, their eyes fixed on me as I resume my pacing.

"Poppy," Nate says, his voice causing me to stop and meet his eyes. "Tell us what happened?"

I take a deep breath and blow it out through my cheeks.

"Well… I'm not sure what Xander has shared with you all about us. But he found out that…" I pause and bite my fingernail, unsure how to come out and tell them the next bit. Maybe if I just show them. I move across to get my phone, knowing that as soon as I show them a photo of Alex they will know.

I can feel their eyes on me as I walk over to the bed and retrieve my phone. I swipe through a few images to find a close up of Alex. I stare at it for a moment, my heart melting with love for my little boy. I see Xander's dark eyes, his familiar smile, and his thick, dark hair.

I turn my phone around, letting Ace see the screen. His gaze shifts downward, eyes focused on the photo before him. His expression changes in an instant as a flicker of realization crosses his face.

"Fuck," he says, snatching the phone from my hand and studying it.

"What?" Theo asks, leaning into Ace so he can see what's on the screen. "Holy fuck," Theo looks up at me.

"I honestly thought he knew," I tell them. "I texted him all those years ago, but he threw his phone in the lake and never got them."

"What's happening?" Nate says, looking at Theo.

As Ace passes him the phone, I observe the moment when Nate connects the dots.

Ace's phone rings and he quickly reaches into his pocket to silence it, declining the call.

"I honestly thought he knew," I repeat, not wanting to be judged by them.

"He didn't know, Poppy," Ace says. "I promise you, he did not know. If he did, he would've been there. He once said if he ever had a kid, he would never be an asshole like his father. That he'd love his kid just like his mom loved him."

I move over and sit on the edge of the bed, unsure how to process that information. Tears come to my eyes at the thought that if he had known, he would have been there. I tell myself I should have tried harder, but that little voice of reason chimes in to remind me there was no way I could have let him know because I didn't have his new number. Plus, I didn't know he had thrown his phone in the lake.

"Tell me, Spitfire, what went down when you told him?" Theo asks.

"He had no clue what I was talking about at first. He was shocked, then he got pissed and just walked out without saying anything."

"Yeah, that sounds like Xander," Ace says.

Ace's phone rings again, and this time he answers it. "Yeah. Reg, just go. We'll meet you there." A pause. "I don't fucking know. Just leave a car, and we'll be there soon." He ends the call. "We need to go." Ace gets up from the couch.

"What if he doesn't show up for sound check?" I ask.

"We can still do it without him. Theo thinks he can sing, so if he's not there, Theo gets his chance to show us," Nate says, coming towards me. "How are you holding up in all of this? Are you okay?"

"Yes," I tell him, tears coming to my eyes, and I hate that I am showing so much vulnerability in front of them.

"It will be fine, Poppy," Nate says, pulling me in for a comforting hug. "Things will work out. Trust me. We all know Xander needs time to process things. It's just how he is. He takes off so he can work shit out." He pulls back to look at me. "Come on, you're not staying here alone. You're coming to sound check."

"I don't know," I add, wondering if I should even go, especially if Xander is pissed and doesn't want to see me. Plus I didn't want to be on the brunt of Reg's fury if Xander didn't turn up. Because I know I'll say something I can't take back. "But what if Xander doesn't want to see me and I'm there during sound check?"

"Yeah, right," Theo spits out with a laugh.

I turn to look at him, unsure if he's being sarcastic or if he's just messing with me like he does with everyone else.

Ace holds the door open and glances back over his shoulder. "Come on Poppy. If Xander's there, he'll probably want to see you."

I scoot over, grab my handbag, and join Ace as we exit the room, with Nate and Theo close on our heels.

On the way down in the lift, Theo throws out questions about Alex.

Half an hour later, I'm sitting off to the side in the stands of the stadium. The sound check is already two hours behind schedule, and still, Xander hasn't shown up. Kit sits with me, chatting about something related to the band's schedule, but I'm distracted and not really listening, so I just nod. My focus is on the stage where Theo is messing up the first song. Whoever told him he could sing should've kept their mouth shut, because he sounds like crap.

Reg got all worked up when he saw Xander wasn't with us when we arrived.

Once Reg started yelling at me, Nate lost his cool and told him to go to hell. Reg then took off with Neil and a handful of the security crew to locate him and drag him back, no doubt. I saw Neil's loyalty firsthand when Xander went missing, so I'm confident he won't say anything about where Xander might be.

When Kit points to the left, I turn my head. My heart races when I see Xander coming towards me. I am relieved to see him, but there's a part of me that hopes Reg isn't back, because if he is, he'll be here soon, shouting for Xander to get his ass on the stage.

I watch him approach, unaware that Kit has already left until I straighten up in my seat and notice her empty chair.

"I'm sorry, Princess," he says, sitting in the seat next to me, his voice trembling with sadness, his eyes filled with hurt as he looks at me.

"No, Xander, I'm sorry," I add, swallowing over the thickness in my throat.

"Stop." The pure agony cutting into the sharp lines on his face renders me speechless. "None of this is your fault. My actions have caused a world of hurt. And I need to make things right between us." He peers up at Theo belting out a song, and his mouth smirks. "The fucker told me he could sing." He turns in the seat, so he's facing me, to give me his full attention. He lifts his hand and pushes my hair back behind my shoulders, and I can see he's open, his shield is down, and I see the real Xander, the exposed one, the one with all the scars, the one who let me in all those years ago.

"I wish I'd been a better man back then. But I fucked up the day I left you, and I've been regretting it ever since. But the fact that I left you pregnant and alone, I'm just so pissed off with myself for doing that to you. To you, Princess. That's what hurts the most. I'm sorry you had to do it alone. It hurts to think that all this time I've had a son out there and I didn't know."

"I'm sorry." The tears come to my eyes. "I honestly thought you didn't want anything to do with us. And then I saw you with all those girls and I thought you'd moved on."

"Shh!" he presses his finger to my lips, silencing me. "Most of that stuff was just Reg and the label trying to get more eyes on the band. But none of that matters now. That's not important. This is."

Remorse squeezes my heart when I see pain flicker in his eyes. "Too much time has been lost already because of what I did. I know I can't change what happened, but I want to make it right for you and Alex. If you give me a chance to make it right, I'll walk away from all this right now."

It shocks me that he would give all this away for us, the thing he has worked so hard to get. "Xander, I don't want you to do that."

"But I want you, Princess. I know I've never said that before because it scared the hell out of me, but I've always wanted you. And I want Alex. And if I have to give all this up to have the both of you, then I will give it up in a heartbeat. I've already lost you once, so I know exactly what matters and what doesn't. I don't plan on losing you again. Just tell me it's not too late and that you still want me, despite what I did."

He swallows as he stares at me, waiting for my response. Hearing his words, expressing that he wants us, the both of us, causes an overwhelming surge of emotions within me, that makes me want to cry.

"No, Xander, it's not too late."

Before I can utter another word, he lifts his hand and weaves his fingers through my hair. With a firm grip, he pulls my face towards him and his lips crash against mine. The kiss is filled with so much passion that I lose all concept of time. By the time we pull apart, I'm left totally breathless.

Chapter 58

Xander

After spending some time reflecting in the park, I knew I had to make things right. Now, as I sit here with Poppy, I can hear Theo in the background, completely butchering another one of my songs. Although I know I should step in and put a stop to it, as I'm certain my ears will soon bleed, I know this moment with Poppy holds greater importance. Resolving this issue is my utmost priority because it is what truly matters to me. It is what my heart truly desires - the chance to create a family with the woman I love and to establish a deep bond with my son.

Screw everything else. I've worked my ass off to get where I am, while Poppy has put hers on hold. I haven't told her how I feel yet. The words are right there on the tip of my tongue, ready to say, but I hesitate and can't get them out. Why is it so ridiculously hard to say those three simple words aloud?

"You need to stop running away whenever things get tough, Xander," Poppy says.

I realize that this has been my issue all along - evading problems and attempting to hide from reality, hoping that things will miraculously resolve themselves.

"I know. I promise, Princess, no more running away. You have my word. Does Alex know about me?"

"Yes. He knows that the second half of his name is the same as yours. That's why I called him Alexander. So he had a little piece of you, even though you weren't there."

Tears well in my eyes upon learning that she included my name with our sons. It makes me realize she never hated me the way I thought she did. She would never have included my name in our son's name if she did.

"What else have you told him about me?" I ask.

"Only that his daddy is working very hard. And one day soon, hopefully, he'll meet him."

"I want to meet him," I say, more tears forming in my eyes. The dark scars that I carry are no secret to Poppy; she's seen them before, and I don't care if she witnesses this side of me. "I may not have a clue about being a father, but I want to be there for him as his dad."

A stray tear spills down Poppy's cheek and I lift my hand and gently wipe it away with the pad of my thumb.

"Poppy," I whisper, my voice heavy with sorrow. As I gently cup the side of her face with my hand, I move closer. "I hate myself for hurting you. Let me be the guy I should've been years ago. Let me be the one who should've stayed and told you how I feel."

"I would like that."

The gentle touch of my lips to hers feels like a pledge of what is yet to come.

"Can I see a photo of him?" I ask, curious to see if he takes after Poppy.

She smiles, grabs her phone, clicks through to find the photo, and then hands it to me.

A stray tear spills down my cheek when I see Alex. His eyes, jawline, and hair color are an exact reflection of mine. He looks just like the photo of me that my mom kept on her bedside table.

"I'm sorry I wasn't there for you, little man," I say to the image on the screen. "I promise to make it up to you now." I run my fingers over his tiny face, taking in every precious detail. It's as if I already know him somehow. It's like he's the same little boy I once was, full of happiness and love. But the difference is, I had the love of both a mother and a father back then. On the other hand, Alex has been without a father for years. I can't help but wonder if he's ever asked about me. And if he has, I wonder what Poppy has told him.

"He's beautiful isn't he?' Poppy says.

"He is."

Reg's loud voice sounds and I hand Poppy back her phone.

"Why the fuck are you not up there?" He says coming towards us.

I quickly stand up, completely ignoring the arrogant dickhead. Taking Poppy's hand in mine, I guide her away from him, striding in the opposite direction.

There is no way this asshole is coming between us. Nothing is ever again. This is my family, and a true man fights for his family to make it work.

I ignore the asshole's persistent rants, even when he continues to follow us and interrogate me about my whereabouts. But I refuse to engage in his game, fully aware that any interaction will only lead to another complaint he will make to the label, accusing me of disappearing once again. However, now that I know the truth, I couldn't care less about his accusations. If I had to choose between fame and family, I would give all of this up in a heartbeat. It's a no-brainer when it comes down to it.

Listening to him, I'm fully prepared to confront Reg if he dares utter a word to Poppy, like he usually does.

To my surprise, he remains silent. I can't help but question the reasoning behind Reg and Ace's insistence on bringing Poppy along for this tour. Sure, there have been times when I've gone off the radar to clear my mind, but most of the negative attention in the media is stirred up by Reg. My outbursts have mostly been in response to false stories printed in the papers or online. I've often clashed with the label over their demands, but my anger was primarily fueled by Poppy being exposed to all that untrue nonsense. I never wanted her to witness any of it, nor did I want her to believe she was just some casual fling. Her presence on this tour allows me to confront the heaviness of leaving her behind. Now, I can finally deal with all the stuff I've been avoiding for years.

"Where are we going?" Poppy asks as I guide her around the back area of the stage and down the side corridor.

"I can't bear the sound of this fool butchering my songs anymore. If he keeps going, I might just jam a pencil in my ears."

Her laughter fills the air, a familiar and comforting sound that brings a smile to my face.

As soon as I step onto the stage with Poppy, her hand tightens its grip on mine. Nate's drumming abruptly halts the moment he lays eyes on me, and Ace's guitar playing suddenly stops.

"Thank fuck," Ace says. "I never want to hear that asshole sing another word as long as I live."

"Hey, it wasn't that bad," Theo comments, approaching and taking his usual spot, ducking his head and slipping his guitar strap onto his shoulder.

Lewis, the sound guy, steps forward. "We're already behind, and Reg is on my ass about the time, so let's just wrap up with the last song," he says, turning away.

The final song, the one that has haunted me for years, now belongs to the fans. But with Poppy by my side, I want to create another special memory for just the two of us. I reach out and take Poppy's hand, pulling her across the stage.

"What are we doing?" she asks, and I hear the worry in her voice.

"We're going to sing," I reply.

Poppy yanks her hand from mine and shakes her head, desperate to create distance between us. But I quickly wrap my arm around her waist and draw her closer to me. I am aware of the watchful eyes of the other three band members as they observe our intimate exchange. Leaning in, I softly whisper into her ear, "Princess, this song is ours. The moment I heard you sing it, I felt something powerful, even though I couldn't understand what it was at the time. It shouldn't belong to the fans, so let's reclaim it as ours."

"But I don't sing anymore, Xander. I haven't for years," she whispers.

It saddens me to hear her say that, especially since she has more talent than some of the singers signed to the label.

"It's just the two of us here, Princess. The guys won't judge you. It doesn't matter how you sound, just sing it with me."

I lean forward, running my face along her neck, and gently plant a soft kiss against her skin. I know how much she used to enjoy this gesture, especially when she's caught up in her thoughts.

"But what about Reg?" she asks, her concern evident.

"Fuck Reg," I respond firmly. "If he causes any trouble, I'll handle it."

I truly mean every word - I'm ready to face him head-on the instant he says anything because this is important to me. I'm determined to reclaim this song as ours, to recapture the essence of what we had all those years ago.

As she catches my gaze, she hesitates briefly before nodding, recognizing the determination in my eyes. I lean in and plant a gentle kiss on her cheek, then shift my attention to scan the band, the sound crew, and the onlookers who are all observing our interaction. Taking Poppy's hand in mine, I lead her over to the microphone.

With a nod, I signal to Nate that we're ready for the song. I notice Ace's expression, as if he's bracing himself for yet another rendition of a terrible song. Little does he know, Poppy has an incredible singing voice, a secret I've kept from him. Only Theo is aware of her talent, as I shared it with him one night. Considering Theo's tendency to reveal secrets, it's highly probable that Nate knows as well.

The beat permeates the air, and Ace and Theo seamlessly merge with the music. I'm unable to look away from Poppy as she watches me lean into the microphone, ready to sing the opening line. I sense her nervousness, her hand trembling in mine. Gently, I rub my thumb along the back of her hand, hoping to reassure her. With a nod, I give her the signal to sing the second line, and she does so effortlessly. Despite her long absence from singing, her voice remains flawless, with that seductive and captivating tone that never fails to enthrall me. I urge her to continue, line after line.

As she grows more comfortable with the microphone, I scan the crowd and notice people standing there, undeniably amazed, curious to know who possesses such an extraordinary voice.

I glance over at Theo, who purposely avoids making eye contact. He, along with Ace and Nate, are completely absorbed in watching Poppy as she passionately delivers the lyrics of "Creep." Just like when she had mesmerized me with her voice and vulnerability on the street, she now demands the attention of everyone present.

Damn, this girl can sing. She owns the stage, and I know if this place was packed right now, she would effortlessly captivate every single person in that crowd. However, I know Poppy. That's not her style, no matter how exceptionally talented she is. She never sought the spotlight; all she ever wanted was to use her music to make a difference for children.

As the song concludes, she looks over at me, her smile radiating pure joy, and in this moment, my heart swells with pride for her.

"Fuck!" Ace says, coming forward. "I never knew you could sing like that."

Poppy's cheeks flush, as if someone has caught her doing something wrong. I pull her close, wrapping my arm around her.

"How was it?" I ask, eager to hear her thoughts.

"Now I understand why my dad loved it so much. Thank you," she says.

CHAPTER 59

Xander

We're heading back to the hotel. Poppy is sitting on one side of me, while the ever-annoying Reg occupies the other. I intentionally made sure there's a significant distance between him and my princess; she doesn't deserve any of his unnecessary rants. Across from me, sit my ever loyal brothers. I've witnessed countless times how they've stood up and told Reg to back off whenever he started targeting Poppy. That's what I admire about them - their loyalty and their willingness to defend what belongs to us.

"So, have you managed to fix the shitstorm you created?" Ace says to Reg, his voice tinged with annoyance.

"I'm dealing with it," Reg replies, focusing on his phone, fingers swiftly typing as if drafting an email. His demeanor exudes indifference, downplaying the seriousness of the matter.

Keen to distance myself from the ongoing chaos, as I consider it more of a Reg problem than mine, I contemplate taking a stand against the label. If necessary and if I am once again unfairly accused for something I have not done, I'm willing to give a press interview to address the issue and set the record straight. However, right now, my priority is shifting away from the controversy to focus on something more important - my son.

I turn my head to Poppy, who is peering out the window. I lean in, and she notices right away, turning her attention to me.

"Can I see more photos of Alex?" I ask, eager to see more of my son. I want to learn as much as I can about him.

She retrieves her phone from her bag and unlocks it. Within seconds, a smile spreads across her face as she shows me a photo of Alex.

"There are plenty more in there," she says, giving me her phone.

I take her phone, eager to immerse myself in every detail and catch a glimpse into my son's life.

As I gaze at the image of the little boy, my attention becomes captivated. He symbolizes the essence of my newly discovered world, one that revolves around a son whom I am only just beginning to know. Despite the physical distance separating us, there is an emotional bond that constantly pulls me closer to him. His smile, captured in the photograph, resonates with a profound sense of familiarity. The strands of dark hair framing his eyes evoke a growing connection that intensifies with every passing moment.

Inside the cramped vehicle, I am acutely aware of the watchful gazes of those around me. Everyone, except for Reg, is keenly observing my every reaction as I delve into these precious glimpses of my son's life. I swiftly swipe the screen, eagerly anticipating the next chapter immortalized in these captivating images.

I stare at the moment captured on Poppy's phone —a photo of Alex sitting on her lap, both of them bursting with laughter. His head is nestled against her chest, while she holds him tightly, their shared happiness emanating from the image. I can't help but wonder what caused this laughter, the special connection that ties them together in that frozen moment. Curious to get a better view, I zoom in on the screen, fixating on their expressions.

As their expressions become clearer, a rush of emotions engulfs me. My eyes water as I realize the reality of all that I have missed out on through the years. The genuine warmth and connection captured in that photograph serve as an immediate reminder of the irreplaceable moments that have slipped through my fingers.

"So, Poppy, I had no clue you could sing like that," Ace comments. "Why didn't you ever perform at school?"

"I don't know. I guess I was already getting noticed for all the wrong reasons with Jade. I didn't want to attract any more attention to myself, I suppose," Poppy responds.

"Who taught you to sing like that?" Nate inquires.

"My dad," Poppy responds. "He was in a band."

"Oh yeah, I remember Xander mentioning that when you gave him the guitar," Ace recalls, bringing up the previous conversation about Poppy's father being in a band. The mention of the guitar exchange seems to tie everything together in their discussion.

As the car arrives at the hotel, I hand Poppy her phone. Before any of us can even unbuckle our seatbelts, Reg promptly opens the door and steps out. Ace looks at me briefly before shifting his focus to Theo and Nate.

"I bet the mess still isn't fixed," says Ace. "The asshole just doesn't have the balls to tell us."

"Yeah, but at least he's not bugging us," Theo says, trying to find a silver lining and acknowledging the break from that difficult asshole.

I slide across the seat and step out. The rest of the band patiently waits for Poppy to exit. Together, we make our way through the side entrance, where a kind staff member holds the heavy doors open for us. Once inside, we head towards the elevators.

As we walk forward, I notice Poppy fidgeting and tugging on the bottom of her shirt, clearly anxious about the attention we're receiving. This behavior is familiar to me, as it stems from the many times when Jade used to criticize her appearance, which always made her feel uneasy. I wish she could understand that none of that matters anymore. She is truly beautiful, and I will remind her of that every single day for the rest of our lives.

Jade's hurtful words, which were nothing but fucking lies, have left a lasting impact on Poppy. I can see how she still gets super nervous when people stare at her, still carrying all those emotional scars.

A groupie, or to be more precise, a cougar who really should know better, approaches us. Neil quickly steps forward, blocking her path. Theo abruptly halts, causing Ace to slam into his back. I can't help but smirk when I hear him complain in his usual grumpy way.

Partaking in flirtatious encounters with anyone who comes his way is a regular part of Theo's routine. The rest of us rarely give much thought to the groupies, unless we're in the mood for a bit of fun. Or in my case, when I sought to escape the thoughts of Poppy and find solace in the haze of alcohol and getting my dick sucked.

"Hey there, sweetheart," Theo says, approaching the middle-aged woman. "What's your name?"

Neil stays behind, while the other three security guards come with us as we continue walking to the elevator.

"Does Theo always act like that?" Poppy asks, glancing over her shoulder to see what he's doing.

"Seriously, every single time," Nate replies, shaking his head. "He shamelessly flirts with everyone."

The elevator doors slide open, and we all step inside. Nate holds his arm out, preventing the doors from closing as we wait for Theo.

"Hurry up, asshole," Ace mutters under his breath.

"Let's just go," I add impatiently, tired of always waiting for Theo to catch up.

Nate withdraws his hand, causing the doors to close. However, before they shut completely, we catch a glimpse of Theo turning to join us. Regrettably, it's too late; the doors are already closing, and no one makes an effort to prevent them from shutting.

"You do realize I'll never hear the end of it now," says Nate.

"Just tell the idiot to cut it out with the flirting," Ace says, casually slipping his hands into his pockets. "We'll have a band meeting in my room tonight after the show."

"I already have something planned," I tell him, taking out my phone.

"Yeah, man. Theo is pretty keen to hook up with a groupie tonight. You know how he is," Nate says.

"Well, tomorrow, meet me in my room at..." We all wait as he checks his phone. "Noon. We have nothing on then. We have a few things to discuss."

Quickly, I tap into my contacts and bring up Kit's number. I type out the following text:

Xander: Hey. Can you sort out a car for me after the show tonight? I need Neil to be there. Can you also see if a burger place can stay open late? I don't care how much it costs.

I slip my phone back into my pocket, determined to make things right with Poppy. We've never really had a proper date; most of our time together was spent at her place. The only exception was that one time at a burger joint in a not-so-great part of town. I knew it wasn't the best choice, but it was all I could afford back then. While I would love to take Poppy to a fancy restaurant, I know that's not her style. I remember that she enjoys a good burger and a laid-back atmosphere. That's exactly what I want too - to share a meal, relax, and have a meaningful conversation, just like we used to. Tonight, my goal is to address any unresolved issues because there's no way I'm letting her slip away again.

My phone pings and I quickly check the message.

Kit: Sure. I'll find something. Have a good night.

Kit is truly incredible. Every request I've made has been effortlessly fulfilled. It's a shame Reg can't adopt Kit's helpful attitude instead of constantly criticizing me.

Exiting the elevator, I slip my phone into my pocket. When I notice Poppy rummaging through her bag for her room key, I wrap my arm around her waist, pulling her close to me. "There's no need for that. You'll be staying in my room from now on."

"Xander," she says.

Keeping her snug against my chest, I guide her forward.

"I've been clear about wanting everything, Princess, and I mean it. I want it all." Placing a tender kiss on the side of her neck, we move towards my room.

As I insert the card into the lock, I effortlessly unlock the door to my hotel room. Holding the door slightly ajar, I signal for Poppy to enter. However, instead of stepping inside, she hesitates in the foyer, eyeing me.

"What's wrong?" I ask, dumbfounded by her intense gaze.

All I desire is for her to come inside so we can explore the naughty thoughts consuming my mind. Yet, it's clear that she's preoccupied with her thoughts.

"Take your time, Princess," I say, trying to be patient. "Or you could let me know what's holding you back."

She maintains eye contact with me for a brief moment before finally finding the courage to speak. Her voice carries a hint of hesitancy as she addresses me.

"So, when you say you want this, it's not just a tactic to lure me into your bed. And then, after the tour, you'll disappear like you did before. Because I can't bear to go through that again. I won't, Xander."

Her face reflects the uncertainty she's feeling, perhaps due to our previous encounters or my tendency to avoid difficult situations.

I know I need to tell her that my intentions are real and this isn't some line to get her into bed. It's no longer just about sex, it has evolved into something much deeper.

Man up asshole and tell her how you feel about her.

Boldly, I reach out and firmly grasp her hand, pulling her into the room.

Startled, she lets out a cry of surprise as I swiftly close the door behind us. Pressing her against the door, my hands rest on either side, creating a profound sense of intimacy. Our eyes meet, her blue gaze locking onto mine.

"Princess, do you truly believe I said those words just so I could fuck you?"

She gazes up at me and swallows. It's clear that she's attempting to maintain a façade, but I can sense from her breathing that all it would take is a kiss and I'd be balls deep in her. But I hold back because I don't want any more confusion.

"I want everything with you, Princess, and that means having you in my bed every fucking night for as long as I live. Do you want me to prove it?" I lean back, removing my shirt over my head. I observe her gaze shifting towards my chest. Her eyes widen, with shock as she takes in my tattoo. "I believe that says it all."

I know how crucial it is to tell her those three words, even if it's tough for me. I want her to know my feelings are real, without judging me for my past. My deepest desire is to bare my soul and lay it all out for her to see.

Struggling to control the lump in my throat, I fight against the feeling of being suffocated by the words left unspoken. Get your shit together, asshole. Just tell her how you feel.

"In the past, I never told you this, but I need to say it now." Swallowing hard, I can feel the words right there on the tip of my tongue. Yet, for some reason, I hesitate. *She won't laugh in your face, you idiot. She's different from all those others, like my father who was supposed to love me.*

Gathering my courage, I open my mouth and just go for it. "I love you." I continue, disregarding the shocked look on Poppy's face. "I've always loved you, Princess."

With a gentle touch, I lift my hand and brush her hair behind her ear, noticing her mouth agape in surprise at my confession. But I can't stop now. I need her to understand that she means everything to me.

"Before I left, I was in love with you. As the years went by, my love for you has deepened. I've learned the hard way in recent years that life just isn't the same without you."

Despite her eyes beginning to water, I press on.

"I may have fame and wealth, but they cannot fill the emptiness in my heart that has persisted since the day I fucking walked away from you. Only you, Poppy, have the power to fill that void. I want you. I want Alex. I've said it before, and I'll say it again—I would trade all my accomplishments in an instant to have both of you in my life. No more games, no more hiding my feelings. I am fully committed now. That's it, Princess—I am laying my heart bare for you."

She moves towards me, pressing her lips forcefully against mine. The gentle glide of her tongue sparks a surge of intense heat, causing my knees to weaken. I wrap my arm around her waist, guiding us backward across the room until we both tumble onto the bed. With eagerness, I claim her mouth while she wraps her legs around me, longing for closeness. The sensation intensifies as we grind against each other. Breaking away from the kiss, I prop myself up on my arms, ensuring not to crush her. She takes deep, steady breaths as she gazes up at me, her eyes filled with awe.

Her hand reaches up, gently caressing the side of my face. "I love you too," she declares, and those words, so unexpected, bring tears to my eyes.

As she holds my gaze, her fingers trace down the side of my face, creating a comforting and familiar sensation. I close my eyes, relishing in her touch. When

I open them again, Poppy's lips meet mine in a fiery kiss. My heart races as she alternates between tender kisses and sensual strokes of her tongue. With my calloused fingers, I slip them under her shirt, causing her breath to hitch. Pressing my hard cock against her, she lets out a sexy moan that always ignites my desire.

CHAPTER 60
Poppy

As he grips the edge of my shirt, he wastes no time in swiftly removing it along with my bra, igniting a rush of warmth that pulsates between my thighs. I gasp as he gently sucks on my nipple, the sensation sending waves of pleasure through my body. Within seconds, he effortlessly flips us over, placing me on top, and forcefully tears off my skirt and underwear. Straddling him, I feel the magnetic pull between us.

"Christ," he whispers, his eyes brim with longing as he gazes at my naked form. His fingers lightly trace down the side of my breast, coming to rest on my hip. "You're still so fucking perfect, Princess."

His words wash over me, bringing a sense of calm.

I tug at the waistband of his jeans. "I want these off now," I demand.

A sexy grin appears on the corner of his mouth as he replies, "You always were my fucking dirty little princess."

He watches my every movement as I undo the button and zipper on his jeans. "Lift," I instruct as I get up off him. When he complies, I pull down his jeans and boxers, checking out his hard cock as it springs out, softly brushing against his stomach.

Lying back on the bed, he puts his hands behind his head and watches me. My eyes immediately are drawn to the ink gracing the left side of his chest and trailing up his shoulder. It's a captivating musical staff adorned with beautifully sprawled notes. However, what truly surprised me when I first saw it by the door was the vivid red poppy flower, accompanied by the elegant black script that reads, "You are special." And I know exactly what he is referring to. It's in response to those lyrics, to the song that is ours.

"I told you, you weren't just some chick I fucked," he says.

As my fingers trace down his chest, I notice goosebumps forming beneath my touch. And then, I see it - delicately written between the musical notes, my name. It's small, yet intricate and beautiful. Overwhelmed, tears come to my eyes. What I see goes beyond words, beyond belief. He's been loving me for real, just like he told me today. This man who can have any woman in the world has chosen me. Me.

I have always loved him deeply, and held onto the hope that one day he would feel the same way about me. When he initially mentioned his feelings for me after finding out about Alex, I couldn't help but have some doubts. I thought he might just be using one of his typical lines, trying to convince me to sleep with him. I feared that once the tour was over, he would leave me as he had done before.

However, now that I see my name permanently inked on his body, it solidifies the fact that he had loved me all along, just as I had loved him.

As he lies on the bed, his eyes cast downward, observing me closely, I lift my hand and touch him, tracing my fingers along the prominent vein on the underside of his cock, savoring the rhythmic pulsation beneath my touch. Feeling bold, I lean forward and slide my tongue along it.

He lets out a groan while lowering his hand to his sides. His hands clench, as though he's fighting the temptation to run his fingers through my hair and instruct me to open my mouth so he can feed me. His nostrils flare as I repeat the action.

"Poppy," he utters, his voice filled with affection. I adore the way he pronounces my name as if I am his entire world.

A surprised squeal escapes me as he pulls me into his embrace, claiming my mouth with a passionate kiss. The intensity of his lips against mine reminds me of the familiar Xander I know, leaving me craving for more. Unable to resist, I gently bite down on his bottom lip, yearning for a deeper connection. His kiss grows stronger, his tongue tracing the contours of my lips, pleading for entrance. As I part my lips, I feel his self-control waver.

With a deep groan, one hand cradles the front of my neck while the other holds firmly onto my hip, anchoring me in place as he intensifies the kiss.

My senses ignite, causing me to whimper as I eagerly respond to the intense strokes of his tongue. I crave more of him, yearning for his taste, his scent, and the way he passionately kisses and caresses me.

A gentle pinch on my nipple elicits a hiss, urging me to grind against him. It feels like a switch has been flipped, reigniting desires that have been dormant for years, since the last time we were together like this, when I could freely embrace my deepest longings. I'm incredibly aroused right now, to the point where I could scream. Gasping for air, I break away from the kiss and softly whisper, "I want you to fuck me."

His expression shows how badly he wants me, as he grabs my hips and guides me closer, his cock teasing my wetness. He grabs my ass, signaling for me to rub against his erection.

"You don't have to ask to get off on my cock, Princess. Just fucking take it, you dirty girl."

My stomach gets all knotted up as I feel the intense sensation every time I slide across his long shaft. Oh, my God. Every bump and vein feels as if it's designed just for me to bring intense pleasure.

"Christ," he breathes out as I glide along his length. "Your pretty pussy is drenching my cock." The heat in his eyes intensifies as he grabs his cock. "Rub it on your clit," he says.

I wrap my fingers around him, taking control.

His eyes lower, fixated on watching my movements. "That's it," he whispers, with teeth clenched while I trace the delicate area.

A pleasurable moan escapes my lips as I indulge myself further.

"Feel good, huh?" he says.

"So good," I say, but it's not just the sensations that have me enthralled. It's the way he gazes at me as if I'm the most alluring woman he's ever laid eyes on. I've seen the tabloids showcasing the stunning women he's been photographed with, and I know I'll never measure up to them with the way they look. Yet, the way he looks at me makes me feel truly beautiful.

Xander's lips part slightly and the desire in his eyes tells me he's into it.

Moaning, I increase the speed of rubbing his cock against my clit. The sensation is overwhelming. I'm incredibly wet and on the verge of coming.

"Fuck, I can feel you throbbing on my cock," he breathes out, tilting his head back, eyes closed, hands gripping my hips hard. "You're so close," he says.

And now I want it even more. "I need you inside me when I come," I confess.

He abruptly opens his eyes and sits upright, pulling me closer with his arm around my lower back. His deep, husky voice sends electrifying shivers down my spine as he whispers, "I want my cock buried inside you too."

Goosebumps ripple across my skin, igniting a deep desire to explore every inch of his body.

Our eyes lock as he slowly enters me, stretching me to accommodate his every inch.

"Fuck, you feel so good," he murmurs, sliding his thumb down to pleasure my clit while I ride him.

His kisses ignite a fire within me. The pleasure intensifies as waves of pure bliss cascade through me, one after another.

"Oh my god," I gasp.

A deep growl escapes his throat as my pussy tightens around him, reaching the peak of my pleasure. His forehead rests against mine, his strong chest rising and falling, as if he, too, has just experienced his release. In a daze, I lean against him, my mind clouded with bliss.

He wraps his arms around me, pulling me in so close that there's no space left between us. It's difficult to put into words the intensity of what I'm feeling right now. His breath softly lands on my face as our foreheads stay pressed together. I see the restraint in his features as he weaves his fingers through my hair, as he meets my gaze.

My heart quickens as I absorb the distinct features of his face, the piercing intensity in his eyes, and the clear torment etched on his expression. It's clear that remaining motionless while he's still inside me is agonizing for him, yet he restrains himself to fulfill my desire. I lean forward, resting my lips against the shell of his ear.

"I need you to fuck me and make me yours."

He gazes at me for a moment, before his hands firmly grab my ass, a look of desire masks his face, causing any self-restraint to vanish. Abruptly, he withdraws from me, and my heart sinks, feeling betrayed by the sudden loss. In an instant, I'm lying on my back. The look in his eyes is undeniably menacing like a predator closing in on its prey.

"You already belong to me, Princess," he proclaims. He drops to his knees in front of me. "Now fucking spread your legs."

As soon as I do, he eagerly leans in, skillfully using his talented tongue to pleasure me, making me moan softly. As he explores my most sensitive areas, his hand glides up my body, playfully teasing my nipple. The sensation is so incredibly pleasurable that it almost makes me purr. It's as if he's memorized every single pleasure spot. With a playful touch, he circles my clit, driving me wild with desire. Growing impatient, I instinctively move my hips against his face, begging, "Xander, please, just fuck me."

He laughs, leaning back and grinning at me. I can see my wetness on his chin, and he doesn't bother to wipe it away.

I groan in frustration. Asshole.

"How badly do you crave my cock?" he asks, his voice low and seductive. I'm fully aware that he is taunting me, making me work for it.

"What do you think, asshole?" I remark, digging my nails into his scalp and dragging his face back to my pussy.

His laughter sends pleasurable vibrations through me when he kisses my pussy. "You want it that bad, huh?"

I bite my bottom lip, my gaze fixed on him. All I can manage is a nod as his thumb softly circles around my clit.

"You're so fucking wet," he remarks, moving his hand away and aligning the tip of his cock with my entrance. "Take a deep breath," he whispers, leaning forward to place tender kisses along my stomach. And then he thrusts forward.

"Oh, fuck," I gasp, my mouth dropping open in surprise.

Rising onto his knees, he firmly holds onto my hips. I tremble with anticipation as he pulls back before thrusting into me, over and over again. His hold on my hips is so tight, that I know there will be marks when this is done. The way he fucks me, the way he consumes me, and the pleasure he sends through my body cause my legs to tremble.

"Xander," I whisper, my hand stretching out towards him, consumed by a powerful longing that I struggle to fully grasp. All I am certain of is that my desire for him surpasses anything I have ever yearned for. His gaze, so penetrating, completely captivates me. I am amazed by the sheer intensity with which he looks at me.

"I love you," he whispers, his movements gradually slowing. The palpable energy between us transforms into something tangible, something undeniably real. As he fucks me, the rhythm builds and it feels so good it makes my toes curl.

I lift my hips, meeting his deep thrusts, adding to our fiery dance. With every penetration, I let go, getting lost in the rhythm. My hands glide down his back, loving the strength of his muscles as they flex with every thrust.

"Xander," I moan.

Every time he slides into me, I feel myself unraveling. He embeds himself deep within my very essence. He has never fucked me like this before. It's like he's starving for my touch, but can't satisfy his craving. A sudden realization strikes me. He wants to dismantle the barriers that separate us. This is the Xander I remember, unguarded and vulnerable. He's inviting me to take the plunge with him into the depths of his soul. I trace the stubble on his jawline, marveling at his breathtaking beauty. His dark brown eyes meet mine as he holds me close, cherishing the moment and sealing it in his memory forever. He's not just physically inside me, it's so much more profound than that. It's everything

I've longed for, this connection with him. Xander Williams doesn't just fuck, he worships with every fiber of his being.

As our fingers intertwine, he lifts one of my hands above my head, while his other hand explores the space between us, tending to my sensitive clit. Every deep thrust draws out a whimper, bringing me closer to the edge. I part my lips, intending to plead for a moment's respite, but I end up moaning. I bite down on my bottom lip, attempting to stifle my moans, but it's pointless. My grip on the sheet tightens as I feel my orgasm approaching.

"Fucking hell," he says.

His next deep thrust takes me by surprise, and I release in an intense rush, my primal moan echoing through the room.

Xander suddenly freezes, his expression transforming into one of genuine concern. "Are you okay?" He asks.

"So much better than just okay," I whisper, my voice barely audible.

His ragged breaths, uneven and raw, give way to deep moans as he thrusts in and out of me. Pleasure contorts his sharp features as he shudders through his release. I can feel his breath warm against my chest when he collapses against me, and I lovingly thread my fingers through his damp hair. He holds me tightly, unwilling to let go as he catches his breath. After a few lingering moments, he lifts his gaze to meet mine.

"Fucking hell. I've replayed our earlier days in my mind for so many years, but it was nothing like this." His mouth twists into a vulgar grin. "So, is it clear now that you're mine? Because this time, there's no fucking way I'm letting you go." His eyes lock onto mine, filled with intensity as he awaits my response.

My breath stalls as his hand glides over my ribs and gently brushes against the curve of my breast, finally coming to rest on the organ threatening to beat its way out of my chest. "Fuck I've missed you."

Chapter 61

Xander

I'm drenched in sweat by the time we reach our last song tonight. All night, I've looked over to see Poppy in her short skirt standing in the wings, watching me pour my heart out on stage. Usually, when groupies shout out their explicit desires, screaming out all the dirty things they want to do to me, I play along, reveling in the attention and fueling their desires with provocative gestures. But tonight, none of that matters. All I can think about is the girl standing on the sidelines, the one I can't wait to take back to the hotel room and do all the dirty things that are on my mind. I give her another one of my trademark smirks, knowing it makes her blush, hinting at what awaits her once this performance is over. She fidgets and squirms, and I can imagine that if I were to walk over there and run my fingers along her slit, she would be wet. Wet for me.

Even after all this time, despite my many faults, she continues to see the good in me. Out of all the women in the world, she's the one I've been longing for and desperately yearning for all my life. She is everything to me. It wasn't until I walked away that I realized no one could ever compare to her and what we shared. It's unbelievable that even after all these years, our connection remains unchanged. What does that say about us? That I found the love of my life when I was just seventeen—a foolish, ignorant teenager who failed to recognize what he had.

Afterward, I plan to take Poppy out on a date.

I never had the means to do that before, and looking back at the arrogant asshole I used to be, I probably wouldn't have even considered it because I didn't realize how much she meant to me back then. Tonight, I want to find a quiet spot where we can have an uninterrupted conversation away from Reg and the others. This will be our first performance out of the five shows we have in Sydney before we get back on the bus and head to Brisbane.

Despite being here for almost three weeks, we haven't explored the country because of our demanding schedule and the label's obligations, which is something I want to address in tomorrow's meeting in Ace's room.

We need some downtime.

We're constantly traveling the world, yet none of us have truly experienced any of it. And what better way to do so than with Poppy by my side? I want her to know that I'm prepared for any adventure that life may throw at us. I'll strive to be the best version of myself for both her and Alex.

I make my way back to the mic for the final song of the night. I used to hate this time of the night when all the memories would come flooding back. But now, as I prepare to sing mine and Poppy's song, it fills me with so much gratitude. This song has been my life, filling my heart with love. Love that started when my mother taught me the lyrics. Love that grew for the girl on the street who would change my life forever. I long to return to that special place where we sang together on the rock, connecting with my mother once again.

Now, singing this song in front of seventy thousand people in this stadium, all I feel is gratitude for the blessings in my life. It all stems from this song, like a tapestry woven with the threads of my life.

I'd ask Poppy to come out here and sing it with me, but I know she'd freak out. It took every ounce of courage for her to sing it earlier today.

"Okay, Sydney, you know the last song. Sing it with me," I yell, extending my arms wide.

The crowd erupts in excitement as I turn to Theo, who begins counting in the band. The music starts, and I grab the mic from the stand, singing the first line. Holding the microphone out to the crowd, they belt out the next line, and then the next. I stand there in awe, listening to the thousands of voices filling the air, singing the song that has shaped my life.

Ace comes over, his fingers effortlessly gliding across the strings. Surprisingly, a huge smile adorns the typically grumpy asshole's face.

"How amazing is this!" he says, redirecting his focus to the crowd, their phones held up to capture the last moments of the night.

And he's absolutely right. It's the best fucking high being up here in the spotlight, with the audience hanging onto my every word.

I join in on the chorus and continue singing the rest of the song. As the song comes to an end, the cheers intensify, giving me a surge of adrenaline. This is what I live for. That exhilarating rush. The spotlight. The music.

"Goodnight Sydney. Keep it real."

Ace, Theo, and Nate come up to stand beside me. Together, we stand there in awe, basking in the thunderous cheers emerging from the packed stadium. We lift our hands and wave out to the ecstatic crowd before making our way over to the right side of the stage. As usual, I am the first to exit the stage, with the boys following closely behind. I'm not exactly sure why they've always done that, but it's become a tradition they simply continue to uphold.

As I make my way across the stage, my gaze meets Poppy's, and a smile graces her lips. Closing the distance between us, I wrap my arm around her waist, bringing her in close so I can plant a kiss on her lips. I love it when she makes that soft whimper. It always puts a smile on my face when I kiss her like that.

"I need to go do the meet and greet," I say, pressing my forehead against hers. "But once that's done, I want to take you out on a proper date."

She looks up at me, her expression filled with surprise. "A date?"

"Yes," I nod. "I've never taken you out on one before." I lean in to press a kiss to her lips before intertwining our fingers and guiding her toward the green room. This is where I'll leave Poppy while I do the meet and greet for those who brought backstage passes.

However, before I do anything else, I need to find a fresh shirt. The one I'm currently wearing is soaked with sweat and clinging uncomfortably to my body. I usually ask Kit to make sure there's an extra shirt in the stockroom, which is conveniently next to the green room.

Up ahead, as I lead Poppy down towards the greenroom, I see the long line of dedicated fans. Tall barriers separate them from the side corridor near the stage. This is where Poppy has been standing all night, observing from the wings of the stage. Good thing they can't see where we are.

As I enter the storeroom, I take off my wet shirt and quickly grab a clean, folded one from the stack. However, the voices of the waiting fans still reach us.

"I heard Xander has his dick pierced," one voice says.

"Well, I heard he prefers blondes," another groupie chimes in.

"I don't care. I just want him to fuck me. I bet he's good at it."

I see the pissed-off look spreading across Poppy's beautiful face. Seeing her jealous makes me grin. I can't help but move in closer. "It looks like my groupies want me," I tease.

"Asshole," she says, pushing me away.

I can't help but laugh, enjoying the jealousy that seems to consume her. Leaning in, I gently place my hand on her neck and plant a soft kiss on her lips. I fight the urge in my body. I'm dying to kiss her and whisper something dirty that'll make her go wild. But if I give in, I won't be able to resist bending her over and fucking her senseless. Not here. Later. There are some things I need to show her first, things that will make her see that it's not just about sex.

"Just so you know, I never fucked any of them, no matter what you've read in the papers. It's just a scheme from Reg and the label for publicity." I reach up and tuck her hair behind her ears, my heart pounding against my chest. "They might want me, but you're the only one who gets me."

Her gaze transforms into one of fiery desire and lust, causing me to laugh as I feel myself growing aroused. "Soon Princess. I promise. Date first. Talk second and fuck later. God, I never thought I'd ever be saying that."

"Who the hell are you and what did you do with that smug asshole, Xander?" she smirks.

I can't help but laugh as I take her hand and lead her into the green room where Reg and the band are waiting for me.

"Well, it's about time," Reg says, a hint of frustration in his voice. I can't help but notice his gaze shifting towards our intertwined hands. If he fucking starts anything, there will be hell to play.

"Leave him alone, man," Nate says. "Just get on with the meet and greet, so we can get the fuck out of here."

I nod at Nate, acknowledging him. It's amazing how my brothers always have my back. Well, except for that one major mistake I made two years ago when I got high and passed out at a bar during our tour. You wouldn't believe the things these groupies do to claim they've slept with a celebrity. Thank God Ace showed up just in time. He took her phone and deleted the video she was recording.

After signing dozens of tits, having multiple photos taken with girls and some guys, some who were a bit too hands-on, it's time to leave. Throughout the night, I keep an eye on Poppy, who stands to one side, observing the interactions between the band and our eager fans, and others who've snuck into the room. All night I'm on alert, wondering if Reg is up to his usual tricks, trying to create a scandal that will skyrocket our sales once again.

Theo is his usual flirty self, while Ace stands off to the side, never cracking a smile. He poses for a few photos and signs autographs without uttering a word. He needs to lighten up. Back in school, he was never like this. However, as time has passed, he has become grumpier.

As I'm about to leave, I notice Ace sitting on the couch, engrossed in conversation with Poppy.

Meanwhile, Theo is busy charming a curvaceous blonde, who, based on past experiences, will probably be the girl the guys spend the night with.

I grab a bottle of water from the table, quickly gulping it down before I make my way over to Poppy.

A smile lights up my face as I watch Ace burst into laughter in response to something Poppy said. It's rare to see that asshole smile, but knowing that my princess had a hand in it brings a smile to my face. They both look up at me as I come to a stop in front of them.

"You ready?" I ask, curious if she's as hungry as me.

"Yeah," she says, getting up.

"Don't fuck all night," Ace says, getting up from the couch.

"Screw you, bro," I say, taking hold of Poppy's hand. I quickly shoot a glance at Neil, who's at the back of the room, and give him a nod.

He returns the nod, letting me know Kit has already briefed him on tonight's plans. He makes his way towards the door, opening it for us to leave the green room. I step forward, holding Poppy's hand, fully aware that the few remaining groupies are watching my every move.

Neil takes the lead, scanning the area for any potential threats. Eventually, we reach a narrow corridor, and he opens a side door. Descending a flight of stairs, we find a black SUV parked, its engine already running. The driver kindly opens the door for us, and Poppy hops in, making room for me to join her.

"So, where are you taking me?" Poppy asks.

"We're going to a burger joint that's staying open just for us," I say to her.

She presses the button on her phone and the screen lights up. "It's past midnight," she says, a look of shock crossing her face.

"For the right price, people will do anything. Plus, I need to talk about a few things, so we might as well enjoy a burger."

"What kind of things?" she asks, with a hint of concern in her voice.

As we come to a stop at a traffic light, I take a glance out of the window. There's this young couple totally lost in a passionate kiss against a brick wall.

As the car starts moving again, I look back at Poppy, who's staring at me, waiting for me to answer. "There are a few things I need to tell you," I say, pulling her closer. "I've got a few questions I should've asked when I first saw you."

I refrain from adding too much to this conversation because Neil and the driver can hear everything I say. What I want to discuss with her is private, just between the two of us.

She nods, then her gaze shifts to the window. And I know her mind is racing once again. It saddens me to know I've caused her this doubt.

In my eyes, she is the epitome of strength, yet self-doubt often plagues her.

After another ten minutes, the vehicle slows down and eventually comes to a complete stop.

"Where here, Mr. Williams." The driver says.

I hate being called that name because it reminds me of my asshole father. But I choose to ignore it because the driver is unaware of that, as he's never worked for us before. He switches off the engine, then promptly gets out to open the doors for us to exit.

Neil's standing on the sidewalk, checking out the deserted street. There's only a handful of people walking around. Since it's a Wednesday night, the streets are noticeably quieter compared to the buzz of a Friday or Saturday night.

Getting out of the car, I grab Poppy's hand as Neil heads towards the burger joint. Neil taps on the door and waits, scoping out the place. Eventually, the door opens and Neil enters, taking a quick look around to make sure there's no media waiting. When everything looks fine, he gives me a nod and steps out of the building. Hand in hand, Poppy and I go into the restaurant.

"Welcome Mr Williams. Miss," a man in his early thirties greets us. "My name is Walter. I'm the owner of this place." He's got a buzz cut and loads of tattoos on his arms. His eyebrow and lip piercings make him stand out from the typical burger joint owner.

"Thank you, Walter, but please call me Xander," I interject, not wanting to be referred to by my last name for the rest of the evening.

"Hello," Poppy says, smiling, as she extends her hand to Walter.

Returning the smile, he shakes her hand. "Now is there a specific place you'd like to sit?" he asks, gesturing towards the empty restaurant.

As I glance around the area, I can't help but admire Kit's choice in restaurants once again. The walls are adorned with posters and music memorabilia, creating a nostalgic atmosphere. It somehow reminds me of the first time I entered Poppy's bedroom. "We'll take that booth over there," I gesture towards a secluded area, far from the bustling kitchen, offering us a hint of privacy. Not to mention, the booth's curved seat allows me to easily slide closer to Poppy, creating an intimate setting.

"Alright, follow me," Walter says as he grabs two menus.

Poppy walks ahead, and I take this opportunity to admire her figure. I've always had an appreciation for a nice ass, and Poppy's is undoubtedly the best I've ever seen. It's absolutely perfect. My excitement stirs at the sight of it, but I remind myself to stay focused. I can't let my desires interfere with what I need to tell her. Tonight, I need to keep my wits about me. I can indulge in her later.

Poppy slides onto the leather seat, accepting the menu handed to her.

Deciding that I don't want to sit across from her, I slide in beside her. This way, I can be close to her and touch her whenever I please. Walter hands me a menu, but I don't bother glancing at it.

"What would you recommend?" I inquire.

"The burger with everything is a favorite among our customers," he suggests.

"All right, I'll go with that, along with a side of fries and a glass of coke." I return the menu and glance at Poppy.

She meets Walter's gaze and says, "I'll have the same."

I fucking love how she eats like any ordinary person, unlike those girls we've worked with over the years who only nibble on celery sticks.

Before Walter turns around, I quickly add, "And could I get two more of those? One for the big guy by the door and the other for the driver of the black SUV parked out front."

"Sure thing," Walter replies.

Left to ourselves, I steal a glance at Poppy and find her examining the environment. Her eyes take in the many framed music posters that adorn the walls—Nirvana, Alice in Chains, Sound Garden, Silverchair, and many others.

"This place is nice," she comments, looking back at me.

"Yeah, it is."

"It kinda reminds me of that time you took me for a burger when I was hungover. Do you remember that?"

"Yeah," I recall. I refrain from mentioning that every time I've ordered a burger with the band, that memory resurfaces.

Walter returns, carrying our drinks.

"Thank you," Poppy says. "Are you a music fan?"

Walter grins, "Yeah, I'm in a band. The frontman, actually." He glances in my direction. "Not as good as you, man. I'm so honored to meet you and have you here in my restaurant."

"So you manage a restaurant and still play in a band," Poppy inquires.

"Yeah, we snag a few gigs here and there, but it's more like a hobby now. We didn't achieve our dream of hitting it big, but I suppose that's how it goes."

Curious, Poppy probes further, "What kind of music does your band play?"

"Yeah, we're a rock band, and we used to write our own songs. I still do. I guess it's in my blood. But most of our audience these days prefers covers. So, I suppose it's come down to that."

"Can I hear any demos of the songs you've written?" I ask.

"Yeah. Why?"

I grab my phone and extend it towards him. "Put your number here and send them my way. We'll be on the lookout for an opening gig for the tour program next year. If you're the right fit, are you guys interested?"

His eyes widen as he takes hold of my phone. "Hell yeah, we'd be interested. Thanks, man," he says, adding his number and handing it back.

I quickly send a text so he has my number. "Shoot me something and I'll run it by the band."

"Thanks, Xander. I definitely will," he smiles, reaching out to shake my hand. "Thanks for the opportunity, man."

"No problem."

"Well, I'll be back shortly with your burgers."

As he walks away, I glance at Poppy and notice a huge smile on her face. "You know you made his day, right?"

"Doesn't sound like they got their lucky break like we did when we first started out," I add, reaching for my drink to take a sip.

"Xander, share with me the story of how you got your big break. When did you get signed by the label?"

I know it's hard to talk about when I left her, but we need to talk about everything if we want our relationship to succeed. I settle into my seat, position myself to face her, arm casually slung over the back of her seat.

"When Ace and I left, he found us this rundown apartment to rent. We were trying to save money because we didn't know how long it would take to start making money from our music. This apartment was the worst I've ever seen—rats, mice, and cockroaches everywhere."

"Yeah, I know the feeling," Poppy says, grabbing her drink and taking a sip. I pause, wondering what she means by that comment. "Go on," she prompts, encouraging me to continue.

"I got a job as a kitchen hand in this old burger joint, while Ace was serving tables in some other rundown restaurant. One night, Ace crossed paths with Nate and Theo, who were in the same shitty apartment building. They were also there, going after their dreams, and something just clicked. They joined our band, and Ace organized a few gigs. Next thing we knew, we were rocking out to packed crowds and getting a loyal fanbase. Eventually, a record label approached us."

Walter comes over, carrying two plates. A towering burger stands proudly, accompanied by a generous serving of fries, and two remingtons hold tantalizingly zesty orange sauce and classic ketchup.

"Enjoy," he says, giving us a smile, and leaving us to our meal.

Poppy stares down at her meal. "I have no clue how I'll get my mouth around this."

I lean in, moving my lips to the shell of her ear. "Trust me, Princess, your mouth works wonders," I whisper.

She turns her head, and I notice a rosy blush on her cheeks.

Chuckling, I move my arm from behind her and grab my burger, taking a delectable bite. The taste is heavenly. I'm unsure if it's the most exceptional burger I've had in a long time or if the sheer delight of enjoying it with Poppy amplifies the experience.

"Is it good?" she asks.

I acknowledge with a nod, savoring the last hints of sauce on my lower lip as I run my tongue over it. Poppy's eyes track my tongue as it moves along my lip, gathering the last traces of sauce. When she meets my gaze, I smirk and give her a wink.

"You're still a cocky asshole, you know that," she remarks. I catch the sassy glint in her eye before she shifts her focus to her burger.

I keep my eyes fixed on her as she takes a big bite, her mouth wide open. After setting the burger down, she looks at me, still chewing. At that moment, I notice a mischievous sparkle in her eye and a trickle of sauce on her chin. A sudden desire compels me to lean forward and lick it off her chin, but she beats me to it by wiping it away with her fingers. Then, with a wicked grin, she slowly brings one of her fingers to her mouth and sensually sucks the sauce from it. As she does, her cheeks hollow out, and she playfully winks at me. With a loud sound, she pops her finger out of her mouth, then teasingly inserts another digit. The process repeats, accompanied by a seductive moan. I'm fucking turned on. My dick is hard by the time she removes her finger from her mouth. Then she throws a mischievous grin my way.

"Well played, Princess," I remark, chuckling.

Can't deny the sexiness of the woman by my side. She not only challenges me but also pushes me to be a better man, and I just want to give her everything in this life. I know we need to talk about our future after this tour, but her finger-licking seduction is seriously distracting. This once playful vixen has grown into a captivating seductress. I've never been a worshiper, but seeing the woman she's become, I'd gladly kneel for her. She's fierce, always pushes me, and she's fucking sexy. I just want to get this conversation over with so we can go back to the hotel room and fuck all night.

Shifting my focus from her, I set my half-eaten burger aside on the plate in front. Slowly, I reach for my coke and take a sip.

"What's on your mind?" Poppy asks.

"There are a few things I should have asked already," I state, placing my glass back on the table.

"Such as?" she says, wiping her fingers on her napkin.

"You never got the chance to pursue your dreams like I did," I remark.

"No, I didn't. But I wouldn't change the outcome because it gave me our beautiful little boy," she responds.

Her words bring tears to my eyes. "I regret not talking to you that night when I called. I really wish I had," I confess.

"We can't change what's happened, Xander. But I don't understand why you called me but you wouldn't talk," she questions.

"Because I knew I'd hurt you. I understood I wasn't good for you."

"That's not true, Xander. You've always been good enough. I just wish you could see that."

"I truly believed that what I did was for the best."

"But I needed you."

"I get that now," I add, watching her pick up two fries and put them into her mouth. "I've mentioned that I'm in, and I mean it."

"Yeah, I still don't know what exactly that means," she says, shifting her focus on her plate.

I extend my hand, softly gripping her chin and guiding her face back to me. "It means I want a life with you and Alex. I want the family we've created. I want it all." She gulps when she hears what I'm saying. "You're my one and only, Poppy. I wanna get to know my son and be his dad. I want us to be a family. If you'll have me, then I want to give you and Alex the world. I have the means to do that now."

"Xander," she whispers.

My heart pounds in my chest, filled with the overwhelming fear that she might reject my plea. At that moment, my lungs tighten, making each breath feel like a struggle, but I push through. "I can't get rid of the regret I have for leaving you. But what I really want is a future with you and Alex. Just tell me you want it to."

"I do want it, Xander. Of course, I want that."

"Then let me take care of you and Alex. Let me do what I should have done all those years ago. Let me do that for the both of you."

She gazes up at me with misty eyes and nods. "I would love that." Leaning forward, she kisses me, and if Walter weren't about to join us any minute, if we were alone, I would solidify my promise by having her naked on this table, savoring her instead of finishing the half-eaten burger still on my plate.

I keep my eyes on her as she turns back and picks up her burger.

"Promise you'll do something for me, Princess," I add.

"What's that?" she asks.

"Do you still want that dream you spoke about?"

"To run a music academy to help disabled children."

"Yes."

"Of course. One day maybe, I'll get a chance to do that," she says, before finishing what's left of her burger.

"Is that why you agreed to do this job? Was the money going towards something like that?"

"No. It was to buy a home so Alex and I could move to somewhere better than where we currently live."

Her words hit me harder than a punch. While I've been living a comfortable life, I never even considered what her life has been like raising my son on her own.

"Damn it, Poppy. Is that what you were referring to earlier with that remark about run-down apartments?"

She holds my gaze for a moment, and under my intense stare, she answers, "Yes."

"Where do you live?"

It takes a few more agonizing seconds before she replies, "On the far east of town. The burger place you took me to is just around the corner."

As I sink back into the chair, I grapple with the harsh reality of how everything has unfolded. That part of town used to be the roughest, a place that both Ace and I would dread during our younger days. And now, it's the very place where Poppy and my son call home. The mere thought of it nearly shatters me.

My appetite fades away as I push my plate aside, struggling to comprehend how she ended up in such a situation.

Poppy wipes her mouth with a napkin, and all the while, I still can't wrap my mind around the circumstances that brought her to live in this place.

"Can I ask how you ended up there?" I turn and see her watching me.

"I couldn't stand living with my mother anymore. She was saying things to Alex that I didn't want him to hear?"

"Like?"

"It was mostly about you. But where we live isn't that bad. I have Mrs. B who lives across the hall, and she's like a grandmother to Alex. She watches him for me, so I don't need to pay for a babysitter when I go to work."

I sit up straight, resting my elbows on the table and burying my head in my hands.

A wave of relentless voices in my head keeps reminding me of the countless mistakes I've made and how I always end up hurting those who care about me.

"Xander," Poppy says, and I lift my head when I feel her hand on my arm. "I did what I had to do. It's not as bad as you think."

"I know you did," I say, hugging her tight, finding solace in the fact that our past is behind us. Whatever she and Alex desire, they can have it all, as everything I possess belongs to them now. I hold onto her a little longer before releasing her, my lips brushing against the top of her head in a gentle kiss.

"So, are you ready to meet your son?" she asks.

A blend of excitement and nervousness surges through my body as I smile and give her a nod.

She takes her phone out and swipes the screen, then presses a few buttons. Holding out the phone for a video call, I hear it ringing.

After three rings, Poppy's mother's face appears on the screen. Once she sees me next to Poppy, I see her body language instantly change.

"Hello, Mom, could you please put Alex on the phone?" Poppy says firmly.

I watch in silence as her mother pauses for a moment before she speaks. "Do you think that's a good idea?"

I can't help but hear her tone, the same tone she used on me that day when she called me a worthless lowlife and predicted that I would ruin her daughter's life.

"Please, just put him on. I really need to talk to him," Poppy says, her tone firmer this time.

It's clear that time hasn't healed the strained relationship between mother and daughter.

Her mother rotates the phone, placing it on a counter, and for a moment, I think she's hung up until I notice the seconds ticking away on the screen.

Poppy gives me a smile. "Are you ready?"

I nod, my heart beats frantically in my chest at the thought of meeting my son.

The phone turns around, but it's not Alex, it's Poppy's mother.

"You shouldn't be doing this, Poppy," she says.

"Just put him on, Mom."

Her mother continues to gaze at Poppy through the phone, and at that moment, I notice a small face appearing in the corner of the frame. It's as if he's curious to see who his grandmother is talking to. As soon as my eyes meet his, I am overwhelmed by the sight of a little version of myself with those same dark eyes. My heart begins to race so intensely that it feels like it might explode from my chest.

"Mommy," he says, in his sweet voice and accompanied by the biggest smile.

A warmth washes over me, unlike anything I've ever felt before.

While lost in my thoughts, I suddenly realize that Poppy's mother is no longer in the frame.

Alex's smile suddenly fades and his brow furrows as he focuses on me. I smile when I notice, he holds his brows and his mouth the same way I do when something is confusing.

"Do you know who this is?" Poppy asks.

"Yes, it's Daddy," he replies with a smile.

When he calls me that name, it tugs at my heartstrings, almost bringing tears to my eyes.

"Hello, Alex," I say.

"Hi, Daddy."

My heart melts for this little boy; it's as if I've traveled back in time, reminiscing about the days when I had a loving mother who meant everything to me.

"Are you almost done with your work, Daddy?"

I recall Poppy's words, mentioning that she informed him about my busy schedule and our impending meeting.

Glancing at Poppy, I find her smiling, watching the interaction as I smile down at my son.

"Yes, I'm just about finished. I'll be home soon."

"Have you seen a kangaroo yet, Mommy?"

I'm smiling so much that the muscles in my cheeks ache.

"No, I haven't seen one yet."

"What about a koala? Have you seen one of them?"

"No, not yet," she replies, "but if I do, I'll take a photo so you can see it."

"And see if you can get one that has a baby on its back."

"Come on, Alex, it's time to go," I hear Poppy's mother say through the phone, standing somewhere nearby.

"Gran said I have to go."

I hear the disappointment in Alex's voice, and I wish I could tell the old bitch to fuck off.

"Alright, sweetie. You be good for Gran, and I'll see you soon. Love you."

"I love you too, Mom. Bye, Daddy."

"Bye, little man."

Poppy's mother comes onto the screen. "Can I talk to my daughter alone, please?"

Poppy takes a deep breath and releases it in a huff, as if frustrated. Within seconds, the video call transitions to a voice call, and Poppy brings her phone up to her ear. I refuse to let that witch destroy the emotions coursing through me after finally having the chance to meet and speak to my son.

However, despite her mother's best efforts for a private conversation, her loud voice still penetrates through the phone.

"Do you really think that was a good idea, Poppy? After everything he put you through. He'll just leave you, and not just you this time."

I'm irritated by her words, so I pull my plate back towards me and finish my cold burger. The best thing to do is to fill my mouth with something so I don't tell the old bitch what I think of her.

"It's not your decision, it's mine and I'll decide what is best for my son. He's our son. He should know his father," Poppy retorts.

"When it happens again, I won't be there to pick up the pieces like the last time."

Poppy lets out another sigh. "Yeah, well you weren't there the first time either, no matter what you think. Goodnight, Mother." She ends the call and places her phone down on the table. I can tell that she's pissed. "I'm sorry she ruined that moment for you," Poppy says, leaning into me and resting her head on my shoulder.

I lift my arm and wrap it around her. "Don't worry about it. Nothing could ever ruin this moment."

Poppy straightens up as Walter approaches.

"How was it?" he asks.

"Best burger I've had in a long time," Poppy replies, with a smile on her face.

"Yeah, man, it was great," I add, standing up and grabbing my phone to pay the bill.

I give him a generous tip for not lingering and respecting our privacy.

"Send the demo and I'll call you to let you know our decision."

"Thanks, man. You should have it sometime in the morning," he says, walking us over to the door. "I appreciate the chance." He unlocks the front door and opens it.

Neil stands there, right where I left him about two hours ago.

Poppy says bye to Walter, then she goes over to the car and gets in while I shake his hand. Neil, who walks Poppy over to the car, comes back and waits for me, keeping an eye on what's going on around us. As soon as I get in the vehicle, the driver closes the door behind me.

I wrap my arms around Poppy, bringing her close. Leaning back, she rests her head on my chest, the sound of the car engine providing a comforting backdrop as we make our way back to the hotel.

CHAPTER 62

Poppy

I'm so pissed at my mom. It's not just about her ruining Xander's long-awaited meeting with his son. It's also about all the secrets she kept from me. Since Xander told me he returned to the house that morning, my anger at her has been steadily growing. If only she had listened to what he said that morning, instead of bombarding him with hurtful words, the outcome might have been different. Doing everything by myself made my life so much harder than it could have been. Her impact on my life has been significant over the years, and this is just one more example.

Xander has made it clear that he loves me, and his tattoo serves as a permanent symbol of his feelings. I'm not sure how any of this will work between us, to be honest. Xander lives a totally different life than what I m used to. As a rock star, he spends months on the road, traveling from one city to another on his never-ending tours. I'm uncertain about how Alex and I will fit into his life. He's told me he'd give everything up for us, but I don't want that. He's living his dream, and he's worked his ass off to make it come true. There is no way I could ever ask him to do that. I know him inside and out. Music is his lifeblood. I understand, because I used to feel that way too.

Lying in bed next to Xander, feeling his hand secure around my waist as he pulls me close, I'm wrestling with the practicalities of our future. The upcoming start of Alex's school adds another layer of complexity; it won't be easy for us to simply pack up and leave when Xander goes on his tours. Despite my strong desire for a meaningful relationship with him, there's a lurking fear deep down that my heart might break again. The idea of not surviving this heartbreak is crushing.

As his arm tightens around me, I feel the warmth of his embrace and the softness of his lips as he kisses my shoulder blade. "What's bothering you, Princess?" he asks, sensing the inner turmoil I'm experiencing.

"What makes you think there's—"

"Because I know you better than you think." His lips curve into a smile, and he playfully nibbles on my earlobe with his teeth.

"I'm just uncertain about how this will work. You're a rock star, always on tour, and surrounded by countless girls who are more than willing to fulfill your every desire on a daily basis. You claim you've never slept with them, Xander, and I believe you. But deep down, I worry that one day you might grow tired of me and be captivated by some beautiful girl. I have a feeling our relationship is headed for disaster. I don't know. Maybe it's because I've heard my mom go on and on about how my dad hooked up with every groupie he met."

"Princess, I've got it all - music, fame. But... I still feel like a worthless nobody, just like they all thought I was. I still-"

"I never saw you that way," I cut in.

"I know. You were the only one who believed I could truly make it. You and Ace. And now, I have everything. Yet, there's still something missing in my life. And that something is you, Poppy. You're the one absent thing." He holds me tighter in his arms. "Everything I own is yours. Even this fucked up thing inside my chest. And those groupies you mentioned who are up for anything, before you, they would have been everything I wanted to get my dick wet. But I didn't go there with them. I knew that if I gave in and fucked them, then all the moments we shared would mean nothing. I didn't want to cheapen what we had by fucking them because they didn't truly want me. They only wanted the name, the fame. That's all it would have been. And yes, there were many times when I let them suck my cock to get me off, but it never went any further than that."

We lay in silence for the moment, his thumb gently tracing circles on my hip, as if waiting for me to say something.

"I'm afraid to let you back in," I finally admit. "I'm terrified that everything will crumble, because I can't bear to have my heart shattered again. I can't go back to those nights of crying myself to sleep. Not just for my sake, but for Alex too."

"I may fuck up. It's a part of who I am. I know I'm not perfect, Princess, and I'll piss you off sometimes. I was a coward for walking away from you before, but this time, I promise I won't leave or hurt you or our son. Give me a chance to prove myself." He props himself up on one elbow and gazes down at me. "Let me be the man I should have been all those years ago."

While staring into his eyes, I pause to think about his words. I search for the truth, the unwavering commitment hidden within them. It's not often you see Xander being so open and honest about what he wants. He s let me see all that's in his heart.

"Okay," I add. "But you can't fuck with us because it's not just my heart on the line this time, it's our son as well."

"You can trust me, Poppy. I won't ever do that shit again," he says, leaning in, gently pressing his lips against mine, as if sealing his promise with a kiss. As his kiss gets hot and wild, I feel a crazy rush of electricity as his hands explore my naked body.

Chapter 63

Xander

After taking a shower together and making Poppy come on my cock two more times, I hold her hand and guide her towards the door, aware that I am running late for my meeting with the guys.

As much as I desire to stay in this room and make up for lost time, I know I have to go, as my brothers are expecting me.

I lead her down the hallway till we get to Ace's room, just two doors away.

I knock on the door and it swings open right away, and there greeting us is Theo instead of Ace. As he smirks, his eyes dart down to our intertwined hands, revealing his intention to fuck with me once again. That's just his nature.

"Took you long enough, dickwad," he says, turning and heading back into the room.

Upon entering the room, I spot Ace and Nate seated at the table, deep in conversation.

As I get closer, I see a bunch of papers neatly stacked in front of Ace, along with a big notepad and pen. He's been working hard on something. That's the reason we chose him to represent the band. Ace knows his shit. Ever since we lost our songs, he's all about reaching the ins and out of the legal details.

The moment Poppy lets go of my hand, I come to a sudden stop. I can tell she's feeling a bit awkward, thinking this is just a band meeting. But whatever we decide in this meeting is gonna affect her too, because I need to tell my brothers that I need to slow down. If the label gets too demanding and keeps me away from my family, I'll give it all up for her and Alex.

I slide my hand around her waist and stand behind her, holding her close against me. I couldn't care less what the guys watching me like creepy stalkers think. They're probably curious since they've never seen me like this with anyone ever. Not even when I let my guard down at Nate and Theo's party, just a month before we signed with the label. Okay, they were there in the room when I got a groupie to suck my cock, but that was it. I never let her touch me anywhere else. Like all the other groupies after that night, I only let them blow me to get off.

"Xander," she says, turning her head to look up at me. "I'll just sit on the couch. It's a band meeting."

"Come on over, Spitfire," Theo says. "It's all good. I've got a spot right here if you're interested." He pushes his chair back and pats his lap, inviting her to sit. Then he gives me a smart-ass grin.

"Fuck off, Theo," I grumble, annoyed. "No chance she'll be anywhere near you, asshole."

Theo bursts into laughter, and I catch Nate smiling at our playful exchange. As always, Ace maintains his grumpy demeanor.

I grab a chair and pull Poppy onto my lap, placing my hands on her hips, hoping she'll choose to stay there.

Theo and Nate are grinning like crazy as they stare at me. Seriously, don't those fuckers have anything better to do besides creeping on me? Sick, twisted assholes.

"Alright," Ace says, flipping through some papers on the table. "I've gathered a ton of information. I had Anita review the contracts we signed, and she pointed out a clause stating that if we decide to leave, the songs we've recorded and produced with the label will remain with them. This means we will never be able to play any of those songs in public again."

"But those are my fucking songs," I blurt out, feeling disappointed that some of the tracks were about the girl sitting on my lap. At the time, I didn't know what I was writing, but now that I do, I refuse to let the label own them. Those songs are mine, a reflection of how Poppy broke through my defenses and saw the real me. "How the fuck do we not have the rights over them?"

"Because of the clause in our contract that states..." Ace grabs the notepad and reads from it. "Any songs recorded under the label are the property of Victory Records. We all signed it." Ace looks around the table.

"So, what does that mean for us?" Nate queries.

"It means we're pretty much at their mercy," Theo remarks. "They practically own us."

"Not necessarily," Ace interjects.

The room falls silent as Ace's piercing gaze sweeps across the group, capturing everyone's attention, before finally settling back on me.

"You mentioned you've been writing songs and have enough for four albums."

"Yeah, so?" I respond, still pissed by the loss of my songs.

"I was thinking, once we're back home, we can check them out, record as many as we can, and then go off on our own."

"But we've lost all those songs," Nate states.

"Yeah, but think about it. How often do we play those songs anyway? I think on our set list for this tour, there's only one. The rest is our new stuff," Ace points out.

"Yeah but still that's our biggest hit to date," Theo says.

"So, what exactly are you proposing, Ace?" Nate asks.

"We should take a break and record Xander's songs. Then we can pick which ones go on an album and drop two albums a few months apart. By doing this, we can leave our old stuff alone. In the meantime, Anita is on the lookout for a loophole in the clause so we can get our songs back. Our sound is what it's all about, not the shit the label forces on us. Plus, we could use some downtime. With everything going on with Xander, it would give him a chance to bond with Alex and reconnect with Poppy. I think taking a break will be good for all of us. Then, maybe in about six months to a year, we can think about touring again. What are your thoughts? We all need to be fully in on this. You know the rules."

Nate leans back, arms crossed, and looks at the group. "We've been doing this for four years, always on the go. I'm grateful for what we've accomplished and the money we've made, but I'm fed up with being just a puppet for the label to stick their hand up our asses. We don't get a say in what happens. We've seen the world, but what have we really seen? Stadiums, hotels, buses, and interview rooms. It's irritating. Our days are jam-packed with radio and TV interviews, then we perform, then hit the road again. Let's tell Reg right now that we're done with that shit. I'm in Sydney for fuck sake. I've always wanted to climb the Sydney Harbour Bridge. And that's never gonna happen with the schedule they give us. So, I'm with Ace on this one. They've been using us, and we need to stop it.

"Yeah, he's right," I say. "We only get time off between tours or when we have to learn some idiot's new song that doesn't even match our style. Or it's time wasted in the recording studio or some damn interview with me trying to fix some messed up shit I'm accused of, all because of Reg and the Label. From now on, everything changes. Starting with the interviews. Why the fuck do the four of us have to do it when one person could do it. When the four of us are there, we only answer a couple of questions anyway, when one of us could just do the whole fucking thing. We should share the interviews around so we can do whatever the fuck we want. And we'll make sure it's over the phone. That way, we can do our own shit, and at least see a bit of the country we're in. I fucking love you guys. You're my bros and I love the music we create. Not that shit they make us play, but our music. But I can't keep going on like this, not now when I have other factors to include in my life." I give a smile to the beautiful girl on my lap before shifting my gaze back to the boys. "I have a son who I have four years of catching up to do. My girl and I need to build a life together. I've lost so much of that life already. And I don't want to give this up, but if we stay with the label, I'll have to. Family comes first for me, not the damn label."

"But I don't want you to give it up for us, Xander," Poppy says.

"I understand, Princess, but it's what I want." I plant a gentle kiss on her cheek, then shift my gaze back to my brothers.

All three, seated around the table, exchange glances with one another.

"So it's settled then," Ace says. "We go out on our own."

"I don't want you guys to decide just because of that," I explain. "I'm just saying I can't keep dealing with the way they manipulate us all the time. It would crush me if I lost what truly matters to me again." I don't have to say anymore. The boys know exactly what I'm talking about.

"I think we should break away and go solo," says Nate. "Our band wouldn't be the same without its frontman. Xander Williams is the heart and soul of Broken Oasis. I swear, I'd quit if one of my brothers weren't here making music with me."

"I agree," Theo nods.

Nate and Theo shift their gaze towards Ace.

"Don't worry, man," Ace says. "After witnessing all the messed up shit on this tour, I'm the one proposing we break free. Plus, I wouldn't want to do any of this without you guys. It's who we are, a broken bunch of assholes who understand each other. Nothing can ever break that bond. And as time goes on, our lives are bound to change. We can't keep going on like this for years under the label. It's better if we record our own music and have control over it. So, are we all in agreement that this will be our final tour under the label?"

"I'm in," I say.

"Me too," says Nate.

"Let's do it," says Theo.

I give Poppy a big squeeze, relieved that I can finally put all my energy into building a life with her and our son, without the constant pressure of the label. When Ace talks, I lean my chin on Poppy's shoulder, eager to hear what else he has to say.

"Okay," Ace says, picking up the pen and jotting a few words down on the notepad. "Starting today, let's make it clear to Reg that only one of us will be doing the interview." He takes out his phone and taps a few buttons. "Kit has two radio interviews this afternoon and two tomorrow."

"Wait a sec," Nate says, whipping out his phone. "First, I wanna see when I can do the bridge climb. There's a few spots in the morning," he says, looking up. "Anyone interested?" He looks at Theo. "I know you won't be, since you're afraid of heights." Then he gives Ace and Poppy a look, and finally me.

"Yeah, I'll go," Ace says.

"Xander, Poppy," Nate inquires.

"Nah, I wanna go to the zoo," I say. I've heard Alex ask Poppy twice now if she has taken any photos of kangaroos or koalas, and I've been trying to figure out how to make that happen with our hectic schedule. So now I can arrange that for them.

"I'm going with Xander," Theo quickly blurts out, flashing me a smile. By the way he's looking at me. I know he's waiting for me to object, thinking he's intruding on my time with Poppy, but I can't refuse him when I know how much he loves animals. I can't even count how many times I've walked into his house to find him watching Animal Planet. The dude would never forgive me if I told him he was not welcome.

"What do you say, Poppy?" Nate asks again. "Wanna join Ace and me for the bridge climb?"

"I'm not great with heights either. Besides, Alex has been asking if I have any photos of kangaroos and koalas, so I'll go with Xander and Theo."

Nate turns back to his phone, presses a few buttons, and then places it face-down on the table. "It's booked for six in the morning," he says, glancing at Ace.

"Okay, then that means Nate and I will handle the two radio interviews this afternoon," Ace states. "Theo and Xander, you guys will take care of the ones tomorrow. Is there anything else I should inform Reg about, besides mentioning that this tour will be our final one under the label?"

"Can they potentially sue us?" Theo asks.

"According to Anita, no, they can't, because our contract doesn't specify a length of time. So, we're not breaking any rules there. It only states that any music produced by the label is theirs. As long as we don't play the ones copyrighted to them, they won't be able to sue us."

"Can I be there when you let that asshole know we're done with his crap and the labels too?" Theo asks.

"Why don't we hold off for now?" I butt in. "There are still twelve days left on this part of the tour, so you know how it's gonna go down. Reg will keep acting like a school kid. Let's just tell Kit that one of us will handle the interviews from now on, and we can do it over the phone instead of going into the studio. And if Reg brings it up, that's when we'll come clean. He might not even notice it with all the shit he's got going on right now."

"Okay," Ace says, "but as soon as he starts on Kit, that's when we tell him."

"Deal," Nate agrees.

"Hold on, let me make sure I've got this right. I have a free day today and tomorrow." Theo glances around the table. "Hey spitfire, come see me in my room?"

I open my mouth to tell him to save that shit for his groupies and cougars he flirts with, but Poppy beats me to it.

"Well, since I'm already seeing you... Theo, I hate to say it, but you're just not doing it for me."

I notice his smug grin transform into a huge smile as he gazes at her. He clearly appreciates her strength, just like I told him years ago. Nothing seems to shake her. His attempts to flirt are falling flat with her. He can't get under her skin like he can with me.

"Leave her alone, idiot," Ace says as he gets up from the table. He quickly taps a few buttons on his phone before making his way to the other side of the room. "Hi Kit," he says, then heads towards a bedroom.

"When you come to the zoo tomorrow, make sure you bring a disguise so that no one recognizes you. And seriously, don't hit on anyone while we're there," I say firmly. If he ruins my day of taking photos for Alex, there'll be hell to pay.

"Seriously, you think that wig and hat hide your identity?" he smirks.

"Yeah, they get the job done. Just make sure nobody knows it's you."

Ace returns. "It's done. I've informed Kit to let me know if Reg causes any trouble."

"How did she take it?" Nate inquires.

"Fine. She couldn't understand why they set up the interviews like that, anyway. So, it's not a problem."

"I'm fucking starving," Nate says, getting up from the table. "Come on, let's go down to the bar, celebrate, and grab something to eat.

I give Poppy a little tap on her leg, signaling for her to get up.

"Give me the lowdown on my little nephew, Alex," Nate says, casually putting his arm around Poppy. It's all good because it's Nate. But if it was Theo, it'd be a whole different ball game because he's such a flirt who always loves getting under my skin. Nate's loyalty is unmatched. He wouldn't even think about hitting on another guy's girl. He knows how much Poppy means to me, and he and the guys already see her as part of our family.

Theo comes over, stands beside me, and watches as Ace opens the door for Nate and Poppy to leave the room.

"You've got it all, man. You've achieved everything you've ever wanted - the dream life, our music, the girl, and the family we've always longed for. I'm happy for you, bro." He playfully slaps my back.

I turn to face him, ready for his usual smartass cocky smirk. But he's really being sincere.

"Thanks, man. My only job now is not to fuck it all up."

"Nah, she's more forgiving than that," he laughs, slapping my back again. "You've already fucked up big time, and yet she still wants you. I don't get it though. Not when she could have me whenever she wants, but hey, each to their own." His smart-ass grin comes out and the fucker just can't help himself.

"Are you two assholes coming or what?" Ace, the grump, says, still holding the door open for us.

Theo is the first to move forward. "Yeah, alright, Mr. Personality," he replies. "Wouldn't hurt to crack a smile once in a while."

CHAPTER 64

Poppy

The next morning, we're all pumped and ready for our trip to the zoo. I can't help but smile as we wait for Theo to arrive. Xander sits next to me in the foyer, wearing his blonde wig and red cap. When people walk by, they can't help but stare at his crazy outfit. Makes me wonder if his eccentric outfit attracts more attention than if he were simply being himself.

My mom once again complained about Xander talking to his son last night. Seeing their bond grow makes me feel all warm and fuzzy inside. It's clear that Xander is just as eager as I am to connect with our son every evening. I'm pretty sure my mom will make things even more difficult when they finally meet face-to-face.

This morning Mrs. B messaged me to let me know her daughter passed away. And that she was sorry that she wouldn't be able to care for Alex as her family needs her. I swiftly responded, assuring her it was fine and expressing my condolences for her loss. This news really saddened me, and all I could think about was how I wished I could be there by her side, offering her comfort, just like she is always there for me.

I'm not looking forward to the conversation I need to have with my mother tonight. I need to ask her if she can take care of Alex for the remaining time I'm away.

I wonder if there will be any restrictions put in place for her to do it, like Xander not having anything to do with his son. But if it comes down to that, I'll just go home. I'm sure Xander will lend me the money if it comes down to that.

Glancing down at the floor, my mind is occupied with our conversation last night and how excited Alex was when Xander told him we had plans to go to the zoo today to see the kangaroos and koalas.

Xander leans back in his seat. "What's wrong, Princess?"

I lift my head. "Just thinking."

"About?"

"Alex staying with my mom until I get back. Initially, I thought it would be okay with Mrs. B looking after him, but now..."

"Now you're worried about him."

"Yeah, you could say that."

"I've been thinking about that, too. Not about him being with your mom, but about meeting him. I thought maybe we could fly back home during the five-day break while they set things up in New Zealand."

"Seriously?"

"Yeah, why not? I can't wait to meet him. Plus, I wanted to talk about a few things."

"Like?"

"Besides your mom living there, is there anything holding you back in that crappy town?"

"No, I lost my job."

"Just a thought, but how about you and Alex come live with me in my house? What do you think?"

We both divert our attention to a person standing in front of us and the moment I look up, I'm on the verge of bursting into laughter.

"Fucking hell," says Xander.

Standing in front of us is Theo, sporting a completely ridiculous disguise. He proudly displays a thick, seventies porn stache, which compliments the hideous sideburns. To complete the outfit, he rocks a black cap, letting his wavy, dark shoulder-length hair peek out.

"What do you think?" he queries, turning his head from side to side, so we can evaluate everything.

"Did you just get off some seventies porn set," Xander says.

"Why? What's wrong with it?" Theo runs his finger over his mustache.

"You look fucking ridiculous," Xander says.

"Can't look any worse than you, asshole."

"Are we good to go?" Xander asks, getting up from his seat.

Neil comes forward and takes the lead, and I can't help but notice the big guy is smirking at Theo. He walks ahead, leading the way toward the car Kit arranged for us.

The car swiftly transports us from the hotel to Circular Quay, passing by the bustling city streets. Our next adventure begins as we board onto a ferry that will take us to the zoo. Throughout the entire journey, Neil stays close by, keeping a watchful eye on all of us.

Unfortunately, Theo's stomach churns uncomfortably during the ferry ride to the zoo, prompting us to move outside in search of relief in the refreshing breeze. As we step outside, I am immediately captivated by the sparkling, glimmering water, its surface mirroring the radiant glow of the sun. I gaze towards the Harbour Bridge, the iconic structure stretching across the water, and ponder if Nate and Ace are still strolling along its majestic path. Xander stands right beside me, and together we take in the breathtaking view of the picturesque landscape. Meanwhile, Theo sits behind us, constantly grumbling for the remainder of the journey.

As we arrive at the zoo, the sounds of laughter and chatter fill the air, while the sight of children running reminds me of Alex. I wish he could be here with us, savoring every moment of this experience. I wish he could witness it all—the kangaroos and the koalas that he adores so much, instead of just seeing them in a photo. I want to give him everything. I want him to have a life where he can follow his passions. To grow into a young man knowing that the world is full of endless opportunities. That's my wish for him as he continues to grow - that he embraces every opportunity that comes his way.

Xander and I stroll through the zoo, hand in hand, while Theo, our knowledgeable guide, effortlessly educates us about every animal we encounter. I wonder if he had a similar love for animals as a child like Alex does.

As we spend our time here, heads turn as people catch glimpses of the guys in their amusing disguises. Unable to resist, I take a photo, a keepsake that will always bring a smile to my face.

When we reach the Australian animal enclosure, I eagerly feed pellets to the kangaroos. Xander grabs his phone, capturing them as they eagerly munch on pellets in my hand.

Throughout it all, Xander eagerly shows me the photos he's taken, each one capturing a moment of pure happiness that he knows will bring joy to Alex. Seeing Xander like this, the desire to create these precious moments for our little boy fills me with deep gratitude for his dedication to our family.

As we continue to explore the exhibit, we spot a few Koalas peacefully snoozing high up in the towering trees. Unfazed by the challenge, Xander continues his quest until he discovers one close enough to capture on camera.

By the time Xander finally captures a photo he is satisfied with, our stomachs rumble with hunger. It's lunchtime.

Xander takes hold of my hand and guides me back along the path towards the main entrance. Walking beside him, Theo engages in conversation about their upcoming radio interviews this afternoon. Before their discussion shifts towards branching out on their own, Xander mentions to Theo that he has Walter's demo on his phone and that he should check it out because it's really impressive. By the sounds of it, Walter might get his big break after all.

Watching Xander and seeing the man he has grown into makes me proud. He's such a kind and caring person, always thinking of others. He's changed so much from the boy I remember. It's common for fame to inflate egos, but with Xander, it's clear that he's motivated by more than just that. He strives to be the best version of himself, and I genuinely admire that. I genuinely like the person he has become.

As we arrive at the eatery, Neil takes the lead, carefully surveying the surroundings before kindly holding the door open for us to enter. The place is bustling with people, the aroma of the rich food mixing with the lively conversations. We skillfully navigate through the crowd, hoping to find an unoccupied table. After what feels like an eternity, we finally spot one and I quickly take a seat, feeling a wave of relief wash over me as I finally give my tired feet a well-deserved break.

After Xander consults with Neil and me about our food preferences, he and Theo head off to place the order, while Neil remains at the table with me. As we engage in small talk, our conversation revolves around the animals we've encountered during our time at the zoo.

Xander and Theo waste no time and swiftly return, balancing large trays of mouthwatering food. Burgers, fries, donuts, drinks. It all looks so good. While we eat, we pass around our phones, sharing the vibrant photos we snapped earlier in the day.

After finishing our meal, we venture outside, searching for a shaded spot in the grassy area to escape the heat. While Xander and I enjoy the cool shade, Theo momentarily vanishes, leaving Neil to stand at a respectful distance, giving us privacy, his gaze fixed in the direction Theo went.

"Thank fuck," Xander says, sitting on the grass. "I finally get you alone," he says, as he grasps my wrist and guides me to sit between his legs. "I swear that idiot never stops talking."

As I sit down, he lovingly wraps his arms around my waist and gently pulls me back, so I am nestled against his chest.

"You wouldn't change him if you could," I say, a smile forming as I think of Theo and his quips.

"Nah, probably not," Xander says, his warm breath tickling my neck, as he gives me a gentle kiss.

We stay quiet, taking in the scene as people walk by.

"We should visit this place again, but with Alex next time." suggests Xander.

"Yeah, I'd like that," I reply.

As I turn my head to look at him, his lips meet mine in a tender kiss.

When I turn my gaze back, I spot Theo making his way towards us, balancing three enormous ice cream cones - two chocolate and one strawberry. He savors the sweet taste of the strawberry-flavored one before making his way over to Neil, offering him a chocolate cone. Then he comes over.

"Here you go, Spitfire," he says, offering me the last chocolate cone.

"Thank you," I say, leaning forward to accept it before it dribbles down the side of the cone due to the heat.

"Where's mine, asshole?" Xander asks.

"You have that interview in a few minutes," Theo responds, sitting on the grass next to us.

"Shit," Xander says, leaning to the side so he can retrieve his phone from his pocket. "I forgot about that."

I savor a mouthful of chocolate ice cream, letting out a groan of pleasure. Xander observes me closely, smirking, and I know exactly what's running through his mind.

With a smile, I offer him a taste of my ice cream. His mischievous gaze remains locked on me as he leans closer. As I observe him licking the ice cream, I can decode all the inappropriate thoughts running through his head.

His eyes widen in surprise as the burst of chocolate flavor overwhelms his taste buds.

"It's good, isn't it," I remark.

"Yeah, I'll get one after the interview." He leans forward to kiss my cheek before he gets up.

"Don't worry, fucker," Theo says, a mischievous grin spreading over his mouth. "I'll show her a good time."

Annoyed by Theo's antics, Xander doesn't even have time to respond before his phone rings. Xander swiftly swipes the screen and brings the phone to his ear, shooting an intense glare at Theo. Despite the tension, Theo still laughs out loud.

As we indulge in our ice-creams, Xander distances himself from us and the noisy crowd.

"You make him happy, you know," Theo speaks up. "He was the biggest pussy when I first met him."

I tear my gaze away from Xander and shift my attention to Theo.

"So, what's the deal with you two now?" Theo inquires. "Have you sorted everything out?"

"So, what's the deal with you and Nate? You don't hear me asking about that?"

Theo laughs out loud. "Okay. I'll give you that one." He takes a few more bites of his ice cream, leading me to believe that's the end of the conversation. But then, he surprises me by speaking up again. "He told me all about you," he confesses.

"He told you about me?" I can't help but wonder just how much Theo knows about our shared history.

"Yeah, but not at first," he says, while licking the ice cream melting down the side of the cone. "Back in the day, Nate and I threw these parties just to have a good time, and I gotta admit Xander was a real hit with the ladies. But he had no interest in hooking up with them. Instead, he'd just get completely hammered. Honestly, I thought he might've been in the closet and didn't want anyone to know."

I can't help but burst into laughter.

"So I asked him, and that's when he told me about you. It finally made sense why he couldn't hook up with chicks. I got it because I'd been there. I told Nate because I knew he would get it since he went through something similar." He pauses, his voice catching a bit. "There you go, Spitfire. I've got the whole backstory." He goes back to eating his ice cream.

"Back it up. You walked away from someone too. What is it with you guys?"

He shakes his head. "No, we didn't let her go. She died suddenly." His gaze shifts, and I notice his eyes start to water.

"Oh, Theo, I'm so sorry," I say.

"It's alright, Spitfire." He looks at me and offers a small smile. "No way you could've known."

I pause for a moment before bringing up another topic. "I noticed that you and Nate seem to have a close connection. I saw you in his bunk bed."

With his ice cream now finished, he shifts his position, stretching out his legs and crossing them at the ankles. He then leans back, propping himself up on his elbow. "I was wondering if you saw that. Just to clarify, there's no romantic thing going on between us. We don't fuck each other or anything like that. Nate is like my rock. Despite my tough childhood, he has been my best friend for as long as I can remember. We practically lived next to each other growing up. Whenever I couldn't handle my nightmares, I'd secretly go to Nate's house.

After a while, he started leaving the window open for me, knowing I needed someone when my mind went crazy. I was just a kid, around nine. So, I'd crash in his bed. Having him by my side was comforting because I knew I had someone I could trust and I wasn't alone. Even now, those nightmares pop up, but having him around helps me cope. It helps me get through them."

Theo's story touches my heart, as it reveals a side of him that contrasts to his usual cheerful demeanor. It's hard to believe that someone so happy could have experienced such a challenging childhood, which has evidently had a lasting impact on him.

Reflecting on my upbringing, I realize that my life has never been as tough as his. I only had to deal with an overbearing mother who projected all her insecurities onto me, nothing compared to what this guy must have gone through.

But Theo bears the scars of that childhood. Growing up a few houses away from Xander, I witnessed the hardships he faced and how he continues to grapple with feelings of low self-worth. It's truly heart-wrenching to imagine what Theo must have endured in his life.

"Well, I'm glad you have Nate," I add.

"Me too," he says.

We both look up as Xander approaches. He exhales deeply, a frown evident on his face indicating that something is bothering him.

"That doesn't look good," Theo says as he sits up.

Xander joins us, plopping down on the grass next to me. He stays silent for a moment, his intense gaze fixed on the ground.

"Don't worry, man, she didn't fall for my charms," Theo says teasingly, attempting to lighten the mood.

Xander lifts his head and looks at Theo. "It's out. Reg didn't do shit to keep it quiet. They asked me about the fifteen-year-old girl."

"Fuck, bro," Theo says as he leans forward. "What did you say?"

"I told them everything. That our manager set it up, you know, like he's been doing for years just to get some publicity. I didn't hold back. I even texted Ace to give him a heads up about what went down and that the label might reach out to him because shit is about to hit the fan."

"What did Ace say?"

"I haven't heard back from him yet," he replies.

"We should go and sort this shit out now," Theo says, and I hear the worry in his voice. "We should get together and come up with what I should say because they'll ask me the same questions later. Fuck." He looks down at his watch. "I've got an hour and forty-five minutes. We need to sort this shit out." He's up on his feet, ready to go.

Xander and I stand up.

Neil takes the lead as he walks ahead.

"Poppy and I have to go to the gift shop to grab a few things," Xander says, slipping his hand into mine. "Then we'll sort this out, Theo," he reassures, patting him on the back with a comforting touch.

CHAPTER 65

Xander

After my recent phone interview with one of Sydney's top radio stations, I know there will be consequences. The news is bound to spread like wildfire. I was completely honest and firmly rejected any insinuations about my involvement with the young girl that could damage my reputation. My heart goes out to Theo. He's got his interview later today and now that the media have wind of what happened, he'll be bombarded with questions. Theo's right. We need to come together and work out how to tell the truth about what's been happening with the label all these years.

It's time to reveal that it's been Reg who sparks the headlines, painting me as a rebellious rocker with a carefree attitude. This portrayal is far from the truth. I never wanted Poppy to think I was a player or that she didn't matter to me. Unfortunately, the media has painted me in a different light. Whenever they get a hold of photos of me standing beside beautiful women, including models and celebrities, they always write some bullshit article that portrays me as a womanizing rockstar.

It's annoying how people have been misrepresenting me all these years, so let's set the record straight. Especially now, I don't want the media distorting my relationship with Poppy, making it seem like she's just another name on a long list of women I've supposedly banged. That's why I feel like I have to come clean about what Reg has done. Once he's sorted this shit out, I plan to give an interview upon my return home, setting the record straight for everyone to hear.

Reg's bullshit has once again ruined my day, abruptly cutting short our enjoyable visit to the zoo. I was enjoying every moment I spent with Poppy, and her infectious smile, as I tried to capture as many photos of the animals as I could for our little boy. But the way the media hounded me with questions during that interview, I know we need to go and prepare ourselves for the shit storm that is coming our way.

With Poppy on my left, holding a stuffed kangaroo and a koala for Alex, and Theo on my right, burdened by his two hefty bags, we make our way to the carpark. Earlier, I sent a quick message to Kit, filling her in on the incident and asking her to arrange a speedy car to pick us up.

The three of us squeeze into the back, while Neil sits in the front passenger seat. As the car moves, I remove the cap and blonde wig, running my fingers through my sweaty hair. Theo does the same, peeling off his fake mustache and sideburns. I'm about to burst into laughter when I see his bright red sunburned face, with the white outline of a mustache and sideburns. But before I can tease the fucker, my phone pings.

Ace: Fuck. I thought that asshole was handling it.

I quickly type my response.

Xander: We're on our way back. Theo's stressing about the interview. Can you come back?

Ace: Yeah, we're on our way now. We'll meet you in your room as soon as we arrive.

I put my phone back in my pocket.

"Was that Ace?" Theo inquires,

"Ace and Nate are on their way. We'll sort everything out," I confirm.

Theo nods, then pulls out his phone and starts scrolling through it. I quickly steal a glance at Poppy, who is quietly observing Theo.

"Man, it's all over the news," Theo states, before tossing me his phone. There are two photos, one of me and the other showcasing the girl that Reg was supposed to take care of. The headline boldly declares, "Band manager arranges 15-year-old for frontman."

Poppy leans in beside me, eager to see what Theo has discovered. As I start reading more headlines, a wave of emotions washes over me. It's always the same shit with the media, never getting any of their fucking facts straight. All I can think about is the second I see Reg, he's gonna get a fucking punch to the face for dragging me into his mess once again.

"What are you going to do?" Poppy asks.

"I have no fucking idea," I state. "He's always dragging me into shit like this. None of it has any truth to it. Well... except the one time I trashed that hotel room. That was legit. But everything else is fake."

I give Theo back his phone. I notice his leg nervously bouncing up and down as he continues scrolling. "This is really bad, man. It's fucked. I'm not sure I can handle this," he confesses.

I can see that he's on the verge of losing his shit. It's evident from his restless fidgeting and the way he bites his bottom lip. To an outsider, it would seem as though he's a junkie desperately searching for his next fix. Normally, Nate would step in, easing his tension. But without Nate here, I don't know what to do. When we hang out, we're usually chilling, laughing, and drinking beers. Not this. Maybe I should shoot Nate a text and fill him in so he can help Theo calm down?

Right when I'm about to text Nate, Poppy's voice breaks the silence. "What did you get from the gift shop?"

As soon as Theo meets her gaze, I notice a distinct change in his mood. He places his phone on the seat next to him and reaches into one of the bags. Excitedly, he pulls out a small elephant and proudly shows it to Poppy. Then he unveils a gorilla, a giraffe, and a kangaroo. Passing them to her, I observe their interaction, and it's as if he has effortlessly returned to his usual self.

"I've got something for the little guy," Theo says. "I hope it's okay?" He withdraws a plastic Hippo head on a long stick, with a lever at the bottom. Pulling the lever causes the Hippo's mouth to open and close. Theo proceeds to give Poppy a quick demonstration.

"He's going to love it," she says, with a smile.

Right then, it hits me - my band brothers are going to fully embrace Poppy and Alex. Alex will have three uncles who, without a doubt, will shower him with love and care, simply because he is a part of me.

Theo consistently shows off all the shit he bought at the zoo - magnets, snow cones, and an array of other treasures. As we approach the hotel, Theo regains a sense of calm and composure, thanks to the influence of my princess, adept at handling situations where Nate would typically take charge.

Once we get to my room, Theo gets all worked up again.

"Where are they?" he asks, anxiously checking his phone. "I only have forty minutes left before I have to do this."

"Don't worry, man. I'll handle the interview," I volunteer, hoping to ease Theo's burden.

A sudden knock on the door captures our attention. Poppy rushes over, and opens it, expecting to find Ace and Nate outside. However, to her surprise, it's Reg who stands there, his tone indicating clear displeasure.

"Where is he?" he snaps at Poppy, forcefully barging into the room. As his eyes meet mine, his expression darkens. "What the fuck have you done?" he accuses, approaching the table. "Lionel just called me and he is absolutely livid."

"Yeah, well, I'm not fucking thrilled either, asshole. It's out, and I won't take the blame for some shit I didn't do, especially not this," I retort.

Another knock prompts Poppy to open the door, this time it's Ace and Nate.

"Why is he here?" Nate asks. "I thought this was supposed to be a band meeting."

"Yeah, it is," I proclaim, my voice laced with frustration. "The asshole just walked in."

"What's going on?" Reg asks, scanning the room. "Are you really having a band meeting without the band manager?"

"Reg, listen the fuck up," Ace says, moving closer to the table. "I just talked to Lionel, and I told him straight up that this is gonna be our final tour with the label because of this problem. Lionel and I agreed that it's on you to fix this problem. He suggested you handle Theo's radio interview." Ace glances at his watch. "Time is running out, Reg. You have thirty-five minutes to sort this shit out, and if you don't, Lionel knows we'll go to the media back home and expose the truth."

I can't believe how Ace just put Reg in his place, and judging by their expressions, neither can Nate and Theo. It's really impressive to see the big guy in action, being assertive, and finally standing up to the label.

Reg scans the four of us, then his gaze lingers on Poppy.

Stepping forward, I know I'll lose my fucking shit if he starts on her.

"Reg, it's time for you to go and fix this shit," Ace says, giving off an authoritative vibe. "Or would you prefer me to call Neil to show you the way out?"

In the intense face-off between Reg and Ace, Reg's phone starts ringing.

"You should answer that," Ace calmly suggests.

Reg grabs his phone from his suit pocket, turns, and heads for the door. We all just stay there, watching him leave with the phone pressed up against his ear. As soon as the door clicks shut, our attention immediately returns to Ace.

"Yeah, man," Nate says. "You showed that prick whose boss."

I move over to Ace and give him a congratulatory pat on the back before heading over to the fridge, wanting to grab a few cold beers to share. Seeing Ace like that reminded me of the time when we were younger, not letting anyone control us.

"I don't have to do the interview," Theo asks.

"Nah, let that asshole handle it," Ace responds, making himself comfortable at the table. Nate and Theo take their seats and join him.

"Did you talk to Lionel?" Theo asks, beating me to the question.

"Yeah, he did," says Nate. "And man, it was fucking awesome. He didn't hold back at all."

As I turn around, holding a few beers in my hand, I spot Poppy sitting on the armrest of the couch. I get she might feel like she's imposing sometimes, but I really want her here. The fact that the guys actively include her is a clear sign that they share the same sentiment.

As I distribute the beers, I find a spot next to Poppy on the couch. With a twist, I remove the lid and offer her the cold beer. She takes a sip before giving it back to me.

"So, what was his reaction when you told him everything that happened?" I ask, casually tossing the bottle top towards the bin in the corner.

"He was furious at first. He said if we stayed with the label, he'd find someone else to replace Reg. But I made it clear that it was more than just that. We wanted more time off, the freedom to own our songs - you know, all the stuff we've been talking about."

"And how did he react to all of that?" I inquire, casually taking a sip from my beer.

"He said he would come back with an offer," Ace says.

"Maybe whatever he offers won't be all bad," Nate suggests. "We can check out their proposals, set our terms, and see if they can meet them. Let them take care of the hard stuff."

"Yeah, we'll check out their offer, but I don't think they'll give us the freedom we want," says Ace. He then shifts his focus to Theo. "Alright, spill it. What happened to you today?"

All attention shifts towards Theo as he scans the group. "What do you mean?" he inquires.

Thanks to Theo's sunburnt face, the distinct mustache-shaped white outline, and his disproportionately large sideburns, it's clear what Ace is referring to.

"Just look in the mirror, dumbass," Ace says.

Theo rises from the table and walks to the elegant mirror hanging on the wall. I catch sight of his smirk and our eyes meet in the reflection. "This will definitely give the groupies something to talk about," he says.

Ace, with a roll of his eyes, reaches for his beer while I can't help but smile and shake my head. Meanwhile, Poppy bursts out laughing.

"Don't encourage him," Nate says, smiling, as he grabs his beer.

CHAPTER 66

Xander

Talking to Alex each night is the one thing I always look forward to, as it adds a spark of joy to my day. It's truly incredible how much love I already feel for this little boy, despite having just met him a few days ago. Whenever we talk, I can't help but notice the clear disdain and hatred in Poppy's mother's expression as she watches me interact with my son.

Despite Poppy's insistence that it's an issue solely between us and our child, the disapproval continues to linger. In the past, the previous version of myself would have easily told her to fuck off without a second thought. Though I still feel the urge, I resist the temptation, knowing I need to be a positive influence for my son now.

Throughout my life, there have been people who have looked at me as if I am worthless, the same way Poppy's mother does. However, having Poppy and Alex in my life has filled that void. They make me feel worthy, like I mean something. Now I know my behavior needs to be better.

After the recent media interview that brought up questions about the fifteen-year-old girl, Ace has assumed the role of the band's decision-maker, while Reg has taken on the main responsibility of handling the ongoing barrage of inquiries from the media.

Ace recently had a conversation with Lionel, who suggested that once Reg resolves the situation, he will depart on the next flight that becomes available. None of us have taken part in any radio or television interviews since the incident took place, and surprisingly, it's been to our advantage. We'll have time to do all the fun stuff we've been missing out on.

From what I gather, Lionel doesn't appear to be excited about us leaving the label, even though he hasn't officially made an offer yet. Ace believes that there might be something on the table once we return home, but at least Reg is no longer constantly pressuring me or giving any attitude to Poppy. That's a plus.

As the curtains draw to a close on yet another night's performance, fatigue begins to take its toll on me.

Our next destination is Brisbane, and tomorrow we begin a two-day journey, opting for the scenic route and making stops at the towns where our interviews were initially planned.

With Reg now taking care of things and working to fix the mess he made, we now have the opportunity to discover the charm of these small local towns. We can visit the cozy restaurants and friendly pubs, enjoy a few beers, and meet so many warm and welcoming people. I genuinely love the relaxed atmosphere that Australia offers.

On our final evening in our room, before we head back to the cramped bunk beds on the bus, I plan to fully embrace the comfort of the hotel room's king-size bed. It's the perfect chance to engage in my favorite activity - getting my girl naked and pleasing her.

As we ascend to the top floor in the elevator, Poppy remains quiet, her thoughts elsewhere. Her mind is consumed by the conversation she had with her mother earlier, while we were driving back to the hotel. The constant disapproval and scrutiny from her mother regarding my relationship with my son not only impacts Poppy, but it also affects me. I struggle to understand why her mother can't just stay out of it.

I wrap my arm around her waist, pulling her closer to me. Her eyes lift as my knuckles softly brush against her jaw while she studies my face.

"Don't worry, Princess, everything will work out," I assure her. "In a little over a week, we can finally be a family." The mere thought of it brings me immense joy. It's the kind of loving family environment I have always longed for, particularly after the heartbreaking loss of my mother.

She nods, her blue eyes fixed on mine, and not a single word escapes her lips. As the elevator doors part, Neil, steps out, leading us towards our room.

It has been another long night, but it was worth it. Poppy had such a great time at Walter's burger place, I reached out to him again. And guess what? He was incredibly accommodating! One thing I really appreciate about him is that he's not one of those guys who likes to stare; he respects our privacy. Those moments of uninterrupted closeness, just the two of us, hold a special place in my heart. Don't get me wrong, I love spending time with my bandmates and the camaraderie we have, but I also crave those quality moments with Poppy.

Walter was thrilled when I told him I had shared his demo tape with the guys. They were all excited and agreed to it, and we will stay in touch regarding the tour plans. It feels amazing to have the means and resources to help others now. That's the most fulfilling part of being in the spotlight - the ability to make a positive difference in other people's lives.

"Thanks, big guy. I really appreciate it," I say to Neil as I open the door to our room.

Poppy smiles at him, "Goodnight, Neil."

"Goodnight, Poppy," he responds, and every time I witness their interaction, I can't help but notice a gentle smile adorning the big guy's face. In all the years he's been with us, I've never seen him like this. His tough exterior hides a more tender side.

As we step into the room, Poppy's breath catches when I pull her closer, pressing her against the door. Our lips touch, sparking a fire inside her, and she passionately wraps her arms around me, matching the intensity of my kiss. She's the addiction I've always yearned for, a desire I've held onto. My grip on her hip tightens as she digs her nails into my scalp, both of us wanting more. With my arm wrapped around her waist, I guide her backward towards the bed.

When we reach the bed, I lower her onto the soft mattress and lie on top of her. I'm so turned on and I grind my hard cock against her. She lets out that soft moan that I fucking adore.

"Fuck. You make me lose my mind, Princess."

I'm fighting the urge to rip the clothes off her body and fuck her right now.

As I press my lips against her jawline, her eyelids flutter close. I gently graze my teeth along the velvety curve of her neck. The scent she exudes is absolutely intoxicating.

"Brace yourself for a wild night. We're gonna be in bunk beds for two nights, so I'm gonna make the most of it by fucking you all night long." I feel her shiver under my touch, and it brings a smile to my face.

I slip my hands under her shirt and strip it off her. Planting a tender kiss between her breasts, I slowly make my way to her erect nipples.

"This needs to go," I suggest, playfully tugging on the lace of her bra.

She reaches behind her back to unclip her bra, forcing her tits into my face. Feeling restless, I teasingly bite her nipple, a mischievous smirk on my face as I grow increasingly impatient. The only thing I crave is skin-on-skin.

I take in the sight of her semi-nakedness. She's just as gorgeous as before, and her tits have gotten a little bigger, but fuck, they're still flawless.

She lets out a soft moan as I playfully circle my tongue around her hard nipple. Enjoying the sounds she makes, I shift my attention to the other one, well aware her eyes watch my every move. Her next moan brings a smirk to my face. I fucking love it.

As I glide my lips along her body, I press delicate kisses down her skin until I reach her belly. With a gentle touch, my fingertips trace the silvery stretch marks just below her belly button.

She's tense, as if she wants to shield them, as though she fears I'll only see her imperfections. When she tries to cover them, I grab her hands to make her stop.

"Never hide them, Princess. You're beautiful to me. You always have been," I say, softly caressing her skin with my fingers. "Did you get these marks when you were pregnant with Alex?"

I pick up on her hesitation, her eyes searching mine, and then she takes a deep breath and gives me a slight nod.

I tenderly place a kiss on her stomach, on top of her stretch marks. "I love you, and I love your body. You're perfect just the way you are."

Letting go of her hands, I observe her closely as she moves them to her sides. My gaze returns to the stretch marks, and I feel a deep affection, a reminder that she carried our child.

I treasure how her body bears the evidence of nurturing our son. I wish I could have been there to experience the joy of feeling her stomach as our son grew, to kiss it, and to witness the beauty of her body transforming with the creation of life. My son, the little guy who already holds a piece of my heart. She has given me the most incredible gift one person can give another.

I unbutton her jeans, carefully undoing the zipper and sliding them down her hips. Within seconds, I'm on my feet, removing her jeans from her legs.

As I toss them aside, I stand there checking her out. She lies on the bed, gazing up at me, her long blonde hair cascading around her like a halo, accentuating her flawless features. Her gaze fixed on me as I slowly remove her panties. She fidgets slightly, and I can't help but wish she didn't have any insecurities. If only she could see herself how I see her - perfect in every possible way.

"Jesus, look at you." My gaze sweeps over her naked body. 'You're so fucking perfect.' I trail a finger down her wet slit. "Open, show me that pussy." I'm getting all excited as she opens her legs. "Wider," I whisper, my voice rumbling with a gravelly tone. "Show me everything, Princess." Lowering onto my knees at the foot of the bed, I lick my lips and zero in on her pussy. "I'm gonna make you come so fucking hard." That's the only warning I give her before I glide my tongue over her clit.

She lets out a desperate, needy sound, that makes me smirk.

I lick a heated circle, then playfully flick her clit, eliciting soft whimpers as she basks in the overwhelming sensations.

Her moans of pleasure fill the room as she tightly clenches my hair, her fist forming a firm grip.

"Fuck yeah, you've always liked that," I tell her before sucking on her clit, listening to the wet sounds that escape my mouth. "Keep making those sexy noises," I say, going deeper, passionately devouring her.

As I introduce a finger, she lets out a muffled moan, her body responding to the rhythm of my tongue against her sensitive spot. When her hips arch, it takes the experience to a whole new level.

"Xander," she breathes out, and though we've only just begun, I can sense she's almost there. I slip in another finger, teasingly withdrawing them before easing them back in.

"Oh, God," she moans, her voice laced with a seductive breathiness that I've always found sexy.

When I sense that she's on the verge of exploding, I remove my finger and plant a soft kiss on her thigh. She lifts her head and stares down at me.

"Xander, I was so close," she confesses and I hear the disappointment in her voice.

"I know," I reply with a smug smirk before giving her clit another lick. "Eyes on me," I tell her when she glances up at the ceiling.

"Are you planning on tormenting me the entire night?" she asks.

"Why do you want something from me?" I ask, grinning mischievously, while lazily giving her another lick.

"Yes," she moans.

This time, I stay there, savoring the taste with slow, gentle licks that leave her dizzy with pleasure.

'Xander,' she says all breathy as she pulls hard on my hair. I can't help but think that when she removes her hand, I'll be left with a bald spot. She's focused on me as I flick my tongue on her clit.

"Oh God, please, I beg you not to stop this time, or I'll die."

I suck harder on her swollen clit while my fingers curl inside her. Finally, she lets go, shamelessly grinding against my face, her moans grow louder and more desperate.

My tongue and fingers find that spot that always drives her wild. A sharp cry pierces the air. She's incredibly vocal, and I adore how I can manipulate her, treating her body like a musical instrument, skillfully moving my tongue and my fingers to produce each sexy sound. It's seriously the hottest fucking thing I've ever seen.

All the teasing and anticipation of building her up is completely worth it. I take pride in the overwhelming, mind-blowing orgasm that crashes down on her.

I continue to savor her taste even after she comes, causing her body to shiver.

When she can no longer bear it, she yanks my face away from her pussy. I can't help but grin, knowing that I've reduced her to a whimpering mess.

"That was fucking hot," I say, before pressing my lips against hers. "Taste yourself," I whisper, and she eagerly responds, engaging in a passionate kiss that allows me to explore her mouth with my tongue. It's hot and demanding. Just the way I like. I love the way she effortlessly mirrors my every movement, making me crave her even more.

As soon as she attempts to reach for the button on my jeans, she lets out a tiny squeal as I flip us over on the bed so that she's on top. When Poppy gets down on her knees, I lift my hands behind my head, eager to watch my naked princess unbuttoning my jeans and pulling down the zipper. She quickly removes my jeans and boxers, and I can't help but watch the way her eyes zero in on my hard cock.

"Kiss it," I command her.

Leaning forward, she presses a soft kiss onto the glistening tip, playfully teasing me like I did to her before.

"More," I say. "Kiss it the way I kissed your pretty little pussy."

She obediently opens her mouth and licks up the creamy droplet forming on the tip. A soft moan escapes me as she circles her tongue around it.

"That's it," I say, all breathy as she teasingly explores the tiny opening. I let out another groan, urging her to do it again.

As she takes the tip into her mouth, my throat constricts. I firmly hold the base of my cock, while my other hand glides through her soft hair.

"Open wider," I instruct. I slowly feed her my cock, gradually stretching her mouth around me. My jaw clenches as she takes me deeper, so deep that I graze the back of her throat.

Despite all the times I allowed groupies to pleasure me orally, none of them compare to the sensation of Poppy's mouth. I used to close my eyes and imagine it was her, but it never felt quite right.

'Fuck,' I add, closing my eyes when she gags.

With a grunt, I pull all the way out, causing a string of saliva to appear between us. 'Do you know how fucking sexy you look right now with my cock in your mouth?" I thrust inside again, loving the way my body coils, the way my dick pulsates on her tongue, the way she sucks hard.

'Christ, I want to fuck your face.' I hold her gaze, a feral sound escaping me, as I feel I'm losing control.

"Do it," she says.

I firmly hold on to her hair, providing her with a brief warning before forcefully thrusting in and out of her mouth, my actions growing more intense, more wild. When I feel her throat relaxing, I increase the speed.

'You like the taste of my cock, Princess.' Saliva drips from her chin and tears well up in her eyes as she nods. 'Show me how much you like it.'

Rising to her knees, she devours me completely. Her suction grows stronger, intensifying the pleasure. A deep, primal moan escapes me as I thrust into her mouth, fully aware of her desire to please me.

"Fucking hell." I thrust my hips forward. 'You're gonna make me come, Princess?" She moans around my cock as I increase the speed. I can feel my muscles straining. I'm on the edge. So fucking close. Just one more thrust does it. I let out a groan as waves of pleasure shoot through me, as I release my warm essence into her throat.

"Swallow it," I tell her. "Take it all like the dirty girl you are."

As I ride out my orgasm, Poppy shows no signs of slowing down, eagerly letting me savor every moment of pleasure. Fuck I love her. Love her with all my heart.

"Good girl," I say, pulling out of her. Leaning in, I kiss her, tasting myself. "You're fucking perfect. I love the way you suck my cock." Rising from the bed, I wrap my arm around her, helping her up from her knees. I lead her towards the bathroom, ready to indulge in another session with my filthy princess.

CHAPTER 67

Poppy

Although I'm feeling sore between my legs after a long and wild night with Xander, I wouldn't want it any other way. I can tell you, that man sure knows how to please a woman. Although walking is uncomfortable, I know I'll long for his gentle touch tonight as he lies across from me in the narrow bunk bed.

I'm pretty sure Xander could tell I was feeling down last night because of my mother constantly interfering and her belief that she knows what's best for me in my life. I know Xander could sense it by how quiet I had been on our way to the hotel. When he surprised me by going back to Walter's restaurant to grab a burger, I couldn't help but smile from ear to ear. It's incredible how, despite being apart for so many years, Xander has become so in tune with my emotions. He used to have a sense of when I felt insecure or experienced similar emotions, but now it feels as though he can almost read my thoughts. He understands me on a deeper level than I ever thought possible.

The countdown is on. With just a little over a week left before Xander, and I fly home so he can meet our son, I'm filled with excitement to see my little boy again. The ache of missing him is so intense that it feels like a part of my heart remains in the States. Xander and I have spent countless hours discussing every detail of our future together, a future that I thought would never happen.

The idea of sharing our lives as a family and moving into Xander's house fills me with immense joy. It's the life I've always dreamed of - the three of us together. However, as the years passed and Alex's birthdays came and went with no acknowledgment from Xander, it felt distant and unattainable.

My doubts grew even stronger when I came across tabloid images of Xander with models and actresses. But after spending five and a half weeks with the band, I know the truth. Reg would manipulate Xander like a canvas, painting vivid stories to generate media buzz about the band. Now I realize how foolish I was to question Xander's love for me. All these years, his love for me has remained unwavering. The way he interacts with our son further solidifies my belief that we are on the path to creating a strong and loving family.

Yesterday evening, Xander informed the band that he will be flying back home after their final concert in Brisbane. He explained to them that Kit has organized a flight for us to head back to the States and reassured them he would be back in time for sound check in New Zealand.

I was stressing about how the band would react to their frontman's absence, especially as they start their tour in a foreign country. They were super excited for Xander to see his son.

I really like the guys in the band. Surprisingly, all the guys have a newfound sense of joy now that Reg is no longer around. I can't help but laugh at the way Ace's annoyance grows as Theo continues his mischievous antics. Nate is such a sweetheart, with his kind and caring nature.

Just last night, I had the pleasure of observing Nate in the green room. He was engaged in a conversation with a young boy, who was merely nine years old, accompanied by his parents. The sheer excitement radiating from the boy at the opportunity to meet his idol, Nate, was truly overwhelming. My heart swelled with warmth as the boy shared his dream of emulating Nate, confidently stating that he could flawlessly match Nate's beat to all of his songs. But the most heartwarming moment occurred when Nate handed the young boy his drumsticks. The pure joy and happiness emanating from that little boy nearly brought tears to my eyes.

As the guys gather in our hotel room to work on the specifics and rehearse one of Xander's new songs, I text Kit and invite her for a drink. Kit, along with Neil, are always up for a drink.

Catching up with Neil and Kit they tell me about rumors going around about Reg. It seems that Lionel told Kit that Ace was in charge of the band until he found a new manager. And that every request from the band is to be fulfilled. It seems like Lionel is taking the boys seriously. I suppose he would, especially when the label's main money maker is on the verge of leaving.

Neil revealed to me today that witnessing Xander's connection with his son has served as a source of inspiration for him to forge a similar bond with his own son. He asked Kit for assistance in locating his son, hoping to reconnect with him. Despite knowing it might be too late, Neil remains hopeful. However, he's concerned that his son may reject him, especially since his stepdad has played a large part in raising him.

Kit also informed me that once the band is done in Australia, Lionel instructed her to book Reg on the earliest flight back, which happens to be the same one Xander and I will be on. However, there's a catch - the label will cover the cost of our tickets, but they insist on Xander and me flying first class, leaving poor Reg to endure the cramped seats of economy. Right now, Reg has no idea, and Kit will probably have to handle his complaints when he finds out about the seating.

Standing in the left wing of the stage, the powerful sound of the crowd's thunderous roar fills the air and sends shivers down my spine. As Xander commands the stage, the energy in the air becomes palpable, buzzing with eager anticipation. The way he effortlessly connects with the eighty thousand people here is truly mind-blowing.

Singing in front of people always makes me feel anxious, but for Xander, it's as if he was born to do this. Back in our teenage days, I could picture him singing in front of thousands of people, and now, witnessing him on this stage, there is no way I would allow him to sacrifice any of this for us.

As another song reaches its end, I watch him take deep breaths, his gaze sweeping over the crowd. He makes his way across the stage, where Nate sits behind his drum set, eagerly waiting for Xander's cue. Xander takes a drink before returning to the microphone. I've memorized the band's set list and there are only two more songs left before the climactic final performance.

In the past, hearing him sing it would stir a hint of sadness. However, now it symbolizes so much more. It's true what he says. It's our song. Despite the fans claiming it as theirs, it will always be ours. It's the thread that connects us in our special way.

Casting a glance my way, Xander flashes that sexy smirk.

A hush falls over the crowd as eighty thousand individuals collectively hold their breath. With eager anticipation, we all wait to see what he's about to say.

"We have a new song to share with you," he announces.

The crowd's excitement reverberates with a deafening crescendo, filling the air with a powerful roar. The moment Xander raises his arms, the crowd grows quiet as they hang onto his every word.

"This song is special to me because I wrote it during a really hard time in my life. I felt the absence of someone special. So, this song goes out to anyone who's felt the heartbreak of losing the most important thing in their life."

The crowd erupts in cheers, and the stadium is bathed in the glow of thousands of phones as Xander turns his head and signals to Ace. Ace effortlessly glides his fingers over the strings, creating a tender melody that gains momentum as Nate and Theo join in.

Throughout the entire song, Xander keeps glancing at me, his gaze lingering, before turning back to the crowd to continue singing. The song is so powerful and moving, evoking a sense of sadness and emotion. It undoubtedly captures the moments and feelings he experienced when he left all those years ago.

As I listen to the lyrics, tears start flowing down my cheeks because of the songs raw and vulnerable nature. It feels as if he has truly let his guard down. The moment the song ends, the crowd erupts into a thunderous chorus of cheers, the sheer force of the sound vibrating through my entire being.

Standing with a smile, Xander extends his hands, immersing himself in the atmosphere. He turns his head to his bandmates, all of them sporting smiles as they soak up the energy from the crowd. This is their essence, what they thrive on - being seen as godlike, living out their dreams of reigning supreme in the music industry.

I am in awe as I observe them. That broken boy from the past, the one who resorted to stealing chocolate bars to survive, has undoubtedly made it, just as I always knew he would.

In the midst of the crowd's ongoing cheers, Nate begins to count in the next song, and the setlist continues according to plan.

As always, a nervous energy sets in whenever it's time for the last song. My anxiety heightens as I observe Xander grabbing the stool and my dad's guitar, slowly making his way toward the microphone. It's a poignant moment, not only because of the emotional connection to the song and my deep affection for this man, but also because a part of my dad is up there on that stage. He's living out a dream that always held a special place in my father's heart - performing in front of thousands of people.

"This one is for us, Princess," he says, his eyes meeting mine. In that instant, I sense the undeniable love he has for me. It emanates from him, erasing any doubts I once had - a love that I once questioned and never fully grasped. But now, I will never doubt it again, not with the sincerity in his eyes and the heartfelt way he expresses his love for me.

As he sings the opening lines, a serene and somber atmosphere settles in the air. The voices of the crowd merge, generating a harmonious sound as if all eighty thousand people in the stadium have congregated for this one moment. Their combined singing overpowers Xander's voice through the speakers. It transforms into their song, a moment they all rejoice in - a shared encounter that belongs to every single one of them.

I take a few steps to the side to get a better view of the crowd. Their phones are raised high, illuminating the air with flickering lights as they passionately sing along with Xander. I know that this is a moment that I will remember for the rest of my life.

Turning my head to look at Xander, I see Ace, Theo and even Nate with drumsticks in hand moving forward to stand beside him and witness this incredible sight. With arms draped over one another's shoulders, they form a tight-knit brotherhood, fully embracing the profound significance of the moment they have brought to life.

As the song nears its end, Nate seamlessly returns to the drums, while Xander delivers the final chorus with an epic flare, marking the last show in Sydney.

The stadium pulses with an electrifying energy, echoing with thunderous cheers.

"Thank you, Sydney. We love you!" Xander declares, before putting the microphone back into the stand. The rest of the band members come forward and stand next to Xander.

Amidst the enthusiastic cheers, they graciously wave to the crowd, expressing their gratitude one last time before making their way off the stage. Xander takes the lead, and the rest of the band effortlessly follows suit. It's a common sight - they consistently walk behind Xander, as if he effortlessly commands the stage. However, there is no trace of envy or ill will among them, only a sincere and deep respect.

As soon as Xander reaches me, he gently lifts me up and embraces me tightly, pressing his lips against mine in a passionate, intense kiss. It's overflowing with raw emotion, leaving me momentarily breathless.

As the band members pass by, they warmly pat him on the shoulder before heading to the green room for the meet and greet. The dynamics in that area have also changed since Ace took charge. The absence of the pressure that Reg used to exert is noticeable. Even though groupies still seek moments to hook up with the band, it feels more relaxed.

I still feel uncomfortable when groupies offer their breasts for Xander to sign, but I understand it's part of being a rockstar. I observe as he flashes his signature sexy grin, takes photos with them, and gives away merchandise. But what I have noticed is when he's finished mingling with them, I see the disappointed look on their faces knowing that they won't be with Xander tonight. Above all I trust him. I never want to end up like my mother.

When the meet and greet is over, Neil guides all of us towards the tour bus. Reg is already inside, engrossed in his laptop, not bothering to acknowledge us as we all board. The guys exchange a look, suggesting that the upcoming trip to Brisbane won't be a pleasant one due to all the tension caused by Reg.

"If you're riding on this bus with us, Reg, don't expect to get the good room," Nate says, walking past our bags at the front of the bus, where they are always placed when we board.

We all stay there, watching Nate, wondering what he's doing as he moves towards Reg's room. From the corner of my eye, I catch sight of Reg turning his head to watch Nate. Not a single word leaves his mouth as Nate enters his room.

As I peer through the open doorway, I see Nate snatching Reg's bag from the bed and fling it out the door, landing at Ace's feet. Without wasting a moment, he retrieves the expensive suits that are hanging in the compact closet before making his way out of the room. "This room is no longer yours," he declares, casually tossing the suits onto the couch. "It's now reserved for family. Our family."

Reg stays silent, his attention returning to his laptop. I notice him swallowing.

"Xander and Poppy, you guys are family. Why don't you guys take the room?" Nate suggests.

"I'm happy to sleep in the bunks," I say, not wanting any special treatment since I'm not the big money maker here. I'm not the one out on that stage, pouring my heart out every night for the adoring fans.

Xander steps forward, grabs our bags, and claims the room.

"Well, I guess that settles it," I say, making my way towards the room. "Thank you for the room."

Xander grabs my hand and pulls me into the room.

Wasting no time, Xander closes the door and pulls me down on the double bed. As we lie together, he wraps his arms around me and snuggles his face in the crook of my neck. "I love you," he whispers, holding me close. He's been telling me that every day since he confessed his love for me. And every time he says it, I just fall harder for him.

"I love you too," I tell him, and the loving look he always gives me when I say those words is something I will always treasure.

In the days that follow, Xander and I find our connection growing stronger as we engage in meaningful conversations and make it a priority to speak with our son every night. I can see the love and excitement reflected on Alex's face, just as it is on Xander's.

During our journey to Brisbane, we make our customary stops at unique little towns along the way. Ace proposes that it is now Xander's turn to step into the limelight and reveal the truth of what happened. As Xander conducts all the interviews for the next two days, the guys keep me entertained. Theo and I take the opportunity to explore the local ice cream parlors, while Nate ventures out to discover the local restaurants. We all, including Xander, have a delightful lunch together. Sometimes, it's just Ace and me strolling the streets, browsing through the shops. Despite his usual grumpy demeanor, he attempts to engage in small talk. It's a bit awkward, but I appreciate his efforts.

What truly stands out is that Xander is the one who holds the band together.

With each passing day, I feel a surge of excitement as we get closer to reuniting with our son. But bringing back all the stuff we've collected is gonna be a real challenge. With the long-awaited reunion drawing near, Xander's emotions are a whirlwind of eager anticipation and nervous apprehension.

During our stay in the hotel in Brisbane, Xander plans a few intimate dates just for the two of us. Being a fan of simplicity, he surprised me one night by ordering room service as soon as we got back to the hotel.

While we enjoyed our meal together, we indulged in a binge-watch session of The Real Housewives of Beverly Hills. The trip down memory lane brought tears to my eyes, and Xander laughed before he gave me a loving hug. That's when he confessed he's addicted to the show, which earns him some playful teasing from the guys back home. Xander also said that he has hooked Theo on the show, and the two of them often share beers while watching the entertaining antics of the Beverly Hills bitches.

Sometimes I pinch myself just to check if this is real. My life was completely different just six weeks ago, crazy right? I never imagined being so happy. I love this guy more than I ever thought possible. Along with my son, he is everything. It's truly mind-boggling that the person I once saw as using people to get what he wanted, and my longtime school crush, turned out to be the one who loves me deeply and makes me feel whole. It's funny how life works out sometimes.

Chapter 68

Xander

By the time we finish performing and make our way off the stage, I can feel the sweat dripping down my face and soaking through my shirt. With our final performance in Brisbane over, our Australian tour has come to an end. This country will forever leave a lasting imprint on my heart as the place where I discovered everything I ever yearned for.

Ace mentioned that I don't have to attend the meet and greet tonight because of our flight, but I really want to. Despite all the drama in the media, my fans are still my top priority. They are the ones who have given me this incredible life. And now that it's not just groupies in the greenroom looking for a quick fling, I genuinely enjoy engaging with those genuine fans who are excited to meet us.

Last night, Walter texted me and said his band snagged tickets to the Brisbane concert and they would all be there. I invited them to chill with us backstage in the green room after the meet and greet. I told Kit, and she made sure we had plenty of beers and food to share with everyone.

They seem like a great group of people, always laughing and supporting each other, just like our own little family. Three guys and a girl. Although, I have a suspicion there's a love triangle going on between Walter, Kyle, and Sofie, with both guys vying for her attention. We ended up chatting about music until the early hours of the morning.

I'm genuinely surprised that Theo was actually interested in leaving the groupies behind for the night in order to connect with another band. Perhaps us going out on our own could be a positive thing for Theo, encouraging him to start taking things more seriously.

As I make my way down the long hallway towards the green room, my eyes instinctively search for Poppy. Throughout the night, I found myself repeatedly looking towards the side of the stage, only to remember that she remained at the hotel, managing everything and ensuring we left nothing behind.

Kit has arranged for a car to pick me up in twenty minutes, which will then take me to the hotel and eventually to the airport. Thank God we don't have to share a ride with Reg to the airport.

The thought of finally meeting Alex is causing me to feel uneasy. Even though we've talked a lot, I'm kind of nervous about meeting him in person. I'm stressing about not meeting his expectations as a dad. Also, I'm scared of fucking it up. I have no clue what Poppy's mother has told him about me. Has she portrayed me as a worthless jerk who abandoned his mother because I didn't want him? One thing I know for sure is that I want a life with both of them. Throughout the years, I've realized I'm nothing without my girl, and now that I have a son, I know I'm nothing without him too.

Just before we enter the green room, my bandmates wait for me by the door. When I approach, they lift their heads. It's strange seeing them like this because usually it's just Ace who waits for me. It's kinda strange to see Theo and Nate waiting because they're usually in there, with Theo mainly checking out the groupies.

"What's going on?" I say, coming to a stop in front of them.

"It's gonna feel strange traveling to another country without you," Theo says, and I can feel the sentimental vibes creeping in.

Damn, this is the last thing I need right now. I look at Ace, and his fake smile tells me he'll miss having me around.

"Shit, you're making it seem like I won't be back."

"We're just gonna miss you, man, that's all," Nate says.

Theo steps forward and hugs me, slapping my back in a brotherly way. "We care about you, man. We understand you gotta do your thing, and we're really happy for you. Since we might not have a chance to say goodbye later, we're saying it now."

"Okay, but I'll be back in five days," I reply, giving him a friendly pat on the back.

"Yeah, I know. But It's gonna be different. Who am I gonna fuck around with now?"

"Hurry up, asshole, we need to say our goodbyes too," Ace urges Theo.

Theo takes a step back. "Let us know how your meeting with the little dude goes."

"I will."

Nate steps up and gives me a hug. "Hope it all goes well, man."

"Thanks," I say as he breaks away from the hug. I throw Ace a glance. "Can you do me a favor and watch my guitar? I don't want it to get damaged or lost."

"No problem. I'll throw it in with my stuff. Don't sweat it, it's all good." He studies me for a moment. "Remember when we got wasted on my old couch in the garage? Where we'd chat about having a family someday."

I nod.

"We always said we'd be there for our kids, loving them and not messing up like our dipshit dads. And now, here you are, actually doing it, dude. You're gonna rock this whole dad thing. I'm so proud of you, man!" He reaches out his hand and pulls me into a tight, brotherly hug.

I'm getting all choked up by what Ace just said, tears and all. Hearing him say he's proud of me hits me because no one other than my mom and Poppy has ever said those words to me before.

Stepping back, I hear Nate sniffle. As I glance over, I see him wiping tears from his eyes. "I don't want to hear shit from any of you fuckers, got it," he warns, his eyes scanning the group.

Theo, always goofing around, casually throws his arm over Nate's shoulder. "Aww, you're such a big softy."

As I watch them, the full magnitude of this moment becomes clear to me. Despite our diverse backgrounds, we have formed a strong bond as a unified family. Our achievements are tied together, and I'm sure our bond will remain unbreakable.

A door abruptly swings open behind Theo, and Kit appears, casting a glance in our direction.

"Sorry," she says, sensing the tension between us. "They're getting a bit restless." She takes a quick look at me. "I thought you were going back to the hotel." Kit checks her watch, then looks at me. "The car's waiting out back to pick you up. If you step in here, you won't make it out in time, and Poppy's likely waiting for you at the hotel."

"Well, I guess I'll see you guys in New Zealand," I say, glancing at everyone. They all nod in agreement, and a tinge of sadness washes over me as I turn away from them. Walking down the hall, I feel their eyes still on me as I embark on the next phase of my life.

CHAPTER 69

Poppy

After catching a connecting flight and loading our bags into the hire car that Kit organized for us, I can't help but feel excited. In just about ten minutes, I will finally get to see Alex.

Throughout the plane ride home, Xander has been unusually quiet. I've tried to get him to open up about how he's feeling, but it feels like he's locked his emotions away. I'm not exactly sure what's going on with him.

I haven't informed my mother that I'm coming back today. There is no way I can face another lecture about how I'm making the biggest mistake by letting Xander back into my life. I've reached a point where her negativity has become unbearable to me. We are a family, and nothing in this world will ever take that from us.

"What does it feel like to be back in your hometown?" I ask Xander as we turn onto the street where we both spent our childhood years.

"It's kinda weird, honestly. I never expected to come back, but here I am, returning for the second time in just ten weeks."

As we pull up to the curb, Xander parks the vehicle out the front of my mother's house. I can't help but notice that his eyes are locked on the house two doors down, its lawns overgrown and its windows covered with boards. Without saying a word, he turns off the engine.

"It's even more run-down than I remember," he observes.

"Is that the reason you've been so quiet? Is it because of coming back here and having to relive everything?"

His eyes meet mine and I see his expression change.

"What if I fuck it up? What if I have no clue how to be a dad to Alex?" he says.

I can see he's struggling just by the way he swallows, his throat tight and tense.

"You won't, Xander," I reassure him.

"Poppy, you don't know that. I'm fucked up."

"But I know you. I know you love that little boy with every ounce of your being. I've seen it."

"I'm completely clueless about how to be a dad."

"I didn't know how to be a mom either until I became one," I say, gripping his hand. "I've seen how you two hit it off every time you interact. It's clear how much you love him. That's all that matters. I understand it's scary. I was terrified at the idea of having a child as well. But you can do it. You'll get through it, and each day it gets easier. Xander, there's no way you could ever mess this up. Trust me."

"You always have a way of doing that. You always see the best in me," he says, gently brushing my hair away from my face. "That's one of the things I adore about you, Princess." Leaning closer, he presses his lips against mine.

As he reaches for the door handle, he lets out a shaky breath. "Alright, let's do this," he says, opening the car door.

The moment I step out of the vehicle, Xander is right by my side, hands tucked in his pockets, gazing at my mother's house. I can't help but wonder if he's reminiscing about all those moments we shared - the meals we enjoyed together while indulging in our favorite show.

He opens the front gate and holds it open for me to walk through. Just as we are about to reach the steps leading up to the front porch, the front door swings open, and there's my mother.

Without uttering a word, she closes the door behind her. The second she turns around, her eyes lock on Xander. Her intense glare means trouble is coming.

"What is he doing here?" she spits, her scornful words cut through the air. She stares defiantly at Xander, her eyes piercing through his soul.

"Well, hello to you too, Mother," I say, sarcastically.

Standing firmly on the top step, my mother peers down at us, her gaze filled with intimidation, asserting her authority and making it clear that Xander is not welcome here. I wonder if she used the same tactics on the day he returned all those years ago, that morning when he attempted to approach her.

"I want you off this property immediately, or I'll call the cops," she says to Xander, still refusing to acknowledge my presence.

"Mom!" I shout, desperate for her to stop this behavior right now.

Xander is my future, and she needs to accept that we're a family now. I haven't had a chance to let her know that Xander didn't know about Alex, because I want to talk to her first about what she's done and how it's impacted my life. If I go into all the specifics, I'll completely lose it with her, and I don't wanna risk that, especially if Alex can hear us. That's why I think we should discuss this in private.

"It's all good," Xander says, turning to me and planting a kiss on my cheek. "I'll wait by the car."

"But-"

"Don't worry, Princess. Just come back out when you're ready to go." He gives my hand a comforting squeeze, then he walks down the path and exits through the gate.

Shaking my head in disbelief, I can't believe my mother could treat Xander that way. I move forward up the steps, passing my mother. Her habit of demeaning him, and disregarding his importance, infuriates me more than anything. It wouldn't kill her to treat him with some respect.

She follows me into the house, complaining all the way.

"Why is he here? Has he pulled the wool over your eyes again? I thought you were smarter than that after what happened last time."

I stop and face her. She's so close, I almost hit her. "You're the reason he left last time?" I spit, my anger making my words loud and forceful. "Why didn't you tell me he came back that morning?" She stays silent, but the look on her face says it all. "Oh yeah, I know all about that and the nasty things you said to him."

All of a sudden, the back door screen bangs shut, and tiny footsteps echo through the house.

"Mommy! Mommy!" Alex sprints ahead and jumps into my embrace, tightly wrapping his small arms around my neck and drawing me near. As his cheek presses against mine, I can feel the coarse texture of sand sticking to his damp skin. Leaning back, a broad smile spreads across his face, and I can't help but be reminded of Xander by the striking resemblance.

He then looks around the room. "Did Daddy come too?" he asks, his voice filled with hope. It's baffling how my mother can still have a problem with Xander being here, even after witnessing moments like this.

"He's out the front," I tell him.

Alex wriggles free from my arms. As soon as his feet touch the floor, he bolts towards the front door.

"Don't go onto the road!" I shout before he bolts through the front door. When I hear the screen door slam, I turn back to face my mother. I'm ready now to have the conversation I've been longing for ever since I found out Xander had returned that morning.

"I can't believe you lied to me. All these years, you made me think I didn't matter to him. But the truth is, he came back here that morning to tell you how he felt about me. He was even planning to ask me to go with him when he left."

"Oh my god, I can't believe this. So, if you meant something to him, where has he been all these years?"

I don't appreciate her harsh tone, so I respond in a similar manner. "He didn't know about Alex."

"Oh, don't be so foolish. I never raised you to be that way."

"There is no way you could ever understand what we have," I spit, turning and making my way down the hall to grab Alex's things so we can get out of here.

My mother follows, but I have no clue where Alex has been sleeping. So I head straight to my room.

"You're making a huge mistake!" She shouts, behind me.

"No, the biggest mistake I made was listening to you and letting you fuck up my life."

"And what happens when he leaves you again? I won't be there this time."

"You were never there for me, anyway."

Opening my bedroom door, I see Alex's bag on my bed. His neatly folded clothes sit on the dresser next to it.

"You're constantly pointing the finger at me for everything that's gone wrong."

I suddenly stop and face her head-on. "That's because you're the one to blame for most of the things, especially this. Every time I don't go along with what you want, you get all mad and start telling me what to do. I thought distance would fix things, but it just made me realize that nothing will ever change between us."

I make my way over to the dresser, collecting Alex's clothes and neatly packing them into his bag.

"Just so you know, Alex and I are leaving. Xander invited us to move in with him, and I've accepted his offer." I don't know why I'm even bothering to tell her that. Maybe to make her believe that she's mistaken about Xander and he wants both of us.

"You'd be a fool to do that. He'll only break your heart again, and not just yours, but the heart of that little boy who already idolizes him."

I pause packing Alex's clothes and give her a quick look. "You can either be happy for us and accept my decision, or you can choose to stay here and be upset about your life, not knowing your grandson."

As I quickly grab Alex's shoes from the floor, I glance back up to find my mother standing there arms crossed tightly over her chest, her lips pressed together in a display of anger.

"I want you in our lives, but it's difficult hearing you criticize the one I love. Please, just accept my decision and be involved in our lives." I stand there, desperately hoping she understands my desire for her to be a part of both my and Alex's life, and how grateful I am for the time she has been spending with him recently. I want us to keep our relationship going, free from judgment, just like a mother and daughter should be. "What do you say? Do you think we can put everything behind us and make a fresh start of it?"

"Are you staying with him?" my mother asks.

"Yes, Mom, I am staying with Xander. I love him. I always have."

Upon hearing my response, she moves towards the door. Just as she's about to walk out of the room, she turns to look back at me. "When he breaks your heart again, don't expect me to be here for you or Alex."

Her words sliced through my heart, leaving a sharp, lingering ache of rejection from someone who is supposed to love me. Sitting at the edge of the bed, I am left speechless, my mind racing to process her words. It's hard to believe that she would simply walk away from us like that, especially after forming a close bond with Alex. I could feel her becoming colder and more distant over the years, but I never imagined she would become so heartless.

Rising from the bed, I grab Alex's bag and exit the room. With a determined effort to hold back tears, I make my way towards the kitchen, hoping to find my mother. To my disappointment, she is nowhere to be found. Feeling a wave of sadness wash over me, I pick up the opal necklace, a heartfelt gift I had purchased for her in Australia, along with a thank-you card where I expressed my deepest gratitude for her kindness in looking after Alex. Placing them on the kitchen counter, I can't help but feel a tightness in my chest, as if carrying a burden that grows heavier with each step towards the door. The dam finally breaks, and tears cascade down my cheeks.

CHAPTER 70

Xander

Leaning against the car, my arms folded over my chest, I watch Poppy enter the house, her bitch of a mother following behind. Despite the years that have passed, she still has a strong animosity towards me. I thought maybe she'd have chilled out a bit by now, but no, she still hates me and treats Poppy like crap.

I wanted to tell her to fuck off, but I held back. I didn't want to interfere with Poppy and her mom. Plus, I've seen them clash in the past and I know Poppy won't take any of her shit. She's always been tough and resilient like that.

As I wait, contemplating what's happening inside, my gaze shifts to the house two doors down. I can't help but wonder if my old man is in there. He's probably already at work, that's if he still has a job. But the way he approached me last time I was in this shithole town and asked me for money makes me think he might be jobless. That's his problem. I couldn't give less of a shit about him or his fucked up life.

The house looks more run-down than I remember. Maybe the way I'm living now has made me see it as even more run-down than before.

In a split second, I snap my head back around as I hear the front door open, and there he is - the little boy I've only seen on the phone.

"Daddy! Daddy!" he yells with excitement as he bounds down the front steps.

My heart races when he calls me that. Powerful emotions swirl through me and it finally clicks. Poppy's words make sense. I'll do whatever it takes to protect my boy. I already love him, even though we've never met.

I step away from the car and approach him. Once I cross the gate, he jumps into my embrace, his little arms wrapping around my neck, holding on tightly until our cheeks are pressed together. I feel regret for all the moments I've missed with him, but I vow to never let that happen again. From now on, he and his mother are my entire world.

"You came back with Mom," he says, leaning back a bit to look at me. I'm totally focusing on his face, checking out all the tiny details - he's got my eyes, my nose, the same face shape, and his dark hair is the same shade as mine. He's a spitting image of me, and I have the photo to back it up - the one my mom treasured by her bed.

Seeing him makes me feel all sorts of emotions I've never felt before. Tears form in my eyes as I cradle this tiny clone of myself in my arms.

"Can I see the pictures of the kangaroos?" he requests, his curiosity piqued. "And don't forget the koalas too."

"Sure," I say. "Let's go back out the gate first, and I'll show you." Carrying him, I step back through the gate, making sure not to draw any more attention than what had already transpired earlier, just in case Poppy's mother notices me on her property.

When we reach the rental car, I gently sit him on the hood, letting his legs dangle down over the side.

I reach into my pocket for my phone and casually lean against the car, wrapping my arm around him to prevent him from falling. With just a couple of taps, I pull up the gallery of photos from our zoo trip.

As I hand him the phone, I watch him intently as he looks at the photos. He carefully studies the image and then, using his tiny fingers, he swipes to the next one, thoroughly inspecting each photo along the way. Then he pauses on a particular image - the one capturing Poppy with her radiant smile as she holds a handful of pellets, feeding a kangaroo. Out of all the photos I took of her during our trip, this one is my favorite.

He studies it for a few more moments, then looks up at me with a smile that is exactly like his mother's. Seeing it brings warmth to my heart, knowing that he is a special mixture of both of us - a flawless combination of his parents.

"Did you feed them?" he asks.

"Yeah, we did."

"Do they tickle when they eat?"

"No, but sometimes you can feel their slimy tongue on your palm."

He screws up his face and then glances back at the photo. Using his fingers he zooms in as if trying to focus on what's on Poppy's hand. "What are those?" he asks.

"Pellets. They sell bags of pellets so you can feed the animals. There are these huge birds that look scary and are always there, waiting to be fed," I tell him, as he looks up at me. "They look pretty weird, with their long necks."

"Are they kind of like ostriches," he asks.

I nod.

"They're emus."

"Yeah, that's right," I say, impressed by his extensive knowledge. Poppy had mentioned his deep love for animals, and it's clear that his wealth of knowledge is truly remarkable. I am confident that he and Theo will hit it off effortlessly. Their mutual passion for animals is bound to forge a profound bond between them.

"Do you have any photos of the emus?"

"Yeah, there are some in there," I reply.

He goes back to my phone and keeps swiping through more photos, asking more questions about the zoo.

We immediately raise our heads at the sound of the front door opening. Poppy walks down the front steps, holding a bag in her hand.

I carefully help Alex down off the hood of the car and move him onto the footpath. "Hey Alex, don't go near the road. Just stay here, okay? I'm going to help Mommy with the bag," I tell him.

"Okay," he says, not bothering to take his eyes off the screen.

Approaching Poppy, I can't help but notice her red eyes, as if she has been crying. It breaks my heart to see her like this. After taking the bag from her, I gently lift her chin, urging her to look at me. As I scan her face, she forces a smile, but I'm not fooled. Something has happened in that house, something that has deeply upset the strongest person I know. It pains me to witness her in such a state.

"Oh," she suddenly says, "I forgot to get Alex's car seat."

"I'll handle it," I reassure her, eager to take charge and shield her from the constant turmoil caused by her mother.

"Xander, it's only going to bring more trouble."

"I doubt getting our son's car seat will make her hate me any more than she already does. Let me handle this, Poppy. You can trust me. I won't cause any trouble. You don't have to go through this alone anymore. Let me support you."

She nods as if granting me permission to get the seat.

Taking her hand, I lead her out the front gate to Alex, who is still completely absorbed in the multitude of photos.

Once Poppy reaches Alex, she crouches down beside him.

"What are you looking at?" she asks, her arm wrapped around his waist as she leans in to see what has caught his eye. I watch their interaction for a brief moment, appreciating the way Poppy is with our son. It's a connection, a bond, that I'm grateful to be a part of.

Heading to the car, I place Alex's bag in the trunk next to ours. As Poppy entertains Alex with some photos on her phone, I walk back through the gate and make my way to her mother's parked car in the driveway. I just wanna see if Alex's seat is still in there. Even though Poppy is upset, I don't really care if her mom calls the cops on me for stepping onto her lawn. I also don't care if her mother's car is unlocked. It won't stop me from getting my son's car seat out without her permission. I'll just deal with the consequences when they arise.

As I near the vehicle, my gaze falls upon a child car seat through the rear window. I try to open the door, only to find it's locked. My focus switches to the front door and I start making my way there. But then my attention suddenly changes when I see movement in the backyard.

As I make my way around the back of the house, I catch sight of Poppy's mother in her garden. She's wearing gloves, a large sunhat and diligently tending to her rose garden with clippers in hand. It's so fucking frustrating how she can just act like her daughter hasn't been out there, upset and crying.

I go through the side gate and head towards her. As I approach, she turns and I lock eyes with her fiery gaze. Her body tenses up and her lips get thinner. Despite the temptation to confront her, I resist the urge to speak my mind. I really want her to know about Poppy's amazing musical skills, But, I quickly dismiss the idea, knowing deep down that it won't make a difference. Her hatred for musicians and music is so strong, that no matter what I say, her opinion will remain unchanged.

Despite these intense urges, I restrain myself. It shouldn't be up to me to tell her how amazing her daughter is. If she hasn't realized it by now, she never will. Besides, I'm devoted to becoming a better man for both Poppy and my son. Rather than voicing any frustrations I may have had in the past, I opt to keep my thoughts to myself.

"We need to grab Alex's car seat," I say to her, trying my best to sound polite. All I want is to tell the raging bitch that her rude behavior will only bring her loneliness in the end.

She turns away from me as if I haven't spoken.

I keep my eyes fixed on her as she walks towards the small wooden table positioned beneath the towering tree. While I wait for her to say something, my gaze sweeps across the yard, and a rush of memories floods my mind. My eyes then shift to the outdoor setting where Poppy and I have shared countless steamy moments. Every time it rained, I would take Poppy's hand and ask her to dance for me. I loved watching her move in that sexy way, and it was fucking hot when she'd let herself embrace her sexuality. I make a mental note to get her to do it again the next time it rains. One of the guys can look after Alex. Suddenly, Poppy's mother's voice breaks through my memories.

"You know you're no good for them," she says, casually tossing her gloves onto the table.

"You've said that already, and thanks to you, I made the stupidest decision of my life. Your words won't convince me to do that again."

"You'll break both their hearts because that's what you do," she declares with a sharpness in her voice as if she finds it difficult to engage with someone she views as inferior.

"You're wrong. You were wrong before, and you're still wrong. When I returned that morning, it was to tell her how much she meant to me, more than you would ever know."

"And just because you have all that fame, you believe you're any different. Deep down, you'll always be insignificant. Sooner or later, she'll realize she's not good enough and you'll find someone better."

"I don't give a fuck about your opinion. Poppy's opinion is the one that counts. I've loved her for years, so no matter what you say, I know I deserve her. I'm not that stupid kid anymore, who thinks that I'm not right for her. She's my family, they both are, and if you keep treating her like shit and push her away just because she wants to be with me, then you'll be making the biggest mistake of your life."

She pauses for a moment, her eyes narrowing as she carefully processes my words. But, unsurprisingly, my words have no effect.

"Once you get the car seat, I want you off my property."

I observe her for a moment, noting her confident posture that seems as if it's trying to silently provoke me. I don't take her bait, instead, I turn away, my hands shoved into my pockets, as everything I desire awaits for me out the front of this house.

It angers me that this woman could treat her own family like that. Poppy is more than enough for me, and she always has been. Despite being famous, I know I can get any woman I want. So why can't she see the way Poppy completely owns my heart? Why can't she get that through her fucking head?

As I make my way back to the front, Poppy's head rises and she glances at me. However, her attention quickly shifts to the front door as her mom emerges. Her mom remains on the front patio, watching me as she unlocks the car. With her gaze fixated on me, it feels as though she's ensuring that I won't steal anything, which brings back memories of my teenage years when people would watch me, assuming that I was up to no good.

After releasing the straps and grabbing Alex's car seat, I shut the rear passenger door. Almost immediately, the car doors lock and the lights flash. Without uttering a single word to Poppy or Alex, she turns and walks back inside the house.

As I return to my family, it suddenly dawns on me that Poppy and I have had similar upbringings. Although Poppy may have had a more comfortable home and always had plenty of food to eat, she never received an ounce of love from her mother. We both had shitty parents. Thankfully, it's something that our son will never have to go through.

Moving out through the front gate, Alex rushes over and slips his tiny hand into mine. We walk together towards Poppy, who stands there observing us. I can't help but notice the warmth in her smile as she watches Alex gazing up at me, his own smile beaming.

Within minutes, the car's engine roars to life, and we're on our way, bidding farewell to the shitty memories of our childhood homes. This part of the journey is taking a toll on me. The thought of going to Poppy's place and seeing where she's been living all these years really bothers me. It will be painful to see their dwelling on the wrong side of town, especially since I've been living a life of privilege. It'll only serve as a constant reminder of the foolish decision I made all those years ago. But thinking about the past won't do anything. All that matters is the future. But I can't deny that it will weigh heavily on my emotions.

Driving to the opposite side of town, seeing the familiar sights and hearing the sounds trigger a wave of memories. It evokes a sense of nostalgia, reminding me of the times when Ace and I would venture into this area, mostly during the day, unless we had a hankering for burgers or were on the lookout for casual flings with girls.

I listen to Alex as he tells Poppy about everything that has happened during her time away. The way they interact is truly magical. It is clear that Poppy possesses extraordinary qualities as a mother, and you can feel the love between them in every single moment. Being able to see this is truly remarkable, all thanks to the amazing woman sitting next to me.

As we drive past the burger joint, memories flood back of the countless times Poppy chauffeured me around in her beat-up old car. I can't help but wonder what became of that old green shit box, the witness to so many precious moments - like our first sexual encounter and the countless adventures we embarked on together, exploring every corner of the town.

"Take the next right turn, and then you'll spot a big apartment block on your left," Poppy instructs, indicating the upcoming street.

After some time, we finally arrive at the parking lot of the apartment block.

"Look, there's one right there, next to my car," she points out, gesturing towards the empty parking spot beside her old green car.

"I can't believe you still have that thing," I remark, stealing a glance at the car as I pull up beside it. It appears even more dilapidated now than it did before, if that's even possible. My gaze remains fixed on it long after I switch off the engine. Does this mean she was financially strapped and couldn't afford to replace it? I ponder whether she had enough funds over the years for the repairs.

Aware of Poppy's watchful eyes on me, I pivot my head and observe the rundown apartment block.

"I'm sorry, Princess. I'm sorry I didn't know," I apologize, feeling the sorrow deep in my chest. It's hitting me hard to see the stark contrast between their way of life and the way I've been living.

She reaches out and grabs my chin, redirecting my gaze towards her. "Don't do that. Don't blame yourself. If you had known, things would have been different. I had no choice but to do what was essential for our survival at the time."

I nod, understanding her words, yet my heart still aches at the thought of the agonizing ordeal she had to endure.

She opens the car door and gets out. As she opens Alex's door, I suppress my guilt and get out of the vehicle. Heading towards the trunk, I retrieve our overnight bags. While we haven't told Alex about our plans, that we are all living together, Poppy and I have already talked about spending the night in her apartment to sort out some things. This way, the removalist I've arranged can transfer her belongings to my house smoothly.

Looking at her current living situation, I'm not sure if it's a good idea for us to stay here tonight. I'm not so much concerned about the building as I am about the safety of the area. But I'm gonna stay quiet and not share my concerns since this is the home Poppy worked so hard to give Alex.

As we step into the rickety old elevator, its unsettling sounds make me worry it could malfunction any second. I quickly scan the wall for a maintenance inspection tag to check when it was last serviced. Suddenly, with a mechanical crank, the elevator abruptly stops on the twelfth floor and the doors slide open.

Alex is the first one to race out.

"Alex, wait up!" Poppy calls out, stepping out of the elevator and searching through her bag for her keys.

Keeping my eyes on Alex, I watch him race down the dimly lit corridor. The flickering light at the end contributes to the unsettling atmosphere, reminiscent of a scene from a horror movie. He stops at a door, positioned roughly one-third of the way down, and leans against it, patiently waiting for us to catch up.

When we reach the door, Poppy swiftly inserts the key and unlocks it. Alex promptly dashes inside.

Upon entering the apartment, I notice subtle remnants of the life she once had. Despite the limited space in the main room, it's evident that she has created a comfortable home for Alex. I move further into the room and put Alex's bag on the worn-out couch. Alex takes off and disappears down a hallway.

While Poppy locks the door, I take in the room, seeing the many music posters that used to hang on her bedroom wall. On the left, I spot the stack of vinyl records that we used to enjoy together, but I can't help but notice that their number has dwindled. I then glance at the guitar, casually resting against the wall, and start searching for her favorite keyboard. But it's nowhere to be found. I look at Poppy and see her silently watching me.

"I know it's nothing fancy, but it's home," she says.

"Where's your keyboard?" I ask, glancing around again to make sure I didn't overlook it.

"I had to sell it. Alex was sick and I needed the money."

My heart breaks when I hear that. I know how much that keyboard meant to Poppy. She must've seen the hurt on my face, because she comes over, wraps her arms around me, and rests her head on my chest. I wrap my arms around her, silently promising that she will never have to go through that hardship again.

Footsteps echo down the hall, and Alex returns to the room, holding a book in his tiny hands.

"Daddy, can you read this to me?" he asks, racing towards the couch and leaping onto it.

A smile of pure happiness spreads across Poppy's face as she takes a step back, creating enough room for me to join Alex on the couch.

Sitting down, Alex scoots closer and hands me the book. When I look at the book, a grin spreads across my face as I see a cartoon monkey clutching a banana in its hand.

"Your mom told me you love animals," I tell him, flipping the book open.

As I read the first lines, I'm reminded of my mom reading to me. I always loved how she'd switch up her voice for every character. Mirroring her, I do the same, and it makes Alex smile. I notice Poppy standing nearby, with a smile on her face, as she observes our heartfelt interaction.

CHAPTER 71

Xander

Through the entire night, I lay beside Poppy, holding her tightly in my arms. The noises coming from inside the building and the constant sirens made it impossible for me to sleep.

With just one day remaining before I have to fly back to New Zealand, there is an overwhelming amount of things to take care of.

The movers confirmed they'd be here at ten to pack up Poppy and Alex's stuff, so we didn't miss our flight at noon. Kit gave me the good news that Lionel is lending us his private jet to fly home to save time. And she also mentioned that we have a new band manager for our time in New Zealand. I know Lionel is doing everything to keep us with the label, but I can't wait to go out on our own.

While I never asked Poppy what happened in her mother's house yesterday, I can see that whatever it was has deeply affected her. She tried to fake a smile for me and Alex, but I could see right through it. I get shitty parents. My asshole father is like the poster boy for fucked up parents.

The crack in the blind allows a soft, golden light to filter into the room, filling it with a warm glow. The sound of footsteps hitting the wooden floorboards reaches my ears.

Alex must be awake.

With utmost care, I gently adjust Poppy's position to free my arm without interrupting her peaceful sleep. Putting on my boxers and jeans, I head out to meet Alex.

When I step into the family room, I see Alex on the couch, a glass of milk in his hand, watching cartoons on the television. The moment he lays eyes on me, a smile breaks out across his face, and I can't help but notice the milk mustache on his upper lip.

"What are you watching?" I ask, moving further into the room.

"Bluey," he says, diverting his attention back to the show.

I glance at the television and notice a talking blue dog. I sit with him for a moment, watching it briefly before I get off the couch and go search for some coffee.

While I wait for the coffee to brew, I make my way over to the many boxes that Poppy packed last night. Curiosity got the best of me when I asked her why there were fewer vinyls than before. Reluctantly, she confessed she had no choice but to sell a few of them in order to cover the bills. It's painful to hear she's been struggling all these years and had to sell the things she loved. There's something I haven't shared with her yet. I haven't told her about the grand piano that sits collecting dust in my house. Now I wonder if I subconsciously bought it for Poppy, not knowing the twists and turns our lives would take.

Never in a million years did I expect my life to unfold the way it has. Reflecting on the younger version of myself, the one who craved it all, the fame, the fortune, and the groupies, I now realize just how naïve I was. Even if I hadn't achieved success in this industry, I would have continued creating music no matter what. However looking back now, I understand that a desire to prove all the assholes wrong, to show them I was not some worthless piece of shit like they thought I was, fueled my initial drive. People like Poppy's mom, who still hold disdain for me, can simply go to hell. I've accomplished tasks that exceed my wildest dreams.

I have a job that brings me immense joy. I love being able to create music and travel the world with my band of brothers, my chosen family, who would go to great lengths to protect me. Above all, I have my own family - a woman whom I have loved for years, and she has blessed me with the most precious gift imaginable. I am deserving of it all. Though I couldn't see it back then, I now know that I am so much more than what they think and how they treat me.

Upon hearing the sound of Poppy's voice, I turn around. "Hey sweetheart," she says, making her way over to Alex still seated on the couch.

"Hey Mom," he says, his gaze fixed on the television.

Poppy moves over, planting a kiss on the top of his head before reaching for the empty milk glass sitting next to him on the couch. When she approaches me, a radiant smile lights up her face.

Her sleepy eyes and unkempt hair only add to her beauty, making her look even more enchanting.

As she places the empty glass in the sink, I notice her gaze lingering on my chest, her eyes fixated on the tattoo she adores tracing with her fingertips in bed. At first, she may have questioned my declaration of love. However, her doubt vanished the instant she laid eyes on her name forever engraved on my skin.

She wraps her arms around my waist, resting her cheek against my chest. As I hold her close, I can feel the warmth of her body melting into mine, creating a sense of deep comfort.

"What time did you wake up?" she asks, tilting her head back to look at me.

"Not that long ago," I tell her. "Just made a fresh pot of coffee."

She rises up on tippy toes and kisses me before turning away. "I'll get us a cup."

My gaze drifts down to admire her ass in those tight sleep shorts. Last night, all I wanted to do was get her naked and sink into her, but with Alex in the next room and the paper thin walls, I knew it was best to just hold her. However, tonight, when we get back to my place, I'll indulge in all the dirty things I want to do to her. Need to get my fix before I fly out for a week without her by my side. It's killing me to imagine not having her there with me, not being able to touch her. I've endured years without physical contact, but now, seven days seems unbearable compared to all those years.

As Poppy grabs two coffee cups from the cupboard, I move over and lean against the kitchen counter. "Are you nervous about leaving everything behind and moving somewhere new?"

She turns her head and stares at me while holding the coffee pot. "Why... are you having second thoughts?" she asks.

"No. Never. I want this for us, for our family," I tell her.

"So, what do you actually mean?" she asks, going back to pour our coffees.

"I know that you have your mom here, as well as Mrs. B," I say, accepting the cup she offers me. I take a sip, tasting the bitterness on my tongue. Despite its unpleasant taste, I do my best to drink it, realizing that tomorrow, when Poppy wakes up, all she has to do is press a button to have a perfectly brewed coffee, unlike this awful crap.

"My mom told me straight up that if I didn't do what she wanted, I meant nothing to her. Mrs. B won't be around. She texted me saying she's moving to help her son-in-law with the grandkids. So, there's nothing left for me here. I'm happy we're finally doing what we should've done ages ago." She turns and leans against the counter across from me. "What makes me nervous, though, is being in your house without you being there."

"It's not just my house anymore, Princess. Looking back now, I realize that when I designed it; I had this vivid image of us sharing a life in it."

"How so?"

"The media room has this huge ass TV. Even though the designer said reclining seats were a good idea, I wanted a couch. I wanted to recreate the times we spent watching The Real Housewives together. Since Theo watches it with me sometimes, I had to get him his own chair. It was weird having him sit next to me since we used to make out on your mother's couch. And then, there's this grand piano, perfectly placed for me to watch you play while I chill on the couch."

"You have a grand piano?" she asks, her face lighting up with a smile.

"Yeah, even though I suck at playing it, I had to get one. When they were drawing up the plans, I insisted on having a grand piano as the centerpiece of the open living area. I mean, I could just relax on the couch and listen to the sound of you playing, like how I used to sit on your bed and watch you create magic on your keyboard. It was this morning when I realized that everything around me seemed perfectly designed with you in mind. I know I have to leave early tomorrow morning, but remember, this home is the one I built for us. Do whatever you and Alex want to make it feel like home for the both of you."

"Xander, I—"

"No, please listen. My main priority isn't the house. You and Alex are what truly matters to me. Paint his room with animals all over the walls if you'd like. It doesn't bother me. My only desire is for the both of you to be happy."

"But we are happy. We don't need extravagant expenses to be happy, Xander."

Right from the start, I've always admired that quality in her. At first, I assumed she was privileged and spoiled, hence the nickname Princess, but she has since shattered that assumption with her actions.

"Okay, but if you need anything while I'm away, just say it."

"I will," she says. "But we probably won't need anything."

Her eyes speak volumes. I can see the unconditional love she has for me. I've never had someone look at me with so much love. In the past, girls have desired me, and I recognize that familiar look—the one that hints at their desire for me to fuck them. Back in high school, Jade, Savannah, and all those other girls used to cast that lustful glance my way. Groupies look at me because I'm Xander Williams, the front man for Broken Oasis, but the look in Poppy's eyes is genuine, brimming with love, and it shows that I am her everything.

"Mom, I'm hungry," Alex says as he comes over.

We both glance at him and as I let go of Poppy, Alex tugs at my arm. As I lift him up, Poppy's smile widens, her eyes sparkling with happiness.

"How about I make us pancakes?" suggests Poppy.

"Yes," Alex says, full of excitement.

"Alex, why don't you go get dressed? We have a big day today," Poppy says, turning her attention to the cupboard as she gathers the ingredients to make pancakes.

"Daddy, can you come with me?" he asks.

"Sure," I say, gently setting him down on the floor.

Without wasting a moment, he dashes off down the hall to his room. I didn't get the chance to see his room yesterday. While Poppy packed a few things, I played silly games with Alex to keep him entertained. Last night when Poppy tucked him into bed, I didn't want to interrupt their special moment between mother and son. After reading Alex another book on the couch before his bedtime, I said my goodnight.

"I'll be back soon," I say, making my way down the hall.

I walk in and find him rummaging through a couple of packed boxes.

"What are you looking for?" I ask as he pulls stuff out of a box.

"Just some clothes," he says, tossing a stuffed gorilla on the floor.

"Hold on," I cut in. "I don't think Mom put them in there."

He stops and stares at me.

Taking a quick look around the room, my gaze lands on a chair in the corner, where I notice a pile of neatly folded clothes. "Are they the ones?" I ask, pointing in that direction.

His eyes lock on the direction I'm indicating, and he immediately sprints towards it. Something in his room catches my gaze, luring me towards it with curiosity. Holding the metal photo frame in my hand, I settle onto the bed to examine it. The photo immortalizes a moment from years ago, showcasing a younger Poppy and me in our youthful glory, beaming at the camera. The memory hits me like a wave - I was at Poppy's place, and she wouldn't let me off the hook until I smiled for the photo. I can't forget how she made silly faces, and I just had to smile.

To my surprise, she had kept this photo for all these years and gave it to Alex. No wonder he recognized me the first time I met him. Despite all the mistakes I made and the challenges Poppy endured, she never harbored any anger towards me or portrayed me negatively to our son. Instead, she included me in his life, making sure that he knew who his father was.

If only I could go back and tell my younger arrogant self, not to be a selfish asshole, that the key to true happiness is this incredible girl and the life we'd have. Don't turn your back on her, because she doesn't deserve to be abandoned. The way she sees you differs completely from how others see you. In her eyes, you are an exceptional individual who means the world to her.

"We should pack that as well," Alex says, walking over and taking the photo frame from my hands. He puts the frame in the box, then picks up the gorilla and puts it on top.

"I'm going to help Mommy with breakfast," I say, making my way to the door, and giving him some space to get dressed.

While Poppy skillfully flips the pancakes, I make my way over to her. I wrap my arms around her gently from behind, pulling her closer, and plant a kiss on her shoulder. "Thank you," I say appreciatively, my voice filled with gratitude.

"What for?" she asks, her gaze lingering on me as she casts a glance over her shoulder.

"For simply being you, and for including me in Alex's life."

CHAPTER 72
Poppy

Alex sleeps peacefully on the four-hour flight, undisturbed by the hum of the plane's engines.

Meanwhile, Xander eagerly suggests reliving our mile-high club experience from our unforgettable flight that took off from Australia. I am initially hesitant, but Xander's alluring touches gradually wear down my resistance. That man seems to have committed every one of my pleasure spots to memory.

As soon as our plane touches down and we load our bags into the town car, a wave of nervous energy washes over me. Xander mentioned his lifestyle has changed and that he specifically designed the house with me in mind. This statement fills me with a mix of curiosity and unease as we venture into this unknown chapter of our lives.

With Alex sitting between us, Xander and Alex engage in lively conversation, filling the journey with their laughter. I shift my attention to the window, and I am immediately taken back by the luxurious houses that adorn the street.

"Are you alright, Princess?" Xander asks, concern in his voice.

"Yes, how much longer?"

"Not far now. Just up ahead."

The driver pulls up and parks in front of a pair of impressive black metal gates. Xander's window smoothly slides down, and I watch as he enters a security code, causing the gates to swing open, granting us passage.

We continue down a long driveway.

As we approach, my eyes widen at the sight of three grand double-story houses side by side, no fences separating them.

"That one over there is Nate and Theo's," Xander says, pointing to the farmhouse-style double-story house on the left, complete with spacious front patios. It truly is a sight to behold.

"And that one over there is Ace's," he points to the right, indicating a magnificent two-story house made of dark brick. It's adorned with tall white pillars that extend up to the second floor. It's grand, exceeding my expectations of what I thought Ace would have chosen for himself.

"And this one is ours," he points to the one in the middle

"This is your home," I ask.

"Our home," he says, correcting me.

As we drive up the circular driveway, everything goes silent. The view through the front window is absolutely stunning.

Before us stands a two-story house, painted in pristine white with elegant black iron accents. The front porch, which wraps around the entire house, immediately catches my attention, complete with a generously sized swing. In my mind, I can already imagine myself leisurely swaying on that swing, enjoying the beauty of the setting sun. The house exudes a formal charm, yet it also has the cozy essence of a farmhouse, incorporating simple elements. Surrounded by meticulously maintained gardens, its allure is truly captivating. I can sense Xander's subtle touch in the design of this house, a testament to his refined taste.

"Is this our new home?" Alex asks, his voice filled with unmistakable excitement.

The driver brings the car to a halt and carefully parks it in the spacious, circular driveway encircling the trio of houses. Xander assists Alex in getting out of his car seat, while the driver kindly opens my door, allowing me to step out.

"I'll get our bags," Xander informs the driver, considering that we only have one medium-sized overnight bag with essential items until our belongings are delivered tomorrow. "You can bring the car seat and place it by the front door," Xander says, his hand disappearing into his pocket as he takes out some cash and hands it to the driver.

Meanwhile, Alex joins me and stands by my side as I look up at the house. While I knew he made a lot of money from his music, I never imagined it would be enough to afford such an impressive place like this. I am genuinely thrilled for him. It brings me joy to know that he did all the things he said he would.

"Come on," Xander urges, taking my hand and guiding me towards the house. "Come see your new home."

When Xander opens the front door, he places our overnight bag in the spacious foyer.

The interior of the house is just as breathtaking as its exterior. The walls are a gorgeous shade of gray with fancy black iron decorations. Adding to the overall elegance, the tiled floors glisten and reflect the light. The twelve-foot ceilings further enhance the feeling of spaciousness in this grand house. I am truly at a loss for words.

Xander leads us into the house, and that's when I immediately notice the magnificent grand piano positioned in the center of the room. This thing screams luxury and money.

The urge to play intensifies, as I recall the vibrant atmosphere of the piano bar in Adelaide, urging me to run my fingers across the keys. Releasing Xander's hand, I eagerly move towards it, my fingers itching to caress the velvety smoothness of its glossy surface.

With each touch of the keys, I'm filled with a sense of excitement and anticipation, knowing that the music will soon come alive under my fingertips once more.

Raising my head, I pause to survey the room, and my gaze lands on the couch that Xander had mentioned earlier. Positioned perfectly, it offers an ideal vantage point to observe me playing the piano.

As my gaze moves towards Xander, I can't help but notice the way his lips curl into a smile, mirroring my own in awe of the piano.

"It's beautiful," I comment.

"I thought you'd like it," he says, smiling at me before shifting his attention to Alex who stands beside him. "Are you ready to see your room?"

"Yep," Alex replies excitedly, beaming with joy.

"Come on, I'll give you the grand tour," Xander says, grabbing my hand.

As we stroll through the big, fancy kitchen, I notice the sleek white countertops and black accents that add a touch of elegance. Moving forward, we come across an elegant dining room. Inside, there is a long, black table set for twelve guests, exuding an air of sophistication.

We make our way up the grand wooden staircase, feeling the polished handrail beneath our fingertips. The full-length windows offer awe-inspiring panoramic views, showcasing the beauty of the surroundings. Xander then gestures to a bathroom located just across the hallway. He then comes to a halt in front of a closed door.

"Are you ready to see your room?" he asks Alex.

With a nod from Alex, Xander opens the door. The astonishing sight of a massive blue shark with its mouth open greets us, revealing a mattress. This is Alex's bed. It is an impressive spectacle, unlike anything I have ever seen.

"Cool, Dad," Alex yells, racing forward. He leaps into the shark's mouth and lands on the mattress.

Stepping forward, I join Xander by the doorway. We stand together, watching our son's face light up with joy as he explores his brand-new bed.

"I think he likes it," Xander says, turning his head to glance at me.

"Yeah, he certainly does. When did you set all this up?" I ask, scanning the room. That's when I spot the large kangaroo and koala over in the corner.

"I arranged the bed before we left Australia, so that way it was all set for Alex when we got here."

"I wondered where the kangaroo and koala got to."

"Yeah, Kit sent them back for me. Come on, there's something I'd like to show you," he says, eagerly grabbing my hand and guiding me down the hall to a room two doors down.

The spacious room immediately grabs my attention, with its large king bed adorned with black silk sheets. On the right side of the room, there is an enormous walk-in closet, while right beside it, there is a stunning bathroom boasting a generously sized egg-shaped bath. The large panoramic windows offer impressive views of the extensive gardens, while the sight of the mountains just adds to the beauty. I can already imagine myself sinking into the warm, scented bubbles of the tub while looking at the breathtaking scenery. Once again, I find myself at a loss for words, completely captivated by the scene before me.

"This is where the magic happens. Where you're gonna scream my name every night," he whispers in his gravelly voice, as he pulls me towards him. "So, Princess, what do you think? Do you like it?"

Looking out at the majestic, mountainous landscape, a surge of admiration fills me, reflecting on his incredible feats. Despite coming from a life of poverty, he has reinvented himself and become a man to truly admire.

As I turn my head, our eyes meet. "I'm incredibly proud of you. Just look at everything you have achieved."

"Thank you, Princess," he says, his voice slightly strained.

I know that my words have left a lasting impression on him, shaping his thoughts and emotions. He tightens his arms around me, drawing me nearer to his chest, while his face stays nestled in the curve of my neck. We stay that way for a while, as he breathes in the familiar scent of my perfume, his eyes slowly closing.

"Mommy!" Alex yells from somewhere out in the hall.

Xander lifts his head and releases his grip on my waist. He pokes his head out through the doorway.

"Mom's in here, buddy," he says.

Whenever Xander speaks to Alex, his tender tone melts my heart. It's as if his walls have crumbled, leaving him exposed and receptive, not only with Alex, but also with me. Xander has shed his tough exterior, the one he always wears to shield himself, and the person he reveals is truly remarkable, with a caring, loving, and kind nature. The boy he used to be, who had a guarded and cold demeanor, always prioritizing his desires without thinking about the aftermath, has transformed into something entirely different. Standing in his place is a man whose kindness and love radiate from him, but only towards us. Only for Alex and me.

Xander steps aside, creating a clear path for Alex to enter the room.

As Alex rushes into the room, my gaze catches sight of the book in his hands.

Overflowing with infectious enthusiasm, he eagerly yells, "Dad got me a whole heap of animal books!" With delight, his face beams, radiating joy and excitement, as he proudly presents the book for me to examine.

When I look up at Xander, I am met with a heartwarming sight - his smile says it all, overflowing with happiness and satisfaction as he watches Alex with sheer delight.

With a gentle tug, Alex pulls me towards the king-size bed.

I lower myself onto the bed beside him as he opens the book. After showing me a few pages of the picture book, he looks over at Xander, who is casually leaning against the door, watching our interaction.

"Dad, can you read me one of the stories tonight?" he asks.

"Of course, buddy."

Alex gets up and races out into the hallway. "This place is awesome!" he yells, his voice echoing through the house.

Xander looks at me and smiles. "Just wait until he sees the pool," he says.

It hasn't escaped my attention that these last few days Xander's smile has become a permanent fixture on his face.

Xander takes care of ordering pizza for dinner, and we get comfortable catching up on the latest drama of The Real Housewives, while Alex continues to explore our new home.

As bedtime draws near, Alex bids me goodnight, and Xander heads upstairs to read him a bedtime story. However, it has been over an hour since then. I hope Alex didn't convince Xander to read more. Alex always has a tendency to request another book or two before going to sleep.

With the empty pizza box in one hand and a wineglass in the other, I make my way back to the kitchen. I toss the box into the recycling bin and give my glass a quick rinse before heading upstairs to see what's going on.

Climbing up the wooden staircase, I strain my ears for Xander's voice as he reads to Alex, but all I hear is silence. As I step into Alex's room, I notice Xander sleeping with a book gently resting on his chest. It's a heartwarming sight, with both of them peacefully sleeping in Alex's brand-new bed, their faces relaxed and content. I wish I could freeze this moment in a photograph, but I left my phone on the kitchen counter.

I'm unsure whether I should wake him up since he has an early flight tomorrow. Lionel has arranged for him to use the label's private jet, which will fly him to New Zealand in the early hours of the morning.

Choosing not to wake him, I delicately lift the book from his chest. At that moment, his eyes slowly flutter open and meet mine. A drowsy smile graces his lips.

"I'm sorry. I didn't want to wake you," I say, not bothering to lower my voice. Once Alex is asleep, the whole house could crumble, and he wouldn't even budge.

Xander takes a quick look at Alex, then sits up and scoots down to the end of the bed and gets out through the shark's mouth.

"No, I'm glad you did. I have something planned for us tonight, and it doesn't involve reading books," he whispers.

"Don't worry about whispering," I say, as I go over to add the book to the stack Xander got for Alex. "He doesn't wake once his asleep."

"Great," he says, coming over and grabbing my hand, pulling me towards the door. "Time's running out, so I gotta make every second count. Because I want to hear you scream my name while I fuck you senseless."

As I enter the bedroom, he suddenly pulls me towards him, and I can feel his hard cock through his jeans as he pins me against the wall. Our lips collide, igniting the air with an electric charge. My heart races as I surrender to the intensity of his kiss, losing myself completely. His lips trail down my neck, prompting me to tilt my head, granting him access. I can't help but moan when his teeth graze my skin.

"Fuck, I love it when you do that."

Without even glancing at him, I can sense his seductive smirk, as if a wave of desire is washing over me and leaving goosebumps on my skin. He gives my neck a few soft kisses, each one leaving a lingering warmth before he pulls back to look at me.

His hungry gaze roams over my face, making me feel completely exposed. As he brushes my long hair behind my ear, a primal desire awakens, and then he kisses me with such force it steals my breath away.

My heart races as his fingers find the hem of my shirt, effortlessly sliding it off and tossing it aside. I'm mesmerized by the intensity in his eyes as he focuses on my black lacy bra. He lifts his hand, delicately gliding his fingers over my taut nipple beneath the lacy fabric, before leaning in and teasing it with his tongue, tracing enticing circles around it. I let out a moan as the sensation electrifies my entire being.

"Stay still," he says, lowering himself to his knees. He leans in, never breaking eye contact, and gently kisses my stomach, including the stretch marks I dislike.

I am filled with a sense of excitement as his hands explore beneath my skirt, his fingers playfully tracing along my thighs, eventually sliding my panties off with ease. Once they reach my ankles, I step out of them.

With a sly grin, he quickly stuffs them into his pocket. "These are coming with me," he declares.

"Pervert," I tease.

He flashes me that sexy smirk that instantly melts my heart. His attention then shifts to unzipping the side zipper of my skirt. When it falls to the ground, I step out of it. He casually tosses the skirt over his shoulder while keeping his eyes on my pussy.

"Touch yourself," he whispers seductively, moving closer, he presses a kiss to my most sensitive spot. "Let's see how good you can make yourself feel. Dance for me like you did in the rain," he looks up at me with those gorgeous, dark eyes.

I smile, treasuring the memories of those intense moments when I would completely surrender, free from any worries about the way I looked and all my insecurities about my body. All I could focus on back then was Xander's adoring gaze, as if I were the most beautiful thing he had ever seen - a gaze that remains unwavering even to this day.

"Go sit on the bed," I tell him.

He leans in and plants a quick kiss on my pussy, then flicks his tongue for a quick lick before he stands up.

"Asshole," I say, seeing that smug grin on his face, knowing he did that just to mess with me. Although I really want to, I resist the urge to yank his hair and tell him to please me with his tongue.

Approaching the bed, he takes a seat. His intense gaze gives me such a rush, making me feel alive and incredibly excited. I love how he looks at me like I'm his entire world.

With a swift motion, I fling my bra to the side and take a step forward, strategically positioning myself just out of his reach. I watch as his eyes move over me, pausing on my pussy, my breasts, and finally my face. When he breathes in, his nostrils get wider. The intensity in his eyes speaks volumes, conveying a suppressed desire that he really wants to fuck me.

I move in my own slow, tantalizing rhythm, egged on by the way his tongue comes out and wets his lower lip. His eyes follow my every move as I trail a finger down my stomach and down further, teasing him as I pause on my pussy before moving back up.

As he watches me, he rests back on one elbow and strokes himself through his jeans.

As I explore my body, Xander never takes his eyes off me. I notice his breaths becoming uneven, a sign that his self-control is slipping. Intrigued by my power to witness him lose control, I continue to test his limits. I want to see how far I can push him, so he boldly takes what he craves without hesitation.

Excitement and desire electrify every cell of my body as I slide a finger into my wetness, and I let out a hiss.

His jaw tightens as he watches me pleasure myself. I tilt my head back, close my eyes, and completely surrender to the incredible feeling. Then I sense Xander on his knees in front of me.

"Move your hand now." His words resonate firmly in my ears, leaving no room for negotiation. I immediately surrender to his command.

Startled by a sudden, sharp tug on my ankle, I let out a small squeak of surprise. When I look down, his handsome face is just inches from me.

"Don't move," he says, his voice all smooth and rough, while the fire in his eyes gives me chills. My whole body craves his touch, but it never comes.

His eyes lock with mine, and with a swift motion, he lifts my leg and positions it effortlessly over his shoulder. Now I wish I'd stayed over by the wall because once he devours me, I won't have the strength to stay upright. That's what this man does. It's not just about him fucking me, he worships every inch of my body. As he lowers his face, zeroing in on my pussy, I'm getting more turned on as I wait for him to touch me.

It's like a shiver down my spine when his fingers graze my inner thigh. A tightness settles across his face, a sign of his self-control. My senses get sharper, and my heart starts racing as he moves in closer and skillfully uses his tongue.

Damn, his tongue on my skin is so captivating, like pure bliss, arousing me with every intentional stroke. I can't help but moan when he touches me like that. As he lifts his gaze, he watches me while his tongue traces a teasing path along my inner thighs.

Every time he glides his tongue over a new spot, he gives it a little kiss.

With every touch of his tongue, he knows just how to push me to the edge. I close my eyes tight and grip my hands at my side, desperately trying not to ride his face the second his tongue touches my clit.

"Xander," I say, my voice barely a whisper when his teasing gets too much and his tongue avoids that sensitive spot.

He knows exactly what he's doing, giving me that cocky grin, making me want it so much more.

"Please," I gasp, biting my lip so hard it actually hurts. Finally, I feel his touch where I ache the most. My thighs quiver as he delicately explores the contours of my most intimate area. A potent blend of arousal and wetness engulfs me, leaving my senses in a state of blissful surrender.

Xander abruptly stops, then takes in a long, deep breath to capture the essence of my scent. The deep, primal sound he makes causes my nipples to stiffen and my heart to race.

"Xander," I squirm as he slowly trails his tongue along the length of my folds. While he skillfully teases, his eyes never leave mine, and I can't help but make some weird, strange noise. Overwhelmed with pleasure, my grip on his hair tightens when he changes direction, tormenting me with deliberate, torturous circles of his tongue.

He stops again, and the way he torments me makes me feel a mix of both love and hate. I let out a tense breath and I catch sight of a smirk spreading across his face. He's purposely being an asshole. Teasing me brings him a great deal of enjoyment.

"Tell me how much you want it, Princess," he says.

I let out a groan, and he smirks back at me.

"If you don't finish what you started, I'll ride your face," I say.

"Fuck, that's gonna be hot," he says, leaning in and licking my clit.

The sensations he's giving me are driving me insane and I whimper like crazy. Waves of pleasure hit harder and harder and I can't help but tilt my head back and get lost in this incredible feeling.

As I run my fingers through his hair, I feel the soft strands between my fingertips, gripping tightly as I succumb to the overwhelming desire and grind against his face. The idea of him stopping is unimaginable. I crave the electrifying sensation of his touch and the pleasure he brings me.

My legs quiver as he circles and teases my sensitive spot again and again. "Oh, my god, Xander," I yell, as he expertly applies the perfect amount of pleasure. I'm close, so close. I tighten my fingers in his hair as my orgasm hits.

I take a few seconds to pull myself together and collect my thoughts. Once I do, I look down at him to find him staring up at me, giving me that cocky look like he just broke the world record for giving me the best orgasm.

"You're so fucking hot when you do that," he says, placing a tender kiss on my pussy.

Standing, he claims my mouth with his own, igniting a fiery connection between us. As his tongue invades my mouth, I willingly submit, savoring the familiar taste that lingers within.

When he pulls back from the kiss, his chest rises and falls as if he's struggling to catch his breath. I watch his tongue glide across his parted lips, savoring the taste of me in his mouth. Then he turns and as he walks over to the bed, he pulls off his shirt and then effortlessly sheds his jeans. Sitting down, he rests back on one elbow while his other hand strokes his hard cock, catching my full attention.

"Come here and ride me, Princess," he demands, giving me a heated look.

I can't help but check out his flawless body, that tattoo on his chest, and well, everything else. He's the epitome of sex, the fantasy of every girl, and he's mine. Mine to fuck and love until the end of time.

I move forward, but I have no desire to ride him just yet; instead, I want to savor the anticipation and have a little fun with him first.

His eyes watch as I approach and kneel in front of him Knowing how much he enjoys watching what I do to him, I use my fingers to spread the pre-cum from the tip of his cock. Then I lift them to my mouth and lick them clean.

The sound of his deep groan brings a smirk to my face.

"Fuck, that's such a turn-on," he says, grabbing his cock in his hand. "Kiss it."

I lean in and give it a passionate kiss, mixing it up with some gentle sucking.

"Damn!" He exhales, as I sensually lick the tip, savoring his flavor. "Open," he commands in his deep, rough voice coming from deep within his chest.

As I open my mouth, he slides his cock inside, inch by inch. I feel my lips stretching wide, and the sound of his groan echoes in my ears as I trace my tongue along the underside of his shaft. With a forceful motion, his hips surge forward, pushing deep into my throat and holding it there for a moment, before sliding back. I suck harder when he does it again, making him go deeper until I gag.

When I get on my knees, he moans with pleasure and it's mind-blowing that I can make him feel that good.

"Damn, you look fucking hot with my cock in your mouth."

He thrusts forward, making me gag, and I hear his sexy moan - feel his cock throbbing on my tongue. I reach out and touch his balls, making it feel even better.

His thigh muscles tighten and he lets out a low growl. He's almost there, but then he pulls out before I can keep going.

"Get your ass up here," he says, pulling me towards him.

Our lips meet and I feel the strength of his arms as he pulls me closer, my body straddling him. He grabs his cock and positions me so he can push inside.

We both let out synchronized moans when he slides in. His eyes slowly shut, as if savoring the sensation.

"Ride me, Princess," he whispers, his voice filled with longing, giving up control to let me satisfy my body's desires.

Every time I move, the feeling gets more intense, as I shamelessly grab what I want and need at this very moment. Xander's eyes watch my face, taking in every brief expression of pleasure. As I adjust my hip motions, a mischievous smirk forms on my lips when he lets out a moan. His hand firmly grabs my ass while the other playfully tweaks my nipple. My heart races as I escalate my actions, moving faster. He's holding me tighter as the pleasure kicks in.

"That's it, let go. Fuck me like there's no tomorrow."

With a strong mix of desire and heat, I can't help but close my eyes and tilt my head back, savoring the intense sensations.

"Oh my god," I moan, the pleasure growing as I increase my pace, riding him stronger and harder. I'm almost on the brink of falling apart.

"Are you almost there? Because I'm about to..." I can't even finish the sentence before I moan and tighten around him. I'm trembling all over from this mind-blowing orgasm. I can barely breathe as waves of pleasure rush through me, moving with each thrust, as I continue to ride his cock.

Xander pulls me towards him, his lips meeting mine as he eagerly deepens the kiss. A guttural moan comes out of him as he finishes, spilling his seed inside me. He wraps his arms tightly around me, pressing his face to the curve of my neck, as I fuck him slowly and ride out our orgasms.

I feel movement as if someone is lying beside me in bed. The morning is in full swing, evident from the light seeping in through the windows. Exhaustion lingers, a consequence of the activities Xander and I indulged in last night, leaving me with no doubt that I'm going to be sore today.

With a hint of curiosity, I crack open one eye, half-expecting to see Xander, who may have overslept and missed his flight. However, to my surprise, it's Alex who is staring back at me.

"Hello, Mommy," he says, smiling.

"Hello, sweetheart," I reply, wrapping my arm around him.

I hear a sound, like paper rustling and I worry that he might have one of his new books in the bed with him, so I shift him to find the source of the noise. But it's not a book, it's a sheet of paper. I grab it and unfold it.

Princess

I left my credit card on the kitchen counter. Use it for whatever - supplies, plans for Alex's room, or anything else.

I wanted to kiss you goodbye this morning, but you looked so beautiful sleeping in our bed that I didn't wanna wake you.

I'm happy, Princess. I'm so fucking happy, and it's all thanks to you and Alex. Not gonna lie, the idea of not seeing you both for a whole week is already breaking my heart. I already miss our time together and I haven't even left.

Call me anytime, day or night, if you need anything. Or if you want to show me something else, I'm up for it. I've never tried phone sex, so that can be fun.

I love you and Alex more than anything in this world.

Xander.

CHAPTER 73

Xander

A sudden knock at the door causes me to jolt awake.

"We'll be landing in thirty minutes, Mr. Williams," announces the new air hostess, using that detested name of mine.

When I don't respond, she knocks again.

"Fine, I got it," I grumble, amazed that I managed to sleep through the entire flight. But then again, it's not surprising considering the lack of sleep at Poppy's old apartment and then the events from last night. I desperately needed to catch up on two days' worth of sleep.

Rushing through a shower, I quickly get into my seat, ready for the plane to land, all the while glancing at my phone. My phone buzzes, and a message from Kit appears, informing me that a car will be arriving soon to pick me up. The message also includes a list of tasks that I need to attend to. However, I momentarily set those thoughts aside as I fixate on a photo Poppy sent me. It captures her and Alex happily enjoying breakfast in the kitchen, and I'm completely absorbed in the moment. My heart yearns to be back home with them.

As the plane starts descending, the roar of the engines fill the cabin, and soon we touch down onto the runway, jolting slightly. As I disembark, I make my way towards the waiting car, its engine humming softly.

In no time, I'm at the hotel, in the elevator, keen to get to my room.

Stepping out of the elevator, I am greeted by the heartwarming sight of my bandmates lounging on a spacious couch in the hallway, each one absorbed in their phone. The sound of the doors opening immediately captures their attention. I can't help but notice the genuine smiles that appear on each of their faces as they turn to look at me.

Theo is the first to get up. He puts his phone away and comes towards me.

"Finally, you're here!" he says, giving me a brotherly hug with a friendly slap on the back. "How was it?"

"It was great," I tell him.

"Good to hear," Theo replies, stepping aside to let Nate and Ace take their turn.

They each give me a heartfelt hug, their embraces filling me with a profound sense of camaraderie before we all begin our journey down the hall toward my room. As we make our way there, they pelt me with questions, eager to know everything.

"What's the little guy like?" Nate asks.

"He's amazing, the most remarkable kid I've ever met," I reply, sliding the card into the door lock and patiently waiting for the green signal before pushing it open. "He has a real passion for animals. He and Theo will instantly connect." I walk in, casually tossing my belongings onto the generous queen-sized bed as the guys make themselves comfortable on the couch.

"Perfect. He can join me when I watch the documentaries," Theo says with enthusiasm.

"Yeah, he'll enjoy that."

"How did the move go?" Ace inquires.

"Poppy's stuff hadn't arrived by the time I left," I answer, walking over to stand in front of the three of them. "You wouldn't believe where they were living; it broke my heart." I glance at Ace. "Do you remember that burger joint we used to go to?"

He nods.

"It was two blocks past that."

"Damn," Ace says, shaking his head.

"What does that mean," asks Theo.

Before I get a chance to respond, Ace cuts in. "That area is pretty rough. Xander and I would always avoid it when we were younger because of the neighborhood."

"Yeah, but Poppy seems strong," Nate comments.

"Yeah, she is," I say, pulling out my phone to show the photo Poppy sent earlier today. It hits me that I've become one of those guys who excitedly talks about their family. But honestly, I don't fucking care. These two people have become my everything. And hey, if the guys weren't interested, they wouldn't have asked.

I hand the phone to Ace, who takes a moment to study it. "Fuck, he looks like you," he remarks, passing the phone to Theo, sitting beside him.

Nate leans in to get a better look.

"I know, but I see bits of Poppy in him too," I say.

I keep my eyes fixed on Theo as he studies the photo, half expecting a playful remark from him about Poppy. It's his way of playfully trying to provoke a reaction.

"You know, you once said you never really noticed Poppy until you got to know her. That's crazy, man. She's absolutely stunning. I definitely would have noticed her," Theo comments.

"You notice everything that walks on two feet," Ace points out. "Poppy went unnoticed in school. We were more into hooking up with the easy girls. And then Xander just stopped. You know, I always had a feeling something was going on between you and Poppy, but I wasn't sure what it was back then."

"I know you did. I didn't say anything because I wasn't sure what it was." Theo hands me my phone. "So, what's been happening while I was gone?" I ask. "Kit messaged me to let me know that we have a new band manager."

The three guys exchange a look as if silently communicating with each other.

"What?" I ask, but before anyone can respond, there's a knock on my door.

"I'll get it," Theo says, hastily getting up from the couch, as though he's trying to avoid answering my question.

"Can someone please tell me what the fuck is going on?"

The door opens, and I hear a female voice. "Good, everyone's here."

Stepping inside I see a tall woman wearing six-inch heels, a tight-fitting dress, cleavage spilling out over the top, and her long red hair cascading down over her large tits. While she is undeniably attractive, but her heavy makeup is not to my taste. I prefer the natural look that my princess possesses. Scanning the room, her eyes lock on me, and with confidence, she strides over.

I can't help but notice the way her eyes slide over me like a predator sizing up its prey.

"Oh, great! We finally have the chance to get to know each other. I'm Veronica. But you can call me Ronnie," she says, pausing for a moment in front of me. Then, she turns her attention towards the couch where Theo has just settled back down. "I guess you could say that I'm already acquainted with some of the other band members. Well, at least two of them," she adds.

I glance over to see Ace is purposely not making eye contact with her. He focuses his attention on everything else but her. It's clear he's already fucked her. Similarly, I notice Theo's not flirting or saying anything offensive, which leads me to believe that he, too, has already crossed that line.

She turns her attention to me again, staring up at my face. "Wow, it's no wonder women are obsessed with you." She reaches out her hand and gently glides her finger down my chest, pausing halfway. "You truly are a looker, aren't you? And that mouth of yours, I bet it can do some amazing things."

Who the fuck is this woman? "Remove your finger now before I fucking break it," I warn her.

She keeps her finger there, testing my limits.

"What the fuck do you want?" I say, shoving her hand away.

She smirks, like it's all just a fun game to her. If this bitch was a dude, he'd get punched in the face for trying to mess with me like this.

"Now that you're done playing house, we need to talk," she declares, turning away. Her smart-ass comment really pisses me off.

All the guys immediately glance my way. Right before I can tell her to fuck off out of my room, Nate speaks up.

"You don't know shit about anything, so shut your mouth. I've already told you we don't need a band manager," he says, shooting Ace a look, who stays silent.

Don't tell me he's back to being a pussy again like he was with Reg.

When she sits on the armrest next to Nate, he jumps up and shifts to the end of my bed, like he's trying to put some distance between them. His behavior makes me wonder if it was just Theo who fucked her.

"We have sound check in a few hours," she says, her eyes once again checking me out.

"Yeah, we're aware. This ain't our first fucking gig," I tell her.

"You're a feisty one, aren't you?" she remarks with a grin. "I like that."

"Is there anything else? If not, then get the fuck out of my room," I say, opening the door for her to leave.

She gets up and strolls over, not taking her eyes off my face. "You'll come around. They always do. Just ask your bandmates," she smirks, her hand skimming over my chest as she walks out.

Closing the door behind her, I walk back into the room and halt in front of the couch. "What the fuck happened while I was away?"

"It's great to have you back, man," Nate responds.

I give him a quick glance.

"Hey, don't look at me. I didn't fuck her, even though she was keen on it. It was these two assholes that were thinking with their dicks."

"Ace," I address. "Theo."

They both look up at me.

"I'm sorry, man. You saw how she was," Ace says. "Plus, I needed to get laid."

"So, what? Now that your dick's been taken care of, you're back to letting them walk all over us."

"No. I've talked to her several times about stuff, but she... well, she just won't listen."

"How many times have you fucked her, Ace?" I ask.

He gives me a look but doesn't say anything.

"Answer the fucking question, Ace."

"Three."

"Theo," I say, turning to look at him.

"Just the one time."

"Yeah, but she keeps showing up and trying to get him to go with her. I straight up told her to fuck off and stop bothering us," Nate says from over on the bed.

"She's acting more like a groupie than a band manager," I state, before I turn my attention to Ace. "Give Lionel a call and tell him we don't need her."

Ace gets up and pulls out his phone. All of us watch him as he dials Lionel's number. As it starts to ring, he walks over to a quieter spot to deal with the call.

"Has this been happening since she arrived," I say, looking at Nate, seeing he's the only one who will give me answers.

"Yep, pretty much. When she showed up and introduced herself, we were in Ace's room, chatting about stuff. She was flirting with Ace all night, just like she did with you then, and when things got intense, Theo and I bailed."

I can hear Ace talking in the background.

"This crap needs to stop right now. If you're looking for some action, there are plenty of groupies out there. Ronnie, or whatever the fuck her name is, is off-limits, okay? We can't deal with another band manager making a scene in the media."

Ace walks over to us. We all give him our attention.

"What did he say?" I ask.

"She stays. As long as we're here on this tour, she ain't going anywhere."

Annoyed, I plop down next to Theo on the couch.

"But that's not all," he says. "Lionel offered a chance to get our songs back."

For a moment, I set aside my irritation and lean forward. "Wait, what do you mean by getting our songs back?" I inquire, pressing for more information.

Ace gives us all a look before answering. "He's got a new contract ready for us, meeting all our demands. The only catch is we have to sign it before the tour ends. Once he emails it, I'll have Anita give it a thorough review."

I take a moment to reflect on what Ace has just disclosed. I want my songs back, they are mine, not theirs. I'm the one who bled my soul out when I wrote those songs.

"We need to shut down this thing with Ronnie right now," I say to Ace. "You saw the fucking chaos that Reg caused. We can't have another band manager causing scandals, and you know it."

"Yeah, I know," Ace says.

"So, how do we handle her?" Nate asks. "If we're stuck with her until this tour is over, we better figure out a plan because that bitch has zero sense of boundaries."

I reach into my pocket and pull out my phone, dialing Kit's number. As I do, my brothers watch me and I can see the puzzled expressions on their faces, wondering what I'm up to. After two rings, Kit finally answers.

"Hey Kit, what's up?" I inquire.

"Not much, why? What do you need?"

"Could you come to my room and bring Neil with you?"

"Sure. We'll be there soon."

I end the call and set my phone on the couch next to me.

"What's happening?" Theo asks.

"We need to come up with a plan to keep her away. Who better than Kit and Neil?"

"What kind of plan?" Nate asks.

"Let's see if Kit can change our schedule."

"And Neil?" Theo asks.

Hearing a knock at the door, Ace wastes no time in opening it for Kit and Neil.

"How was your trip back home?" Kit asks as she walks in and sees me sitting on the couch.

"It was fantastic," I answer.

"And how about meeting the little guy?" Neil asks, stepping further into the room.

"It was fucking awesome. I was scared shitless at first, but damn, it was worth it," I admit, knowing about Neil's effort to reconnect with his son.

"That's great, Xander! I'm happy for you," Neil says, smiling.

"So, what do you need help with," Kit asks, always ready to get things done.

"Our new band manager," I say.

"Yeah, what's her deal?" Kit says with a smirk, and I think she's aware of our problem.

"We need to give each other some breathing room. Sadly, she's sticking around until the tour's done."

"So, what are you thinking?" Kit asks.

"Any chance we can change our schedule and let her keep running to the old one? Can you make it work?"

Kit grabs her phone and starts tapping away. "Let me check. Tomorrow, you guys have two radio interviews, both by phone, so that won't be an issue. You can do them from wherever you are." She bites her bottom lip and taps on another screen. "I can reschedule that; it's not a problem. And those two should be fine. Yeah, I think we can do that," she says, looking up. "The only thing that might be a problem is the meet-and-greet after the show. I can also see about moving sound check forward by an hour?"

"Yeah, that would be great."

Kit presses a button, shifting her phone to her ear she moves to one side.

"So, what do you want me to do?" Neil asks.

"Do whatever it takes to distract her."

"Sorry, boss, she's not really my type. If you're asking me to fuck her, that's definitely not happening."

I grin at the big fella, respecting that he has standards. The other guys laugh out loud.

"He's better than you two idiots," Nate says, giving Ace and Theo a look.

"I don't want her anywhere near us. We can't stop her from being in the greenroom tonight, but let's make sure she's not in the same car when we get picked up later. That sort of shit. Just take care of those sorts of details," I tell them.

"Yeah, I got this," he says with a smirk, like he might actually have fun.

Kit returns, stashing her phone in her pocket. "The guys are already there if you wanna do sound check now. Everything's ready."

I look at Theo, Nate, and Ace, and they all nod, telling me they're good to go. "Yep, sounds good."

"Sure," Kit says. "Just give me five minutes to sort out transportation. When you're ready, go out the back and someone will be there." Kit taps her phone, makes a call, and leaves the room.

What I truly admire about Kit is her exceptional professionalism. She avoids unnecessary drama, unlike some people. She remains unaffected by the starry-eyed effect that newbies often succumb to when they join the label and meet us. It's as if she sees us as real people, just like Neil has done over the years when I take my late-night walks to clear my mind.

"Do I stay here and keep an eye on Ronnie, or come with you guys for sound check?" he asks.

"You should come. That way, she won't suspect anything," I suggest.

"Will she give Kit a hard time when she finds out things have changed?" Theo asks.

"Don't stress over Kit," Neil says, looking at Theo with a grin on his face. "I've seen big guys totally lose it when Kit gets in their faces. She may be tiny, but she packs a mean punch. The new band manager doesn't stand a chance against her, believe me."

"Shit, I'd love to see that," Theo remarks.

"Yeah, same here," Neil laughs, right before he walks out the door.

Now that it's just the four of us, I face the guys. "Both of you, stay the fuck away from her," I tell them, looking directly at Ace and Theo. Their heads move simultaneously, nodding in unison.

Sound check goes well. Ronnie is a no-show. It's incredible how refreshed I feel after just a five-day break and coming back to what I truly love. When I'm lost in the music, taking it all in, and feeling like I'm on top of the world. With everything I have now, my life feels whole and complete. However, even though the music brings me joy, it can't replace the deep longing I have for those two special people who own my heart. I wish they were here with me.

While the sound team is busy fiddling with buttons and cables during breaks, I daydream about the other side of the world. I wonder what Poppy and Alex are up to—maybe they're unpacking now that the movers are done. Is Poppy's old green car in the garage or out front?

Once sound check is finished, Ace proposes that we all go out for a bite to eat. We've never really chilled with the crew before, but I'm really enjoying getting to know them. Kit finds a spacious venue that can comfortably fit all seventeen of us. Since it's only four in the afternoon and the restaurant isn't busy, they happily close their doors, allowing us to have our gathering in private.

As we wait for our food, I feel the need to call home and check in. Sadly, the time difference prevents me from doing so.

While glancing at my phone, I notice a missed call from Poppy, which must have occurred during soundcheck. I listen to the recorded message. I hear Poppy and Alex saying goodnight and telling me they love me. The message is so touching, it brings tears to my eyes. When I look up, I see my band brothers have been watching me the whole time.

"How does it feel to have it all?" Nate asks, beer in hand.

"It's fucking amazing," I respond, placing my phone face down on the table. "But there's this feeling that something is going to go wrong like I'm gonna fuck it up. Or some higher power comes and tells me I don't deserve any of this."

"But you deserve it, man," says Theo.

"Thanks, bro. Maybe you should try it," I say.

Theo steals a glance at Nate, and in that moment, an unspoken conversation flows between them. Doubt creeps into my mind, making me wonder if I said something inappropriate.

"We had someone just like Poppy," Nate says. "You know, someone who was a big deal to us in the past. Sadly, she's no longer around. She died."

"Fuck man, I'm sorry," Ace says.

I'm speechless. The idea of Poppy not being in this world would destroy me. My heart goes out to them. I look at Theo and see him with his head down, focused on his glass, wiping away the condensation with his thumb.

All I want is to hug the clever jokester and say sorry. The same goes for Nate, but I don't want to cause a scene and make people notice our intense conversation. There's so much noise and laughter from the other tables. I don't want to be a buzzkill.

"What was her name?" I ask, curious to learn more about the girl who was so important to them.

Theo glances up at the sound of my voice and replies, "Bianca."

Nate places his beer on the table and grabs his phone. Within seconds, he hands it to me, eager to show me the girl who held such significance in both their lives. As I look at the screen, I see a younger Nate with longer blonde hair. Theo looks the same, just with a more youthful, almost teenage-like face. Between them stands a beautiful girl, her dark hair cascading in beautiful waves. What grabs my attention are her dark brown eyes and a smile that just radiates pure happiness. They all smile together in a selfie. The smile on Nate's face in the photo is unfamiliar to me, unlike any I have seen from him before. Could this be the reason why he's so serious now? Perhaps life's challenges have taken its toll on him, weighing heavily on his heart.

"Music was her thing," Theo says. "She absolutely loved it. One of the most talented guitarists I've ever come across. No offense, Ace," he says, directing his gaze toward Ace.

"None taken, man," Ace replies.

"I thought you knew, Xander," Theo says, giving me a look. "I told Poppy about Bianca at the zoo."

"Nah, she didn't say a word to me. Bianca was stunning." I pass Nate back his phone.

"Yeah, she totally was," Nate says, gazing at the photo before he turns off his phone and shoves it back in his pocket.

We take a moment to sit in silence, enjoying our beers. as the sound of laughter comes from the other tables around us. It's great to see everyone gathered here, instead of the band always being isolated, like when Reg was in charge.

Once the food arrives, the talk switches to the wild adventures the guys have had in New Zealand. Theo's cracking up as he describes Nate and Ace's epic disguises for their adventure. They all go into detail about their trips, sharing the incredible sights and unforgettable experiences they had together.

Chapter 74

Poppy

Xander has been gone for only three days, and I'm going crazy without him. Despite talking twice a day, once with Alex, and later having a more intimate conversation with just the two of us, involving a bit of phone action. Xander's dirty talk has always been a turn-on, but damn, when he gets explicit about what he wants to do to me, it's next level.

Xander filled me in about Ronnie, who won't quit hitting on him. Just last night, right after the concert, she showed up at his door, saying she wanted to chat. Instead of opening the door, Xander had Neil come over and ask her to leave. The guys' new plan is to get Neil to kick her out when she shows up. Poor Neil. I feel sorry for him for having to deal with her shitty antics. But I tell you, if I ever come across that bitch, she's gonna regret hitting on my man.

Xander's day trip pics are always a riot, especially with the guys' hilarious disguises. But none of them can beat Theo's crazy sideburns and over-the-top mustache. Without Reg, they're having a blast exploring more of the country they're touring. And in turn, I send Xander photos of Alex and me as we go about our days.

We've made ourselves at home in this beautiful place. I haven't had a chance to hang my posters yet, the ones from my old bedroom. I'm kinda lost on where to put them because I wanna make sure it's okay with Xander. Especially with all the music awards proudly displayed on the walls, highlighting his success with diamond, gold, and platinum albums.

During the afternoons, Alex and I enjoy spending time together in the pool. Afterward, we head indoors, where I indulge in some baking, and Alex tries to learn his dad's songs on his guitar. There are many moments when I see him, completely engrossed in his guitar, hunched over with the instrument resting on his lap. His mouth slightly contorts in concentration, reminiscent of Xander. When Xander's back, Alex wants to play one of the band's songs on his guitar to surprise him.

Whenever my son talks about his dad, I can see the love in his eyes. Despite the difficulty I faced at the time and over the years that followed, I know now that leaving my mom's house was the best choice, particularly when she began speaking ill of Xander. The father-child relationship is something I've always held sacred, and I would never want it to be tainted. I felt compelled to tell Alex about his dad, even though Xander had not been a part of his life at that point. The last thing I wanted was to follow in my mother's footsteps, witnessing the chaos she created with her hurtful words and actions towards my father.

Every day, I am uncovering the world of music that I have missed out on for so many years. The sound of the piano resonates through the air as I lose myself in the melodies that effortlessly come to life under my fingertips. It feels as though a beloved old friend has resurfaced, granting me a renewed sense of liberation and emotional release, just as it once did before.

As I navigate through this journey, a powerful urge emerges within me to aid children who face difficulties in communicating, especially those who cannot speak. The aspirations I once had for my life are resurfacing. I realize now that my mother's perception of me does not define who I am. I have the potential to surpass her expectations and become so much more than she thinks.

Chapter 75

Xander

I'm counting down the days until our reunion. Seeing the photo Poppy just sent me of her and Alex by the pool, I really wish I could be there with them.

Tonight's our last concert, but I can't wait to hop on the plane and head home.

I can't wait to wrap my arms around my girl and give my son a big hug. Introducing Alex to the guys is something I'm eagerly looking forward to. They're curious about him, asking questions about home every time I hang up.

While I love my job and it fulfills all my aspirations, my love for them surpasses everything.

I've thought about the future and how I see myself moving forward with my family and the band.

Now it's time to tell the guys what I want. Despite Ronnie's annoying attention-seeking behavior, I'm willing to part with my beloved songs, even if it's gonna hurt like hell. It's important for us to venture out on our own.

Anita told Ace that the offer was really tempting, but the contract said Ronnie would stick around as our band manager.

When Ace told Lionel again that we didn't want her here, he just brushed it off, saying we got everything we wanted. Lionel also mentioned he's keeping her in the role as a favor for an old college buddy and suggested he have some fun with her if she's up for it. It hit me that she might be a cunning groupie, scheming to get close to one of us for her own gain, like some gold-digging hussy.

That's why tonight, I've told Neil to stand guard at the green room door and keep her the fuck away, so we can have our meeting before the show begins. Theo and I are patiently waiting for Nate and Ace to join us at the meeting I requested today. Today Ace and Nate were off exploring, so Theo and I ended up at the cinema. It's great to do normal things like everyone else. But when the lights came back on, I had to suffer through wearing that scratchy wig and cap again.

"It's kinda sad that this is the last show, huh?" Theo says.

"Yeah, but I really want to go home."

"I get it."

The door swings open, and Nate and Ace walk in, all dressed up for the show. With the opening act nearing the end of their set, I know I have to hurry.

"What's up?" Ace comes over and sits beside me on the couch.

"I want out."

"What the fuck?" Nate says.

"Not the band, dumbass. I wanna quit the label. Let's go out on our own. You guys only stuck around to help me get my songs back, but I'm fine with letting them go."

"You sure about that?" Ace asks.

"Yeah. Just think about it." I lean forward in the seat. "The label claims they're meeting our requests, but they're not really. We don't want Ronnie, but we have to deal with her because Lionel owes someone a favor. He's not giving us what we want. What if we need to make another change down the line for something else? Will he be on board with that or is it gonna be like the Ronnie thing where we don't get a say?"

"There's no guarantee he'll listen to us," Nate points out.

"Exactly. That's why we go out on our own. Make a few albums. Get someone we trust to be our band manager and we have the final say in everything."

I stop when I hear raised voices coming from the doorway, where I put Neil. Ronnie's loud voice clearly shows she's pissed about not being able to enter the room.

"So, what does everyone think?" I ask, bringing my focus back to the group.

Ace nods in agreement. "I'm on board with that."

"Yeah, me too," Theo says.

I turn to Nate.

"As I've mentioned before, I'm fully behind whatever decision you guys make. Broken Oasis wouldn't be the same without any of us, so count me in."

"Alright, it's settled. We're going out on our own," I say, getting up. I head towards the table at the back, swiftly grabbing a bottle of water while still listening to the commotion coming from the other side of the door.

"When should I inform the label?" Ace inquires.

"Let them sweat it out," says Nate. "They don't give a fuck about what we want, so let's make them wait a few weeks."

Lowering the bottle after consuming half of its contents, I catch Ace's glance and nod in agreement with Nate's statement.

Suddenly, there's a knock on the door, and it swings open. My attention shifts to see Kit walking into the room, with Neil still standing guard at the door, stopping Ronnie from entering.

"You guys are on in five," Kit informs us.

"Thanks, Kit," Nate replies.

Afterward, as she makes her way back to the hall, I see the smirk on Kit's face before she closes the door behind her.

"Alright, guys, let's go out there and give it everything we've got. Let's make this the best performance of our lives. And then we can all go home," I say, huddling with my brothers.

Grins light up their faces as we exchange hearty slaps on the back, fueling our adrenaline for the ultimate performance.

Advancing towards the door, we follow Nate, who takes the lead. With the door opened, we step out, guided by Neil as we make our way towards the stage. Despite Ronnie not being directly in my line of sight, given her persistent stalking qualities over these past days, I'm certain she's nearby, even if she remains unseen.

After giving it our all, we're left exhausted and sweaty as the show comes to an end. I'm cracking up as I see the crowd lose their shit when Nate throws his drumsticks - they adore those fucking little things.

Before I go into the green room, I quickly change my shirt and do my usual routine for this time of the night. I grab the phone and call home.

Alex's cute face appears on the screen.

"Dad," he says with a grin, sounding just as excited as he does every night when we talk.

"Hey buddy," I reply. "How's it going?"

"Good. When are you coming home?" he asks eagerly.

"I'm flying out tonight, so I'll be home tomorrow."

"Guess what? I have a surprise for you?"

"Really? What is it?" I ask, grinning.

"No, I can't tell you it's a surprise."

"Hey," Poppy says, leaning on Alex's shoulder to get a good look at me.

"Hey, Princess," I say, checking out her gorgeous face.

"I'm looking forward to you coming home," she says.

"Me too."

"Me and Mom are gonna go for a swim soon," Alex says.

It brings me joy to know that they're enjoying the house and making it their own. It was my intention all along when I had to leave - I wanted them to feel like it's their home just as much as it feels like mine.

"You know what? Maybe I'll join you for a swim tomorrow," I say.

"Yes. I'll show you my cannonball and how much water I can splash on Mom," says Alex.

"I'm dying to see that. Then I'll show you mine and you'll see how much more water I can splash on Mom," I say.

With a mischievous glimmer in his eyes, Alex turns his head towards Poppy, letting out a giggle.

"Oh yeah. Well, you better prepare to get wet when I show you how much I can splash you guys," Poppy says, with a big grin on her face.

"Sure, Mom," Alex says, rolling his eyes. "You hardly got me last time."

Their playful banter brings a smile to my face.

Lifting my head, I catch sight of Kit standing not far from me, it's time for me to join the band in the green room.

"Well, I gotta run," I say, feeling sad about all the moments I'll be missing with them. "I'll see you both tomorrow. Love you," I say, the words just now effortlessly flowing out. Every day, I make sure I tell them that.

"Love you too," they both say, and it never gets old hearing them say that. I hang up, put my phone in my pocket, and walk toward Kit, who's watching me.

"We're almost home," she says, and I can sense she understands how much I long to be with the people I hold dear, especially with all the times she's been fetching me to come to the green room this week.

As I sit on the flight back home, I'm constantly glancing at my phone, counting down the hours until we reach our destination. But it feels as if time is crawling at a painfully slow pace.

Just trying to kill time, I strum a few chords on my guitar, but my thoughts are elsewhere. Theo looks restless like he's trapped in his thoughts again. Chatting about random stuff has proven to be the most effective way to help him clear his mind. Since that day at the zoo, I've discovered the secret to helping him unwind.

"Let's write a song together when we're back home," I suggest.

"Seriously?"

"Yeah, why not?"

"What if it turns out shit?"

"No big deal. We'll just write another one. I've got a bunch of crappy songs that will never get recorded."

"Really?"

"Yeah."

"Yeah, I'll give it a try," he says, getting comfortable in the chair and looking more relaxed. I notice that his legs are no longer bouncing up and down. "I can't wait to meet Alex. Can we meet him when we get back?"

Theo, plus all the guys have been so keen to meet Alex. They've been bombarding me with questions about Alex since I've returned.

"Yeah, I was thinking of inviting you guys over as soon as we're back home, so you can meet him and see Poppy again."

"Yeah, I'm in," he smirks in response. "You know, seeing Poppy again, and..."

"Alright, keep it to yourself," I smirk back, knowing that Theo, always playful and ready to fuck with me, is back to his relaxed self.

"I might give you a hard time, but honestly, I'm really happy for you and I wish I had what you've got," Theo confesses, his leg bouncing up and down again.

"One day, it might happen. You never know."

"I doubt it. Especially when no one else even comes close, you know?"

"Yeah, I get it."

"Thought you would."

Hearing him open up deeply touches my heart. Could Theo's fear of letting anyone in again be the reason for his flirtatious behavior? Is he afraid of letting someone in because of the pain he's experienced?

Taking a moment to observe him, I offer some advice.

"When you write your song, tap into that feeling. Feel it right here." I tap my fingers against my chest. "That's your song, man. Write it for Bianca."

He's giving me the once-over, obviously pondering the suggestion I just dropped.

"Do you think Nate can help?" he asks.

"Sure, you and Nate can come up with the lyrics and I'll help put them together if you want."

"Thanks, I'd appreciate that. Well, I guess I'll try to get some sleep," he says, getting up from the couch. "You should do the same. We still have a while before we land."

"Yeah," I say, fully aware of the fact that we still have over ten hours left until we touch down. "I'm just too excited to sleep."

Theo walks towards the door, and as I hold my guitar, my fingers effortlessly start strumming. A melody emerges, carrying me away and causing time to swiftly slip through my fingers.

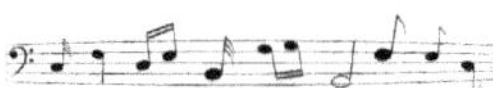

The moment I step off the plane, a surge of excitement rushes through me, reminiscent of the joy I experienced as a child before my mother passed away. It evokes memories of those exhilarating Christmas mornings when I would eagerly rush to see what Santa had brought. I can't wait to see Poppy and Alex. It's like my whole body is buzzing.

On the flight, I'm the only one who hasn't slept.

The SUV ride home takes forever, but the second Ace puts in the security code to open the gates, I'm bursting with energy, ready to bolt out of the car just to get there faster. This overwhelming desire to be home is an entirely new experience for me, and the wait is driving me crazy.

"Hey guys, come meet Alex," I say as we start moving through the gates.

"Now," Ace says with a grin, showing how stoked he is.

"Yeah, let's do it."

"Hell yeah, I'm in!" Ace says.

Nate and Theo share excited smiles, eager to finally meet the little guy they always ask about.

As the car drives up our long, circular driveway, I can't contain my excitement.

Before the driver even opens the car door, I'm already out and rushing up the front steps. I don't even look back to see if the guys are with me. My only focus is finding Poppy and Alex.

As I step through the front door, I leave it open for the rest of the guys to follow. The air is filled with the delightful aroma of freshly baked cookies, instantly evoking memories of our teenage years when Poppy would often indulge me with her homemade treats.

But I don't get far into the house when I hear an excited voice.

"Daddy!" Alex shouts, sprinting towards me and leaping into my arms.

"Hey, little man," I say, holding him tight.

As I peek over Alex's shoulder, I spot Poppy approaching, rocking that beautiful smile.

"Hey, Princess," I say, moving closer to her.

The sensation of coming back home now holds a deeper, extraordinary meaning.

I lean in to kiss her, wanting to give her so much more - more like the dirty thoughts that have been looping through my head since I left. But with Alex in my arms, I restrain myself and settle for a simple kiss. There will be plenty of time for that, because I'm not leaving anytime soon.

As Poppy takes a step back, her attention turns to the guys standing behind me.

Theo greets her with his usual grin. "Hey, Spitfire."

She rushes over and I watch as she warmly hugs each of them, welcoming them home.

As I move closer, Alex stares at the guys, clearly wondering who they are.

"Guys, I'd like you to meet Alex," I announce as I introduce them. "Alex, these are your uncles." The moment the words escape my lips, I can't help but notice the proud expressions on my three brothers' faces.

Except for Nate, who grew up in a stable family, Theo and Ace have never been a part of a loving family structure. I know that being acknowledged as Alex's uncles will undoubtedly fill them with a profound sense of pride, something they will treasure deeply.

Theo's the first one to step forward. "Hey Alex," he says, offering his hand. "Just call me Uncle Theo."

"Don't freak out the kid," Ace says, stepping up next to him. "Hey Alex, I'm Uncle Ace."

"Yeah, like that's not creepy," Theo says, laughing.

The clicking sound of heels on the tiled floor instantly grabs our attention, causing all of us to turn and gaze towards the foyer. Ronnie comes forward, her wide smile giving off a feeling of being welcomed as if she's an integral part of our family.

"How did she get past the gate?" Nate questions.

"I'll call the cops. Nate, contact security," Ace says, reaching for his phone.

Nate quickly grabs his phone and takes a step forward, attempting to prevent her from progressing any further into the house. However, she effortlessly dodges him and proceeds towards Poppy.

"We haven't been introduced yet," she says, offering Poppy her hand.

Poppy looks at me, raising an eyebrow like, 'Who the fuck is this woman?' I'm about to hand Alex to Theo, to protect Poppy from this crazy bitch. However, Theo quickly steps forward, positioning himself between Poppy and Ronnie, effectively creating a protective barrier.

"Why the fuck are you here?" Theo demands, his voice brimming with anger. In all the years I've known him, I've never seen him act like this before.

Ace and Nate both quickly turn around, holding their phones up to their ears, as if Theo's loud voice has shocked them, too.

With Poppy safe with Theo, I turn Alex away from the commotion. However, he squirms in my arms, eagerly wanting to see what is happening.

"I want to introduce myself because I'm curious to know who has captivated the attention of our frontman. As the band manager of Broken Oasis, it's my responsibility to stay informed about these things," Ronnie says.

Nate steps forward, slipping his phone in his pocket. "They're on their way," he announces, moving towards Theo. No doubt the guys will haul her ass out, but then again, the crazy bitch might have them up for assault if they touch her.

"So, you're the new band manager," Poppy comments, stepping around Theo and Nate, before giving me a quick glance. "That's her?"

I filled Poppy in on all her crazy antics—what went down in New Zealand, Ace sleeping with her, and her non-stop flirting with Theo. I've also filled her in on all the crazy shit this bitch has pulled trying to get into my hotel room.

"Yes, I'm their band manager. What other reason would I have to be here?" Ronnie confirms.

Poppy takes a step forward, positioning herself directly in front of Ronnie. Despite the significant height difference, with Poppy being a foot shorter, she maintains an unwavering gaze fixed on Ronnie.

"Alex," Poppy says, not breaking eye contact with Ronnie, who's still holding out her hand, waiting for a handshake.

Without skipping a beat, Alex responds, "Yes, Mommy."

"Go to your room and get that surprise that you want to show your dad, okay?"

Nate and Theo watch with curiosity, wondering what is about to happen. Poppy's piercing gaze, coupled with her confident stance, leaves me with no doubt that some serious shit is about to go down.

I carefully place Alex down, but Poppy remains motionless, her eyes locked on Ronnie. The room falls silent, except for the sound of Alex's footsteps and the muffled voice of Ace coming from somewhere in the room.

As soon as Alex exits the room, a sharp gasp escapes Ronnie's lips. Poppy seizes a handful of Ronnie's hair and yanks her face closer, their faces now just inches away from each other.

"You seriously think you can hit on someone else's man, bitch?" says Poppy, yanking Ronnie forward, completely ignoring her pleas for mercy.

"The cops will be here any minute," Ace says, joining us guys as we watch Poppy drag Ronnie towards the front door.

"Fuck, this is hot," Theo says.

I have to fucking agree. It's so hot watching my princess put this psycho groupie bitch - wannabe band manager in her place.

The four of us move forward. No way we're missing out on watching this. I look over at Nate and Theo and see them grinning like crazy.

Hunched over, Ronnie's heels click on the tiles, filling the room with an echoing sound. "Just so you know, I won't hesitate to report this to the label," she warns Poppy.

"Go for it," Poppy says, sounding unimpressed. "And I'll gladly expose you for the pathetic groupie you are." Poppy reaches the door and forcefully swings it open. "Now get the fuck out." With a strong shove, she propels Ronnie out through the open doorway.

Ronnie stumbles out but quickly regains her balance. Without delay, she proceeds to fix her disheveled hair, smoothing it back into its original style.

"If you dare touch him again, or even think about checking him out, you'll regret it."

I've never seen Poppy so protective before, and I have to admit, I fucking love it. I always sensed her unease whenever Jade and those other easy chicks would constantly hang around me. But she never did anything. But now that she is aware of my true feelings for her, everything has changed. She's become possessive, and I'm totally into it.

Plus, it's awesome to see Poppy dealing with a situation that I, as a man, couldn't quite handle. Ronnie needed someone to be assertive, to speak up, and to tell her that boundaries were being crossed. She never listened to any of us, so hopefully now that this shit has gone down, Ronnie finally knows her place.

Making sure Ronnie doesn't come back in, Poppy stands guard by the door.

"I'll head out and wait for the police," Ace states, stepping forward. As he approaches Poppy, a smile brightens his face, and he gently pats her shoulder to express his approval. Just as he makes his way out, two security guards suddenly appear.

"Holy shit, Spitfire, that was hot," says Theo, his face lighting up with a wide grin.

As Poppy turns around in the foyer, I make my way over to her. "Fuck, I love you," I confess, sealing it with a hot kiss that leaves her breathless.

Epilogue

Six Months Later

Xander

We're all at Theo and Nate's place. Well, everyone except Poppy. She's at home, completely engrossed in her online Child Psychology course. When I returned from my tour in New Zealand, Poppy told me she wanted to go after her dreams. I'm proud that she's finally pursuing her passion. Poppy has been an incredible mother to Alex, always putting him first, despite facing financial challenges. Now is her time to focus on herself, and it's my turn to step up and be the dad I've always wanted to be. I fucking adore every single minute of it. That little boy owns half my heart, and his beautiful mother holds the other.

Over the past five months, we've cut ties with the label. Given all the chaos caused by Ronnie, we couldn't trust Lionel. Honestly, going out on our own has been the best decision we've ever made, now giving us a new sense of freedom. We're thrilled about it. Finally, we're making the music we want and our original sound is back. Just the other day, we recorded an amazing song, with a mix of powerful melodies and heartfelt lyrics, as a tribute to Bianca.

I have to share something with you. The day Nate and Theo came over to my place to show me the lyrics they had written together, I almost fucking lost it. It was truly an emotional moment for me, witnessing how much their beautiful girl meant to them. It all makes sense now why they are the way they are. Theo's flirty behavior, Nate's serious demeanor, and their shared desire for casual hookups are a way to numb the pain of dealing with the loss of Bianca.

I understand completely, for there is no one in this world I could ever love other than Poppy. I never want to know the anguish and heartbreak they have experienced. Because of this and with each passing day, my appreciation for the countless blessings in my life deepens.

"Okay, everyone got it?" I say, hoping these guys are actually paying attention for once, even though they're focused on trying to beat Alex at Mario Kart.

"Yeah, we know. You've said it a bunch of times," Ace replies, straining to glance around me at the television as I step forward.

The race ends and the three guys slump back into the lounge, disappointed. Alex leaps up, cheering triumphantly for beating all three of them again.

I have to admit, watching my five-year-old son consistently kick these guys asses makes me incredibly proud.

"Poppy and I are going out for dinner at seven, so make sure you're all there by eight-thirty for the opening," I tell them.

"Yeah, we get it. And before you tell me again, I've already got Alex's black suit," Theo says.

"Listen Xander. I know we fuc-," Ace pauses and looks over at Alex sitting in between Nate and Theo before he continues. "We mess up sometimes, but you don't have to worry about this. I promise you we've got this."

"Dude, if you're this nervous about the opening, imagine how freaked out you'll be when you propose one day," Nate teases.

"I really want things to go well. It's important to Poppy," I explain.

"It will," Ace says. "It's kinda annoying how you don't trust us with this shit."

With all eyes focused on me, I quickly meet their gaze. I nod, knowing they're right. Settling onto the chair to the side, I become a spectator as the four of them enthusiastically engage in another round of Mario Kart.

Ever since Poppy started her course, these three guys have been instrumental in helping me with my plans. Their assistance has been crucial in locating the perfect spot for Poppy's non-profit organization. The commitment shown by each of them in this project is truly impressive. They went all out to lend a hand, and each of them chipped in a million towards it. It shows how much Poppy and her cause means to them.

Ace took it a step further by contacting Kit and Neil to see if they wanted to help oversee the project.

They both came willingly, switching to our record label in an instant when they saw how easily someone could be promoted without a particular skill set. I don't think either of them were enthusiastic about working with a certain groupie who had a habit of being over-clingy. And I can't really blame them, considering the circumstances.

After Alex crushes the guys for the third time today, I say my goodbyes.

While Poppy's in her online lecture, I sneak off to our room and lay the fancy dress Kit sent this morning onto the bed. Poppy's unaware, and that's the plan. I want everything to be a surprise for her. I was stressing about Alex letting it slip, but so far, he hasn't. Grabbing my phone, I shoot Poppy a text.

Xander: When you finish, I've got something to show you.

I notice the bubbles appearing, and I patiently wait for the message to arrive.

Princess: You already showed me it this morning.

With a smile, I recall all the dirty moments we shared in the shower this morning. I swiftly type out another quick message.

Xander: I'm down to do those steamy shower moments again if you want, but it's something different.

Princess: What is it?

Xander: Can't tell you, it's a secret.

Princess: Okay. I'll be there in ten.

I set my phone aside and make my way to the bathroom for a quick shower.

After freshening up, I smoothly slip into my expensive suit. As I finish dressing, Poppy enters the room. She immediately spots the stunning blue backless dress lying on the bed, then glances in my direction. I can't help but notice the way she checks me out.

"What's happening?" she asks, moving over to inspect the dress.

"We've got a date," I tell her, taking her shoulders and turning her around. "Go get in the shower." I give her ass a playful slap. "And don't bother asking where, because I'm not telling you."

While she's in the shower, I stand at the door, checking her out through the glass panel watching her lather soap onto her skin. It's fucking hot, watching her like this. Despite the overwhelming desire to join her, I fight against every fiber of my being to stay where I am.

After forty minutes, Poppy emerges, her dress hugging her figure and her long blonde hair falls in elegant curls down her back. She's absolutely stunning. Despite her usual preference for casual attire like jeans or a skirt, tonight is a special occasion, and she's dressed accordingly. This event holds great importance, especially since our band has utilized its connections to invite potential sponsors and media outlets to cover the opening.

When we walk out the door, there's a limo waiting for us. It'll take us to the fancy restaurant I've reserved tonight. I made sure to have burgers on the menu because they're Poppy's favorite. I've got everything sorted for a special evening for my princess.

Seated in the quiet restaurant, Poppy takes in the hushed atmosphere and scans the vacant tables. "What are we doing here?" she asks.

"We're gonna have burgers," I say.

She smiles. "Yeah, I don't think they serve burgers here."

"They do, I checked," I tell her, feeling the ring box in my jacket pocket, right by my heart.

The guys have no clue I'm popping the question tonight. That's why I've been incredibly nervous. I've been freaking out about every tiny detail, wanting everything to be perfect, including the vibe and the moment I pop the question. I want her to remember this night forever.

As the server makes his way towards our table, a smile brightens his face as he warmly welcomes us. "Can I start you off with something to drink?" he kindly inquires.

"I'd love a bottle of your best champagne," I say, wanting to try something different than my usual beer or Jack Daniels. I really want to spoil Poppy with something fancy, especially because this occasion is so important. Besides, I've always wanted to say that iconic line we always hear in movies.

Poppy's gaze lingers on me, her intuition alerting her to something amiss. "Xander, what's going on?"

I remain silent, observing as the server returns with a bottle of champagne. He presents it to me, and uncertain of the proper protocol, I simply nod and ask him to pour two glasses. Throughout this entire exchange, Poppy's gaze remains fixed on me.

As soon as the server leaves, Poppy bursts into laughter. "You're way out of your comfort zone, pretending you know all this," she says while laughing.

I burst out laughing, knowing how fucking stupid I look, sitting in this fancy restaurant, pretending to be someone I'm not.

I stare at her while she wipes the tears of laughter from her eyes.

"I wanted tonight to be special," I say, pulling out the ring box from my jacket pocket.

The moment she notices it, her hands instinctively rise to cover her mouth in surprise. I stand up from my seat and move towards her. Her eyes follow my every step. I kneel on one knee and open the ring box, offering it to her. I don't give a damn how cheesy this might seem, what really matters to me is this incredible woman and how she's changed my life, in the past and now.

"Poppy, I used to think love wasn't real. That it was nothing more than a fabrication, a mere illusion created by people. But then, that night, when we crossed paths on the street. I encountered a girl who only saw her imperfections. On that night, I witnessed your strength, your beauty, and the pain you carry."

As I continue, I notice tears coming to her eyes.

"Looking back now, I realize that what I felt was love. I've been totally and madly in love with you ever since. Having you in my life completes me, and I never want to experience the emptiness of not having you by my side again. Let's keep living this beautiful life we're making together. Princess, my heart has always belonged to you, and now I want to make it official. Poppy, will you do me the honor of becoming my wife?"

"Yes," she says, her voice trembling as the tears stream down her face.

Taking the ring from its box, I take her hand and gently slide the ring onto her finger. Knowing that Poppy prefers simplicity over extravagant bling, I opt for a classic design featuring an emerald stone and five tiny diamonds arranged in a simple pattern.

As I lean in for a kiss, I see the pure happiness on her face, reflecting the same joy I feel inside. Looking back on the tough journey that got us here, it's clear that all the obstacles we conquered were crucial for reaching this significant point in our lives. Even if it meant enduring that pain all over again, I would willingly embrace it just to have the privilege of being by her side.

We enjoy our burgers and savor every drop of champagne. During the meal, I notice Poppy frequently looking at the ring on her finger. We exchange loving kisses, engage in deep conversation, and become so captivated with each other that we don't even realize the server has already cleared our plates. This is how it has always been with her - being in her presence feels effortless, knowing that I never have to justify my value.

Then it's time for us to move on to the next part of our night. I have to admit, I'm incredibly nervous about this next step. It has been her dream for as long as I've known her, and I want it to exceed all of her expectations.

When the limo pulls up to the curb, I see Poppy's wide-eyed expression as she looks out the window, taking in the swarm of media and the red carpet in front of the grand building.

"What are we doing?" she asks, looking at me.

"There's just a formal function we need to attend tonight," I say, ignoring the rapid fire of camera flashes.

"But you're no longer with the label. What's this event?" Right before she looks out the window, I see a hint of worry on her face. I bet she's freaking out about her imperfections and how the media might portray them. I fucking hate that bitch Jade and her crew for planting doubt in her mind. If only she could see herself through my eyes. If only she could see how fucking perfect and beautiful she really is.

"It's our event," I say, trying to ease the tension I can see building up in her body.

"Our event?" she says, her brows furrowed. "I don't understand."

"Come on." I grab her hand and tap the glass, signaling to the driver that we're good to go.

As soon as we step out of the car, the cameras begin to flicker, momentarily blinding us while the media eagerly capture snapshots of our arrival.

Amidst all the chaos, a guy with a microphone calls out, "Xander, over here!"

With a tight grip on Poppy's hand, we make our way towards the eager media. Despite the smile on Poppy's face, I can sense the underlying worry in her eyes.

"Can you tell me about tonight's charity?" the guy asks, holding out a mic for me to answer.

Smiling, I know exactly how to play it up for the media. "Sure. The charity we are supporting tonight is the Poppy Williams Music for Children Foundation." I glance towards Poppy to gauge her reaction. Her eyes widen in surprise, and the tears start pooling. "From the moment I met Poppy, she has been passionate about musical therapy to help children."

"What exactly is music therapy?" he asks.

Even though I already know the answer, I turn my head to give Poppy a chance to respond.

She takes a deep breath and smiles before explaining, "Music therapy is a technique that promotes the growth of social skills, communication, motor skills, and cognitive abilities, all while engaging in interactive music programs."

I am amazed, watching as she confidently tackles a few more questions.

The reporter then shifts their focus back to me. "You mentioned Poppy Williams. Does this mean the frontman of Broken Oasis is officially off the market?"

"Yes, that's correct. She's the one, always has been. We're not married right now, but it's definitely in the cards," I reply.

"So, you could say we're the first ones to report this exciting news," the reporter says.

"Yeah," I say with a chuckle. "I guess you could say you're in the know since we just got engaged tonight."

Moving forward, I know allowing the media more chances to ask questions could potentially turn our wedding into a media frenzy. They will stop at nothing to chase the initial scoop.

Amidst the chaotic clamor of other reporters yelling for an interview, we press on, seizing one final chance for a photo opportunity before entering the building. As we step into the foyer, there's a noticeable shift in the atmosphere — a sense of calm takes over.

Poppy turns to me. "Xander, I can't believe you did this for me," she says, her voice choked up, tears pooling in her eyes.

"I'm committed to you, Princess. And so are the guys. This is a team effort. We all wanted to see your dream come true, just like we've been able to live ours."

"Are the guys inside?" she asks, brushing away a tear.

"Yes, and Alex is there too," I say, glancing up to see Kit and Neil standing by the door. Poppy remains unaware of their recent hiring because I wanted to keep tonight as a surprise.

I nod at Kit, indicating for her to go ahead. Kit, accompanied by Neil, comes forward.

"Whenever you're ready, they're all set for you," Kit tells Poppy.

Upon hearing Kit's voice, Poppy turns around. "Kit!" With a burst of excitement, she rushes over to Kit and wraps her arms around her, squeezing tightly. Afterward, she proceeds to Neil and embraces him as well.

"Congratulations," Neil says.

As she lets go of the hug, I extend my arm towards Poppy, and she intertwines her fingers with mine. Together, we walk towards the double wooden doors. I can already imagine tears forming in her eyes as soon as she sees Alex, Ace, Theo, Nate, and his family. And let's not forget about all the musical instruments generously donated by the bands we've worked with over the years, thanks to the unwavering dedication of Ace, Theo, and Nate.

Just as we're about to walk in, Poppy looks at me.

"I never thought it was possible to love you more than I already do, but every day you continue to surprise me, Xander Williams. How did I ever become so lucky to deserve someone like you?"

Her words bring tears to my eyes, confirming that I hold a special place in her heart and validating that I am worthy of her love.

<u>Get your bonus story to see what happens next for Xander and Poppy!</u>
At https://dl.bookfunnel.com/hmfovw17bv

Ace's story is Next

Sixty Days of Summer – Out Now

About the author

Eve Campbell writes steamy romance novels that capture the excitement of love. Her books feature broken characters and draw readers into a world where even the most damaged hearts can find passion and healing.

Join my Facebook Readers Group – Or find me on Social Media to keep up to dates with any new releases.

Five Summers - ISBN 9781923416031